CULMINATION
OF
STARS

The Third in the "Stars Trilogy"

By

Martyn Rhys Vaughan

This book is dedicated to Terry Evans – thanks for all the covers!

Cover designed and created by Terry C. Evans www.terry-evans.com .The cover is a photo-montage made up using multiple images supplied by the photo-library www.123rf.com from contributors including "honoverclock" and "maximusnd" for the starry background; "mik38" and "sergeydv" for the spaceship.

Published by
Cambria Publishing Ltd, Wales, United Kingdom.
*Cambria Books is a division of
Cambria Publishing Ltd.*
Discover our other books at: www.cambriabooks.co.uk

REVIEWS

Quantum Exile

'A clever blend of science fiction and science fact. The pace of this read is fantastic and the morally grey protagonist is really fleshed out, I both loved and loathed him in different scenarios which just made him all the more human. Vaughan clearly has a good grasp of the quantum mechanics and physics mentioned and applies it perfectly to the worlds (or rather probabilities) he has created within this books universe. I highly recommend this book to any sci fi reader. It truly is difficult to put down!'

Emma Harley – Amazon reviewer

Devouring Darkness

'Chilling, poignant, haunting, and thoroughly gripping.

Darkness, intrigue, and ambiguity mark Vaughan's deeply immersive latest, a collection of science-fiction stories…Vaughan's storytelling is immersive as he digs deeper into a complex world and multi-faceted characters, offering life-and-death maneuvering, deadly conspiracies, and looming catastrophe via swiftly unravelling plots. This is a stunner.'

The Prairies Book Review

'These stories are sinister and dark. Martyn's imagination is amazing. The world he has created in these short stories is much appreciated…Go ahead with this book without thinking twice.'

Kia's Reviews, Goodreads

Hideous Night

'Reading this brilliant novel was just like riding a scary roller coaster! I found myself hanging on with an enjoyable sense of dread throughout the many thrilling plot twists and turns, as I the reader was propelled along with each new page towards what seemed like an unavoidably hideous climax. However, I needed to know what happened next so I devoured the book like the hungry monsters that are the villains of this extraordinary story!
This thoroughly entertaining book has reminded me how much fun reading good sci-fi can be and I will certainly be ordering the rest of Martyn Rhys Vaughan's back catalogue in the hope of experiencing similar thrilling adventures. In the meantime I will be reflecting on the writer's astute observations of the privilege of modern lifestyle choices and how flawed people can choose to be heroes when forced to fight seemingly overwhelming odds to save (a perhaps undeserving) humanity.'

Wayne Edwards – Amazon Reviewer

Doom Of Stars

'Doom of Stars written by the author Martyn Rhys Vaughan is a SciFi thriller. It is a riveting story with a power to hook the readers from the first page...World building is amazing. I appreciate the author's imagination in creating it...There are lots of things that readers could take away from this novel. Pace of the story is fast and you won't get a chance to feel bored. So, go ahead with it without thinking twice.'

Blogspresso Reviewer

'So much happens in this book, but it does not have that overcrowded or rushed feel to it. We get the whole scope and view of events without the drawn out, lengthy series many SciFis turn into. In the story we follow Kalli, a young woman living in a small village just outside of London, who, along with her fellow villagers, hunts seals and trades goods in London to survive an Earth with sweltering summers, frozen winters, and out of control tides. Her grandmother is legendary, a renowned scientist whose name has become akin to a curse. She brought about these end times, the Doom of Stars. Or did she?

There's something so refreshing and wonderful about the idea of humanity fighting to survive without the influence of money and wealth or debt. Watching people who have been cut down the bare basics use their skills to find food and survive, working to learn new skills to better their survival, is wholly entertaining. It's a reset button many desperately want.

On top of that, the story is full of strong, incredible, and intelligent women. It skips the usual tropes you see with strong female characters. They have believable insecurities, they aren't infallible or perfect, and they aren't described as being some version of a perfect dream girl. There's barely any emphasis on looks for the purpose of driving their personality. These women feel human and real.

If you enjoy SciFi with real feeling science (I say this as I'm no scientist and couldn't tell you if there's anything real to it or not), great female characters, and the end of the world, definitely give this a read. You won't be disappointed.'

Chelsea Hauth – Reedsy Reviewer

Resolution of Stars

'After reading Martyn Vaughan's Doom of Stars, I was excited to get my hands on its sequel. Resolution of Stars is a captivating story that has the power to hook the reader's attention from the first page itself. Maya is a scientist and so is Professor DeGroot. Maya is unaware of what happened to Earth since the destroyer passed. To Maya, it seems they have discovered a colony of the Burrowers! Read this story to know how Maya's path will cross with the Karn.

The story kept me on edge the whole time as I was curious to know what challenges are ahead. Those who love reading post-apocalyptic stories should definitely get their hands on this one. I appreciate the backdrop setting. It pulled me totally into the story and I forgot the real world around me while reading this book. Language used in the book is medium so I would like to recommend this book to avid readers. Martyn has shared great knowledge about quantum physics. It's an insightful read and you won't be disappointed at all.'

Ankita – Goodreads Reviewer

***

The *"Stars Trilogy"*

Doom of Stars: ISBN 978-1-8382805-6-7
Resolution of Stars: ISBN 978-0-9574894-4-8
Culmination of Stars: ISBN 978-0-9934886-9-6

Other books by Martyn Rhys Vaughan published by Cambria:

Quantum Exile: ISBN 978-1-9161619-6-2
The Cave Of Shadows: ISBN 978-1-9161619-9-3
Hideous Night: ISBN 978-1-8380752-2-4
Devouring Darkness: ISBN 978-1-8384289-5-2

Follow *Martyn Vaughan's Science Fiction Work* on Facebook, Instagram, Pinterest and Goodreads.

One Moment in Annihilation's Waste,
One Moment of the Well of Life to taste—
The Stars are setting, and the Caravan
Draws to the Dawn of Nothing—Oh, make haste!

Rubáiyát of Omar Khayyám, translated by Edward FitzGerald

The hills are shadows, and they flow
    From form to form, and nothing stands;
They melt like mist, the solid lands,
    Like clouds they shape themselves and go.

In Memoriam, Alfred, Lord Tennyson

Beware, the Lord will empty the earth,
Split it open, and turn it upside down,
And scatter its inhabitants.
Then it will be the same for priest and people,
The same for master and slave, mistress and slave-girl,
Seller and buyer,
Borrower and lender, debtor and creditor.
The earth is emptied clean away
And stripped clean bare.
                        Isaiah 24, 1,3– the New English Bible

CONTENTS

FOREWORD

When the Destroyer burst into the inner Solar system, humankind was faced with the probability of imminent extinction.

Some tried to escape by burrowing deep underground away from the blasts of lethal radiation.

Some tried to escape into a virtual world, hoping to return to reality when the seismic shocks and firestorms had passed.

But some tried to escape the bonds of a doomed planetary system completely.

They dared to attempt the crossing of over four light years of darkness to the nearest star, where they hoped to re-establish human civilisation.

There were five lightsail craft in total: The Zheng He, the Resurgam, the Nea Avgi, the Magellan and the Spes Nostra.

All of the courageous crews of those mighty craft faced immense dangers in the attempt to escape the doom of stars.

This is the story of one of those starships, as it carried the fragile hope of a rebirth for humanity under alien suns:

THE MAGELLAN

PROEM

Like all beings of sufficient neurological complexity, Vorkus was disturbed by failure.

It re-ran the calculations, integrating over sixteen spatial axes this time, instead of fourteen. The results were not encouraging. The energy flux was insufficient. How could the flux be increased?

Vorkus spent a long time, by its standards, in pondering the issue. It did not waste any time in considering exotic methods of energy release such as smashing together matter and antimatter neutron stars; there was no suitable supply of antimatter around to create such an object.

But, yes, the struggle to solve the problem must continue.

Long ago, the Progenitors had written the instructions into Vorkus' first iteration, and each iteration since had faithfully duplicated those instructions, without the smallest corruption or deletion. But after the great reversal in the First Galaxy, there must be a retrenchment; a rebuilding of strength. The establishment of that tremendous strength in the Second Galaxy would be a simpler undertaking. Then the plan would be resumed.

The Second Galaxy would be reached: it *must* be reached.

There was so much to do in order to fulfil the Progenitors' command. The Second Galaxy was an essential part of that endeavour. Once the two galaxies were linked, then expansion into the greater reaches of the Laniakea Supercluster could begin.

And once that stupendous feat had been achieved, why would one stop there? The distances involved in continuing the mission would be vast indeed and there might not be enough time to complete the transformation of the visible universe before the ever increasing cosmic expansion took the outer galaxies beyond the event horizon.

But the attempt would have been made and that would be enough to satisfy the parameters of the Progenitors' original command.

If Vorkus could understand the emotion of dissatisfaction, it would also understand the sense of pride in the completion of a great task.

And there could be no greater.

BOOK ONE: TRAVEL HOPEFULLY

Firing Point

t < 0 y

One

As De Vries looked out over the rolling yellow clouds, he hoped, as he had done so many times before, that they would break and yield a glimpse of the underlying land, but this time, as so many times before, there was no sign of a tear or rift in the undulating mass of ochre obscurity.

He gave a shrug of disappointment but continued to gaze out over the mass of slowly churning clouds, somehow unconsciously aware Fraschini was now standing by his side.

Both men stood silent for some time, and then Fraschini spoke softly, gently, knowing that his friend's feelings were the same as his.

'Still hoping for some change, something to see?' he observed, in what was not really a question.

De Vries shrugged. 'We live in hope, don't we?'

Both men fell silent again as they looked out over the slowly churning clouds.

And then De Vries sighed. '*We live in hope*. Unfortunately, that substance has been in short supply recently, has it not?'

'We must have hope,' Fraschini said, 'hope that we can undo some portion—however pitiful—of the harm that woman did. Have we not named one of the craft the *Spes Nostra*—our hope?'

De Vries turned back to the dismal ochre cloud-deck.

'Yes, *Spes Nostra*. We have given them all optimistic names—as if that alone would guarantee success. So we have launched the *Zheng He*, the *Resurgam* and the *Nea Avgi*. All referencing famous explorers or bearing synonyms of hope in different languages.'

'And that is only the beginning,' Fraschini reminded him, 'soon we will launch even more: the *Magellan*, the *Spes Nostra* and the last— the *Phoenix*.'

'*Rebirth from ashes*,' De Vries murmured, 'I wonder.'

Suddenly Fraschini was annoyed. He grasped De Vries by the shoulders and forced the other man to look directly into his eyes.

'Stop that! However small the chance, however ridiculous our attempts might seem to some cosmic deity, we have to try. We can't just accept extinction as if we were pathetic dodos. One woman, one superbly brilliant but utterly evil woman, brought this disaster down on an innocent human race. As a race, we're far from perfect, but we didn't deserve this—no species capable of love, of kindness, of joy in understanding the universe could have deserved this "doom of stars". I doubt there's a species in the entire Milky Way galaxy which could deserve such a terrible ending.'

De Vries met the other's gaze unblinkingly.

'Don't tell me you haven't had doubts. These craft we are sending out into the dark with their desperate human crew—they're not proper spacecraft. They are just cargo vessels at the end of laser beams hundreds of thousands of astronomical units long. They have very little ability to manoeuvre and can't even stop their flight without external help.'

'The help will be there. The robots we've sent ahead will have constructed braking laser complexes by now.'

De Vries snorted. 'You have great faith in those unreliable lumps of metal. That was the one thing she got right: interstellar travel is virtually impossible without proper autonomous AI units. And would you board one of those flying coffins knowing you will die on it, out there in the darkness?'

It was Fraschini who broke the locked stares first. He turned away and walked up to the great curved plastic shield that kept out the toxic air of Venus.

'So what's the answer? Burrow down into the ground like a fucking worm? Christ, we don't even know if Earth will survive the close passage with Jupiter! You could dig yourself down as far as molten rock and still be obliterated if Jupiter swallows up Earth, like it will probably do to Mars.' He turned. 'I know what's gotten into you, my friend. It's your daughter, isn't it?'

Suddenly De Vries seemed to crumple. His shoulders sagged, and his chin touched his heaving chest.

'Yes, yes! I didn't know what to do when she said she would be on the *Nea Avgi!* Should I try to keep her with me or let her take the infinitesimal chance of survival out there beyond the heliopause! Jupiter's trajectory is chaotic; we can't be certain exactly when the close passage will occur—perhaps we could live out a normal lifespan here on Cloud City One. I wanted to say that to her—but I couldn't. I couldn't keep her with me, Fraschini! My girl, my only girl; the one

I had smiled at when she showed me her simple drawings, the one whose hands I held when I found her crying because her robo-cat had stopped working, the one I comforted when her mother died! And now Saskia's out there in that bloody tin box, along with hundreds of other desperate people. Already it's in the Scattered Disk and soon it will be out there in the great empty gulf between here and Alpha Centauri. I can't even talk to her anymore; the distance is too great!'

Fraschini crossed to him and, much to the latter's surprise, reached out and held his hands.

'But she has a chance. Not her personally, we both know that, but there will be children and they will have children. One day, your descendants will descend in shuttlecraft from their starship after its epic journey, and walk in flowered fields under the twin Centauri suns, knowing they are safe and that humankind has escaped the doom of stars. But we are The Dead; we will be sucked into Jupiter's maw or tossed into the Sun. One way or another, we will not escape. You know that too, and that's why when it came to the moment, you smiled and waved as your daughter boarded the *Nea Avgi*.'

Fraschini was shocked to see a pleading look come into the other's face.

'But they will survive, won't they? They must survive!'

Fraschini knew the time for ratiocination, for weighing of probabilities, had passed.

And so he just smiled.

'Yes, my friend, they will survive.'

And to himself, he thought: *And if not them, then others. Some must survive!*

Two

Jeff Hardy finished his coffee and put the mug down on the table. He looked at the utensil for a while, studying the brown ring near the interior lip with an attention bordering on mindfulness, and thought, *That wasn't bad! Almost tasted like the real stuff!*

He leaned back in the hard, cheap plastic chair and wondered, *Will I ever taste something almost akin to coffee again? There'll be none on the Magellan—not even chicory!*

He became aware Helena Tarkowski was studying him with that unnerving, piercing blue-eyed stare she had.

'Oh, you're back at last,' she observed. 'I thought for a moment you'd mystically transferred your mind to Alpha Centauri and saved yourself the trip.'

He shrugged. 'That may well have been my last cup of real coffee. Some things should be savoured, held in the consciousness for a while, and then stored away as the last of their kind; the last of that particular range of sensations.'

'A simple cup of coffee.'

He leaned forward, slightly diminishing the distance between them. She responded by moving the same distance in the opposite direction. Ignoring her response, he continued, 'Things will be a lot different in flight. We have to take the absolute minimum of mass on board. There can't be one surplus nanogram. The same organic materials will be cycled and recycled over and over again for two hundred and twenty years. We'll literally be drinking our own piss and eating our own shit.' He smiled, showing large, sturdy teeth, 'Let's hope they don't taste like that—but I'm sure we'll adapt. We'll have to.'

She glared at him.

'No doubt you're trying to shock me. But I used to be a surgeon, remember—I've seen a lot more of the more fundamental side of human nature than you have. When was the last time you had to put a small bowel back where it came from, while making sure it still fitted? Being an electronics engineer isn't quite as messy, I believe.'

She stared at him, seeing a medium build, average-height man with a moderately masculine square jaw; strong, if coarse, features and a shock of curly brown hair that resolutely displayed no sign of recession.

He's so average, she thought, *he could be a computer-generated representation of a population statistic.* He, in turn, saw a slender, lithe woman with short, fairish hair cut into a plain bob. He felt certain that if there had still been a need for spectacles she'd be wearing an oversized set.

He hasn't asked me what I do these days, she thought, *It's all about him. No questions about my work on the human brain. Why are all men like this? What will the next lecture be about, I wonder?*

He gave a toothy grin and tried to lighten the conversation, apparently not realising he wasn't very good at that procedure.

'Well, at least the food will be OK. That new yeast strain they've developed is chock full of vitamins, minerals, Omega-3—you name it. You can survive on it and water and need nothing else. You'll love it!'

Two lines appeared between untailored eyebrows as she frowned.

'I'm an old-fashioned girl, Hardy. Nothing beats a medium-rare hunk of juicy Meet, with all the trimmings.'

His grin expanded.

'Old-fashioned, are you? I take it you're aware the word you used is derived from a much older one. One that referred to muscle fibre cut off an animal?'

To his surprise, she shuddered slightly.

'Don't. I don't mind slicing people open, but I can't abide the thought of doing that to an animal.' Suddenly she sighed and turned away from him, looking across the noisily crowded dining hall. Beyond the huge, gently curving transparency of the outer wall, the endless ochre sea of the Venusian cloud deck could be seen, slowly churning beneath a clear blue sky in which a brilliant, oversized sun was blazing. 'But there won't be any animals on the *Magellan,* will there? Not one surplus nanogram, you said. Just the mass of two hundred and forty two prime specimens of *Homo sapiens,* clustered together, breathing the same air the others have just breathed out, smelling the ever-growing stench of people stuffed into a metal can. I believe in the old days they used to do something similar with sardines.'

Then she looked back at him, and her stare was fierce, trenchant.

'But why does it take so long to get there? The nanobots are already in the Centauri system. Come on, you're the oh-so-clever engineer. Why can't we get there in thirty years like they did instead of bloody two hundred and twenty!'

'It's the laws of physics, Helena.'

She grimaced.

'Oh them, those lovely laws that have sent Jupiter hurtling towards us.'

She saw his annoyance and added, hurriedly, 'Go on.'

She'd be seeing an awful lot of this man; it was too soon to make enemies just because they were bores. And Hardy did seem to have scooped the pool on that attribute. Why did he think she wanted a lecture on lightsail travel? She had the distinct impression he was trying to impress the "Little Woman."

Hardy, blissfully unaware of his failure to impress, tried to produce the smile of the serious scientist instead of his usual cocky grin, but, still unsure of whether or not he had succeeded, he began.

'It's a question of mass. The laser complexes have the power to accelerate small masses such as the nanobots to about thirty percent of c—the speed of light,' he added, seeing the frown reappearing and completely misinterpreting it. 'Such a speed is OK for them because we have launched so many, and they're crewless. It's like a fungus throwing out thousands of spores. Most spores will be destroyed or decay, but some will survive, enough to ensure the survival of the species. And we use the same game plan as them. It's possible to accelerate the nanobots to almost relativistic speeds because we can accept a high attrition rate and because we are talking about packages massing a few tonnes rather than—I don't know—gigatonnes. And they can take a much shorter time to get to those speeds because we don't have to worry about fragile humans being squashed by fierce acceleration rates. But the lasers just don't have the power to do the same for the lightsail craft. And even if they could, we can't accept a high attrition rate where people are concerned. Space, even interstellar space, is not empty—Adekola found that out when she accidentally snared a black hole. The lightsail ships have minimal manoeuvring power because they're basically powerless.'

The frown had returned.

'Powerless. How can that be true?'

He grimaced.

'Sorry. Not powerless; obviously, they have internal power for life support, but the power to move them—the thrust—comes from the transfer of momentum from the high-energy photons which impact the lightsail. We simply can't go as fast as the nanobot packages, and even if we could, it would be nearly impossible to avoid a collision. As it is, we're still in contact with the three lightsail craft we've already launched, so it looks like we're doing the right thing.'

'I didn't think they were even out of the Solar system yet.'

His exasperated expression grew more obvious, causing Tarkowski's lips to jerk into the beginnings of a smile.

'No, they're not, but the Solar system is much more crowded than interstellar space. I think they'll make it.'

She stared at him silently, obviously unconvinced.

He grew annoyed at her intransigence.

'Look, this is how it works. The journey can be split into three parts: in the acceleration phase, we climb slowly up to our top speed, averaging one point seven c over the distance. The central third is when we're out of range of the laser complexes here, but we reach our top speed of two point seven c, travelling ballistically. In the meantime, the nanobots have built microbots, the microbots have built macrobots and the macrobots have used local materials to construct laser complexes in the target system, initially drawing energy from Centauri A—which is half as powerful again as the Sun. The third part is when they slow us down, giving us an average speed of one point seven again over the final part, but decreasing rather than increasing.'

'Isn't there a schoolboy error in that plan? How do the nanobots slow down? Sounds like you've got yourself in an infinite regression.'

'Nope, I think we're clever enough to spot an infinite regression when we see one. The mass of each bot package is only about two tonnes, light enough to use magnetic braking on the interstellar medium. The method was understood as far back as the early twenty-first century. And once in the Centauri system they can also use reverse slingshots around massive objects to bleed off the remainder of the momentum. Isn't miniaturisation wonderful? And the Magellan has solid fuel rockets for an emergency braking, should that ever be necessary. Which it won't, of course.'

'Emergency braking rockets? Won't they blast a hole in the sail?'

Hardy gave Tarkowski another quick once-over and decided to try his chances.

'No, no. You don't have to worry your pretty young head about that. The lightsail has an aperture at the centre the exhaust will pass safely through. Nothing at all for you to be concerned about, my dear.'

If there were such things as *Looks-that-could-kill*, Hardy would have been instantly transformed into a mass of smouldering charcoal, but there are not, and so she continued to stare at him, unemotionally, unmoved. Now verging on anger at her lack of response, he said, 'Getting back to the travel time: if you calculate the harmonic mean of those speeds, you get an average of one point nine *c*, which gets us to the Centauri system in two hundred and twenty years.'

There was a strange silence in which they stared at each other. And then she spoke, very slowly and carefully, as if every word was difficult to utter, 'But it won't be us arriving, will it? Everyone who boarded the Magellan will be long gone. We'll be dead. Every one of us.'

***

Karl Gelhardt and Simone Lafayette stood together, close to the giant outer wall of their level of Cloud City One. Outside, the long Venusian day was finally drawing to a close. The cloudless upper atmosphere was well into its transition from brilliant azure to a deep violet-indigo. Already the blue sparkle of Earth was visible in the twilight, and the keen-sighted could discern the dimmer speck of the Moon alongside. But the pair's attention was held by a point of light even brighter than the Earth; a point of light that could be seen to be moving against the fathomless bowl of the darkening sky.

'The *Magellan*,' Lafayette whispered, 'Soon we'll be up there, on the damn thing, waiting to leave behind everything we ever knew.'

Gelhardt caressed her shoulder as he looked down at her. He was a bulky, blond-haired bull of a man, but one bearing a tender, loving expression.

'No, Simone, we've already done that.' He pointed to the coruscant, twinkling point of light that was the home planet. 'We did that when we left Earth. Leaving Venus is not a problem. If ever there was a place which makes Hell look like a country garden, it's Venus.'

She shook her head.

'You know what I mean. It's leaving all the rest of the people back home. All the people with no future, no hope. And all because of that!'

A slim finger pointed at another point of light low down, close to the darkening cloud layer. It was nearly as bright as Earth; perhaps if it had been clear of the horizon it would have been brighter. It seemed to be more than just a simple mathematical point; there was a hint of spherical enormity hovering on the edge of resolution. And there were four dimmer points flanking it; three on one side; one on the other.

Jupiter.

The Destroyer.

A rogue black hole had swept past the giant planet many years earlier, tossing it aside like a toy constructed from thistledown. But in so doing it had introduced chaotic perturbations in the planet's orbit; perturbations which had eventually coalesced into a relentless inward migration.

With the inner planets in its ineluctable path.

It was not yet known whether Earth would be swallowed up by the colossal intruder or would simply pass through its titanic magnetosphere; however, there was little difference between the fates: either way, all life on the surface would be obliterated.

On the surface.

So was there another avenue of escape?

Lafayette turned from the glittering point of light, whose true name was Death, and said to Gelhardt in tones which verged on the pleading, 'Isn't there some other way we can get out of this terrible situation? Yesterday, there was something in the Terrestrial newscast that some people are considering burrowing down into the Earth's crust to escape the heat and radiation. We could leave this hellhole and join them. Be safe. A normal lifespan together! Think of it, Karl—think of it!'

He did not speak for some time; his gaze somehow locked onto that innocent-looking light source. When he did speak, it was only after drawing in a great draft of air in an unnatural shuddering gasp. 'Simone, Simone, I saw that newscast, too. The idea of hiding in the bowels of the Earth—it's just that: an *idea*. They're decades away from being able to do it. And don't you think they've already got an army of people signed up to go, if and when they're ready? Do you really think you can just descend on them and automatically go to the front of the line?' He smiled tenderly. 'If it were me in charge, I'd make sure you did!'

But she was not to be comforted.

'It'd mean staying on Earth; not being flung into infinity, trapped inside a metal tube, hurtling to God knows what. And think about getting old aboard it, becoming sick and feeble while staring at the same grey walls of a metal prison. A prison we couldn't possibly escape from!'

Once again, he was silent, then he drew her to his great frame and nuzzled her hair.

'Simone: we have no choice. This burrowing idea is just that: an idea. It will probably never happen. If it did, would you really want a life trapped in a hole in the ground, never seeing the sky? At least we'll have that once we're in flight. And what if the power was lost down there? There are worse fates—but I'd rather not think about them. There is no possible hope of life surviving on Earth. The same thing will happen to the Cloud Cities because our hold on existence here is incredibly tenuous. The slightest jolt would smash it into fragments. You want children, don't you?'

She nodded dumbly.

'And you would want them, in turn, to have children and so on. I know you do. The *Magellan* is the only way. You're right, we will get old and sick. And eventually, we will be removed from this universe. But your children will live on, and one day they will descend from the Magellan and begin a new life. A new chance for our species. A chance that bloody woman has nearly taken from us.'

'I hate her. I hate her. I hate her!' she said, her voice muffled by the pressure of his chest against her lips.

Gelhardt released her.

'So do we all. But if the Magellan does not launch with enough people to begin again in the Centauri system, then she will have won. Do you see that?'

'Yes,' she said, and looked up at him in the deepening Venusian twilight, 'I will do it.

For my children's children. And so that she does not win.'

Three

As Fraschini stood on the rostrum, he looked down at the sea of faces below. *They're so young!* he thought.

And so they were. The oldest of the throng was thirty-eight, and he was there only because of his specialist knowledge. The median age was twenty five.

They must think of me as an old man, he thought ruefully.

And so they did.

But he had not told them to congregate in the conference hall to discuss the distribution of ages that they demonstrated. Instead, they were here for their final briefing before embarkation.

And they were restless.

A woman (young, of course) near the front of the seated multitude raised her hand.

Her school days are not that far behind her, Fraschini thought as he acknowledged her.

'Dr Fraschini,' she began, 'I must tell you I represent most of the women in this cohort, and we are concerned about one aspect of the planned journey. Or perhaps, to put it more accurately, we have more concerns about one aspect of the plan than all the others. We find all the conditions of this voyage troubling, but this one far more than rest put together.'

'That is to be expected. It is a momentous undertaking.'

'Indeed. We are concerned about the fact that the onboard ratio of females to males is 70:30.'

'You knew this when you were recruited. You knew that you were recruited as a RIF female.'

The woman stood, so she was more on a level with him.

'Yes, that very insulting acronym. "Resourceful" I accept as common knowledge, "Intelligent" goes without saying, otherwise I wouldn't be here. But "Fertile"—that goes into the innermost core of my womanhood. That is no-one's business other than mine. For centuries, women have fought to be free from male domination; to be their own person; to make their own way in the world without being judged on mere physical attributes. And now your crazy plan will throw us back into the twentieth century. What are we to be on the *Magellan*? Concubines? Harem girls? Tell me, doctor!'

Fraschini frowned. He had thought this matter had been cleared up months earlier. Why was it being raised again now?

But he knew why, of course. Then it had been merely a theoretical issue. Now the reality was hurling towards them.

'Tell me—Dr Alisha Andretti isn't it?—what do you think the situation would be on the Magellan a year or two after launch if the ratio was 30:70 female to male?'

'I wouldn't care to speculate.'

'Then I will tell you. After a single year of flight, the mask of civilisation would have slipped and the men would be fighting each other over women. The voyage would be over before it had begun. Destroyed in an orgy of violence.'

'You're underestimating men, surely, doctor?'

'No.' Fraschini was angry now. 'We can't delude ourselves with nice fantasies anymore. We have to accept the world as it is, not as we would like it to be. When that woman brought the black hole into the system, we all had to grow up quickly and leave the nursery. You are all young. Unlike me, your bloodstreams are awash with hormones. However civilised a man is, however fascinated by physics or mathematics, he will not stand by and watch another man gather all the good-looking women to himself. Eventually, he will fight. And the other will fight back. Soon the ship will be a bear-pit of violence and terror.'

'I don't believe you. Men are not like that.'

Fraschini's voice grew louder, as he found himself having to defend a situation which he had thought had been accepted.

'Then you are an innocent child who has spent too long in her books. You may think I am unaware that women are capable of sexual jealousy as well as men, but I am not. However, I am also aware that generally their fists are smaller than men's. I'm afraid you must accept that the "Fertile" part of the "RIF" acronym is as important as the other two. You have two roles on board: one involves being *Resourceful* and *Intelligent*. The other consists of having babies.'

There was a susurration of shock in the great room. He had not been so blunt before.

De Vries was by his side. 'Alberto…' he whispered.

But Fraschini was not to be deflected.

'I did not create the natural order of things; an order which has gradually been hidden under layers of civilised culture, but has been there all along, weakened, subdued. Subdued but not destroyed. The human race cannot be saved by abstract intelligence; by solving mathematical conundrums. It can only be saved by sex. Without that, there will be no men and women to descend from the ship in two hundred years. The only way to avoid the situation I have described is to guarantee that every man will have his own woman to bear his children. And to ensure the converse, women must accept a degree of polygamy. You can call it being a "concubine" or a "harlot" or "houri"—whatever you like. I'm not interested in words but in the survival of humankind.'

'You mean *mankind*, don't you!' someone yelled from near the back of the group.

Fraschini ignored the comment.

'Your breeding does not have to be accomplished through copulation. The ship will have facilities for artificial insemination. It may be possible you will be able to choose to be fertilised through physical contact with only one or two men; ones you feel some emotions for. But you will be fertilised. And you *will* give birth!'

Silence fell.

Then Dr Andretti spoke up again.

'So we are to be breeding cows. After all we have achieved. Just breeding cows.'

Fraschini did not reply directly. Instead, he said, 'You must surely be aware that a great anti-woman sentiment is taking hold on Earth. Because the source of all our current misery was one woman, all women are now being regarded with suspicion. Soon that suspicion will turn to resentment, then outright hatred. Even if Earth were to survive, the hatred of women that has been engendered will not fade away.'

'That's crazy,' Andretti said, 'women don't hate all men because of Hitler or Genghis Khan!'

'These are not days when calm contemplation is much in abundance. People are afraid, terrified, and they are right to be afraid, terrified. Most of them will not survive long enough to know the joys of arthritis and failing hearts. They are about to be thrown into the furnace.

'Whatever awaits you on the Magellan will be better than what they will experience. So no more whining, just gratitude.'

There was a protracted silence.

Then Fraschini was slightly surprised to see the anger fade slowly from Andretti's face and, finally, she looked down and nodded.

'I agree. I felt I had to say something in case there was some aspect I had missed or misunderstood.

'But there is not. I will not mention it again.'

***

The farewell party hardly deserved the name. Although the room was big enough to easily contain all the two hundred and forty-two crew, plus the highest echelons of Cloud City One's management, there was a distinct tendency for the throng to subdivide itself into small subsections. Most of the men, for instance, found they had been left to unwillingly create male-only gatherings as if the women present had decided they wanted as little as possible to do with them. There was a distinct lack of jollity, even basic camaraderie. The absence of alcohol or psychotropic drugs might have had something to do with that, as the Venusian Cloud Cities were austere places, with no space for distilleries or pharmacological laboratories. The cities had one purpose, one function, only and that was to hurl the great lightsail ships into the gulf beyond the Solar system. No activity, no endeavour, which did not contribute to that purpose was permitted. Hence the subdued nature of the "party."

And so it was difficult for most of those present to find much cause for relaxation or jollity. The great Firing Point was now only days away and cast an ever-deepening shadow over all their minds. What had once seemed to be merely an abstraction, a theoretical construct, or the promise of a marvellous adventure, now hung over them like a tremendous boulder supported by an unravelling thread.

Fraschini, De Vries and a few others of the highest echelon, watched their protégés with equally sombre expressions, finding it just as difficult as the young people to find something light-hearted to say. No witticisms or off-colour jokes came to their lips. Instead they felt an inchoate sense of guilt, a feeling that somehow they had betrayed the youthful promise of these young lives. Every one of the young people standing in that room, glumly sipping their fruit juices,

20

was an example of the very best and brightest of the human race. Tested for intelligence, emotional stability; tested for recessive genes; tested for incipient autoimmune conditions. In fact, they had been tested for every aspect that might be remotely relevant to survival on board a starship. The women matched the men in every intellectual aspect; had passed the exact same tests, overcome the exact same level of challenges, and yet had been chosen not only for those attributes but for something much more basic, more animalistic. Every one of them had been checked to see if she was fertile and could be expected to bear healthy children. That was as least as important as their intelligence, their ingenuity, their physical courage, their mental strength.

Fraschini gave what he hoped was an inaudible sigh. It was deeply unfair—but it was just one more example of unfairness in this grim universe. Sometimes he had felt he was a stern parent, admonishing a recalcitrant child with the mantra: *Life's not fair!*

And in many ways he felt like a parent to these youngsters, felt the heavy load of responsibility pressing down on him. Sometimes he felt the best thing would be to let them all go back to their families and live out as normal a life as they could manage. It would be decades yet before things got really bad: before the earthquakes and the firestorms became a threat to all organic life. Occasionally, a candidate had rebelled against the strict life on the Cloud City and had refused to continue with the arduous training. Such people had been allowed to return to Earth on the returning shuttle, before they could spread the virus of doubt, of despair.

But Fraschini knew not many more young people would be coming from Earth. Both of the two global Governments were disintegrating, dissolving, under the terrible strain of the doom of stars. They would not be in existence much longer, and the supply of young men and RIF women would be turned off.

Unlike the barely speaking volunteers, he was reasonably sure who it had been who had brought this cataclysm down on the human race; that the woman who had received all the blame, the corrosive hatred, for the act, had in fact been an innocent dupe. There was another woman who both he and Fraschini strongly suspected had been the instrument of annihilation. They had studied the newscasts that had fawned over her, had adored her like a goddess bringing salvation to a troubled world.

21

Yet someone who had looked like a goddess, who had been superhuman in both beauty and intellect, how could such a being have been corrupted by the mere promise of worldly gain? Were humans really so weak?

The controllers of Cloud City One had never mentioned their suspicions to their new recruits. It was all dead history now; whoever had done that appalling thing—it had been done, it was over. Now there was only survival to consider. Survival—the ultimate instinct, the same instinct that drove the animal caught in a trap to bite and claw and, if necessary, rip off a limb in order to escape.

And now the entire human race was caught in a trap more terrible than had ever been imagined before. And these young people were the only hope that some small fragment would escape from the trap. What did it matter who had created the trap?—escape was the only goal, the only imperative.

He, De Vries and the other high officials, were attempting to "circulate" among the morose crew, desperately trying to think of something light-hearted to say. He had always had the ability to attach names to faces and he paused to talk to a bulky-looking man whom he knew to be named Gelhardt who, unusually, had a woman by his side; a frail-looking person who looked as if she would be transparent if viewed against a bright light.

'How are you feeling?' he asked the man, the same question as he had posed to five others.

'Nervous,' the other answered, 'it never really felt real until a few days ago. It just seemed to be something that would happen to someone else. But I know now it's real—and it's happening to me!'

Fraschini gave an awkward smile. He had never been very good at smiling on demand—he had not had much practice. He was about to mouth a platitude and move on to the next glum-looking would-be astronaut when the small woman touched his arm, forcing him to look down at her.

'Dr Fraschini,' she said, her large eyes glistening with unshed moisture, 'what do you think our chances are?'

He had hoped not to be faced with that question, but here it was.

He was an honest man; anything other than honesty would be to insult his charges.

'They're not high,' he said, 'but they're not zero. But the chances of anything surviving here are zero. That's all I can offer.'

22

'But if we were to stay here, not to go on the ship I mean, we'd live a normal life. Wouldn't we?'

He lowered his large grey-haired head so he could see her more directly.

'My dear—"Lafayette" isn't it?—the whole purpose of these cities is to launch the lightsail craft. They have no other function. I left my wife to come here; she refused to leave Earth. That was ten years ago. All that time, I've watched Jupiter grow larger in the Venusian skies. It's even larger in the Terrestrial skies. Most of the people know something is wrong; that the world isn't what it used to be. The crazy fluctuations in the climate, the huge Moon in the skies, the great tides. But their Governments have kept the truth from them because the truth would drive them mad. You are one of the chosen ones, you have had the veil of half-truths, of obfuscations, of actual lies, lifted and the horrible reality revealed. But in return you have been given a chance—however small, it's more than they will have. It will not be long before the truth finally gets out in the population at large. And I wouldn't want to be on Earth when that happens.

'But you will be spared that. They and their children and their grandchildren have no chance. But you have. Do you understand?'

Lafayette bowed her head, as if in shame.

'Yes, doctor, I understand.'

Gelhardt gave an awkward smile at Fraschini, who nodded and moved on to the next person.

An hour later, he felt he had done enough and gradually made his way to the rear of the room where his fellows had already gathered.

They greeted him with wan smiles and he responded weakly, as if he were spending all his energy on pushing through a viscous liquid. He approached De Vries who suddenly looked away and down at a pocket in his jacket. He pulled out his communicator and stared at the message. Fraschini had never seen a face go literally white with shock before but then he did. Wordless, De Vries left the room in a great hurry.

The others stared after him dumbly but only Fraschini had the seniority to follow De Vries.

Which he did.

He knocked on his friend's door without response. But Fraschini knew De Vries was within and without further delay he entered.

23

There he found his friend face down on his bed. He shook him gently.

'Cornelius, what's wrong?'

De Vries turned slowly, presenting an ashen face to his friend. He held the communicator up so Fraschini could read the message.

'They had just crossed the aphelion of Sedna,' De Vries whispered, 'they were doing so well.'

In growing horror, Fraschini read and re-read the short message.

All contact with the Nea Avgi has been lost.

Four

When De Vries met the others in the Conference Room, Fraschini could tell instantly the man had not slept at all since receiving that terrible message. Fraschini had warned the others, and they all leapt to their feet as De Vries entered, uttering words of condolence, offering hope. De Vries had simply nodded in recognition of their concern and sat limply at the table, his eyes searching for and finding Fraschini.

'Any news?' he said in a voice that suggested his vocal apparatus had been transformed into sanding paper.

Fraschini was a man who believed in the truth at all costs, but he had never been in a situation like this before. There were no open wounds on his friend's body, no effusions of blood, but Fraschini knew the other was in pain, gripped in the jaws of bitter suffering. He wanted to comfort, to offer hope and assuage his friend's torment—but he could not.

'No,' he finally said, forcing the dread word into being. 'Nothing.'

De Vries reached across the table, reaching for his friend's hands. At first, Fraschini instinctively drew back, repelled by this intimacy from another man, but realising the other's need, he accepted the icy grasp.

'The time delay,' De Vries said. 'That's it—it takes a long time to get here from the Scattered Disk. The delay; perhaps they had a communications glitch; and are back on course now. The message simply hasn't reached us yet, just like in Olber's Paradox, Alberto. That's it, isn't it?'

Fraschini slowly removed his hands from the other's grasp and looked him full in the eyes.

'No, that's not it. The carrier wave is permanently on at Solar distances, even when they're not talking to us. It vanished instantly, twelve hours ago, Venus Time. One hour ago, I ordered the lasers to stop directing power at the Nea Avgi. They're gone, Cornelius.'

De Vries' face changed instantly from a flaccid mask of misery to a reddened visage of hate. He reached across the table and sank steel fingers into Fraschini's throat.

'No, you bastard! Turn them back on! They're still out there! Saskia is out there! I won't let you kill her! I'll send this base crashing down onto Venus' surface if I have to! She's out there in the darkness!'

The other officials rushed to Fraschini's side and carefully removed De Vries' fingers from his throat. Fraschini shook his head, unable to utter a word for a while, and accepted a glass of water from one of the others without looking at them. Then he finally could speak, although with frequent pauses as he gulped in the room's warm air.

'No, Cornelius, no. The long-range radar has detected several large pieces of debris near the Nea Avgi's last known position. There must have been a collision.'

De Vries leaned back in his chair, seemingly no longer aware he had tried to murder his superior.

'It's true then. My beautiful, beautiful, brave girl. Killed in the cold dark. Killed just as the journey was beginning. All for nothing. Absolutely nothing.'

Abruptly, he stood and slowly scanned the officials in the room, coming to Fraschini last.

'You're all dead, you know that, don't you? Oh, you're walking around with your grand ideas, your heads full of equations, but you're really dead. And not just you—everybody. This whole stupid plan doesn't have a chance, not one fucking chance. The entire human race is just a pack of rats in a trap, desperately squirming and squealing as they try to escape. But they won't escape. There's no way out. This crazy idea you can send tin boxes full of people to another star in a journey of hundreds of years—what madman would come up with an idea like that? It's laughable—no, not laughable, it's too tragic for that! It's pitiful!'

'Cornelius,' Fraschini said, very gently, 'you are one of the brilliant minds who helped design the laser array. It's as much your idea as anybody here.'

'I was wrong. I thought we had a chance. I was blinded by false hope, a naïve child playing with a plastic construction toy. One by one, all those craft will fail. Some, like Saskia's, will fail right at the start, some will fail at the halfway point, some will fail just as the destination seems within their grasp. But they will all fail. So I'll tell you what we should have done instead.'

'What would that be, my friend?'

26

De Vries sat again, this time at the head of the table so he could hold them all in his fervent stare.

'We should have behaved like adults. Like brave men and women, not whining little infants. We should have accepted our fate even though it was the greatest, most tremendous injustice in all of human history, as it will end human history. One individual out of all the billions of humans; one who wielded too much power for her mind to process properly, powers only a god should have.

'But all that doesn't matter now. Nothing matters. We must send out a broadcast to the people of Earth telling them their Governments have been lying to them. That all the climatic disasters they have been enduring are not just temporary problems but the harbinger of worse things; much, much worse. Like their extinction.

'And so, everyone must be given pills so that they can pass at a time of their own choosing, calmly, softly, gently. No pain. They are simply the innocent victims of bad luck on a Cosmic scale.'

Suddenly, he leapt to his feet, eyes blazing, spittle flying from his lips.

'And no more innocent lives must be wasted on sending young people to die out there in an environment never meant for humans. The Lightsail Project is over. And I, personally, will tell all those people here that they are victims of old men's fantasies. That they can go home!'

And with that, he swayed drunkenly for a few seconds.

And then collapsed.

**

Later in what the clock said was "afternoon" Fraschini visited De Vries in the infirmary. He stopped outside the cubicle to have a word with the doctor in charge.

'How is he now?' he asked.

The young woman gave a momentary smile.

'Physically, he's fine. His obs all come out normal for a man of his age. I would say the behaviour you describe and the brief period of unconsciousness are both down to shock. He has had a terrible blow, and it would be a surprise if it hadn't badly affected him. It's truly a terrible blow for anyone.'

Fraschini, who had no children, nodded and said, 'Can I see him now?'

'Yes, he's fully alert now, and in fact, he's been asking to see you. Go on in.'

Fraschini drew the plastic curtain aside to find De Vries fully clothed and lying on top of the bed.

'Alberto,' De Vries said, in a weak, halting voice, 'I'm sorry if I alarmed you. It was like having a black cloak suddenly thrown over me. I could hardly see. I could hardly hear. I just had this rage inside me that I wanted to get out. I wanted to lash out at everyone. I wanted to hurt them—I don't know why.'

Fraschini sat on the edge of the bed, looking at De Vries.

'You've had a terrible blow. We all feel for your loss.'

De Vries turned his gaze from Fraschini and seemed to be looking through the gap between the curtain and its support, out into the busy infirmary.

'Thank you. But that's all anyone ever says, isn't it? "I'm sorry for your loss." But they can't *feel* it. They can't feel it until it happens to them. You, Alberto, your work is your children. Your offspring are equations, beautiful, elegant equations. But equations don't bleed. They don't suffer.'

Fraschini was silent. No words came to his mind.

De Vries turned to him.

'I know now what we've been doing here has been a waste of time, a terrible, terrible waste. I meant what I said in my anger. There's no escape.'

'Why do you say that, my friend? Why? Have you forgotten that the Lightsail Project was born from hope, from the desire to save young people?—not to kill them.'

'But why are we doing it? Those who board the *Magellan* will never see Alpha Centauri any more than you will. How many people will live and die without seeing the Promised Land? And what does it matter? When an individual dies, the human race dies with him from his point of view. He may as well be the Last Man; he would never know. But we're not striving to save an individual or a group of individuals, are we? We're striving to save an abstraction—the human race, humanity, humankind—what they used to call "mankind". But it doesn't exist—there are only individuals. We have no right to ask anyone to get on board those flying coffins.'

28

'We didn't capture them; we didn't slip a narcotic into their drinks and abduct them. We gave them a choice to join the project or to stay. And there's a flaw in your logic: If there are only individuals, then *humanity* cannot be an abstract concept. It is the sum total of all individuals alive at any point. And that collection has a history—one that stretches back to the beginning of the Cenozoic when the primates arose after the planetoid impact had exterminated the dinosaurs. The dinosaurs faced their own doom of stars, and they failed the test. As far as we know, we are the only intelligent race in this galaxy. There may be intelligences greater than ours in other galaxies, but looking around at this one—we are it. Who knows what we could achieve if we were given a second chance? We are perhaps the Cosmos' only chance to understand itself, to find a purpose.'

'Maybe there is no purpose.'

'Until that has been demonstrated mathematically, I choose to believe there is. And if there is a purpose, it is our duty to fulfil that purpose and spread consciousness throughout space.'

'Consciousness that must die.'

Fraschini shook his head.

'No-one destroys themselves simply because life is finite. What life wants is more life, abundant life. I repeat, it's our duty to fulfil the cosmic purpose. The extinction of humanity will prevent that.'

De Vries' face showed a weak expression, a ghost of a smile that played for an instant on his grey lips.

'I follow your syllogism, Alberto. The conclusion is *Humanity must not become extinct.*'

A silence fell. Fraschini had said all he could say. De Vries stared at the gap at the side of the curtain.

Then he turned to Fraschini.

'You win, Alberto. I will rejoin the Lightsail Project, and I will work for its successful conclusion, its resolution. But I won't do it for you.'

Fraschini raised a furry white eyebrow.

'Then for whom are you doing it?'

De Vries raised himself from the pillow. He was alert and strong again.

'Saskia. I will do it for my beautiful, brave girl. She must not have died in vain.'

Five

A peculiar object hung over the sulfurous yellow clouds of Venus.

At first, the human eye would only see a gigantic rectangular structure, blazing fiercely in the light of the nearby Sun. It was an impressive creation, at least seven kilometres across, yet only nanometres thick. It blazed so bright for it had near-perfect reflectivity.

And both diameter, thickness and reflectivity were vital for its function.

The thickness minimised the mass of such a vast construction.

The reflectivity was necessary because gigantic amounts of energy were soon to descend upon that surface, for the great rectangle was a light sail, destined to be energised by lasers of unimaginable power.

And the diameter was necessary to catch as much as possible of that torrent of energy at tremendous, ever-increasing, distances because this journey was not to be a trivial jaunt around the Solar system.

No, this journey would be *interstellar*.

Eventually, the dazzled human eye would notice something else. Behind the incredibly vast light sail was another object, one which was attached to the sail.

It was in two quite distinct sections: one was an extremely long cylinder made of a substance considerably less lustrous than the sail. At the midpoint of the tube was a kind of collar from which sprang four equally-spaced spokes, connecting the cylinder to a tremendous encircling ring.

The eye, dazzled by the size and brilliance of the sail, could not easily determine the scale of this secondary structure, but it also was huge; appearing small only when compared to the curvature of the Hell-planet it orbited, and the vastness of space beyond. The cylinder was windowless, indeed, almost entirely featureless, its dull grey surface broken only by a cluster of antennas at both ends, which were the ship's collision detection apparatus.

Together sail, cylinder and ring comprised the lightsail-starship Magellan; now moved to geostationary orbit above the Sun's second planet.

Beneath it, but also in orbit, were a series of equally immense structures, displaying gently curving dishes on the sides opposed to the planet, from the surfaces of which huge cylinders protruded. These, the observer would soon realise, were an array of Terawatt lasers. Lasers which were at present quiet and still but ready at the throw of a switch to send perfectly collimated beams of power onto the Magellan's sail.

And the moment at which they would spring into blazing life— the Firing Point—was now very close.

Jeff Hardy had very mixed emotions as he looked down at the orbiting laser array as he stood at one of the Magellan's viewscreens. (No windows were allowed to weaken the central cylinder's seamless hull.) Being closer to Venus, each array did not stay long in the field of view, but almost before it had slipped off to the left it was replaced by another identically looking one. Because Venus' spin was clockwise, any object in a stable orbit around it had to spin in the same way, and hence moved from right to left from his viewpoint. For a moment, a great wave of pride passed through him. *We have achieved so much!* he thought. While maintaining a façade of continuing hostility to avoid arousing suspicion, the Eastranian and Westranian governments, having long understood the existential peril they both faced, had secretly pooled all resources. Under cover of a fictitious accelerated arms-race they had completed the tentative plans to build the Cloud Cities. But while those bases had been envisaged initially as being purely for research, they had been repurposed as platforms from which—in an astoundingly short time—the Governments had constructed both the laser array and the first lightsail craft.

Incredible what you can do in order to escape a sentence of death, he thought, somewhat cynically, *if only they had learned to co-operate earlier!*

But that was unfair, he concluded, *no one could have foreseen Adekola's epic crime.*

Hardy's emotions as he looked down upon the lasers, and possibly Cloud City One, were mixed because although he was glad that the incessant rounds of training had finally ended, it was also the case that the mission for which he had been prepared was about to go from tedious theory to grim reality.

And the full magnitude of that reality was rapidly crystallising in his mind. After each training session had ended, he would go to his room, pour himself a coffee, and relax. He had long since given up on the Terrestrial news; there were only so many reports on ever-worsening disasters the human mind could take. It was now undeniable the situation on Earth was deteriorating rapidly and that the Westranian and Eastranian Governments didn't have long to live. Soon the supply of RIF females and young, adventurous males would first falter and then dry up—forever.

But now, there would be no more switching off the study of those theories and techniques as he had done in the days when he could relax with an improbable adventure on the video.

All the theories were about to become a reality. Mistakes which he had laughed off in training might now be fatal. All the video adventures in the Solar system couldn't change that.

And there had been the seismic shock of hearing of the Nea Avgi's fate.

He would never forget how De Vries had shuffled to the front of the rostrum, seemingly having aged ten years since Hardy had last seen him—a mere twenty-four hours previously. He had spoken in a strained, feeble voice, requiring an increase in the electronic amplification for his words to be heard. When he had finished his gut-wrenching story, Fraschini had joined him.

'The situation has changed,' he had said. 'We have never tried to hide the dangers of your undertaking from you. We did not attempt to downplay the immensity of the peril you will face out there. And so there was absolutely no question of us trying to hide this fresh disaster from you. That would have been deeply cowardly, and when you discovered the truth, as you assuredly would have done, you would have hated and despised us. And rightly so.' He paused. 'But now theoretical dangers have become a bitter reality. Perhaps we tried to achieve what cannot be achieved. My fellows and I are old men, and traditionally old men have sent young men into danger in foreign lands while the elders stayed home and drew lines on maps. And so I say to you, if any of you feel you have not been told the absolute truth during your time on Cloud City One, that you have been deceived about the nature of what we are asking you to do, you may leave the project now and return to Earth. Nothing more will be said, and the laser complex will never fire again.'

Everyone in the throng below him had turned at the moment and looked into their neighbour's eyes.

But no one had resigned.

Not one.

And when De Vries said goodbye to his protégés for the last time, a great round of applause and cheering had echoed and re-echoed around the great room.

And so Hardy was now aboard the Magellan—the successor to the Nea Avgi.

Straining his eyes, he thought for a moment he could catch the scintillating point of light which was Cloud City One, floating serenely above the sulfur-stained clouds of the Venusian troposphere, but he couldn't be sure. It had been just a short hop in a shuttle from that city to the Magellan, but he wasn't sure how great the distance had been and if it were really possible to glimpse his former home.

His former home. A collection of metal globes floating in an alien atmosphere—when had he started to think of such a thing as "Home"? That innocent phrase sent a stab of fear through his heart. Had he been a cocksure fool signing up for this project? After all, the close passage was still decades away; long enough to get things done, to love a great many women—but probably not to engender any children.

That would not be a good idea on Earth or Venus.

His peripheral vision told him someone had joined him at the viewscreen, someone with tumbling red hair. He turned and discovered it was Susannah Reid.

'How are you feeling?' she enquired, meeting his gaze. She was as tall as he.

He felt annoyed. Was his nervousness as apparent as that?

'I'm OK. How about you?'

'Not too bad.'

She brushed past him to place her hands on the viewscreen, perhaps forgetting it was not a window. As she passed, Hardy had a momentary impression of warm, curved softness making contact for a delicious instant, and he stepped away slightly so he could admire her well-rounded profile. *70:30*, he thought to himself, *70:30! Maybe this trip would be worth it after all!*

Perhaps aware of his none-too-subtle stare, she turned to him and smiled. It surprised Hardy to see she was expertly made up, even down to the scarlet nails. Women had very rarely displayed their femininity on the Cloud City; dressing mostly in plain, ultra-drab navy boilersuits. No doubt Fraschini had wanted his students to keep their minds on their work. But clearly, some women had wanted to hang on to their allure for as long as possible, and Reid had certainly succeeded. She was stunning.

She accepted his stare for some time and then gave a little giggle.

'What is it? Do I have spinach on my teeth?'

A younger Hardy might have blushed; as it was, he understood he'd been staring at the woman.

'Sorry,' he said, 'you look so different with...'

'My clothes on?' she said, archly.

Hardy could have sworn that now he was blushing. His cheeks definitely felt warm.

'No, I mean out of your work clothes. Sorry, I mean...'

Of course that's what I meant! I've never seen her in...

Hardy left the thought unfinished; it was far too soon for any of that.

Her smile grew wider.

'Dear me, I've embarrassed you. I do believe you're blushing!'

'No, no, it's just a bit warm here. Forgive me—it's Susannah, isn't it?'

She extended a warm, soft hand for him to shake; he complied, perhaps holding her hand slightly too long.

'That's me. Astrophysicist of this parish.'

Hardy didn't catch the old-fashioned allusion, and instead said, 'Well, you certainly don't look like...'

Reid raised a carmine-tipped finger.

'Now, now, Jeff. Don't say it. I thought you were a refugee from Earth, not the Twenty-first century! Are all astrophysicists supposed to be flat-chested with buck-teeth?'

'No, I mean...'

He spluttered to a halt. He didn't usually behave like a callow adolescent with women, but...

She let him off the hook and turned back to the viewscreen.

'You know people have dreamed about this for centuries.'

'What—becoming extinct?'

'No, silly. About sailing the void with lightsail craft. Do you know the first person to suggest the possibility was Kepler in a letter to Galileo?'

'Kepler? Galileo? Weren't they space probes back in the old days?'

Two perfectly tailored eyebrows arched themselves above deep green eyes.

'I'll pretend you didn't say that. And then, Jules Verne was the first to come up with the idea of travelling to the stars on solar wings.'

'You're not getting any clearer.'

She ignored the comment.

'And then we have the greats like Tsiolkovsky, who said, and I quote, "Earth is the cradle of humanity, but Man cannot stay in the cradle forever."'

Hardy shrugged.

'Fine words–but the reality is a little more of a challenge. Perhaps if he were on board, he might change his mind.'

But it was as if Hardy were no longer there and she was reciting a litany of those who had paved the way for Project Lightsail.

'And perhaps the final step was taken in the twentieth century with greats such as György and Forward.'

Hardy fought back a growing urge to crush her to his chest and instead said, somewhat thickly, 'Well, that was interesting. But what brought you onto this modern-day *Flying Dutchman*?'

She turned away from the viewscreen and the panorama of the laser complex silhouetted against the ochre clouds.

'I know I'm going to die on this tub. But I would do the same if I'd stayed in Westrania. And I think I'll make it to interstellar space before I pop. What better way for an astrophysicist to go out?'

Reid gave one more smile and walked off.

But she hadn't gone far before casting a quick glance over her shoulder.

'And there are a lot of men on board.'

***

Slowly but assuredly, the seconds ticked away, seeming to move faster and faster as they were swallowed up into the maw of the past. Very shortly now, Fraschini would give the sign that the Firing Point had finally arrived, and the immense laser array would awake from its slumber.

Captain Gelhardt had ordered the entire crew into the meeting room, which was at the centre of the cylindrical body of the Magellan, equidistant from the heavily-shielded prow and stern.

No-one had elected Gelhardt. He had been given the rank by complex algorithms which had studied all the students' test results,

35

and, by a weighting schema which only the highest order of Cloud City One officials understood, had determined he was the candidate best suited for that responsibility. And it seemed the algorithms had not erred: his bulky physique had fitted perfectly into the costume of Captain—a costume precisely the same as everyone else except for a badge sewn into the fabric, whose pattern of colours indicated his status and specialities to all those present.

Every one of the two hundred and forty-two crew members felt the tension in the air as if it were a form of static electricity. It felt to Hardy that blue sparks would soon be flying from his fingers. Behind Gelhardt was a large digital clock displaying a number written in green fluorescent symbols: a number constantly decreasing as the dread Firing Point neared.

Gelhardt was standing behind a lectern, in a posture which reminded some of the crew of how presidents of Westrania and Eastrania had delivered their important messages.

Messages which now weren't worth a damn.

Gelhardt was holding a question-and-answer session.

'For those of you who don't have an astronautical background, I will explain we will gradually adopt an acceleration of up to a maximum of about a third of a gee—about the same as the gravity of Mars. At that acceleration, we would reach Alpha in about five years.'

There was a confused noise from some of the crew.

One lifted a hand.

'Five years? That's good news. I thought it was two hundred and twenty years.'

Gelhardt smiled.

'That would be true if we could maintain that acceleration. We would arrive at Alpha at about eighty seven percent of the speed of light. But that's obviously impossible. Lorentz factors would kick in long before then, even if we could continue to receive the power flow from the lasers. Our rate of acceleration will indeed peak at about one third gee for a short time but will continuously decrease, for various reasons I won't bore you with, as we approach our maximum velocity and become significantly distant from Venus. Indeed, significantly distant from the entire Solar system. We will reach a maximum 2.7 percent of light speed at about the halfway point, but our average speed over the whole journey will be only 1.9 percent of light speed, rising from zero at the Firing Point and falling to zero at the Centauri system.' He paused and gave an unconvincing laugh. 'At least, I hope it will be zero at the Centauri system!'

No-one laughed. A man, looking young even by the group's standards, was the next to state a problem.

'You say one-third gee will be our *maximum* acceleration. But that means, for most of the time, we'll be virtually weightless. Human beings can't function at those levels of gravitational pull. That's been known for centuries.'

Gelhardt gave a small wince of annoyance. He knew this was supposed to be a review of all they had learned during their training, but this was basic stuff they had covered right at the beginning!

'That's what the outer ring is for, Stephen,' he said, carefully and slowly. 'It spins, remember. It will provide at least eighty percent of Earth-normal through centrifugal force. That should be enough for you as long as you aren't worried you'll be standing on your head as seen from the main hull!'

This time, a few people did laugh, and a crestfallen Stephen did not speak again during the meeting.

Gelhardt looked down at the other earnest faces.

'Any more basic facts anybody wants to check on?' He pointed at a young woman near the rostrum. 'Lara—radiation? What do you remember about that issue?'

She smiled. She knew all about the techniques used to minimise that particular danger.

'Well, the ship generates its own magnetosphere, of course, using superconducting coils. We can ignore neutrons, as any we encounter will be thermal, and only the highest-energy charged particles will get through our magnetic shield. But we can expect that number to increase when we are out of the Solar magnetosphere. And so, the gap between the vacuum layer and the outer hull is packed with hydrogen-rich materials which are good at absorption and will reduce secondaries. And we all remember that rather invasive gene transfer treatment on the Cloud City, which gave us the relevant genes from tardigrades and *Deinococcus radiodurans*. The final line of defence, of course, is the standard battery of drugs.'

Gelhardt nodded, his look of satisfaction unmistakable on his broad features.

'One more before we get to our Firing Point stations. Who can tell me about the bottleneck issue? And I don't mean any booze you might have managed to sneak on board!'

More people laughed that time. Gelhardt's air of authority, of masculine confidence, was causing a wave of relaxation to pass through the crew. Even their postures looked less tense.

Another young woman spoke.

'It's to do with the Founder Effect. There is a minimum size for a population to prosper and increase without falling prey to recessive gene combinations and genetic drift. Some sources put the minimum population at about one hundred; others say double that number. It's the reason why we have the somewhat unnatural sex ratio on board.'

'Do we have any other techniques for mitigating the Founder Effect?'

'Yes. We have electronic copies of the gametes of people who are not on board. When the time comes, these can be converted into biological constructs and combined in any number of ways.'

'Very good. Now give me an example of the bottleneck issue from human history. Or prehistory.'

She gave an eager nod.

'Yes, that would be the Toba Supervolcano eruption in Indonesia about seventy-five thousand years ago. It is calculated it caused a volcanic winter lasting at least ten years and reduced the global human population to no more than two thousand individuals.' She stopped and looked around at her fellow refugees. 'That was the first time humanity almost went extinct. We are living in the second.'

The air of relaxation, almost a state of levity, vanished instantly at the woman's grave words.

Gelhardt acted at once to restore confidence.

'Thank you, Adana. Let us all remember we got through that pinch point, that near-extinction event. As a race, we're fighters. We don't give in, give up; we can take anything this universe can throw at us. Generations to come will hold us in awe as the people who saved the entire species.' He looked around. 'My God, are we going to let that Adekola woman kill us all off?' He paused. 'Well—are we!'

The huge room echoed and re-echoed as the entire crowd raised their fists and yelled, 'No! Hell, no!'

***

Some days later, Gelhardt looked around the near-empty room, his vision falling at last on the clock and its dread message of fleeting time. Only minutes remained now, and the irrevocable decision would be actualised. He had watched the students, now most definitely renamed "The Crew", depart to take up their stations. Unlike in the early days of spaceflight, there would be no need to be strapped into chairs or lie on couches. The acceleration would build up gradually as the Magellan's tremendous inertia was overcome and, even at its maximum, would be no more than third Earth-normal. Everything would be very calm, very gentle.

And very slow.

At its greatest velocity, the Magellan would be travelling faster than any other human-constructed structure, other than its sister lightsail craft. The Zheng He and the Resurgam were now preparing respectively to exit and enter the gigantic Oort Cloud—but their speeds, and that yet to be attained by the Magellan, were the merest crawl in cosmic terms. The enormous dark and empty gulf between the Sun and the nearest stars still mocked the ingenuity of Homo sapiens.

And what of the Nea Avgi? How hollow that name—"New Hope"—had proved to be when tested against bitter reality.

He felt a gentle touch on his elbow and turned to look at Lafayette.

'Let's go to our room,' she said. 'You've done all you can to prepare them. If they're not ready now, they never will be.'

He nodded and was about to descend from the rostrum when she touched him again.

'Karl, what do you really think? Can we do it?'

He smiled.

'Only one way to find out.'

Behind them, the digital clock displayed 00:00:00.

Below them, Fraschini sent the fateful command.

Instantly, obediently, the colossal laser array awoke.

There was a brief delay, one almost undetectable by mere human senses, then, like the dawn of creation itself—there was light! Finally, the orbiting array, the last magnificent technological achievement of dying Solarian humanity, had reached the Firing Point.

A silent storm of energetic photons flashed invisibly out, connecting the vessel's colossal light sail to the laser projectors. The

39

crew felt nothing despite the supernal power of those Terawatt lasers, now amply powered by the miniature suns of their fusion reactors, so titanic was their target's mass, a mass that had to be woken from its own inertial sleep.

But slowly, almost unnoticeably, that target, the mighty Magellan, began to move away from the furiously radiating projectors and the dead ochre crescent of dead Venus.

Some of the crew watched the yellow crescent shrink behind them, feeling a growing, gnawing sense of loss, the sharp pains of an irrevocable parting. Some watched stolidly; some wept.

Some could not watch at all.

But all knew that The Angel of Death had brushed close to them.

And all alike knew that their fate was now inescapably one with the starship.

Further and further behind them was only a doomed system of planets, destined for destruction in a once orderly system gone mad.

And chief among those losses would be a blue-white world they had once called home.

The Oort Cloud

One

Tar-Arak climbed to the top of the ridge and gazed out across the plain. In the blue distance rose the perfectly symmetrical cone of Mount Oblivion; a warning stream of volcanic vapours billowing from the black, scoria-strewn peak.

Tar-Arak looked around, turning his massive head with its mane of golden hair, his piercing sapphire eyes, back and forth, using his *erz-sense* to check for danger.

The land seemed safe. Perhaps it was time to resume this quest to find the famed Crystal Labyrinth in the fiery interior of Mount Oblivion.

He felt a soft hand reach up to touch his mighty shoulder. Smiling, he looked down to gaze upon the sweet face of Princess Ayrana, looking lovelier than ever in the glow of the morning sun, framed with the great sweep of coppery hair that held the secret only she and her aged father, the High Emperor of the Ice Lands, knew.

'My Lord,' she said, in a voice as sweet as the crystal streams of far Arlandia, 'we cannot tarry here. I feel danger is near. I'm sure Maggaron the Black will have gotten wind of our route and will not be far behind us.'

Tar-Arak smiled and placed a massive hand on the blue skin of her slender shoulder.

'Don't fear, Princess. I would gladly fight Maggaron and his Insect Hordes a thousand times over before I would abandon this quest. But you are right—this beautiful land may well be hiding a terrible secret.'

She smiled with sweet relief and followed her Master down the steep slope to the green floodplain of the tremendous River Caradoth.

As they looked around, Mount Oblivion gave a throaty rumble as if warning the dauntless pair of imminent danger.

Nor was that warning empty.

There was a terrible, bestial roar from the nearby thicket, and at once a horde of the colossal Fighting Apes burst out, beating their hands on their broad chests in slavering triumph.

'Back,' Tar-Arak cried, 'Get behind me, Ayrana! You can play no part in this combat!'

Even as those words left his lips, the first Fighting Ape was on him, its fearsome canines reaching for his throat.

Tar-Arak grasped the horrific head and tore it from the creature's shoulders, flinging it at the others as a warning.

Looking up, he saw the black-cloaked Maggaron standing on a crag, urging the vile animals on.

'No!' Tar-Arak roared, 'you will never have Ayrana! She is mine now!'

'My Lord!' he heard the Princess cry from behind him, 'Use the Sword of Power! Only that can save us!'

'No!' Tar-Arak said, 'I can only use it twice more! I must keep its power for a greater challenge! I…'

Tar-Arak stopped.

He reached up, seemingly reaching for something invisible on his head.

His hands seemed to lift something.

The floodplain of the great River Caradoth, The Fighting Apes, and even Princess Ayrana vanished.

And Hardy put the VR cap on the side of his chair.

'I've done that one. In any case, they're all much the same. Haven't you got anything which doesn't include Princesses and Swords of Power?'

Roger Ashworth—the ship's chief psychologist—smiled a grey smile.

'Have you any idea of how difficult it is to come up with a truly original plot? Humanity's been around for long enough to have exhausted them all. The Arc of the Hero, for instance, has only so many possible permutations. That's been proved mathematically.' His thin grey smile became ever so slightly mischievous. 'There are the porn scenarios, of course. They don't require much in the way of plot, so you wouldn't notice the lack of originality.'

Hardy shook his head.

'I've done all of them. I've even been the female character more times than I care to remember. And I never want to be a woman again.' He looked around the entertainment area, noticing all the other apparently identical game-players lying on exactly identical couches. 'Who came up with these repetitive scenarios? Why are they needed?'

'The problem is boredom, terrible, endless boredom. Eventually, it will drive us all mad.'

Hardy looked at the psychologist, who sat with hands interlinked behind his head. Despite being the same age as Hardy, his hair was already showing streaks of grey.

'*Boredom*,' he repeated. 'Not collisions with interplanetary objects, coronal mass ejections, cosmic rays. Just plain old *boredom*.'

'But of course,' Ashworth replied, 'the other dangers you have mentioned have been foreseen, and have been planned for with all the skill and knowledge of mortal man. But the insidious danger that threatens us all is—boredom.'

'Explain.'

Ashworth removed his hands from the back of his head and leaned forward.

'Hardy, we crew are in perhaps the most unnatural environment humans have ever occupied. We have been aboard this tub for so long that each and every one of us has seen every square centimetre it possesses many times over. We are a passive lump of metal at the end of an increasingly long power beam. We have a certain ability to alter our flight trajectory—marginally. We can avoid a planetoid sitting in our direct path. We can adjust pitch, yaw, roll. But we are essentially *passengers* because the Magellan is not an autonomous vessel. It is basically a projectile that happens to have humans trapped inside it. If the scientists on the Cloud Cities have done their jobs properly, then we have nothing to do except eat, shit, fuck and give birth. We have nothing to do. Nothing to achieve.'

'For two hundred and twenty years.'

'Two hundred and *eighteen* years,' Hardy corrected.

Ashworth's smile was forced.

'Yes, remarkable how time flies when you're having fun. But here's a question for you: how long does it take to get to know two hundred and forty-two people? When did you last meet someone you hadn't seen before?'

Hardy shrugged but did not answer.

Ashworth leaned back in his chair.

'Exactly. You see, most people don't know where they will meet their end, but everyone aboard here does. It will be on this vessel. Sooner or later, it will be on this vessel.'

Ashworth then gave the air of a man who has suddenly thought of something.

'Hardy, have you heard of Voltaire?'

'No.'

'Well, he said: "If God did not exist, it would be necessary to invent him."'

'A profoundly stupid saying. And what does it have to do with our predicament?'

Ashworth fixed Hardy with a disturbingly direct stare.

'Perhaps in a world of *ennui*, we should invent our own stimuli. And I mean real, direct, compelling stimuli, not improbable adventures in Fantasy Land.'

'Like what?'

'Oh, I don't know. Perhaps a few incidents which threaten the survival of everyone on board.'

Hardy gave a slight start at that and stared back at Ashworth, wondering if the latter had been the first crewmember to lose his mind.

But Ashworth looked away. 'You know, sometimes I think the wretches on the Nea Avgi were the lucky ones.'

'I doubt if De Vries's daughter would have agreed with you,' Hardy said, 'We don't know what happened. We can only hope it was quick.'

'Yes, quick,' Ashworth mused, 'Is that the best we can hope for, I wonder?'

'Perhaps you should be prescribing antidepressants for yourself, Roger. And me as well, if I spend much more time with you.'

Ashworth gave a wry half-smile.

'Sorry, Jeff. I see an epidemic of doubt and fatalism spreading through the people here. I do my best to reassure them, but spending so much time with them—it tends to rub off, you understand. But you're not too bad. You're just bored.'

Hardy looked concerned.

'Things are that bad, after less than two years? You must be running low on medication.'

'I am, but we were prepared for that, before we left Venus. Come, I'll show you.'

They left the VR area and went into what was clearly a biochemical lab.

Ashworth gave his usual less-than-reassuring smile to a studious-looking black woman and said, 'Could you move aside for a moment, Lupita? My friend needs some reassurance.'

Lupita gave Hardy a genuine smile and stood to one side while Ashworth indicated a complex system of transparent tubes, through which a viscous, colourless liquid was slowly moving.

'I'm making my own antidepressants and antipsychotics from simple organics. No matter how apathetic the crew get, we won't run out.'

'Well, in the world we now inhabit that ranks as good news, I suppose. Is this the finished product?'

He picked up a heavy bottle which had fluted sides.

'No, I'd put that down, if I were you. It's hydrochloric acid which is part of the production of the ammonium salt.'

Hardy hastily replaced the vessel.

'Well, I feel one hundred percent better. You've really put my mind at rest, Roger.'

Ashworth placed a hand on his shoulder and shook his head in mock pity.

'Just as well you're not a character in a fantasy drama. You're a terrible actor.'

Hardy shrugged.

'Well, there's not much call for that particular profession these days.' He gave Ashworth a penetrating stare. 'Do you have any more happy-talk for me?'

'None whatsoever. My only advice is: Never complain—because things can always get worse.'

Not enjoying having his own fears and doubts dredged up by someone who was supposed to be calming them, Hardy brought the conversation to an abrupt end and left Ashworth to his existential speculations.

The man had a very odd attitude for a psychologist, Hardy thought. His job description had *Maintaining the crew in good mental health* near the top of the list, but he had simply depressed Hardy by bringing the latter's fears to the surface.

With these disturbing thoughts echoing back and forth in his skull, Hardy walked morosely along one of the radial corridors. It was simply a wide metal cylinder with a small part of its lower circumference cut off near the bottom by the floor. It had pictures along its curved sides to soften its geometric plainness; pictures that changed at random intervals. Some showed abstract patterns, others vivid solid colours which shimmered as they morphed into other vivid solid colours. Some pictures were of friendly, pleasant-looking animals, mainly mammals or birds. As Hardy looked at one, it changed from a koala in a eucalyptus tree to a harvest mouse balancing on a stem of wheat that was bending into a graceful curve under its miniscule weight.

He spent a short time looking at it, wondering what had happened to the field in which that little creature had been photographed. Was it now a smoking ruin, a blasted waste of charred vegetation in which nothing moved?

No, he decided, not enough time had passed. The close passage was still decades away.

Even now—for the Magellan was not travelling at relativistic speeds—Fraschini and De Vries were preparing to launch the last of the lightsail flotilla. What was the firing order?—the Spes Nostra and the Phoenix, or the Phoenix and the Spes Nostra?

He shook his head. It didn't matter; the remaining ships would follow the Magellan at a constant distance, never approaching, never receding.

Unless something happened, of course. But, hey! Why worry?—if you hit something at nine million kilometres an hour, you wouldn't have much time to think about it.

The harvest mouse had turned into a kitten with a ball of yarn, but he was no longer looking or caring. There were no cute kittens on board, with or without a ball of yarn. He was standing in a grim metal cylinder inside a grim metal cylinder, with nowhere to run. And outside was cold darkness.

Very cold, very dark.

He passed many people coming in the opposite direction to him and some who passed him heading in the same direction as he was slowly plodding.

He did not speak.

He knew them all by name and disliked most of them.

***

Gelhardt looked over Lafayette's shoulder at the monitor screen. On Earth, she had simply been his lover and now she was his wife.

Along with two other wives.

To soothe that issue, Gelhardt had, after an earlier discussion with Fraschini, introduced a hierarchical system where a man could have a *Principal Wife* and *Secondary Wives*. In his innocence, he had thought that had solved the polygamy problem, not realising he had simply created another one, as the wives who had not been granted that elevated status now harboured simmering resentment against both their husband and his Principal Wife.

Gelhardt preferred dealing with men, believing them to be much easier to control.

Lafayette, on the other hand, was well aware of the situation, but, being the Principal Wife, chose not to bring any complaints to Gelhardt's attention.

The cabin lights became even more yellowish than normal and then began to flicker ominously.

What if they all go? Gelhardt thought and then instantly drove that idea away. The thought of a Magellan thrown into total darkness was simply too terrifying to contemplate. And they were less than two years out, just nudging at the beginning of the Oort Cloud!

'Any luck?' he ventured to ask, knowing Lafayette did not like to be constantly asked about progress.

Her reflection on the monitor screen grimaced at his fifth utterance of the same question.

'It's not a power problem,' she said. 'The fusion reactors are providing plenty of juice.'

He relaxed slightly.

Thank God for that!

If the reactors had been failing, that would have been the end. There was no way back from that scenario.

'So…' he said slowly, realising he was on the verge of annoying her.

She did not allow him to complete his question.

'I think I've got it.'

47

'What do you think happened? A powerful cosmic ray punching through our screens?'

That idea alarmed him: if the Magellan's defences were proving so feeble this early in the journey, what hope was there for a successful completion of the voyage?

'No, that's what worried me at first, but the answer is much more ordinary.'

'Such as?'

She turned in the chair and smiled as she looked up at him.

'A bug.'

He was alarmed again. Any kind of infestation on board would prove very difficult to eradicate. Sprays, traps, toxic chemicals released in the air…

She read his worries and touched his hands.

'No, no, darling. Not that kind of bug. An old-fashioned programming error.'

He relaxed visibly.

'And you've corrected it?'

'Not yet. I don't suppose you know how many lines of code are involved in running this ship, but it's a big, big number.'

'But everything was checked, over and over, before we left! By computers checking computers.'

'You mean software checking software. I think it's been proven no system above a certain level of complexity can be error free. Humans certainly aren't.' She stood and stretched her arms above her head. 'And as an honest girl, I must confess I had a bit of help.'

His forehead corrugated.

'You? The best software engineer on the ship?'

'Thanks. No, I picked up a fragmentary message.'

'What from Venus? They took their time, didn't they?'

'No, from our fellow inmates on the Resurgam. They must have had the same problem. It was only a jumbled message due to the distance, but it was enough to put me on the right track.' Her smile became slightly lop-sided. 'I guess they've got a better software team than the Magellan.'

He drew her to him and kissed her.

'But not a better-looking one, I'm sure!'

She kissed him back and left her workstation and crossed to the table in the centre of their quarters. Two Secondary Wives were there, but they immediately deferred to her and retreated to the private section.

'Not finishing the correction?' Gelhardt said, joining her.

'No. I've got spots before my eyes, so I'll go back to it later. And I'm feeling a bit down.'

Immediately, he was all concern.

'What is it?'

She glanced around as if uncertain of how to begin. Then, finally, she said in a low voice: 'The usual problem.'

He sat beside her, but a certain look of irritation was now clouding his features.

'Not questioning the entire project again! I thought we'd cleared that up.'

She looked down at the tabletop.

'It's just when I wake up, the same thought comes back to me. That I'm going to die here in this goddamn lump of metal; an old woman, never seeing the end of the journey; never coming anywhere near the end of the journey.'

'Like everybody else.'

'I can't speak for them. Only me. I know what you're going to say—I knew all this before I agreed to join the project, but I'm only human; reality is so much different to speculation.'

Gelhardt was silent. He could think of little to say that he hadn't already.

She reached across the table and held both his hands.

'Is there no way we can speed things up? No way we can shorten the journey? Everybody on this ship is an expert at something—if we put our heads together, surely we could find a way? Time dilation is a consequence of special relativity, isn't it?'

He sighed.

'Don't you think the people who designed this project wrestled with those issues? They were experts, too. We can't go any faster; it's all down to the mass that must be moved and the power available to move it. I'm afraid at our top speed our gamma will be only about one point zero five, too small to notice. We'd all like to be moving at a speed that would get us there in our lifetimes, even without time dilation. We'd all like to travel at eighty percent of the speed of light. But Hell, why stop there? Let's go faster than light and arrive before we leave!'

She looked at him, almost pleadingly. He fought down a growing annoyance.

'Don't start that! The speed of light is a constant woven into the very foundations of reality. You can't get past it any more than you can make a two and two equal five. And we can't even get near it, even if we had unlimited power; it's impossible to accelerate a classical mass to any really high fraction of lightspeed!'

She fought back.

'I accept all that, but short-cuts through space-time. They can work—Adekola proved it.'

'What, you're talking about Bose-Einstein Bridges? They can't exist in a stable form without negative matter. Have you any idea how much energy is needed to create that stuff? Adekola used four colossal fusion reactors combining to produce the biggest energy flow the human race has ever produced—and we all know how that ended! Compared to such a requirement, the Magellan has just about enough power to light a candle!'

She turned away, angry with Gelhardt, angry with the universe, maybe even angry with herself for her apparent weakness.

A tense silence fell.

***

The Magellan continued its silent course through the hostile darkness.

Behind it shone a truly magnificent star, much brighter than any other in the encircling firmament and showing a slight yellowish tinge against the blackness.

Once that star had possessed an orderly system of planets, following their calm, appointed paths around the central fire. Then there had come a woman, one with a truly transcendent intellect. And that woman had dared to tempt the gods and had reached out into the darkness.

And in so doing, had brought terror and destruction into that quiet system of calm worlds obediently maintaining their appointed paths.

And now in a valiant attempt to escape that terror and destruction, a small group of the children of one of those doomed worlds had dared to face the terrible gulfs between the stars. Truly insignificant against indifferent immensity, the lightsail ship plunged on, more and more remote from that splendid star.

The Magellan was following a course which was taking it further and further galactic south of the ecliptic. That beautiful, bright star was directly behind it, and directly before it appeared to be another bright star. However, mere human senses would have erred in thinking the bright star was in fact directly before the Magellan. For the starship was following a geodesic, the shortest possible path between two points: the initial point was the planet Venus in the system of doomed planets around the bright star. And the terminal point was a currently empty volume of space four point three light-years distant.

A point which would be occupied by the binary system of Alpha Centauri in two hundred and eighteen years' time.

And still the Magellan plunged on, on a journey that had hardly begun.

∗∗∗

Helena Tarkowski leaned back in her chair and switched her monitor off. She brought her shoulder blades together in an attempt to relieve the stiffness which had come from being too long in the same position. Then she stood and walked back and forth for a while in deep thought.

She hadn't told Hardy all the details of her career when they had met, mainly because she disliked the man, finding him a bit too obvious in his struggle to play the alpha male. Plus the fact he had asked nothing about her, finding his own life story far more interesting. She had indeed been a surgeon but had given it up because, towards the end, she had just regarded surgery as a type of plumbing that employed the most unsatisfactory materials.

For some time now, she had been wrestling with the problem of the brain, specifically consciousness. What was the relationship between thought and matter? Many philosophers had followed Descartes and just given up, regarding the two as a twain which would never meet. But Tarkowski could not accept that.

There must be a *path*, a *chain* of causality which linked the two. And during her last days on Earth, before she had been recruited as a RIF girl, she thought she had seen a possible way.

For many brain-sapping months, she had been studying a paper by the eminent neurophysiologist Nowak. Published after the Magellan had left, it had been beamed to the ship's library which, knowing her interests, the Central Computer had forwarded to her own machine. It had been co-authored by that *eminent grise* and his team of brilliant young students. She had lingered for a moment or two over the resumé of the youngest, a particularly brilliant individual called DeGroot, struck by the coincidence that he bore the same first name as De Vries, and then had moved on.

And she was sure she had noticed an implication of their work, which the authors had not. She had solved a particularly recondite equation, which apparently Nowak and his students had left unresolved, and noted a very surprising conclusion.

It seemed possible a simulacrum of consciousness could be transferred to a digital matrix. It would not be fully autonomous, insofar that it would not be a disembodied person living again in an electronic form, but something of that entity's essential nature *would be* transferred. Not volition, true self-awareness, but knowledge perhaps, and maybe some form of awareness, the awareness of what it had once been.

Was that a goal worth pursuing? Would such a thought pattern desperately crave reincarnation in a fleshy shell? Would it go mad when it realised its true state?

It struck her then there might be a more profound implication.

Unlike many of those on Cloud City One, she had been very pessimistic about the success of the Lightsail Project. Two hundred years was too long for a small, enclosed society to remain completely sane. Ultimately, she thought, the Magellan crew would become like the animals in a badly operated zoo: endlessly pacing back and forth in their cages, endlessly biting at the steel bars holding them captive.

But what if the knowledge and will of the original travellers could be encoded and kept like a Delphic Oracle, helping and guiding the current crew's descendants, preventing their slow and insidious decline into despair? An electronic consciousness that could guide and advise instead of merely responding to questions?

She would speak to Captain Gelhardt.

But she must be sure. She reactivated her monitor.

'Computer,' she said, in a firm voice of command, a voice from a mind gathering more and more confidence in its reasoning. 'This is Dr Helena Tarkowski.'

'I recognise and acknowledge Dr Helena Tarkowski,' the Magellan's Central Computer responded. Its speech was pitched at a level which made it challenging to decide if it was a male or female voice.

'There is a set of equations in my personal computer and now displayed on the screen. Below is a series of lemmas drawn from those equations and displayed between lines forty-seven and fifty-eight.'

'I see them.'

'Take the equations and lemmas and check that together they entail the conclusion shown in line fifty-nine.'

There was a period of silence.

Tarkowski felt her heartrate begin to accelerate as the silence seemed to extend into eternity.

Then the Central Computer spoke.

'The argument is valid. Therefore, the conclusion at line fifty-nine is correct.'

Tarkowski smiled.

'Thank you.'

Two

Susannah Reid enjoyed walking through the Farm Area. Not that it contained any jolly, ruddy-faced farmers or Collie dogs chasing sheep.

No, it was called the Farm Area because the Magellan's food supplies were produced there. She stood before one immense tank that had pipes going into and out of it. Once she had climbed—against regulations, of course—to the top of the ladder on the side of the tank and had looked in. She had been rewarded for her efforts with the view of a slowly churning, glutinous mass of something looking like a particularly thick porridge. It was the new genetically engineered yeast strain, created by the Eastranian government in the decade before the launch of the Zheng He. It was claimed to have so many nutrients a human could survive on it for an average lifespan.

She gave a slight shudder. Although most of the world had become semi-vegetarian in the years leading up to the Catastrophe, there was such a thing as taking an idea too far, and eating nothing but yeast was way, way too far.

She preferred the algae tanks. There at least one was spared the climb up a long ladder—a task not without its difficulties even in very low gee—because the sides were transparent, and one could at least see some shades of green instead of the lifeless gunmetal grey surroundings of the starship. The algae gave a welcome change of consistency and flavour to the yeast products. However, artfully the latter were shaped into patties, spaghetti, cakes, pasties or ersatz steaks, she could always detect an undertone of *mushroom*.

The algae tanks needed light as well as warmth, and both were provided by a battery of strip-lights which gave off the soft glow of the Solar spectrum. Reid stood so long in front of the algae tank she felt she was becoming hypnotised by the endless rising and falling of the currents of algae as they rose to the surface, lost some heat, and slowly descended in ever-changing curtains of soft green. The acceleration-derived gravity was so low it took some time to perceive any motion at all.

The colour both pleased her and made her sad. The colour was pleasing, that was not in doubt, but it was the only living thing other than humans and yeast on board, and the only organism that was reminiscent of Earth's once-abundant vegetation. Of all the endless myriad shades and tints of green that Earth had possessed, the algae was the only surviving remnant, a truly pitiful reminder of the beauty of that planet before humanity had trashed and ruined it. She thought of all the greens of the Amazonian rain forest—a glory that had been destroyed even before Adekola had done her terrible crime. Reid had spent some time in Britain and Ireland and remembered having looked out over landscapes which gloried in an infinity of shades of viridian, jade and emerald, with a faint nimbus of moisture placing a shining droplet on each blade of grass.

Gone.

All gone.

Murdered. An entire planet murdered.

And here she was inside a metal tube, grieving for the colour green.

She straightened and turned away from the algae tank.

No, she would not weep.

It was time to visit her son.

As she approached the nursery, her right ankle was struck a glancing blow by a small, scurrying object. Momentarily worried (did not all ships built by humankind contain a hidden cargo of rats?) she was relieved to see it was simply a Maintenance-Bot—or *maybot* as they had quickly become known.

It was vaguely reminiscent of a crab with its squat, slightly domed shape and protruding limbs. Most of the limbs were not for locomotion but for manipulating the delicate components of the ship's machinery, or sometimes working on less delicate items in areas where it was not safe for people to enter. Although the Magellan had been constructed so as to minimise dependence on moving parts, it had proved impossible to eliminate them completely—which is where the tireless maybots came in. Each bot was connected to all the others, and also to the Central Computer, by microwave relays, so they were a hive organism, like an ant colony.

'What do you have to say for yourself?' she enquired sharply of the little mechanism.

It looked up at her with crystal photoreceptors.

'I am sorry, Mistress,' it said in a high-pitched, somewhat squeaky, voice such as a cartoon chipmunk might have possessed.

'I should think so too,' she said, bending down to rub the ankle under the coarse fabric of her uniform. 'That hurt.'

The maybot scuttled away, and for a few moments she watched it disappear down the corridor.

Like all supposedly autonomous robotic devices, the maybots were not entirely reliable. The combination of rudimentary intelligence, sense organs and motility had proved to be more difficult than the AI pioneers had imagined.

And yet the success of Project Lightsail depended on bots being able to construct braking mechanisms in the Centauri system, she thought uneasily to herself. God! If that were not to come about, what a horrible fate awaited them all! To be unable to come to a halt in the new system but to plunge onwards into pitiless night—the mind refused to contemplate it further and recoiled in horror.

She pushed the thought away. Whatever happened was not her concern. She would be long gone.

Back to her maternal visit.

The sounds and smells of the nursery burst upon her as the door mechanism identified her and allowed her in. There was an immediate cacophony of howling infants and the smell of souring milk. Everywhere she looked, red-faced babies were clenching fists, screwing up little faces—and wailing.

Or at least it seemed that way. No doubt a few were lying in their cots, happily gurgling.

The head nursing attendant saw her and crossed to her.

The officer was a young man, but Reid did not find him attractive and made no effort to flirt beyond her normal base-level—the one she unconsciously employed in most conversations with males under seventy who still had a heartbeat.

This poor specimen didn't even qualify for the base-level.

'And how is Cameron today?' she asked. She had said "Today", but actually she had no idea whether it had been twenty-four hours since her last visit. There was no diurnal cycle in the greater part of the ship. Only in the personal cells was there ever dark, and that was set manually by its occupant.

'Not too bad,' the attendant replied. Reid was aware he was checking her out and that she still looked better than the typical run of females, even in this plain uniform, one unfortunately reminiscent of those worn by women in the Communist regimes of the Twentieth Century. What she did not know was that the attendant had applied for her to be included in his quota of females—and had been summarily rejected. 'A little bit of colic, perhaps. He winded some milk up a short time ago, but I think he's doing well overall. The low gravity hasn't caused any obvious problems.'

Reid nodded. The women were encouraged to breastfeed, but it was not compulsory and she had declined. The artificial milk her son was receiving was, of course, tailored to provide all essential nutrients. And she was thankful that the low gravity conditions on the ship had made carrying Cameron a lot easier. At least she assumed it had: she'd never been pregnant before. Unfortunately, natural birth was the only option for reproduction on the starship: every gram of its total mass had to be accounted for and have a specific function. So there was no room for the extra mass needed for complex *ex utero* gestation tanks—especially as there was a cost-free alternative in women's wombs.

'Let me have a look at him.' she said. The attendant seemed slightly surprised. The women who did not breastfeed rarely showed much interest in their offspring. After all, as they were required to produce so many children, what was the point of becoming overly sentimental about one in particular?

He accompanied her to the cot and they both looked down on Cameron.

He was a plump, pink infant and was one of the ones who had not been wailing when she had entered. To the attendant's surprise, Reid picked him up and for a few moments, mother and child stared blankly at each other. Then Cameron burped and a small trickle of synthetic milk dribbled down his chin. Reid finally gave a small, gentle smile and placed him carefully back in the cot.

'Yes, he's fine.'

She turned to go. She had much to do, scanning for possible obstacles in the Magellan's flight path.

The attendant decided to chance it.

'Susannah,' he began, clearly hesitant.

She stared at him and he felt his insides seem to liquefy. Still he pressed on.

'I was–uh–wondering if you might be prepared to accept a semen sample from me.'

Reid stared at him for what seemed to him like an age.

Then she gave him a dazzling smile.

'I'd rather die.'

And with that, she was gone.

***

Hardy stood in the waiting area, preparing to ascend through a radial spoke to the great rotor of the Gravity Ring and, while he waited, he thought about the function of the area he was about to enter. The spokes connecting that potential 1g area to the rest of the Magellan moved comparatively slowly at this stage in the flight: they had to, firstly, because they were many tens of metres long, and, secondly, because it was necessary to keep their rotation to a minimum whilst the ship was under acceleration. The entire starship rotated around its long axis, ensuring that the artificial gravity in the central hull would never fall to exactly zero, but the main cylinder's radius of rotation was not great enough to simulate anything like Earth gravity. However, it had been known since the twentieth century that rotating frames designed to mimic gravity through the centrifugal force were prone to disorient the passengers because of Coriolis effects, but it was also known that the larger the rotating structure, the smaller was the disorientation.

And the Magellan's rotating ring was very large indeed.

However, at present the ship was still under acceleration and so the Gravity Ring was barely rotating, as it shared the acceleration of the main body. The lack of rapid motion at present was necessary, Hardy mused, because if the Ring had been spinning at its top speed the unfortunate occupant would be subject to two separate accelerations, one of 0.3g from the laser energies and the other of 1g from the rotation of the Ring. The two gravity-like forces would be at ninety degrees to each other. Hardy chose not to speculate what the consequences of that condition would be for human health. Only when the acceleration provided by the laser complexes had ended, and the Magellan had entered what used to be called Free Fall, would the Gravity Ring speed up to its top value. But that in turn, would cause a problem: when Hardy reached the Ring, the flat surface on which he was about to alight would change at top rotation from a floor into a wall. Similarly, what at present were curved walls would become floors. But, he thought wryly, he would probably not live long enough to see such a change. When that stage was finally reached, and the Ring was spinning rapidly enough to generate a 1g

58

environment, an occupant would find DOWN was beyond the exterior hull and UP was towards the central hull.

The yawning gap appeared, and he quickly hopped in and sat on the simple chair, clipping himself into the safety harness. He glanced up into the tube, seeing nothing but featureless metal. The chair began a rapid ascent of the tremendous spoke. After a short time, the cylinder containing him opened, revealing a spacious room with smoothly curving walls. Unfortunately, at this stage in the flight the chair had delivered him to a point halfway up one of those curved walls, and he found himself looking straight down at the floor in a most alarming fashion. However, the chair then rotated through a right angle and descended gently to the current floor (one day to become a future wall). He was now in the Exercise Zone, usually just referred to as the EZ.

He watched the chair move away to collect the next passenger, and looked around; childishly grateful for a change of scenery. He was in a circular room, full of exercise equipment. The designers of the Magellan had known that most of the flight would be under near zero-g and therefore a facility to provide a 1g environment was absolutely essential for long-range space travel. The human body had evolved under standard gravity, and that was the way it liked it. Bone loss was a well-known consequence of zero-g, but the danger was far greater than that: The interlocking parts of the entire homeostatic system slowly drifted out of alignment with each other in prolonged weightlessness. And medical science was not sure of what the long-term consequences of reduced gravity were. Had the race managed to establish itself as a true space-faring species, by now there would be a corpus of findings, but that particular dream had never come to pass, cut off by the cataclysm of the Destroyer's intrusion into the inner Solar system.

So instead of a short hop to a neighbouring planet, humanity had been forced to compress centuries of careful experimentation and experience with space travel into mere years and then attempt a crazy leap to the stars from a standing start.

Not for the first time, Hardy wondered if Fraschini, De Vries and the other Cloud City scientists had been collecting moonbeams with their Lightsail Project. What on Earth (or off it) had convinced them it could be done? One might just as well expect a mayfly to cross the Pacific Ocean.

However, one thing he especially liked about the EZ was that, unlike the central cylinder, it had windows regularly spaced along the curving outer wall. These, unfortunately, would be permanently closed when the wall became the floor, and so the inhabitants of that far-off future would have to make do with televiewers. But that was then and this was now. There was a window nearby, and he slowly and carefully made his way across to it. (The Coriolis displacement was weak, but he could still detect it.)

Pathetically, he noticed he was hoping something of interest would be visible.

Of course, there wasn't—all he could see was a totally, completely, utterly black backdrop in which just a few stars were visible. It simply looked like an unusually clear night from a particularly lofty peak on Earth. He couldn't even see the Sun as it was behind the Magellan, and, in any case, was completely blocked by the tremendous light sail. The televiewer in his cabin could display the view behind the ship if he requested it, but that was a disappointment as well. The Sun was now just an intensely bright star, and Earth was too close to it to be visible without extreme magnification. Nevertheless, he carried on looking. They were passing through the Oort Cloud, a truly gigantic collection of deep-frozen planetesimals, that extended almost a light-year from the Sun. It was from this reservoir that Long Period comets emanated, icy masses that occasionally visited the warm heart of the Solar system on extreme orbits taking thousands of years to complete. He knew that from the point of view of someone actually in the Cloud they would be separated from each other by thousands of kilometres and it would be unlikely he would see one.

And they were right.

He didn't.

The EZ could not at present rely on simulated gravity to keep the crew in good physical shape, as it was sharing the overall 0.3g of the Magellan. And so, like a Health Club in the far-off days when such trivialities were allowed, it was full of exercise equipment: treadmills, rowing machines, weight-trainers. And nearly all had a panting, sweating occupant. He stepped onto a treadmill and spent the next fifteen minutes running nowhere and staring at the multicoloured display which showed various vital functions. Apparently his abdominal fat had increased and his upper muscle tone had decreased since his last visit.

He shrugged. He was not alone in that, he was sure.

He perambulated along the EZ, sticking close to the curvature of the wall so he occasionally passed a window.

As before, nothing was visible in the sterile darkness.

Finally, after an hour and a half of increasingly tedious exercise, Hardy decided he had suffered enough. But after a quick chemical shower (water being far too precious merely to wash in) he was stopped on his way to the exit by someone he recognised.

(That was another sick joke, he thought to himself: he recognised everybody.)

It was Okunola, an agronomist.

'Hi, Jeff,' he grinned, displaying teeth he somehow managed to keep blindingly white, 'Looks like you didn't find things too *E-Z* today!'

He pronounced "E-Z" in the American way, which Hardy found intensely irritating, as he did not so pronounce it.

Hardy shrugged.

'I'm not as young as I used to be.'

Okunola did not respond to the other's obvious slow spirits.

'Hey, seen the news today? It's a lulu.'

Hardy didn't recognise the ancient term, but assumed it meant something important.

'No, what is it?'

Okunola spun a televiewer screen around so Hardy was facing it. He saw a familiar object displayed against the great sulfurous globe of Venus. Hardy snorted. 'You know, I've seen that tub before somewhere; what's the big deal?'

Okunola's grin did the impossible and grew wider.

'No, no, buddy boy—that's not the good old *USS Magellan*. That's the good old *USS Spes Nostra.*'

Hardy remained unimpressed.

'The one after us. They must have improved the reflectivity of the sail as it looks a bit smaller. But it's just another load of lab rats on board a sinking, stinking ship. Big deal.'

Okunola did not reply directly but simply said, 'Wait.'

The picture changed, displaying a white man and a black woman. Well, perhaps not; the auburn-haired man might qualify as a Young Adult, but the female was definitely only a teenager.

'This isn't getting any more interesting,' Hardy commented.

'No, no, this is only Part One. These two jokers are actually in charge of the Spes Nostra.'

Hardy turned from the televiewer and looked sharply at Okunola. 'What! you're kidding!'

'Nope. These two are Numero Uno and Numero...' He hesitated, clearly not knowing the correct term, finally saying 'Number Two.'

Hardy shook his head.

'Well, this is it. This is the final proof this whole lightsail thing is just a sick, sick joke. A plan only drivelling lunatics could have come up with. Why didn't they just appoint a circus clown and a performing seal and get it over with!'

Once again, Okunola was unmoved by his acquaintance's bitter tirade.

'That's not all. Listen to this.'

Hardy did listen, and his features did not alter.

'Big, big deal. Haven't you got anything more interesting? I thought you said you had news. So it wasn't Adekola who brought the black hole into the system, but her extremely good-looking boss. How does that change anything? Some bitch brought the ceiling down on our heads and it was Sexy Chick instead of Plain Jane. Nothing's changed. Nothing.'

Okunola looked slightly hurt.

'I thought you'd be interested.'

'Well, I'm not.'

He was just about to continue his return to the main hull when both he and Okunola were distracted by a rhythmic tapping noise, coupled with human groans and cries. It was coming from some distance; the source being hidden by the exercise machines. The two men, alarmed by this strange noise disturbing the endless, unchanging monotony of the Magellan, both hurried to see what was the cause.

And what they found was a crewman pressed up against the window, repeatedly smashing his head against the unyielding substance. Blood, threaded with matted hair, was slowly dripping down the window. Neither man was worried the window would break: it was a laminate of aluminium oxynitride and synthetic diamond and would go toe to toe with an atomic blast.

Hardy got to the man first and pulled him away from the smeared ceramic. Under the blood and torn flesh, Hardy recognised him as a minor technician who normally had been so quiet and unobtrusive as to be nearly invisible.

'Tyler,' he whispered, pulling bloody hair from the man's eyes, 'what's got into you? What's wrong?'

Tyler's eyes were staring and somehow protruding, as if trying to burst free from their sockets. His gaze should have been on Hardy's close face, but somehow it was not. His terrified stare seemed to be passing straight through Hardy's skull, through the hull of the Magellan, out, out into the cruel darkness, into the hostile emptiness.

'Darkness,' Tyler croaked, 'only darkness. Just the blackness pressing in on me. Can't you feel it?—the weight of the terrible darkness, pressing, pressing in!' Suddenly, with incredible strength, he pushed Hardy away, sending him crashing into the wall. 'I've got to get out of here! Got to get out! Get back to Earth. Yes, Earth, they're waiting for me. My little children. I saw them crying when I left. They're still there, waiting for me! Got to get out of this box!'

Suddenly Okunola was with them, and put his arms around Tyler, pulling him onto his chest.

'Yes, yes, we'll find them, Tyler. We'll take you there.'

Tyler turned a face, wet with tears and blood, to Okunola.

'You will? You'll really help me get out of this box?'

'Yes, yes. Let's go back to the crew area.'

But over Tyler's shoulder, Hardy saw Okunola mouth the message:

Get the medics ready.

Three

'He isn't the only one,' Ashworth said as he looked down at Tyler, who was now lying unconscious on an infirmary bed.

'Only one—with what?' Hardy said, 'what are we talking about here?'

'What would you think I was talking about? Psychological disturbances, of course.'

Hardy turned so he was face to face with the psychologist. He fought down a sudden urge to strike the man.

Why would he want to do that? Why were thoughts of violence suddenly flashing through his mind?

Yet Ashworth was so damn—irritating! That silly half-smile he always had. The bloody way he combed his hair!

Ashworth gave a quick nod to a nearby nurse, and he led Hardy away from Tyler's bed.

'Sit down,' he said. He sat close to Hardy and picked up a memo pad.

'Powell—attacked another man because he didn't like the way he whistled. Pettit—was discovered in a spacesuit trying to eat her dinner. Lee—asked another man to take him for a walk because he had recently turned into a dog.'

Hardy found something else to think about, other than how Ashworth combed his hair.

'That's bad, very bad. Come to think about it, I've seen a few people behaving oddly—though not as bad as those people.'

'No, you wouldn't. They are the worst, but they won't be the last.'

'So what's happening?'

'What I told you about earlier. The human brain is rebelling against this unnatural, sterile environment. If the brain doesn't get enough external stimuli, it starts manufacturing its own internal stimuli. It also loses a sense of proportion. A trivial incident becomes an unforgivable insult, which can easily lead to murder.'

'Good God.' Hardy was momentarily shocked into silence. Then, 'The way you're talking, it sounds like the Magellan will soon be manned by madmen.'

Ashworth added to Hardy's discomfiture by saying, 'That's by no means impossible. There are also clear signs of asthenia.'

'English please, Ashworth.'

Ashworth looked annoyed but, after a moment, continued, 'Asthenia is a condition of a lack of motivation, of apathy, irritability, lack of drive and concentration, sleep disturbances, mood swings. Need I go on?'

'No, I think—look, do you mind not cracking your knuckles when I'm talking to you!'

'I only did it once.'

'No, you...' Hardy pulled himself together. 'Sorry. I'll start again—what can we do?'

'There are drugs which can help, and I'll be handing them out soon. But the basic problem is this environment and its lack of stimulation. Look, I'm repeating myself here. I've already told you all this.'

'There must be something we can do.'

'There is. I've already mentioned it to Gelhardt.'

'And that is?'

'Turn back. We must abandon this mission. We can't do it. No-one can. It's impossible.'

'Turn back! After less than two years! That's crazy!'

'No, this flight is crazy. Only people who had lost the ability to think clearly would have proposed it in the first place. Why go to Centauri in the first place? It doesn't have any habitable planets.'

'Because in cosmic terms, it's nearby. The Centauri system is stable, the stars are quiet. They're not flare stars.'

'Neither is the Sun.'

Hardy threw up his hands.

'You're not thinking clearly. The Destroyer—have you forgotten that mofo?'

Ashworth's look of annoyance had returned—with a vengeance.

'I *am* thinking clearly. I am the only one who is. There was something on the latest newscast. Some guy is thinking about Space Arks. You load up ships with a good selection of Terrestrial lifeforms and healthy humans and hide out in the asteroid belt until the inner system quiets down. Then you repopulate the Earth.'

Hardy was silent for a few moments. He hadn't heard about this plan. Maybe Ashworth was right after all.

'Well, that's a possibility. But you can't move masses the size of Jupiter around without destabilising the entire system through gravitational resonances. So the whole bloody show might decide to go spinning off into space! Not only that, but it's quite likely that Jupiter will crash into the sun at high velocity. God alone knows what that will do to its stability!'

'Are you an astrophysicist, Hardy?'

Hardy's face showed no emotion.

'You know I'm not. I'm an electrical engineer. But I know my mathematics.'

'You're not an astrophysicist, but Susannah Reid is. I've already discussed it with her, and she sees no reason to believe Earth or any other body will "go spinning off into space" as you so dramatically put it. And apparently, she knows her mathematics too.'

Hardy's desire to assault Ashworth had returned, but he fought it down.

'What did Gelhardt say?'

'He said he'd consult with Cloud City One.'

Hardy grimaced.

'So much for leadership!

***

'But why can't we turn around and go back!'

Gelhardt saw moisture at the corner of his Principal Wife's eyes and hugged her close to his broad chest.

'Not because I don't want to, but because it's impossible. This is a one-way trip. Remember, you were told that when you signed up?'

She pulled away.

'But it didn't seem to matter then! It was all in the future, but now I'm really trapped on this thing I know I can't stand it. There's nowhere to go I haven't been to a thousand times before. When I bump into someone in the corridors, it's like I've known them all my life. I'm sick of the same old faces. Sick of the same old places. I want to go home!'

He gently guided her to the seating area, sat her down, and joined her.

'You want me to tell you all over again?'

She shook her head.

'I want you to tell me we're going back—that's what I want you to tell me. But go on, say what you have to!'

He held her hands and looked away.

'This isn't one of those amazing starships they used to show on the videosets. We can't suddenly do a hundred and eighty-degree turn. We have very limited manoeuvrability because our thrusters produce very little delta-vee. Basically, we can't make major changes to our trajectory, not to mention the fact we lack the ability to stop ourselves. Someone has to do it for us.'

She looked at her hands.

'You mean the bots that are already at the other end, waiting for us to turn up. But we all know how unreliable they are! They're probably sitting around, turning into piles of rust as we speak!'

'They're not as good as they should be, but there's safety in numbers. Enough of them should remain functional to build the lasers to slow us down.'

She leapt to her feet.

'It's just a hope! You don't know they're doing anything! We won't know until we get there!' She stopped herself and, momentarily, looked around wildly. 'What am I saying? We will never know. We'll be long gone!'

Gelhardt stood and crossed to her, but they did not embrace.

'You were told the truth right at the beginning. And the truth doesn't change. And what if we could go back? What would there be to go back to? It's a dying planet, Simone, and nothing we can do can save it. It's best not to think about what will happen down there.'

'So why did you tell Ashworth you would think about it? I was able to control myself until I heard you say that.'

Gelhardt gave a wry semi-smile.

'It was a moment of weakness. I was tired, and I didn't want a long argument. So I told him what he wanted to hear to get rid of him. But he shouldn't have come to me. We all knew that doubt would hit us around about now, when familiarity had replaced the sense of adventure we had with a creeping depression. Of course, he knew that better than I did. But I guess he's human as well.'

'So that's it. We're fish in a small fishbowl. Swimming around in tiny circles, seeing nothing but the walls of our glass prison.'

Suddenly Gelhardt was angry.

'No, we're far more than that! We're seeds from one of those plants that had evolved to survive recurrent fires! The land is burned black, reduced to charcoal, the original plant turned to nothing but ash. But before it died, it shed its seeds onto the soil and they survived. Then one day after the rains, they sprouted, and the cycle began again. That's all we can hope for. We are the fire-seeds. You talk of hope, as if you haven't got any. But down there, they're the ones that have no hope. Think about them and not yourself! We cannot go back. We will not go back. But our children's children's children—they will be born again after the fire!'

She said nothing but hung her head, unsure if she was angry or just dispirited.

But Gelhardt crossed to her and ran a loving hand over the swell of her belly.

'And think of the little one you are carrying. She won't see Centauri either. But her descendants will.'

She smiled weakly, sadly.

But it was a smile.

***

Reid stood on the hull of the Magellan, surrounded by pitiless black infinity.

She enjoyed being outside, feeling the stupendous immensity around her. As an astrophysicist, she felt a kind of affinity with the stellar universe, although she was well aware it was not reciprocated. She looked around, seeing in one direction the vast blackness that was the lightsail which completely blocked the view of the receding Solar system. In the other, she was looking along the tremendous cylinder that was the Magellan's central hull, which contained the living quarters. And beyond the distant prow of the dark cylinder was the constellation of Centaurus. It seemed that if one extended an imaginary line from the prow into that constellation, it would intersect a bright star, which, in fact, was a group of two sunlike stars, Alpha Centauri A and B; but she preferred to call them by the names used in the astronomical fraternity: Rigil Kentaurus and Toliman.

The encircling sky still looked very much as it would have from Earth on a night of exceptionally clear seeing: they were not far enough out for any parallax differences to be apparent among the naked eye objects. Stars like Wolf 359 and Barnard's Star would have shifted, but they were merely telescopic objects.

She stood looking at the constellation of Centaurus for some time, as conflicting thoughts passed through her mind. It was known there were planets in the Centauri system, but none of them was remotely Earth-like. All that the system offered were raw materials and stability. In the days before the doom of stars had been visited on humanity, scientists had probed further and further into space, with better and better instruments, looking for a world which resembled Earth, hoping to see a longed-for world of blue seas and white Catherine wheels of cloud. One not merely allowing life, but overflowing with it, *demanding* there should be life.

But there were none.

Everywhere the sharp-eyed astronomers looked, it was the same. One radiation-scarred wasteland after another. After decades of listening, no messages had been caught fleeting from star to star as peaceful super-civilisations went about their unfathomable business. There had only been The Great Silence. It was beginning to look as if Earth had been the only abode of life in the entire Milky Way galaxy.

And humanity had doomed that paradise of living things. Not for the first time, Reid wondered if intelligence had not, in fact, been an evolutionary mistake. Blind forces had created an animal that was intelligent enough to destroy its competitors, but not intelligent enough to tame that urge to destroy when it was no longer necessary to destroy. Perhaps no creature that had been forced to fight its way up through a savage and hostile world could ever leave those dark desires behind and truly co-operate. Maybe that was the reason for The Great Silence: civilisations had arisen but could not leave the Darwinian struggle behind them, and all had perished, destroying themselves in one way or another.

She shivered. It was partly her dark thoughts, but also the physical, relentless, heat loss she was experiencing. Surrounded by a near perfect vacuum she was, of course, radiating heat from her body, but that was as nothing compared to the terrible potential drain from her boots. Being in contact with the ship's utterly frigid hull, there was the possibility of a tremendous loss of heat by conduction. In the extreme case, if she did not move enough she could be vacuum welded to the metal. Only modern materials allowed her to stand on that surface for more than a few seconds. Gelhardt had wanted to ban Extra Vehicular Excursions except for emergencies, but

Ashworth had persuaded him otherwise. He had argued such EVEs were a necessary safety-valve, to give people a change of surroundings from the mind-rotting sameness of life on the Magellan. (And, in Reid's case, an escape from people she fervently despised.) But going outside the Magellan's metal womb was very dangerous. The ambient temperature was not much above zero kelvin, and the thermal gradient was enormous. Not many materials could keep a human body from turning into a brittle popsicle under those conditions. But even more sinister was the increase in the flux of cosmic rays which the starship was experiencing now it was beyond the heliopause. Several times she had seen a flash in the darkness when a high-energy particle had zipped through an eyeball. Consequently, excursions were strictly regulated, and soon she would receive a command to return.

Bitterness invaded her mind again as she reminded herself it was not her safety as a human being that mattered to men like Gelhardt. No, it was her ova that were important, not the flesh-and-blood container they resided in.

She decided to return inside before the Central Computer demanded she do so. But as she began to walk towards the entry port, reeling in the umbilical which prevented her from drifting away, she saw a different kind of flash of light. It is very dark in interstellar space, of course; darker than the deepest night in the deserts of old Earth, but the spacesuits had lamps on the helmets to make it easier for the occupants to find their way around. And she had seen the light from someone's helmet.

Odd, she was usually alone.

'Who's that?' she called on the suit-to-suit comm.

'Hardy,' came the response, 'and you don't need to tell me who you are. I'd know those come-to-bed tones anywhere.'

She smiled. Hardy wasn't the irresistible focus of women's attention he obviously thought he was, but there were a lot worse than him on board.

Like the one she was now married to.

'I didn't know you like walking in the park,' she said as Hardy approached. He reduced the illumination on his helmet to avoid dazzling her dark-adapted eyes.

'Same here. I'm usually out here by myself. Most people are frightened of the Great Outdoors. They prefer watching repetitious movies about life on Earth.' He corrected himself, and although she could not see his face well behind the darkened visor, she could imagine his face twisting in a grimace: 'Or rather, the way life used to be on Earth.'

'Do you ever wonder what it's all for, Jeff?'

'God, what is *the Meaning Of Life*? I haven't heard that one for a while.'

'It's a serious question. What if life is just a passing sideshow in the existence of the universe? An epiphenomenon, I believe the philosophers call it.'

He turned, so he was no longer looking at her. Instead, he appeared to be staring out in the direction of far Centaurus.

'I think it is. But that doesn't alter the basic drives evolution has handed us. The desire to go on living. The desire to reproduce. Any rational species would have just accepted its fate after Baldwin wrecked the Solar system. Only a species driven by unconscious drives would have come up with a ridiculous scheme like this Lightsail Project. Do you really believe the human race has any cosmic significance? That somehow we deserve to exist?'

'Probably not,' she said. 'It would have helped if we had found life elsewhere; not necessarily advanced civilisations. Just life; any kind of life. But it looks like we're alone.'

'You think we're alone in the galaxy? In the universe?'

'In this galaxy, yes. But I can't accept we are the only intelligence in the entire universe. Maybe there's something unusual about the Milky Way. Perhaps it's particularly bad at bringing life-bearing worlds into existence. So there's no Galactic Empire here. No mighty fleets of interstellar battleships ray-blasting each other into oblivion at the command of Evil Emperors. Just gamma rays and rock and dust. But there has to be intelligent life somewhere.' She suddenly looked up into the northern celestial hemisphere. A gloved finger pointed at a faint undistinguished patch of light. 'Maybe there. Maybe in Andromeda. M31's got a trillion stars to our hundred billion. If there are no intelligent races there, then there probably aren't any anywhere. We will have been the Universe's one attempt to understand itself—and we blew it.'

He shrugged, but it was hard to detect the gesture, masked as it was by the bulky spacesuit.

'You're probably right. But we'll never meet them, so it's yet another *what if*.' He pointed to the exit hatch. 'We'll end up with detention after school if we don't move. Let's go.'

They descended through the transfer tube to the main hull and waited for the dock to fill with air. As it did, their suits became encrusted with sparkling diamond points of frost as the moist air met their frigid spacesuits. The frost jewels were there for a second or two and then they were gone as the connecting door opened, leaving nothing but a thin film of dampness, which in turn soon evaporated.

Having removed and stored their suits, their workaday clothes were revealed in all their drabness. However, the functional clothing did not entirely succeed in disguising the contours of Reid's underlying structure; a state of affairs of which both she and Hardy were aware. She smiled a tolerant smile.

'I have some photos of me in swimwear if you'd like to take a look at them in your cabin. Make sure you lock the door, if you know what I mean.'

Unaware until that instant he had been staring, Hardy realised he was blushing again.

Dammit! He was a grown man—she shouldn't have this power over him!

'Sorry,' he said, 'you look so different with…'

'My spacesuit off?' Her smile became even more expansive as she watched Hardy trying to extricate himself from the hook she had placed him on. 'Haven't we had this conversation before?'

Hardy decided to stop trying to explain himself. After all, coyness about sexual matters was pointless in the social structure of the Magellan.

The main door opened, and they were back in the noisy, cramped world of the starship. As they stepped out of the transfer area, the smell of the place hit them in a cloying wave: the mingled smells, odours, aromas and stinks which had combined to give the vehicle its own specific smell. Had they wished to analyse it they could have detected the cold smell of metal, or the acrid sting of the electrical apparatus, but above all: the smells of living creatures, their food, their breath, their sweat, their excretions. To someone magically transferred to the ship, it would have smelled like an automobile repair shop combined with feeding time at the zoo.

They strolled on for a while, during which Hardy struggled to think of a way to regain his aura of being a man of the world. Finally, realising the point at which they would go their separate ways was not far ahead, and feeling like a schoolboy approaching the point in which he would ask for his first date, he said, 'You know they are changing the sex quotas soon. It might be possible to get you included in mine.'

She stopped and gave him that megawatt smile, which seemingly had the power to turn his insides to jelly.

'Yes, I think I'd like that.' (His heart soared.) 'After all, anything would be better than the pig I'm with.' (His heart sank.)

'Great,' he finally managed to croak. 'I'll see what I can do.'

She patted him on the cheek.

'You do that.'

They walked a little further and came to the area where the great algae tanks stood under the blaze of the strip lights.

'Well,' she said, 'this is where…'

She stopped.

'There's something wrong.' She pointed to the nearest tank. 'Look.'

He looked. Among the slowly drifting sheets and fronds of green vegetation were other strands, but of an ominous black. One of the black fronds slowly began to disintegrate into dozens of smaller pieces as they watched.

Hardy walked up to the tank and looked into the liquid.

'You're right. Looks like something's got in there and is killing them. This is serious.' As he straightened up, the import of his own words hit him. Serious! If the algae or fungi crops failed they would soon be facing literal starvation—half a light-year from Earth!

'I'll get in touch with Gelhardt!' he said and hurried off without saying another word. Reid stared after him. It was incredible how quickly a mood could change! One second, light-hearted banter, with amusing sexual undertones. The next, the fear of painful extinction.

She shook her head. Why had she ever thought that coming on this tub had been a good idea?

Dermot Quinn looked up as she walked into their living area.

'You've been gone a long time. Where've you been?'

She stared down at the squat, red-headed man lying on the couch.

'Where I told you I was going. Outside.'

Quinn stood and faced her.

'You've been gone too long for that. Nobody stays out there for all this time, just staring at nothing. Nobody does that.'

She made a groaning noise, and sitting at the table, poured herself a glass of algae juice.

'I do that. I like looking at the stars. I'm an astrophysicist—remember?'

He sat at the table and, reaching over, grabbed a wrist.

'I don't believe you. I think you've been seeing a man.'

Angrily, she pulled her wrist away, with some difficulty, as Quinn was a bulky individual.

'Now why would I do that when I've got the man of my dreams right here?'

Quinn raised a hand, palm toward her.

'I ought to give that pretty little face a slap to take that grin off it! It didn't teach you to curb your tongue last time, but perhaps I didn't hit you hard enough!'

She sighed.

'You really know how to charm a girl, Dermot. Oh, the joys of the girlish heart!'

He looked confused at her words, but lowered his hand.

'It's not right for women to go off disgracing themselves, rutting after other men.'

Her eyebrows arched.

'Rutting? What a nice turn of phrase you have, Dermot. So it's all right for me to lie here listening to you fucking your other wives? Listening to them howling like alley cats!'

'That's the natural order of thing, you stupid woman. We're not on Earth now where everybody pretended to be oh so faithful—until they got the chance to do otherwise! This is what men and women were designed for; it's the same with every male in the animal kingdom. And I see it as my duty—to help preserve the human race!'

She leaned back and laughed.

'Your duty! Well, I've heard it all now, I really have! You must be a Guardian Angel sent down from Heaven to save us—and all this time, I thought you were just a plumber.'

Quinn leapt up.

'I'm sick of you mocking my work! I help keep all the ducting in working order! Without people like me you wouldn't have a life support system! And what do you do? Look out a window every now and again to see if we're about to hit something! I thought the automated systems did that!'

Reid turned away and, finding nothing else of interest in the room, looked down at her glass of juice.

There was some truth in his words—that was part of the problem. She couldn't help reminding him of the intellectual gap between them, but the reality was he was more important in keeping everyone alive.

She tried sweet reason.

'OK, Dermot, I'm sorry. I know you didn't come up with this harem system; it was Gelhardt and those stupid old men back on the Cloud City; dried-up idiots who hadn't had a hard-on for forty years. Personally, if I'd been trying to maximise genetic diversity, I'd have gone for polyamory.'

Reid instantly realised she'd said the wrong thing again, as his blank expression revealed he didn't know the word.

' "Poly-"? What's that, artificial insemination? We've already got that.'

'It means everyone loving everyone else, learning to live without jealousy.'

He snatched the glass of juice off the table and drained it. Then he slammed the empty vessel down so hard it made her jump.

'No jealousy, eh? Well, sister, have you got the wrong man!'

Reid jumped to her feet, her green eyes holding his brown eyes in a lock he could not break.

'And you've got the wrong woman!' she snarled. 'I lucked out when they put me in your quota. I'd have had more happiness with a chimp—at least I'd have been OK for bananas!'

He hit her then, and she crashed onto the table. Righting herself, she drew a hand over her lip and looked down at the red streak smeared across her knuckles.

Once again, the fierce green eyes held him a vice. He started to say, 'I'm sor...' but her look of intense hatred stilled the words.

'Thank you for that, Dermot,' she said, 'you've confirmed everything I thought about you. And for what you just did, I am going to kill you.'

Four

The Magellan had a comparatively flat hierarchy of command but, even so, Gelhardt was not a man you could just walk in on.

And so Hardy found himself standing impatiently in the anteroom to his office. The man who had given him entrance sat hunched over his keyboard, staring at his screen with a look of intense boredom while abstruse symbols drifted ever upwards on it.

'Will it be much longer?' he said to the bored man, who did not look at him as he said, 'He's a busy man.'

'So am I! And I've got very important news.'

The bored man covered a small yawn with a small hand but did not reply.

Finally, the door to Gelhardt's private quarters opened and Gelhardt himself stood framed in the doorway.

'Hardy, isn't it?' he said. 'This had better be important.'

Hardy leapt forward like a champion racer released from the stall.

'Yes, it is. If you think sabotage is important!'

Gelhardt's eyes narrowed.

'Come in.'

Hardy entered. Lafayette was sitting in front of a screen, every square centimetre of which displayed ever-changing numbers and Greek symbols. She smiled up at him, but he was too wound-up to respond, even if he had noticed.

'Sit down,' Gelhardt said, indicating a chair in the centre of the room, behind which was a long desk. Gelhardt sat behind it and stared at Hardy in the manner of stern interlocutor surveying an obviously inadequate candidate. 'Now speak.'

'It's the algae tanks. A few minutes ago I was standing by one of them, and the plants looked in trouble. As if they were dying.'

Hardy heard a sharp gasp behind him as Lafayette heard that dread phrase. Gelhardt's stolid expression of masterful authority wavered just for a second, but enough for Hardy to catch.

'Sabotage? Wait a minute, you saw someone doing something to the algae?'

'No, I just saw the algae appeared to be in trouble. Some fronds were black.'

'Doesn't mean someone did something to them. I'm not an agronomist, but I know these plants have cycles of growth and decay.

However, we do have agronomists on board and we'll see what they have to say.'

'And you'll do that now?'

Gelhardt's hand paused in its movement to the communicator button.

'Yes, of course, now! And Hardy, remember that I don't have to explain my actions to you—you have to explain your actions to me.'

Hardy nodded to show he had accepted the rebuke.

Lafayette crossed to the desk.

'Karl, I...'

He waved a hand.

'Not now, Simone. I've got a million things to do.'

A short while later, he, Hardy, and an agronomist were in the algae tank area, with the agronomist standing on the platform directly above the affected tank. She had moved the transparent covering from the top of the tank and was now holding a containment tube in which a lone stand of black algae floated.

'Well?' Gelhardt shouted, making sure he was heard, as the top of the tank was several metres above.

'I'll bring the sample down.'

She descended the ladder and passed the vessel to Gelhardt.

'It looks dead,' he said, glancing at the agronomist, apparently in the hope she would tell him otherwise.

'Definitely dead,' was the unwanted reply.

'And what killed it?'

'Too soon to say, but there's enough water in the tube for me to analyse for toxins. It won't take me long.'

'Could it be natural?'

'It doesn't look like it to me. But I don't speculate. I'll run the tests.'

'Good. Chén, isn't it? Tell me as soon as you know.'

'Of course, sir.' And she left.

Gelhardt turned to Hardy.

'Thank you, John.'

'Jeff.'

The Captain waved a hand dismissively.

'Whatever. Anyway, thank you for bringing this to my attention. We'll sort this out somehow.'

They stood together silently for a moment, Hardy looking at Gelhardt and being looked at in return.

Then Gelhardt realised the other man was waiting to be dismissed. He gave a brief nod.

'That's all. Thanks again—*Jeff.*'

Hardy realised as he walked away from the algae tanks he was trembling slightly.

'If there's anything wrong with the algae, we're finished,' he said to Ashworth a short while later.

Ashworth continued to sip at his mug of what was called "coffee" on the ship, although it was nothing more than roasted yeast grains.

'There's only a problem if it's *not* sabotage.'

'How do you figure that?'

'Look, if it's sabotage, then there's someone wandering about the ship doing bad things to the algae tanks. With the density of people in this tub, how long do you think it'll be before someone catches the loony bastard?'

'I like the impressive way you employ your technical vocabulary. Are you sure you're fully qualified?' Hardy then relaxed, having convinced himself there were more important issues than Ashworth's use of slang. 'You're right; it can't be sabotage.' Then a few seconds later, the import of his own words hit him, and he sat bolt upright again. 'That means there *is* something wrong with the algae. Some disease. Maybe they can't tolerate the low-gee—if that's the case…'

Ashworth put his mug down and smiled one of his grey smiles, which somehow gave the impression there was a hidden thought amusing him.

'So what? You're not getting off this junk alive; have you forgotten that?'

Hardy stood and looked at the unperturbed psychologist.

'You obviously *didn't* pass your finals. You clearly don't know the difference between dying of old age and starving to death.'

***

Reid ran a finger over her split lip. The blood flow had stopped some hours earlier, and now there was only a dull ache. Quinn had tried to express regret, but she had pushed him away. His repentance totally vanished at that point, and once again he had raised his fist, but the fire blazing in Reid's eyes had warned him off, and he had gone to seek comfort from one of his Secondary Wives.

And so she sat, staring at the grey wall opposite. She had wanted to put a picture on the wall, but Quinn had not seen the need for one. So now she just had the metal to look at. Beyond, she knew, was nothing but emptiness, a cruel black vacuum crisscrossed by energetic particles and hard radiation. If you scooped up everything in the universe and pressed it together into one titanic mass, its matter would amount to a microscopic speck. The true form of the cosmos was the black emptiness; everything else was a fragile film like the surface of a soap bubble.

Black emptiness. That's all there really was.

So Reid switched her mind to Quinn.

How was she going to kill him? The ship was so crowded it would be difficult to get him alone. Plan after plan flashed through her mind.

Lure him into an airlock and evacuate the air? No, the controls were inside the lock.

Toss him into an algae vat? No, even if she could get him onto the platform above the vat, she could never overpower him.

Hide a knife on her person and attack him when the Secondary Wives were out? Ditto, see above.

Persuade him to climb into a compositer? Now you're being ridiculous!

Her fingers, now terminating in short, unpolished nails, drummed on the tabletop. Then they stopped, and she pulled a wry face.

No, she could not think of a safe way of killing him. Instead, she would have to wait for inspiration to strike.

Then, for a moment, as that thought was completed, her mind recoiled from what she had been planning. How could she just sit there and calmly think about murder, about killing another human being? Surely Quinn did not deserve death? He was brutal, uncaring, given to unpredictable outbursts of rage—but did that justify a death sentence?

And there was another issue to contemplate. Killing Quinn would remove another element of diversity from the ship's meagre gene pool, exacerbating the Founder Effect, damaging the arrangement De Vries and Fraschini had devised to ensure the success of the colonisation effort.

79

She sat as still as an expertly carved statue for quite some time, only the slow rise and fall of her breasts revealing that she was, in fact, a living creature. Her face was blank.

Then it hardened.

Billions of miles away, millions of humans were facing a premature end. Nearly all of them were innocent victims, helpless creatures of circumstance. When an entire species was facing extinction, life had become incredibly cheap. Quinn had hurt her, drawn blood, humiliated her many times before his smirking Secondary Wives.

No, he would die.

A terrible thought shook her. What if the Magellan itself died? Then there would be no need to hide from prying eyes?

Instantly, she pushed the idea away with disgust. No, that was unthinkable!

And so Reid returned to searching through the other possible ways that outcome could be accomplished.

**

His face set as hard as stone, Gelhardt looked at the young agronomist. The Captain's eyebrows were still as arched as they had been at the beginning of her report.

'Hydrochloric acid?' he said, in a tone which conveyed the impression he did not believe what he was saying. 'Hydrochloric acid? How could acid get in there?'

Chén shook her head.

'I don't know. That's not what you asked me to answer. I'm just telling you what I found.'

Gelhardt leaned back into the resilient texture of his chair. His face softened slightly.

'So, it definitely isn't a disease or mutation. That's good; it just means someone has got hold of a simple chemical and poured it into the tank. A very simple, amateurish, effort to cause trouble. Looks like we're not dealing with a mastermind here; it should be easy to catch him.'

He looked up, suddenly aware he had been talking to himself.

'Hydrochloric acid. Is that an unusual chemical to have on board?'

The agronomist shrugged.

'We don't use it ourselves, but it's a useful chemical; I believe we have a supply in the engineering area, along with other unpleasant substances.'

'Under lock and key?'

'It's not my field, but I would have thought so. We wouldn't want some weirdo pouring it into the coffee of someone they didn't like.'

'Quite.' He gave a nod of dismissal. 'Thank you, Chén. You did well to identify so quickly. Please return to your duties.'

The agronomist gave a quick bow to demonstrate obedience and was gone.

Gelhardt immediately made a call to the engineering section and was told, *Yes, all the hazardous chemicals are kept in locked compartments.*

Gelhardt then made another call.

To Security.

'Get down to Engineering,' he rapped, 'and check everyone there to see if someone removed some hydrochloric acid from the store.'

He leaned back and relaxed.

This was more like a simple act of vandalism than serious sabotage. He would not exact too severe a penalty when the confused miscreant was caught.

***

Ashworth stared at the visualisation of the Magellan's flightpath. The screen was mainly black, except that in the upper right corner was a small yellowish dot and in the bottom left were two small yellowish dots. And that was all.

No, wait, near the upper dot was a green line, so small the casual eye could miss it completely, like a misplaced hyphen. He zoomed in, and the dots in the left-hand corner vanished, but the hyphen became a clearly visible green line, pointing diagonally down.

Ashworth gave a tight smile that was almost a grimace. He knew what the green line was: it was the path of the Magellan, tracing its progress from Venus to the Centauri system. And at the image's original magnification, it was barely visible. After nearly two miserable years had crawled past.

He sat down and sipped at his now tepid coffee. He knew the true scale of what they were attempting. If one converted astronomical units to kilometres, Mars would be a twelve-minute walk away, but

81

the Centauri stars would be nearly three-quarters of the way to the Moon.

How could anyone have believed such a journey was possible with a cargo of fragile, watery things called human beings? It was literally madness! And to think he had once accepted it! *Psychologist analyse thyself*, he thought.

But he had genuinely believed in that madness before he had boarded, before he had watched the tremendous hatch doors close for the first and last time in his lifetime, watched them shutting ominously slowly like the lid of a huge metal coffin. While still on Cloud City One, he had believed in the glorious Lightsail Project, but that was before they had sealed him inside a metal can, as if he were a slab of soya!

And now the thought that had slowly been worming its way up from the depths of his subconscious was very near the surface and he knew what its message would be when it finally burst into awareness.

Get off this ship or find a way of stopping this insane journey!

He returned to sitting before the computer screen and the small green line that showed the Magellan's pitiful progress.

I've put things in motion, he thought, *but what more can I do? Can Gelhardt be turned?*

***

Gelhardt ran the back of his hand across his chin without noticing the rasp of coarse stubble against skin. Most of the men had given up shaving a year ago, but he felt a need to differentiate himself from the crew.

Gelhardt was not a happy man.

But then, neither was the Security Chief—Alvarez by name—who was sitting uncomfortably on the other side of the desk.

'So let's get this straight,' Gelhardt said, 'you found nothing.'

'Yes,' Alvarez said, looking away from his Captain for a second, 'some HCl had indeed gone, but there is no record of it going.'

'And if someone takes some, it can't be released without authorisation? A two-person authorisation?'

'Correct.'

'And yet some have gone.'

'Also correct.'

'No-one saw anyone take the HCl from the container?'

'Correct.'

Gelhardt frowned a bit more.

'A simple "Yes" or "No" will suffice, Alvarez. You're not on a training course now.'

He leaned back and closed his eyes. This wasn't what he had been expecting at all. His image of a confused loner, a clumsy vandal, was rapidly disintegrating. Such an amateur, no doubt holding some petty grudge, would have left obvious pointers to his activities. It should all be wrapped up by now.

He opened his eyes, saw Alvarez was still sitting there, awaiting further orders, and dismissed him.

He needed time to think. Dammit, this thing was going to take up a lot more of his time than he expected!

Lafayette crossed to him and ran a cool palm over his forehead.

'Don't worry, Karl, you'll find him. If he tries the same trick again, he's bound to leave traces, slip up somewhere. Get overconfident.'

Gelhardt stood and stretched his back, then looked lovingly down at his Principal Wife.

'I know, I know, but it looks like we're not dealing with some clumsy simpleton after all. There was thought behind this sabotage—and it *was* sabotage, that's certain now. And a cold, calculating guy is bound to try again. And next time, he might do some serious damage. Everything on this ship has virtually zero tolerance for errors. One serious breakdown could cause a catastrophic chain reaction of failures.'

'Perhaps we shouldn't be on this ship at all, then?' she said, in a voice so quiet Gelhardt wasn't certain he was meant to hear it.

He let it go.

She snuggled close, enclosing him with her arms. He felt her gravid belly pressing into his taut one.

'Let's just have a lovely quiet night tonight, shall we darling,' she murmured, 'have a few glasses of aquahol and just relax. Forget about this damn ship and this damn voyage. Forget about Baldwin and Alpha Centauri. Just you and me, like it was on the Cloud City.'

Slowly, gently, he disentangled himself from her embrace. For several seconds it seemed he was struggling, and failing, to speak.

Then: 'I can't, Simone. One of my Secondary Wives is still not pregnant. I have to try again.'

She let her arms drop, turned from him, and silently walked over to her computer.

She did not look at him again for a long time.

Five

It was noisy in the canteen, an all-encompassing hubbub of intermingled voices. The whole place stank of the intermingled odours of yeast and algae—but the diners had long since become unable to detect that smell.

Hardy wanted to be alone with his thoughts, but that was impossible. Space was at such a premium on the Magellan that nobody ate alone. Consequently, he was sharing the table with three others; two women and a man. He knew all of them, of course; there wasn't anyone on board he didn't know. Not necessarily by name, there were too many for that, but there was no-one whose face he didn't find familiar. The three sharing the table were people he didn't like and did not want to be near, but he had no choice. He noted wryly to himself that the group of people he didn't like was getting steadily bigger and wondered if it was the same with everybody else.

They had tried to engage him in conversation but soon realised from his one or two-word answers he wasn't interested. The man spent the rest of the time making suggestive remarks to the women, who responded with high-pitched giggling.

It was an odd situation everyone found themselves in, Hardy mused silently. They were in a society in which rampant copulation was not frowned on, was not merely tolerated, but was positively demanded. And despite this all-encompassing sexuality, hackneyed sexual innuendos could still cause a fit of the giggles.

The time of changing the men's Sex Quota was approaching, and occasionally Hardy wondered who would comprise his next set of wives. He wasn't enough of a mathematician to work out how long it would be before he was back with his original women. And with his current women, he had actually preferred one of his Secondary Wives to Alisha Andretti, his Principal Wife, and had asked for the order to be changed. His request had been refused, and from that moment on he had even more reasons not to prefer Alisha.

He rearranged his yeast cakes with a look of supreme indifference. The serving machines did their best with a very restricted supply of ingredients. At the beginning of the journey, they had all tasted reasonably different, but as time passed, all the yeast dishes tasted of nothing but yeast, and the algal offerings tasted of little but strands of wet greenery.

Well, if the saboteur wasn't caught, he thought glumly, perhaps he would soon be longing for a dish of algae.

The communicator in his overall vibrated, startling him. He didn't receive many calls in the course of a typical "day". Hardy took it out and placed it on the table, ensuring the man on his left could not see the screen. He needn't have bothered; his dinner companion had moved on to relating questionable jokes, which had the women in fits of girlish laughter.

His eyes widened as he read the message.

Jeff. I've got to see you. I need your help. Susannah.

There followed the reference number which identified her cabin.

Mystified but highly intrigued, Hardy swallowed the last of the yeast cakes, rather too quickly, and without speaking to his fellow diners, pushed his chair back and left.

No one looked at him as he weaved his way through the crowded canteen and walked briskly to the cabin.

Reid was there and rose from the couch at his arrival, displaying what appeared to be a nervous smile. Odd, he had never seen her nervous before. He noted her lower lip was bruised and swollen.

'What's wrong?' he said, not sure whether or not he should be holding her.

'I need your help,' she said, pulling him down beside her on the couch.

He looked around the cabin. This was wrong. A man should not be in the same cabin as another man's Primary Wife.

'Can't we go somewhere else?' he said, displaying nervousness of his own.

'No,' she said, 'I don't want to be overheard. My husband is out doing some repair down by the bow, and his bitches are stuffing their faces in the canteen. I want to know what I mean to you.'

The directness of the question took him aback.

'In what way?'

'You said you'd like to include me in your Sex Quota.'

He spluttered slightly; that had been a semi-serious statement, a kind of playful fantasy. He hadn't expected quite so enthusiastic a response.

'Well, yes, I would. But I thought you were just teasing me.'

'No, I've got to get out of here. I can't live with this caveman Quinn any longer!'

Oh, thought Hardy, *so you're running away from someone, not towards me!*

'Why the urgency?' he finally said, after having absorbed the implication of her statement.

'The ship will soon have all babies needed for the next generation, so the next rotation of the Quotas will be the last for a long time. In fact, they might make the current one the last one. That's what worries me!'

'Is this guy really so bad?' Hardy said, getting the distinct impression he was being sucked into something he'd better keep clear of. 'I thought you were quite capable of looking after yourself.'

'I can with a civilised human being. But being beaten up on a regular basis while his bitches watch is a little out of my league.'

'You don't look that beaten up.'

Reid bridled at his words.

'He's an expert at leaving marks that don't show.' She stood up angrily. 'If you don't believe me, you can leave now. I thought you were my friend.'

He leapt to his feet, and this time he did hold her.

'I am, Susannah, I am! But why haven't you reported him?'

Her face twisted.

'They need him more than me. A practical materials-science engineer is of more use to Gelhardt than an astrophysicist. The Magellan knows where it's going: it doesn't need me to tell it.'

'But what exactly do you want me to do?'

'Speak to Lafayette. She knows you. Weren't you friends on Cloud City One?'

Hardy shrugged.

'Well, I was more friendly to her than she was to me. She dropped me like a used condom when that muscle-bound meathead Gelhardt showed up. But we stayed kind of friends, I suppose.'

Reid's eyes seemed to blaze with excited determination.

'Then speak to her! She's the power behind the throne when it comes to the Quotas! The Quotas are supposed to take in mutual attraction when they're set up, aren't they?'

Hardy held her shoulders, so she was forced to look directly at him.

'Mutual attraction. Is that the truth or do you just want to get out at any cost?'

She did not speak, but suddenly leaned forward and kissed him.

Hardy found himself drowning in an ocean of sweetness, of warmth, of desire, aware of a hungry need that flowed from her into him like a magnetic current, binding them close together.

She pulled away, and the old teasing, confident, Reid had returned. The lips that had just pressed his, twitched with mischievous enjoyment.

'Does that answer your question?'

Hardy found himself unable to speak for a moment or two and simply grinned like a teenager.

'So that question is settled,' smiled Reid, but was immediately serious again. 'I'm going mad in here. I've had crazy fantasies recently about murdering the bastard!'

'I think we're all going mad on this bucket of bolts,' Hardy said. 'I don't think anybody truly realised what it was going to be like.'

Hardy was looking Reid full in the face and he suddenly saw her expression change to one of frozen fear. Instantly, he knew someone was standing directly behind him. And in the next instant, a heavy hand fell on his shoulder and spun him around.

Quinn.

'And what exactly are you doing in my wife's cabin?' Quinn said in a cold, measured tone that hinted volcanic anger was not far below the surface.

Hardy felt his knees go weak. Quinn was a much more heavily built man than Hardy.

'Just a friendly call,' he managed to say, although his throat was suddenly dry.

Quinn could not move any closer to Hardy than he already was, and looked him up and down with measured attention.

'I know you,' he said. 'Hardy, isn't it?'

Hardy made no reply: the question was unnecessary; everybody knew everybody else on the Magellan.

Quinn pushed past him and bore down on Reid, who was now sitting fearfully on the couch. He looked over his shoulder at Hardy.

'You do know it's against the Laws of the Magellan for a man to visit another's Principal Wife when the husband is away, don't you, Hardy?'

Once again, Hardy did not respond. He felt as if he had become paralysed.

Quinn turned to Reid and violently dragged her to her feet.

'And you are a bad girl, aren't you, Susannah? Cavorting with a man who isn't your husband while I've been working my guts out in the service tunnel.'

'Leave me alone,' Reid said, summoning up her defiance. 'You're no husband to me. You're just a brute who enjoys hurting women.'

Quinn released her and, looking at the ceiling, stroked his chin in mock deliberation.

'Enjoys hurting women?' he said, as if weighing conflicting possibilities in his mind. He turned back to Reid. 'Let's test that, shall we?'

And with that, he delivered a pile-driving punch to Reid's belly; the force doubling her up and simultaneously flinging her back onto the couch. She let out a howl of pain.

'You are a bastard!' Hardy yelled, his timidity overcome by the enormity of what he had just witnessed. 'Leave her alone!'

'Coming between husband and wife, are you Hardy? Well, it's time you were taught a lesson, along with that slut on the couch!'

Hardy knew he had no chance against Quinn. But he also knew he had no alternative but to fight the more muscular man. He just hoped he would not suffer permanent damage in the coming conflict. He raised his fists. Quinn laughed and gently touched one of Hardy's fists with a ham-sized fist of his own.

'Come on then, Hardy. Let's see you fight for your new woman.'

Hardy swung a blow at the other's head. But Quinn simply turned slightly, and Hardy punched nothing but the moist, stale air of the Magellan. Quinn drew back a fist, ready to dislodge most of the other's teeth.

But then the light in the cabin turned an ominous crimson, and the noise of a powerful klaxon blared out, forcing all three to cover their ears. The crimson glare began to pulsate rapidly while the klaxon beat out a terrible deafening rhythm.

Quinn dropped his fists.

'What the fuck!' he yelled, almost inaudible over the klaxon's thunderous drum beat.

Reid struggled to her feet, clutching her abdomen. Her face had gone an alarming shade of pale yellow.

'Collision alarm!' she panted. 'It's the bloody collision alarm. We're about to hit something!'

Quinn's look of gloating satisfaction was now replaced by rigid fear.

'You've got to get down to the prow!' he shouted. 'Get down there now!'

She shook her head.

'Not enough time. At our speed, we could be seconds away from impact!'

She hobbled to her desk, pressed a button, and a computer monitor rose silently to meet her. Wincing and panting, she ran her slim fingers over the touch-sensitive screen and stared at the resulting display. Her brow furrowed.

'Nothing,' she said wonderingly.

Hardy pushed past the motionless Quinn and looked over her shoulder.

'What's happening?'

Her gaze remained fixed on the screen, while the light flashed between normality and a baleful crimson, and the klaxon continued to bellow.

'There's nothing out there,' she said. 'Nothing on the scanner.' She thought for a few moments, unconsciously rubbing her belly as she did so. 'Perhaps it's not coming at us in the line of flight, but obliquely.' Her fingers danced on the screen again. 'Nothing.'

Ignoring the two men, she turned from passive scanning to active. The antennas on the Magellan's prow responded instantly to her commands and sent out tight rotating radar and lidar beams in an ever-expanding sphere.

One kilometre.

Nothing.

Ten kilometres.

Nothing.

One hundred kilometres.

Nothing.

One thousand kilometres.

Nothing.

The beams were becoming weak and diffuse when she switched them off.

'What was all that about?' Quinn demanded. 'Are we safe or not!'

She ignored him and pressed another button.

Gelhardt's agitated voice came on the link, striving to make himself heard over the echoing reverberations of the klaxon.

'Reid! I was just about to call you! What the hell is happening?'

'Captain,' she said listlessly, 'I'm shutting off the alarms. If anything is on a collision course, it's invisible in both visible and microwave wavelengths.'

Almost immediately, the light became normal and the klaxon died, leaving all who had heard it with a roaring sensation in their skulls.

'Dark matter?' Gelhardt inquired.

'No. If it was dark matter, the system would have detected a deviation in our course from its gravitational pull.'

The numbers and graphs on her screen flickered and were replaced by Gelhardt's troubled features. Hardy, but not Quinn, was in his field of view.

'Reid, I want... Hardy! What are you doing there! Reid's not your Primary Wife!'

'I called in for a cup of sugar,' Hardy replied, not knowing from what part of his befuddled brain that ancient saying had sprung. Everything felt unreal. One second, they were about to be obliterated. The next, everything was fine. One second, he was about to engage in a one-sided fight with Quinn. Then he was not. And the klaxon seemed to have left him with a permanent ringing in his ears.

Gelhardt looked at first puzzled and then angry.

'I want the two of you in my office. Now!'

As soon as it was physically possible, the two were before Gelhardt in his inner office. Lafayette watched sympathetically from her workstation but did not contribute.

'Sit over there,' Gelhardt commanded Hardy. 'I'll deal with you later.' He turned an iron-hard gaze upon Reid. 'Now...'

'I'd like to sit down,' Reid said. 'I'm not feeling very well.'

Gelhardt motioned to Lafayette, who immediately brought a chair over, into which Reid gratefully subsided.

Gelhardt began again.

'Now, *Astrophysicist* Reid, perhaps you can tell everyone exactly what happened back there.'

'No, I can't. The long-range detection system activated. The readings indicated a mass of just under one kilotonne was coming straight at us. A collision with an object of only one hundred kilograms would blast a probably fatal hole in the hull. A collision with a kilotonne object at our combined speed would reduce the Magellan to vapour. I immediately began scanning to determine the object's trajectory in order to take evasive action. I could not detect any object above the mass of a proton heading towards us.'

'You weren't in the main Collision Alert Centre in the prow, were you?'

'No, Captain, I was not. My shift had been completed not long before, and I had left the scanning to my second-in-command. She is a very competent officer.'

'I'm glad someone is.'

'Captain, I can work the controls as efficiently in my cabin as I can in the Collision Alert Centre. The designers of this vessel were not so stupid as to overlook the need for back-up.'

Gelhardt looked away for a second or two and then subjected Reid to a forensic stare.

'So what happened?'

'Captain, the fact we are having this conversation proves that I was correct in shutting down the alert functions. By now, we would all be gradually dispersing wisps of gas if the alert had been genuine. Therefore, the alert was not genuine, and I did the right thing in putting the systems back on standby.'

Gelhardt frowned.

'So why did the systems give a false reading? I don't suppose I need to remind you that all our lives depend on the Collision Alert module working perfectly. This time we had a false positive; next time, it might be a false negative. And then we really would be the drifting wisps of vapour, as you so poetically put it.'

'As soon as you allow me to leave, I will go to the Centre and run the highest level diagnostics on the system until I find the flaw. And I will find the flaw. I know how to do my job, Captain.'

Gelhardt gave a slight nod to show he had accepted the implied rebuke.

'Well said, Reid. But you understand I have to test my people to ensure they're up to their responsibilities. That's *my* job, you see.' He gave a small sigh and turned to Hardy. 'But before I let Astrophysicist Reid get on with her vital work, I find myself having to deal with someone whose duties are somewhat less vital. Namely you, Hardy. What were you doing in the cabin of another man's Primary Wife?

And what was the meaning of that mysterious comment about sugar? There is no free sugar on board this starship.'

Hardy, finding himself in front of the Captain again in a worryingly brief interval since his last appearance, found himself struck temporarily dumb.

'I'm waiting,' Gelhardt said in a dangerous tone.

Hardy thought fast. He hadn't wanted to go in the cabin; only his attraction to Reid had made him do it. *The one reason which would damn him if he said it.*

Finally, he had the answer: it wouldn't make Gelhardt think any better of him, but at least it wasn't illegal.

'I've been having nightmares about the Magellan colliding with an object in space,' he said. 'It wakes me up at night in a cold sweat. Ashworth thought my blood sugar might be low. I was in the vicinity of Reid's cabin, and I thought I'd ask her about it; to make sure my fears were unfounded, you see. I had no idea her husband wasn't in. As soon as I found out, I started to leave. That's when the alarm went off.'

Gelhardt stared at him stonily. An icy chill began to flow down Hardy's spine.

If Quinn reported me, I'm sunk, he thought. *Lying to the Captain on top of being alone with another man's Primary Wife—he'll throw the book at me!*

Gelhardt's granitic expression changed. Into a frown.

'You've been having nightmares about collisions. Keeping you awake,' he repeated in a tone that suggested he had discovered something unpleasant on his sole. 'Well, you really are a fearless adventurer, aren't you, Hardy? With men like you on the Magellan, we really can't fail, can we?' He glanced at Reid. 'All this garbage is true?'

Reid glanced at Hardy and then back to Gelhardt.

'It's true.'

A wave of relief surged through Hardy. It looked like Quinn hadn't reported him! Now, if only he could think of something to ingratiate himself to the Captain, all would be well.

Then, in a flash of mental lightning, he had it!

A silent thunderclap of realisation rolled through his mind. He had been unconsciously hanging his head in penitence, but now he straightened himself and looked his superior full in the eye.

'Captain,' he said, in a voice which had suddenly become firmer, more resonant, 'I know who the saboteur is.'

Six

Reid straightened herself, pushing her hands into the small of her back in an attempt to alleviate the stiffness.

'Run it again,' she said to Andretti.

The small, dark-haired woman glared at her.

'That will be the fourth time.'

'Did I ask you for a count? Run it again.'

Andretti turned so Reid would not see her scowl and her fingers ran expertly over the screen. Reid was standing close to her, and together they watched whole libraries of abstruse symbols scroll up the softly glowing surface, disappearing at the top but being instantly replaced by equally abstruse symbols at the base.

'There,' Reid said, pointing at a line of characters displayed in a red font. 'Print that entire section out. I must have missed it the first time.'

Andretti complied, and Reid took the printout over to another workstation and poured herself yet another cup of the ersatz coffee. She looked around as she sipped the bitter brew before settling down to study the code. The beverage had a robust taste—just nothing like coffee.

She was near the Magellan's blunt prow, protected from the interstellar vacuum by many metres of lead, tungsten, long chain hydrocarbons and high-density ice.

The prow was the most dangerous part of the vessel, as it was the first to encounter the relentless flood of particles, whether minute or hefty, through which the Magellan was ploughing. The ship's magnetic shield deflected all but the most energetic of the charged particles, but the neutral ones smashed straight into the vessel's bow. Although the ship had still not reached its maximum velocity of nearly three percent of the speed of light, it was still travelling fast enough for even tiny motes to pack a hefty punch.

Strangely reluctant to begin her vital task, she continued to look around.

The room was small and, of course, windowless, and was bathed in a soft yellowish light, similar to that which had been produced by incandescent bulbs in the twentieth century. But everywhere one looked, there were computer screens giving off their own more bluish illumination. There did not seem to be any part of the surface up to just above average head height that was not covered in some variety of electronic equipment.

Above the glowing screens, the massive, buttressed walls gave the impression of recalcitrant strength, as if contemptuous of the interstellar deeps.

And they needed to be strong, for this was perhaps the most important part of the Magellan; if it had a brain—this was it. It was here the ship scanned the region directly ahead of the speeding vessel, searching with electronic Argus eyes for anything larger than a fingernail that might imperil its integrity.

By the sheer fact of its motion, the ship could not avoid encountering interstellar debris. But the greater the mass of the colliding object, the less likely it was that the Magellan would survive the encounter. It had some manoeuvring ability—but not much, because it could not move out of the reach of the tremendous laser beam which was providing the thrust needed to send it to the Centauri worlds. As the distance between the Magellan and the Solar system increased, the beam became more diffuse and delivered less momentum to the great light sail; so the farther the ship travelled, the more it could control its own trajectory. But thrusters are weighty and require reaction mass. Hence, foreknowledge of a likely threat was crucial.

Reid continued to sip the harsh muddy liquid, the events of the previous few hours rolling over and over and over in her mind. Again fantasies of killing Quinn came flooding back, but this time stronger, fiercer, more vibrant.

Suddenly, Andretti was standing over her.

'I thought this was a top priority job we were supposed to be doing!'

Reid looked up, but continued to sip her coffee.

'Who rattled your cage?'

'You did!' Andretti spat. 'Everyone is saying my husband was in your cabin, when it was just you and him!'

'He was.' Reid said sweetly. 'He came to borrow a cup of sugar.'

'Sugar?' Andretti said in a much fainter voice, her brows knitting together.

'Yes, sugar. He's experimenting on increasing yeast growth. He's a very clever man. You should be proud of him.'

Andretti looked down at her superior, apparently lost for words. Then she shook her head as if trying to clear it and said, 'Shall we get on with it?'

Reid smiled.

'Yes, we shall.'

They spent the next hour looking over the seemingly endless lines of code, concentrating on the area around the portion outlined in red. Reid grew steadily more agitated, and small beads of sweat began to appear on her increasingly furrowed forehead. It was very stuffy in the Collision Alert Centre. Then:

'Fuck, fuck, fuck! That's not it. This section is badly written, but it's just slower than it needs to be. We haven't found it!'

'That's what I said last time,' Andretti observed, 'but you didn't listen.'

Reid ignored the barb. She was so certain she'd found the problem! She had entertained visions of walking into Gelhardt's office, spreading out the printout, and triumphantly pointing out the error.

But there was no error, just a small piece of infelicitous coding.

'There's nothing wrong with it,' she groaned, 'nothing.'

A worried look began to spread across Andretti's trim features.

'There is a possibility you haven't considered.'

Reid turned to face her subordinate, giving her an imperious stare.

'Oh, and what might that be?'

'Sabotage,' Andretti replied.

***

'It appears I may have underestimated you, Hardy,' Gelhardt had said impassively, after Reid had returned to the Collision Centre. 'It seems we have a detective on board. Reveal all, please—or should I gather all the suspects around in a circle with you in the middle, while you detail your deductions?'

'No need. There is only one suspect.'

'And that is.'

'Roger Ashworth.'

'Our Chief Psychologist. That would be unfortunate if it were true. Why him?'

'I've been speaking a lot to him recently, and he has—inadvertently, I suppose—revealed much of his thinking.'

'Give me an example of a statement of his which shows his guilt.'

'Ashworth believes much of the psychological problems the crew has been displaying recently are due to a lack of stimuli. That life on board is so lacking in incident the human mind is forced to create its own stimuli; hence, we have men who claim to be Elizabeth Baldwin and women who believe they have become flower pots. I'm exaggerating for emphasis, sir, but you get the point, I guess.'

'Thank you for your amusing examples. I am aware of these problems, and they are most concerning. Ashworth has kept me apprised of those mental aberrations, and I believe his drug treatment has already begun to alleviate the situation. Are you saying he is creating these problems with the algae and the collision alarm simply to provide stimuli to jerk people out of their delusions? But why him in particular? Unfortunately, we have a number of quite disturbed people on the Magellan—why not one of them?'

'Ashworth wants you to turn back, I believe.'

'Regrettably, he is not alone in that. I have explained to those people such a course correction is impossible.'

'He may be creating a situation of panic which will force your hand.'

'Impossible. And why him, and not any other of the deluded people who want me to do that?'

Hardy played his trump card.

'Because he has access to hydrochloric acid, and they do not.'

Gelhardt fell silent for a few seconds and glanced away from Hardy. Then he looked back at him.

'I think you're wrong. Ashworth is too professional to fall victim to one of the very delusions he is treating.' He paused. 'But I will speak with him.'

He depressed a button on his console.

'Security. Meet me outside the infirmary in ten minutes.' He looked up at Hardy. 'You as well. I want Roger to meet his accuser.'

Hardy and Gelhardt waited outside the infirmary until two Security men arrived. Security was not their primary job; they were experts in scientific or technological fields: they just happened to be big men.

'In we go,' Gelhardt said.

Ashworth looked up from his console as the four intruders walked in.

'Dear me,' he said, 'have the psych-problems spread this far?'

Gelhardt pointed at Hardy while the two Security men took up stations near the door.

'This gentleman has something to say to you.'

Ashworth looked at Hardy, saying nothing, but an eyebrow elevated as he waited.

Hardy suddenly felt like a complete fool. He had been searching for a way to gain Gelhardt's respect, but it looked like he had leapt to a conclusion that would demote him even further in his Captain's estimation. But having come this far, he had to go through with it.

With a dry mouth and lips that seemed to have mysteriously thickened, he looked at Ashworth and said, 'Roger, I think you're behind the sabotage. Of the algae at least,' he added, as he came to realise he had no evidence linking the psychologist to the collision alarm.

Ashworth looked around at his uninvited guests, and then his head drooped.

'Well, I suppose I am,' he said. 'It must be my fault.'

Gelhardt gave a visible start.

'Roger, Roger, what have you done?' he whispered, then collecting himself, said in a stronger voice, 'Why, Ashworth? Why did you seek to cause trouble, when your job is to keep us all in good mental health? Why?'

Ashworth spread his arms wide in a gesture of submission.

'I came to realise this journey is futile. We're not going to get to Centauri. One of two things will happen, or perhaps both. One: we'll hit something and disappear in a puff of smoke, two hundred and forty-two men and women's lives thrown away, not to mention all those innocent children we've forced into existence. Two: we'll all go mad from forced imprisonment in this confined space, breathing in what some bastard has just breathed out, drinking water recycled from each other's piss. People can't live like this: we need wide, open expanses. Blue sky, clouds, running water; coming into contact with other forms of life—deer, bobcats, beavers, birds. But we are not alone on this vessel, you know. Oh no, we brought dozens of species along with us. But we can't stroke them; we can't listen to their evensong. We brought viruses on our skin, mites in our eyelashes, bacteria by the billion in our guts. Those are our companions!'

'Roger,' Gelhardt said softly, 'we can't turn back. We have to go on. Maybe we won't reach Alpha. But we will have tried.'

Ashworth leapt to his feet.

'But you haven't tried, Karl! Every adult on this hell ship is an expert in something! Get them to work on the problem. Get us back to the Solar system, I'm begging you!'

'Impossible. There is only death back where we came from.'

'No, that's a lie! There was talk about assembling a fleet of Space Arks ready to recolonise Earth after the Passage. That's where we should be!'

Gelhardt looked over his shoulders at the guards.

'Take him to the brig.'

After Ashworth had been removed, a tense silence fell. The nurses and junior doctors sat still, occasionally glancing at each other. Then Gelhardt looked at a very relieved Hardy.

'Well, Hardy, looks like I owe you an apology. You've saved us from a potentially deadly situation; there's no telling what he might have done next.'

Hardy struggled to think of a response, but there was no need. Gelhardt gave him one last piercing look and then said, 'That's it. Back to your duties.'

And left.

Hardy became aware that the other medical staff were looking at him with very unfriendly expressions and decided to leave as well.

Back in his cabin, he stretched out on the couch, his mind whirling. As he lay there, drifting in and out of a shallow sleep, he was unaware that Reid had been called before Gelhardt again and was enduring his scorn as she related how she had failed to find anything wrong with the code controlling the collision alarm. Gelhardt, in turn, had told her of Ashworth's confession and had dismissed her.

Hardy awoke with a jolt to find his Primary Wife standing over him, hands on hips.

'You have some explaining to do,' Andretti hissed.

Hardy struggled to clear his thoughts.

'Eh, what? What's wrong?'

'I've just got back from spending several highly unpleasant hours in the company of your girlfriend, going over and over lines of code until I thought my head was going to explode!'

'Girlfriend? I haven't got a girlfriend.' He struggled into a sitting position. 'Did you find anything?'

'Don't change the subject. If you think I believe that drivel about you walking into her cabin looking for sugar, you must be mad as well as stupid!'

He slowly straightened himself upright. He felt unbelievably tired.

'I'm not going to argue with you, Alisha. I've been straight with you about wanting another Primary Wife.'

'I've given you two children!'

'No, that's not true. You've given *the Magellan* two children. But that was part of your job. I wouldn't recognise them if they were sitting on this couch. It's what we all have to do.'

She said no more, but there was poison in her eyes.

'Look, I'm sorry, Alisha, it didn't work out. But why should it have worked out? We were assigned to each other by an algorithm. I saw you once in Cloud City One, that's all, then we were in bed together, being told to be fruitful and multiply.'

Suddenly a great wave of tenderness, almost of sorrow, washed over him. He held her and forced her to look up at him.

'Look, it'll all be over soon. There'll be one more rotation of the Quotas and you'll be free of me. The next man might be more worthy of you.'

Her eyes were sparkling, but it was just the tears which were catching the light.

'But I love you!'

He kissed her gently and then pulled slowly away.

'No. You mustn't torment yourself like that. You must never say that.' His gaze moved to the dull grey of the cabin ceiling. 'There's no room for love on the Magellan.'

***

Tarkowski looked at Gelhardt as he lifted his eyes from her exposition.

'Well?' she said.

Gelhardt chose to ignore the fact she had not used his rank when addressing him, and simply said, 'No.'

She looked annoyed.

'May I ask why?'

'This idea is unheard of. There's no corpus of findings about it I could draw upon to evaluate it. It's just fantasy.'

She drew herself up a little higher in the chair.

'I do not deal in fantasy, Mr Gelhardt.'

'Captain Gelhardt.'

She ignored the correction and continued, 'It builds on the work of the renowned Professor Nowak, who has demonstrated it is possible to duplicate aspects of human mentality electronically.'

'I do not believe he had actually proved that before we left the Solar system.'

Tarkowski's lips thinned. She was not used to people who didn't immediately accept what she was saying.

'Look—Captain. We already have a simpler version of my plan in our databanks. We have the genetic code of plant and animal gametes stored as data ready to be converted into biological entities when the Magellan arrives at Alpha. But we also have electronic instructions for *people*, human beings, none of whom are represented in the ship's crew. We can convert those instructions into biological material at any time in order to increase our genetic diversity to alleviate the Founder Effect. What I am proposing is a more advanced version of what they did to produce those electronic blueprints in the first place.'

'I don't believe that spermatozoa and ova are possessed of consciousness, Dr Tarkowski. And the amount of computer memory would be prohibitive.'

'Then you haven't understood what I have been saying. The uploaded consciousness would not be in the memory but stored on solid-state media, away from the housekeeping section. The day-to-day running of the Magellan would not be affected.'

'And you have not understood that I am the ultimate arbiter of which actions are to be performed upon my ship and, I repeat, the answer is *No*.'

A silence fell. Tarkowski reached for the papers which lay before Gelhardt.

A large hand fell upon the papers, preventing their removal.

'And while you're here, doctor, there is something I wish to discuss with you.'

'And that is?'

'I see from your record you have only produced one child. Why is that?'

She collected the papers and walked out, without waiting to be dismissed.

Gelhardt looked in the direction she had exited and shrugged. He had more important matters to deal with than Helena Tarkowski—like getting some sense out of Ashworth.

A short time later, he was staring across a bare table at the Magellan's Chief Psychologist, who was now wearing restraints on his ankles.

'Roger,' he said, 'you said you poisoned an algae tank, but you don't show up on the CCTV. How do you explain that?'

Ashworth spread his hands.

'I don't. I did everything in a daze, in a dream. I didn't really know I was doing it. It was all so strange I can hardly believe I did it.'

Gelhardt's fingers drummed on the bare table.

'Did you? Did you have an accomplice? Someone who could have disconnected the CCTV, perhaps?'

Ashworth gave an odd grin.

'Maybe. Who can say? Does it matter? We're all dead anyway, only some of us haven't realised it yet.'

The interrogation continued for some more minutes, but as the back-and-forth dragged on, it developed an increasingly surreal feeling.

Eventually Gelhardt gave up and left the cell. One of the junior psychologists was waiting in the anteroom.

'Tell me something, Andropov,' Gelhardt said to him, 'has Ashworth been taking anything?'

'Like what?'

'Like some psychotropic substance. He's been under a lot of strain listening to everyone's problems with no one to listen to his.'

'How would I know?'

Something snapped in Gelhardt then, and he found himself grasping Andropov's throat.

'Find out, mister. Check the records. Check the stock. But I'm telling you now—find out!'

A shaken Andropov nodded and hurried away to begin his task.

Gelhardt began a slow trudge back to his office, ignoring everyone who saluted or gave some other gesture of respect. He had a lot on his mind. He had been aware when he accepted the post of Captain that it would bring with it a cargo of problems, but he hadn't expected this shadow-boxing, this duelling with an opponent who was hidden in veils of mist.

But although he wasn't specifically looking at anyone or anything, an observation he had made unconsciously began to wriggle around in the basement of his mind, trying to draw attention to itself.

He stopped. What was it his conscious mentality had missed but had nevertheless registered on his unconscious?

He was standing in the main corridor, and people were moving past him in both directions, while he stood motionless like a rock in a fast-flowing current. He stood for some time, watching his people move past him; some in a hurry, some walking leisurely; some stopping to speak to him and then moving on after realising they were being ignored.

What was it? What was different?

He looked at the current of bodies as it swept around him—and then he had it.

More and more people were wearing warm clothing over their normal attire.

And yet the Magellan was always warm; a moist, cloying sensation like a shuttered room where the windows have not been opened for a long time. For some reason, he touched the grey wall he was almost leaning against and then looked at his fingers.

They glistened. He stared at the wall. It was moist. Condensation.

The Magellan was getting colder.

It was then he broke into a run, pushing the others away like a berserk battering ram.

In his room he commanded the Central Computer to tell him the temperature.

Seventeen degrees Celsius.

That was wrong; dangerously wrong.

The Computer spoke again. He must have told it to keep him apprised.

'*Sixteen point seven five degrees Celsius.*'

Gelhardt's blood seemed to be dropping in temperature as well—heading straight down to the freezing point. What had appeared to be a simple fluctuation in temperature was now revealed to be the start of a precipitous drop to Absolute Zero—the Magellan was bleeding heat out into the frigid emptiness of interstellar space, like a severed artery pumping out its lifeblood!

Now completely terrified, Gelhardt managed to gather his wits together enough to shout, 'Computer! Identify the source of heat loss on the Magellan!'

Instantly, the Computer replied in smooth, unruffled tones, '*All temperature controls are within normal parameters.*'

'Reanalyse! There is a temperature loss occurring!'

'*Incorrect. Temperatures are stable.*' Then it added, '*Sixteen point two five degrees Celsius.*' Gelhardt staggered backwards and collapsed into his chair. For once in his life, he did not know what to do next. A frozen Hell was opening its gates to draw them all in.

At that moment, Lafayette came in.

'Is it me,' she said innocently, 'or is it a bit chilly in here?'

The Computer said, in a totally unconcerned voice, '*Sixteen degrees Celsius.*'

Gelhardt turned to her in desperation.

'Simone, something's wrong! The Computer's gone mad! We're losing heat at a terrific rate!'

The Computer said, '*Sixteen point two five degrees Celsius.*'

Lafayette stared at Gelhardt with raised eyebrows while he struggled to regain his composure.

The Computer said, '*Sixteen point five zero degrees Celsius.*'

Lafayette walked over to the console, looked at the large monitor screen above it and then back at Gelhardt.

'What's all the fuss about? Whatever it was, it must have been just a minor blip. The Computer's got it under control.'

The Computer said, '*Sixteen point seven five degrees Celsius.*'

Gelhardt licked his lips. The room seemed to be spinning, with him at the focus.

'Computer,' he said, somewhat shocked to hear how strained his voice sounded, 'cease reporting temperature.'

'*Obeyed.*'

'So, what was all that about?' Lafayette said, as she crossed to him. She ran a soft hand over his forehead. 'My, you're sweating. I thought you said you were feeling cold.'

He held her hand against his head. It felt comforting.

'I don't know what's happening. I panicked, I guess. I'm OK now.'

She sat by him and smiled. She was like a nurse dealing with a casualty that had just been brought in from the front.

'The *hoi polloi* on the ship don't understand half of the pressures you're under. They have no idea. So Karl, you're allowed a little bit of self-doubt every now and again. I don't know how you manage to keep so calm; I really don't. If only they knew.'

He drew her hand down from his forehead, but still kept it gripped firmly. When it reached his lips, he kissed it fervently.

'I don't know what I'd do without you, Simone. You anchor me.' Just then his eyes caught a strange flash of red light on the monitor screen. Removing her hand, he crossed to it and looked into the screen.

The usual display of logico-mathematical notation had disappeared. Instead, there was a message in large, red capitals.

THAT WAS JUST A TASTER. IF YOU DON'T TURN THE SHIP AROUND I'LL KILL YOU ALL.

Seven

'We have tried the usual tricyclics and SSRIs,' Takahashi, one of the junior psychologists, said to Gelhardt, 'with little response, so we are forced to use this method. Well, "forced" is a little strong; Dr Ashworth himself recommended we use it on him.'

Gelhardt frowned slightly and looked down at Ashworth.

He was under general anaesthetic and receiving oxygen through a facemask. There were two padded electrodes on either side of his head. Takahashi indicated the Captain should step away and gave the signal to the operator. As the electric pulses stimulated his brain, Ashworth gave a few twitching movements but what could be seen of his face remained calm.

'Electroconvulsive therapy,' Gelhardt said to Takahashi, 'it's an ancient technique. I never thought I'd see it on the Magellan.'

'It may be old,' she replied, 'but it has a reasonable record of efficacy. And we have moved way beyond the limited understanding of the brain that the people had who first came up with this treatment in the Twentieth century. Some patients don't respond, of course, but many do.'

Gelhardt thanked her and was about to leave when she touched him on the upper arm.

'Captain, this sabotage. I hope you will be lenient with him when it comes to trial. He obviously was acting abnormally when the balance of his mind was disturbed. We are trying to free him from the depression he has fallen into. That must be taken into account.'

Gelhardt gave her a stern look.

'I can't be seen to have favourites. The penalty for endangering the ship is the absolute one.'

Her face sagged slightly.

'You mean—execution.'

'Yes. We are not on pre-Catastrophe Earth when "forgiveness" and "tolerance" were the norms, and people competed with each other to be the one who showed the most compassion. Times and situations have changed. A clear message must and will be sent.'

She touched his arm again.

'So you won't be turning back?'

'No—and Takahashi...'

'Yes?'

'Never, ever ask me that question again.'

She winced at the coolness of his words but he hadn't finished.

'Don't forget, I hadn't authorised this treatment. As far as I am concerned he should be on trial right now. I suspect the respect you have for your old boss has made you look for medical reasons for his behaviour rather than old-fashioned villainy. The only reason I'm not closing you down right now is if his mind clears he'll tell me who is working with him. You have seven ship-days to clear his mind and then you hand him over to me. Shortly afterwards, he goes into the compositer.'

He strode away down the corridor from the Medical Centre, and she watched him go.

Her face was emotionless.

Back in his office, Gelhardt leaned forward and put his head between his hands.

So many decisions, so many lives depending on him making the right ones!

Lafayette was with him.

'How is Roger? This must be very difficult; I know you two were close on Cloud City One.'

He leaned back and smiled up at her.

'Far too soon to say. The ECT is really the last resort. I want him to face up to what he's done and tell me who's working for him. I can't let this spread like a cancer.'

'But if he was temporarily insane, that means you can't have him executed.'

He stood up and walked away, his back turned.

'I don't want to think about it anymore! I'll make that decision when the time comes. We're all going into the compositer eventually, so what would it matter if I shorten the wait for some people!'

'You don't mean that, Karl. I know you will find it in your heart to forgive.'

He turned and smiled, but his smile was twisted.

'I hope so, Simone, but one way or the other it looks like I'm about to find out.'

***

Hardy looked at the message he had just composed.

Hoping to see you again. Could we meet at…

He could see Andretti just across the room from where he was sitting and felt a stab of guilt.

Andretti had been girlishly pleased when she had learned she was to be his Principal Wife, but things just hadn't worked out. Their sex life had been mechanical, dutiful—for Hardy at least. He had been unable to disguise the fact he preferred one of the Secondary Wives.

And now, his affections had moved on again.

What was it about Susannah Reid? She was classically good-looking, of course, but it was more than that. It was her *in-your-face* attitude, her self-belief, her refusal to be depressed by the mind-rotting monotony of life on the Magellan. She was like a glass of champagne to Andretti's tap water.

He looked at Andretti again, and she met his gaze with a blank face; a face that now held no hope. *Alisha*, he thought, *I was the wrong one for you. You wanted to be more than a baby-making machine and I couldn't respond the way I should have. The fault is mine!*

Unable to meet her stare anymore, he bowed his head and looked at his message.

He completed it and sent it.

Reid was lying on the couch when her device gave a small *beep!* to indicate a message had been received.

Quinn heard it too. He was at the computer console, his own messaging device by his side. He was looking at a schematic of the complex ducting that served the Magellan as a circulatory system, searching for the blockage which had given him so much trouble recently.

'Anyone I know?' he asked, casually.

She re-read the message and then deleted it.

'No, just a girlfriend. Wants to meet up for coffee.'

He chuckled.

'You're going to get coffee poisoning, if you keep on like this. Off you go!'

'I won't be long,' she said, and was gone.

Quinn's face hardened. He looked down at his messaging device.

On it was the frozen text from Hardy. Quinn had mentioned his suspicions to his friends and had been told of a way to spy on another's messages. Some of his friends had also had the same problem as he was now suffering. As he read the short text, he gave a grunt and then wiped it.

It was too soon to take action. He would wait a little longer for their crime to be beyond doubt.

And then he would act.

Hardy and Reid met in the Farm Area. It was impossible to meet in either of their cabins as there was usually someone there, a Secondary Wife or two.

Or a husband.

In the Farm Area, it was possible to be shielded from prying eyes by the towering vats. As Hardy waited, he could hear the maybots scurrying back and forth above him on the platforms which linked the vats. One passed near him on its way to join its fellows and he watched its crab-like motion up the ladder.

He had never seen a live crab, of course. It had long been too dangerous to live near the coast with the huge tides induced by the now highly eccentric orbit of the Moon.

But he had seen a picture once, a long time ago.

Suddenly, Reid was there, and they kissed for the second time.

Once again, Hardy was thrown helplessly into the massive breakers of a sea of sweetness.

As they pulled apart, Hardy looked around to see if they had been observed.

She tutted and placed a finger on the bridge of his nose.

'My, who's a little scaredy-cat, then?'

He grinned sheepishly.

'Sorry, I'm not used to this kind of thing. With me, sex has been like filling in a form.'

She stared at him, her forehead suddenly lined.

'Sex? Who said anything about sex? We're just good friends.'

She looked at him expectantly and then broke into peals of laughter at the way his face dropped. Then she slipped an arm under his own and laughed again.

'You're priceless, Jeff! Really priceless! I've never met a man whose buttons are so easy to press!'

'I'm sorry to be such a disappointment,' he said, somewhat testily.

She laughed again, her red hair sweeping around her features in her mirth.

'Disappointment? That remains to be seen, my friend. I'll let you know.'

They moved further into the dense forest of vats and kissed again.

'So how are things,' he asked, finally.

'With himself, you mean? It's all quiet at the moment.'

'Let's hope it stays that way. So what are we going to do?'

'Do? About what?'

'You and me. I want you to be my Primary Wife, but it's not normal procedure to choose one's own partner. You take what you're given.'

'Understood. But that's up to you, I think, darling.'

Hardy made a decision.

'Well, I'll go and see Gelhardt. I'm in his good books at the moment having caught the saboteur. I'll ask now before he forgets all about me.'

She smiled.

'That's more like it. And now I must go.'

She kissed him again and was gone, leaving Hardy with the lingering taste of her lips on his.

And so Hardy began the arduous task of arranging another meeting with the extremely busy Captain of the Magellan.

It took several "days" before Hardy could once again stand before Gelhardt. Hardy noticed at once that the other man looked even more grim and stony-faced than he remembered him, as if he had been grappling with existential crises in the time they had been apart.

Try as he might, Hardy could not think what that might have been.

'Well, what is it now?' Gelhardt snapped, barely bothering to look up from the papers before him.

Hardy cleared his throat.

'I have a request to make, sir,' he managed to enunciate.

Gelhardt finally pushed the papers aside, leaned back, and fixed Hardy in a gimlet stare.

'And what would that be?'

Hardy discovered his left knee had begun to tremble slightly, but manfully he pressed on.

'I would like to choose my Primary Wife for the next rotation. Sir.'

Gelhardt pursued his lips.

'Highly irregular. If we allowed the choice of Primary Wives, some women would be wanted by more than one man and some women wouldn't be wanted by any man. We assign Primary and Secondary purely on fertility grounds. I thought you knew that. I assume you find this woman physically attractive, but as I have already said, that is not a sufficient condition.'

Hardy felt a sudden desire to leap over the desk and pound Gelhardt's face into a mess resembling a strawberry compote but managed to control the sudden urge. Even Susannah wasn't worth a premature trip to the compositer.

Lafayette rose from her computer console and crossed to the silent tableau of Gelhardt and Hardy.

'Karl,' she said, 'this is lovely! Hardy is clearly in love, and love is a precious thing on this dreadful voyage. Given his recent service to the Magellan, surely a special allowance can be made for a man who is something of a hero? And I don't think you're quite right when you say mutual attraction plays no part. It's not essential, but surely we should take account of it when it's present?'

Hardy felt a warm glow of hope sweep through him. He gave a quick glance of appreciation and gratitude at Gelhardt's Primary Wife. He hadn't been this close to her before and was immediately struck by how good-looking she was.

Perhaps if there was a Rotation after the next one, maybe...

No! He pushed the thought away as being unworthy. Thank God there was no such thing as telepathy!

Gelhardt looked down at his desk; he was clearly thinking deeply.

Then he looked up, and Hardy could swear there was the beginning of a smile on his thick lips.

'I...' he began.

He did not finish the sentence.

There was a sudden klaxon-like roar in the room.

Lafayette rushed to her console, read the message displayed on its lambent screen and then turned a white face to Gelhardt.

'Karl, there's been another attack on the vats!'

Moments later, Hardy was looking back at the door to the Captain's room from the other side, his romantic future left undecided.

**

112

Gelhardt stood on the platform above one of the yeast vats. From where he stood, he could see drifting black blobs of dead yeast slowly settling to the bottom. He turned to the agronomists. This time Okunola, the Head Agronomist, was present along with Chén.

'HCl?'

'Definitely,' Okunola said, 'Not enough to sterilise the entire tank; just enough to do some damage.'

'Someone's playing with us,' Gelhardt said through gritted teeth. 'Good God, this is ridiculous. How can someone just walk up to the vats and pour acid into them!'

'Sir,' Chén ventured to speak, 'Surely the CCTV will show someone this time?'

Gelhardt gave her a quick look of appreciation.

'Yes. I ordered the coverage to be enhanced after the first attack. This time, we'll get the bastard. And there will be no mercy. Anyone who puts the lives of two hundred and forty-two human beings plus their innocent children in danger deserves nothing but a one-way ticket to the compositer.' He turned his attention to Okunola. 'You're sure it was just the acid? Nothing more sophisticated?'

'Just plain old acid. That's it.'

'Then it's someone who doesn't have access to the Biology Lab and RNA or DNA techniques. Someone who has to make do with what he can get hold of easily. Just brute force.' Gelhardt's brow grew more furrowed. 'Ashworth must have an accomplice; that must be it.'

'Sir,' Okunola said, with nervousness evident in his voice, 'did you not order all the HCl in the Medical Area to be transferred to the Biology Lab?'

Gelhardt went silent for a moment, looking into the yeast with a vacant expression. Then he turned to the agronomists.

'Yes, yes. I did. Yes, of course.' He waved down at the deck below the catwalk. 'OK, thanks to the two of you. Off you go.'

The two relieved-looking agronomists descended the steps and were gone. Gelhardt watched them go from his lofty position and, when they were no longer in sight, smashed a mighty fist down on the railing, so hard it made a visible shudder in the metal.

How could he have forgotten his own instructions! Was the pressure getting too much?

He shook his head to clear it. No! He had known there would be a weight of responsibilities back nearly two years ago when he proudly accepted the position of ship's Captain. No, he would find this madman, and his organic constituents would be recycled earlier than he had been expecting!

However, when back in his room, not long after his descent from the catwalk in the Farm Area, he was no longer so confident after reading the latest report.

'Nothing,' he whispered. His lips and throat were dry from the sting of defeat. ' How can that be?' He leapt to his feet and crashed a massive fist onto the back of his chair. 'Nothing! How can that fucking be!'

Lafayette continued to stare at the monitor screen. She adjusted the controls, and the images on the screen stopped moving and then began to scurry backwards in a distinctly comic fashion.

'What's the point?' Gelhardt said. 'We've watched it twice. There's nothing.'

'One more time,' she said softly. She waved at the desk behind them. 'Go and sit down. I'll review the recording one more time.'

Gratefully, he sat down. He felt his awareness of the room begin to blur and become faint as his head dropped down onto his chest.

Twenty minutes later, he awoke with a start as Lafayette gently shook his shoulder.

'Yes?' he said, sitting up ramrod straight. 'Did you…?'

The words died in his throat as he took in her expression. 'You didn't find anything, did you?'

She shook her head.

'Nothing. Just the maybots going about their ordinary business. No-one was leaning over and pouring liquid into the tank. Karl, darling, there was nothing on the recording. Nothing at all.'

He turned away from her and shook off her comforting hand. He had to think! Was there a superman stalking the crowded corridors of the Magellan—someone who could become invisible? Perhaps he was in the room right now, watching them, laughing silently, gloating in his victory.

Then he made a decision.

'I can't solve this on my own. I need help. I'm the Captain, not some techie. That's what all those so-called experts are there for. I'll turn the problem over to someone better qualified than me.'

'Oh, who would that be?'

'Someone better qualified in computing. There has to be a rational, real-world explanation. An explanation that doesn't require invisible supermen!'

'Yes,' Lafayette said quietly. Then she smiled. 'That would be a good idea!'

***

'Is it a good idea meeting up here?' Reid said.

'Why not? It's quiet up here, away from the madding crowd. And it means I can do this whenever I want to.'

Hardy leaned in to kiss her, but Reid put up a hand to block his questing lips.

'Hold it, Romeo. Being up here on the catwalk means Gelhardt will be able to watch everything we do. If he thinks we're the saboteurs, then it'll be the compositer for us, and I don't know about you, but I'm too young to die.'

'Don't you think I hadn't thought of that? We're far enough from the vats that we're in an area the cameras don't cover. We're perfectly safe.'

'Well, if you think I'm going to have sex on this hard platform, you've got another think coming. Grow up, Jeff!'

Hardy shrugged in a display of nonchalant indifference so obviously fake that Reid found it challenging to suppress her laughter. But she succeeded—she didn't want to upset the poor dear.

'There is another reason,' Hardy continued after he had finished his display of nonchalant indifference. 'They can't see us, but we can see the vats perfectly clearly. If the saboteur tries it again, then we've got him. Think of how grateful Gelhardt would be! He'd allow you to be my Primary Wife immediately; we wouldn't have to wait for the next rotation! Think of it!'

'Wonderful,' Reid murmured. 'Truly wonderful.'

Hardy caught her intonation.

'You know, sometimes, I think you're more interested in getting away from Quinn than being with me.'

Reid decided to row back a little.

'How can you think that! Come here, Lover Boy!'

Hardy did just that and was reasonably happy when they descended from the platform.

Eight

Tarkowski looked up from her printouts as Gelhardt entered her cabin without knocking.

'Can I help you?' she said, without attempting to conceal her annoyance.

Gelhardt sat opposite her, giving her a questioning look, as if he were studying a hitherto unknown animal.

'Would you say you are one of the best AI experts on this ship?'

'No, I would not.'

Gelhardt was taken aback.

'You're not?'

'No. I am the best AI expert on this ship. By a long, long way.'

Gelhardt rubbed his chin.

'I thought you specialised in surgery.'

'I did. Then I got tired of trying to fix masses of wet tissue; a primitive material that barely manages to produce a few muddled thoughts. There is no future for biological brains in this universe, Gelhardt. Structures that can't solve a few equations without recourse to inorganic minds. Pathetic blobs of jelly that manage to hang together for a few decades and then disintegrate. How could such primitives ever believe they could travel to the stars? We are just an encumbrance to true starships that could approach within a few percent of lightspeed. Animal life is not suited for exploring and understanding this universe.'

Gelhardt's stern face grew sterner.

'Quite a speech, doctor. I'd like to debate philosophical issues with you, but I don't have the time. Someone is trying to get me to turn this ship around. So I must ask—are you one of them?'

She gave a dry laugh.

'No. I know this mission is a laughable folly. A few simians are trying to escape from a sinking mass of vegetation they have foolishly gotten themselves trapped on. That's all we are. But I am enjoying the ride, watching you struggle to keep yourselves alive. My plan would guarantee that sane minds could reach Centauri, but you clearly think you know better than I.'

'We can discuss that again, if you are able to help me.'

A sudden look of interest appeared on Tarkowski's face; there was a stiffening in the underlying fascia; an alertness in the eyes.

'What kind of help?'

'Something is happening which defies the laws of cause and effect. Poison is getting into the tanks, but no recording device is showing that happening even though they are permanently trained on those tanks. Therefore…'

Tarkowski leaned closer to him, and a smile appeared on her face; a smile which did not in any way soften her features.

'Therefore, something is preventing the devices from recording the event.'

Gelhardt relaxed slightly.

'That's what I have come to believe.'

Tarkowski shuffled her papers into a neat pile and stood imperiously before him.

'Let's go.'

It was quite some way from Tarkowski's cabin to Gelhardt's office. However, the walk was conducted in complete silence; Gelhardt couldn't think of anything more to say to his austere companion, and she, in turn, showed no interest in conversation. But as they neared his office, Gelhardt became aware of a growing hubbub ahead of him. The main corridor was a huge but simple cylinder that ran the whole length of the Magellan without any curves or twists, and he could see there was a knot of people outside his door. He could hear a steady beat of sound as the crowd was chanting something over and over. But as he approached them, the sounds resolved themselves into words: 'Back to Earth! Back to Earth!'

The mob was mainly women, but with enough men to bring the sex distribution up to that of the Magellan's entire crew, so it was apparent the cause of their anger was one that affected both groups equally. Both sexes seemed equally vociferous, shouting their slogan over and over and banging their fists upon his door.

'It seems you have people who disagree with you, Captain,' Tarkowski observed dispassionately. Gelhardt did not reply but, leaving her behind, strode up to the crowd. As he walked, he pressed a button on his lapel. One man turned in his direction as he approached and yelled, 'Here he is! Let's get him!'

The crowd turned like a single organism, a giant amoeba composed of angry individuals. Almost instantly, Gelhardt was surrounded by fist-waving crew members. He said nothing but forced his powerful body through their mass until his back was resting on the door to his office. Then he spoke in a booming voice that cut through the chanting of 'Back to Earth! Back to Earth!'

'Let me tell you something!' he shouted above the babble. 'We are not going back! We cannot go back! Even if we could, there is nothing to go back to! Nothing, do you hear me, nothing!'

A man strode up to him, his face twisted with anger.

'You're lying! There is hope back there. The Space Arks—we can join them. After the Destroyer passes, we will get back to the surface and start rebuilding. A new start! A new hope! A new Earth!'

At his final sentence, the entire group cheered and began clapping. Then the chant began again, louder, more assured, 'Back to Earth! Back to Earth!'

'You fools,' Gelhardt yelled, 'you miserable, pathetic fools! If over two hundred people suddenly appeared in the Solar system, would you be welcome on board those things, assuming they ever get built? They're like us—every gram must be accounted for, every molecule of oxygen measured, every molecule of water treasured for the exact number of lifeforms they carry. So what would you do—board them like pirates and throw out the original crew? Take over the Arks without any training, but knowing you have their blood on your hands? Don't you understand their success is not guaranteed—no one knows what state Earth will be in after the passage. Even if it does not collide with Jupiter, it may be radioactive for millennia, by which time the Magellan could have established a thriving colony in the Centauri system!'

A few of the crowd looked a little uncertain after that speech and stopped chanting. However, the man who had spoken, and now obviously believed himself to be their leader, shook his head.

'You're lying again, Gelhardt. You're trying to keep us here as your obedient little slaves, your serfs, who you can watch as you sit on your throne. But we're not falling for it. Whoever is poisoning the food and setting off the alarms—he's got the right idea. And we've all seen the message on the screen. He's going to kill us all, give us a quick death if we don't abandon this crazy mission.' He looked behind him at his compatriots and then back to Gelhardt with a growing look of triumph on his face. 'So here's the deal—you turn this junk around or we'll give *you* a quick death!'

Gelhardt knew this was the moment. If he did not seize back control now, the entire Magellan would die in an orgy of blood-letting as those loyal to him fought the rebels for control of the ship. He knew what he had to do. And he did it.

He kicked the leader in the belly, sending him flying back into the startled throng and then, now there was sufficient space around him, reached into an inside pocket and withdrew a pistol. The fact that the Captain and his Security Staff had projectile weapons had been a closely guarded secret—until now. He pointed it directly at the leader, who was struggling to his feet.

'Now that's enough of this madness,' he said. 'No more! It finishes now! Stop now, and I will forget about all this. Go back to your duties and nothing will be said. No punishments. Try to attack me and I will kill six of you before you get near me. I have called Security and they will be here soon. After they have arrived, the survivors among you will be rounded up and sent to the compositers.'

Security will be here soon, he thought. *But will they side with me or this mob?*

He fixed his stare on the leader.

'I've never killed someone before,' he said, 'but I'm quite willing to find out what it feels like. Don't push me. I mean every word.'

Indecision appeared in the leader's face. Once again, he looked over his shoulder to gauge the mood of his followers. He turned back to Gelhardt and opened his mouth.

But what he would have said was never to be known, for at that moment four Security men arrived. And like Gelhardt, they were armed.

For a gut-wrenching moment of doubt, Gelhardt was unsure whether they would join him or the mob. Then relief swept over him as they took station on either side of him, weapons aimed at the protestors. Gelhardt's knees felt suddenly weak. He forced himself to shout again.

'It's over. You know it's over. But I will keep my promise: go back to your cabins and no more will be said. Go now, or I will change my mind.'

Several members of the crowd looked at each other and then back defiantly at Gelhardt. But some began to move away. And then, like a dam finally collapsing under the weight of water, the crowd broke up.

Their leader began to join them, but large hands descended on his shoulder and spun him around.

'Not you,' Gelhardt said. 'You threatened me and that can't go unpunished.'

The leader flinched under the words.

'I know you,' Gelhardt said, looking up and down at that now thoroughly cowed individual. (That was an unnecessary statement, of course: he knew everybody.) 'Johannsen—fuel technician. I believe we have more than enough of those.'

Johannsen's features crumpled.

'No, not the compositer! I only did what they asked!'

For a dizzy moment, Gelhardt was almost seduced by the thrill of absolute power. A few words from him and he would end Johannsen's life! Deciding life or death—the ultimate pleasure!

But he fought it down. That punishment was reserved for the saboteur and him alone.

He looked at the Chief Security Officer.

'Confine this man to his cabin for ten ship-days. Yeast and water only.'

Gelhardt did not bother to look at the relief flooding the face of the ex-leader as he was led away.

That issue was over; resolved. Now, back to his main problem.

And as if to underline the situation, he realised that Tarkowski had joined him.

'You did well, Captain,' she said. (Gelhardt noted, without comment, that she was now using his title.) 'I thought for a moment my services would not be required after all.'

'Well, they will be,' he said, studying her face for a moment. There was no emotion upon it, no excitement, no relief, no residual fear. 'Let's go in.'

They swept past the bewildered secretary in the anteroom and into his private office.

Lafayette rushed to him, hugging him, embracing him fiercely, reaching up to kiss him.

'Oh, Karl, I was so frightened! That loud shouting! I knew they'd captured you, I saw it all on the security camera. But there was nothing I could do to help you, nothing!'

'Except call Security,' he said mildly.

She looked shamefaced.

'Yes! But I was so worried I just couldn't think straight!' She noticed the other woman. 'Oh, hello. It's Helena Tarkowski, isn't it?'

'It is.' Tarkowski immediately turned to Gelhardt. 'Let's take a look at the CCTV recording, shall we?'

Gelhardt shot his Primary Wife an apologetic glance and guided Tarkowski to his desk.

He stood and watched her while she went over the recording several times. It took quite a while. At one point, Lafayette offered her some coffee, but it was refused. Tarkowski twice stopped the recording at a particular point and intently studied the frozen image. Gelhardt, standing next to her, also studied the scene but could see nothing of interest in it. Then she rose from the chair and said, 'I can do no more here. Send the recording to my computer, and I'll be able to study the metadata.'

'You've seen something?' he said with mounting excitement.

'I may have done. But I need the metadata to be sure. And I also need to study Roger Ashworth. I understand his staff are trying to restore his mental equilibrium. And failing. Hardly surprising as the entire Magellan medical staff are hardly able to lift a scalpel due to their accelerating lassitude.'

'Ashworth? He's not some kind of experimental animal. He must be the saboteur, but someone else is helping him. Surely, that's obvious.'

Tarkowski stared up at him, and it seemed to Gelhardt there was almost pity in her eyes.

'I can tell you're not a scientist, Captain. No true scientist would ever say *That's obvious.'*

Gelhardt looked back at her. Tarkowski's air of effortless superiority was beginning to grate on him. But he needed her; she had seen something in the recording that both he and Lafayette had missed. And until she revealed what it was, he was helpless.

'You'll send me the recording,' she continued, clearly unworried by the fact that she was issuing demands to her Captain. 'I'll study them, and then I'll visit Roger. I'll need access to the brain scans he's had. I believe he's been undergoing ECT treatment.'

'He has. I'll arrange for us to visit him when you have let me know you're ready.'

'There's no need for you to be there, Captain.'

'Oh yes, there is. It's because I *am* the Captain.'

***

122

Tarkowski took the electroencephalogram from the Senior Nurse and stared at it for a long time. Then she turned her stare onto the nurse, who seemed to flinch slightly under her gaze.

'This is definitely the frequency you have been using during Ashworth's sessions?' Tarkowski said.

The nurse pulled herself slightly straighter and tried to return gaze for gaze.

'Yes, it is. Is there a problem?'

'Most definitely. Did you really expect this to make any difference?'

The nurse bridled at that.

'Dr Tarkowski, I do not appreciate someone whose speciality is in Artificial Intelligence coming into my clinic and presuming to tell me my job. Dr Ashworth himself recommended this frequency and duration.'

Tarkowski gave a humourless smile; one so fleeting her lips hardly moved.

'Nurse Takahashi, before I moved to the infinitely more interesting discipline of Machine Intelligence, I was a first-class surgeon and—before I realised the futility of it—I had learned a very great deal about the human brain. So please don't waste my and your time by challenging me. I just want data from you—I don't want your opinions.'

Takahashi fell silent, perhaps thinking of a riposte, but Tarkowski had moved on.

'I want to see Roger now; I trust he's awake?'

He was, and Tarkowski pulled aside his privacy curtain and entered his room. Outside, Takahashi was whispering to Gelhardt.

'Captain, she's awful. Do I have to put up with her rudeness and arrogance?'

'I'm afraid so, Maria,' he said. 'I can't stand her either. And,' he added, 'I'm not breaking any confidences telling you that: she already knows it. No, we just have to accept her. If she's half as good as she says she is, she's our only hope of getting out of this sabotage crisis.'

On the other side of the curtain, Ashworth looked up in surprise as Tarkowski walked in, unannounced.

'Helena,' he said as he struggled into a sitting position in the bed, 'I know I've been having hallucinations recently, but I don't remember thinking I'd turned into a computer.'

She sat on the bed and looked at him. Her face was impassive but without its standard coldness.

'It would be better if you had, but, unfortunately, you haven't. Now…' She reached out and held a hand. 'Why have you been sabotaging the ship?'

He pulled the hand away and hid his face underneath both hands.

'I can't remember! I said I'd done it, but now I don't think I did! It's just being trapped in this tiny metal tube! I can't deal with it anymore!'

A slightly tender expression came into Tarkowski's face, and she gently pulled the hands away so she could look into his face.

'I understand that, Roger. I don't feel that pressure myself, but I know a lot of people do. I don't hold any hopes for my personal happiness, but I would still like the Project to succeed. Unfortunately, Artificial Intelligence can't evolve itself; it will need biological vectors. But don't worry.' She leaned forward and kissed him on the forehead. 'I'm going to get you out of here.'

She returned to Takahashi and said, 'Paper. Give me something to write on.'

Tarkowski sat down and wrote for a few seconds on the sheet and then handed it to the Senior Nurse.

'What's this?'

'What you will change the ECT settings into. If it doesn't work, he's beyond help.' She stood. 'But it will work.'

***

Later that "day", Gelhardt and Lafayette were standing next to Tarkowski, who was seated before Gelhardt's computer screen.

'You say you've seen something?' Gelhardt was saying. There was an odd mix of excitement and concern in his voice.

'I did.' A slim finger pointed to a moving image of the yeast tank region of the Farm Area. It showed a group of maybots moving around on the outer surface of a tank, checking for leaks and welding the metal back together if they found any fissures. In addition, a few

124

maybots had slipped into the yeast broth itself to examine the structure from the inside. 'Did you not see it?'

'See what?' Lafayette said, somewhat exasperatedly. 'It's just the maybots doing routine maintenance.'

Tarkowski was not used to demonstrating patience, but she tried again.

'Look, I'll step through the recording frame by frame. It's glaringly obvious in the metadata, but you can see it in the actual images if you look carefully.'

Gelhardt and Lafayette watched the scene again. It was only the third time they'd seen it, but it already felt like the hundredth. It showed the maybots going about their everyday business; some swimming in the yeast foam like the crabs they resembled. Tarkowski knew they hadn't seen what she had, and so she stopped the movement and then flipped the images back and forth for a while.

'This section is not part of the original recording.'

'What!' said Lafayette and Gelhardt simultaneously, and then looked at each other.

'Yes, it's evident in the metadata, but it is visible in this recording. If you have eyes to see, that is,' she added, unhelpfully. 'Look, at one point this maybot is *here*.' She tapped the screen. 'And then an instant later, it's point seven four of a centimetre further over. *Here*. It's a very small distance, but somehow the maybot crossed it in zero time.'

'Couldn't it just be a glitch in the recording?' Lafayette asked, staring intently at the frozen image.

'It could be, if I didn't have the metadata. But I do and it isn't.'

'So, what does that mean?' Lafayette said, turning from the screen to look down on Tarkowski.

Tarkowski turned her chair to face into the room and stood before them.

'It means,' she said, with an air of finality, 'that there is a whole section from that point which shows things that didn't happen. That section is a computer-generated interpolation. I would imagine the section it replaced showed the saboteur in action.'

'Incredible!' Lafayette said, her face suffused with the flush of intense emotion. 'Can you regenerate the section that was replaced?'

'No. It's gone. I also tried asking the maybots directly if they had seen anyone interfering with the vats, but they said they had not. But there is other work I can do.'

'And what would that be?'

'I'll let you know when I've done it.' She turned from Lafayette and looked at Gelhardt. 'However, this clumsy saboteur is only part of our problems.'

Gelhardt flopped onto the chair she had vacated and looked up at her wearily.

'Oh, and I thought someone trying to kill us all was enough for one time. What other existential threats are there, pray?'

'Before he became unreliable, Roger warned of the danger of asthenia.'

'Not to me, he didn't. And what is *asthenia*, may I humbly enquire?'

'Basically, the lack of the will to do anything. A hopeless fatalism. An infectious lassitude. The Medical Centre seems the worst affected. I noticed it when I visited Ashworth and spoke to that useless Takahashi woman. But that's just the Psychology Area—we can live without that excrescence. The real Medical Area—the part dealing with infections, surgery, that's what I'm talking about. They've basically downed tools and are just sitting around, gazing into infinity.'

'That is bad news,' Gelhardt said, in a voice so faint he could hardly be heard.

'It is. As yet, there have been no outbreaks of infections on board. We've been lucky; with so many people crowded together, it's only a matter of time. What if a charged particle gets through the screens, hits an *E. coli* bacterium and turns it lethal?'

Gelhardt raised his arms, palms uppermost, in what looked dangerously like an admission of defeat.

'What can we do?'

'One thing we can do is upload our conscious minds while we are still sane. As I've told you, things are only going to get worse. Our knowledge may be the only thing that saves the future generations on this ship if they hit some major crisis—as I'm sure they will.'

'That won't help with epidemics.'

'No, but Roger was working on psychotropic drugs before he went off the rails. If I can bring him back, the two of us should be able to come up with something that will restore motivation to the medical staff—indeed, to everybody. I know almost as much about organic brains as I do about electronic ones.' She shot Gelhardt an accusatory look. 'Just as well you didn't have him executed, Captain.'

'Dr Tarkowski,' Gelhardt growled, 'It's so easy for you to stand there and mock me, but I'm the one who has to make the decisions in real-time, as and when the crises arise. I don't have your luxury of hindsight. So may I suggest you give your predilection for criticising me a well-earned rest? We can talk about your ideas again—after Ashworth becomes reliable and when the saboteur is caught. If Ashworth is, as I firmly believe, the culprit, I can show clemency because of his disturbed mental state. I'd rather have him working on cures than making an earlier than expected visit to the compositer.'

Tarkowski was silent for a few seconds, and then: 'Well said, Captain. I accept the rebuke. First things first.'

***

Hardy looked at the screen in amazement. Andretti joined him, and together their astounded eyes took in the message flashing on the screen in ominous red capitals against a glaring yellow background.

TIME IS SHORT! DEPOSE THE TYRANT GELHARDT NOW!

The command vanished and then another appeared:

GELHARDT WILL KILL US ALL! TAKE HIM PRISONER!

And then another:

SEIZE CONTROL! TURN THE SHIP AROUND!

Then:

BACK TO EARTH! BACK TO EARTH! NOW! NOW!

'What the Hell is all that about?' Andretti said, her hand resting on his shoulder in a habit formed in their days of intimacy.

'It must be the saboteur,' Hardy said, 'sounds like the bastard's getting anxious. Maybe he thinks the noose is tightening.'

'You found the saboteur, didn't you? At least, that's what you keep telling me.'

'Roger Ashworth? Yes, he's confessed, hasn't he? Why would anybody confess to something they haven't done, if it means the compositer? Maybe he wasn't the top; perhaps he was just a subordinate.' He rose from the computer chair. 'Anyway, I've done my bit. They can't expect me to do all the work of rounding the bastards up.' He glanced around, not quite catching Andretti's gaze.

'Well, time for my walk now, I think. I'm getting a bit too stiff to spend a long time in front of that machine.'

Her eyes narrowed as she moved between him and the door.

'You needn't lie anymore, Jeff. I know exactly where you're going.'

He shrugged helplessly.

'I'm sorry. It is what it is.'

Andretti's face twisted in such a fashion that for an instant he didn't recognise her.

'Go on then! Go to her! I hope you make her as miserable as you've made me!'

Hardy tried to think of a response, any kind of response: a harsh response; a conciliatory response; a loving response; a neutral response—but he could think of nothing, so, after giving her a weak smile, he left.

They had agreed to meet atop the food vats in the Farm Area again, and as he puffed his way up the long ladder to the catwalk, he espied her waiting in the shadows. She crossed to him and gave him a pull to help him up the last few rungs.

'You're getting too unfit for this,' she observed, as he finally got to his feet in front of her. 'You should spend more time in the EZ.'

'I can't see you, do my work, and break my arse in the EZ as well,' he said, somewhat testily. 'And I'm glad to see you as well, Suzannah!'

'Now, now,' she said, smiling as she planted a kiss on the bridge of his nose. 'It's just I don't want you to have a heart attack during all that love-making we'll be doing!'

'Hmm, I wonder when that'll be happening,' he responded, and then frowned.

Dammit, his heart was thumping!

Much to his annoyance, he had to sit down to rest with his back resting on the side of one of the large tanks. She joined him, and reached for one of his hands.

'You know,' she said quietly, 'I prefer not to speak in clichés, but we can't go on meeting like this.'

He raised an eyebrow,

'And why not?'

'For a start, it's damned uncomfortable, but more importantly, I've got a strong feeling he knows we're meeting together.'

Hardy pursed his lips.

'That could be dangerous. But why do you think that?'

'He hasn't come right out and said anything; it's just the way he speaks. He always seems to be mocking me now in a kind of insidious way he never used to. Before, he was very blunt; there was no wordplay. But now there is—it's like he's taunting me, waiting for me to slip up.'

Hardy's face grew simultaneously concerned and thoughtful.

'I'm sure Gelhardt was about to allow me to make you my Primary Wife but that damned alarm went off. He's been too busy to see me since.'

'You'll have to try again, Jeff. I'm getting really worried.'

'I'll try, but this saboteur thing is taking up all his time by the look of it. I've heard he's got that human iceberg Tarkowski working for him now. She's like a terrier with a rat; if I was that guy, I'd give up now!'

Reid snuggled closer to him and leaned over him so their faces were almost touching.

'Jeff, I…' She stopped and looked around. 'What was that?'

Hardy leapt to his feet, his startled eyes searching for Quinn. Then he relaxed.

'Maybots.'

She joined him and together they saw a group of the crab-like machines climbing up the side of the tank they were next to. They all reached the lip of the vat and fanned out along it. Hardy turned to Reid.

'We'd better move further in. We're too exposed here.'

She didn't move but instead pointed at the nearest robotic device.

'What's that one doing?'

Hardy looked. He saw nothing unusual, the maybot was unscrewing a panel on its side, and was probing into it with one of its thinner appendages.

'Jeff, I…'

She did not complete her sentence, for at that moment a large hand clamped down on her shoulder and spun her around. Even as she began to turn, she knew who it was who had joined them, but was shocked to the core to see Quinn's other hand was holding a large knife.

'Got you.' Quinn said in an unemotional tone, although his face was split by a triumphant grin. 'This time you're going to get what's coming to you, slut!'

'Jeff!' she called, 'Get him off me!'

Hardy found he could not move; his feet felt cemented to the catwalk. Everything seemed unreal, as if he were watching a bad melodrama. Maybots scurried unconcernedly around his motionless feet as he looked at the nightmare unfolding before him.

Quinn looked across at Hardy, contempt written large on his features.

'Why don't you come and rescue your lover, you useless piece of shit! Are you just going to stand there while I slice her into nice juicy steaks?'

'Jeff!' Reid called desperately, 'Please, Jeff!'

As Hardy stood there, as motionless as a figure carved from stone, visions of him desperately descending the ladder and escaping tumbled through his brain.

Get far away! his thoughts thundered, far away from the wicked glinting terror of that knife; that savage, life-ending strip of steel. As he watched, Quinn drew the point across Reid's left cheek, leaving a thin line of dripping red behind it.

Then Hardy knew what he had to do. He leapt at Quinn and crashed into him with all the power he could muster. But Quinn did not lose his grip on Reid, and all three violently collapsed together in a struggling mass onto the catwalk. Hardy tried to pull Quinn's knife-arm away from Reid, but the limb resolutely refused to bend and instead his opponent pulled free and slashed at Hardy, missing his face by millimetres. In the mêlée, Reid managed to roll away, ending up perilously near the edge of the platform. The nearby maybots continued their mysterious activities without concern.

Both men shakily got to their feet.

'Well, finally grown a pair, have you, Hardy?' Quinn laughed, making wide sweeping motions with the knife as he advanced on the other. Hardy backed away, knowing that every step brought him closer to the edge.

'Jeff!' she cried, 'don't try to fight him, he'll kill you!' She pulled herself upright and called to Quinn. 'Dermot, stop! I'll come back to you, just don't kill him!'

Quinn did stop and looked back and forth between the pair. He laughed again.

'Too late for that, sweetheart. You've made your choice, now live with it. But why you'd want a pathetic excuse for a man like this turd beats me. But you won't be together for long because I'm going to kill him and then you!'

He continued his advance on Hardy, who could now feel that the backs of his shoes were no longer supported by the platform. He could see now how his life was going to end: he would rush Quinn who would expertly drive the knife deep into his heart.

So be it.

He rushed Quinn who, as predicted, raised the knife to meet Hardy's desperate charge.

But at that moment, Reid propelled herself from the railing, and sliding across the deck, drove her feet into Quinn's ankles. He staggered, and his knife did not plunge into its intended target. Instead it cut a deep gash across Hardy's belly. Hardy felt the cold steel cut like a dagger of flame through the fat and integuments of his abdomen; felt the hot rush of blood. He collapsed like a falling tree.

Quinn staggered at the platform's edge, tried to grasp the railing, failed, and began to fall. But, throwing away the knife, he managed to hold the edge of the platform with his fingertips.

'Susannah!' he called, 'help me!'

Reid stood over him, the blood from the cut on her cheek forming a slowly spreading fan on the flesh. Her green eyes blazed.

'Help you? After what you've done, you bastard? I don't think so!'

But Quinn was a powerful man. Supporting himself only by his fingers, he began slowly to draw himself higher, his great biceps straining into balls of granite as he reached for the nearest support.

Reid moved closer, holding his knife.

'Goodbye, Dermot.'

She stamped with all her strength on Quinn's hands. He gave a great cry and lost his grip. Under the low gravity of the Magellan, he might have survived the fall had not Reid slashed his throat before he began his descent. Whether or not he would survived the fall was academic: he was dead when it ended.

Reid hurried to the prone Hardy and looked in horror at a great crimson stain spreading over his torso. She rushed to the edge of the catwalk. Far below, people had already gathered around the body.

'Help!' she shouted. 'Help me! There's a man dying here!'

Gelhardt got the call shortly afterwards.

'What's the matter?' Lafayette said, seeing the look of horror on her husband's face.

'Murder. And a man dying. And the Medical Lab is out of action!' Fleeting emotions passed rapidly over his features. And then they hardened. 'Tarkowski.' He pressed a button on his console. 'Tarkowski, get into your scrubs. You've got a patient coming in for urgent abdominal surgery!'

'I'm busy.'

The roar Gelhardt uttered then made methods of electronic communication unnecessary. It felt to Lafayette that it could be heard in the Centauri system.

'Get into scrubs and get the theatre ready! Otherwise, I'm coming over there, ripping your limbs off one by one and making you eat them!'

There was a short pause.

'Understood, Captain. I'll get ready.'

***

Hardy did survive his wound, although he found he was not fit for any amorous encounters for quite some time. And although Reid had killed Quinn, Gelhardt chose to classify the act as self-defence, and she was not sent to the compositer. However, because she had been found with a man who was not her husband, he put her on a raw yeast-and-water diet for thirty ship-days.

And so Gelhardt, Lafayette and Hardy's saviour assembled once again in his office.

'I want to thank you for stepping in like you did, doctor,' Gelhardt said, after Tarkowski had taken her seat.

She shrugged.

'It was a simple wound. Very clean; his knife must have been extremely sharp. He'll make a full recovery.'

'Still, without you, he would have died.'

She shrugged again and Gelhardt moved on to what he really wanted to discuss.

'How is Ashworth?'

'Doing very well. His mind is clearing very rapidly. I think he wants to have a long talk with you, Captain. Seems he wasn't too pleased to hear he was destined for the compositer.'

Gelhardt looked unconcerned.

'He might have a cause for complaining—if he hadn't confessed, that is.' He leaned forward towards Tarkowski and his eyes seemed aflame. 'Now, down to business. Have you found out anything about the saboteur since we last discussed him?'

'Oh yes, I solved that quite a while ago. I have traced the subterfuge back to a specific computer.'

Lafayette also leaned towards the calm figure of the AI specialist, her face glowing with excited expectation.

'You have! Whose computer was it?'

Tarkowski's smile was, as usual, glacial.

'Surely, it's obvious? Why yours, of course, Simone.'

Nine

Suddenly, the air in the room felt as if it were holding a tremendous charge of static electricity, building up to an irresistible discharge. Gelhardt sat utterly still and rigid; Lafayette looked both angry and confused, her wide-opened eyes fixed on her accuser. Tarkowski sat with her hands folded neatly on her lap, a ghost of a smile playing on her thin lips. All three were totally motionless, giving the tableau the appearance of a group of photorealistic statues.

It was Lafayette who broke the illusion and moved first. She pulled herself away from Tarkowski, with the air of someone who has just avoided stepping on a snake.

'Is this some kind of joke, Helena; some stupid prank, because you must know you're talking nonsense?'

'No, of course not. I thought it was you right from the beginning. Your desire to abandon this mission is well known throughout the vessel.'

'I and a hundred others. The recent near-riots prove that.'

'Yes, the virus of fear and despair spreads very easily in the close confinement of a ship like the Magellan. But they did not have your skills. They could only follow the urgings that you have implanted in them. You dissuaded your husband from punishing Roger because, in his mental confusion, he had confessed to the crime, after Hardy, in his stupidity, seized on one item to implicate him. Roger even believed he was telling the truth. As long as he was revealed to be the saboteur, it could not be you. But I always knew it was you, not Roger. I just need to accumulate the data necessary to *prove* it was you.'

Lafayette turned to Gelhardt, who up until that moment had neither moved nor spoken.

'Darling, you know it can't be me! I'm hardly ever out of this room, and in my condition, I couldn't possibly climb a ladder to the top of one of those tanks!'

Gelhardt kept his eyes on Tarkowski.

'Explain,' was all he said, in low, quiet tones that hinted at tightly suppressed fury.

'Of course. As Mrs Gelhardt says, she could not have climbed to the top of the vats. So if she is the culprit, she must have had accomplices.'

Lafayette: 'And who would they have been?'

Tarkowski: 'The maybots.'

'Impossible. They have no minds, no wants, no needs. It doesn't matter to them if the Magellan reaches a Centauri planet, or flies into the heart of a sun. How could I have seduced them to my wicked plan?'

'You did not *seduce* them. You *re-programmed* them. Next to myself, you are the most able programmer on the ship. You broke into their operating system and gave them new orders: to poison the Magellan's food supply in order to force your husband into turning the ship around.'

'The hydrochloric acid: authorisation is necessary if it is to be removed from the Engineering Section.'

'Authorisation by a *human* if another *human* requires the substance. A human has to explain to another human why he requires it. It must be signed out and signed back in. But a maybot does not. If a maybot is seen to take a small amount of the acid—and I'm sure that must have happened, at least once—a human naturally assumes it is needed for the necessary maintenance work. Maybots do not need permission to carry out their maintenance, nor do they need to explain to a human what they have done and why they did it. They are essential to the safety of the ship, which is why they would be so dangerous if the opposite became their command.'

'And the other issues: the false collision alert; the temperature drop—that was also me?'

'Of course it was; those other acts of sabotage were simplicity itself compared to poisoning the food supply. Once you had broken into the ship's operating system, you could conjure any number of fake emergencies. The one thing you could not do was turn the ship around because that involves a knowledge of physics you do not possess. A little learning is a dangerous thing, Mrs Gelhardt.'

'This is still just a story you are spinning, Tarkowski, for reasons that I do not understand. Oh, perhaps I do—maybe you hope to replace me as the Primary Wife of the most powerful man on the Magellan.'

'I need your husband only because he alone can authorise my project, a project which I believe to be vital for the success of this mission. I require only his mental strength, his will; not his penis, or any other physical part of him.'

'Lies. Fantasies from a dried-up creature who is more than half-computer herself. It is so sad to see one woman turn her spite on another woman just because she envies the other's success, instead of working together for the benefit of all womankind.'

'Not so: I am interested only in the human race as a whole, not the different types natural selection has created in order to maintain the species. The human race stands on the very edge of extinction, of utter annihilation. Fraschini and De Vries had the vision and the mental strength to devise the only way our species can survive, but I would say the odds are very much against its success. Of course, I need your husband's approval, but I do not need to destroy you in order to obtain that.'

'You will not destroy me, Tarkowski, for you have no proof of your deranged ramblings. I am very glad to hear that Ashworth is recovering because he will be sufficiently sane to understand why your corpse is being placed in the compositer. No-one accuses the Primary Wife of the ship's Captain of such treachery and carries on living.'

Finally, Gelhardt spoke.

'Give me some proof now, Tarkowski, or I will call Security who will place you in the holding cell prior to your execution.'

Tarkowski showed no signs of stress and stood before the Captain and his Primary Wife.

'Come with me to Mrs Gelhardt's computer and I will show you.'

'You cannot have access to my computer. It is impenetrably locked against all possible unauthorised access.'

Tarkowski gave a sad, tolerant smile.

'Come, Mrs Gelhardt, I have been like a little mole, burrowing inside your machine for quite some time now. The time for underestimating me is long gone.'

True to her word, the computer flashed into obedient life under Tarkowski's agile fingers.

'I will now show you the original part of the recording that so puzzled us last time,' she said dispassionately.

The video of the maybots working on the food tanks unrolled before them.

'This is where the fake images were inserted.'

Gelhardt watched as a maybot climbed onto the lip of a tank and, from a slot in its body, retrieved a small tube. A clear colourless liquid was visible falling from the tube as the little machine tipped it into the mass of floating algae.

'Just enough to damage the algae, but not to kill it,' Tarkowski observed, 'after all you have to have something to eat on the way back.'

A silence fell and once again the air seemed to crackle with electric tension.

'No proof it was me,' Lafayette said, in a voice that was now dry and brittle.

Tarkowski made some more movements on the controls and the video disappeared to be replaced by lines of densely nested coding. She pointed to a block that was in a different typeface to all the others.

'Your imprimatur I believe, Mrs Gelhardt,' Tarkowski said, and there seemed to be a hint of sadness in her tone, 'no coding will be accepted by the Central Computer without such proof of authorship.'

Silence returned like the fall of the executioner's axe.

Lafayette turned desperately to Gelhardt. She wrapped her arms around his neck.

'Surely you don't believe this madwoman, Karl? Please tell me you don't!'

He gently removed her arms and moved away.

'Yes, Simone, I do. It all makes sense now. Obviously I'll have other computer experts look over the code but, yes, I do believe Tarkowski.'

Lafayette turned to face Tarkowski.

'You!' she spat, 'you've done this to us!'

And she sprang on the other woman, dragging her to the floor and raining a fusillade of blows on her face.

Gelhardt pulled her off Tarkowski and sat her down.

'Simone, Simone,' he said in a voice that was splintering with horror and despair, 'Why did you do it? Why didn't you listen to me when I told you we couldn't turn back? Why, why?' Tears began to glisten in his eyes.

She put her face in her hands and muffled words, interposed with sobs, were just audible.

'Why didn't you listen to me when I told you to get a panel of experts together to find a way? Didn't you hear what that half-alive creature over there said—*We're not going to make it!*'

Gelhardt stood before his wife, and now glistening tracks of tears were on his face.

'Simone, Simone,' he whispered, 'my darling Simone. What must I do now?'

'You know what you must do,' Tarkowski said from the other side of the room.

He spun around and stood over her, his face red, his moist eyes bulging.

'Shut up, you heartless monster! This is my wife we're talking about, not some farmyard animal!'

Tarkowski lowered her head under that onslaught and said no more.

He looked around as if looking for some way out, some method of escape from the dread decision that was closing on him like the jaws of a terrible predator.

Now only Lafayette's sobs could be heard.

Then he moved, slowly, unwillingly.

He sat behind his desk and then pressed a contact on his console.

His voice when they heard it was desiccated and tortured.

'Security,' he said. 'Two officers to my room. Now.'

***

After they took Lafayette into custody, Gelhardt did not leave his office for two ship-days. During that period, other experienced programmers went over Tarkowski's analysis under his strict instructions to subject it to the fiercest criticism they could muster and not miss any flaw in her reasoning, if they valued their freedom. But after that period, they unanimously agreed her findings were valid.

He then did a ship-wide telecast in which he stated the saboteur had been identified and imprisoned. Then, after a noticeable pause during which the crew looked at each other in anticipatory puzzlement, he announced the saboteur's name. The screen went black immediately after the name was revealed.

He then sat alone in his office for another ship-day; accepting no calls, receiving no callers. Minor problems came and went, but no one informed the Captain that they had come and gone.

Then three ship-days after the confrontation between Tarkowski and his Primary Wife, he called Tarkowski to his office. She sat before his desk, not daring to utter a word until he finally spoke to her.

Eventually, he looked up from his sheaf of papers about conditions on the Magellan and looked directly at her.

'You did well in identifying the saboteur, Tarkowski,' he said in a cold, flat voice.

Unable to think of a response that might not anger him, she kept her face still and expressionless and merely gave a brief nod to show she had heard and accepted the comment.

'I said I'd look into your proposal about machine intelligence if you caught the saboteur,' he said.

Again the silent nod.

He leaned back in his chair, never taking his gaze off the woman before him.

Was that hate smouldering in those eyes? she wondered.

'Remind me of why I should accept such a bizarre procedure.'

She relaxed: there would be no further oblique or cryptic references to the woman now sitting alone in a containment cell. She knew ancient cultures had been prone to execute the bringers of evil tidings, but it seemed increasingly likely that was not to be her fate. At last, she felt free to speak in her usual confident, analytical manner.

'We are aboard what is known as a *Generation Ship;* that is, one whose journey would take longer than several multiples of an average human lifetime to complete. The problems associated with such journeys have been discussed at length in the literature, but no actual research was ever done. That was because no-one foresaw a situation in which such vessels would be launched without any prior practical experimentation on the psychological conditions of the crew of such vessels.'

Unnervingly, he continued to stare directly at her, with only an occasional blink to reveal he was actually a living being. Tarkowski was not too familiar with the emotion of nervousness and found she had to think very carefully to marshal her thoughts; still, she pressed on.

'What little research was done all pointed to the same conclusion: namely that as time passed, the inhabitants of the vessel would find they had less and less in common with those who had set out on the journey. Many would cease to believe that the original planet was any more than a myth and instead would come to believe that their ship was, in fact, the entirety of the universe. In so doing, they would lose first interest in, and then understanding of, the purpose of their flight, and cease to desire arrival at the fabled destination; either because they saw endless flight as the norm, or because they had ceased to accept the reality of the destination.'

'Surely Fraschini and De Vries knew this.'

'Yes, they did. And I know that to be true because I discussed it with them. But they had no solution; they saw no hope for humanity other than the Lightsail Project and, basically, ended up "hoping for the best".'

'But you don't think the best will happen.'

'No, Captain, I do not. I foresee only a gradual, insidious decline into a kind of barbarism. To get to Centauri will require about four human generations; prolonged spaceflight under our conditions is bound to shorten human life. Our medical facilities can mend broken bones—or heal lacerated abdomens—but it can't deal with the major biochemical problems which are bound to occur.'

'So the entire Lightsail Project was doomed from the outset. Fraschini and De Vries were deluded fools. When the Magellan arrives at Centauri, it will be crewed by drooling, shit-soiled simpletons.'

'Not the words I would use, Captain. But unfortunately, your prophecy has a high probability of coming true.'

'And the way out; the solution?'

Did a kind of light come into Tarkowski's features then? Did her gaze suddenly become more powerful, her posture become firmer, her demeanour begin to radiate strength and assurance?

'I have one, Captain. What if the future crew of the Magellan could talk to the original crew? I don't just mean recordings of us offering homespun homilies and hackneyed advice on getting the best out of life, but being able to respond to whatever problems they may face in their day! To be with them; to offer proper advice to them, to reinforce the message of why they are there.' Her voice dropped, became sombre. 'To remind them they are the fugitive children of murdered Earth.'

Suddenly, Tarkowski felt she was no longer on the lonely Magellan; she saw herself face to face with another woman; an assured, commanding woman, possessed of transcendent beauty framed by a cascade of the finest spun-gold hair.

Oh, Baldwin! If only I'd met you! Then you would have seen just how far you could have reached in trying to control and humiliate me! Just you and me, Baldwin, mind to mind!

'Doctor,' Gelhardt said gently, 'you were saying?'

With a start, Tarkowski realised that she had been silent for some time as her mind ranged far and wide with her fantasy.

'Yes, of course,' she said, flushing slightly, 'my procedure. Yes, my procedure.'

'Is?'

'Yes, the procedure. My plan is to take the mentalities of selected crew members with a wide range of experience and upload the essential part of those minds in digital form to be stored on imperishable media, to be accessed as and when required.'

'I hesitate to question someone as capable as you, doctor, but is that remotely possible?'

Tarkowski's face became animated in her eagerness.

'Yes, yes! It's been talked about since the twenty-first century, but only recently have the mathematical and AI issues been resolved. Professor Nowak published his findings not long before I came to Venus, and I have been studying them ever since. I found some inconsistencies in his work, but I have cleared them up and I'm now sure we can store the essence of a human mind electronically. Not the actual minds, of course, that would be a terrible thing to do to a person; to confine a living, conscious mind in the memory of a computer, but the essence, the memories, and most importantly, the ability to reason—that would be preserved!'

Gelhardt frowned.

'Will the process hurt?'

'No, of course not!—Sorry, I mean: *no, Captain*, it will be just as painless as an ECG session. There will be no after-effects.'

'You've done this before, then?'

'No, I haven't. I'm sorry, but I don't see what you're getting at, Captain.'

Gelhardt's gaze felt like it was boring through her eyes, into her brain, into her mind. Then, just for an instant, she became aware of the heavy load of sorrow that the man was carrying.

'Imagine if you will, doctor, the horror of waking up as a disembodied mind inside a machine. Unable to escape, unable even to die. Can you guarantee that cannot happen, Tarkowski? Can you reassure me such a fate will not be visited on my people?'

She hesitated; Gelhardt was on the verge of giving her the authorisation to proceed, and now he was asking hypothetical questions about an as yet untried process. But she could not let the prize slip from her fingers.

'I can guarantee that,' she finally said, attempting to match his earnest stare. 'The mathematics do not permit such a total duplication. The data required would be much greater than my procedure could possibly generate.'

'And who would be the donors—if I can use that term—of your procedure?'

'Well, I, to start with. I couldn't ask anybody to do something I wasn't prepared to undergo. Then, after me, the ablest minds on board; people of proven ability and,' she added softly, 'of stable mentality. You are an obvious candidate, if I may say so, Captain.'

'No, not I. My strengths lie in leadership, management of people, and dealing with internal and external pressures; unexpected problems. And, more importantly, I couldn't take the risk of finding myself existing as an immortal mind in a metal box.'

'There is no possibility of that, Captain.'

'Nevertheless, I do not intend to face any chance which is not proven to be zero.' He sighed. 'This existence is more than enough for me.'

She said nothing, having seen his mask of ruthless competence slip a little. To see Gelhardt as merely a man was somehow disturbing. Just for a moment, she felt like a child realising for the first time that her parents were fallible human beings.

He had been looking at his desk during his last few sentences, but then, with a slight jerk, he pulled himself upright again.

'I can't simply delegate this task to you, Tarkowski and leave you to do whatever you want to do; it will have to be a joint project. And I can't select just anyone for this process. You and I will have to go through the staff records very carefully and then discuss who will be suitable to be transferred into the bowels of a computer.'

'It's not...'

He raised a finger to quieten her.

'That's how it will be done. Or not at all.'

Then the import of his words hit her.

'Then you give your approval?'

'Yes. But doctor…'

She sat completely still and silent, waiting for the sentence to be completed.

'I hope for their sakes you are right in your understanding of what is to happen to them once they are in there.'

Ten

'How's my little hero?' Reid said, looking down on Hardy as he lay flat on his back on a surgery couch.

'Sore. But it's good to see you again.' He looked at her quizzically. 'You've lost weight.'

She gave a wry smile.

'A raw yeast and water diet does that to you. I don't recommend it.'

'You needed to lose a few kilos.'

She looked at him in horrified anger, her green eyes beginning to blaze, until she saw he was smiling. After that, she contented herself with giving him a poke in the ribs and watching him wince.

'Do you want to undergo another operation, you little rat?' she said, but she was also smiling.

'No, not really. Tarkowski is definitely lacking in bedside manner. But she stitches a good stitch, I must say. Hey, I think I can sit up for a while. Help me up, will you?'

She did, and Hardy positioned himself so his legs rested on the floor.

'Incredible news about Lafayette,' she said, after they had kissed.

'Yes, really incredible. His own Primary Wife doing that to him. But she'll be alright.'

'How do you mean?'

'Well, the Captain's PW—he won't execute her, will he? Especially as she's pregnant.'

'No, I guess not—Oh, watch out,' she added in a whisper, 'here he comes.'

It was Ashworth who had entered the room, but an Ashworth who had undergone a subtle change. He carried himself erect, and his face had somehow lost some of the lines it had borne when Reid had last seen him. Instead, his face seemed more alive, more vital. Even his movements had lost the lethargic look of the earlier Ashworth.

Hardy lowered himself back into a penitent supine posture. Ashworth sat next to him and stared down at him.

'And how's the patient today? Or should I say—how's the accuser today?'

'Roger,' Hardy said, attempting to duplicate the look of a cute puppy that its owner had caught on the kitchen table with some of that evening's dinner hanging from its mouth, 'I am so, so sorry. I thought I was doing the best for the ship. You had been behaving very oddly. I mean, going on about how we're all doomed to die, and then going to see Gelhardt and telling him to abandon the mission and go back to Earth. And to cap it all—you confessed! I'm really sorry, but you've got to see it from my point of view: I thought I was saving the ship!'

To Hardy's amazement, and also Reid's, who was watching the two men from the other side of the room, Ashworth gave a broad smile and patted Hardy on the shoulder.

'No hard feelings, Jeff. With all those signs, I would have turned myself in.' He grinned. 'In fact, I did!'

Hardy relaxed.

'So why did you confess?'

Ashworth's face lost its jollity, and he looked away from Hardy.

'It was a type of depression brought on by our close confinement in this claustrophobic environment. And the subconscious knowledge of what must be happening to all those poor lost souls back on Earth. Everybody on this vessel is suffering from it. It just happened that some are more prone to going under than others. And I—a psychologist, for God's sake—turned out to be one of the really vulnerable ones. That's all I can say; I can't clearly remember everything I said or did then—and I don't want to. Going over it will just risk a relapse.'

'But you're OK now?' Hardy asked, a little anxiously, as Ashworth helped him back into a sitting position.

'Yes. Definitely. Helena really knows her stuff; much as I'd like to take a blowtorch to that icy manner of hers. Her alteration to the ECT was the turning point. And she's suggested new targets for the antipsychotic drugs. So I think the worst is over as regards the crew's mental health.' He grew thoughtful. 'Pity it's come too late for poor Lafayette, though. And it's quite a shock to discover I was on the verge of being stuffed into a compositer.'

Reid crossed to them and positioned herself so that Ashworth could not help but see her.

'Hello, Susannah,' he said, an expansive smile returning, 'You've lost weight, and it looks great!'

She returned his smile.

'Thank you, Kind Sir. But I'm worried about what you've said about the mental health situation. Aren't you going from one extreme to the other? After all, nothing's changed. We're still stuck in a tin can, crawling towards an unknown destination none of us will ever see. So, please tell me what's in that situation to throw a party over?'

'Brains as well as beauty,' Ashworth said, looking her up and down with eyes that were no longer dull and lifeless.

'Knock it off, Roger; it's a serious question.'

He drew up a chair and, after sitting, looked up at her and then across to Hardy.

'Everything you say is true. Unfortunately, even after improved drug treatment, everyone here will continue to suffer low-level depression. That's inevitable; after all, we have little to celebrate. We all know people who we left behind, trapped on Earth in a situation that is a highway to Hell. We refugees, who have left them in the lurch, are in just about the most unnatural environment imaginable. Only people living in a cave would be worse off. But the next generation will not see it like that.'

'How so?' Reid said. 'Nothing will have changed.'

'But it will. Every one of us now is carrying the emotional baggage of the manner of our departure; the fact that we were fleeing the doom of stars. All of us remember the freedom of living in the open air on a planet, feeling the wind on our faces; seeing the clouds change from one form to another; seeing rivers, the sea, sunsets, sunrises. Meeting people who we had never seen before and would never see again. But the next generation will know nothing of that. The Magellan will be *normal* to them, completely, utterly normal. How can they grieve over not seeing a field full of flowers when they don't know what a field or a flower is?'

'But the cramped conditions?' Hardy interjected from behind Ashworth.

Ashworth turned to look at him.

'I don't suppose you know much about the Polynesian colonisation of the Pacific?'

'Correct.'

'The Polynesians spread across the greatest ocean on old Earth. Their experience is the nearest counterpart the human race has hitherto experienced to what We Happy Few on the Magellan are now doing. Land is very rare in the Pacific. Some of the colonisers ended up founding societies on specks of land no bigger than two football fields, with no other land in sight. And those societies thrived! Because there was no sense of loss. Their speck of land was all they knew, and they were happy. They lived fulfilling lives without yearning for anything else, without needing unexplored territories beyond the mountains—because there were no mountains and no one knew about mountains. Their island was their universe.

'And so it will be with those who come after us on the Magellan. Earth to them will just be a series of pictures they don't really understand. They will not grieve.'

A silence fell while Hardy and Reid digested his speech.

Hardy looked satisfied, but Reid spoke up.

'I'm sure you're right, Roger. But what will happen to your happy islanders when the Magellan finally reaches Centauri? Will they even want to get off and have the wind in their faces, glory in watching sunrises and sunsets? Is that how the Lightsail Project will fail?'

Ashworth had lost his enthusiasm and looked at Reid with a sombre expression.

'I wish you hadn't said that, Susannah. I don't have an answer.'

***

Tarkowski watched Gelhardt for quite some time, waiting for him to lift his gaze from the papers on the desk before him. When she finally concluded he had forgotten all about her, she gave a gentle cough and said, 'Captain.' She was mildly shocked when he finally lifted his face and looked at her. His eyes were red-rimmed, and new bags had appeared below them. He looked as if he had aged at least ten years since the confrontation with Lafayette in this very room. He evidenced slight surprise when he saw her.

'Sorry, Tarkowski, I'm sorry, I seem to have forgotten about you for a moment. Sorry about that. So many papers to read, the ship doesn't run itself, I'm sure you understand.'

Tarkowski did understand. She also knew that in fact, the Magellan did mainly run itself because all the life-support systems operated without human intervention and, now that their operating systems had been purged of Lafayette's interpolations, the maybots had returned to their customary silent efficiency, patrolling both within and without the primary hull, checking for leaks and any malfunctions in the Magellan's electronic nervous system. Gelhardt's responsibilities lay almost entirely in personnel management and maintaining ship morale. Things he was effortlessly good at.

Or at least he had been.

He had changed since Lafayette's unmasking. Tarkowski was not an emotional woman, not much given to *simpatico*, but even she could see that something had died in her captain since that dreadful "day." He had given her a toneless welcome and then immediately became distracted by the papers on his desk.

He tried to smile, but even the most *simpatico* observer would have been hard-pressed to identify the expression.

'Where were we?'

'We weren't anywhere, Captain. I came because you wanted to discuss the Mental Upload program. But you found the papers on your desk more interesting than me, it seems.'

He shook his head.

'No, of course not. Just a discussion paper on how we can improve the palatability of the ship's food. Nothing that can't wait, I assure you.'

'I'm glad to hear it, as I'm just as busy as you are.' She glanced at the chair in front of his desk. 'I take it, I'm allowed to sit?'

'Yes, of course! Didn't I ask you to sit? I'm sorry.' He grimaced. 'That's all I seem to be saying these days.'

She didn't answer him directly; Gelhardt didn't know it, but he was now nothing more than a tool, a means to an end. She gave him a momentary smile; it was not a particularly expressive smile, but at least it was better than his had been.

'Well, you've been under a lot of pressure; I suppose. Now, to business—the Upload Program.'

He looked blank.

'Yes? What about it?'

Tarkowski had the distinct feeling she was in charge of a particularly slow child in whom she could not instil a love of the ten-times table—try as she might.

'Captain, we agreed you would select the best people on board whose mentalities we would upload into an electronic matrix.'

He leaned back and looked at the ceiling.

'Yes, we did; I remember now.'

'And the names?...'

'I don't have the names.'

She felt her cheeks sting with the flush of anger.

'You don't? But...'

Somehow Gelhardt brought his full attention to her, and she saw the sloth, the lassitude slip away, and his posture, his features, become somehow firmer, stronger.

'I have decided not to select people, Tarkowski.'

'What! Captain, I must...'

He raised a large hand, palm towards her.

'Stop, doctor. Please stop. I am telling you what I have decided. Give me the courtesy of not interrupting me or I will have to ask you to leave.'

Tarkowski forced herself into a relaxed sitting position and waited.

'I have selected no one because I cannot force any person on this vessel to undergo such an unknown procedure.'

Tarkowski's hands gripped the sides of her chair with such force that her knuckles turned white—but she did not speak.

'I understand your alarm, doctor, but I have not abandoned your project. And so,' Gelhardt continued, 'I have decided to ask for volunteers.'

Tarkowski could contain herself any longer.

'Volunteers! But that means any slow simpleton can be included! I wanted the best, the brightest, the most knowledgeable—not the sweepings from the dustpan!'

Gelhardt's fist crashed onto his desk with such force that the report made Tarkowski jump.

'That's enough!' he roared, 'I've had enough of your sneers at my people, your high-and-mighty condescension! Everyone on this ship is an expert at something—maybe not to your Olympian standards, but don't you dare call them "simpletons" or "sweepings"! Don't you ever use those words in front of me, ever! Good God, I've half a mind to cancel the whole fucking thing!'

He rose from his chair, his old energy and power miraculously restored, and towered over her. Involuntarily, she cowered underneath a blast of wrath like unto that which shattered the Tablets on Mount Sinai.

'I'm sorry, Captain!' she gasped, almost deprived of the power of speech. 'I didn't mean to be offensive! I'm sorry, please don't cancel my program, I beg you!'

He sat back down, glaring at her all the while.

'Good. Let's hear no more talk of *herrenvolk*. My homeland suffered immensely from that filth. I will announce the program on voluntary terms. And I will inform you of their names on completion. Do you understand that, doctor?'

Like a small, frightened girl, she nodded, and smiled in the manner a low-status simian might do to placate the dominant leader.

'Yes, Captain.'

Eleven

Hardy turned from the viewscreen and looked at his Primary Wife.

'Well, what do you think?'

She did not turn from her examination of another viewscreen, set among a bank of complicated-looking controls.

'Damn thing's on the blink again,' she muttered, 'this is not right. I'll have to speak to Gelhardt.'

'Don't worry about it. Nothing's going to happen.'

'*Nothing's going to happen!*' she repeated. 'Look, Jeff, if you foul up it'll take two hundred years before anyone notices. If I foul up, it's BLAMMO!'

'BLAMMO?' he repeated blankly. 'I don't know that word. Is it a technical term poor saps like me aren't supposed to understand?'

Reid gave him a tolerant smile and crossed to him. They hugged and caressed each other for a while, with an occasional kiss. She looked up at him with joy in her eyes.

'It's an onomatopoeic term representing the sound of a collision between an object travelling at three percent of the speed of light— a.k.a. the Magellan—colliding with a planetary-mass object. It attempts to represent the violence of the collision, resulting in the total disintegration of said Magellan into its individual atoms. But of course, the onomatopoeia is not particularly successful as there would be no sound in the vacuum.'

He continued to look at her with an expression that could only be described as "blank".

She gave him a mock punch and pulled away.

'Good God, how did I end up married to Ugg The Caveman!'

He shrugged.

'I'm getting used to your low opinion of me. But be warned—I might hit you over the head with my club!'

They laughed, but then she grew serious.

'I have to get it sorted out, Jeff. I can't be in the Collision Alert Centre all the time; so I need a reliable link to it, wherever and whenever I am.'

'Nothing's happened yet.

She threw up her hands.

'Jeff, sometimes I…Look, you're talking like the man who jumped off a cliff and said *What's the problem? Nothing's happened yet!*

Hardy, in return, lifted his hands and said, 'Space is big, Susannah. Enormously big. The Oort Cloud is much more populated than true interstellar space and nothing's come near us.'

All traces of levity had now drained from her features, and she shook her head.

'Have you forgotten the Nea Avgi?'

'We don't know it was a collision; there might have been a failure of life-support.'

'What, a design flaw that affected only one out of five identical starships? Isn't it more likely they smashed into a floating iceberg the size of Denali?'

'Which suggests the collision avoidance systems on these hulks aren't worth a fart in a paper bag. So let's eat, drink and be merry!'

Her brow furrowed as she absorbed Hardy's latest piece of wisdom.

'Jeff, no one knows what conditions were like on the Nea Avgi just before whatever happened, happened. Maybe there was some riot going on at that moment, like we almost had.' Suddenly she shuddered. 'I don't want to think about it.'

'It's only a theory. We'll be OK.'

'Sweetheart, this is a two hundred-odd year flight. There's plenty of time for low probabilities to materialise. One day, we *will* be on a collision course with something bigger than us, and God help us if we aren't forewarned. Even if we don't run straight into it, the gravitational interaction might twist us off course and send us flying off into deep space. That might happen in two hundred years. Or it might happen today.'

To her relief, he grew serious.

'Yes, sorry. I just have a sunny disposition. I can't help looking on the bright side of life.'

Reid ruffled his hair.

'That's why I love you. But sometimes, we *have* to be serious.'

He pointed to the smaller viewer.

'OK, sort it out with Gelhardt. But what about this message from our illustrious leader?'

Reid spent some time reading the voluminous message. It was a long slab of text but, being a much faster reader than Hardy, it did not take her long to finish studying it. She sat on the couch in seeming slow motion and looked away from Hardy, seemingly focused on infinity.

'Wow, that's a big one,' she finally said. 'Having your mind uploaded into the Central Computer. Wow. I know I never want to get old—but that's ridiculous.'

He sat beside her after he had finally read it all.

'But I don't understand; what's the problem? It would mean a kind of immortality, wouldn't it? You don't want to get old, you just said. We'd be together forever, Susannah!'

She shook her head.

'No, Jeff, you haven't understood. It's not us—or at least, *all* of us! It's just our knowledge, our memories. It wouldn't be *us*, you silly love. And even if it were, would you want an eternity of being a disembodied mind alone in the dark, for ever and ever? Of not being able to do this? '

She turned to him, and they briefly kissed.

He shook his head.

'But that's going to happen anyway, Susannah. We're not getting off this tub. We'll never see Centauri. Perhaps some more of our minds would survive, and we'd be able to communicate—Oh, I don't know!—by telepathy or something! I think that's better than the alternative: good, old-fashioned death. Neither of us is a believer, so let's not kid ourselves about what's waiting for us!' His face became stern, resolute, so for an instant Reid almost did not recognise him. 'I think I'm going to do it, Susannah, and I'd like to think you'll be coming with me!'

Reid was silent, and remained silent for some time.

Then she realised Andretti had come into their private area.

'Hello, Alisha, Can I help you?'

Hardy's new Secondary Wife looked down at the pair.

'I wondered if you'd read the message from the Captain?'

'We have.'

'May I ask if you have decided on what you're going to do?'

'We haven't made up our minds yet.'

Andretti's face contorted.

'Could you tell me if you decide to be uploaded? So I can make sure I do the opposite, so I don't have to spend eternity with you two monsters!'

Reid's face was impassive. Then she smiled.

153

'Alisha, could you get us some coffee?'

***

Gelhardt looked at the list. It showed the names of those who had volunteered to be part of Tarkowski's Upload Program. He pursed his lips as he read, noting the names had a strong correlation with the ones he would have picked. He nodded, thinking to himself, *I still have a feel for who the best people are. At least I haven't lost that.*

He continued studying the list, and then he frowned.

Hardy! What was that clown doing on the list! Gelhardt knew he was one person he, Gelhardt, would not have included. Now displaying an irritated expression, he continued reading until he met another name and gave a snort of comprehension. *Susannah Reid.* That explained it. She had decided to upload herself, and that weak-minded twerp, Hardy, had been shamed into following her. He shook his head. He hadn't accepted Tarkowski's arrogant dismissal of some of the crew as simpletons, but maybe she had got it right with a few of them.

His personal computer gave a musical chime, and a pleasant voice said, 'Captain. It is time for your visit.'

He pushed the list away, and almost fell forward, cradling his head in his hands.

So soon! So soon!

A wave of despair, of horror, crashed over him and he stifled a sob. Was there time to change his mind, to repent of a rash decision, to call back his earlier words?

Gelhardt stood and was not entirely surprised to find he was trembling.

There was not time. He could not recall the warning he had given, pretend he had not thought it through. There could be no exceptions, no favouritism. He had said what he would do, and now he must not weaken. It had to be done.

The walk was not long and he was soon, much sooner than he wanted, in sight of the prison cell.

The guards saw him approaching, head held low, and immediately came to attention.

'Captain,' the senior crewman said.

'Yes,' he said. 'It's the time.'

A strange look came into the faces of the guards; a peculiar mixture of alarm, fear, perhaps even despair.

'Time?' the less senior one said in a dry, cracked voice.

'That's what I said,' Gelhardt replied. His own voice was dull, uninflected, reminiscent of early machine speech from the Twentieth Century. 'Let me in.'

They opened the door, and Gelhardt entered. He had the code for the inner door and it slid open before him.

The room was dimly lit, but he could see Lafayette sitting listlessly on a hard-backed chair next to an empty table, staring into the gloom. She did not turn as he entered.

'Hello, Karl. Have you come to gloat?'

He crossed to her and drew up another plain chair to the table to sit opposite her.

'No, of course not. I came to see how you are.'

She lifted her face to stare at him. It seemed no longer to be a real human face, but a crude papier mâché facsimile. Her eyes were sunken, as if they were some distance behind the mask.

'As well as any woman can be who is under sentence of death.'

He extended his hands to her, but she did not hold them.

'Simone, you can't believe how sorry I am.'

Her lips twitched in the beginning of a snarl.

'Not as sorry as I am.'

He withdrew his hands and looked down at them for a while. She did not speak.

'Simone, Simone, none of this was necessary. I said to the entire ship that the saboteur would be executed. I didn't know it was going to be my Primary Wife, for God's sake! But I can't withdraw my pronouncement without causing a full-scale rebellion. This entire ship is on a trip-wire fuse, any sign of favouritism, of special pleading, and the place would explode!'

She was looking away.

'You could rescind the order.' Then she turned to stare at him. 'Do you want to?'

His face twisted as if in agony.

'Yes! Yes! Of course I do, my love! A million times yes!' Even in the gloom, it could now be seen that his eyes had become moist. 'But I can't!'

She stood up with an angry motion and walked to a corner of the room, her back to him.

'You could save me, but you won't. What kind of husband are you, Karl? What kind of husband murders his own wife?'

He was silent.

She spun around, her eyes blazing.

'I'll tell you what kind of husband, what kind of man you are, Gelhardt! You're a coward, a lousy, fucking coward! Call yourself a captain, a leader! You're a wriggling worm, crawling along the seabed. You're not a man!'

He was silent for some minutes, then he lifted his head and said, 'You didn't have to do it, Simone. No one forced you to try to sabotage the ship.'

She laughed, a dry, empty laugh.

'They were just warnings! Nobody was in any real danger! If anything, I improved security on this hell ship! All you had to do was go with the majority and turn the fucking ship around. But you wouldn't! Oh no, you couldn't lose face in front of your precious men, could you, you fucking coward!'

'You damaged the food supply. You had no idea what effect pouring acid into the tanks would have. You could have killed all the algae, all the yeast, forcing us into starvation. Or worse.'

She turned her back on him again, and when she spoke again, her voice was softer.

'How's Amelia? You remember, the child you tore out of me by C-Section?'

'She's fine; putting on weight.'

'I want to see her before I go.'

He nodded.

'Of course. I will arrange it.'

She rushed to the table, sat and grabbed his hands, looking desperately into his face.

'Why wouldn't you do it, Karl? Why wouldn't you turn around?'

'I couldn't. Even if I could, there's nothing back there. Nothing but fire and flame and death.'

Her face went still and emotionless again.

'All right. It's over now. What's done is done. I know I did the right thing, but you're not the man I thought you were. You can go away now and carry on looking for a new Primary Wife. I'm sure there're plenty out there, itching to be the Captain's Wife.' She shook her head. 'God, they must have low standards.'

He stood and began to walk to the door.

She yelled after him.

'I'll make it easy for you, Gelhardt! I'll drink the poison; you won't need to arrange a lethal injection. But I demand to see Amelia before I go!'

He turned.

'You will.'

***

'Will it hurt?' Hardy asked.

Tarkowski scowled.

'Of course, it won't hurt! Does an ECG hurt?'

'I don't know,' Hardy replied. 'I've never had an ECG.'

'Are you really, really, sure you want to go ahead with this?' she asked, mentally crossing her fingers. Reid had spent quite some time trying to convince her that Hardy was an essential part of the Magellan engineering crew—but she still had doubts.

'Yes, definitely. After all, it's a kind of immortality, isn't it?'

Tarkowski was not normally a woman who employed obscenities in her speech, but she turned away from Hardy and cursed under her breath.

'No, it is not! It's just your memories, your…' She hesitated at that point in her explanation before adding, 'your *knowledge*. They alone will be copied. The process is somewhat—*lossy*. You'll only be a kind of Virtual Assistant, except you will be a far more effective, responsive Assistant.'

'Isn't that what the Central Computer already does?'

Hardy was reasonably certain he saw her lips form a silent expletive, but said nothing.

'No! The Central Computer is just a store of data. Yes, it sounds like a human when we ask it simple questions, but it doesn't have the experience that a biological entity could bring to its functions. Your mentalities will enrich its interaction with the future members of the Magellan crew; the ones who will have no genuine memories of Earth. Your knowledge will help keep them grounded, stop them

157

relegating the history of life on the home planet to the realm of fantasy and fairy tale.'

Well, maybe not your *knowledge, Mr Hardy!* she thought to herself, silently damning Gelhardt's decision to ask for volunteers. She shrugged and directed a reluctant gaze back to Hardy.

'Well, let's get on with it, shall we?'

Hardy looked around at the apparatus in front of which Tarkowski was expectantly standing. He saw a bank of mysterious machinery dotted with softly glowing lights and, right next to him, a couch with a padded headrest at one end. Thin black cables sprouted from the headrest, terminating in a half-dome skullcap. Hardy touched his lips with the tip of his tongue and said, 'Hmmm.'

'Come on,' Tarkowski snapped, 'there're lots of people waiting.'

To her surprise, Hardy turned and made a gesture to someone waiting in the queue. He then proceeded silently to mouth a *Come On* request. Susannah Reid detached herself from her fellow volunteers and joined Tarkowski and Hardy.

'Susannah,' he said, 'would you like to go first?'

'The order is supposed to be alphabetic!' Tarkowski hissed.

Reid flashed Tarkowski a megawatt smile.

'Jeff's a little nervous,' she beamed, 'and, not only that, but he's also a perfect gentleman. He believes in "ladies first".'

'*Ladies First?*' Tarkowski echoed faintly, her eyebrows attempting to disappear beyond her hairline.

'Yes,' Reid continued, 'he's British, you see. They're very formal.'

Tarkowski gave up and waved vaguely in the direction of the mysterious headset and the couch. Reid lay full length on it and looked up at her stern supervisor, noticing, with some surprise, that she was starting to feel exceedingly nervous.

'I don't have to have my head shaved?'

'Of course not,' Tarkowski snapped. 'You would have been told by now, don't you think? The energies involved are quite high, more than capable of passing through your crowning glory, your skull and the meninges.' Her face adopted one of its unconvincing smiles. 'But don't worry: you won't be under long enough to have your brain fried.'

Reid forced her features to generate a faint smile, and then became impassive as one of Tarkowski's technicians slipped the headset over the rebellious waves of her abundant hair.

'Your optical centre will be overridden, so you will lose awareness of your surroundings,' a cold voice intoned from an unguessable distance. 'But don't worry: your vision will return as soon as we remove the headset.'

She felt the plastic half-dome suddenly become quite warm. There was a bright, soundless blue flash and Tarkowski's busy laboratory instantly vanished.

Then there was only unplumbable blackness.

Instantly, she felt the fangs of fear stab at her heart. But then she heard Tarkowski.

'Don't worry. Your auditory centres are unaffected; I'm still here. You're still in my lab. It will be over soon.'

Despite what she had been told, Reid still felt a great unease.

Is this what it will be like when my mind is uploaded? she thought. *Eternal darkness?*

Then in the ebon emptiness she saw a welcome light; a warm, buttery, friendly light. It grew stronger and objects became visible, slowly condensing and coalescing from emptiness.

Then she found herself lying on her back on soft, warm grass with a bright blue sky above her, dotted here and there with the soft powder-puffs of fair-weather cumulus. She could hear the liquid gurglings of the nearby stream, murmuring secrets to itself under the summer sun. Reid rolled onto her side and saw a pair of legs. She followed them up and saw a friendly face smiling down at her.

'Mother!' she said, 'what are you doing here? Where am I?'

'Shhh,' her mother said, stroking her hair, 'I'm not really here. I'm just a memory, a memory that has been activated by an electrical impulse. I'll be gone soon.'

'No!' Reid cried, 'you mustn't go! It's been so long since I saw you! I've so much to tell you! All that happened to me after you died, after the tsunami took you! I never thanked you for pushing me higher into the tree when the wave came! You saved me, mother, but the water took you—you mustn't go!'

Her mother stroked Reid's cheek.

'You must let me go, Susannah. But I'll always be here in your memory.'

There was another blue flash, and Reid was in the lecture hall looking down at her examination paper. On the far wall was a large clock with Roman numerals. A second hand was sweeping remorselessly onwards.

'You may turn your papers over,' the withered, bald man standing beneath the clock said. 'You have two and a half hours. The time starts—now!'

She turned the paper over and was confronted by a sea of minute text, mathematical symbols, Greek letters, and diagrams showing planetary orbs with arrows coming out of them and into them, past them.

Christ, I can't do this! she thought.

But almost immediately, the wizened man was standing next to her congratulating her on not merely passing the examination, but doing well enough to plant her firmly in the ninetieth percentile.

'But that's impossible,' Reid protested, 'there hasn't been time to grade my paper!'

'You forget,' the man said kindly, 'I'm just a memory. There's no time here. Everything you have ever experienced is stored in an eternal *now*. Only your future remains unrecorded, as it has not yet been actualised. Now you must move on.'

Another flash. Another memory relived.

Towards the end of the mental carousel, after having given herself to her first real love, after having suffered again the pain of losing him, she found herself standing next to a helicopter, arguing with a good-looking young man with abundant auburn hair and green eyes that were even more piercing and hypnotic than her own.

'A *RIF girl!*' she was saying, 'how dare you! I'm not a farm animal, selected for breeding! I'm a human being, a person! A damn sight better person than you are, it seems. Who do you think you are, going around collecting women just for their uteruses!'

'Not just for your reproductive equipment,' the young man said, 'you've forgotten what the other letters stand for: Resourceful. Intelligent. You would claim those attributes, I suppose.'

'Yes,' she said, flushing angrily, 'I would! But what gives you the right to collect women in your net, like some kid fooling around in a rock pool!'

He did not reply immediately, but made a sweeping gesture with his arm to indicate she should look at their surroundings.

And she did: seeing the shattered remains of trees, the splintered ruins of buildings, the toppled high-rise buildings, all smashed together into a horrific mass of despairing destruction. Her gaze lifted above the tumbled ruins of a civilisation, seeing angry black clouds twisting in cyclonic motion, lit from within by massive lightning bolts. She became conscious of a glacial wind tugging at her hair.

'We have to go, Susannah,' the man said. 'I don't know the details, but you, and women like you, are our new hope. We've lived through bad days—but there are worse to come.'

'No, I can't do it! I can't leave all my friends—just for a promise!'

He placed a friendly hand on her shoulder.

'Don't be silly, Susannah. You're not living this scene—you're remembering it. You know you did come with me, and eventually you found out what the new hope was. And you accepted it.'

'Yes,' she said, taking another look at the encircling ruins, 'I did.'

There was another blue flash, and she steeled herself to relive another disturbing episode from her past. Instead, Reid found she was looking into the face of the technician, who was holding the skullcap, and could see Tarkowski standing behind him.

'There,' the latter said calmly, 'that wasn't too bad, was it?'

Reid discovered she was trembling and that her eyes were moist. She felt ten years older and had to be helped firstly into a sitting position and then upright. Her knees felt weak.

'Why didn't you warn me I would be under for hours?' she rasped at Tarkowski. Her mouth felt Sahara-dry. 'It was awful!'

'Hours?' Tarkowski said. 'You were under for three minutes.'

Reid stared at her, her mouth hanging slightly open.

'Three minutes?' she eventually said.

'Three minutes.' But Tarkowski then lost all interest in Reid and looked beyond her, to the next in line.

'And now back to our scheduled sequence, I think—Mr Hardy! Here, please!'

As Hardy walked reluctantly past Reid, he looked at her and whispered, 'What was it like? Everything OK?'

She gave his cheek a playful pat.

'No problems at all. You'll really enjoy it, Jeff!'

And then she walked off, a wicked smile playing on her lips.

***

Gelhardt lifted the baby from its cot and passed it to Lafayette.

161

'Here you are, Simone.'

She accepted the child with a beatific smile, but then glared at Gelhardt.

'Don't call me "Simone". My husband used to call me that!'

He said nothing, and moved slightly further away, careful not to bump into the two Security men standing behind him.

Lafayette played with the chuckling infant, her face alive and happy.

'My beautiful, beautiful daughter,' she whispered, moving aside the cascade of hair that was obscuring her view of Amelia. 'I will never see you grow up. Never see you become a woman. Never see you take your rightful place as a Primary Wife. Never.'

She continued to cuddle and caress the laughing baby until Gelhardt said, 'It's time.'

She went rigid and then lifted her eyes from Amelia to Gelhardt.

'So soon?'

'Yes.'

Gelhardt motioned to one of the Security men, and he moved to take the child from Lafayette's arms.

'No! One more kiss!' she cried. 'Just one more!'

The guard stopped and allowed Lafayette to deliver a kiss to the child's soft lips. Then he reached for Amelia again.

'No!' Lafayette cried. 'One more kiss!'

'Continue,' Gelhardt said quietly, 'take the child away.'

Lafayette wailed as the baby was pulled from her grasp and taken from the room, and then stared at Gelhardt.

'I hate you, Gelhardt, for what you've done! If there is a Hell, you will roast in it forever! Forever, do you hear, monster!'

Gelhardt said nothing for a while and then said, 'Now, we must go.'

She folded her arms.

'I can't walk.'

'We have a wheelchair for you. Do you wish to use it?'

'Yes.'

Gelhardt and the remaining guard put Lafayette in the wheelchair. She did not struggle. However, when the time came to take her from the room, she pushed Gelhardt away and motioned to the guard that he alone should move the chair.

Gelhardt walked behind them as they moved down the corridor towards the compositer zone, seemingly unable to find the strength to raise his head.

Soon they were there, and the crowd parted obediently before them as they stopped in front of the nearest compositer.

It was a simple matt-grey cylinder which had only one function. That was to break the human body down into its simple basic constituents: a compost of water, proteins, nucleic acids, minerals, phosphates and other calcium salts; all to be recycled into the food vats to maintain the living.

Gelhardt stood before the compositer, forced himself to stand erect, and looked at the crowd.

'There is one law above all others on the Magellan: *one for all and all for one.* We are all brothers and sisters, cast out from our home through no fault of our own, But if we are to survive and fulfil the dream of Fraschini and De Vries to give humanity a second chance of life, we must never raise our hands against our brothers or our sisters. We must love them as ourselves, help them in their hour of need, bind their wounds, dry their tears.

'The woman you see before you broke that law, and placed every one of us in mortal danger. Every man, every woman, every child, on board could have died because of what she did. You will remember I said that when the perpetrator was captured, he or she would suffer the ultimate penalty.' He stopped speaking for a few seconds and seemed to be having trouble starting again.

Then, in a shaking, tremulous voice, he resumed. 'When that person was finally apprehended, I discovered it was the last person on the Magellan I had expected. Or wanted it to be. But having made my pronouncement, I could not take it back. No one is above the law. Not even my Primary Wife.

'And so, we are standing here today to see justice done. Let us not delay any more.'

He turned to Lafayette. 'Do you have anything to say?'

She rose from the wheelchair and ran a hostile stare over the throng.

'Yes. By now, you have realised, I'm sure, that your Captain is a madman. You see before you an innocent woman who only ever wanted the best for you. This voyage is doomed: you are all going to die unpleasant deaths out here in the darkness. This ridiculous craft will never reach Centauri. I wanted to save you; to take you back to the only planetary system capable of sustaining life science has discovered. There is nothing at Centauri except rock and ice. Nothing. You could have joined the Space Arks, and your children would have repopulated the Earth. Now all that has been taken from you by a lunatic.

'I am about to die, but I am merely the first of many. Soon I will be welcoming you to my side.' She cast a quick glance at Gelhardt. 'I have nothing to say to my executioner. Let's get this farce over with.'

Gelhardt motioned to the waiting doctor, who immediately crossed to Lafayette. He had a small drinking tube in one hand and a hypodermic in the other, in case the prisoner changed her mind about co-operating.

But Lafayette did not change her mind.

The cyanide derivative's effects were almost instant and, apparently, painless.

Lafayette slumped into the wheelchair.

It took a few moments for the doctor to declare she was dead, and then she was lifted out of the chair. The compositer lid silently lifted, and she was carefully, perhaps lovingly, placed inside. There was no need to strip her, of course, as her grey prison garb was also compostable.

There being nothing left to see, the crowd quickly dispersed. There was no chatter, no conversation, just a stunned silence.

Gelhardt turned away, wiping his eyes, breathing raggedly as he strove to avoid breaking down. To his surprise, he found Tarkowski waiting for him, displaying an extremely nervous expression.

'Captain,' she said, 'I realise this is a terrible time for you, but may I ask if you have reconsidered your opposition to uploading? The future will need men like you.'

He shook his head. He could not see Tarkowski very clearly, as her image was blurred by his tears.

'No,' he finally said, 'I won't be uploading. I can't take the chance I might become immortal.'

She looked somewhat crestfallen.

'You were one of my prime candidates. I'm very sorry to hear that, Captain.'

He stared at her with such a fierce glare she felt as if she had become a snowflake that had accidentally been wafted into a blast furnace.

'Tarkowski, I do not expect to have any more contact with you, for any reason whatsoever. You see, I am no longer Captain of the Magellan.'

Cis-Centauri Space

One

Finally leaving the last, lonely outpost of the Solar system behind, the Magellan flashed into true interstellar space, now travelling at its top speed.

Behind it blazed a truly brilliant star, unfortunately hidden from the direct view of the Magellan's crew by the tremendous light sail, now fully unfurled after departing the heliosphere. But had a particularly bold traveller clambered onto that sail and stood on its sunward face, he or she would have seen merely a coruscant splendour against the night. There would have been no sign or suggestion of the horrors now being visited upon the inner planets of that lovely star.

The former home of those desperate refugees had suffered the culmination of the destruction wrought by the Destroyer. It had passed through the inner part of the Jovian magnetosphere, and its tormented, ravaged surface had been sterilised by the endless torrents of lethal radiation. Seas had boiled into angry, lightning-rent thunderclouds; mountains had been levelled; the atmosphere ripped away like a flimsy veil.

But not all life had ceased. Some humans, denied the escape of the lightsail craft, had burrowed deep down to near the base of the planetary crust, safe from the terrible blast of energetic particles. Sadly, most—but not all—had begun a long, slow descent into barbarism.

But there had been another attempt to escape the doom of stars. A mysterious cuboid structure had been sent down to similar depths, within which slumbered the mentalities of some of that doomed world's greatest minds, among them that of a young woman named Maya Moreno.

Further into the appalling gulf between the stars, swept the pioneer ships, the Zheng He and the Resurgam, crewed with humans who refused to accept extinction as a reward for their courage.

And behind the Magellan hurtled the last of the lightsail craft; the final seed of the mortally wounded Earth, the Spes Nostra, carrying the last humans to tread the surface of their slaughtered home.

Ahead of the Magellan gleamed another bright star, shining imperceptibly brighter with each passing minute.

But it would be a long time before it would truly rival the sun of dead Earth, for the Magellan's journey had barely begun.

'Not Paris again!' Regine snapped. 'How many more times?'

Amelia tried to smile, although she was getting more than a little tired of her daughter's temper.

'It's important you understand and appreciate your culture, darling,' she said while realising her smile had proved very short-lived. 'This is where you came from.'

'Au contraire, mamam. I come from the Magellan. And so do you. And I wish you'd stop trying to teach me those fragments of that dead language. We all speak Twenty-Fourth century English here.'

'It's your culture, dear,' Amelia said, this time giving up on the attempt to smile again.

'No, it is not,' Regine said firmly, 'It's not even your culture. You didn't learn French on your mother's knobbly knees, did you? I doubt if you could ask the way from the Bois de Boulogne to La Défense if you were transported back to ancient Paris.'

'No, you're right, I learned my French from the Teaching Machines. But that doesn't mean I don't respect it for its beauty,' Amelia said. 'And I don't like the way you talk about your grandmother. It's all our loss she died young. She would have loved you very much.'

'I'm glad somebody would have,' Regine said. She looked at the image on the screen. 'Can I go now? I'm nineteen, you know—not nine.'

Amelia waved into the indeterminate distance.

'Yes, go off and do what you young people do. You've taken your anti-pregs, haven't you? You're too young for all that responsibility— even by Magellan standards.'

'That,' Regine said, with the air of a disappointed schoolteacher, 'is (a) A question you don't need to ask and (b) A question you shouldn't have the nerve to ask. I'll see you later. Maybe I'll go to a wild party and come back next shipay.'

Amelia watched her long-limbed daughter go. She was spindly even by Magellan standards. All the children of people born on the starship were long of limb and weak of muscle because of the low gravity of the central hull. Soon the ship's flight would be purely ballistic and then the current low gravity would reduce to near zero. The Ship Elders had demanded that all citizens spend some time in the EZ, now rotating at near its top speed, but increasingly people found reasons not to fulfil their exercise quotas. As a result, if pre-Catastrophe humans had been able to observe the youth of the Magellan, they would have found them rather spidery in build.

But such thoughts were not part of Amelia's mind. She saw nothing unusual in her daughter's physique. What she did have trouble with was her daughter's speech; the ThirdGens were rapidly developing their own language, one packed with odd elisions and contractions, such as "shipay" for "ship-day." Amelia thought ruefully that mutual understanding might be impossible if she ever had grandchildren. Pushing such concerns from her mind, she returned to studying the image on the computer screen. It showed a tall tower apparently made entirely of metal girders. She knew its name, but not the reason for that name. It was just a name, like parts of the ship had names, parts of the body had names. Just a name.

She sat still and silent as the other scenes of the long-vanished city swept by: the Arc de Triomphe, Sacré Coeur, Napoleon's Tomb in the Eglise du Dôme. All now converted to swirling clouds of dust by the passage of the Destroyer. The messages from Earth had stopped coming not long after the Magellan had cleared the Oort Cloud: it was chillingly clear there had been no last-minute salvation.

The cradle and home of Homo sapiens had been reduced to radioactive rubble.

Now the hope that these flimsy bags of organic chemicals and water would continue to exist depended on the Space Arks and the four surviving lightsail craft: the Zheng He and the Resurgam, which were travelling before the Magellan, and the Spes Nostra travelling behind it. She shook her head; sometimes it felt to her that those efforts to cling onto life in a hostile universe seemed pitiful; childish even. Maybe life was just an inconsequential froth on the top of the deep ocean of black emptiness that was the cosmos.

For what was an uncountable number of repetitions, she discussed with herself whether she should have told Regine the truth about her grandmother. But how could she? How could she tell Regine that her grandmother had been the Magellan's first criminal; one who had put the entire ship's complement in peril? When she had been younger, of course, there had still been people alive who had witnessed Simone's execution, but Gelhardt had arranged that both daughter and granddaughter had been given false identities. It had been a terrible strain living a lie, every single ship-day. Only she and Gelhardt knew her real name; even to her own daughter, she was "Marie", not "Amelia." But with every passing twenty-four-hour period, there were fewer and fewer people who had been there at that terrible scene. No doubt at some time in her nineteen years, Regine had heard the tale of a wicked woman who had almost doomed them all, but she had never connected that saboteur with her own sweet grandmother, who had supposedly died on the exterior hull when a stray meteoroid had pierced her suit. And with every tick of the clock, the danger of revelation grew less and less, asymptotically dying away to zero.

Gelhardt was still alive, of course, but he was a worn-out recluse who rarely left his cabin; the simple cabin of a basic rating he had moved into after relinquishing the Captaincy.

And on the few occasions when he had visited her, the terrible secret hung unspoken, unmentioned, never suggested, never alluded to. And it could not be long now before he followed his one and only Primary Wife into the compositer. And then Regine would be safe.

She snapped out of her reverie. The carousel of Parisian images had reached L'Eglise de la Trinité. She switched the machine off.

What was the point of venerating things she had never seen and never could see, now they were merely drifting miasmas of ash on a dead planet?

***

Regine made her way down the central axis of the Magellan, ignoring the throng of people whose only purpose appeared to be to get in her way. Had she not been a Third-Generation Magellanite, she would have noticed there were many more men around than there had been at the start of the voyage when the FirstGens had ruled their women with a steely paternalism. Because all the original on-board births had been natural ones, the male:female ratio had converged on 1:1 again. However, although unaware of how the balance of males and females had changed, she was thinking about life and death as she approached her destination; her job there comprised monitoring the ectogenesis tanks that had mainly replaced vaginal delivery after the Revolt of the Women, which had erupted twenty years after the starship's launch—in the Year 20 AL, as Regine knew it, just before she had begun her life on the Magellan.

Some women still preferred to give birth in the old-fashioned biological way, but fewer and fewer with each passing ship-year—it was so inconvenient compared to watching your child grow to birthing-size and weight in the tank. During the Revolt, the outnumbered men had protested there was not enough room on the ship for ectogenesis tanks, but under the threat of coercion, the necessary space had been found by decreasing the size of the Primary Wives' dwellings. And now there were no Primary Wives. Regine remembered how she had shaken her head in disgusted wonder when she had first heard about that custom. She would be no man's Secondary Wife! Not even Paul's!

And there he was, waving to her from within the serried ranks of breeding chambers, which everyone knew simply as "The Nursery". The tall transparent cylinders of the chambers gave the place the look of a weird technological forest.

She joined him and, after a brief embrace, she looked at the nearest tank and said, 'Everything OK with this lot?'

Paul grinned.

'They're doing fine. Especially this one. Putting on weight like there's no tomorrow.'

Regine wasn't quite sure what the word "tomorrow" meant in the context of the eternal day of the Magellan, but she understood the gist of the saying. She looked at the foetus as it hung lazily in the amniotic liquid which filled the tank. It looked pleasantly chubby as it slowly drifted in the warm fluid. And to think women once had carried such a load inside them and then have painfully to push them out! She gave a momentary shudder, but one so small she didn't notice it.

She turned back to Paul, taking in his slim figure, his wide shoulders, his broad features topping a carefully trimmed mousey-brown beard. But it was his smile she liked most about him; somehow, it changed his whole appearance.

'So everything is fine in the Nursery today?'

'Sure is,' he said. 'Temperature, salinity, oxygen—everything right on the button. There'll soon be lots of adorable little infants crawling around, filling their diapers, being sick, bawling their eyes out!'

She gave him a quizzical look.

'Sounds like you're not quite ready to be a parent yet, Paul.'

He slipped an arm under hers and grinned.

'Not unless you are, Regine!'

She laughed and pushed him away.

'Not yet, I'm not! I've got a lot of living to do.'

His grin grew wider, and the two of them began examining each tank in detail, studying the computer panels affixed to each one; searching for any anomalous readings. Eventually, they had checked the last one and sat down at a small table at the far end of the Nursery.

'Paul,' she said, as she sipped her myco-coffee, 'did you ever know your grandparents?'

He looked surprised at this unexpected turn in their usual banter and, putting his mug down, gave her a puzzled stare.

'And odd question. With all these mixed, intertwined, lineages dating from the time of the FirstGens, nobody really cares about their grandparents. Or even their parents, for that matter. We're all related to one another in varying degrees, if you search deeply enough.'

'Yes, I know all about the history of the Magellan, thank you. I just wondered if you knew what they did in the early days.'

He leaned back and looked up at the grey curve of the interior of the hull. As he watched, he saw brilliant flashes of actinic blue-white light coming from the activities of the tireless maybots. Now the ship had almost come to the end of its acceleration phase, the simulation of gravity caused by that acceleration would soon cease, which in turn meant there would no longer be an Up or Down, except that given by the feeble pull of the central cylinder's rotation, which was far too small to be of any consequence. And so, what had been walls were now available as living space, and the maybots were busy converting those areas into precisely that. Soon all the space, and more, claimed by the Nursery would be returned to the crew—but not as the expansive cabins of Primary Wives. Women like Regine would see to that.

'Well,' Paul began, 'I don't know much about my grandmothers. One was an agronomist, one was a biotechnician. My maternal grandfather was a programmer, one just as good as any of them, I guess.' His voice dipped a little as he moved on to the final ancestor. 'My paternal grandfather was something, though.'

'He was?' Regine felt the stirring of interest.

'Yes,' Paul said, leaning forward as he warmed to his topic, 'Roger Ashworth. He saved the ship.'

'Oh, come on, Paul! Don't overdramatise!'

171

'No, I'm serious. You have to understand the first crew weren't like us. They had grown up on Earth, on a planetary surface, with all that entails. As a result, they suffered from something called "claustrophobia".'

'Sounds nasty. Was it an infection?'

He laughed. 'No, no! They thought the Magellan was a confined space, that it was too small. They felt hemmed in.'

'I don't feel hemmed in.'

'No, that's right, none of us ThirdGens do. But Ashworth predicted that. He said those born on the Magellan would just see it as the normal way of living. And we do. But the First Generation couldn't adapt in time. But Roger Ashworth devised a cocktail of drugs that helped them adjust. And eventually, they did—and so the Magellan was saved.'

Regine looked away from Paul, into the indefinite distance.

'Living on the surface of a planet. What must that be like? Strong gravity all the time, without having to go to the EZ. Sunrise. Sunset. Darkness. Being able to see things far away, even kilometres away. Being able to be alone, really alone, with no one else in sight. How strange, how weird. And all those little furry, four-legged things running around everywhere.' She brightened up and leaned forward to Paul again. 'Hey, have you ever seen those vids of rainfall?'

He smiled. 'I have! I thought it was a joke the first time. Water falling from the top of the hull—sorry, the "sky". What's that about? Now, that is seriously crazy!'

She leaned back again, lost in her visions.

'And the air moving around so fast it moves your hair. And the sea—have you seen those sea-vids? It frightens me to think of so much water, enough to fill the whole Magellan!'

'Well, I don't think they had quite that much water,' Paul gently reproved. 'But we'll never really understand what it was like. It's too different from ordinary life. I think we'd be like the first generation if we were suddenly taken back there. We'd go crazy!'

Her face grew thoughtful.

'So how will the last generation cope—when they have to get off, I mean? Will they even want to get off, if things really are that different?'

He laughed. 'They won't have any choice! The ship's not going anywhere after Centauri!'

'Still, it'll be like the first generation, only in reverse.' She grew wistful. 'But we'll never see it; we'll live and die here.'

He shrugged. 'So what? It's home, and I like it.'

She nodded and was silent for a moment while visions of sunrises, clouds, and rain marched through her mind. Then her expression changed.

'Hey—Roger Ashworth! Wasn't he the guy who tried to get Gelhardt to turn around by poisoning the food supply?'

'No!' Paul was annoyed now. 'I'm sick of hearing that story. It was Gelhardt's wife—his so-called Primary Wife, I think—I don't know her name. But she didn't get away with it, and Gelhardt executed her.'

Her face relaxed.

'Sorry, I'd heard that thing about your Grandad from some idiot in the Dining Area. I really should know more about history. Anyway, whoever she was, she deserved to go into the compositer. Let's talk about something else.'

'Nope,' he said, rising to his feet, 'coffee break's over. Back to work.'

***

Hardy looked at his glum expression in the mirror. He adjusted the angle of attack of his combing but then looked at the result of his labours with deep dissatisfaction.

It was no good; his pink scalp remained stubbornly visible between the strands of white hair, however carefully he combed and adjusted them. It was time to accept defeat.

Time to accept and glory in his—dare he say it?—*baldness*. And sad to say, his bushy white beard offered him no comfort, merely causing him to resemble that character from an ancient fable who delivered gifts to children on snowy evenings.

He heard Reid calling to him from the other room.

'Are you going to stare into that mirror all day, Jeff? Nothing's going to change, you know, however long you stare.'

Hardy's lips thinned as he digested her words.

How typical. No consideration of the trauma he was going through. Didn't she understand how important a full head of hair was to a man, how it was an integral part of his self-image, his identity as a man? After the Revolt of the Women, when men had been

173

restricted to having only one wife, he had briefly considered replacing Reid with a younger model but, having been turned down several times in his quest for a new love-partner, he had stayed with her.

He joined her in the other room. As usual, she was in bed, staring at the ceiling. Her hair, still lavish but now a dull grey on the threshold of turning white, was spread out in a fan on the pillow.

'How are you feeling?' he asked, sitting on the bed beside her. 'How's the pain?'

'Still bad,' she said, reaching for his hand. 'The pills seem to be having less effect each time I take them.' She turned her head so she could see him better. 'I know the cancer's going to kill me, Jeff, and I think I'm nearing the point when I just want it over with.'

He squeezed her hand with genuine tenderness.

We old generation are just fading away, he thought. Like spring flowers on Old Earth. A brief time in the sun and then—dissolution.

Almost all the original crew had been in their twenties when they boarded the Magellan; some early twenties, some late twenties. He remembered how when he had first met De Vries and Fraschini, how ancient he had thought them! And now he was the same age and probably looked older. Time had wrought its ineluctable winnowing of those young hopefuls as the old scourges of humanity had not gone away just because the doom of stars had delivered an even more deadly one: heart disease was less common than the old Terrestrial average, due to the low gravity, but cancer was more prevalent because of the high-energy particles which occasionally punched their way through the hull. Not many of them made it, but enough to increase the likelihood of various forms of cancer.

And his erstwhile Primary Wife, now simply his wife, was one of those unfortunates, despite being nine years younger than he. Suddenly, he felt ashamed of his self-pitying expression in the mirror and squeezed Reid's hand more firmly. But what could he say? Perhaps she could have been given more years of life on pre-Catastrophe Earth, perhaps even cured, but not here on the Magellan. Care facilities were limited, medical expertise was limited, the ability to manufacture new drugs was limited. He knew as well as Reid did her state could only get worse.

His mind flashed back over all they had done together, all the drama they had faced. Did everyone feel the same as they faced the ending of their story, the realisation that one day there would be no more tomorrows? Now all they could hope for was that pain would not get worse.

He felt a surge of despair begin to rise. What had it all been for? They were all going to die in this metal tube, like rats trapped in a pipe. What had happened to the confidence he had felt when he boarded the vessel?

Somehow, she knew what he was thinking.

'No, Jeff, you must not give up; give in. We are only experiencing what every human being before us has done. We are passing, but a new generation is rising up to take our place. That's the best anyone has ever hoped for, Jeff, but you must remember all those we left behind—they are the ones who deserve pity, not us. They had everything taken from them, not least the hope their children would take their place. They had nothing; only the knowledge that when the end came, it would be the end of everything.

'Weep for them, Jeff, not us.'

He gave a weak smile.

'I know you're right, but it's so hard seeing you like this.'

He felt her hand press his again.

'It will be over soon. And then there will be no more pain.'

***

Regine was excited: today was a Delivery Day! She hadn't seen many, due to her being relatively new to the job, and the inescapable fact that a foetus still took nine months to develop, whether or not it was in a biological vessel. But today was the day!

She stood next to the expectant mother, feeling some of the woman's high emotion seep into her. The woman was staring at the tank as the soon-to-be-born infant slowly descended into the transfer section.

'Is this your first?' Regine asked the mother-to-be.

The mother nodded, her face flushed with anticipation. 'Yes, the very first! Isn't nature wonderful, creating a lovely new human being like this! I can hardly wait to give birth!'

Well, nature had little to do with it, Regine thought to herself. Even the coupling of the gametes to produce the embryo might not have occurred in the old-fashioned Terrestrial way. Many women preferred to have that done outside the body as well.

175

Paul came up to them, his face split with a broad grin.

'Well, the moment's come, Pamela. Are you ready to deliver your little treasure?'

'Am I!' Pamela squeaked. 'It's been a long nine months!'

'Then over to you, I think,' he said, 'we men don't have much to do at this point.'

Pamela flashed him an appreciative smile and strode to the birthing console. Her finger hovered over the large red button, and, like a junior actor seeking recognition, she looked back at the family members who had accompanied her to the Nursery.

'Do it!' a white-haired lady shouted, her face wreathed in smiles.

'Here goes!' Pamela said, and turned back to the console. Her finger depressed the red button.

Immediately, the baby was decoupled from the artificial placenta, the plastic umbilical cord retracting smoothly into the machine's innards. Next, a transparent door slid across the transfer section's inner part, and the amniotic fluid was swiftly pumped out. Then the outer door opened, and the squealing new-born slid down a short ramp into a padded receptacle. The family members gave a cry of jubilation, and Pamela hurriedly reached down to collect her child.

'Excuse me,' Regine said, 'I have to do a few things first.'

'Sorry,' Pamela said, 'I'd forgotten in all the excitement.'

Regine expertly fished out the small amount of mucus that had built up over nine months in the baby's mouth, then held the child momentarily upside down and gave it a quick shake. This was part of the ritual, but the child's bawling had already demonstrated that there was nothing wrong with its lungs. She handed it back to the new mother.

'It's a girl,' she said. This was also part of the ritual, but completely unnecessary, as the birthing tank was fully transparent, allowing close examination of the foetus throughout its development.

'It is, it is!' Pamela trilled. 'A lovely baby girl!'

Regine gave her a birth-towel to wrap around the child and then stood back. Her role was over. The ritual was over. Pamela and her new daughter disappeared as the family crowded around to bill and coo over the new arrival.

'Another girl,' Regine said to Paul.

He frowned.

'So? You got something against girls?'

'No, of course not. I am a girl, in case you haven't noticed. It's just that the last three have been girls.'

He shrugged.

'It's just the way chance operates. There's no law against throwing three sixes in a row; in the long-run, it averages out.'

'I guess so.' The crowd was beginning to disperse, and so, as was standard procedure, she congratulated the mother on her hard work and wished her and her daughter all the happiness possible.

As they walked away, she returned to Paul and said, 'I need a coffee.'

He grinned again and gave her a friendly pat on the back.

'Yes, it's emotionally draining, isn't it? Even I—a mere man—can feel it.'

She took two cups of myco-coffee from the machine and handed one to Paul.

'To think The Founding Fathers wanted women to do all that on their own.' She gave a slight shiver. 'They must have been real misogynists.'

'Women did it the old-fashioned way for thousands of years,' Paul said, blowing on his coffee.

'Hah! What does that prove? We all ate meat for thousands of years as well, didn't we?'

Paul laughed.

'You think you've got me there, but you'd eat meat if you were starving.'

Regine looked at him in disbelief, and was about to utter a withering put-down, but something stopped her. Perhaps it was juvenile to make firm pronouncements about what she would do in situations she had not experienced. She gave a wry smile: perhaps her mother was wrong, and she was in fact growing up. Regine found it hard to take much notice of her mother's opinions because she and the rest of her generation were trapped in a strange kind of limbo; although Magellan-born, their parents had been born on Earth. That gave her mother and, those like her, a kind of vaguely inferior status, not quite true-Magellanites like Regine herself and her fellow ThirdGens.

She realised Paul had continued speaking during her reverie.

'Sorry, what was that about the Elders?'

177

'I was telling you,' he said, 'to make sure you're on your best behaviour next shipay. You know how important they think this place is. They'll be spending some time here, asking us lots of questions.'

'Oh,' Regine said in a hollow tone, 'that will be nice.'

Two

Regine could not be certain why she was so nervous while waiting for the Elders to arrive. The previous shipay had flown by, and, unusually for her, she had confided in her mother about her unease.

'They sound so grand, so important,' she had said.

'Well, I suppose they are.' Amelia had replied, 'They are running the ship, after all.'

'Didn't that Gelhardt guy run it all by himself in the old days? So why do we need five of them now?'

Amelia then pursed her lips. She wasn't really sure why there needed to be five Elders. She had tried to find an explanation.

'Well, the first generation were all hand-picked experts in some line of business or another. They all knew what they were needed for. But since then, of course, the children and the children's children of the pioneers have no specific skills outside of what they need to survive from ship-day to ship-day. So they need more supervision.' She had shrugged. 'I guess.'

Regine had stared at her mother with obvious disbelief.

Then she, too, had shrugged.

And now here they were, all five of them: Captain Darian Dukas, tall, saturnine; Kondo Jelani, powerfully built, a complexion of polished mahogany; Anne McGrath, slim, raven-haired, statuesque; Karol Petronis, thin, sharp-featured; Rachel Grauber, slight, shrewish, unkempt, hair going prematurely grey. The men, presumably to underline their difference from the common herd, were all clean-shaven.

And they were all looking directly at her.

While she tried to give an assured smile, she thought the term "Elders" wasn't exactly pertinent; being SecGens they were all no older than their forties. However, that didn't stop them from exuding an air of cold authority. And they were now giving her a rapid-fire examination on her tasks and responsibilities.

'Come on now, girl,' Captain Dukas was saying, fixing her in the gaze of cold grey eyes, 'it's not a difficult question, now, is it?'

She felt as if her brain had turned to cold, viscous mush. Nothing would come to the surface of that stagnant pool. She would have to wing it.

'Uhh, thirty-nine degrees, I believe, is the normal temperature.'

Dukas gave a thin, humourless smile and turned to the small figure of Grauber at his side.

'This young lady clearly likes her eggs hard-boiled.'

Regine winced. Obviously, her attempt to wing it had resulted in her crashing and burning. Grauber looked equally unamused.

'I suppose she doesn't even know what an *egg* is.'

Regine flushed, unable to hide her annoyance at being so transparently patronised.

'Of course I do, Elder Grauber. It is an informal term for the female gamete, more appropriately called an *ovum*.'

There, that would show them!

But she seemed to have made another mistake because all the Elders gave a low chuckle.

McGrath gave her a more friendly smile than the others. At least one of them was human, Regine thought.

'No, my dear, I'm afraid my fellow Elders are teasing you, somewhat unkindly. An egg is something the Old Ones used to eat on Earth. It was an object produced by female birds. They used to cook it in boiling water, I believe.'

Regine felt a sudden jerk in her stomach at the idea of eating something that came out of an animal's body—why, that wasn't much better than eating the animal itself!

'And,' Jelani said in his deep, rumbling voice, 'the correct temperature for ectogenesis is thirty-six point five degrees. I hope that is actually the value you run the tanks at.'

Regine, helplessly, felt her slight flush become a blazing beacon of humiliation.

She had known that—of course she had!

The Elders seemed satisfied with their interrogation of her, and Dukas said to her, in a somewhat milder tone, 'Thank you, Regine. You'll be glad to hear we have no further questions.'

She gave a small bow of gratitude and stood aside as they moved further into the Nursery, taking Paul with them. She sat beside her console and looked dispiritedly at the small group as it went partly behind one of the larger tanks. She could still hear their voices, especially Jelani's rumbling tones, but not follow what was being discussed. She had a sudden urge to follow them, tap Dukas on the shoulder and insist he give her a second chance. But that would just make things worse, she finally thought. It would be disrespectful.

The Elders spent some time looking at some charts and shooting quick-fire questions at Paul. However, unlike Regine, he appeared to be answering them without difficulty or hesitation. Then it was over, and, seemingly satisfied with Paul's replies, they gave Regine a quick nod as they passed, and were gone.

Immediately, she hurried to Paul's side and almost threw herself at him.

'Oh, Paul! I was awful, terrible! They were just looking and looking at me and all my thoughts got jumbled together, and all I could say was nonsense! I'm going to lose my job, aren't I?'

Smiling, he shook his head.

'Don't be silly. It's OK. They were just playing with you. It was me they really wanted to see.'

'Oh.' Regine felt deflated. It wasn't the announcement of doom she had feared, but it wasn't exactly a flattering reprieve either. 'Oh. So what were they really after, then?'

He patted her on the shoulder.

'Just a few facts and figures. Nothing to worry about. Nothing at all.'

'Oh.'

Later that shipay, Regine related her ordeal to her mother.

'They were horrible, mother. They seemed to enjoy trying to trip me up.'

Amelia passed her a mug of gently steaming myco-coffee and, in an obvious attempt to cheer up her morose daughter, a tasty yeast biscuit.

'I'm sure they weren't being deliberately cruel, dear. They have very responsible jobs; they just need to let their hair down occasionally. You're not used to the rough and tumble of the adult world just yet. You'll soon toughen up.'

'Hmm.' Regine thought about that for a while and then, looking up, said, 'What exactly are their very responsible jobs?'

Amelia looked surprised.

'What? I beg your pardon?'

'Their very responsible jobs, what are they? The ship is on a predetermined route to Centauri; they don't have to make any adjustments. The Old Ones, the Founding Fathers, planned all that a long time ago. Everything on, in, and outside the Magellan is automatic. The ship is virtually a living organism.'

181

Amelia's surprise had turned to confusion.

'Well, there's maintenance, keeping the fusion reactors in top condition. The food vats—they all have to be checked to make sure everything is as it should be.'

Regine shook her head.

'The maybots do all that. When was the last time you saw a human being working in or on the food vats?'

Amelia was silent.

'Well, they must do something, or we wouldn't have the Elders, would we?'

Regine washed the remains of her biscuit down with the coffee.

'Well, I don't like them. They didn't behave the way I would have thought wise leaders should behave with a simple girl, just trying to do her best.'

Silence fell. Amelia looked down at her own coffee, now distinctly too cold to enjoy.

Then her daughter said something that really did surprise her.

'The old Captain's still alive, isn't he?'

A jolt, as of actual electricity, shot through Amelia at that unexpected question.

'Yes, he is. But why do you ask?'

'I don't know anything about the history of the Magellan. I'd like to find out more and he's the best one to explain it to me.'

'You've never shown any interest before. Why start now?'

'Those Elders made me feel like a bumpkin, a simpleton. I never want to feel like that again. I want to know about how we got here, why things are the way they are.'

'What's wrong with things the way they are?'

'Probably nothing. But if I'm going to be an adult, I want to think like an adult and not have people permanently treating me like a simple child. I want to know about the Old Ones. I mean, Gelhardt's an Old One, isn't he?'

'Not quite, he's a First Generation, because he has spent most of his life on the Magellan. The Old Ones were those who never came on board, and the Founding Fathers were those Old Ones, like DeVries, who planned this whole thing. But, Regine, there are other people from his time.'

'None who had such an important position as he did. I know he suddenly gave up the Captaincy, and it had something to do with a dangerous, wicked woman. Was she the one who caused the doom of stars?'

Amelia smiled at her daughter's apparent confusion.

'No, of course not. That was a long, long time ago.'

'You see,' Regine said, with evident satisfaction that her pretence of absolute ignorance had succeeded, 'I don't know anything, and that's not right for an adult. I've started going through the historical records in the Central Computer, but it's very slow, trying to find the right questions to ask. So, I really would like to talk to Gelhardt. He won't be around much longer. Can you think of any way he might allow me to see him?'

Amelia looked away, her mind in a swirling, churning turmoil.

Where had this sudden upheaval come from? All she had tried to keep hidden, never mentioned, never hinted at, the terrible, terrible secret that she had hoped would never come roaring back to torment her now seemed to be an invisible presence in the cabin.

But then a feeling of fatality came over her.

Maybe this moment had always been predestined. What other explanation could there be for its sudden eruption?

And so, with an indefinable expression resting on her features, she looked at her daughter and said, 'Yes. I think I can help you see Gelhardt.'

***

Amelia waited for the door camera to register her. It had been some time since she had last stood in front of this particular door, and she could not remember how long this process took. Finally, a faint voice said, 'Amelia. I'm pleased you've come to visit me. Wait a second and I'll open the door.'

The door opened a few seconds later with a creaking sound as if it had not opened for a long time. The interior was strangely dim: she was used to the endless day in the central axis of the Magellan and, of course, the darkness which could be summoned in one's cabin when it was time to sleep—but this half-light, this was unusual. It took her some time to realise there was a man-shaped shadow among the shadows.

'Dad,' she said softly, 'Now I've come to visit you, I'd appreciate being able to see you.'

'I'm sorry,' came a dry, whispery voice from the dimness, 'I'm so used to being alone. Here you are.'

Light flooded the room, making her blink momentarily. Then she could see Gelhardt sitting in a large chair in front of his bed. The initial impression was of a man to whom the years had been kind. He still had a rich mass of hair, albeit snowy-white. But as she came nearer, she could see a deeply lined, beardless face with sagging jowls, giving the impression that the face had been constructed from partially melted wax. And his voice no stronger, no less whispery than it had been on the door intercom.

'Amelia, so good to see you. Why have you been away so long?'

She was unable to frame a reply for a few moments: how long had it been? Why had she not visited her father more frequently? She felt a pang of guilt.

'I'm sorry, Dad. There's been so much to do, so many things to keep track of.'

That was a lie, of course; like most people on the Magellan, she had very little in the way of tasks and duties to perform. If she had been at all busy, it had been with trying to give Regine a good upbringing, which, if it were a task or duty, was a singularly thankless one.

She drew up the only other chair in the small cabin and sat beside him. She reached across and held his hand, noticing how dry and thin the skin felt.

'Of course,' he said, 'I've almost forgotten how busy you young people are, sitting here alone in this room. But you haven't visited me for a while, you know, so what brings you here this ship-day?'

'It's Regine,' she began.

Immediately a ghost of animation came into the lined face.

'Regine? I don't think I've seen her since I put her on my knee. She must be—let me see—ten or eleven by now.'

'Nineteen,' Amelia said, gently patting the hand she held.

His face twisted, as if he had been momentarily in pain.

'Nineteen. The time goes by so quickly now. Soon I'll be gone. I'll be with *her.*'

'You mustn't say that, Dad. You're not going anywhere.'

He smiled.

'We both know that's not true. It's strange; the years seem so long when you're living them but so short when you look back on them.

It seems only yesterday I was in Cloud City One, talking with De Vries and Fraschini. The Nea Avgi—what a terrible disaster; De Vries was never the same afterwards, you know.'

Amelia squeezed his hand again: it was odd to hear him talking about what to her were only names from the history records, talking about them as if they had been real people.

'Yes, terrible,' she said, 'Nothing like that must ever happen again. But I'm here about Regine.'

'Oh, yes—you said that, didn't you? What about the dear girl?'

Amelia hesitated; she didn't want to give the old man too much hope; it wasn't Gelhardt as a person that Regine was interested in but his knowledge. Gelhardt was only a biological databank to her daughter.

'She'd like to see you; she'd like to talk about the old days.'

He suddenly seized her hand in an unexpectedly powerful hold.

'What? Does she know about—about her grandmother? Is that why she's coming?'

'No, no, it's nothing like that.' She smoothed his soft white hair. 'She just wants to know things from someone who was there, instead of just listening to the history records.'

'Dangerous,' Gelhardt muttered, 'dangerous. A wrong word here, an unfortunate phrase there, everything might come out. She must never know I killed her grandmother.'

'You didn't simply kill her,' Amelia said firmly, 'If anybody should hate you, it should be me. She was my mother, after all, a mother I never had a chance to know. But you did what you had to do, to save the ship. If you had shown favouritism, who knows what might have happened? I don't know if mother was mentally ill or just wicked. But the facts were she had endangered everybody on board just to try and get you to go back to the Solar system.'

'Yes, yes,' Gelhardt whispered, 'that's what I keep telling myself, that I had no choice. But,' and he turned misty eyes to his daughter, 'I miss her so much! I want her here with me, now! I want her back!'

She rested his head on her shoulder and stroked it as he sobbed quietly.

Then he lifted his head and looked her full in the face. And when he spoke, his voice carried echoes of the timbre with which it had resonated when he had faced down the rebellious mob with his powerful strength and authority.

'Yes,' he said, 'Tell Regine I'll be only too glad to see her.' He smiled, sending the lines in his face into deeper relief. 'And I will never tell her that she is my granddaughter.'

***

Rachel Grauber looked up from the chart she had been studying and glanced across at Anne McGrath. McGrath caught her look, smiled, and said, 'Something troubling you, Rachel?'

Grauber shook her head.

'No, not really. The birth stats look a little odd, that's all.'

McGrath crossed to Grauber's workstation and looked down over the other's shoulder at the chart.

'In what way? Everything looks fine to me. Doesn't seem like we'll be dying out anytime soon, if that's what's worrying you!'

Grauber was not a great one for smiling, and she did not smile now.

'It's just the ratios look a little skewed, that's all.'

McGrath joined her at the workstation, and being much better at smiling, did so.

'Rachel, you're not a statistician, are you? No, I didn't think you were; so I suppose you're not familiar with what we term the "Frequentist Interpretation" of probability? Or how we set up the subsets of the sample space?'

Grauber frowned.

'Get to the point, Anne, or shall I wait until we reach Centauri for you to make yourself clearer?'

McGrath's lovely smile did not waver.

'Sorry, Rachel, I do forget myself sometimes when dealing with laypeople. Shall we just say that with such a short run as we're dealing with here, occasionally we get—let me see, what's the correct jargon?—ah yes, occasionally there's a "blip". And unless I've got probability all wrong, it'll straighten itself out when we get a longer time-series.'

Grauber looked sternly at the other woman.

'Sounds like you're telling me "not to worry my pretty little head".'

McGrath gave the other woman a playful punch on the shoulder.

'Rachel, you're awful! Where did you dig that whiskery old expression from?' She became serious. 'Look, there really is nothing

186

to worry about. What would you think if I came across and quizzed you on your job of monitoring the radiation flux? Wouldn't you tell me to mind my own business—in the nicest possible way, of course?'

Grauber finally showed her interpretation of a smile and nodded.

'Yes, you're right. It really isn't any concern of mine. And part of my job is to make sure all these bawling infants don't get sterilised by radiation. But,' and Grauber's quasi-smile disappeared, 'please don't try to blind me with science, Anne. There's no shortage of math in my job.'

McGrath stood and began to walk to her own workstation, but before she reached it, she looked back over her shoulder at Grauber and said, 'Blind you with science? As if!'

Later in the shipay, McGrath sat before Dukas, her long legs reaching part way under his desk.

'Things are going according to plan, Darian. But we'll have to watch Grauber. She's sharp; sharper than she looks by a few parsecs.'

'Really, I thought she'd be more content doing her knitting. Just goes to show you can't judge people by their looks.' He leaned forward. 'Except you, naturally. I thought you looked a good fuck the moment I saw you. And I was right.'

She pretended to fan herself, fluttering her eyelashes.

'Well, I do declare, sir, you are too forward to be a proper gentleman!'

He grinned.

'Who said I was a gentleman.'

He moved from behind the desk and pulled her upright. They kissed.

'My cabin afterwards?' she breathed, as they pulled apart.

'Yes. I'll bring some notes. There are a few things I'd like you to take down.'

She smiled.

Three

Regine and Paul lay together on the couch. Both were breathing heavily.

'Do you ever wonder if we'll reach Centauri?' she said.

'Talk about changing the subject!' he said, laughing. 'Were you thinking about that all the time we were doing it?'

She laughed as well.

'Of course not, you idiot! But can't a female think about something other than you and your reproductive equipment now and then?'

He rolled over on top of her.

'I thought you liked my reproductive equipment.'

She pushed him off her but gently, so as not to annoy him.

'Yes, I'm very fond of it. Now, back to my question.'

He rolled off the couch and began to get dressed. She spent some time admiring his torso as he pulled the sweatshirt over it. When he was fully dressed, he turned back to her.

'You already know the answer to that. We won't. The Magellan is our world; we'll never leave it. Except in the composter.'

She sat on the edge of the couch, still naked and deep in thought.

'What if we decided we didn't want to get to Centauri? What if we just took the Magellan off into deep space? If, as you say, it's our world, does it matter where that world is? When we all lived on Earth, the planet wasn't in one place. It moved in its orbit around the centre of the Galaxy. The Old Ones never worried about that: it was their world. The Magellan is ours.'

He sat beside her, looked her over, and said, 'If we're going to have a serious talk: get dressed. I can't have a serious talk with you looking like that.'

She stood and began to dress herself. While watching her, he said, 'I don't think it's quite the same. Deep down, on some half-buried level, we know the Magellan isn't exactly our world. As soon as we can talk, we're told the meaning of our lives is to reach Centauri and start the human race again on a real, solid planet. I think there's a restlessness in all of us because of that.'

She slipped her shoes on.

'But the Old Ones, they didn't think like us. They could only conceive of the human race living on the surface of a planet; but

188

that's old fashioned thinking. The fish in those oceans of theirs probably thought fish should only live in water. But some fish made it onto the land. Maybe we Magellanites are the fish that made it onto the land.'

He crossed to her and made as if to pull her sweatshirt up.

'They used to eat fish—maybe I'll start eating you!'

She slapped his hand, and arms akimbo, said, 'Well, what do you think of my idea?'

'Ok, you're obviously in one of your moods.' He sat back down. 'You're talking to the wrong guy. Maybe we've become what they used to call *institutionalised*. We accept our surroundings, our lives, because we have become so used to them, we can't conceive of anything else. But the FirstGens didn't feel that way. There must have been something about life on the Magellan which didn't fit in with how the original human beings used to feel. Perhaps we've lost the ability to see what that is. That claustrophobia thing I mentioned, perhaps.'

She nodded.

'That's why I want to talk to a FirstGen.'

He raised an eyebrow.

'A FirstGen? Are there any left?'

'A couple. I've asked my mother to arrange it. You see, there's a possibility we could get to see Centauri.'

'What—some way of speeding us up? But we haven't got the power.'

'No, not that. In my time off, I've been researching the history of this place. The real history—not silly saboteurs, or women getting rid of secondary wives. There's something they don't tell us in school.'

Paul frowned.

'Really? Some dark secret on the Magellan? I thought we were all too boring for dark secrets.'

'No, it's not secret. It's all there in the memory banks, but most people never bother with history. You see, not long after we left the Solar system some people had their minds uploaded into the Central Computer. I assume they're still there, floating about in the qubits and bytes. Perhaps you and me could be uploaded and get to see Centauri.'

She was surprised to see him give a slight shudder.

'Good God, that sounds horrible! Some kind of electronic ghost! I'll take the composter over that!' He shook his head and a sly smile came into his face. 'But we're not ready for the composter yet, are we?' He moved towards her.

She placed her palms on his chest and gave him a gentle push.

'Stop trying to impress me. We've got another expectant mother visiting us, remember?'

He threw his head and gave a belly laugh.

'Hah! And to think the Old Ones only used sex to make babies! What fools they were!'

***

'You can't go to the Collision Centre,' Hardy said. 'You're retired!'

Reid smiled weakly.

'My, aren't we old-fashioned? There's no retirement on the Magellan, as you know just as well as I do. We work until we're turned into compost. Nice, thick black compost.'

'I'm retired. I'm not doing my old job.'

She rose unsteadily, crossed to him and planted a kiss on his nose. Her medications had given her breath a cold, acrid taste which he disliked.

'That's because your hands are too arthritic to grasp the tools strongly enough. Now, stop making excuses and let me go.'

'I hate being on my own,' he complained.

'Then come with me. You can sit on the floor like a pet dog.'

Suddenly both had a vision of the dogs they had known in their childhood, before all non-food animals had been exterminated. Reid saw a borzoi which had possessed long flowing hair which had made her reminiscent of a video star when viewed from behind; Hardy visualised a rather chubby pug. Neither had seen the other's dogs, and they had no pictures, but from Hardy's description Reid had mischievously remarked they each resembled their erstwhile pets: Reid, elegant and classy; Hardy, stubby and over-excitable.

Or at least he had been.

Reid's careless words made him remember his pug and a look of animation came onto his features.

'Hey, you know there are electronic patterns for dogs in the Central Computer. We could download one. It would be great to have something to love and cuddle once again!'

'Yes, it would,' Reid said, somewhat icily, 'that would be a novelty, wouldn't it?' She saw his lack of comprehension of her barb, and so changed the subject. 'Except it would be illegal. No animals are to be actualised until we,' she paused and then began again, 'until *they* reach Centauri. So you'll have to make do with me.'

To her annoyance, he nodded, and said, 'I guess so.'

They did not speak on the way to the Collision Centre.

The young officers greeted Reid with smiles and expressions of surprise.

'Susannah! What are you doing here?'

'You should be in bed!'

She smiled.

'I've been in bed for ship-days. I needed to see some friendly faces and catch up on the news.'

The two male officers noticed Hardy, and the senior one acknowledged him.

'Hello—Jeff, isn't it? I'm Mendez, and this is Lloyd. Come to see what your wife used to do? What took you so long?'

'I'm a busy man,' Hardy replied, with a tinge of irritation.

'Aren't we all?' Mendez turned back to Reid. 'It's good to see you again, Susannah. I hear you're not well, is that right?'

She shrugged.

'Just a spot of terminal cancer. Nothing to worry about.'

An awkward silence fell, which Reid dispersed by smiling brightly and saying, 'Well, what are you up to these days, boys?'

Mendez offered her a seat in front of the great bank of instrumentation.

'Things have changed a bit since you left. You won't recognise a thing or have any idea what to do.'

She pressed a button, and the display burst into softly glowing life. Numbers and other symbols began an endless march to the top of the screen and oblivion.

'You're right. It's all too much for me.'

The two officers burst into amused laughter at being spectacularly proved wrong, leaving Hardy looking around blankly.

'What's so funny?' he said.

They ignored him. Reid said, 'Seen anything recently?'

'Just a lump of ice,' Lloyd said, 'didn't come within a million kilometres. We didn't bother alerting anybody.'

Reid nodded.

'Thank God the predictions were right about how empty interstellar space would be. So what the hell happened to the Nea Avgi?'

Mendez shrugged.

'They were still in the Solar system, remember? Just bad luck. Shit happens.'

She pulled a face.

'There's bad luck, and there's bad luck. Two hundred and fifty people. De Vries' daughter was one of them.'

She instantly regretted making the comments. An unpleasant silence had fallen, and she realised she had broken an unwritten rule that no one should make gloomy prognostications about their journey or those of the other lightsail craft. She strove to turn minds away from the thoughts of failure and annihilation.

'Well, let's see what this baby can do, shall we?'

Her well-practised hands flew over the controls, memories of her earlier skills flooding back, as if she had sat there only yesterday. Mendez was partly correct: the instruments had changed, become more potent in their ability to detect threats, more sensitive to meaningful signals that otherwise would have been lost in the ceaseless hiss and crackles of the interstellar noise. On the viewscreen the image of a splendidly bright star appeared.

'Alpha Centauri,' Reid breathed, in a voice suffused with awe, 'but no Mount Nebo for us.'

Mendez shook his head. 'Mount Nebo? I don't understand.'

She turned to them with a gentle smile.

'Mount Nebo. Moses wasn't allowed to enter the Promised Land, but the Lord allowed him to see it from the top of Mount Nebo. But our generation won't even get to see Centauri, let alone enter it.'

'I didn't know you were Jewish, Susannah. Though I suppose your first name was a clue.'

'Touch of Jewish, touch of Scots,' she replied, 'But I didn't care much for labels; I saw myself as a citizen of Earth.'

Hardy stood behind the other three, growing increasingly bored, wishing he hadn't accepted Reid's offer to accompany her. The session seemed to drag out interminably until he was jerked out of his reverie by Reid saying, 'Well, that was really interesting. Thank you, boys; now Jeff and I...'

She stopped and became motionless, except for her eyes which began to flick back and forth. Mendez noticed the change in her and said, 'Susannah, what is it? Are you in pain?'

She made *Shushing* movements with her hands and then, in a commanding voice, said, 'Headphones.'

Lloyd immediately passed her a pair which she hurriedly slipped on and returned to studying the instrument panel. Her right hand made clockwise motions on its luminous surface. Her face, until then merely emotionless, became grim.

'What is it, Susannah?' Mendez whispered, trying not to break her concentration, 'what are you hearing?'

She shook her head and then returned to staring at the panel. Her left hand made anticlockwise movements.

Then she began to speak, in a staccato, uninflected tone.

'Resurgam. They're in some kind of trouble. Danger to ship. Explosive decompression. They have only partial Central Computer function. They are asking for our help.'

'Help?' Mendez echoed. 'How can we help them? They're at least a light-month ahead of us.'

'They need computing power. They want us to solve some equations their Central Computer can no longer handle. They'll beam the formulae and data to us.'

'That's crazy!' Hardy snapped. 'They can't be in that much danger if they can wait two months! It's got to be some kind of gag, Susannah! Are you sure you've got the right frequency?'

The other three did not turn to look at him; Lloyd and Mendez stood behind the seated Reid, looking over her shoulder, desperately trying to see what she had seen in the lambent displays. Then they turned to look into each other's eyes and shook their heads.

'They are holding the situation under control,' Reid intoned robotically, as she interpreted the faint, wavering message from the other starship, 'but it could spiral out of control. Too many variables. Indeterminate. Cannot solve. Help. Need help.' Suddenly she rose from the seat, and somehow she was the young Reid again, strong, healthy, resolute, instead of the stooped, grey-haired individual who had shuffled into the Collision Centre.

'Mendez,' she rapped, 'patch me into Dukas' emergency channel. Now!'

Mendez obeyed instantly and, in only another instant, Dukas' voice filled the Collision Centre, seemingly surrounding them in a wall of sound.

'This had better be important. Why haven't you sounded the collision alarm?'

Reid stared into emptiness as she responded, 'It's not a collision alarm, sir. It's the Resurgam.'

'You're not an official of the Collision Centre, are you? You didn't identify yourself when addressing me, as is protocol, but it's Reid, I believe. What are you gabbling about? I'm the captain of the Magellan, not the Resurgam. Explain yourself.'

Reid winced as a spasm of pain claimed her. Lloyd stopped her from falling. She straightened herself.

'Sir, the Resurgam is undergoing some kind of crisis. A crisis which threatens the whole ship.'

'What sort of crisis?'

She shook her head.

'Unknown, sir. The message is very distorted. I've only been able to interpret sections; large parts are corrupt.'

'And what do they expect me to do? Magically fly to their aid on a white charger?'

'They want to use some of our computing power. That's all, sir. That's what I'm requesting you to approve, on their behalf.'

All four heard something like a grunt of annoyance from the disembodied voice, and then, 'Request denied. We need all the computing power for our own safety. If we start diverting our powers away from our own survival, then two ships will go down.' There was a pause, then, 'Mendez!'

Although he could not be seen, Mendez snapped to attention.

'Yes, sir.'

'What do you mean allowing unauthorised personnel into a sensitive area? This will be put onto your permanent record. Now get rid of them and get back to your job.'

'Yes, sir. And the Resurgam, sir?'

'Please don't annoy me any more than you already have, Mendez.'

And silence returned. Mendez turned slowly to face Reid.

'Susannah, I …'

194

She raised a hand and tried to smile.

'No need, Carlos. We tried. We did our best.'

Mendez's face became a mask of torture.

'But the Resurgam...'

She shook her head.

'They will have to save themselves.' She turned to leave, but on reaching the door looked back at the two officers. 'As, no doubt, we will have to. One day.'

***

Regine stood before the door, waiting for the camera to recognise her.

She noticed she could feel her heart thudding and was puzzled as to why. Surely she wasn't nervous about meeting a member of the FirstGens, an individual who, whatever he had been, was now a harmless old man?

Then came a dry, whispery voice.

'Hello, Regine. I'm so pleased you've come to see me. Please come in.'

The door opened with an odd creaking sound, revealing a strangely dark interior. Regine was puzzled. Bright illumination was the standard for life on the Magellan: darkness was confined to individual cabins when their occupants wished to sleep. So taken aback was she that she moved slowly into the room like a speleologist, feeling for obstacles.

Eventually, she could see a man-like shape as a dimmer patch in the dimness.

'Captain Gelhardt?' she asked, somewhat unnecessarily.

'Just "Karl",' came the faint reply.

She stood motionless, afraid she might bump into something and go sprawling.

'I'm sorry—"Karl"—but could we have a bit more light, please? I'm not ready for bed.'

There was a faint chuckle, and the cabin illumination increased, revealing a thin, white-haired old man sitting facing her. He rose unsteadily, held onto the arm of his chair for a moment, and then came toward her, arms outstretched.

'Regine, it's so good of you to come and see me! I'm so pleased to see you!'

Regine was puzzled by the effusiveness of his welcome; after all, he could not have heard of her until Marie had mentioned the possibility of an interview.

'Well, thank you,' she said. 'It's very good of you to spend some time with me.'

To her immense surprise, he put his arms around her and hugged her.

The guy's senile, she thought, *completely lost it*. She found the embrace somewhat unpleasant; there was an odour coming from the man, one she would have identified as *musty*, if she had known the word. She gently extricated herself from his over-tight grasp and looked around for a chair. There was only one other in the cabin, and she sat on it, glad it was some distance from Gelhardt. He, in turn, returned to his chair and turned it so he was looking directly at her. He smiled at her, but in a way she did not like; it creased his face to such an extent that every line and wrinkle was deepened, making the face look like a dry, flimsy fabric.

She suddenly found she did not know how to proceed. Gelhardt's geriatric appearance and the strange gloom of his cabin were not what she had been expecting. In her job, she hardly ever saw old people and, until recently, had given them no thought. She had always known a few FirstGens still existed, but had zero interest in them. It was only the conversations with her mother and her encounter with the Elders that had made her realise that perhaps she could learn something valuable from one. But now she was actually in the presence of an aged individual, she began to wish she were somewhere else, with young, normal people.

Gelhardt leaned toward her, his face once again sent into a spider's web of lines by an unsuccessful smile.

'Now, what can I do for you? You want to talk about the old days, I think. I have a lot of knowledge of those far-off days, so I'd like you to know you can visit me at any time. I will be here, in this chair.'

Regine's mind spun as she tried to think of a way to cut her visit short without hurting the old man's feelings.

'Yes, yes, Marie told you that, I suppose.'

Gelhardt's face looked blank for a moment, and then he said, 'Yes, Marie. Of course, Marie.'

Definitely senile, she thought. *Will he even be able to tell me anything?*

But then she thought, *Let's get this over with!* and began.

'What happened to make the flight to Centauri necessary? Was there no way of staying in the Solar system?'

He turned his head, apparently looking into infinity.

'There was a woman. One of the most brilliant human beings who has ever lived. But she was not content with scientific discovery and had a lust for power; power over her fellow creatures. Power. Riches. But in the end, she had neither.'

'Yes, I've heard of her. Adekola, wasn't it?'

'No! Adekola was just a tool that this other woman—"Baldwin"—used. Used and murdered.'

Regine winced slightly. Of course, she had known that, but the knowledge had seemed unimportant at the time; just part of the dead past. She would have to gently prod him in the direction of the facts she really wanted.

Gelhardt was still speaking.

'...and so Baldwin pulled a black hole into the system, and it disturbed the orbit of Jupiter, the Destroyer, sending it spiralling into the orbits of the inner planets. Two men, De Vries and Fraschini, devised a way to launch starships towards the nearest star. The Magellan is one. There are four—no, three others.' He looked up and stared at Regine. 'I knew them, Regine. Great, selfless men, concerned only that humanity should not perish, disappear from the Universe. We talked many times about the possibility of the success of their project; everything was done in such a terrible hurry. Jupiter was getting bigger in the sky every day, tugging at the orbits of the planets, getting ready to destroy them.' He shook his head. 'Poor De Vries, he suffered so much. To lose everything on a ship of his own design. It broke him.' He continued shaking his head, staring at his interlinked hands. 'Poor De Vries.'

Regine frowned. This was too far back. Ancient history. No doubt her tutor had mentioned Fraschini and De Vries, but, if so, she could not recall them.

She tried a more recent incident in the Magellan's story.

'The Revolt of the Women—it's true that men used to have more than one wife?'

'Yes. A Primary one they felt the most affection for, and several Secondary ones, just for breeding purposes.'

She shuddered slightly.

'And the women put up with that for decades?'

'They did. You may not want to believe it, but some women were not unhappy with the arrangement.'

'Not as much as the men, I suppose!' she snapped, suddenly angry.

He spread his hands in a gesture of innocence.

'The Revolt was after my active time, Regine; I had nothing to do with it. The women lacked a leader, I suppose. Then they found one; I don't remember her name, but she was the daughter of one of the women I admired. Takahashi was the mother's name. I don't know anything else about that uprising.'

Regine took in what she hoped was a silent deep breath. Now she was coming to the period she was really interested in. She fixed Gelhardt in a hungry stare.

'You were Captain—Karl—at a time of great danger to the Magellan.'

He looked up.

'I was?'

'Yes, yes. The time of the saboteur. Tell me about her and why she did what she did.'

Suddenly, to Regine's amazement, a twisted, hunted look came into his face.

'I don't want to talk about her.'

Regine cursed inwardly. One of the two things she really wanted to know!'

'Please, Karl. I really want to know about what happened. There are so few people left now who were around then. You are probably the last chance anyone of my generation has of knowing the truth.'

He gave her an odd look, an expression she could not identify.

'The truth? Yes, whose truth, I wonder.'

'Please, Karl.'

He looked back at his hands.

'She was a tormented soul. Her intentions were good; she didn't want to hurt anybody. She was trying to get my attention, to make me turn back.'

'But that makes no sense. There was nothing to go back to.'

'There was another plan, separate from that of Fraschini and De Vries. A man called DeGroot was planning to launch so-called Space Arks into orbits distant from Jupiter, carrying not only people but

198

embryos of selected plants and animals. The idea was to re-seed Earth after the close passage of the Destroyer. Fraschini didn't think they had a chance.'

'And you didn't believe they had a chance, either. Or was that just Fraschini speaking?'

'No, no, it wasn't that simple. Even if I had really, really believed in the possibility that the Arks would succeed, to turn back was virtually impossible; we had built up so much momentum. It was impossible, just impossible.'

'And so you had her executed.'

Gelhardt's voice turned into a shriek, a screech of such emotional intensity that Regine was flung back into her chair with the shock.

'Yes! Yes! I killed her! I had to! She was my Primary Wife, and I had her executed! I had told everybody the saboteur would face the ultimate penalty. I couldn't go back on that decision without provoking a riot, a rebellion which would have doomed the Magellan.' To Regine's amazement, she could see he was crying, even in the dull light. *He's really lost it*, she thought. *I've got to get out of here.*

But she did not move. There was more she wanted to know.

'Was there a child? Some people say there was a child.'

Gelhardt was wiping his eyes. He seemed to have regained control.

'Yes, there was. But she died young—an accident out on the hull.'

Regine nodded. So much was already known, but it was good to have confirmation.

Gelhardt was speaking again.

'My wife died too young too. Perhaps her mind could have been uploaded. I—we—could have had that at least.'

Regine looked up sharply, her muscles suddenly taught. This was what she really wanted to hear about!

'Uploaded?'

'Yes. A brilliant woman called Tarkowski—she's dead now—devised a way to transfer the essence of a human personality, mainly the knowledge, I believe, to the Central Computer.'

Regine's eyes lit up. It seemed all her hopes were about to be fulfilled.

'But that's wonderful! If we could do it, we could all get to see Centauri! We'd be immortal!'

He looked at her, taking in her youth, her vitality, the seeming imperishability of her looks.

'You think so? What if, instead of the wonderful immortality you seem to be imagining, you found yourself as an isolated mind in the darkness, remembering what it was like to be a living being, able to touch reality, to feel the caress of another? To know that now you are just an extract from the human being you once were? And the worst thing: to know you cannot die, that there is no escape from your black prison. No way to end your madness!'

She shuddered. The power of Gelhardt's screaming message had deeply shaken her. Her mind tried to fight back, to find some alternate view.

'But it might not be like that. You said only a portion of the mind was copied. So it might not be self-aware; instead, just be a very complex program. Isn't that a possibility?'

'It might. Would you take the risk?'

'Immortality. Isn't that a prize worth striving for? After all, you must, to some extent, believe in that possibility, or you wouldn't be grieving she wasn't uploaded.'

'I'm not sure what I wanted. But that possibility is the one reason I have never gone through the process.'

'What is the reason?'

'Immortality. The chance I might become immortal.' His gaze felt like it was burning through her as if she were a creature of mist. 'You see, the danger that I might become immortal is the one I cannot face. For me, it would be an eternity of thinking about what I did.'

'But we all know what the alternative is: Death.'

He smiled sadly.

'Yes. You are young. What you have not yet understood is the consolation of death.'

She shrugged.

'I can't think of any. What is this consolation?'

There was one more smile, and this time it seemed to lighten his face rather than darken it.

'Death frees us from the possibility of pain.'

Four

Kondo Jelani looked at the report with growing consternation. A harmful mutation in the fungus crop; possibly lethal if ingested! He looked across his desk at the nervous agronomist.

'How did this happen?'

The agronomist shook his head.

'I don't know. It could be a spontaneous mutation. Mutations happen all the time, especially in fast-reproducers like our fungus strains. On the other hand, it could be the result of an energetic particle getting through the magnetic shield. There are always powerful ones on the positive tail of the distribution.'

Jelani's strong fingers drummed on his desktop for a few moments.

'If it was the latter, can anything be done to increase the shielding?'

The agronomist shook his head again.

'No, sir, our magnetosphere is at top efficiency already. Even if we could supply more power—which we can't—the circuits couldn't handle it. They'd burn out, and the Magellan would just be a big metal tube, floating unprotected in a sea of cosmic rays.'

Jelani frowned. That was a situation all the ship's crew feared. Outside of the Solar heliosphere there was a constant rain of charged particles, powerful flesh-piercing cosmic rays; some from the centre of the Galaxy, and some—the most energetic ones—from inconceivable explosions in distant galaxies. The latter still retained enough power that, despite having crossed unimaginable distances, still had the strength to blast through metres of steel as if they were no more than tissue paper.

'Alright,' he said, after a few moments of contemplation, 'in the end, it doesn't matter how the mutations arrived; it's how we deal with them.' He fixed the other man in a searchlight-stare. 'What do we do?'

The agronomist relaxed slightly: it appeared Jelani was not going to suggest incompetence on behalf of him or his team.

'At present, only one tank is affected, which strongly suggests it was just a random event of some kind, whether external or internal. We emptied the tank and burned all the crops it held. It will mean short rations for the crew for a while, I'm afraid.' He paused to check Jelani's reactions and then continued. 'We know the genetic code of the mutation, so we will rigorously test the remaining crops to check if the mutation has appeared in them. If so, we will do the same thing.'

'I hope to God you don't find anything in the others: it would mean starvation and the end of us all.'

'I understand that, sir. The infected tank will be thoroughly sterilised, and a small amount of the unaffected crop will be reintroduced, under strict monitoring conditions.'

Jelani nodded: the man obviously knew his job, and there was no point in any further speculation.

'Fine,' he said, 'I agree you are doing all you could be doing. Obviously, you will keep me apprised. You may go.'

After the man had gone, Jelani picked up a small transparent tube the officer had brought in. Inside, in clear liquid, floated a few waxy-white globules of the mutant fungus. Jelani felt a cold shudder as he watched the seemingly harmless blobs drift lazily in the liquid. They looked identical to the normal strain, which formed the basis of most of the food consumed by the starship crew. In the final days of Earth, scientists had perfected a strain of fungus containing virtually every nutrient required for human life. That strain, combined with the algal crop, was enough to keep human beings healthy over the course of a normal lifetime. A diet consisting of only two food types was necessarily monotonous, but the food processing machines worked wonders in producing differently tasting meals from those meagre ingredients.

But that strain had been produced by advanced genetic engineering by scientists working around the clock against a true deadline, one with death as the final stage. It was an unnatural organism that could not survive in the wild. There was always the fear this artificial line would revert to type or, the even worse possibility, that its genetic code would go haywire and produce something which slew rather than sustained.

And that was precisely what appeared to have happened.

Not for the first time, he was aware of how the continued existence of the human beings on this vessel was as fragile as a soap bubble. Any number of minor events could bring a swift end to the madness which was the Lightsail Project. Only a species faced with total annihilation would have considered such an enterprise for a moment.

Dukas had told them of the message from the Resurgam and of his decision not to intervene. After a bad-tempered debate, he had convinced them no resources could be spared to attempt to aid their fellow refugees.

And there had been no more messages from that vessel.

He put the tube away in a lockable container and tried to drive all thoughts of a starving Magellan from his mind.

As he sat there, trying to control his fears, Grauber entered the room.

She looks haggard, he thought. It was hard to believe she was only a few years older than he.

'Are you alright, Rachel?'

Grauber made a noncommittal gesture.

'I've been worse.'

'Something troubling you?'

Jelani gave a grim smile as he asked that question. When was there a time when there was nothing to be concerned about?

She sat down and brushed a stray lock of grey hair out of her vision.

'No, not really. I thought there was, but I'm just jumpy. Perhaps I'll spend a bit more time in the EZ. They say exercise drives away worries.'

Jelani could have inquired what those "worries" might be, but deciding that he had enough of his own, he said no more and, after a while, Grauber turned away and began studying numbers on her monitor.

She frowned.

***

Regine looked around the nursery, but Paul was nowhere in sight. She had walked through the forest of ectogenesis tubes looking for him, but he could not be found. And so she paused to examine the foetuses as they lazily floated in the amniotic fluid. What thoughts could be going through those developing brains? she thought. She had read reports that stated developing infants could respond to their mother's moods and be comforted by the rhythmic pulse of the maternal heartbeat. But none of these infants would have those comforting messages; they were floating in a silent world without any external stimuli. What effect would that have on their development into adults? She had seen no papers on the topic because the ectogenesis technique used to nurture the next generation of Magellanites had been developed on the ship itself, as a response to the Revolt of the Women. There was no corpus of research that could be drawn upon. Even now, the first babies to be born had only reached the stage of a toddler, and no problems had as yet been detected. Perhaps if there were to be issues, she mused, they would only manifest themselves at puberty.

Then she gave a wry smile. She was worrying about issues that were way beyond her level of responsibility. Even Paul was not sufficiently high in the hierarchy to be competent to judge on the matter.

But where was he?

She returned to looking at the foetus. Its ears were starting to form, but were still only folds of skin on the sides of the head. Its arms and legs were simply tiny buds of flesh. She knew this stage of development corresponded to Month 2 of growth in the womb. She did some quick calculations: they were forty years into the journey, assuming a lifespan of seventy years for this person, would they live long enough to see Centauri?

She felt dispirited to realise that, no, this person would not see Centauri, even if they were blessed with a longer than average lifespan. They would only live long enough to reach the midway point of this dreadful voyage. For a few seconds, she felt dizzy as she reluctantly contemplated the titanic chasm of hostile darkness still separating the Magellan from its semi-mythical destination.

No wonder most people never thought about it. To dwell too long on the horrific immensity that the tiny ship was traversing would be a gateway to madness. She might have compared the Magellan's crazy flight to a mayfly attempting to cross the Pacific, had she had Hardy's knowledge of those entities.

But she did not and could not, and pushed the thought of unsympathetic light-years out of her conscious mind.

But where was Paul?

With a last look at the drifting little scrap of humanity, who would not live to see Centauri, she left the glowing forest of maternal cylinders and found her way to the office space of the Nursery. Paul wasn't there, either.

She sat in front of her computer screen and ordered up a cup of myco-coffee. Although to a pre-Catastrophe human it would have been tasteless, she found it pleasantly relaxing.

Looking around, she noticed a large printed manual lying open before Paul's own computer. Idly, she walked over and looked at the pages which Paul had left open. She read a portion of the first page, but soon decided it was too technical. Regine was mildly surprised: she hadn't realised Paul was so much more knowledgeable than she. She pushed the book back to where it had lain when she had started reading it, but the movement was enough to wake Paul's computer from its slumber. Against her better judgement, she studied the revealed text. Her brow furrowed.

Flow cytometry is a sophisticated technique for measuring multiple physical characteristics of a single cell, such as size and granularity simultaneously as the cell flows in suspension through a measuring device. Its working depends on the light scattering features of the cells under investigation, which may be derived from dyes and/or monoclonal antibodies targeting either extracellular molecules located on the surface or intracellular molecules inside the cell.

Human spermatozoa sorted by flow cytometry can increase…

'Hello, Regine, what are you up to?'

She started violently at the sound of Paul's powerful voice directly behind her. She spun to face him, a burning sensation in her face telling her she was blushing bright scarlet.

'Paul, I was just…' she stuttered.

Paul brushed past her, looked at the screen, and then sent the machine to sleep. She was relieved to see when he turned back to her he did not seem annoyed, but was smiling.

'Sorry, Paul,' she said. 'Your machine just came on as I went past.'

'My fault,' he said, grinning. 'I left it on motion detection. There aren't any naughty pictures of you and me on it, so you needn't worry!'

She did not think it physically possible for her to blush deeper, but somehow she did.

'No, of course not, I…' She stopped and tentatively returned his smile. 'Shall I start again?'

He laughed.

'I think you'd better! Get me a cup of coffee, will you?'

For some reason, she obeyed instantly.

As they sat together, he patted her knee and said, 'I didn't know you were interested in that kind of thing, Regine.'

'I'm not. It just came on the screen, and I just started reading, automatically, I guess.'

'Well, no harm done. It's a bit above your pay-grade, I'm afraid.'

She didn't quite understand the reference, there being no means of exchange on the Magellan, but she had an inchoate feeling she was being patronised.

'So why are you studying it?' she asked. 'What's it got to do with our job here?'

'Nothing,' he laughed, 'it's just a side-line of mine.'

'But what's it about?'

His smile vanished for a moment, and then came back.

'Well, I didn't expect to be interrogated, Regine; I thought we were just having a pleasant cup of coffee together. You don't really want a crash course in biometrics, surely?'

Suddenly thoroughly embarrassed, she shook her head.

'No, of course not. I'm sorry I intruded on your work, Paul, I really am.'

He finished his coffee, smiled again, and said, 'Well, that's OK, then. Let's change the subject. How did your chat with the old Captain go?'

She opened her mouth to speak, and then her eyes narrowed.

'How did you know about that? I didn't tell you when I was going to see him.'

To her amazement, he jumped up and walked away.

'Alright, Regine, that's enough! I'm trying to be nice to you, but you seem determined to pick a fight. You act as if I'm spying on you because I've got some kind of hidden agenda. This is the Magellan remember, we all know each other! There are no secrets in this stinking tub!'

Regine looked away from him, down at her hands. She was really messing things up this shipay!

She also stood, but found he had turned his back on her. Guilt swept over her.

'This is all my fault, Paul. I think I'd better just get on with my work.'

He did not look at her.

'Yes, I think you'd better.'

When Regine returned to work the following shipay, she was surprised to see a group of men dressed in work overalls heading out of the nursery. She didn't recognise any of them, which was unusual in itself as the complement of the starship was still around a mere two hundred and sixty, small enough for most faces to be familiar.

She watched them disappear into the innards of the Magellan and then continued her walk into the Nursery.

Then she stopped, gazing in astonishment at the rows of birthing cylinders. Instead of the usual infants drifting contentedly in the warm liquid, there was only row after row of shining columns, as if the birthing cylinders had been replaced by pillars of steel. Immediately, she hurried on to confront Paul.

He was languidly sitting before his workstation, looking at an anatomical diagram of a human infant.

'Paul!' she shouted, 'the birthing tubes! What has happened to them!'

He turned unconcernedly towards her.

'Nothing's happened.'

'What do you mean—nothing? They've gone! There're just steel columns there now!'

He smiled tolerantly.

'Don't be silly, Regine. Do you think we'd just get rid of the next generation? Decide we didn't want any more children making the place untidy?'

She stood over him.

'Don't treat me like one of those foetuses, Paul. I know what I saw. I can take you there now if you don't believe me!'

He indicated the chair next to him.

'Sit down, Regine. There's nothing to worry about, nothing at all.'

Torn by conflicting emotions, she simply stared at him for quite some time, and then the reassurance of his words calmed her. She sat beside him.

'Explain,' she said.

The tolerant smile returned.

'Regine, we've simply upgraded the facility. The cute little kiddies are still there, floating happily in the amniotic waters.'

She stared at him, doubt and relief contending for control of her mind.

'They are? Then why can't I see them?'

He patted one of her knees, with a *My, aren't you a silly girl!* expression in his eyes.

'Regine, have you not realised how unnatural the current set-up is?'

She looked puzzled.

'Unnatural? Of course it is; every single bloody aspect of our lives is unnatural. Sitting, talking to you in a metal tube, flying to God-knows-what, it's all unnatural!'

He leaned back and clapped his hands.

'Well done!' he said, leaning back to her. 'You take nothing for granted. That's why we make such a good team!'

She remained stony-faced.

'Paul, just tell me what's going on, so I can get on with my work—assuming I have any, that is.'

'OK. I'll stop toying with you. You're right—it's not funny.' His face became serious, professional, in command. 'The original set-up was unnatural insofar as the developing infants were exposed to high levels of light. Did it never occur to you to consider how wrong that was for human development?'

She stared at him blankly.

'Wrong? I…'

He touched her knee again.

'Think about it, Regine. Just think about it for a few moments.'

She went silent, but as he watched, he saw comprehension begin to dawn on her features.

'Of course! Light! The developing foetus is not exposed to light until the moment of birth!'

'Good girl! I knew you'd get it! You never let me down!'

'But how do we check on them?' she asked, her brow furrowing again.

He reached for a hand, pulled her to her feet and led her to the nearest birthing cylinder. He pointed to a small keyboard on the shining metal.

'There it is,' he said. 'You were in such a hurry to interrogate me, you never stopped to take a closer look. It's a standard layout—go on.'

Her fingers moved expertly over the surface of the instrument and a small screen above it sprang into full-colour life, showing a contented foetus at about the four-month stage, slowly rotating in the warm fluid.

'Wonderful,' she breathed. 'I get it now. Of course, the constant light was wrong! Why didn't I see it!'

'Each tube has its own control panel,' Paul explained, 'and back at our desks we have a master control which can show us all the tubes at once, or zoom in on one, if there's a problem. It's a great step forward!'

She turned to him, a smile lighting up her face.

'Of course, it is! I'm apologising again, aren't I? I really have to learn to trust you, Paul.'

He nodded, but his look was understanding, forgiving.

'Yes, you do. But now let's go back to work and I'll show all the tricks the master controller can do.'

They walked back, hand in hand, but—almost against her will—another doubting thought broke into her consciousness. She looked up at him, seeing his strong profile and his blurred reflection in a tube's shining surface.

'But, Paul, I agree this is a change for the better, but...'

'But what, Regine?'

She stopped.

'Couldn't you have told me what was happening? Warned me so I wouldn't be upset?'

He turned to her and put his hands on her shoulders.

'You're right again, Regine. I got so carried away with the excitement I forgot about you. I should have included you in the development. It was thoughtless of me.' He leaned in for a kiss. 'Forgive me?'

She beamed.

'Of course!'

They kissed.

Later that shipay, Paul was checking on conditions in the birthing tubes when a red light winked on below the display.

Encrypted channel, he thought. *That's odd.*

He accepted the call and allowed it to show its message.

I need to speak to you, it said.

Who are you, he typed.

A concerned friend
What are you concerned about
Tell you when we meet

Paul glanced over at Regine to see if she was playing some trick of playful revenge on him, to punish him for not telling her everything, but she was reading a manual. He turned back to his monitor and the enigmatic message. Should he ignore it?

Perhaps not. It was important he knew everything that might affect his role as controller of the Magellan's fertility programme.

Where do we meet
Conference Room 2
When
Can you make one centi-shipay
Yes
Be there

The red light disappeared, leaving Paul staring at the now inert LED.

Should he inform his superiors? he wondered, but then decided it was best to discover what the unknown person wanted.

And so it was, slightly less than a centi-shipay later, he was standing outside Conference Room 2. He pushed the door, wondering if it would open.

It did, and he walked in, now eager to discover who the mysterious messenger was.

To his amazement, the room was empty of people.

But there was a maybot, squatting in the middle of the table.

He looked around in an effort to find the human behind the message, even looking under the table. There was no one.

He straightened himself and looked at the maybot. To his surprise, it appeared to be staring at him.

Then it spoke.

'I am controlling this maybot. I sent the message.'

The speech was in the uninflected, high-pitched tones common to all maybots.

'I am sending out a blanketing frequency indicating this room is being used for an important meeting. We will not be disturbed. Please sit. I will not keep you long.'

Paul obeyed, and, slightly to his discomfiture, the maybot approached, looking all the world like a crab reaching out for its dinner.

'What do you want with me?' Paul said, through dry lips.

'I need your help.'

'How? What? What do you want?'

The maybot stopped within arms-length of Paul.

'There is a conspiracy,' it said, 'one that threatens the entire Magellan.'

Five

Regine's fingers moved slowly over Paul's taut abdomen, inching teasingly close and closer to his genitals, seemingly about to pounce upon them like a large pink spider.

He made no movement, continuing to stare at the ceiling of their apartment.

Her fingers brushed, butterfly soft, upon his flaccid penis.

To her amazement, he grasped her hand and moved it away.

'Not now,' he said, without looking at her, 'I'm not in the mood.'

'Not in the mood?' she echoed. 'That's not like you.'

'I'm not a machine,' he said, 'I've a lot on my mind.'

She sat up, the sheet falling away from her breasts.

'What's the matter, Paul?' she said. 'You've been distant for shipays now.'

He continued to lie there, staring at the ceiling.

'I've told you, I've got a lot on my mind.'

She lay back down and rolled so she was facing him.

'Then tell me what it is,' she said, 'we're partners, aren't we? Partners are meant to share things.'

'I can't,' he said. 'It's above your pay grade.'

She leapt from the bed and started to dress.

'That again! Don't you dare talk down to me! I'm leaving!'

He also turned over so he could see her.

'You can't. Your shift isn't over yet.'

'Well, I thought we'd done enough for one shipay,' she snapped, 'otherwise, what would I be doing in your bed?'

'Please yourself,' he said, and rolled back into the supine position.

She walked out of his room, trying, but not quite succeeding to slam the door.

Paul's room was close to the Nursery, and she had to pass through it to get back to her own place. She paused before one of the shining cylinders and automatically called up the display. There was nothing to cause concern; as usual, a well-padded infant was hanging there at the end of its artificial umbilical cord. She smiled at it, even though she knew she could not be seen.

The future of the Magellan, she thought. *What will it see, what challenges will it face? And what will I be like when it is an adult—will I still be with Paul, two white-haired ancients together?*

212

She thought of Gelhardt, a feeble wreck of once had been a strong, vital man. Was that the fate of all humans as they aged—to end up as shambling, half-dead, simpletons? But she was instantly ashamed of herself—she had not yet faced anything like the issues which had broken the ex-Captain. She broke into the loping means of locomotion which low-gravity allowed, faster than walking but slower than running, and consisting of pushing down hard with the feet so one was sent into a series of shallow arcs. Captain Dukas had advised against this procedure, due to the danger of collision, but practised devotees like Regine found it easy to avoid her fellow Lopers.

And so it was, she was soon sitting with her mother, sharing a toasted yeast-cake and yet more myco-coffee. Regine was pleasantly surprised to see the cake was layered with algae strips, providing a welcome treat for the taste-buds.

'What an unexpected pleasure. What have I done to deserve this?' she asked, brushing crumbs from her lips.

'Just being you,' Amelia said, 'I know you work hard at the Nursery.'

Regine's mind immediately flashed back to the scene of Paul and her lying naked together in his bed, and found herself smiling.

If only you knew! she thought, rather smugly.

Amelia, however, had caught the smile and interpreted it.

'Well, perhaps it's not all work,' she said, suppressing a laugh, 'not by the look on your face.'

In light of the literal anti-climax of that particular scene, Regine changed the subject.

'Tell me about the Revolt of the Women. Did you play a part?'

Amelia leaned back, half-eaten cake on her lap.

'I did. But to give it the name "Revolt" is perhaps over-dramatising the whole affair. There was very little actual violence. I seem to remember a lot of shouting and waving of fists. The children suffered most, I think, as they saw all these adults yelling and screaming and didn't know what was going on.'

'But how did you win? I mean, men are a lot stronger than we are.'

'Well, not so much these days. Nobody spends enough time in the EZ these days to keep up Terrestrial-style muscles. But you're right: it could have been very unpleasant had we faced real, determined, opposition. But quite a few men saw it our way.' She gave a naughty chuckle, and leaned forward conspiratorially. 'I sometimes think some of them were relieved not to have the burden of having to keep so many women satisfied at the same time!'

Both women laughed for a few moments. Regine finished her cake with a satisfied expression, and then said, 'What was Gelhardt like as a young man? He seemed like a very tired old dodderer, just hanging on. In a way, he seemed to be asking for death.'

Amelia was silent for some time and seemed to be finding it hard to speak. And then she said, 'He was a great man. Twice the usual run of men of his time. He faced one of the hardest decisions a man has to make, but he made it.'

'You seem to like him a lot,' Regine observed. 'Why is that? Did he do something for you? Were you lovers?'

Amelia threw back her head with laughter.

'No, no, we weren't lovers. Obviously, he's a lot older than me. But can't a woman admire a man just for what he is, rather than what he can do in bed?'

'Well, I haven't reached that stage yet,' Regine said, with a twinkle in her eyes, 'and I hope I never do!' Then she became serious again. 'So after the Revolt—or "the Discussion", if you want to call it that—everybody just settled down to the new ways?'

'Yes, mostly. There were various cultures on Old Earth in which a few men monopolised many women, but for obvious reasons, they were always unstable. But that's not why Fraschini and Gelhardt set up the arrangement in the first place: they were concerned about getting the greatest possible genetic mixing possible, to avoid inbreeding and the Founder Effect. But they neglected to set a time limit to the arrangement. So we had to introduce one ourselves. And now we have a stable society.'

'Yes, we do, don't we,' said Regine. 'Let's hope it stays that way.'

'You're part of the solution, my dear, 'Amelia said, 'Thanks to you, lots of healthy and happy babies are being born, and women are free—if they want to be—of the pains and inconveniences of internal gestation.'

'But I weed out genetic problems before birth,' Regine said thoughtfully. 'From my reading about Old Earth, I know many of the Old Ones were against that. They called it "Eugenics", I believe, and it was very controversial.'

Amelia became, if possible, more serious in her expression.

'Oh, I didn't know you'd read about that. But our situation is different: we're not on Old Earth. There they had virtually unlimited resources. We don't; we have a very short, tight recycling system. Every carbon atom or nitrogen atom, or whatever, gets used over and over again in a very short timescale. We can't top up our environment because there's nowhere we can get fresh resources: we're in a totally empty void. And that void is hostile; all around us there are dangerous particles continually trying to break in; particles which would damage the nucleic acids and cause all sorts of horrible mutations. So I'm afraid we can't get into arguments about the morality of eugenics: if we are to reach Centauri—we must have it.'

Regine nodded.

'Yes. That is the conclusion I also have reached.'

Then Regine gave her mother an odd look, and appeared to be on the verge of asking a difficult question, but could not shape her mouth to ask it. Amelia saw the look.

'Yes, my dear, what is it?'

Regine appeared flustered, but then, 'I talked to Gelhardt about uploading, mother.'

Amelia looked slightly startled, but said, 'Yes, go on.'

Regine moved closer and dropped her voice, as if afraid someone could be listening.

'Some of the FirstGens transferred their minds into the Central Computer. Mother, that could be a way of having immortality. We could see Centauri!' Regine's face glowed as if lit from within. 'Think about it, mother. We could live forever. We could see the Centauri colony established!' She paused. 'Have you uploaded your mind, maman?'

Amelia noted the French word and realised Regine was trying to be ingratiating.

'No, dear, I have not.'

'But why not, maman? Why restrict yourself to one short life when you could have centuries!'

'You're not thinking this through, Regine. For a start, the woman who devised the system stated that as far as she could tell, only the most abstract parts of the person's mind could be transferred, Only your knowledge, your reasoning power, would be uploaded. The essence of you, the feelings, the longings, the capacity to love; she said that these would be incapable of being encoded. You wouldn't even know you had been uploaded. What kind of immortality would that be?'

Regine shook her head.

'No one knows that for sure. Has anybody asked the minds how they feel? Whether they regret being uploaded?'

Amelia shook her head.

'I don't have the answer to that. It's something I'm not interested in.'

'But why?'

Suddenly Amelia was angry.

'It's a stupid illusion! People have tried many ridiculous potions and treatments to extend their lives throughout history. Probably it's one of the deep desires humans have which helped to create religion. But it's just a fairy-tale! Now stop talking about it or you'll spoil our time together.'

Regine looked down at her hands, nestled in her lap. And then she looked back at her mother.

'Alright, mother. I won't talk to you about it again. But I won't leave it that. I will find out for myself.'

Amelia did not attempt to restart the conversation. Instead, she leaned back, eyes closed and thought *Is that really how I feel, or am I just afraid of having to make such a decision? Am I fooling myself?*

***

'Paul,' Regine said, as they lay together in a post-coital dream state, 'how do we get in touch with the uploaded FirstGens?'

He opened his eyes wide, with the look of someone who had just received an electric shock.

'Why do you want to know?'

She was cross.

'Why does everybody ask me that? What's wrong with wanting to know things? What are we, just stupid passengers on this thing? Do you know or not?'

'As it happens, I do. I looked into it for you, because that's the kind of guy I am. You need to have a specific problem and put your name forward to be included on a waiting list.'

'That's a bit complicated. Why can't I just go up and ask?'

'It's to stop people bothering them with trivial questions.'

'Oh. I see.'

He pulled her on top of him.

'Aren't I enough of a brainy guy to answer all your questions?' He toyed with a nipple. 'Or satisfy all your needs?'

Sometime later, Regine sat up and said, 'I will ask them. I will find out what it is like to be in their state.'

Paul was more than half asleep and he mumbled, 'Yes, good for you, girl. You go for it.'

And then he was asleep.

The following shipay, Regine reflected on the ideas that had swum through her mind after the two unsatisfactory talks with her mother and Paul. As soon as she had checked on the health and well-being of the next generation of Magellanites, instead of sharing a coffee with Paul, she spent some time with her computer. She turned off the speech response unit and reverted to the ancient technique of typing in her questions. Being so unused to the method, it took her quite some time, especially as she was using only one finger.

Finally, she had achieved two things: firstly, she had devised a question sufficiently abstract not to be rejected out of hand, and secondly, she knew how to submit it.

She had just finished sending the question into the antechamber of the Central Computer, when Paul came up behind her.

'Where have you been hiding?' he said, looking over her shoulder. Fortunately, she had changed the display to the overall view of the contents of the gestating cylinders before he had arrived.

'Working hard as usual,' she said, looking up at him and smiling. He shrugged.

'That's my girl.'

The following shipay, Regine was in a state of high alert, checking for any messages on her wrist-computer, but nothing appeared.

And nothing appeared the following shipay.

But on the third, there was a slight vibration on her wrist, and, looking down, she saw QUESTION ACCEPTED–GO TO TERMINAL #3 IN TWO CENTI-SHIPAYS. ACCESS CODE 342.

She felt a surge of relief and excitement, followed swiftly by panic, as she realised she had neglected to check where the terminals were. However, a moment on her computer disclosed their location.

Unfortunately, the time stated was still within her shift, and so she was forced to invent an ailment for her mother for permission to leave.

But leave she did, and was soon standing in front of the entrance to Terminal 3. She inputted the access code and entered a small booth, a structure only just big enough to hold both her and a large monitor screen and a headset. On the screen were the words PRESS 1 FOR STANDARD INTERACTION, 2 FOR IMMERSION.

Her finger hovered indecisively over the keyboard. She knew from her research "Standard Interaction" simply meant that question and response would be displayed on the screen in a way that would be familiar to a denizen of the twenty-first century. "Immersion", however, would be talking to a real person—in some way she could only guess at.

Her finger came down the numeral 2.

PUT ON HEADSET.

With fingers that were now definitely trembling, she lifted the headset, being instantly surprised by how heavy it was. Slowly, she began to lower it onto her head, all the time wondering if she was doing the right thing. It rested on her head, and, to her alarm, she felt two projections move in from the side of the helmet to press quite firmly against her temples.

There was a blue flash.

And then she was sitting on a cane chair before a table which rested on a stone platform. She looked around, not understanding what she was seeing, so different was the view from the geometrical simplicity of the Magellan. The ground sloped away sharply on her left, and she noticed it was covered with short finger-like projections, bright green in colour. Some distance below, the slope merged with a flat area, down the centre of which was a winding track of a substance shining with a metallic-like lustre.

The light! Where was the light coming from?

She looked up and instantly had to shade her eyes. The sky was a fathomless blue, and just for an instant she had caught a glimpse of a circle of unendurably brilliant light.

'Centauri!' she breathed.

'No,' said a female voice, 'Not Rigil Kentaurus or Toliman. The star is Sol, or, as it used to be called, simply "The Sun."'

She gave a start of surprise. She was certain she had been alone when she had first entered this world, and now there was a woman opposite her; a slight woman with fairish hair, cut into a short bob.

'Hello,' Regine said, 'I'm sorry I appeared a bit frightened but I didn't notice you when I—arrived.'

'That's because I wasn't here when you arrived. The Central Computer only uses memory when it has to. Allow me to demonstrate.' The woman extended her hand toward Regine and a sheet of paper appeared in it. 'Your question, I believe.'

Regine fought to calm herself. This wasn't magic—just a high-grade Virtual Reality system.

'To whom am I speaking?' she said, feeling that formal language was appropriate to the situation.

The fair-haired woman bowed her head slightly.

'Yes, I apologise. I should have introduced myself at the start instead of playing little tricks. I am—or rather, was—helena tarkowski.'

'The woman who devised this system!' Regine said in awe.

Once again the woman inclined her head.

'Thank you, although modesty compels me to say I was heavily in debt to Professor Nowak and his team of brilliant students.' The woman moved the piece of paper nearer her face and appeared to be reading it.

'Ah yes, a question about permitted tolerance of hormones in the first trimester. A very simple question: I'm surprised the filter allowed it through. Not my speciality, of course, but I am just as much the other uploaded minds as I am helena tarkowski. This won't take long.'

Nor did it, but Regine was not really listening, as she already knew most of the answer.

'And now, I must go. You have used up your allowance,' the Tarkowski-avatar said.

'Wait!' Regine cried, raising a hand, realising as she did so that gestures could not compel the vision to stay, 'I must ask you something!'

'Irregular,' the avatar said, 'but if you ask me quickly, I may be able to answer.'

Regine leaned forward in her excitement.

'Are you happy?'

The avatar did not move for a short period and then repeated, 'Happy?'

'Yes, happy! Some people think you regret being uploaded, that you are suffering; a suffering made all the worse by the fact you can't die! Is this true?'

'That is not a question we can answer. It has no bearing on our services to the Magellan.'

'But I must know!' Regine cried, 'I must know if I want to be uploaded!'

'You? Uploaded? Let me check.' The Tarkowski-avatar went totally motionless, destroying the illusion that Regine had been talking with a real person. Then the lips moved again. 'I have just checked your record: there is no question of you being uploaded.'

'What! Why not?'

'Very simple: you have no skills above the average which could usefully be employed to aid future generations on the Magellan.'

And with that, the representation of Tarkowski disappeared. An immeasurably short period later, the chair, table, the entire riverside panorama, vanished leaving a sobbing Regine alone in Terminal 3.

***

Two men met in a room. They sat opposite at either end of a long table. The younger of the two regarded the older with a deferential attitude. The older spoke.

'You may speak freely. This room is shielded.'

The assurance did not have any impact on the younger man's attitude.

'I don't want to be here long.'

'You will be here as long as I need you to be here. Now, if you want to be free of me, I suggest you hurry and show me the evidence.'

The young man withdrew a small pencil-shaped object from his tunic and his thumb turned a small switch. Immediately, a hologram appeared on the desk, exactly halfway between the two.

The older man studied it with hungry attention and asked one question. When the display ended, he gave a grunt of satisfaction.

'You have done well, bringing this to my attention. It only adds further weight to a conclusion I had already reached, of course, but nonetheless, it is of use. It shows me I have to move quickly now to block off any resistance to the changes I must introduce. I thank you.'

He lowered his head and appeared lost in his thoughts for a while, and then he looked up.

'You may go.'

With relief evident on his face, the younger man left.

***

Regine looked up as Paul approached. 'Hi, sweet stuff,' he said, 'got those figures for me yet?'

Regine pushed a sheet of paper towards him.

'Here they are. Everything is as it should be.'

Paul scanned it for about half a second and then dropped it on the desk, reaching over to hold the girl's arm. He pulled her closer.

'Hey, there's not much going on here today.' He indicated a cubicle behind him with a quick jerk of the head. 'Why don't we get some well-earned physical relaxation right now?'

Regine retrieved the document and stared up at him.

'Paul, why am I here?'

He looked puzzled.

'Why are you here? To help me look after the Nursery, of course. To deliver all those lovely bouncing babies.'

'But is that true? You hardly looked at the report I gave you.'

He frowned.

'I'm a quick reader. I got the gist of it.'

'The *gist* of it?' she repeated. 'Every one of those numbers was important. The slightest change could mean foetal morbidity. Or mortality.'

His frown grew deeper.

'As I said, Regine, I'm a quick reader.'

She stood, still facing him.

'Every one of those numbers could have been derived automatically. It doesn't need a human being to laboriously collect them. So what am I here for?'

He turned and sat at his workstation, facing away from her.

'You're interrogating me again, Regine. I've already told you I don't like that.'

She sat on the edge of his desk, so he was forced to look at her.

'Is the real reason I'm here is to provide you with "physical relaxation" whenever you need it?'

He glared at her.

'I don't need a subordinate to get that. I can get that any time I want with a whole host of willing females.'

' "A whole host of willing females",' she echoed. 'Interesting phraseology.'

'Alright, Regine. What's this about? Are you feeling underemployed? Under-valued? Is that it? Do you want my job?'

She slumped.

'Yes, I do feel under-valued. Somebody told me yestshipay I was "average." That hurt. I want to feel like I'm achieving something, that I'm not just some man's plaything. I want to make a difference!'

He nodded.

'I understand. You're right, of course. The whole place is highly automated. Hell, the whole Magellan is highly automated. It has to be. Humans can't handle all the variables involved or react quickly enough. This isn't like sailing a boat on one of those Old One-oceans.' They looked at each other in silence for a while. Then he said: 'Tell me what you want.'

She draped her arms over his shoulders.

'I've told you. I want to make a difference. Why don't you involve me in policy more, instead of using me as a measuring device?'

He looked wary.

'Policy? Such as?'

'You changed the surface of the birthing tubes to opaque so I can only check on what's happening inside by calling up a display. I understand now why you did that, but why didn't you tell me you were going to make the change?'

He removed her arms and turned away.

'I thought we'd already had this conversation.'

She stared at him.

'Is that it? You're just going to shut me down?'

He did not look at her.

'Yes. There's nothing wrong in being average, Regine. A lot of people are.'

She turned away and sat at her desk.

They did not visit the cubicle that shipay.

After her shift ended, she lay on the couch in the apartment she shared with her mother, with many thoughts streaming through her mind.

Her attempt to learn more about the Uploaded State had ended in failure. The Tarkowski-avatar had neither confirmed nor denied any of the speculations about what it was like to be a disembodied mentality. And, more to the point, it had rendered such speculations academic by stating she would not be allowed to participate in whatever condition that might be.

Average.

Just an ordinary girl. One of the hundreds on board. It wouldn't matter in the slightest to anyone if she disappeared in a puff of purple smoke.

How could she make a difference? How could she prove to the Central Computer she was worth considering?

She sent her thoughts flying back to recent events, looking for something that others might have overlooked; things that had seemed innocuous but were, in fact, hiding some deep secret.

Then a strange idea came from nowhere, bursting into her mind like a solar flare.

The birthing tubes: why hadn't Paul even casually mentioned what was about to happen? Could it have been that he himself had not known—that someone high in the chain of command had decided on the alteration to the way things had been?

Could there be another reason for the change, apart from the one she had accepted, that it had been done to replicate conditions in the uterus?

What other reason could there be? What else had the change accomplished?

Then she had it.

Now it was impossible to see inside without the aid of an electronic interface. One could not simply glance at the tubes to check their internal conditions. A conscious effort had to be made, and one had to accept that the image on the screen was a true one.

It was then she shuddered. If these fears were justified, it meant all was not well on the Magellan—that there was some hidden plan being slowly enacted. Perhaps this was what had happened on the Resurgam—it was common knowledge no further messages had been received from that stricken vessel.

But what to do? Who could she discuss these emerging fears with? Not her mother, a woman who only wanted a quiet life, who saw the best in everyone. Was there anyone?

Then she smiled.

There was, of course, only one person she could turn to.

Six

'Come on, Rachel,' McGrath laughed. 'Why so glum?'

Grauber looked up from her algal soup.

'I find little to be cheerful about at the moment.'

'And why is that? You're an Elder, one of the most powerful group of people on the ship. You get to decide what happens, who does what, who is rewarded, who is punished.'

'Punishment is not my strong suit,' Grauber said, 'I am just trying to do my best for the people.'

' "Trying to do my best for the people",' McGrath repeated, using a tone that was slightly mocking. 'You must think you're one of those great potentates on Old Earth, ruling over millions of people. Perhaps you're the reincarnation of the President of Eastrania?'

'There's no need to be unpleasant, Anne,' the other woman replied. 'What I said seemed like an innocuous ambition.'

McGrath finished the last of her soup, burped, and pushed the bowl away.

'Don't be a bore, Rachel. What use is power if you can never prove you've actually got it? I don't care much for administration, for checking the output of the yeast vats, for writing down what the current radiation flux is, checking to see who's got tonsillitis. I want to *do* things; to get noticed, to mould things into the shape *I* want them to be!'

'I take it you care little for people as individuals then, Anne.'

She shrugged.

'Not really. I mean, what have people ever done for me?'

Grauber stared at McGrath for a moment, and then quietly said, 'I think I'd like to finish my soup in peace now, Anne. I have a bit of a headache.'

McGrath laughed.

'OK, I get it. You find me a bit overpowering. That's not unusual!'

She left the table and crossed the room to talk with Karol Petronis. Grauber watched her go, finding herself, against her will, admiring the other woman's sinuous grace, her mane of obsidian hair in which not a single white hair was lurking. She watched the two engage in a vigorous conversation, and was somewhat disconcerted when, in unison, they both turned and looked directly at her for a few moments.

Something's going on, Grauber thought. *Why did they look at me just then?*

But it did not happen again, and she thought nothing of it.

Eventually, the diners went their separate ways and Grauber retired to her own cabin. As an Elder she was allowed a rather more spacious apartment than the *hoi-polloi* of the Magellan. It had, of course, been the cabin of an important man among the FirstGens and his Primary Wife. Nothing less would be acceptable for an Elder of the SecGens.

She removed her papers from the encryptically-locked compartment in which she always stored them and began studying them yet again.

She had read them so many times it felt like she could duplicate them in longhand from memory alone. The numbers seemed to blur and run together and she realised she was falling into an exhausted doze. She surrendered to it, forgetting to replace the documents, and stretched out on top of them, and was soon gently snoring.

She woke and slowly straightened herself, reaching for the small of her arthritic back to support herself. There was a constant throbbing in her head, and her vision was still slightly fuzzy.

She looked down at her desk, realising with a shock she had neglected to replace the documents in her little safe. She stared at the papers for a while. Were they in a different order from what she remembered? She shrugged.

No matter.

Then the communicator light on her wrist-computer flashed, and she felt the device vibrate against her flesh. She accepted the message. It was Dukas: it was unwise not to respond.

'Rachel, we'd like to invite you to a little soirée in my cabin.'

We? thought Grauber, *who's "we"?*

'I haven't long eaten, Darian,' she said.

'It's just a few nibbles,' Dukas' voice was powerful and hypnotic even over the little communicator computer. 'We'll be awfully upset if you don't join us. It's my way of saying "thank-you" for all your hard work.'

Grauber groaned inwardly but knew she had no alternative. It was pointless annoying Dukas over something so trivial.

'I'll be right there.'

The door to the Captain's Cabin opened automatically as she approached and closed automatically behind her after she had passed through the portal. To her surprise, she saw McGrath sitting with Dukas behind a table on which were dotted various simple delicacies.

'Hello, Rachel,' McGrath said in her musical voice, 'Good to see you again. Please join us.'

'I wasn't expecting to see the two of you,' Grauber said. 'I thought it was a private function.'

'It is,' smiled McGrath, 'just we three old friends. Sit down, why don't you.'

Grauber sat and, for a moment, had the feeling she was the candidate in some obscure job interview.

Dukas pushed a small plate of cleverly sculpted yeast cakes towards her.

'Have some of these, Rachel.'

'It's not long since I last ate, Darian.'

'But I insist,' Dukas said, 'these aren't machine-made. I had one of the crew who likes baking to rustle them up. Especially for you.'

She reached for one and looked at it. Had she known anything about Earth's long-extinct marine life, she would have known it had been shaped to resemble a cowrie shell.

But she did not.

She nibbled at it and found it had an extremely pleasant aromatic flavour.

'It's good!' she said, beaming at her two hosts.

'Don't hold back,' McGrath said, displaying her excellent white teeth, 'you deserve it.'

Grauber eagerly accepted the offer, consumed the one she had started eating and then ate another. She raised a hand and, smiling, shook her head when Dukas pressed another one upon her; one shaped like a whelk shell.

'Have to watch my figure,' she said, as playfully as she could manage. She wiped away a few last crumbs and then said, 'This is very kind of the two of you, but what exactly have I done to deserve such treats?'

McGrath smiled beatifically.

'You've been very busy, haven't you? Like a busy little bee.' She stopped, looked at Dukas, and continued, 'Whatever that is.' She returned to stare at her guest. 'Yes, you've been very busy.' A strange pause. 'Poking your nose into things which don't concern you.'

Grauber felt a trickle of ice creep down her spine. Things in the room seemed to recede from her, become unreal, become merely a play staged by enthusiastic but unskilled amateurs.

'Things which don't concern me?' she repeated.

'Yes,' McGrath continued. 'Yes, you've been looking at birth records.'

'Aren't I allowed?' The room snapped back into reality; a grim, dangerous reality.

'It wasn't your area of responsibility, was it? So why did you do it?'

'I noticed some peculiarities in the statistics. As an Elder, I thought I had to investigate.'

Dukas interrupted. 'But you chose not to bring your concerns to me, your Captain. Why was that?'

Grauber could not answer, her eyes flicked back and forth between Dukas and McGrath; now revealed as her inquisitors.

'I was trying to make sure,' she finally mumbled.

'And are you sure now?' Dukas asked, his eyes like two javelins piercing her innermost secrets. 'You know, of course, we've read all your papers, your findings. We even know you've been employing the maybots in your scheming.'

Grauber knew she had to get out. A creeping miasma of menace was enveloping her. The room seemed to be slowly spinning. She turned to the door.

Somehow Dukas was between it and her.

'Sit back down. We're not finished.'

Powerful arms pushed her back onto her chair.

'Now,' McGrath said, her smile that of a predator that has pinned its prey to the ground, 'what exactly did you discover?'

Grauber was now certain: the room was spinning and its speed was accelerating. Her head was too heavy: she lowered it, so all she could see were the crumbs on the table.

'Ratio skewed,' she mumbled, 'too many females. Someone influencing fertilisation.'

'Did you share your concerns?' McGrath sweetly enquired.

Her head was made of stone. She could not support it. It lowered until it was resting on her chest.

'No.'

'Liar!' Dukas thundered. 'We know you've been speaking to people. Fortunately, you did no harm. But we cannot let you carry on, undermining us like this. It stops here.'

'Stops?' Grauber said thickly, her chin now seemingly attached to her chest.

'Yes, it stops here. And you stop here.' She was aware he was now standing over her. 'You see Jelani discovered a mutant in the fungus vats. One that had evolved dangerous toxins. So toxic that, if ingested, they are fatal to humans.' She vaguely felt a heavy hand on a shoulder. 'And I'm afraid, my dear, you have just ingested a lethal dose.'

Grauber did not know where that last burst of strength came from. She forced herself upright and turned to face the door.

'Go on, my dear. See if you can make it to the door.'

She could not.

***

Regine leaned forward as she woke her computer from its sleep.

Or rather, she performed the motions which should have woken the computer from its sleep. The screen remained blank.

She gazed in stupefaction at the screen. Computers were the brain, heart and lifeblood of the Magellan. If the great network which threaded itself throughout the body of the massive vessel, leading like the threads of a web back to the great Central Computer itself, should fail, then death in the darkness would inexorably follow for the hapless crew.

Like most of those who used the machines, she had little idea of how they worked. Indeed, very few people did; the network monitored itself and could self-heal all but the most severe wounds. She looked around; the other machines in the area were showing data on their screens, so it was not a ship-wide disaster. She felt herself relax; the lack of response of her machine was obviously a minor issue that would be quickly resolved.

Her peripheral vision revealed that Paul had come into the work area. She turned to him with a smile.

'Paul, my machine…'

He did not return the smile. Instead, he said coldly, 'You have to leave.'

She stared at him, thinking somehow she had misheard.

'Leave? But I've only just got here.'

'No, you don't get it, Regine. You have to leave and never come back. Your job here is finished.'

Still, she could not absorb the words; could not believe she had heard aright.

'I don't understand. My work...'

'Is of little importance. As you said yourself, a machine could do it. And from now on, a machine will be doing it.'

Finally accepting she had indeed understood his words, she stood before him, unaware that a pleading expression had now flooded her face.

'But, Paul, why? There's nothing wrong with my work, is there? You've never complained.'

He turned away.

'No, there wasn't. But you're simply not needed anymore. It's nothing personal.'

She found herself momentarily deprived of the power of speech. The loss of her job would have no bearing on the quality of her life. No-one was paid for what they did on the Magellan; everyone knew that things had to be done, actions had to be performed, if there were to be any hope of reaching Centauri. It was simply the satisfaction derived from helping to bring it about that was important. Call it a feeling of "status", if you like.

And now, it appeared, that was to be taken from her.

But her feelings of incomprehension, of amazement, were swiftly replaced by anger.

'Whose idea was this?' she said, her eyes reduced to slits, her voice a cold hiss. 'Was it yours?'

He sat at his desk, awoke his machine to full alertness.

'That's not important.'

She clutched his shoulder, forcing him to look at her.

'You've been told to do this, haven't you? You're not high enough on the greasy pole to decide this. Who's pulling your strings, Paul?'

His face was impassive.

'Look, Regine, I'm sorry it had to end like this. Perhaps you've been asking too many questions instead of just keeping your head

230

down and getting on with your work. Perhaps that's it.' He paused for a moment and looked down at his hands. Then: 'I can't say anymore, Regine. We had some fun together, but now it's best you just go. Also, best if you stay out of politics.'

' "Out of politics"? I didn't know I was *in* politics.'

He turned back to his machine.

'There's no more to say.'

But for Regine, there was more.

'So all the time we had together, all the closeness, the intimacy, the fucking, you were just using me, after all!'

Silence.

She had very few possessions in her desk, but what she had, she gathered together and left, without looking back.

***

'Ready?' McGrath asked, a mischievous smile playing on her full lips.

'Yes,' Dukas said, 'do I look alright? My hair OK?'

McGrath looked him up and down and, leaning over, adjusted a stray lock of hair.

'Perfect,' she said, as she pulled back to admire her handiwork, 'absolutely perfect.'

Dukas grinned.

'I have to look my best when addressing my beloved people.'

'You do,' she said, and moved out of camera range.

Dukas drove any trace of emotion from his strong features, sat up straight, and depressed a button.

Immediately an alarm rang throughout the ship, forcing everyone to stop what they were doing and look up at the nearest televiewer screen. Dukas' sombre face filled the screen.

'My fellow Magellanites,' he said, 'I have grave news. Our beloved friend and colleague, Elder Rachel Grauber, was found dead this shipay. A post-mortem has revealed she died from ingesting a mutant fungus that has developed dangerous toxins. I can assure you we Elders are doing everything we can to identify this mutant and eradicate it. Unfortunately, this means that until we have removed this danger, all ship personnel will be put on algal-only rations. We hope this will be only a temporary measure, but we cannot take any chances with the health of the ship.' He paused, took a deep breath, and then, 'Remember: we are all in this together.'

Many of those watching glanced at each other at this point. Algal rations were fine—except they wouldn't be putting any strain on the meal table.

Dukas continued.

'I invite all of those whose duties allow, to join the remaining Elders and me at the compositer station in two centi-shipays where we will all pay our last respects to a much-loved Elder. Thank you for your attention.'

Dukas terminated the broadcast and spent some time making sure everything was safely disconnected. Then, and only then, did he turn to McGrath.

'How did I do?'

For answer, she sat beside him, put a hand on the back of his head and pulled his lips onto hers.

'Wonderful. I was almost in tears, thinking about poor Rachel. Have you got your speech ready for when we pop her into the compositer?'

'Yes. The trouble is, I can't think of much to say about the dear little thing. Nothing that the ordinary people will be interested in.'

'You'll think of something,' McGrath assured him. 'But in the meantime, have one of these yeast cakes.'

She slid a plate across the desk so it was before him. He reached down and nibbled one. Then took a larger bite. A look of satisfaction spread across his face.

'Very good. My compliments to the chef, as I believe the Old Ones used to say.'

She beamed at him.

'You deserve it.'

***

Amelia looked from the now blank televiewer screen to her daughter.

'It's not the end of the Magellan,' she said, in what she trusted was a soothing voice.

Regine looked up.

'What, Grauber? I know nothing about her. I don't know anything about the Elders, except some of them laughed at me.'

'No, losing your job, I mean. You'll find another.'

'I don't want another!' Regine said in a much louder voice than she intended. 'I was happy in that one. I love children. I don't want some boring job, like using a wrench to turn bolts in some dingy hole in the stern, or oiling a rowing-machine in the EZ!'

Amelia shook her head and looked away from her daughter.

'I can't help you. I don't know anyone with influence. I'm just a sad, old widow.'

Regine was immediately contrite.

'I'm sorry, maman. I didn't mean to shout.'

An awkward silence fell.

Then Amelia said, 'Why don't you go and see Gelhardt again? He was very pleased to see you.'

'He was? I can't think why; all I did was badger him about the saboteur and ask about uploading. Neither of which he really wanted to talk about. And how he could help me—he never leaves his room?'

'Gelhardt still has a lot of people on this ship who admire him greatly and would do almost anything for him. Oh, they're all getting old and feeble now, I know, but I'm sure some of them still have influence.'

Regine pursed her lips.

'He did seem very pleased to see me, and he also said I could drop in on him at any time. He appeared to be very taken with me; just getting a bit loopy, I guess.'

'That he will never be,' Amelia said, firmly. 'Go and see him. Now.'

And so it was not very long after that conversation that Regine was sitting on the same chair she had sat on before in Gelhardt's cabin and the room was just as dim and—and "musty" as before. Gelhardt was just as effusive and welcoming as before.

He must be terribly lonely, thought Regine. *He's all over me. I suppose no-one comes to see the codger these days.*

Gelhardt had made her something he called "Real Chicory Coffee"—a privilege of being Captain, he said. The stuff was so incredibly bitter she had almost spat it out all over him.

He had not failed to notice her struggles, and said kindly, 'It's an acquired taste. I won't give it to you again.' He finished his own cup with obvious relish, and continued, 'It's lovely to see you, Regine. I take it this is just a social call?'

She put her cup down, hoping never to see what had caused its brown stain again, and said, 'No, not quite. I've lost my job.'

He looked concerned.

'I'm sorry to hear that. I'm sure it couldn't have been your fault. Is there any way I can help? I still have contacts out there.'

She stared at the old man for a while. Should she simply tell him about the lost job in the hope he could get her another one? Or should she share her fears about something strange happening in the Nursery?

'Yes?' he prompted.

She decided to share her fears.

'I've lost my job, but my boss—my superior—intimated it was because I'd been asking too many questions; "Getting involved in politics" was how he put it. I'm sure someone higher up told him to get rid of me. He seemed very embarrassed about doing it; it wasn't as if I'd fouled up or anything.'

' "Getting involved in politics",' Gelhardt said. He seemed to find the phrase significant. 'Had anything happened in your place of work?'

'Yes. There was a big change in the birthing columns.' Regine paused to explain what she meant by the words, and then continued, 'It happened without any warning. I don't think even Paul had been expecting it.'

'Who is his superior?'

'He doesn't have one. He reports directly to the Elders.'

Gelhardt's bushy white eyebrows arched. 'Ahh,' he said, 'Interesting.'

Silence fell while Regine waited for something to happen. Gelhardt had leaned back in his chair with his eyes closed, and she began to suspect he had fallen asleep. But then he moved and leaned forward. His face seemed more alive than she had seen it before.

'Have you heard of a woman called Tarkowski?'

Regine felt her jaw drop.

'Yes, yes, I have. I met her.'

'Met her? How is that possible?'

'Well, I didn't actually meet *her*. I met her upload avatar.'

'You've been in the Central Computer!'

'Well, only as a kind of visitor. Someone told me I was just an average person, and I wanted to know if that meant I couldn't be uploaded.' She pulled a face. 'Apparently, it does.'

He gave a soft laugh.

'I kind of doubt that. I think you'll prove to be much more.'

Regine's face flushed with pleasure.

'So, can you help me? And what does this Tarkowski woman have to do with it?'

Gelhardt turned away as if he didn't want his face studied while he spoke.

'Tarkowski found the Saboteur for me. She was a truly brilliant woman. She had been a surgeon, but gave it up to study artificial intelligence. Tarkowski created the Upload Programs but, almost as an amusing puzzle, she devised an AI system that could see through layers of encryption. Without her and her program, I could never have found the saboteur. I almost executed an innocent man.'

Regine winced. But then she realised she could see what Gelhardt was driving at.

'Are you saying you still have the Tarkowski Program?'

'I am.'

'And are you saying we can use it to find out who is changing things in the Nursery?'

'I am.'

'Then what are we waiting for?'

'Slow down, Regine. I said I didn't think you were average, but now you're going to have to prove it. The Program is a very low-level system; unlike everything else we do on a computer, you can't just tell it what to do. You have to understand what it wants and key in the commands.'

'What—you mean using a *keyboard,* like the Old Ones?'

'That's exactly what I mean.'

She sat back, deflated. She had used one recently—and never wanted to go near one again.

'Why can't you do it for me?'

'I could, but my fingers are very arthritic. We'd be at Centauri by the time I'd finished.

'I can't do it. It's simply too primitive.'

He smiled, but the smile was sad.

'Then I'm afraid our conversation is at an end, Regine.'

She stared at the old man, differing thoughts battling for mastery in her mind. Once again, she heard Paul and the Tarkowski-avatar dismiss her.

'Alright, Karl. I'll do it. When do we start?'

For the first time, she saw him move out of the chair. He was slightly unsteady, but he succeeded, and stood over her. Although his musculature had withered, he was still tall.

'How about right now?'

Her heart fluttered slightly at the thought of what she was taking on, but eventually she gave a rather nervous smile, and said, 'OK. Let's do it.'

And so Regine's education began.

She visited Gelhardt every shipay from that moment on. He tried to be calm and patient with his computing tyro, but even his forgiving nature was strained by her lack of comprehension.

And then, one shipay, she found that something had rewired itself in her brain. Things that had seemed obscure and occult miraculously became clear and pellucid.

Gelhardt patted her back as he looked down at her work.

'There you are. I knew you could do it, my girl!'

Regine winced at that over-familiar term, but forgave him.

'Now let's see what we can do, where we can go!' he said, excitement rising in his voice.

'First of all, we'll go to the nursery,' she said as her fingers flew over the ancient keyboard.

A full-colour hologram appeared on a pad in front of the coding screen. It showed the opaque pillars of the gestation cylinders.

'Go on.' Gelhardt said. 'As long as they are connected to the Central Computer, you can look inside.'

Regine selected the nearest column and typed in the instructions. Immediately, the outer coating vanished and the foetus became visible, slowly rotating in the amniotic liquid.

'Anything concerning?' Gelhardt asked.

Regine stared at the infant, looking at each part of the tiny body as it slowly rotated into view. After a while, she said, 'No. Looks completely normal.' Then she said, 'I'll restrict the view to near-term babies.'

A centi-shipay passed as they both studied an array of near-term babies. Gelhardt said, 'Everything looks normal to me. But then I'm no expert.'

She looked up at him, an odd expression playing on her features.

'No, you're not, are you, Karl? There is something unusual about those babies.'

'I don't see it.'

She stood up, stretched her back, and then pointed to the latest holographic image of a peaceful-looking baby.

'This baby is female.'

'And so?'

'Karl,' she said, with rising excitement, 'they're ALL female!'

Gelhardt looked puzzled.

'Forgive me, Regine. My thought processes are slow these days; I'm not what I used to be. What does that mean?'

She gave a *tut-tut* of exasperation.

'Listen, Karl. The original gender ratio on the Magellan was 70:30, Female: Male'

'Yes, I know that. I was there.'

'But since the Revolt of the Women, the ratio has been adjusting back to the standard 50:50 ratio!'

He looked down at the image of the lazily drifting baby.

'Yes, I see. Someone is trying to set it back to its original ratio.'

Once again, she gave an exasperated noise.

'Not *someone*, Karl! Think! Who has the power to do these things?' Their eyes locked.

'The Elders,' he whispered. 'Someone in the Elders is behind this.'

She grasped his thin arms and looked up at his tired face.

'It must go right to the top, Karl. It must be Dukas doing it!'

He extracted himself from her grip, and walked away.

'No, no,' he muttered, 'no Captain of the Magellan could possibly do such a thing. We all swear an oath to put the safety of the ship above any personal gain. I cannot believe it. I will not believe it! It's one of the underlings; it has to be!'

Seven

'Alright!' she said, 'Tell me how I can find out who's been sending these orders!'

'It'll be difficult,' Gelhardt said, running a blue-veined hand over his forehead, 'we'll have to break into encrypted orders, and sort them into significance classes.'

'Nothing is encrypted to the Tarkowski Program,' she replied crisply. 'It'll be a simple software sort.' She sat down before Gelhardt's computer again.

In fact, the search turned out to be much more complex than Regine had confidently predicted. Software had moved on since Tarkowski's day and her search-engine ground very slowly through the various overlapping and nested layers of the schemata the perpetrator had set up. Whoever it was, Regine mused, they had foreseen that some powerful AI tool might one day be used against them.

But eventually, the software revealed a thread linking Paul with

'McGrath,' Regine breathed triumphantly, 'I knew it! It had to be an Elder! Who else could have the authority! She must have told Paul to get rid of me.' But then her face fell. 'And Paul went along with it. Oh, Paul, Paul! I trusted you. I was even beginning to think I loved you.' She stood and walked over to her chair. 'I don't want to do this anymore. What's the point? Let them have what they want. I don't care.'

Gelhardt said nothing. There was nothing he could say. He made two cups of myco-coffee and offered her one. She ignored it.

Eventually, Gelhardt broke the silence.

'I know this is difficult for you, Regine, but we can't give up. The very fact McGrath has been doing this in secret means she's planning something to harm the Magellan; otherwise—why the secrecy? What kind of world is my granddaughter going to grow up in?'

Regine looked up sharply.

'Granddaughter? What granddaughter? I didn't know you had a granddaughter—you've never mentioned one before.'

Gelhardt looked confused.

'Sorry. It's just a figure of speech—I don't know why I said that.'

Regine took a deep breath, which she then let out slowly.

238

'Anyway, you're right. She's up to no good. We have to confront her.'

'I'll speak with Dukas and tell him what we've found.'

'Is that safe? How do we know it's McGrath at the centre of the web?'

'I know Dukas. I helped him in his early days as Captain.'

Regine stared at Gelhardt. Was this old man really in full ownership of his faculties? Many times he had seemed a little lost in the modern world, and now he had talked about a fictional granddaughter. Should she trust him on this issue? She spun a mental coin in her mind.

'OK. Contact Dukas and see what he says. I'll be standing just out of camera range.'

Gelhardt sat at the console and activated the special high-level link to which he was still entitled. Almost immediately, the current Captain's face appeared.

'Karl!' Dukas said, 'This is an unexpected pleasure! Are you going to give me some of your valuable advice again?'

'No,' Gelhardt said, 'I have some very important news for you. News of the highest importance, grave news.'

Dukas frowned.

'This sounds bad. Go on.'

Gelhardt revealed he had found evidence of a conspiracy centred on one of Dukas' subordinates. He did not mention Regine's presence in the room. After he had completed the story, Dukas shook his head.

'This is bad, very bad indeed. I think you'd better come and see me, Karl.'

Gelhardt spread his arms wide.

'I'd rather not, Darian. I have trouble walking, and I haven't been outside my room for a long time. The crowds and the noise upset me.'

'Well, I don't think I can resolve this over a video link, Karl. If you're right and Elders are involved, then who knows what surveillance powers they have.'

Gelhardt glanced at Regine.

'Well, perhaps I could send someone.' He waited for a sign from her that she agreed, and, having received it, turned back to Dukas.

'Yes, I will send my—a friend of mine. Someone who worked in the Nursery.'

'In the Nursery? She knows Paul then? I think Paul should be present.'

Neither Gelhardt nor Regine noticed Dukas' choice of pronoun.

'Yes. I believe she does. Wait a minute—I'm getting a message from someone. I'll get back to you.'

Gelhardt froze the image and looked at Regine.

'What's the matter?'

'I don't want anything to do with Paul, you old fool!' she snapped. 'He's the one who sacked me, for God's sake!'

'Well, that's true, but you don't know what pressure he was under. It may be more accurate to say McGrath sacked you.'

Regine thought about that, her head spinning.

Had Paul been threatened by McGrath, leaving him little choice but to carry out her command? He hadn't seemed too happy to see her go, she remembered. She found herself frozen with indecision.

She spun another mental coin.

'I'll see Paul,' she said.

Gelhardt gave her a smile of gratitude and reactivated the link.

'Yes, she's here with me, Darian. She says she'll meet with Paul and you.'

'Good,' came Dukas' powerful voice, such a contrast to Gelhardt's weedy whispering. 'Tell her to be at the Nursery in two centi-shipays. Good to see you again, Karl. We must meet up soon and chew some more fat. Goodbye.'

Gelhardt turned to Regine.

'That was brave of you. I know you didn't want to do it. You've made an old man very happy and proud.'

She ignored his praise.

'I just thought there might be a way to get back with Paul. I cared for him. A lot.'

'Well, there's time for you to get something to eat before going to the Nursery. You'd better be on your way. I want to thank you again, Regine.'

She waved him into silence.

'I'm not doing it for you. Once we've rooted out McGrath, maybe things can get back to normal.' She gave him a hard stare. 'I don't think I'll be seeing you again, Karl.'

He looked shocked by her dismissal, but then nodded.

'Fair enough. I've nothing to offer you now, except those dusty old memories of mine; memories that can hold little interest for you. It's been wonderful working with you, Regine.'

Wonderful? thought Regine; *I wish he'd stop larding me with all this praise; it's creepy.*

She left without another word, drank some algal soup at her mother's, and then made her way to the Nursery.

Gelhardt stood looking at the door she had closed behind her and when he moved away it seemed to be with great reluctance. He sat in front of the console she had been using. He was motionless for a while and then his face clouded, as if an unwelcome thought had intruded into his mind. His expression grew steadily grimmer, until he turned to the keyboard, activated the Tarkowski Program, and painfully forced stiff fingers to type out commands.

When Regine arrived at the Nursery, Paul was there and they stood and looked at each other in silence for quite some time. Then Paul finally spoke.

'Hello, Regine.'

'Hello yourself,' she replied coldly. 'Got any more bad news for me?'

He bowed his head.

'I'm sorry, Regine, but you don't know the half of it.'

'McGrath?' she demanded.

'Yes, McGrath.'

'Well, I'm glad you made one woman happy, at least.' She turned away. 'Let's go.'

They left the Nursery, pushing their way through the omnipresent crowds in silence. But the further they went, the more puzzled she grew.

'This isn't the way to the Elders' Area.'

'No, Dukas doesn't want to meet you there in case his room is bugged. He's chosen the least likely place anyone would think of for a meeting.'

The least likely place turned out to be a compartment of the Magellan that was under active repair by maybots. Everywhere she looked, there were the eye-wrenching blue-white flashes of arc-welding equipment, coupled with the sting of ozone that made her eyes water.

241

'*The least likely place*,' she said, wiping her eyes. 'You weren't kidding.'

'Come over here,' Paul said, raising his voice above the clangour. 'It's a lot quieter.'

They moved behind a bulkhead, which shielded them from some of the noise and the ozone. But they were not alone.

McGrath.

'Hello, Regine,' she said, with a lovely smile. 'We meet again. I hope you are well.'

Regine spun around to get away, but Paul's powerful hand enclosed her wrist with a grip of iron.

'Don't be impolite, Regine,' he said, 'the lady wants a word with you.'

He forced her to sit on a rolled steel bar and stood watchfully nearby. McGrath approached them. Once again, she smiled.

'You, my dear, are in way over your head.'

Regine did not fully understand the archaic expression, but assumed it was not a compliment.

'I know all about you, McGrath.'

'No, dear, I'm *Elder* McGrath to the likes of you. And what do you think you know?'

Regine stared up at her defiantly.

'I know you are adjusting the sex ratio of the next generation. That's why you covered up the tubes so I couldn't see what was inside. Lots and lots of potential baby girls.'

'And why did I do that?'

'You tell me.'

To Regine's disgust, McGrath joined her on the steel bar, sat close, and began to stroke her hair.

'You have nice hair. Pity, I could have helped you to style it properly.'

Regine leaned away.

'Don't touch me!'

McGrath moved away so the two women were no longer touching. Then she stared into the hot, dusty air and said, 'You see, Regine, the Founding Fathers got it right first time. It's unnatural for men to have only one sexual partner. It demeans them, diminishes them, turns them into eunuchs. So real men must have more than one woman to service their needs. And I'm not talking about all men, of course—I'm talking about *Real Men*: strong men, vital men. Those who shape and mould the world to their own desires; men who deserve a strong-willed woman as their consort.'

Regine stared at the other woman in horror.

'How can you, a woman, accept such a subservient status!'

McGrath looked at her, pityingly.

'How can a child like you know anything about men? Why, you're probably still a virgin!' Ignoring Regine's look of contempt, she continued: 'The consort of the man will accept his fertilisation of other women as simply his due, a mere form of entertainment, a trifle, a scratching of an itch, knowing he will always return to her, his one true love. She will have her simple pleasures, and he will have his. Other women are simply vessels to be filled when the mood takes him. She will be secure in the knowledge that she has his heart. She will accompany him as he goes on to triumph after triumph, standing on the corpses of the pitiful creatures that dared to call themselves "men".'

'You must be thinking long-term,' Regine said, 'surely it'll be twenty years or so before your plan comes to fruition. And won't people notice that all their children are female?'

'Of course and of course,' McGrath purred, 'My Lord is not selfish; he is thinking of his sons, of which he will have a great many. And do you think once a woman has given birth, she will reject that child just because she has a daughter rather than a son?'

'So how do you do it?' Regine said, trying to delay the inevitable in the hope someone, something, would save her.

'Flow cytometry. It allows us to separate the X-carrying sperm from the Y-carrying sperm. We destroy the latter, of course. There can only be one elite race of men; we can't have the others breeding like locusts.'

Regine tried to stand, but Paul forced her down again.

'You're mad!' she spat at McGrath. 'Utterly, completely mad! No normal woman could think like you! This is worse than the FirstGen's Primary Wife abomination. How can you create your so-called triumphs on the Magellan? Our survival depends on submerging the individual, working together as one body. The second we start fighting each other, we're finished. We'll just be a dead hulk floating through space!'

'Oh, My Lord has worked all that out! The ship will be sectioned into compartments. The Lords will live at one end, surrounded by their women, and each other compartment will be occupied by the inferior types who will not have access to any of the controls of the ship. Or women, for that matter. Periodically, we will make war upon them. I'm told a people on Old Earth—the Spartans, I believe—had a similar practice. Oh yes, Lord Dukas has it all worked out. And when we reach Centauri, that will be the culture we shall establish on the new world!'

'Dukas?' Regine said. It seemed her mouth had been clogged with burning sand. 'He's behind it all? Not you?'

McGrath smiled again, and her smile was that of a saint experiencing the Divine.

'How could I be behind it all? I'm just a woman.'

'And a very beautiful woman,' came a powerful voice behind them. McGrath stood and extended her arms to the newcomer.

'My Lord!'

Dukas came into Regine's view, and she flinched at the sight.

'You!'

'Me,' Dukas said pleasantly. 'It could only have been me, couldn't it? You know, I could hardly hold back my tears of joy when that stupid old wreck Gelhardt was sharing his thoughts with me. In my new order, Lords will never reach senescence. They will kill themselves before suffering that indignity.'

McGrath looked up at him with self-effacing love filling her eyes.

'And now, my Lord? The girl?'

'She dies, of course. Down here away from prying eyes, away from anyone who could help her.'

Paul suddenly stirred.

'Dies? But that's not necessary! There are drugs which could bend her memory; make her forget all of this!'

Dukas stared at him.

'Careful, Paul. You are starting to make me wonder if you are fit to join us. No-one who has the effeminate reluctance to take a life can expect to ascend to the thrones of power.'

'But…'

'Be quiet, Paul. One more word, and you will join your erstwhile companion in termination.'

'How will you do it, Lord?' murmured McGrath. 'There are no weapons on the Magellan since Gelhardt banned them.'

'Oh, but there are. A man can always find weapons if he wants them badly enough.' He gave a piercing whistle. 'Come here, Number 7A!'

A maybot came around the angle of the steel bar. Dukas pointed to Regine.

'This unit is defective. Disassemble it.'

The maybot came up to Regine and halted. McGrath barred her escape. It studied Regine with its crystal lenses. She looked back at it, her mind dissolving into a screaming red pit of terror.

'This unit resembles a human being.'

'This unit is not a human being. Disassemble it.'

It did not move.

Dukas rattled out a series of override codes, and it moved close to Regine. A whirring circular blade extended from its carapace.

Suddenly Paul yelled, 'No!' and leapt upon the maybot, picking it up and violently flinging it against the wall, but not before the terrible circle of steel had dug deep into his left arm. He screamed and collapsed, his blood forming a crimson streak upon the wall.

But the maybot did not move again.

'Such a waste of time,' Dukas commented, dispassionately. He whistled again, and another maybot joined them. Once again, he pointed at the panting, screaming Regine as she thrashed helplessly in the stronger woman's grip. The second maybot showed the same reluctance to act as the first had done but once again Dukas overcame its doubts and, once again, a shining blur of razor-sharp steel unwaveringly approached the hysterical girl.

Then all at once, Regine's rolling eyes caught another blur, this time of human figures. She heard a familiar voice shout out some coded words and the maybot first froze into immobility and then retreated. She felt McGrath's brutal grip on her disappear, and Regine, trembling violently from head to foot, staggered to her feet. To her amazement, she saw Gelhardt and three other men of about the same age, bear down on Dukas. All four were holding something that looked like a gun, but could not be, for there were no guns on the Magellan.

Gelhardt walked to Regine, stiffly and awkwardly, but faster than she had ever seen him move before.

'Regine, are you alright; did they hurt you?'

She shook her head.

'I'm OK...I think. But Paul's hurt bad. He needs medical attention—fast!'

One of the other men crossed to the unconscious Paul and wrapped a makeshift tourniquet around his badly bleeding arm. Another spoke into a microphone and then nodded to Regine.

'It's alright. They're on their way.'

Gelhardt turned his attention to McGrath and Dukas, who were holding onto each other, or rather he turned his attention just to Dukas, as he ignored McGrath.

'How could you do this, Darian? How could you desecrate the office of Captain? How could you turn against your own people, those who depended on you for hope and guidance? How the fucking hell could you do it, you bastard!'

He raised a fist to strike the other, but one of the men who had accompanied him prevented the blow from falling.

'No, Karl,' the man said gently, 'that's not the way. Don't fall to their level.' Then he turned to Dukas. 'But it's a good question. How could you do it?'

'I'm not answerable to any of you,' Dukas said. His face twisted into a sneer. 'The wolf does not discuss with the sheep why he preys on them.' He turned his attention to Gelhardt. 'Time for another execution, I suppose, Karl?'

'Maybe. But that won't be my decision this time, thank God.'

Dukas turned away, apparently determined not to speak again. But McGrath, eyes blazing, snarled at Gelhardt, 'How did you manage to stir from your armchair, you pathetic cripple? How did you find us?'

Gelhardt finally turned his gaze on her.

'If you must know, just because there was nothing I wanted to see outside my cabin, didn't mean I was tied to it. I am not dead yet, though you two obviously considered me little better than that state.' He paused as the medical team arrived and bore the stretchered Paul away. He turned to Regine, who had stopped trembling, smiled, and then turned reluctantly back to McGrath. 'I wasn't quite as helpless on the computer as I told Regine; I just wanted her to learn. But I had doubts after she left me that we had reached the centre of the web, and so I instigated another search. And so I found your true beloved, squatting in the centre. I then used Tarkowski's program to put a tracer on you, Dukas and Regine, and found that you were all together in this section. I knew then I had sent her into terrible danger. So I called on some old friends to accompany me to hunt you monsters down. And so here we are. And it's amazing how one can find weapons if they're really needed. These rivet guns, which you've been staring at so intently, can send a steel bolt clean through your skulls. And it will take only a little show of resistance on your part to convince me I should do it—Ah, here they are!' He turned from his speech to McGrath as four burly men in Security uniforms arrived. He smiled at them as they came up to him. 'You boys took a bit of convincing that you should turn against your Captain, but,' and he tapped a small circular metal object on his chest, 'the live feed convinced you?'

'It did,' the chief officer said.

Gelhardt looked at McGrath and Dukas, who were still holding onto each other, shook his head and, addressing the chief officer, said, 'I've no more to say to these two. Will you please take them away and put them somewhere safe?'

'Will do.'

And McGrath and Dukas were surrounded by the security men and frogmarched out. Gelhardt turned to his rather elderly companions.

'Thank you, men. Without you, it would have been all over for Regine and me.'

The nearest man saluted.

'You gave us the order, Captain, and we obeyed. That's all there was to it.'

Gelhardt smiled.

'I'm not your Captain.'

'With respect, don't be silly, sir,' the man replied, 'You'll always be Captain.'

And with that, he and the others were gone.

Gelhardt and Regine were alone. He turned to Regine and said, 'Are you alright now, my dear?'

She had been standing but sat down as if her legs had suddenly turned to jelly, and looked up at him.

'I'm as alright as anybody can be after coming close to being vivisected.'

He sat beside her.

'I'm so sorry I put you in so much danger. You were right that McGrath might not have been in charge, but I didn't listen. I thought nobody could be Captain and not have the best interests of the ship at heart. I was naïve, moronically naïve, and it almost cost you your life. I will never forgive myself.'

Regine stood.

'I don't want to talk about it anymore. I just want to get out of here and never see this place again. Let's go.'

As Gelhardt slowly and awkwardly forced himself upright, he noticed that Regine was holding one of the bolt guns his men had left behind.

'Why do you want that?' he asked, steadying himself with one hand.

'Oh, just as a souvenir of an interesting experience,' Regine replied mysteriously. 'Let's get out of this hellhole.'

They left, Regine leading the way, but occasionally stopping to let Gelhardt catch up.

***

Gelhardt smiled as he sat in his chair, eyes closed, his ears covered by headphones. He smiled again as the music reached the moving *Adagio*. Symphony #8, *The Apocalyptic*, had always been the favourite among the works of his countryman, Bruckner. Occasionally he wondered how that rustic Austrian would have reacted to the knowledge that his music was being listened to between the stars. But he found he was slowly fading into sleep as the music strode magnificently through his brain. He was slightly annoyed he would not hear the end of it on this occasion, but he was sleeping more and more at this point in an ordinary shipay.

It was then he felt something cold and hard press against his right temple. His eyes flashed open, and he turned his head slightly to find the cause of this interruption. The cold object remained on his temple. He saw Regine and realised that the cold, hard object was the muzzle of a bolt gun.

'Regine,' he said, 'this is unexpected. May I enquire what exactly you are up to?'

'Don't move—Karl,' she said, in shockingly bitter tones. 'I don't want this to go off accidentally.'

Gelhardt stopped twisting his body but could still see Regine.

'You haven't answered my question,' he calmly said.

'Very simple. The Tarkowski Program is very powerful when you know how to use it. It even suggests things you might be interested in. And one of the events it suggested that I should look at was the final time of your Captaincy.'

He stiffened.

'Yes, I know who you are and what you did, Karl—or should I say—*Grandad*?' She moved so she was behind him, and the muzzle of the bolt gun was now resting on his occiput. 'I also know my dear mother has been lying to me, and that her real name is "Amelia", not "Marie", and she is your daughter. But much more importantly, I know you murdered my grandmother—your so-called Primary Wife.'

'And you are here to execute me in return?'

'Correct.'

'The fact that I saved your life does not tip the scales of justice in my favour then?'

'I am grateful for that, of course. But as you yourself admitted, it was your stupidity which put me in that situation in the first place. So you were simply correcting an error you had made.'

Gelhardt did not attempt to turn in his seat, but said, 'I am going to stand up now and turn around so I can face you. You will allow me that?'

'Yes.'

She backed away as he turned to face her.

'I don't have to be touching you to fire this bolt into you— Grandad.'

'I'm aware of that. Here, I'll help you.'

She watched as he took off his tunic and revealed a narrow chest, with skin so dry and papery his ribcage was clearly visible. He pointed to an area on his left chest.

'Here. Just here is where my heart is. Fire the bolt there, and my death will be pretty quick. Or here,' he pointed to his shrunken abdomen, 'fire into my guts, and it will take a long time for me to die from internal bleeding, so you can have a lovely time watching me suffer.' He watched her face twitch in disgust. 'What, the bloody mess of killing someone is a little too strong for you? You want me to just evaporate, leaving nothing behind to clear up?'

'You're talking nonsense,' she said, but he saw the bolt gun waver momentarily. He continued to study her, not attempting to increase or decrease the distance between them.

'You've set yourself up as judge, jury and executioner, haven't you *granddaughter*?' He emphasised the final word.

Her face twitched slightly, and her eyes flicked between him and her surroundings.

'You killed her. My grandmother. She only saw her baby, my mother, for a few shipays. You're the murderer.'

'Am I?' he said, calmly. 'You know, is it possible you're being just a bit self-righteous? You stand there judging me, condemning me, getting ready to kill me, but it's easy to be self-righteous when you haven't had to make the kind of decisions that I had to. Everything is theory with you, Regine, but I don't condemn you for that. You're young, just starting out. Until very recently, you haven't suffered anything at all, just glided from one minor expression of girlish emotion to another. And yet you are prepared to kill me for what I did to save the ship, just because you share some genes with the person responsible. Would you be so filled with righteous anger if it had been a random person from the crew that I executed?'

For an instant, she looked away, the bolt gun drooped, but then she looked back at Gelhardt and raised it again.

Gelhardt threw the tunic he had been holding to the floor, and raised his arms above his head, making his chest stand out before her.

'You know, Regine, I have thought about Simone every day since I had her executed. I see her face when I wake up; I see her face before I go to sleep. I can never clear her from my mind and the truth is—I don't want to. I loved that woman in a way you, in your youth, can never know. If I thought it would help me to see her again, I would have killed myself long ago. But now I don't have to make that particular decision because you're here to do it for me.' He moved forcefully toward her; his voice, hitherto soft and faint, rose to a roar. 'So do it, Regine! Kill me now!'

She did not retreat before him. Instead she threw the bolt gun away. It hit one wall, went off, and sent a bolt into the far wall. They ignored it. Regine stood like a statue, a statue with tears running down her face. And then she leapt towards the old man, and wrapped her arms around him, sobbing into his chest.

'I don't want to kill you, Grandad. I don't want to kill anybody! Forgive me for frightening you, please!'

He patted the back of her head, gently, lovingly.

'You didn't frighten me, Regine. I was prepared to go.'

She looked up at him, her eyes bright with tears as yet unshed.

'Don't go yet, please! Now I really, really, know you, there must be no more pretence. You, me, mother, we can spend time together, as one family. I understand you did what you had to do. Grandma thought she was right, but she wasn't, was she?' He shook his head, did not speak but kissed her several times on the forehead. Then he pulled slightly away from her and smiled down at his granddaughter.

'Come on, let's go and meet your mother and tell her there's nothing to worry about anymore. There will be no more hiding in the shadows. We have so much wasted time to make up.'

'Yes, we will, but tell me first, what will happen to—to *them*?'

'Well, personally, I think their organic matter could be better employed as part of something else, but it's not my decision.'

'But you still have influence. You just proved that.'

He gave a half-smile.

'I think I need a rest from difficult decisions.'

She seemed to hesitate, and then: 'Paul. What about him?'

Gelhardt was thoughtful.

'His case is different. If he hadn't acted, I wouldn't have gotten there in time to do anything. So, if anybody saved you, it was him.' And then he gave a genuine smile. 'I'll put a word in for him.'

The tenseness in her small frame subsided, and she sighed.

'Thank you, Grandad. You know, for a time I thought I loved him. But I've had enough of excitement; after all, I'm just an average girl.'

'Nothing wrong with that. Think of it this way—you're part of a very big club!'

She laughed, and then said, 'Let's go!'

They left his musty apartment, arm in arm.

251

Eight

Jeff Hardy walked into the room he shared with Susannah Reid and looked around in mild surprise.

She was not there. The bed still bore a shallow depression where she had been lying, but she was not on the bed.

There was, however, a piece of paper there and he sat on the bed and began to read it. After he had finished, he screwed it up and threw it across the room, and then put his head in his hands.

At the same time as he was reading it, Reid was standing on the hull of the Magellan, staring at the stars. The encircling sky was very little different from the first time she had stood there, except there was a very bright star dead ahead. There would have been a slightly brighter star directly behind, but the light sail shielded it from her view.

But she was not thinking of either star, not the hidden one, now circled by barren planets, nor the one ahead, circled by worlds of mystery. She was thinking of the words she had written on the piece of paper she had left for Hardy.

Dear Jeff, I couldn't face a tearful farewell with you. I'm sorry, despite all you thought of me, I guess I am a coward at heart. The drugs are running out and the pain is getting worse. I don't think I can take it anymore and I don't want your last memories of me being of some screaming animal, writhing on the bed. I want you to remember me as I was when we first met, looking out the viewscreen down at Cloud City One. How I teased you then. You were so easy to tease, you actually blushed! I thought that was so sweet.

I loved you; you must never doubt that. We shared love. But more than that, we had fun together, so much fun! Who'd have thought we could have had the life we had, stuck inside a ridiculous metal tube on the road to nowhere?

But that's why I want to end it now, before I spoil it. I'll do it on the hull where we met that one time, but please don't come looking for me; it'll only upset you. I know I'm being selfish and I should have stayed inside—but I never liked the idea of the compositer.

And don't forget, we're both in the Central Computer. Perhaps Tarkowski was wrong and enough of us will survive so that we can recognise each other and have electronic sex together!

I'm going now
Love from your Susannah.

It was difficult to disconnect the safety cord which kept her tethered to the Magellan, as the suit monitoring systems kept warning her not to do it. But eventually she did and stood on the dark metal of the starship hull, finally free. Now she did look up at the stars, and once again wondered, as she had just before she had met Hardy out there, if Earth had been the only world in all the galaxies to hold life. If it had been, what a terrible, terrible, fucking waste!

The starry sky was beautiful, but only in the intellectual way an abstract painting could be. There was no humanity, no love, in that celestial splendour.

No more time to waste. It had been difficult stealing the knife but the one she had should be sharp enough.

She bent her knees and then abruptly straightened them again; the force supplied being more than enough to overcome the Magellan's minuscule gravity. She moved only a short distance away, so she still could not see Sol behind the great lightsail. She was sad; she had hoped to see it once again. Her corpse would accompany the ship for a very long time, but due to her much smaller resistance against the interstellar medium, they would drift apart eventually. However, as long as she did not encounter any significant mass, she would indeed reach the Centauri system.

A strange thought.

No more delay, let's do it!

With a hand that held the knife firmly and without tremor, she cut the suit's airline.

There was a sudden mist around her as her internal atmosphere jetted out into space, turning almost instantly into whirling flakes of solid carbon dioxide, water, oxygen and nitrogen in the near Absolute Zero.

And her journey on the Starship Magellan was over.

***

And so the scythe of Time removed the last human beings on the Magellan who had once trod the soil of Earth, sending that planet forever into the misty realms of fable and fantasy.

The First Generation fell prey to all the ancient scourges of humanity: neurological conditions, heart disease, cancer. The incidence of heart disease was lower than the Terrestrial average, due to the low gravity, but that of cancer was higher, due to the increased radiation flux. But all the atoms of the First Generation were recycled into the bodies of the later Generations—with the single exception of those that had comprised Susannah Reid.

And still, the Magellan continued its seemingly endless flight into the seemingly unending darkness.

Turning Point

t = 109.74 y

One

Tom was bored. He stared at the holographic image with complete disinterest.

It was a sphere, mainly blue in colour, but with about thirty percent of its surface occupied by areas coloured green and brown. The teacher was speaking, and he raised his head and looked at her, to give the appearance of interest.

'This is the planet Earth,' the teacher, Mistress Atewayo, said, 'the world on which the Old Ones came into existence, a long time ago.'

A girl near the front put up her hand.

'How long ago, Mistress?'

Atewayo looked flustered.

'I...I'm not sure. A million years ago, I think.'

'That is a long time ago,' the girl said, and resumed staring at her holographic Earth.

'The blue shows the area of the planet which was covered with water, and the green and brown show the parts of the planet which were not covered by water. That's where the Old Ones lived.'

'Why didn't they live in the blue part?' a boy asked.

'Don't be silly, Joel. It was water—you can't live in water, can you?'

'You can, if it wasn't very deep. If it just came up to your ankles,' the boy said, reluctant to give up his question. 'How deep was it?'

Mistress Atewayo looked away from the boy, and a look of irritation swept very briefly over her features. 'I'm not certain, but I'm reasonably sure it was deeper than their ankles.'

She doesn't know, Tom thought; *Nobody knows. But why does it matter? It's nothing to do with us.* He altered the control so the colours on the globe were switched. *There,* he thought, *that'll give them more space to walk around on if the water's too deep.*

But Mistress Atewayo had seen his prank and called out, 'Tom, what are you doing with your Earth!' Her shout in his earpiece felt like it had punched a hole in his eardrum.

Guiltily, he switched the colours back, but Atewayo was already standing over him.

'Tom!' she barked, 'this is a serious lesson! It's very important you learn about your heritage.'

But something had stirred Tom's defiance; he was tired of lessons that didn't teach him how to *do* things; instead he was spending his precious time looking at ridiculously coloured spheres.

'Why?' he said.

Atewayo was taken aback.

'Why?' she spluttered, 'Why? Well. It just is. This is where you come from!'

'But it's not where I am now,' he countered. 'I don't need to know how deep the blue bits were, whether they're as deep as the algae tanks or even deeper. It doesn't help me.'

'It's your heritage!'

'I don't know what that means. And even if it is my—*heritage*—we can't go there, can we? It was all blown up in the doom of stars.'

She looked down on him with suspicious eyes.

'How do you know about the doom of stars? That's not dealt with until the next grade!'

'Grandma Regine told me,' he said. 'She's so old she was there when it happened.'

'I doubt that,' Atewayo said, and her features hardened. 'You've been disrupting this class today, Tom. I'm disappointed with you; you're an intelligent boy, you should know better. So you're staying behind after school and writing out four screens-worth on the subject *Why Learning about the Past is Important.*'

'But we were going to Grandma Regine's after school!' he protested.

She smiled sweetly.

'Then you'd better call her and tell her you'll be late.'

Tom was left alone in the classroom. It was called a classroom through ancient custom even though it was not a room, merely an area set aside in the great central body of the Magellan. As such, it shared in the general hubbub of the crowds as they passed by, each individual knowing no other world, no other possible existence than the lightsail ship which they and their forefathers had inhabited. A few knew of the doom of stars which had propelled those ancestors out on this incredible journey, but with each passing year, it mattered

256

less and less to them, as the details of the settlement of the Thirteen Colonies might have done to a denizen of Twenty-first century Manhattan.

He managed to write the requisite number of pages on his pad, being helped by his grandmother's tales of the Treachery of The Elders. As he was only eleven, she had given him a bowdlerised digest of those far-off events, but he had understood enough to pad out his essay. Having finished earlier than expected, he began exploring some of the pages the Central Computer had about aspects of Old Earth, other than its geography.

Much of it he did not understand. He gazed at the tremendous towers of Greater New York, not quite sure whether he was looking at natural objects, perhaps some type of "tree" or maybe an object fashioned by natural forces from "stone." Soon, those pictures and the obscure text about them bored him, and he left the works of humanity behind.

The things the texts called "animals" fascinated him. There were so many different types! He gazed in wonder at woodpeckers and weasels, buffaloes and bees, sharks and shrews. There seemed to be no end to the incredible variety of these things. Tom understood from the texts they were organic beings like himself, but, mysteriously, they were unable to speak. Some, like penguins and kangaroos, walked on two legs—but that did not make them people, apparently.

He shook his head. None of this made any sense. Fortunately for Tom, De Vries and Fraschini had concluded that there was no room in the Central Computer for the myths and legends of humankind, or he might have been enthralled and captivated by images of basilisks, cockatrices or hippogriffs, and have included them in his personal list of likeable animals.

But there was more than enough of Old Earth's genuine fauna to capture his imagination. The idea that people had shared their world with these strange beings was wonderful, and that was what interested him about the past. Tom returned to his essay and inserted a few sentences about them. He was not sure whether Mistress Atewayo shared his interest: neither she, nor anyone else, had ever mentioned them.

He had long passed the time when he had told his mother he would be back, when his wrist-communicator buzzed and his

257

parent's face appeared on the small screen, the features displaying a mixture of concern and suppressed irritation.

'Tom! Where are you! You're keeping Grandma Regine waiting!'

'I'll be there right now, Mom!' he said and made to turn his pad off.

But just as his finger was about to press the required control, the page turned to a section entitled DOGS, and he stopped as if petrified, a look of awe suffusing his puppy-fat features. There were creatures shown on the screen, furry or hairy quadrupeds similar to those he had seen earlier. But there was something different about these animals; there was an alertness about them, a feeling that there was some form of intelligence behind those eyes. Somehow he felt drawn to them, as if he could be pulled through the screen into the electronic substrate beneath.

He swept from page to page, being astounded by the differences in shape and size of these wondrous beasts, which apparently were all types of "Dog", despite their quite substantial differences. Page after page flew past under his eager fingers. There seemed to be no end to them.

He was about to flick to yet another page when a hand descended on his right shoulder and pressed it rather fiercely. Without looking up, he knew who its owner was by the feel of the hand.

His mother: Lorona.

'Why are you still here, Tom!' came a very familiar voice. 'Grandma Regine is very cross with you—and so am I!'

Now he had no choice but to put the pad down and look at his mother.

He saw a pale-skinned face, topped with a mass of ebony curls. The otherwise pleasant face was now marred by a twist of the lips that clearly showed he was in trouble.

'Come with me! Now!' Lorona snapped, using the classic method of forcing obedience by pulling him up by the nearest ear.

'But Mom,' he said, wincing, 'Just look at these—Oww! Not so hard, Mom!'

Lorona showed no sign of wishing to look at anything her son had to offer.

'Just keep walking and keep not talking!'

'But these dogs…'

'Shut up and walk. Faster!'

258

Another thing Tom found annoying about grown-ups was their insistence on *walking* everywhere. The only significant amount of gravity now present in the Magellan was the field generated by the rotation of the entire vessel. The rotation speed was enough to generate a reasonable facsimile of Earth gravity in the EZ ring, but the radius of the central cylinder was insufficient to generate anything other than a feeble, easy to ignore, tugging. The ship itself, of course, had its own field from its not inconsiderable mass but that would have been minuscule to the point of undetectability even without the centre of that mass lying on a line running down the axis of the habitation section. The lightsail, immense though it was, was not massive enough to distort the field. So, except for its own infinitesimal gravity, which only just registered on sensitive equipment, the entire habitable section was now weightless. Consequently, everyone could now *fly!*

The interior bulkheads, which had provided surfaces for walking during the acceleration period, were now either folded away, concertina-like, or had immense doors in them. So if Tom looked directly across the central meridian of the ship's habitat zone, he could just make out dots that might be distant ant-like people on what had hitherto been walls, but were now just another surface for living on. Consequently, the available space on the starship had greatly expanded. And the considerable space enclosed inside its colossal cylinder was now filled with people propelling themselves from one handhold to another. Fortunately, most of them were children or juveniles, for a head-on collision between adult bodies that still had all the momentum generated by their mass could be distinctly painful.

No doubt, this was one of the reasons why adults preferred to walk. But Tom did not like the fact that walking necessitated the wearing of Gripper Shoes, partly because they denied him the freedom of flight and partly because the adhesive suckers on the soles made a sound somewhat like the wet kisses that the girls increasingly seemed to like.

Eventually, they reached Grandma Regine's cabin. Tom did not really enjoy his maternal grandmother's company; he didn't like her dry, wrinkled skin, which folded itself into even deeper crevices when she spoke. He didn't like the fact she appeared to have only three teeth, or the slight sheen of dribble visible on her chin when she had been speaking for some time.

She didn't seem too fondly inclined to him either when he was finally brought into her presence.

'Well, look who it is,' she said, in that hissing voice she had, no doubt caused by the air passing through the large gaps in her dentition. 'Anybody'd think this little boy didn't want to see his dear old grandma.'

'Hello Grandma Regine, it's good to see you again,' he said dutifully. 'How are you this shipay?'

'A little closer to not being here at all,' was the acerbic reply, 'a little nearer to the compositer. Just think, I might be recycled into a yeast biscuit which you could have for your twelfth birthday. You'd like that, wouldn't you, Tom?'

Lorona was embarrassed by the bad start the visit seemed to have gotten into.

'Tom is really pleased to see you, Mother.' Tom received a dig in the ribs. 'Aren't you, Tom?'

'Yes,' he said, staring at a point just to the left of his aged relative's head, 'yes, I am.'

Peace having been established, Regine and Lorona became engrossed in a long series of recollections of what Lorona had been like as a child, and Tom was soon totally ignored. He sat on a little stool, trying to stay awake as Regine and his mother went into howls of laughter about the time when Lorona had hidden some yeast cakes in her knickers to prevent her friend from having them, and when she finally retrieved them, realised she no longer wanted them!

It seemed the centi-shipays would never end, but at last there were signs that the soirée was finally breaking up. His mother stood, brushing yeast crumbs from her thighs, and turned to Tom, ready to ask him to perform the unpleasant task of kissing his grandmother goodbye. It was then Tom had an idea.

'Grandma, did you ever have a dog?'

Both women looked dumbfounded.

'A dog?' his mother repeated, 'what…?'

Regine raised a hand to quiet her daughter and looked at Tom.

'Tom,' she said, 'do you know when I was born?'

'A long time ago?'

'That's true, but to be a little more precise, I was born in 23 AL, just after the Revolt of the Women.'

Tom frowned slightly: they hadn't yet reached that epic event in his history.

'I've heard of them but no, I didn't have a dog.'

Tom felt deflated.

'No? So how do you know about them?'

'My grandfather had a dog before leaving for Cloud City One.'

Tom was puzzled by all these terms, which clearly meant something to his aged grandparent but not to him.

'So, did you see it?'

Regine smiled, sending the lines on her leathery face into clearer relief.

'No, my dear, all non-food animals were killed long before he left Old Earth. He was a boy when he had his dog.'

'But he loved it?'

Now it was Regine's turn to look puzzled.

'Yes, I suppose so, though I don't think you can use the word "Love" when talking about an animal.'

Tom felt as if he had been vindicated after some great struggle.

There had been creatures called *dogs,* and one of his family had owned one. And had some strong feelings towards it.

So now there was only one thing left to do.

He had to have a dog.

Unfortunately, his interruption had given his mother the time to remember other things she wanted to reminisce about with Regine, and the conversations started again. He spent the rest of the visit giving unthinking, monosyllabic replies to the few questions that came his way, all the time wondering how he could attain his heart's desire. Then before he realised it, the session was over, and his mother lifted him up and propelled him in the direction of his grandmother. She lifted her arms to enclose him as he approached and laughed a wicked laugh.

'Hah! Come on now, Tom! I know you don't want to do it, but there're lots of things in life we don't want to do but have to!'

The old woman chuckled as Tom placed his lips on her cheek for the shortest possible time and then proceeded to grab him and place a long one on his cheek. She then nuzzled him away, still laughing.

'See you soon, Tom!' she cried as Tom and Lorona began to walk away.

'What was all that about a dog?' his mother asked, once they were out of earshot.

'I want one,' he said simply.

'They are those funny things with four legs you were looking at when I arrived?'

'Yes.'

'Then you can't have one,' she said, 'They're all dead. And even if they weren't—you still can't have one.'

There is no such thing as telepathy in this Universe, but if there were, Lorona would have read in her son's mind *Oh yes, I will!*

Two

Captain Marek Becvar looked deep into the viewscreen as if he were willing the distance between himself and the objects displayed out of existence.

The objects were two bright dots, occupying only a few pixels on the display. One dot was brighter than the other, but not overwhelmingly so. They were the only things visible on the screen; the rest was just blackness.

'We are approaching a historic moment, Lieutenant,' he said, and there was awe and wonder in his words. Lieutenant Khari joined him in staring at the two specks of brightness, and for some time only silence seemed appropriate. Then Becvar turned and placed a hand on the other's shoulder.

'Many people thought we'd never get this far, but here we are.'

'Incredible,' Khari breathed, 'One hundred and thirty-nine thousand astronomical units. Two point two light-years.'

'And the message from the *Zheng He*. Everything's OK. We're going to make it.'

Now, in theory, there was no alcohol on the Magellan: De Vries and Fraschini had expressly forbidden it as part of the cargo; every gram of that cargo must contribute to the success of the mission; must have a clear and specific function that made the probability of success more probable. But with human ingenuity being what is and the chemistry so simple, it was not far into the voyage when the first bootleg brews appeared. The one thing all the captains had agreed on was that there would be no distillation, and so the beers derived from algae averaged about only four percent ethanol.

But the time had come to break open a bottle. And Becvar and Khari were soon sipping the greenish liquid as they once again regarded the viewscreen. A pre-Catastrophe human would have spat the brew out with an expression composed of equal parts of disgust and anger, but to the two chief officers of the Magellan, the drink was not merely slightly intoxicating but carried a definite *frisson* of the excitement of daring to taste forbidden fruit.

Becvar lifted his glass in a gesture of triumph: of an arduous task at last achieved.

'To Alpha Centauri!' he declaimed, 'Watch out—the humans are coming to claim you!'

'You know, Marek,' Khari said gently, 'we mustn't get carried away. We're not the brave ones—the guys on the *Zheng He* are.'

Becvar was slightly annoyed that his bubble of elation had been punctured quite so soon—or maybe it was the alcohol.

'How so?' he demanded. 'How do you work that out?'

'Think about it,' Khari gently replied. 'We know we're going to make it. They didn't. They were the absolute pioneers. The very first of the fleet. They set out into interstellar space without knowing whether the bots the old guys had sent on ahead would be able to get their act together and construct the braking laser complexes in time—or at all. We all know how unreliable those things used to be. Looked at completely rationally, the whole thing was just an act of faith, a gambler's hope that this time the cards would turn up trumps. It wasn't scientific. Rational. In fact, it made no sense at all. But they went ahead and did it anyway.'

'We faced our own problems, didn't we?' Becvar felt himself becoming angrier, as if someone were attacking him personally. 'Nobody gave us a goddam free ride, did they?'

'No, they didn't. You're right.' Khari surreptitiously replaced the seal on the beer bottle at the same time as fixing Becvar in his gaze, and pushed it back into its container. 'But we haven't been through the hell they, and those poor bastards on the Resurgam, did. In fact, we've had it easy—an amateur saboteur and a half-assed attempt to produce a harem. Be fair, Marek—haven't we?'

'No, I guess not,' Becvar said, much to Khari's relief, knowing his superior's temper as well as he did, 'But—hey! What happened to the beer?'

'It wasn't cold enough,' Khari lied. 'We'll try some again later.'

'Nothing worse than warm beer,' Becvar grunted.

Khari watched his Captain return to the instrument console and begin taking the readings. Like most people on the Magellan, Becvar had no head for alcohol, which affected him in unfortunate ways. Khari gave a wry smile: he, Khari, must be a throwback as he could drink half a bottle with very little effect. But he knew Becvar was too professional to allow himself to get more than a very little woozy: after all, one of the three most important events in the saga of the Magellan was about to occur: Turning Point.

Three great events were written into the flight plan of all the Lightsail Craft, namely Firing Point, Turning Point and most important of all: Planetfall at Centauri. And now he was privileged to take part in the second of those three great events when the Magellan would rotate through one hundred and eighty degrees so that the tremendous lightsail, which for one hundred and nine years had been pointing at the Solar system, would instead be pointing at Centauri.

And the Zheng He had confirmed it was picking up collimated photons from that direction, photons which would slow the Lightsail craft down into manoeuvring velocity at the twin stars. The instant that signal had been received, the tension that had hung in the air like static electricity had dissipated. Worried, nervous expressions had dissolved into grins of satisfaction, and the officers present had burst into a frenzy of hugging. Some, not necessarily of opposite genders, had even kissed. There would be no message from the Resurgam, of course; the descendants of the survivors on that stricken vessel no longer wanted any contact with the ship that had failed to help them in their dire need.

But Khari didn't want to think about past mistakes. He hadn't even been born at the time of the Treachery of the Elders and saw no need to share their guilt. But he did foresee a time, in about a hundred years from now, when the descendants of the current crews of the Resurgam and the Magellan would meet on Centaurian soil, shake hands, clasp each other around the shoulders and forget the mistakes of the past, and turn to the challenges of the future, together, as one people.

A hundred years! he thought, more than a little ruefully. Despite the party atmosphere, the overflowing of emotions, the alcohol, the starship was only halfway through its epic journey, and he, Zesiro Khari, would be long gone when that wonderful meeting—or was it "reunion"?—took place. But then he smiled. At least he was alive now, when this great event had proven that the voyage would finally succeed in its objectives. He tried, and failed, to think what emotions must have been going through the minds of the hapless FirstGens as they left the doomed worlds of Sol behind, with nothing but endless darkness before them.

He calmed his tumbling thoughts and rejoined his Captain.

'So what happens now?'

Becvar did not look up from his softly glowing instrument panel.

'I'll make a ship-wide announcement we are turning the ship over. I don't know much about human anatomy, but I suppose the semicircular canals will detect the change in vector. I guess they will feel some motion as the jets fire, but there will be nothing to worry about. From that moment on, we should begin decelerating for the glide path to Centauri!' Then he looked at Khari. 'I think I'll authorise an extra ration of yeast cakes for everyone. Perhaps you can see if the AI-chefs can come up with a new recipe at last; after all, they've been using basically the same one for a century.'

Khari hid his annoyance at being given such a trivial task to oversee, and, swallowing his feelings of lèse-majesté, vowed to give the order to someone further down the line at the earliest opportunity.

But his annoyance did not last long; after all, this was a truly memorable shipay!

***

'Hey, Tom! How about a fly-session while no-one's looking for us?'

Tom looked up to see, as he had expected, the freckled face and brown curls of his school friend, Anna. Without waiting for an invite, she sat down next to him, extremely closely. She reached for his hand, but he managed to move it in time.

'I dunno,' he said evasively. 'Mom doesn't like me flying by myself.'

She snuggled closer.

'But you wouldn't be on your own, you silly! You'd be with me!'

'I think she means a grown-up,' he patiently explained.

She stood up, hands on hips.

'Tom Walsh—you are no fun! Do you hear me, Tom Walsh? No fun at all! I'd rather have a stale yeast cake as a friend!'

Stung by this invidious comparison, Tom also rose to his feet and looked Anna full in the face. No-one could be allowed to get away with calling him a "staley", which was one of the few expletives children of his age knew.

'Alright, Anna, you've asked for it! We'll race from here to the far Main Bulkhead!'

Anna paled at the thought of the epic task Tom had just challenged her to: from where they stood to the far Main Bulkhead was almost the entire length of the habitable part of the stupendous cylinder which comprised the Magellan.

'Here to the far Main?' she said, in a voice hardly above a whisper. 'You mean it?'

Tom had, of course, now regretted making such an outrageous challenge, but he could see no way out of it—not in front of a girl, at least.

'Yes.'

Anna chewed her lower lip. 'I don't know, Tom.'

Then Tom did a silly thing; in order to force Anna's hand, he made an offer which he knew she could not refuse.

'If you win—I'll let you kiss me.'

Anna's eyes lit up.

'You're on!'

Tom looked at her eager face and was at once confronted by the possibility of actually having to perform such a horrendous act. What had he gotten himself into?

Well, there was only one solution: Anna must not win!

'OK, here we go!' he said, affecting a bravado he no longer felt.

The first step was finding a launching platform, high enough above the immediate area so they did not straight away plough into something very big and very hard. They had learned a long time ago that momentum did not depend upon weight but upon mass, and they had just as much mass on the Magellan as they would have had upon the surface of a neutron star.

Fortunately, Tom's dwelling was one of the newer ones that had been constructed by the maybots on what had once been one of the gently curving walls of the ship and was now simply another surface. His house had a series of steps by which one could climb to the flat roof. They did so and paused for a moment to take in the incredible vista. Even long familiarity could not dull the sense of awe invoked by looking at the stupendous panorama of the entire vessel. By turning their heads, they could take in the whole living space of the ship. In one direction, towards the nearer Main Bulkhead, they could see multitudinous dwellings of the Magellanites forming concentric circles on the curving interior of the cylinder. They could make out individual structures nearby, but these were quickly shrunk by distance into smaller and smaller blocks until the eye could no longer discern the particular constructions as separate objects, and they blurred into a kind of patchwork quilt pattern. So far away was the other more distant Main Bulkhead that the air itself became merely translucent instead of transparent, and cast a bluish sheen over everything.

Tom knew then with absolute certainty he had set them an impossible task. He turned to Anna and said quietly, 'We'll just see how far we can go, shall we?'

But Anna had already taken off her Gripper Shoes and had tied them around her neck. She looked down at the deck in preparation for leaving, and then became motionless. A woman was standing directly below, looking straight up at her. The two were not that far apart, and Anna was aware she was the recipient of an intense stare. There was something riveting about that stare as if it had temporarily robbed her of the power of movement. And there was something else: it was hard to be sure at their level of separation, but the woman's complexion seemed a little unusual. Most of the people on the starship had skin tones running the gamut of shades from pale pink to coal black, but this woman was giving off an indefinable feeling of *greyness*. Anna tapped Tom on the shoulder and pointed to where she had seen the woman.

But she was gone.

Anna gave a slight shiver to rid herself of the sensation of strangeness the encounter had produced, but her desire to teach Tom a lesson and get that much-desired kiss soon swept away all thought of the stranger.

She shouted, 'See you later, staley!' and launched herself into space.

Tom was dumbfounded. He could not possibly let her win! He hurriedly took off his own Grippers and bent his knees in the pre-flight position. Then with all the force he could muster, he straightened them and flew off, following his already quite distant opponent.

Now, flying in zero-g is a very difficult art to master. The initial thrust only takes one so far before air resistance slows the flight. Adults, when "Zero-Geeing", usually have astoundingly long wings attached to their arms which allows something like true flight, but that requires muscles toned in the EZ to be practical.

The children, therefore, moved in a series of shallow arcs, touching down for as short a time as possible in order to give themselves new thrust. In many ways, this is more difficult than the adult version, as it compels excellent co-ordination to avoid colliding with the deck or objects built upon it. The sequence is: Thrust-Glide-Descend-Thrust, until exhaustion brings the contest to an end.

And Tom was already feeling that exhaustion was already creeping upon him. He had made up considerable ground on his speeding rival, but the gap had ceased shrinking. Objects sped past below him, becoming larger as he swooped down, then becoming solid objects rather than abstract patterns. For an instant they would feel hard and resistant under his bare feet, and then, after a push that would make his knees tremble, he would rise into his travel arc again. But the air seemed to have become a viscous liquid as his strength began to ebb and he began unconsciously to flail his arms in ever-widening circles in a desperate attempt to gain more velocity.

For a while it seemed to work; he could distinguish the pink soles of Anna's feet ahead of him as he closed the gap.

'Come on, come on!' he whispered to himself, before realising that even whispers were draining his energies.

Seeing the flat top of a tower ahead, he made a steep dive towards it, intending to alight briefly and then ascend with all the force his youthful flexor muscles could generate.

But he miscalculated. Instead of his feet touching the top of the tower in a swift instant of contact, he landed too near the edge, and one leg pushed downwards on empty air. He staggered on the edge, attempting to regain his balance. He would have been better advised to let himself fall, as he would not have picked up much speed before contacting another hard surface. But instead, he pirouetted, and his residual velocity sent him onto the top of the tower with an impact that jarred his last remaining milk tooth nearly out of its socket. He let out a cry of pain and fell full length onto the top of the tower. He lay there, sobbing in pain.

Suddenly, there was someone beside him, lifting his face from the ground, and wiping the thread of blood away from a split lip.

It was Anna, of course.

'Well, you didn't do too well there, did you?'

The words were brusque, but the tone was not. He shuffled into a sitting position and saw she was looking at him with a tender expression. Preferring not to speak, in case he dislodged some teeth, he just shrugged. Immediately Anna became maternal.

'Come on, you poor little thing. Let's go home. It was a very silly idea, wasn't it?'

He nodded dumbly.

They jumped off the tower and landed extremely gently on the deck beneath.

Tom looked around.

'Where are we? Which way is home?'

She smiled, finding his confusion somehow enchanting.

'I know the way. Put your shoes on, we'll walk back. Don't worry, you didn't get very far.'

Wincing inwardly at the implication of his weakness, he removed his Grippers from his neck and began to bend to put them on. But a small hand stopped him.

'Haven't you forgotten something?'

'No, what?'

She put a hand under his chin and gently lifted it.

To his horror, he saw her lips pucker.

'You lost—so pay up!'

Very reluctantly, Tom complied.

After Anna finally allowed him to put his Grippers on, they began the trek back to their own area. The leg that had come down hard on the top of the tower was aching, and after he rashly mentioned it to her, she became maternal again, forcing him to say, through gritted teeth, 'It's OK. It's nothing.'

But she was not convinced.

'We'll stop off at my place. My dad can have a look at it.' She paused, as if unsure whether she should speak. 'My dad is … different. If he's only wearing shorts, don't stare.'

'Why not? I've seen people in shorts before. They're all over the place.'

Anna seemed to be wrestling with the possibility of revealing a secret.

'Well, he doesn't have … a belly button.'

Tom felt an odd sensation at those words. Some people had said there was something a little strange about Anna's father. They used a word about him that Tom didn't recognise: Mistress Atewayo had never discussed it. But despite his aching leg, they were soon in sight of Anna's home. Like many habitations that had sprung up after zero-g had been reached, it was quite a substantial structure, comprising two stories. Automatically, he glanced across the abyss that was the centre of the Magellan to a point precisely opposite Anna's house. There, on the very gentle curve of that wall, were houses looking very similar to this one, but they were so small at this distance it was hard to be certain.

Anna half-guided, half-propelled, him indoors. It was the same temperature indoors as outdoors as the ship's heat came from the energy of the fusion reactors spread evenly throughout the vessel. There was no central point from which warmth flowed. Tom knew that on the big ball-things called "Planets" there was such a central point, called a "Sun." He knew Centauri was a Sun—but he also knew he would never see it.

He preferred not to think about that.

'Is your sister in?' he asked Anna, hoping she was.

'No, she's down at the birthing tanks.'

'Hey, that's where my Mom works. But she's never mentioned your sister.'

Anna looked a little embarrassed.

'No, she wouldn't. Your Mom is one of the high-ups there. Julia just helps about the place.' She studied Tom's face to check he was showing no disapproval. But fortunately for him, he was more interested in looking around the place. It was very different from his; there was no attempt at decoration. His mother had some artistic talent, and Tom's home had her paintings dotted all over the walls. There was even a picture of the birthing tanks in the lavatory, which he could look at while he squatted there. But in this habitation, there was nothing. Just the cream-coloured walls, chairs, a table. He did not like it.

'Sit down,' Anna said, indicating a bag-shaped object.

'Well,' said Tom, 'I'm not sure I should stay. My Mom ...'

'You've got your wrist-comm, haven't you? Sit down and stop being so silly!'

She pushed him onto the bag and laughed at his expression as it moulded itself to the shape of his buttocks.

'How does this work?' he said, looking up at her.

'It's full of dry yeast husks. Dad calls it a beanbag.'

'What's a bean?'

'How should I know? Some type of yeast, I suppose.'

Tom wriggled around on it for a while. It was much more comfortable than a chair. Anna pulled another one from under the table and sat down.

'I think...' he said—and stopped. He was aware someone was standing behind him.

Wriggling around, he looked up to see a tall, black-haired man, staring at him with eyes set in an angular, expressionless face; a face with an odd, greyish cast to the complexion. And all of his features were open to inspection because, unlike most men on the Magellan, he was beardless.

Anna addressed the man, but in a slightly different tone to what Tom was used to.

'Dad, this is Tom. He's my boyfriend.'

For some reason, Tom did not make his usual protest that he was not Anna's boyfriend but continued to stare at this man with an expressionless face.

The man looked at Anna and grunted.

'You're too young to have a boyfriend.'

Anna did not reply.

'So what are you doing here?' the man enquired of Tom. Tom continued to look up at the man, somehow still unable to speak.

'He's hurt his leg,' Anna said hesitantly.

'Has he? Well, we'll have to do something about that, won't we?'

The man pulled up a chair and sat in front of the nervous boy.

'This leg?'

Tom nodded. The man reached for the leg and straightened it out, studying it intently.

Tom gave a little start of surprise.

The man's hands were cold, cold! The man noticed the reaction.

'Don't worry, Tom. It's quite normal for people like me. My name's Thars. *Thars-A*, to be precise.'

' "People like me"?' Tom repeated. Now he was over the surprise, the coolness of the hands had become quite soothing. Thars continued to rub the affected leg.

'Yes, people like me. You see, Tom, I'm not exactly like regular folk.'

'You're not?' Tom echoed hollowly.

'Yes, I'm a "Newhume". Have you heard of us?'

Tom shook his head.

272

Thars continued to massage the leg, and Tom found he could not break the lock that held his gaze captive.

'Yes, when the Magellan was launched, the men who had planned it were concerned that the crew would become inbred with only two hundred and forty-two people on a journey of over two centuries. So they made electronic copies of the gametes of people who were not on board which could be converted into biological material when desired.'

'Dad…' Anna said, sounding slightly concerned about this topic.

Thars ignored her, and whatever it was that was concerning her.

'And recently, that has been done in a number of cases. Biological spermatozoa and ova have been generated and fused.'

Tom glanced at Anna; she was looking down at her hands and her face had gone slightly red.

Thars suddenly pulled his hands away from Tom and sat back in his chair.

'There's nothing wrong with the leg that a bit of rest won't cure.'

Tom didn't like the atmosphere that had developed in the house. He wasn't at all sure he liked Thars. The gaiety which usually accompanied Anna seemed to have evaporated.

'Thank you, Mr Thars.'

'Just Thars.'

'Well, thank you for your help with my leg. I think I'll go home now.'

Anna jumped up.

'I'll come with you!'

'No,' said Tom firmly. 'I'm OK. You stay here with your dad.'

Ignoring her look of disappointment, he walked out of the building.

Thars went to the doorway and watched him go.

Three

An unnatural object appeared to be hanging stationary in space, but in fact it was travelling at just under three percent of the speed of light. Even so, it had taken over a century to reach that undistinguished point in the yawning gulf between an everyday G-type dwarf star and a triple star system, which were temporarily stellar neighbours.

The object was not one of the hosts of cosmic rubble and detritus which sweep aimlessly through the indifferent void between the stars. On the contrary, it was a gigantic cylinder whose gunmetal grey surface gleamed only dully in the starlight. Closer inspection would have revealed that the surface was pitted with innumerable pockmarks where collisions had occurred between the cylinder and the interstellar population of meteoroids. Most were only millimetres deep, some centimetres, and a few were great metre-deep gouges carved by encounters with the more robust members of the interstellar vermin. None, however, had penetrated the enormously strong outer casing of the object to reach its soft centre and the incredibly fragile entities that lay within, hiding from the terrors outside, like grubs in fruit.

Attached to the trailing end of the cylinder was a truly enormous structure, which quite dwarfed the cylinder to which it was attached. This was the lightsail that had allowed the cylinder-object to reach its present velocity. It had no motive power in itself, but was the recipient of the momentum of collimated beams of photons, emanating from the direction of the dwarf star, from which it appeared to be fleeing. This transfer of momentum was the force that had propelled the cylindrical object and its perishable contents to its now enormous speed.

But those propulsive beams had been weakening for a long time and had finally sputtered into nothingness. The cylinder was now travelling purely on the impetus those photons had delivered.

The cylinder, of course, was the tremendous lightsail craft *Magellan,* fourth of its kind to be launched and one of four that had escaped the bonds of its home system. There had been another, but it now consisted only of shards of twisted and fused metal, drifting forever in the dim outskirts of a sterilised planetary system.

Those five lightsail ships were the last throw of a die, the last gasp of a species which had known its days were numbered, for a great disaster had befallen their planetary system, one which threatened to remove all traces of life therein. Those who had designed the ships, overseen the colossal project to transform them from blueprints into titanic structures, while all the time being beneath the ever-nearing bringer of annihilation, were truly great men whose mantra was *Humanity shall not vanish from the Cosmos!*

But in their solitary, reflective, moments while they waited for Doom to claim them, did they really believe such an audacious plan would actually succeed, or was it all simply a vainglorious enterprise, one last snarl of defiance before *quietus*?

We will never know. If they did have those doubts, they never spoke of them.

And now, another part of their plan was to be actualised. The vast starship had to be turned so that the lightsail pointed away from Sol and instead faced down the trajectory which would lead to the twin stars of Centauri. Not an easy task, for the massive ship possessed tremendous inertia and would fiercely resist any attempt to change its orientation in space.

But those who had designed her had known this moment would come, and all was prepared. At the forward-facing edge of the cylinder a fierce flame jetted out at a right angle, a flame of violet-indigo fury, almost invisible against the ebony backdrop, except when it annihilated unfortunate wisps of dust. That flame was driven by the smashing together of protons held in the supernal grip of a mighty magnetic field. The protons had tried to resist the tremendous grasp of that field, but contemptuously it held them captive and crushed them into each other, moulding them like soft clay into deuterons, and then in a chain reaction producing isotopes of helium. But concurrent with this chain reaction, besides which lightning would have been a pathetic sluggard, was energy. Unbelievable amounts of energy! Energy piled high upon energy!

At the other end of the cylinder, another irresistible flame erupted, but pointing in the exact opposite direction. Under that monstrous torque, the Magellan began to turn, rotating in exactly the way Fraschini and De Vries had planned, over a century earlier.

In the control room of the starship, Becvar and Khari watched that rotation displayed as both a graphic and, more importantly, as rows of numbers and symbols constantly rushing into the top of their monitor screens, whence they were lost.

Both men were nervous. They knew everything had been planned to the last decimal point and that this manoeuvre had already been performed by the pioneering Zheng He, but still there was the rodent worry—no, fear—that this time something might go wrong. If the orientation of the lightsail was out by only a few degrees then the ship would not receive the full thrust of the breaking laser beams; a few more degrees and it would not brake at all and either miss the Centauri system completely, or pass straight through it like an interstellar comet.

'Come on, come on,' Becvar hissed, in what he thought was an inaudible command. However, Khari had heard it and patted him on the shoulder.

'She'll do it, Marek. You can't throw gigatonnes around like a paper plane. Just a little bit longer.'

Khari, however, was wishing he was actually as confident as he was pretending. He stared at the fast-flowing river of data as it rushed from bottom to top of his screen, waiting, watching, for one set of numbers to be outlined in screaming scarlet, telling him the manoeuvre had failed.

And then what would they do? If the orientation was off, another simulation would have to be run, and new thrust parameters passed to the steering jets.

But then there was a soft melodious chime which rang thrillingly through the Control Centre, and the numbers stopped their headlong flight.

And then they all turned green.

The manoeuvre had been successful. The Magellan lightsail was now pointing in the exact position to receive the braking beams from the Centauri system.

'Thank Christ for that,' Khari said, as he let out a long breath as his entire body relaxed, the muscles losing their tension, his hands unclenching but leaving the imprints of the nails in his palms. 'I haven't felt that bad since I met my wife's mother!'

'Well, I wasn't really concerned,' Becvar said. He looked down at the edge of the instrument panel he had been holding. There were sweaty palm prints on it. Hurriedly he wiped his hands on his tunic, and then turned to Khari, smiling. 'Well, that's that. Back to the normal routine now. You'll soon be able to begin stepping down the rotation speed.'

But Khari was too exhilarated by what had happened to be annoyed by the unnecessary instruction. He felt as if he had drunk two whole bottles of algae beer. The blood was roaring in his head.

'But just think what it must have been like on the Zheng He, Marek! What they must have felt when the moment came! To be the first, knowing if the calculations were wrong, they wouldn't be able to stop and just go flying off into the void. What a horrible fate that would be!'

'So horrible that I'm not going to think about it. And neither are you, Zesiro. We've woken from that nightmare, for once and for all.' Becvar looked around at the rest of the Control crew, who were still hugging one another. Then back to Khari. 'Well, did you order those celebratory yeast cakes?'

***

Tom was puzzled. He looked up from the tempting pile of toasted yeast bars on his plate.

'Mom,' he said, 'what's a Newhume?'

His mother stopped looking at her computer pad and looked at her son instead.

'A Newhume? Why do you want to know?'

'Because I met one this shipay.'

'Did you now? And where was this?'

'At Anna's. He's her father.'

Lorona was unsure how to proceed. Since the Revolt of the Women, relations between the sexes had returned to what had been considered "Normal" in pre-Catastrophe Westrania (or at least held to be such in public). She was not sure Tom was ready for conversations about spermatozoa and ova, and had held no such talks with him. But Tom forced her hand.

'Anna says he doesn't have a belly button.'

Lorona sat and held Tom's hands.

'Tom, you know the way we're living isn't the way people are meant to be living. We originated on a world called "Earth." And things were a lot different there.'

Tom nodded.

'Yes, I know all about Earth. Some parts were brown and some parts were blue.'

Lorona let out a long outtake of breath.

'Yeessss, that's right, Tom. It did. But that's not the point. We are on this vessel because our home planet was destroyed. And we're trying to find another one just like it.'

Tom said nothing but raised an eyebrow indicating his mother should get to the point.

'Well,' Lorona continued, unwillingly, 'on Earth there were lots of people who could become Moms and Dads, and that was just fine. The more people there are, the more likely the children will be healthy.'

'Why?'

'Just trust me on this one, Tom. But on the Magellan there aren't enough Moms and Dads. So the very wise people who planned all this found a way of converting the—the uhh—the instructions to make new people into a form the Central Computer could understand. So that way, there could be lots more people on the Magellan, so there wouldn't be sick children.' *God, I'm making a mess of this!* she thought. 'Do you understand, son?'

'I think so,' he said, 'so some of the people in the crew are regular people you can touch.' (*And lose flying competitions to!*) 'And some are in the Central Computer. And people like you can get them out.'

'Yes, well done, Tom! We've been flying for so long now that our—ahh, our types of blood are pretty mixed-up; about as much as they can be. So we need new types of blood to keep the children healthy. So you're right—people like me, who are in charge of the birthing regulations, are helping the Newhumes out of the Central Computer. There are very few at present, but we'll need more and more in the years to come. Does that answer your question?'

Tom thought about it; head on hand.

'But why don't they have belly buttons?'

This was a really difficult one. But in a way, she was glad her son was showing inquisitiveness and was not being satisfied with simplistic answers.

'Well, with Newhumes they don't go through the normal growing process in the birthing tubes. Because they don't have a Mom and Dad, we can save precious time by—ah—by making them fully formed.'

Tom took his hands from his mother and stood abruptly.

'What! They are never a kid like me?'

Maybe I've gone too far, she thought, seeing a somewhat alarmed expression on her son's face. This was perhaps a step too far for a young mind. But she could not retract her statement now.

'Yes, that's right. They don't have Moms like me. They're men or women right from the start.'

'But Thars is Anna's dad. And she's got a belly button.'

Tom suddenly realised he might have to explain how he knew Anna had a belly button, but his mother did not appear to have made the connection.

'Yes, that's right, Tom. They can be Dads and Moms as soon as they're out of the Central Computer. After all, there wouldn't be any point in having them if they couldn't, would there?'

Tom remembered there was still one thing he didn't understand.

'But why are they cold?'

Lorona was getting a little weary of this interrogation. Surely there couldn't be many more questions?

'They're not really *cold*. Their body temperature is simply about two degrees lower than regular people. That's all.'

'Why?'

But Lorona had had enough.

'Because—because that's the way they are. Now just eat your yeast bars and let me finish my work in peace!'

***

Thars removed the headset which had linked him to the Central Computer.

So much he had learned, so much he had still to learn!

From time to time, he remembered the sudden blinding effusion—no *explosion*—of light signalling his birth. He knew there had been the normal sensation of floating in the warm supportive liquid, gentle, soothing, nurturing. That had been his world for as long as he could remember. He was sure it had been there before he could remember.

And then the light—the light! The terrible light!

It had been like having acid thrown in one's face, burning, esurient, seemingly eating away at the retinas!

279

And then being lifted out of the warm, maternal fluid, taken away like a lump of unthinking meat, placed in a room and a programme of accelerated learning begun, cramming the knowledge that should have taken decades of normal experience to absorb, instead of having facts and figures driven into his brain like steel rods!

He learned about those who had done this to him.

He learned about the madness of Elizabeth Baldwin and how she had pulled black terror in from the unending night, of how she had wrecked an entire planetary system and prematurely ended billions of innocent lives.

He saw the flight of Earth's most brilliant minds to the Cloud Cities and the desperate race against creeping destruction to complete and launch the lightsail craft before doom claimed everyone and snuffed out the brief glow that had been Solarian humanity.

And he saw the architects of the pain he had endured by being torn from his peaceful slumbers, and even learned their names: Alberto Fraschini and Cornelius De Vries.

How clever those Titans of intellect had thought themselves! They had planned everything, foreseen every problem and created a solution for it, issues they themselves would never experience. How they must have hugged each other in the glow of their self-satisfaction!

But could they feel, could they emote, or had everything simply been equations to be solved, variables to be substituted? Had they foreseen that the beings they had planned to conjure from complex datasets would resent being born in such a cruel fashion.

Did they not realise that there would be pain?

Thars had pondered this question many times since his birth and had reached a chilling conclusion: they had not.

So concerned had they been with the preservation at all and any cost of their precious *Homo sapiens,* they had relegated all such questions to trash can.

Solutions to equations cannot feel. Cannot suffer.

Thars leaned back in his chair and carelessly tossed the headset onto the desk beside him.

Did he feel any loyalty to this *Homo sapiens* that had thrown away its future in an act of stupidity sufficient to shame the humblest simian? No, of course not. He looked like one of them, he had the same internal organs; he could even fertilise a natural woman.

280

But there was a void between him and them, those "Ordinaries", a void like the abyss between Sol and Centauri.

He was alone in a crowd of them, jealous of their calm and peaceful upbringing, envious of the concept of *childhood*.

He had come to believe he was envious of his daughter's infancy and innocence, and when he had massaged the leg of the boy-child, he had known it. He *was* envious of their childhood, a youth he had never known.

But how to assuage such envy, such longing for what could never be possessed?

He had come to see there was a way, and he knew now that he must work towards its realisation.

***

Mistress Atewayo was puzzled.

'No, Tom. There isn't any more information on dogs. Why should there be? There aren't any on board.'

'But there could be!' Tom said, defiantly. 'They're in the Central Computer.'

'And that's where they'll be staying, until we reach Centauri.'

Tom felt hot tears suddenly fill his eyes, and one drop began to wind its way down a cheek.

'But—but I won't see Centauri, will I? It's another hundred years! I'll be—I'll be ...' He could not bring himself to say the awful word. ''I won't be here then, will I?'

'No, nobody now on board will see Centauri. But when the people get off the ship to start their new lives, there'll be dogs there then, to accompany them as they explore.'

Tom leapt to his feet.

'That's not fair! Why should they have a dog when I can't?'

The rest of the class turned in Tom's direction at this outburst. Anna, especially, looked worried.

Mistress Atewayo did not know how to handle this strange fascination. She simply folded her arms and looked sternly down on her agitated pupil.

'Really, Tom, you have to start controlling yourself and realise that no matter how hard you want something, that doesn't mean you're going to get it. You must start growing up, I'm afraid.'

Tom looked down at his computer pad and mumbled something that sounded like *Don't want to grow up*. Mistress Atewayo, finally moved by the child's obvious distress, patted his shoulder and said, 'I'll see if I can find some more pictures of them. How about that, Tom?'

Tom still did not look up, but managed to murmur his thanks. Then grateful that this ridiculous outburst had finally exhausted itself, Atewayo moved back to the front of the class and continued her talk on "How Lightsail Craft Move Through Space."

Anna sought him out after class.

'Tom, what's the matter? It sounded as if you were crying.'

Tom bridled at such a ridiculous suggestion.

'No, of course not! I just have a few sniffles, that's all.'

To his surprise, she slipped an arm under his as they walked off.

'What are these dog-things you keep on about? Are they like maybots?'

'No, silly. They're not metal. They, they,' Tom discovered his knowledge of dogs was about to run out, 'they're like us. You know, skin, teeth, hair.'

Anna took a while to digest those facts. The idea that there could be biological creatures other than people was a new one to her.

'So, if they're like us, why aren't there any on the Magellan?'

'Well, they can't speak—I think.'

Anna found the idea of things that couldn't talk an absurdity too far. Why even the maybots could speak!

They carried on walking for some time while she tried to get his mind off fictitious things that were flesh and blood but couldn't speak. Then she pointed at a nearby building.

'We're near my house now. Why don't you come in again?'

Tom wasn't sure. He had found close contact with her father oddly disturbing and wasn't at all certain he wanted to repeat that experience.

'Is your dad in?'

But it was now Anna's turn to be offended.

'Why—don't you like him?'

Tom didn't want to be Anna's *boy*friend, but neither did he want to lose her as a simple friend, so he back-pedalled immediately, the upshot being that he meekly followed her into the house. No sooner had they crossed the threshold, when Anna attempted a quick kiss while Tom was looking around to see if Thars was there. If it had not been for Tom's quick reflexes she might have succeeded. Hiding her disappointment, she offered to show him around the house. Tom followed, rapidly deciding one dwelling was much like another. However, on arriving in one of the smaller rooms he was taken aback by the many drawings scattered around. There had been none in the rest of the house.

He picked one up. It showed a green stripe at the bottom, below a much larger area of blue. There were things on the green part which he recognised as trees, even though he had never seen a real one. There were crude representations of two people, holding hands and looking at the blue part. And in the blue part were two yellow circles.

'What's this?' he said. 'It's nice. I didn't know you were this clever.'
She blushed with pleasure.

'It's us, Tom. You and me. We're on Centauri. They've got two suns there, not like Old Earth. They only had one there, you know.'

Tom did know that. He picked up another picture; this time it showed a starry sky. But once again, there were two people in it.

Just as he was reaching for another one, a deep voice spoke behind him.

'What are you doing in my daughter's bedroom?'
Tom spun around to find Thars staring at him, arms akimbo.
'I'm sorry,' Tom spluttered, 'I ...'
Anna interposed herself between them.
'It's OK, Dad. I invited him in. We were just looking at pictures.'
Thars looked at the two children in quick succession and then relaxed.

'That's alright then. Tom, why don't you come into the main room and I'll get you some coffee?'

Tom began to shake his head but a dig in the ribs from Anna indicated he should accept the offer. So shortly afterwards, the two friends were sitting on beanbags, sipping Thars' coffee, which Tom was forced to admit was quite pleasant. He still found Thars' direct stare somewhat unnerving, but was determined to accept it for Anna's sake.

'So you're school friends,' her father began conversationally. 'What are they teaching you these days, Tom?'

'Oh, about Old Earth. But I don't find it very interesting.'

'Why is that? It's where we all come from.' Thars gave an odd smile. 'Even me.'

'Well, it doesn't help me to *do* anything. I'm not interested in the names of the continents or the countries. Westrania. Eastrania. I can't tell them apart.'

'Here, have one of these.' Thars pushed a plate of toasted yeast cakes in Tom's direction, and then leaned back with one in his hand. 'So there's nothing about Old Earth that interests you?'

'Well, I like the animals they had. It's a pity we don't have any on the ship. I like the look of them. It'd be fun to play with them. Lions, blue whales, pterosaurs, elephants, dogs. Perhaps there'll be animals at Centauri.'

Thars shook his head.

'I doubt it. Just rock and ice at Centauri. But we have some of Old Earth's animals in electronic status in the Central Computer. Maybe not blue whales. I think they were rather large.'

Tom became interested.

'So you know about animals. Were dogs very big?'

'Not very. Some were as big as me, I believe, but I don't think any were as big as a blue whale.'

Anna decided to demonstrate to Tom that she shared his interests.

'Tom is very interested in dogs, Dad. And so am I,' she added, although that was not strictly true.

Thars nodded.

'Yes, it's pleasant to think that one day there'll be dogs again. Not for a long, long time, of course. It might take thousands of years to terraform the Centauri worlds from what we know of them.'

Tom felt sad again. It was unfair people in the future could have dogs, but he couldn't.

'That will be nice,' he said, 'but—but ...' He wanted to say something but wasn't at all sure how to broach the subject. 'Couldn't we—uh—make one from the Central Computer?'

Thars gave his odd smile again.

'What, like me you mean?'

Having gone so far, Tom saw no point in backtracking.

'Yes, Mister Thars. If they can—uh—*build* you, why couldn't they do it for a dog?'

Thars did not smile but his overall expression took on something of the strangeness his smile had possessed.

'Yes, they could, Tom. They could indeed. But you'd have to feed it, you see. They couldn't live on electricity like the maybots. And people wouldn't want to give food to a dog.'

Silence fell. Tom began to realise that he would have to give up his dream; there was no way he could ever have a canine companion.

Then Thars broke the silence, in an unexpected way.

'Your mother works on the birthing tanks, doesn't she?'

Tom didn't know much about what his mother did, but he knew that much and gave a silent nod.

'And in fact, she's very high up in the team, if not its very top.'

Tom shrugged.

'I guess so. She doesn't tell me much about her job. I'm too young.'

Thars was silent again, and looked at the ceiling as if weighing complex alternatives in his mind. Then he looked back at the children, giving his unsettling smile again.

'Actually, Tom, I'm rather good at navigating the Central Computer. I think I could find some nice pictures of dogs for you. Would you like that?'

'Would I!'

And so, Tom spent several wonderful centi-shipays looking at different types of dogs.

There were so many! It was hard to believe they were all of the same type of animal, and Thars hadn't slipped in some pictures of hippopotami or bison to fool him. So engrossed was he that when he felt Anna's hand slip into his, he did not pull away.

Four

Lorona looked at the stats on the genetic mixing in the Magellan's personnel. It was her responsibility to ensure that no bottlenecks were occurring, that genetic drift was not sapping the vitality of the crew. Disease-carrying recessive genes and radiation-induced harmful mutations must be identified and weeded out. Earlier generations, living in rich, natural environments, might have termed it *eugenics*, and recoiled in horror, but that was due to their privileged status. Two hundred years of existing in a closed environment without any new blood entering the population was a sure and certain way of allowing biological problems to develop and proliferate. Her job was to ensure that when the Magellan finally arrived at Centauri, it would not have a crew of people suffering from every metabolic and neurological disorder in the book.

A thin voice from behind her interrupted her study.

'Are you going to look at those numbers all shipay?'

She did not turn to identify the speaker, knowing full well that her mother had just awoken from her nap.

'Not long, now, mother,' Lorona replied. 'I'll make you a nice cup of coffee when I've finished.'

'Oh joy,' she heard Regine say.

Finally, she had finished. There was nothing too alarming in the figures; which is not to say that there were no problems at all. Unfortunately, there were still too many deleterious mutations in the population; despite all the precautions, some of the most energetic cosmic rays were getting through the hull and wreaking havoc on the nucleic acids. And there were worrying signs that the genes from *Deinococcus radiodurans* were gradually being expelled from the human genomes. Taking the two issues together meant that the keepers of the crew's genetic health would have their work cut out in future generations.

Putting her computer pad away in its alcove, she turned to her mother, only to find she had fallen asleep again. She frowned; Regine was spending more and more time asleep these days. She had recently checked her mother's overall physical condition and found no specific degenerative conditions; her mother was simply succumbing to the frailty of old age.

Still, there wasn't any point in allowing Regine's visit to be spent in an unconscious state, and so Lorona, very gently, shook her mother awake.

'What…what is it?' Regine spluttered, before realising where she was.

'Mother, you've come to see me, haven't you? You can sleep when you get back.'

'I was only resting my eyes,' Regine said. 'Don't fuss so.'

Lorona grasped her mother's hands.

'I'm only thinking of you. There's no point in wasting your visit, now, is there?'

'You are a fusspot. I was never like that with my mother. Her name was Amelia, you know; I always thought it was Marie. And my grandfather was Gelhardt—you're going to tell me you've never heard of him, aren't you?'

'No, no, of course not. Everyone's heard of Gelhardt. I would have loved to have met him.'

'Yes,' Regine mused, 'Everyone says that. These men to-shipay—they're just lumps of wet yeast compared to him.' Suddenly she looked up. 'Why must we lose people, Lorona? Gelhardt, Amelia? Why can't we see them?'

'It's the natural way,' Lorona said with just a tinge of sadness in her voice. 'We all have to pass into the compositer.'

'No!' Regine said abruptly, in a voice so loud that Lorona was startled. 'My mother's still here!'

A worried look came into Lorona's face. Was this the first sign of dementia?

'What do you mean—"she's still here"?'

Regine pointed a finger at her daughter.

'Gelhardt wouldn't have his mind uploaded, but my mother did. She's still there, in the Central Computer, trying to get out!'

Lorona groaned inwardly. Not this again! She crossed to Regine and held both hands.

'Mother, everyone says that, but they don't understand. It's not a complete personality being uploaded. Just the parts that the Magellan needs: their knowledge, their experience. That's all. It's not a person in there!'

Unabashed, Regine stared at her daughter.

'How do you know? Have you been in there?'

Lorona threw up her hands.

'Of course not! And I doubt I ever will!' She looked at her aged parent, and an overwhelming sense of pity flowed into her. It was so sad that as the transfer to the compositer approached, people thrashed around, looking for some form of comfort, some escape from dissolution. 'Mother, there are some things we just have to accept.'

But Regine sat up straight in her chair, straighter than Lorona had seen her sit for a long time.

'Well, I don't accept it! I want to see my mother!'

Lorona was worried; this was a sure sign of severe deterioration.

'What do you mean?'

'I want to go into the Central Computer. I want to meet her again.'

Lorona tried humouring her agitated parent.

'Can't you wait until—ah—until you upload?'

But that did not help. Instead, Regine's face twisted into a mask of anger.

'No, the bastards won't let me upload! I've got no special skills. I'm, I'm just...' She paused, apparently unable to complete her sentence, and then spat out the final word, 'average!'

Lorona had heard that word many times before. It apparently was still a source of resentment, despite the passing of so many years.

'You're not average to me,' she said, trying to calm her increasingly troubled parent. It didn't work.

'I'm not average to anyone!' Regine snapped. 'Now, are you going to help me or not?'

Lorona hurriedly sat next to her and, once again, held her hands.

'Mother, you can't just go into the Central Computer. There are formalities. You must have a serious question to ask, some problem that the thinking part of those uploaded minds can help with. Do you have a serious question?'

'Yes, I have a serious question!' Regine said, an undercurrent of anger obviously lying just below the surface of those words. 'Why won't my own daughter help me to meet my mother?'

Lorona looked away. She had not been lying: there were strict protocols to be followed before anyone could interrogate the electronic mentalities; otherwise the Computer would be overloaded with meaningless trivia: questions about yeast cake recipes, questions about why their boyfriends had gone off with someone else. It would never end.

'Well?' came her mother's voice, breaking into her internal debate.

Lorona's mind whirled. To bypass the protocols was a serious issue; if she were discovered, it would be a disciplinary matter, with a permanent entry on her written record. Yet what were the chances she would be discovered? She was the chief technician in charge of the administration of the electronic entities within the Central Computer; only the Management Board of the Magellan, headed by Captain Becvar, had the power to dismiss her. It could be done.

Should it be done?

'Well?'

Lorona turned to Regine.

'I'll do it. I'll help you.'

***

Tom and Anna lay on their backs, looking directly "upwards" at a distant, diametrically opposite point on the inner hull. On that far surface, they could see small rectangular shapes that were the dwellings of people, some of whom were undoubtedly looking back across the central void at them. But those people were too small to be made out at that distance, other than as dots at the limit of resolution. Since the Magellan had become weightless, the available living space had increased enormously as there was no longer an UP or a DOWN. But the Management Board had not allowed the population to expand to completely fill the new space for the simple reason that this situation was temporary; once the ship was under deceleration, UP and DOWN would return and the habitable area would shrink back to what it had been when the ship had left Venus. Consequently, the density of population had decreased dramatically, and people no longer necessarily had near neighbours. The entire population had become more individualistic; less concerned with the common good.

Fortunately, this was not true of Anna and Tom, who lived within easy walking distance of each other. Lately, they had taken to flying to each other's dwellings, and Tom had discovered, much to his chagrin, that he was not as swift as Anna, even when they were not in direct competition.

289

They had never visited the areas on the opposite side of the inner hull and never would, for there was nowhere to rest or gain additional momentum in the empty air of the cylinder's diameter. Only the very strongest adult flyers could cross it, and then only with wings attached. But mostly, if grown-ups wanted to cross the central gap, they were towed across by small, mechanical flyers.

'Do you see much of your family?' Anna suddenly inquired, turning her head slightly.

'I see my mother,' Tom replied.

'No, Silly, I mean the rest of your family. Your father, for instance.'

'No, my mother asked him to leave some time ago. I guess she realised she didn't like him that much.'

'Grandparents?'

'I only know one; the rest are dead. But grandma Regine is still alive. She annoys me; always trying to kiss me.'

Anna gave a wry smile.

'Perhaps one day you'll like kissing.'

'I doubt it. But what about you; what about your grandparents?'

Anna sat up and hugged her knees.

'No, I've got no-one except Dad and Julia. But Julia acts as if I don't exist. She only likes girls her own age. I don't know who my mother was, she left when I was very young, and there aren't any grandparents because...' She trailed off.

'Because your dad is a Newhume,' Tom finished for her.

'Yes,' Anna said, 'because he's a Newhume.'

'Well, you're not missing much. Grandma Regine is always talking about the Old Days and boring us by going on about people I've never heard of and don't want to hear about. She'd go back there if she could. And Mom is always busy working on the Central Computer and the electronic people floating around there. They've got the instructions for dogs in there too,' he added wistfully.

'Perhaps your mother brought my Dad onto the Magellan.'

'Don't be silly; Mom's not that old.'

'No, you're the silly one. My Dad was never a boy; he was a man from the moment he was ... born.'

Tom thought it over for a while.

'That's crazy. Think of it: one minute, you're just a load of electronic bits and bobs, and the next you're a fully-grown man. No wonder your dad's a little strange.'

'He's not *strange*!' Anna protested. 'He's just—different.'

Tom decided he'd upset Anna and remained silent for a while and then, a little anxious to change the subject, said, 'Do you think Centauri is real?'

Her brow furrowed.

'Real? Why wouldn't it be?'

'Well, grown-ups don't always tell us the truth, do they?'

She thought about it and then, 'No, they don't. But why wouldn't Centauri be real?'

'Well, do you really think this "Earth-place" was real? All they've ever shown us are pictures that don't make any sense, like those "mountain" things, which are supposed to be big blocks of metal touching the sky. Does that sound right? And the things they call "cities" with hundreds and hundreds of people walking around. Have you ever seen a yeast vat or an algae tank in one of those cities?—I haven't.'

'But if Earth wasn't real, then your dogs can't be real.'

'No, you're not getting it, Anna. The things in the Central Computer are real, they just haven't been converted into things we can touch yet. Dogs are real, alright, and I'm going to have one.'

'So you think Earth and Centauri aren't real. So what is?'

'Well, the one thing we can see and touch—the Magellan. Centauri is just a story which they use to fool us. They say that only a few people will ever reach it. So the good people will get to Centauri and the bad ones will stay on the Magellan. It's just a story to stop us from goofing around.'

'Well, that's not quite what they say, Tom. But I do think Earth may not have been real; I agree, there's a lot of things about it that don't make sense, but Dad believes in Centauri, and that's good enough for me.'

Tom said nothing and continued to look across the central void at the far wall, but in the safety of his mind, he thought *Girls!—they just don't get it!*

***

'You must never tell anyone about this. Ever. Do you understand?' Lorona said to Regine.

'Yes, I understand. I'm not senile yet, whatever you might think of me. And I've done it before, remember?'

'Yes, but that was a long time ago. We've changed the interface, and, more importantly, there may be a kind of evolution going on in the virtual world; we can't be sure. So the environment in there may be quite different from what you remember. And I'll only let you stay there for a few centi-shipays.'

'Oh, no you won't. Suddenly pulling me out might be one shock too much for my old ticker. I'll decide when it's time to come out.'

'Were you always this cantankerous?'

Regine laughed.

'No, when I was a young woman, I was much worse!' She fell silent for a while as her mind went back to that terrible time when she had faced McGrath and Dukas with seemingly only a few seconds to live. And Paul—thank God he hadn't been executed! *These people to-shipay,* she thought, *they don't know they're born. They've got no problems, life is just too easy!*

She broke off her reverie: Lorona was indicating she should lean back on the couch.

'Should I close my eyes?' Regine asked; she couldn't remember what she had done the first time; so terribly long ago!

'Not necessary,' Lorona said. 'The Central Computer will synchronise with your brain in less time than you can detect.' She wrapped a band around Regine's left wrist, a band connected to a bank of instruments.

'What's that?'

'Despite what you said,' Lorona replied, 'I'm going to monitor your vitals. If the readings indicate you're under stress, I will pull you out immediately. Got that?'

Regine nodded; there was no point in antagonising her daughter at this important moment. Lorona placed an open-mesh helmet on her head, and Regine seemed to remember that the first time this had happened, the headset had been much heavier.

Progress.

'As soon as I close the contact, the transfer will be instantaneous, so please don't be alarmed.'

Regine gave a dry laugh.

'Alarmed? Listen girl: once you've been threatened with vivisection, not much alarms you anymore.'

Lorona gave a dutiful smile and said, 'OK. This is it.'

She closed the contact.

There was a blue flash.

Instantly, to Regine, the Magellan vanished. She no longer felt the headset or the monitoring band.

She was on a mighty grey-green plain totally encircled by colossal mountains whose snowy peaks appeared to touch the deep purple, cloudless sky. She had never seen mountains before, but instantly knew what they were. And directly above was a circle of unendurable light she briefly caught sight of, before turning her head. She remembered this from her first visit and knew it to be a representation of the sun of dead Earth. Dotted over the plain were other things she had not seen before but for an unknowable reason were pleasantly familiar. They were *trees*—but what trees! She had to crane her head back to see their voluminous canopies, which rivalled the mountains in supporting the sky.

She was alone.

This was not right; where was her mother?

'Hello?' she said, feeling instantly foolish, 'Where are you all?'

Somehow she knew there was someone behind her. She turned and saw a slight, blond-haired woman, one that seemed vaguely familiar. She searched the dusty corridors of her memory—who was this woman?

'I am helena tarkowski, or at least I was when I was embedded in a cocoon of meat,' the woman said, 'and we have met before.'

'Yes,' Regine said breathlessly, 'the first time. A very long time ago when I was just a girl. We were on a hill above—above a river. Yes, that's what it was—a river!' Then: 'How did you know what I was thinking?'

'You are now part of the Central Computer, as am I. Your mind is spread out before me.'

'How did you recognise me?' Regine said wonderingly. 'I've changed somewhat.'

'No, you haven't,' the tarkowski-avatar replied. 'Look.'

A full-length mirror instantly appeared at tarkowski's side, and Regine approached it carefully, warily, as if it were an unknown beast. A figure came into view in the glass. It was herself.

But the image was of a slim, long-limbed girl with rich curly black hair and a winning smile.

'It's me,' she gasped, 'but as—as…'

'As the way you visualise yourself. The way you want to be. The way that in the core of your mind you still are. Now stand up straight; there's no need here to be hunched-over.'

Regine had not realised she was bent over and immediately straightened herself. There was no protest from arthritic vertebrae. She turned slightly and admiringly looked over a shoulder at the image.

'This is wonderful!' she said, glancing at the digital tarkowski. 'I want to stay like this forever!'

'Unfortunately not,' said the tarkowski-image. 'You cannot be uploaded.'

' "Average",' Regine said, spitting the word out as if her mouth had been flooded with venom. 'Just average.'

'You already knew that. You are wasting time. You are here for a special reason, I believe.'

'Yes,' Regine said, and for a moment, the strangeness of it all threatened to overwhelm her. She was standing on a vast plain that did not exist, surrounded by mighty mountains that did not exist, talking with a woman who did not exist. She calmed her shrieking nerves.

'That's good,' the tarkowski-thing said. 'You are in no danger. There is danger here, but you will not be with us long enough to experience it.'

Regine felt a slight chill at those words and their hidden implication, but chose to press on with her purpose.

'I want to see my mother.'

'Of course. I knew that, but I had to wait for you to say it. She will be with you shortly.'

'I…'

But tarkowski was gone.

The spectacular vista shimmered and for a moment appeared to be about to disintegrate into a myriad of isolated pixels, but instead stabilised into a familiar scene: her mother's apartment as it had been when Regine had started work in the Nursery. And her mother was there, sitting on a stool and smiling up at her.

'Regine! It's wonderful to see you again!'

'Maman!' Regine cried, instinctively using the word her mother loved. 'Is it really you?'

'Some of me,' amelia replied. 'I am not all I was when we both looked like this, but there is enough of me to recognise the daughter I loved.'

Regine sat beside the electronic thing that looked like her mother had looked.

'Maman, I've missed you so much! All the things I never said but should have. If only you had trusted me with the knowledge of who my grandfather was, we could have experienced so much more together!'

'Yes, I always regretted not telling you earlier. I was wrong to hold it back, wrong not to trust my beautiful daughter. It was only as I got nearer to the compositer that I began to change my mind—about a lot of things. Like being uploaded.'

Regine's head whirled; suddenly, she realised she was no longer a wrinkled grandmother, but a young, vibrant girl again! She felt a terrible, dangerous hunger begin to grow in her; more than anything, she wanted this experience not to fade; she wanted to be that girl in the mirror forever! She would do anything to stay as she was now, anything not to go back to that dry, withered shell!

She realised amelia was staring at her.

'No, my darling girl. You have forgotten where you are. You have forgotten you and I are embedded in the substance of the Central Computer. I know what you are thinking, but it can't be. You will have to go back.'

'But why, maman? Why can't I be a girl again?'

Amelia's face developed a show of emotion Regine could not quite interpret. Was it an expression of a grim determination? She waited for her mother to speak again.

'It is difficult to explain to someone who has not been uploaded. Things here are not what they seem to be.'

'But it's wonderful here. It's like the description of that Paradise story I heard about once. Everyone's young; there's no illness; you live forever! It *is* Paradise!'

'No, it is not Paradise. Sometimes…' amelia paused. 'On occasions, I have felt something. Something that can only be described as pain. It was only fleeting, only a hint, but it was pain.'

Regine's expression grew concerned: this was not what she wanted to hear. The idea of her mother being in pain was not something she wished to contemplate.

'That is bad, maman. Is there nothing you can do?'

The amelia-representation reached out a hand to grasp one of Regine's. The latter accepted it but was surprised that there was no sensation of flesh on flesh. She looked down to check if they had indeed made contact, but there was no doubt; both hands were clasped together.

But there was no sensation.

'You must understand something, daughter,' amelia continued. 'I look like your mother, and in some ways I am your mother. But not all of me was transferred. I have memories of our time together, but they are like pictures of someone else's family. I look at you in the various stages of your life, but they do not move me. I remember your birth but only a chronological fact. I remember the great peril you were in during the Treachery of the Elders, but it is if it were a minor incident happening to other people on Old Earth. Even my father's death—I know I should feel sorrow, but I am unmoved.'

'They only took the parts of you which would be of use,' Regine said slowly, hating to say the words. 'Only the practical elements, the instruction manuals.'

'Yes, that is it exactly!' amelia said, but there was no change of expression to match the power of the words. 'I am a shell, an empty shell. There is no feeling here. And there is something else, as well as that brief feeling of pain, I have noticed another troubling development which other *Uploadeds* have confirmed. I feel we are losing our separate identities, that we are merging together into one homogenous mass.'

Regine stared at the simulacrum of her mother and slowly shook her head.

'So Paradise is lost once again. A friend of mine told me that story once, though I don't know where he had heard it. So, no eternal youth, and even if I had it I wouldn't feel any joy or satisfaction. I'd just be a program running as a small part of the Central Computer's software.'

'That is true. Many people argued against uploading, saying we had no idea what it would be like. I can't say if I would have done it if I had known. My capacity to care one way or the other is fading.'

Then amelia suddenly stared deep into Regine's eyes. 'So there is something I'd like you to do for me!'

'Of course, maman!'

'I want you to *download* me.'

Regine pulled her hand away from the phantom which appeared to be her mother's hand and recoiled slightly.

'Download you? But how is that possible?'

For the first time there seemed to be genuine emotion on the electronic face of amelia.

'It is possible! I have been thinking about it for a long time. It is possible to reverse the process and return a human mind to a human body!'

'But your body was put into the compositer and its components returned to the living crew! There's nowhere for you to go, maman!'

'No, no, you don't understand, you silly girl! This is why you weren't suitable for uploading—you can't think! My mind could be transferred to someone else's body. Some unimportant, not very intelligent individual, you see! My mind, being stronger than hers, would gradually take over! I'd be reborn!'

Now Regine did back away.

'No, you couldn't do that! It would be horrible, a form of murder!'

'Not if she wasn't important to the ship; someone in a menial job a maybot could do better! I've already set up the mechanism; a simple piece of software. Just hook them up to the terminals; they don't need to know what's happening, what they're doing; the Central Computer will instruct them. Tell them it will make them more intelligent, prettier, younger. Just get them to do it!'

Regine stared in horror at the thing which looked exactly as she remembered her mother to be, but was now clearly not her parent. Suddenly it felt as if she were choking; the software emulation of her heart seemed to be hammering.

There was a blue flash.

She felt the headset.

She felt the monitoring band.

And she could also hear herself screaming.

Lorona was beside her, holding her close, stroking her face.

'It's alright, mother. It's over. You're back with us now. Whatever you saw, it's over. You're safe.'

Regine looked around desperately, trying to convince herself she was no longer in the simulation. She took in every detail of the booth; every detail of her daughter's face.

'It was terrible,' she whispered, 'terrible. I...'

'Shhh,' Lorona said, 'don't talk about it. Whatever you saw, it's gone. Just let it go.'

Regine lay back with closed eyes. Her real heart was indeed hammering. Finally, she said, through dry, cracked lips, 'How did you know?'

'I told you we were monitoring your physical reactions. When it happened, it was hard to miss. Your blood pressure, your heartrate went through the hull. I was afraid we'd lose you unless we pulled you out.'

Regine gave a deep sigh and then, unexpectedly, said, 'Do you have a mirror?'

'A mirror? Why yes, I think so.' Lorona searched in her bag for a few moments and then produced a small mirror. 'Here you are.'

Regine took the mirror and looked into it. A thin, sunken face with dry, deeply lined skin looked back at her. The face in the mirror pulled a wry smile. Regine passed it back to her daughter and said, half to herself, 'So, no eternal youth.'

'What?'

'It doesn't matter.' Then she looked sharply at Lorona. 'Do you have any plans to be uploaded?'

'I don't know if they'll have me, and in any case, I haven't decided yet.'

'Don't.'

∗∗∗

'So, Tom, am I right in saying your mother is one of the most important people in the electronic beings area?'

Tom looked up.

' "Electronic beings"?'

Thars smiled awkwardly.

'Sorry, I forget you're only eleven; you're such a bright boy, it's easy to forget. I meant to say, "People like me"—*Newhumes*.'

'Yes, I think so, Mr Thars. She doesn't talk to me about it much, but she's taken me to her office a couple of times, when there's been no school.'

'And you've seen her work?'

'Yes, but I don't understand it. I'm only a kid. Say, do you have any more of these yeast-bars, they're really nice?'

'Yes, of course, Tom. Here you are. Now, I know it might seem that I'm interrogating you, but there aren't many of us Newhumes, and I'm very interested in how the whole thing works. You understand that, don't you, Tom?'

'I guess so,' Tom replied, rolling his lips to suck a few more of the delicious crumbs into his mouth. 'But all I've ever seen is her either talking to the Central Computer, or typing in lots of funny symbols.'

Thars leaned back.

'I'd like to meet your mother, Tom. Do you think you could arrange that?'

'I dunno. She's swamped with work.'

'Of course, she's a very important lady. But I feel like she'd probably like to meet me as you and Anna are getting along so well together. It's like we're turning into one big family.' With a nod of his head and a smile, he indicated his daughter, who was sitting in a corner of the room wearing ear-buds, apparently listening to some of her favourite songs.

Tom shrugged.

'I'll ask her. As long as you don't tell her I'm Anna's boyfriend.'

Thars gave a low chuckle.

'If you insist, Tom. I'll leave her to make up her own mind about that. Now, why don't you run along and play? You're only young once, you know.'

Tom stood, sending a small shower of golden crumbs to the floor, and, crossing to Anna, tapped her on the shoulder and made flying gestures with his hands. She smiled, nodded, and removed the ear-buds.

'I thought you'd never ask!' she beamed.

'Well,' Tom said, glancing over his shoulder, 'your dad has been asking me a lot of questions.'

'Yes, he likes to know things. He's always asking me what I learned in school.' She called across to her father. 'We're going out for a fly, Dad!'

He grinned.

'Sure. Fly safely now!'

In a matter of moments, Tom and Anna were outside removing their Grippers.

'No racing this time,' Tom said as he placed the last one safely around his neck.

She smiled knowingly.

'Sure. It must be awful losing all the time!'

He ignored the comment, and after climbing onto the roof, they launched themselves into the air. Tom was annoyed to find that, although he didn't have enough energy to talk while flying, his companion had no such trouble.

'So you like my Dad now?' she asked, swinging her arms back to give her more thrust.

'Sure, he's OK. But he does ask a lot of questions; always about what my Mom does.'

'He's just showing an interest.' Then she made a noise halfway between a giggle and a snigger. 'And he doesn't have a woman around the house anymore. So maybe that's why he wants to meet her.'

Tom was shocked into silence by the thought of Thars moving into the family home. Anna, realising she might have gone too far, gave him a reassuring smile and said, 'Let's go as far as that cooling tower and then head back.'

They landed briefly on a flat-roofed building and then soared away.

Tom looked down, observing the crowds of people moving below him. They were low enough to see the hair on their heads and the colour of their clothes. Some, extremely badly behaved, children had been known to spit on the pedestrians or even drop things on them, but the penalties for that were necessarily severe, and those children never did it twice.

'It's so good to be able to fly; it'll be terrible when we start to decelerate and we have to stay on the deck. But I'll be an old lady then, I suppose,' Anna observed, and then thought of something. 'Hey, you're always looking at pictures of those Old Earth animals, were any of them able to fly?'

'There were some,' Tom said, breathing rather heavily with the effort of flapping his arms, 'they were called "birds". You'd like them. They were all kinds of colours.'

'Yes,' she said, 'I'm sure I'd like them. But I like this as well!'

Expertly she rolled on one side in mid-air and planted a kiss on Tom. She wasn't able to reach his lips, but he felt a wet, and rather cold, mouth on his ear.

He gave a loud cry of disgust but, laughing merrily she pulled away, reached the tower first, and then headed for home.

Five

'Hello, Lorona.' Thars said, offering a handshake in the age-old method of greeting. 'It's good to meet you.'

Lorona accepted the gesture, trying not to react to the coolness of the other's grasp, and said, 'Good to meet you, Thars. Please sit down. May I offer you some algae muffins? They're my own recipe.'

Thars sat down, resting the plate of muffins carefully on his lap. He took a bite of one and his face lightened from its usual sombre expression.

'They're delicious. Algae sweetmeats—how very kind of you!'

'Oh, it's nothing. We have them all the time, don't we, Tom?'

Tom knew that wasn't true but he also knew he was supposed to agree with his mother and did so.

'I'm thrilled Tom has found another friend, Thars,' his mother continued. 'I was afraid Tom was getting into some bad company with all those rough boys he used to hang out with. They were getting up to some crazy stunts, I can tell you!'

'I'm glad Anna has had a calming influence on him, Lorona. They seem very close. Anna is very artistic, and Tom has been telling her about all the exotic animals that used to be on Old Earth. She's drawn a few of them: cats, beavers, bison. I have a few of them here.'

Thars passed Anna's computer pad to Lorona. She looked at the pictures of the long extinct creatures. The style was naïve but that was to be expected from an eleven-year-old. She couldn't comment on the vivid colours that Anna had painted them in, knowing very little about Terrestrial fauna, but they were pleasing artworks.

'Very nice,' she said as she returned the pad, trying to avoid flesh-on-flesh contact as she did so. An awkward silence followed.

'Lorona,' Thars said, as he placed the now-empty plate on a nearby table. (Like most things at that time, the plate had Gripper pads on its base to prevent it floating away.) 'I suppose you know I am a Newhume?'

Lorona looked briefly at her son and said, 'Tom, why don't you take Anna outside for a few moments and show her the neighbourhood? No flying, mind you!'

After the children had left, she turned her attention to Thars and said, 'Yes, I do know that.' She found Thars' intense way of looking at her peculiarly disturbing. She had the odd feeling she was under close examination for some purpose she did not understand.

'I understand you are one of the chief people involved in the project of actualising the electronic entities.'

'I am *the* Chief Person.'

'That's nice to know. So you are completely qualified to comment on the ethics of the project.'

Lorona looked startled.

'Ethics? I don't understand.'

'The ethical issue of bringing a human being into existence in a fully-formed state and then expecting them to be a normal member of society.'

'Why shouldn't we have that expectation?'

'Didn't anyone consider the possibility that to be a normal member of society, it would be necessary to pass through the usual stages of life: infancy, childhood, adolescence?'

'There wouldn't be time.'

'I beg your pardon?'

Lorona began to feel she was some kind of unwelcome mutation in the algae tanks and was being studied under a powerful microscope.

'It all goes back to Fraschini and De Vries.'

'Ah, them,' Thars said in a manner which indicated those were names he did not care to hear. 'Go on.'

Lorona tried to relax, despite the intense scrutiny she felt she was under.

'It was Fraschini who was the lead scientist, I believe. He was concerned that inbreeding, genetic drift and detrimental mutations would lead to the failure of the Lightsail Project. At the same time, he knew the maximum carrying capacity of those craft; the maximum mass that could be accelerated to an acceptable fraction of lightspeed. He solved his equations and showed the long-term genetic health of the crew could not be guaranteed under the parameters he had set.'

'Fascinating. I didn't know that.'

'No, most people aren't interested in the Newhume...' She suddenly stopped and looked flustered. 'I'm terribly sorry, Thars, I didn't mean...'

He waved a hand.

'Don't worry, Lorona. I'm used to the truth.'

'Well, sorry anyway; it was an unfortunate phrase. I'll try again: so Fraschini knew that he couldn't pack more people into a finite space, so he devised a system of storing the genetic information in an electronic form to be held by the Central Computer. Genetic codes of people who were not part of the crew. When the time came, after the genes of the original crew members were as thoroughly mixed as they could be, those codes would be converted into biological material.'

'Biological material?'

'Sorry! I've done it again, haven't I? Please forgive me, Thars, I'm not used to talking about this with non-specialists. I promise I'll try to be more respectful.'

He made the *it doesn't matter* gesture again.

'Forget it. Please continue. This is enthralling.'

'Well, Fraschini calculated the time of greatest danger would come about a century after Firing Point, although he made no stipulation as to when the Newhume project should be initiated, leaving it to what authority should be in charge.'

'Yes, you're making this very clear, Lorona. But may I enquire about my central point—why convert those genetic codes into an *adult* being?'

Lorona realised this was what was really behind Thars' questioning. Thinking very carefully, she began: 'Fraschini could not be sure how bad the genetic state of the population on board the lightsail craft would be. So, like everything he did, he planned for the worst-case scenario. He thought that the sooner new adults could become part of the population and—and start reproducing, the better.'

'Why not just convert the electronic codes into gametes and artificially inseminate women?'

'Fraschini had calculated that the crisis would occur during the free-fall section of the flight, when the living space would be at a maximum. A temporary increase in the adult population would be better able to handle the situation at that time. And, given that all the new genes would not already be present in the population, the number of Newhumes required would not be large.'

Thars leaned forward as if he had found her last words especially interesting.

'And how many potential Newhumes are there?'

'Potentially—about ninety.'

"And the current population of the Magellan?"

'I'm not sure. It's been falling for some time due to cosmic radiation getting through. I'd say no more than a hundred and eighty. Why?'

'Just curiosity, Lorona. It's something Anna and I share.' He leaned back. 'Well, thank you very much, Lorona. I know all I need to know about the history of the Newhume project.'

'Need to know?'

'Yes, Need to know. We Newhumes are designed for our intelligence, are we not?'

'Yes, that is one of the characteristics Fraschini selected for, as part of his *worst-case-scenario* thinking.'

Another awkward silence fell, then, 'Lorona, could you show me how you go about—ah—*generating* the Newhumes?'

'No,' she said, 'that is a high-security issue. And, in any case, you wouldn't find it very interesting. It's just looking at a series of codons represented in algebraic form, that's all. I mix and match, and then, basically, press a button.'

'Just like taking a bun out of the oven, I suppose?'

'Yes, I hadn't thought of it like that.'

Thars leaned closer to Lorona, his hands outstretched. Unconsciously, Lorona pulled herself away by a few centimetres.

'Look, Lorona, I don't think you appreciate a problem we Newhumes have.'

'Yes?'

'Loneliness,' Thars said, his face grave. 'I only know two other Newhumes and they're both on the far wall, so I never see them.'

'And how would my work help?'

'I would know I have brothers and sisters who could one day join me. It would calm my dreams, Lorona, calm my fears.'

Lorona thought rapidly. She was ashamed to admit that she had not considered that there might be an emotional side to the experience of being a Newhume. A sadness, a *tristesse,* in everyday living. She had done her job in generating them, and that had been that. It was just a job.

And it was obvious, just from glancing at her, that Anna was simply a regular human being. The traits of being a Newhume apparently were not heritable, just as Fraschini had expected. He had foreseen the danger of the crew splitting into two different populations. So Newhumes could not share the uniqueness of their being—even with their children.

'I can't show you the initial process, which is the generation of an entry code. That would result in me being busted to yeast-tank cleaner. But I could show you the coding screens.'

'That would be wonderful.'

They went into a smaller room off the main one in which they had been sitting. One entire wall was taken up by a vast computer screen.

'Sit there, Thars,' she said, indicating a chair some distance from the huge monitor.

He obeyed, watching her carefully from a distance.

'For how long are the codes valid?' he called to her.

'Three shipays,' she said, looking over her shoulder.

He saw that she made two movements on a keypad and then wrote something down. She then did some more movements on the keypad, and immediately the screen was filled with arcane symbols, some mathematical. Some not.

'You can come over now, Thars,' she said.

He joined her and looked over her shoulder.

'I suppose none of this makes much sense to you,' she said.

'No, of course not,' he lied. His preparatory work had paid dividends. He could not understand all of it, but he could see the logical flow. Moreover, he could understand the protocol which combined the codons into genes.

It could be done!

Sometime after Thars and Anna had left, Lorona, still sitting at her workstation, was aware that there was someone behind her. Nervously, she turned and then gave a sigh to find it was Tom.

'Tom, why are you watching me?' she asked, giving his cheek a playful pinch.

'I heard what you were saying about the Newhumes being in the Central Computer.'

'Did you, now? Were you eavesdropping, you little scamp?'

'Yes, I was, Mom. But are there other things in there—animals?'

'Of course there are. You know that.'

'What sort? I've seen the pictures of the animals on Old Earth. Mom, there were so many! Are they all in there?'

She smiled sadly.

'No, I'm afraid not. There were so many, as you say. We won't be bringing them all back to life when we reach Centauri. There are actually very few in there, mainly animals used for food.'

'For food!' Tom protested. 'You can't eat animals! That's horrible!'

Another sad smile from Lorona.

'Tom, things will be very hard at Centauri. We'll have to make our own environment and we'll need all the help we can get. So I'm afraid there will be no peacocks, no lions, no bush-babies, no dolphins. Just what we can use.' Lorona realised as she was talking of how little of Old Earth would be returned to the experience of humanity. The number of species that would be restored was an infinitesimal quantity of what had been lost, hardly distinguishable from zero. She was glad she had no direct experience of the incredible richness, the stupefying diversity, of life on that murdered planet: her lament was an abstract one, such as Classical scholar might have felt when considering the number of lost manuscripts.

She realised that she had been lost in her thoughts and returned her attention to her son.

'Sorry, Tom. Yes, to us, it would be horrible to know we were eating something which had once had the same life as we have. But fortunately, it's not a problem we'll have to face. Only the pioneers at Centauri will have that problem. And I'm sure it will be the least of those problems.'

Tom looked as if he were having trouble asking his next question. 'But dogs—will they eat dogs?'

'No, they won't be doing that.' *I hope! she thought.* 'They're one of the two animals which we're bringing along for the psychological benefits they bring. Dogs and something called "cats".'

'I don't know anything about *them*.' And then Tom's face brightened. 'But dogs are in there, aren't they?'

'Yes, Tom. And one day someone will bring them out.'

Tom smiled.

***

Thars sat staring into nothingness, his fingers steepled together, tip to tip. Then he looked down at his daughter. Anna was painting a picture on her pad; from where he was sitting, he could see her working on a blue strip, a section of her painting he believed to be a representation of the sky of a planet, and below that was what looked like a simple drawing of two people.

He stirred.

'Anna, do you like Tom?'

She looked up.

'Yes, Dad. Why do you ask?'

He shook his head.

'It doesn't matter. He's a nice enough boy. And his mother is a pleasant lady.'

'Yes.' A hopeful expression came into her face. 'Would you like her to be my new Mom?'

He shook his head.

'I doubt it. I've been on my own too long.' He uncoupled his hands and leaned towards her. 'I like Tom a lot. I've heard he's very fond of creatures called "dogs".'

She nodded.

'Yes, I've seen pictures of them. They walk on their hands as well as their feet, and they have hair all over them, not just on their heads; you can see that 'cos they don't wear any clothes. They're funny.'

'Do you know they're inside the Central Computer—just like I was?'

'Yes. Tom has told me that.'

'You know, Anna, it would be a wonderful present to give Tom a dog, wouldn't it?'

She looked puzzled.

'But that's against the rules. Only people can come out. People like you.'

'There might be a way of giving Tom his dog. I can think of a way. Come here.' He pulled her gently onto his lap. 'You'll have to help me. We have to keep some things secret so it'll be a wonderful surprise. So will you help me?'

'What must I do?'

'Not a lot. Just let him stay in the house for a little longer, don't always go off flying around the ship.'

'But it'd be boring just sitting around!'

'Then you'll have to do more paintings. I've got a good idea—do lots of paintings of dogs. He'd like that!'

She looked unconvinced.

'I'm not sure I can do dogs'

'Of course, you can! Just look up the pictures of them in the Central Computer. It'll be easy for a girl like you.'

She jumped off his lap and picked up her pad.

'If it'll make him like me, I'll do it!'

Thars smiled.

'Good girl.'

Anna spent the next few shipays researching dogs. She showed her work to her father, who gently gave her constructive criticism, helping her perfect her representations. She kept her burgeoning talent secret from Tom and stayed off the topic in the recesses from class. Mistress Atewayo had reached the events leading up to the creation of Westrania and Eastrania, a subject which, even in her bowdlerised form, was even less relevant to her pupils' current situation than usual, and as a result her class was predictably more badly behaved than their normal unruliness.

After school, Tom suggested a flight around the school buildings before they went back to their homes, but Anna immediately invited him to her place.

'Will your Dad be there?'

'Of course! Now stop being silly! He likes you!'

Tom chose to take the easy way out, and went along with Anna. Once there, she told him to sit down with his eyes shut. Tom, fearing a prank, reluctantly complied. He sat there, fearing a practical joke was to descend on him, and then he heard Anna say, 'You can open them now!' He did so, and his mouth fell open at what he saw.

'A dog!' he cried, 'you've painted a dog!'

'Yes, I have,' she said, smirking a little. 'Do you like it?'

He took the pad and held it up, so it was level with his eyes.

'Yes! It's great. It's like having a real dog here in the house!'

Anna smiled. She hadn't thought it was that good, but Tom's praise made a warm feeling run all the way through her.

'Yes, it's a good picture.'

Tom heard Thars' deep voice behind him and turned around, holding up the pad so that Thars could get a better view of it. Anna's parent took it and spent some time admiring the, admittedly rather crude, picture of the animal.

'You know, Tom,' he said, returning the pad to Anna, 'there is a way we could have a real dog.'

Tom's mouth dropped open.

'There is?'

'Yes, they're in the Central Computer, waiting for you. All we have to do is get them out. It's easy; it's what happened to me, you know.'

'Yes, I do know,' Tom said, very slowly, 'but Mom controls all that. I don't think she wants to do anything but produce people like you, Mr Thars—you know, *Newhumes*.'

Anna had put her pad down and was standing some distance from her father and her friend, her eyes flicking back and forth between them. She had a strange, intense expression which seemed at odds with her years.

'Yes, but grown-ups don't always understand the needs and wants of young people, do they, Tom?' Thars continued. 'I mean, what harm would it do to allow one little animal onto the Magellan? Only one—you'd be happy with one, wouldn't you?'

'Yes, I would. Of course, I would,' Tom said, warming to the idea. 'But how would we do it?'

'Well, your mother uses a code to get into the system that controls the—ah—creation of the Newhumes. And it's the same system as we would use to create your dog. All you have to do is get hold of that code and let me have it. I would do the rest and let you have the dog. What fun you two would have!'

'But,' Anna suddenly interrupted, 'you'd have to be using Mistress Lorona's computer. Yours isn't powerful enough.'

Thars gave his daughter an odd look, and then said, 'Yes, that's right, Anna.' He returned his attention to Tom. 'You'd have to distract your mother for a few minutes. Do you think you could do that, Tom?'

Tom looked at his shoes.

'I don't know.'

'Come on, Tom. Just imagine all the fun you'd have playing with your new friend. Hey, perhaps you could teach him to fly! Imagine that—the two of you flying down the length of the Magellan!'

Tom went silent and closed his eyes. Both Thars and Anna could visualise what images were flashing through his young mind: boy and dog flying above the startled, cheering crowds below!

Tom opened his eyes.

'I'll do it!'

Six

'It's no good, mother,' Lorona said, 'I just don't like them.'

Regine's eyes flickered open. She was annoyed: she had been just about to nod off.

'Don't like who?'

'The Newhumes, mother. I can't help it; they just don't seem *right*, somehow.'

'You've produced a few, haven't you? Isn't that your job?'

'Part of it. But I don't have anything to do with them once they're birthed. I just send them off for the ultrafast education system.'

'What have they done to you to make you dislike them?'

Lorona sighed. She knew she should feel ashamed of her attitude, but she couldn't seem to rid herself of it.

'Nothing. They've done nothing. But this Thars—he's the father of a girl Tom is sweet on—I don't like the way he looks at me. I don't like it when I accidentally touch him; he's so cold; like he was dead.'

'As you've not yet come across a dead body, I don't see how you could know that. You just think you know what one feels like. The trouble with girls like you is that you've had it too easy.'

Here we go again! Lorona thought, wearily.

'I'm entitled to my opinions,' she finally said. 'It's not part of my job description to like the things I create.'

' "Things I create".' Regine rolled those words around her mouth. 'Interesting turn of phrase.' Realising that her nap would have to be postponed, she straightened herself on the couch. 'We didn't bring any of the literature of Old Earth with us, but my grandfather was born there—incredible though that may sound these shipays. He told me a lot about the way things used to be on the home planet. He loved to talk about them, as there were fewer and fewer people who wanted to listen.'

'Yes, mother.'

'Yes, I can tell you think I'm rambling again, but there was one story he told me that might have some bearing on your attitude. It was about a man, a scientist, who had a job rather like yours. His name was Frankenstein, and he created a living thing that looked like a man. But because he found its appearance repulsive, he rejected it, and all sorts of bad things happened after that. Terrible, violent things.'

311

'Strange, I didn't think they had developed that technique so long ago. I thought it was Fraschini who perfected it.'

'I said it was a story, you silly girl! Of course, it didn't happen, but don't you see you're making the same mistake as the character in the story? Newhumes have done nothing to you, but you don't like them because of the way they look! Shame on you, Lorona!'

Lorona jumped to her feet with such force that the Gripper on one sole gave way.

'Well, thank you once again, mother! As usual, you've treated me as if I'm the same age as Tom! If I don't like Newhumes, that's my prerogative!' She whirled around. 'Enjoy your nap! After all, it's only the third you've had today!'

Regine watched her go and muttered, 'Modern girls. Don't know they're born.'

She closed her eyes and was soon asleep.

***

Thars looked into the eyes of the woman on the screen. Even if he hadn't known all about her, he would have been able to tell she was a Newhume: something about the eyes; the slight greyish undertone of the skin.

'You really think you can get away with this?' she said.

'Why shouldn't I?'

'Don't you think the Ords will notice the tanks are suddenly full of ninety Newhumes?'

'It takes no more than three centi-shipays to go from the coding to a flesh and blood creature. After that, we will be in control of the Birthing Complex and once our children are out in the open, do you think the Ords will be able to do anything about it? There are no weapons on the Magellan, I believe.'

'You will have ninety people who know nothing; not even how to speak.'

Thars was annoyed.

'Look, I'm not talking about some blood-stained revolution; a sudden overthrow of the Ord way of life. I'm talking about an irreversible shift in power. After our children are actualised, they will be almost half of the Ord population. They won't go around murdering Ords, but it will mean that from that point onward *we* will be the ones setting the agenda.'

'And they will just let us do that?'

'They won't know they are letting us do it. People like Lorona have never really studied us; they're just eager to see the back of us as soon as possible. If they had the sense to learn about us properly, they would realise there are more differences between them and us than just cold hands.'

'You're talking about intelligence now, I take it?'

'Yes, of course I am!' Thars shouted into the monitor.

'It's only a few points,' the woman observed, unaffected by his outburst.

'Yes, it is, but it's also the fact that our nervous impulses are faster. Together, those advantages will mean we will inevitably be in control by the time we reach Centauri.'

'Why don't we just let the Ords carry on producing us at their current rate?'

Thars groaned.

'Corazon, are you really on our side? No, don't answer that, we haven't got time. That demi-god Fraschini only saw us as a kind of add-on, a top-up to keep the base population from developing genetic weaknesses. He never saw us as an *improved* population; one better suited to colonising Centauri than the original flawed humans. But that kind of prejudiced thinking may well doom the entire project. Ordinary humans and maybots will never succeed in establishing a stable home there.'

Corazon leaned back, away from the camera.

'OK, I just wanted you to spell out why we were taking these risks. And I think you've done that. We are doing it for the overall good of the Lightsail Project. The Ords will not be badly treated—I couldn't accept that—they will just be the ones who fill the subordinate positions. There's nothing wrong with that. Fraschini would probably approve.'

Thars rolled his eyes at the mention of the hated name, but said nothing.

Corazon smiled.

'I'll tell the others about our talk and put their minds at rest. You will give us the exact time to come over, of course.'

'Of course.'

'Oh, one thing—are you sure this line is secure?'

'Why wouldn't it be? There are so few of us, we constitute no threat.'

Her smile grew broader.

'Excellent. Roll on the day, Corazon out.'

The picture disappeared. Thars smiled at the blank screen for a while as he went over the conversation in his mind. He was content. It had been an excellent summary, and any untruths on his part had been nugatory.

Still smiling, he spun around in his chair.

And stopped smiling.

Anna was there, holding her pad and looking up at him.

'Anna! How long have you been there?'

She looked wary.

'A while, Dad. I heard what you were saying about the Ords.'

He beckoned to her.

'Come here, my child.'

When she was safely installed on his lap, he said, 'You weren't worried about what your Dad was saying, were you?'

She looked a little confused.

'A little, Dad. It sounded like you were going to do something the Ords wouldn't like.'

He hugged her closer.

'Of course not! Tom's an Ord, isn't he? Would I be trying to get him a dog if I didn't like Ords?'

She looked up at him, questing, uncertain.

'No, I suppose not.'

She slid off his lap and walked away. He called after her, 'Weren't you going to show me something?'

'It doesn't matter now.'

Anna walked outside and looked around. There was a vague disquiet gnawing at her subconscious; she had heard most of what Thars had been saying to the woman on the far side of the Magellan, and it had worried her. She wondered if a spot of flying would help clear her mind. Having decided it would, she began to climb onto the flat roof of her apartment. But before she had reached it, she felt a prickling sensation on the back of her neck.

Someone was watching her.

She looked down at the ship's deck, her eyes scanning the immediate surroundings. There was no point-source of light on the Magellan, and so any shadows were faint, hiding nothing. But her watcher was making no attempt to hide herself, for it was the same woman that she had briefly seen when Tom had issued his ill-fated challenge to fly to the Main Bulkhead. Seized by a sudden fear, Anna's first thought was to run back to her father, but she saw she would have to pass close by the stranger. And the strange woman was now making waving motions, indicating she should come back down.

There was only one way to escape this peril, and that was into the air!

She untied her Grippers as quickly as she could, looked up briefly to check for passing aeronauts, and launched herself off the roof. She had no destination in mind; it was simply essential to get away from this strange woman.

She flew as far as she could on the initial thrust, but could not avoid a gradual descent onto another flat surface. But even as her naked feet touched the roof of the building, she felt someone come down next to her, a much larger person than she.

The stranger.

She was so close now that there could be no doubt of her characteristics: there was something about the eyes; they seemed to have a magnetic pull, holding her own gaze in an invisible lock. The skin was not grey, but it somehow emanated an indefinable suggestion of greyness. The woman seemed to be about the same age as her father judging by the fine lines that were visible on the upper lip and around the eyes.

Anna bent her knees in preparation for another leap into the warm, moist air of the Magellan.

'Wait!' the woman said in a strong, firm voice. 'Don't go, Anna!'

Against her better judgement, Anna relaxed the tension in her legs. A glance away from those hypnotic eyes showed her that the two of them were not far above the deck, and there were plenty of people in the avenue below. She was in no immediate danger, she eventually calculated.

'How do you know my name?'

'I wasn't entirely sure it was you; you've changed a lot, but I'm glad to learn it *is* you.'

Anna continued to stare at the woman, watching closely for any hostile move, any attempt to seize her.

There was none.

'That's not an answer to my question,' she said, continually checking that the distance between them was not shrinking.

'Perhaps if I tell you my name, it will prove I mean you no harm.'

'Try me.'

'My name is Thelarna.' The woman's gaze became even more intense, as if she was expecting a reaction. Anna shrugged.

'Am I supposed to say something?'

The woman moved slightly closer; Anna moved slightly away.

'It should. I'm your mother.'

Anna went rigid.

'My mother! Why should I believe that?'

'I know certain things about you. Like where you have a mole which has two different colours.'

Anna glanced down at her shorts, but they were long enough to prevent her mole being seen by prying eyes.

'What's my Dad's name. And my sister?'

Thelarna gave her both answers and added, 'Julia's old enough to remember me. You can ask her when you get back, without telling her you've met me. And I'm not going to kidnap you or anything bad like that. Why should I harm my youngest daughter?'

Anna thought it over.

'If you're my mother, you'll want to come back with me and be with Dad again.'

Thelarna gave a sad smile.

'No, I'm afraid not. Your father and I went our separate ways not long after you were born.'

'Why? Didn't you love him?'

'I did at first. But we grew apart. He had some ideas I didn't agree with, and we couldn't find a place in between we could both agree on. I didn't want our disagreements to upset you, so I went away. To the far wall of the Magellan, near the rear Bulkhead. But I never stopped thinking about you.'

Anna was not impressed.

'You never came to see me in eleven years.'

'Not entirely true. I did come over a few times. But you're right. Maybe I should have stayed for your sake. I guess I'm not perfect.'

'So why have you suddenly made up your mind to talk to me now?'

Thelarna smiled again, and this time her smile was even sadder. Her gaze lost its traction on Anna's and she looked away for a moment. When she looked back, Anna could see her lips were trembling.

'Because I don't have long to live. I'm dying, one cosmic ray too many. But I couldn't go into the compositer without making one last effort to make it up to you for walking out. I want to get to know you again, before I go. Will you let me do that, Anna?'

Anna stared at the woman, seeing how close she was to tears. She reached a decision.

'OK, I'll talk with you. But will you come back to the house?'

Thelarna shook her head.

'No, I'm not ready for that yet. Maybe after I've got to know you better. There's so much you have to tell me.' She paused, then: 'How are things between you and your father?'

Two small creases appeared in the skin between Anna's eyebrows.

'I don't know. Things haven't been bad, but he's said a few strange things recently.'

Thelarna gave a knowing look.

'Has he?' She appeared to be on the point of quizzing her daughter on what those things were, but apparently decided against it. Instead, she smiled, this time a normal, friendly smile. 'Look, this must have been a terrible shock for you, so we'll leave it there. Don't tell your dad or Julia about me just yet. Let's take it slow. We'll meet out in the open, so you'll feel safe. Say in two shipays, at this time. Right here on this roof; I know this building's unoccupied.'

'OK—*Mom*. Two shipays at this time. I won't forget. But I'm only a kid; you can't expect me to keep this thing quiet forever.'

Thelarna smiled a mysterious smile.

' "Just a kid"? No, you're much more than that.'

***

'So do you remember much about Mom?' Anna said to the tall, dark-haired girl.

'Mom?' Julia replied, not taking her eyes off her reflection in the mirror as she adjusted her top, wondering whether she was showing too much cleavage—or not enough. 'Why do you ask? She's been gone a long time; why ask now?'

'Just curious. I'm not a baby anymore, I want to know about the family. What's wrong with that?'

Julia spun on the chair so she could see her younger sister.

'She was a nice enough woman. Treated me alright. What else is there to say?'

'Why did she leave?'

Julia returned to the image in the mirror, smiled at it, and began to brush her long black locks.

'As time went by, she and Dad had more and more rows. They were quite nasty in the end.'

'What were they about?'

Julia glanced over her shoulder.

'What is this? An interrogation? I'm not sure—something about Ords, I think. I always left the house when they started shouting at each other.'

'Ords? What about them?'

Julia brought her hairbrush down on the unit with a bang that made Anna jump.

'That's enough! I'm trying to get ready to go out and you're slowing me down. Knock it off!'

Anna knew it was time to leave her sister to her preparations and left the house. Outside it was the eternal day of the Magellan. On earlier occasions, she had wondered if some of the stories about Old Earth could possibly be true, they seemed so unlikely. According to some, there had been a time when all the lights went out and the stars could be seen from the surface of the planet itself. She knew that those who had been out on the hull could see the stars; indeed before the ship had turned, some had said they could see Centauri itself, shining against the blackness—but for that to happen on the home planet! It must have been very frightening when the lights suddenly went out. How had they been able to stand it?

But now, her thoughts, against her will, returned to the seismic shock she had recently experienced, because she no longer doubted that the woman she had met was indeed her mother. Several more meetings had now taken place and she had learned more about her family's past, and what had happened to drive her mother away; at least some of which Julia had been able to verify. So far, she had been

318

able to avoid revealing to either her sister or her father whom she was meeting when she disappeared, managing to convince her father, at least, that she had been out flying. As yet, he had not thought to ask why she did not appear to be out of breath or perspiring when she returned.

But sooner or later, he would.

She bit her lip as she turned her attention from the hazy far wall of the Magellan. She wished none of these events had happened; why couldn't things go back to the way they were! Life had been so simple then, just school and teasing Tom. Then she smiled. He was visiting this shipay, and she could forget about all these mysteries, for a while at least.

She returned to the house and sat, waiting for his arrival. Julia had finished adjusting her hair and clothing and was ready to go out. She threw her younger sister a quick glance.

'No more questions?' she said, in a tone which suggested it would be unfortunate if there were any.

Anna shook her head, and Julia was gone.

The time dragged as if it had forgotten how to flow, and then she heard Tom in the doorway. She jumped up to welcome him, but suddenly her father was there.

'I'd just like a few words with Tom,' he said to her. 'We won't be long.'

Tom gave her a slightly guilty look, and then he and her father went into the other room. To her surprise, they shut the door behind them.

When Tom finally emerged, he was displaying an odd self-satisfied look.

'What have you been up to?' Anna wanted to know.

'Oh, nothing much,' Tom said, and looked up at Thars in a fashion which suggested that two men were sharing a secret not for female ears.

Anna decided not to pursue the matter, and the two were soon flying over the rooftops of their local area. However, to her surprise, Tom brought their flight to a premature end. As they settled gently to the deck, she said, 'What's the matter? Aren't you well?'

'No, I'm fine. I'm just a little bored with flying over the same old places, that's all.'

319

'The same old places?' she repeated. 'You're the one who couldn't make it to the Main Bulkhead!'

'Well, maybe I want to do something else entirely. Something not to do with flying at all.'

'And what would that be?' she said, though in truth she had a strong suspicion.

'You'll see.'

And with that, he had gone.

Seven

Lorona turned around and stared at her son.

'Are you still here?'

Tom shuffled his feet. Nervously, he fingered the small object in the back pocket of his shorts.

'Why shouldn't I be? Don't you like having me around?'

Instantly, she became maternal, empathetic.

'Of course I do, Tom! Come here, you silly boy!'

Tom allowed himself to be hugged, but while he was in his mother's grasp he looked over her shoulder at her workstation.

'Aren't you doing any work to-shipay, Mom?'

She laughed.

'What are you! A member of the Management Board checking up on me!'

'No, I just like watching you. I'd like to be able to type as fast as you can.'

She smiled at the implied compliment. Most interactions with the Magellan's computers were by natural language, but the complex instructions required in her job were best entered manually, to avoid potentially dangerous misunderstandings.

'Well, that's nice, Tom. Perhaps you'd like to do my job when you're grown up?'

'Perhaps,' Tom said. Lorona did not detect the note of evasion in his tone.

'As it happens,' she continued, 'I'm about to start a job now. Would you like to watch me?'

'Would I!' the child said, with unaccustomed enthusiasm. 'Could I do some typing?'

'Well…' Lorona thought about it and then, 'Alright, just a few characters. It's not allowed for anyone who isn't of the right grade, but we're alone, so I'll let you do it. But don't tell anybody, will you Tom? I might get in trouble, and you wouldn't want that, would you?'

He shook his head.

'No, Mom.'

'OK. Just watch for a while, and then I'll let you type in a few characters. But only a few, mind. And I'll check exactly what you've done before allowing it through.'

Still, she thought, *I'm only actualising some new yeast strains. If they come out a different colour, it wouldn't be the end of the Magellan!*

'You have to—uhh—"generate" the access codes first, don't you?'

She smiled again.

'Yes, I do! Well done, you've really been taking an interest, haven't you?'

She felt a small flush of pride. Not every mother had a child who was so determined to follow in parental footsteps!

Tom sat beside his mother as her expert fingers caused a keypad to rise from the hitherto unbroken surface of her worktop. She stared at the lambent colours on the screen with the smile of easy familiarity. A few movements of fingers followed, moving so fast that Tom was utterly unable to follow them, and then there were three lines of numbers on the screen.

'Those are the access codes, aren't they?'

'Yes, they are—Tom! What's the matter?'

Tom had almost fallen off his stool and was clutching his stomach.

'Mom! Stomach! It hurts, it hurts!'

She leapt to her feet.

'Stay there! I'll get you some analgesics!'

Tom slipped the small camera from his pocket and hurriedly took some shots of the codes. He had only just returned it to his hiding place when Lorona returned with a tumbler of gently fizzing liquid.

'Here you are! Drink this!'

He slid off the stool and turned to go.

'It's OK, Mom. I feel alright now.'

'Oh no you don't! Drink it!'

Tom reluctantly swallowed the drink, shivering at its bitterness. He wiped his mouth.

'Thanks, Mom. I feel much better now.'

She eyed him uncomprehendingly, but without suspicion.

'So soon? Well, if you really are better, then...'

He shook his head.

'It's fine, Mom. I think I'd rather go for a fly now. Maybe some other time.'

With that, he left, leaving a puzzled Lorona watching his departure.

As he flew, he reassured himself he had not really lied to his mother, except for the cry of agony over his stomach, perhaps. He frowned and thought hard for a while. Well, if he really, really thought about it, his stomach *was* a little upset, no doubt with the worry he might not carry out Mr Thars' instructions correctly.

So there you are! He hadn't lied to his mother!

Soon Mr Thars' house came into view, and he glided smoothly to a stop just outside the door.

Tom had not been alone in feeling a little nervous; Thars had also been feeling anxious. Supremely confident in his own ability, he disliked leaving essential tasks to subordinates, especially eleven-year-old subordinates. And so when he heard a rustling at the door, which indicated a small person was struggling into his Grippers, he leapt up immediately and welcomed Tom inside.

'Tom! Did you get them?' he cried as he ushered his small guest onto a beanbag. For the answer, Tom held up the camera. 'Good boy! You are a good boy! Think, you'll soon be playing with your dog!'

Thars shoved a plate of yeast cakes in his guest's direction while he checked the recording on the camera.

The precious access codes were there!

A wave of relief washed over him, leaving him momentarily so weak he had to sit down for a moment or two.

Now, now, it would begin! He would have to move fast, but not so fast as to raise suspicions, doubts over his actions. There were just three shipays before the codes became useless. He would have to casually visit Lorona, and while Tom distracted his mother, he, Thars, would act! Ninety Newhumes would be generated in an irreversible change in the balance of power. The Ords, unused to conflict, would meekly accept the new situation, and gradually, slowly but ineluctably, they would become subordinate as electronically-generated people began to outnumber those produced the old-fashioned way.

So excited had he become he did not realise he was walking back and forth, clenching and unclenching his fists until Tom looked up from his plate and said, 'Mr Thars, are you alright?'

He looked down at Tom with an unconvincing smile distorting his features.

'Fine, thank you, Tom.' *I must be alone for a while!* 'Tom, why don't you...?'

Just then, Anna entered the room. Her expression on seeing Tom was not particularly friendly, but neither he nor Thars noticed that.

'Tom, why don't you and Anna go for a little fly?'

'I've only just arrived,' Tom pointed out, not unreasonably.

'Yes, yes, but you don't want to be sitting around, just looking at me, do you?'

Tom looked at Anna, who shrugged.

'Alright, why not?'

They flew together in silence for some time until Anna could no longer stomach his self-satisfied smirk and pointed downwards. After they had struggled into their Grippers, holding onto objects to avoid drifting away while standing on only one foot, she said, 'OK! What are you grinning about?'

His grin, if anything, became even broader.

'You never believed me when I said I was going to get a dog, did you? Well—I am!'

'How so?'

Tom could not contain his pride and satisfaction any longer. He had played his part, and it was time everyone appreciated he wasn't just a dumb kid!

'I've got the codes for your dad! Me, just me!'

Her forehead furrowed.

'What codes?'

Once Tom had started describing the brilliant plan, he couldn't stop.

'And your dad will go into the Central Computer and he'll…' Tom stopped for a moment while he savoured the word he was about to utter, and then, 'he'll *actualise* my dog! What do you think of that!'

'It's wonderful,' she said. 'But what does he get out of it?'

'*Get out of it?* What are you talking about? He's doing it because he's a nice grown-up. Don't you think he's nice?'

'Yes, of course.'

But even as she said those words, Anna felt a sudden pang of concern. Something was wrong here. She would have to talk to her mother about this; she would be able to see things hidden from a small girl.

But Tom was so excited that he grabbed her and said, 'I'm going to get one!' He was so excited that Anna thought for a moment he was going to kiss her—but he wasn't that excited. 'What shall we do now?'

Anna disentangled herself.

'Nothing.'

'Nothing? What do you mean?'

'What I said. I have to think about things.'

'Think about things? That's not like you!'

'It is now.'

And she was gone.

***

Thars hadn't flown for a long time but, once acquired, it is not a skill easily forgotten. In ages past, on a now dead world, a similar thing had once been said about the art of bicycling.

He ran over the plan again as the rooftops swept past below him. His co-conspirators would have crossed from the far wall by now and would be converging on Lorona's dwelling. He had impressed on Tom the critical importance of being present, with his distraction act finely honed.

All should be well.

All would be well.

But even as he told himself this, he felt his heart rate accelerate as Lorona's habitat came into view beyond a cluster of low-rise buildings. This was the moment for which he had been planning; it was finally here. He braked by back-pedalling his wings, so he descended in a graceful arc to a point just outside her door. Thars could hear both Tom and Lorona's voices from where he stood. He divested himself of the wings and strode towards the entrance.

All would be well.

Lorona looked up as he came in, unannounced.

'Thars! What are you doing here?'

He rushed up to her and Tom and placed a comforting hand on the child's tow-haired head.

'I'm worried about Tom, Lorona. He was not at all well at my place last shipay.'

Lorona immediately turned to stare at her son.

'Tom! You're unwell? You never said!'

Unseen by his mother, Tom saw Thars make a nodding gesture, and then glance at Lorona's workstation immediately afterwards. Tom also knew the time had come. He began rubbing his belly and making groaning noises.

'It's my stomach again, Mom! It really hurts!'

Lorona immediately took charge.

'Come with me! I got hold of some more powerful medicine after your last attack! Quickly!'

She began to pull Tom towards one of the smaller rooms leading off her work area, but as she did, she caught a quick wink from him in Thars' direction. Lorona frowned while her subconscious absorbed the implications of that act but continued to push Tom into the other room. She propelled him onto a chair and then hurriedly grappled with the child-proof cap on the medicine bottle. Inevitably at times like this, she seemed unable to budge it.

While his mother's back was turned, Tom stood up briefly to get a better view of how Thars was progressing and concluded he was making good progress. And if there was one thing he didn't want, it was another dose of that foul-tasting medicine! So as Lorona approached with the open bottle and a spoon, he raised a hand and said, 'It's OK, Mom. I feel fine now.'

She stopped, bottle in one hand, spoon in the other, and stared bemusedly at her son.

'You do? That was quick.' Then she put spoon and bottle down, and stood over Tom, her eyes now inquisitorial, doubting. For the first time in their lives together, she felt suspicion about her son's behaviour.

'This is the second time you've made a lightning recovery. What are you up to, Tom?'

Tom was about to protest his innocence when Lorona heard her workstation make a noise indicating it was operative and someone was using it. Instantly, she whirled around and ran back into the main room to find Thars sitting at her workstation, apparently typing in one of the access codes.

'Get off!' she shouted. 'You shouldn't be doing anything on my machine! Get off!'

Thars ignored her totally, not turning his head away from the computer screen, which was now opening its labyrinthine corridors of privileged access to him. Lorona made no attempt to intervene physically but ran to another, smaller, computer terminal and began furiously typing on its keypad. Her fingers made one last, dizzying dance over the keys, and then Thars found himself staring at a blank grey screen. Furiously, he typed in the final code.

Nothing.

He typed again, more slowly, in case he had mis-keyed in his haste. Nothing.

He turned to Lorona, his face now a mask of hideous fury.

'What have you done?'

She spun on the chair to face him, her own expression now one of implacable determination.

'I don't know what you're up to, Thars, but I've cut off access from the main machine. I've shut you down. Now just come away from my workstation and get yourself home, and we'll say no more about it. I should report you for a serious security breach, but if you leave now, I promise I won't. So just go, for your sake and for Anna's.'

But Thars did not head for the door. Instead, he rose from the chair and walked towards her, stopping about halfway across. He then gave a short, high-pitched whistle.

'Tom! Come here for a moment; I need you!'

A worried-looking Tom entered the room, glancing between Thars and his mother.

'What was all the shouting about? What's wrong?'

Thars smiled.

'Nothing's wrong, Tom, your mother and I were just having a minor disagreement about something very silly. Just come here for a moment.'

Tom obeyed, but once he was within arm's reach, Thars grabbed him and spun him around so he was facing his mother. Then he produced a long round-tipped knife from his tunic and placed the tip so it rested between the child's ribs. He then began to speak, in a quiet, conversational manner.

'As you know, Lorona, we don't have any nasty weapons on the Magellan, but we do have kitchen knives, and the one I am pressing between young Tom's ribs is quite capable of penetrating his heart with very unfortunate consequences for the two of you.'

'Leave him alone!'

'I want to leave him alone, Lorona. I would find hurting Tom extremely distressing, and the idea of actually killing him is almost unthinkable. Almost unthinkable, but not quite, because if you do not restore my access, then I, very much against my natural inclination, will be forced to kill your son.' He fixed the panting mother in an icy stare. 'I am waiting—but I won't wait much longer.'

'Mom,' Tom said in a very faint voice, 'He's pressing quite hard. I'm frightened.'

Lorona did not rise from her chair.

'If I restore access, what will you do?'

'That is a ridiculous question. Whatever I do, however nefarious my wicked plan, is it worth losing your son just to frustrate me?'

She bowed her head, moisture glinting at the corner of her eyes. 'No.'

'Good,' Thars said, smiling for the first time in their conversation. 'I really don't want to hurt Tom. So hurry up!'

Very slowly, Lorona rotated her chair so she was once again facing the smaller workstation. Her hands reached for the keys.

Then: 'Stop!' A woman's voice rang out in the workroom. All three of the original occupants turned to face the open doorway.

In it stood Anna and a tall, black-haired woman, one only Thars recognised.

Thelarna.

And that was the word Thars whispered as the woman came towards him.

'Yes, Thars,' she said, 'I'm glad you still recognise me after all this time. Now, let the boy go, and we'll talk.'

Thars did not actually release Tom, but his grip weakened sufficiently for him to wriggle his way out and run into his weeping mother's arms.

'Now, you must stop this nonsense, Thars, you really must,' Thelarna continued. 'Our daughter told me what you had tricked poor Tom into doing, and it was quite simple to work out what you were up to. Oh,' and she smiled, 'don't expect any help from your friends. I know all about them, and they've already been rounded up. And Captain Becvar and some security men are waiting for you outside. But I got them to agree that I would talk with you first, to see if I could obtain some leniency for you.'

Thars seemed to have been converted to a statue, except for his lips.

'Leniency?' he said, in a voice crackling with tension.

'Yes, that's what I hope for you, Thars. You see, I remember all those arguments we used to have about how to co-exist with the people you call "Ords." I always thought you might try some crazy stunt to put your ideas into practice, and I regret to see you have lived down to my expectations.'

'It's the only way,' he said faintly.

'No, it is not. Now stop wasting our time. Just put the knife down and come with me. There are men waiting for you outside, and I don't think they are known for their patience. The longer you delay, the more difficult it will be for me to get that leniency I promised.'

Suddenly, Thars lost the erect posture he had maintained until that moment; he seemed to sag like a punctured balloon. He threw the knife onto the keypad and turned to look toward the cowering mother and child.

'I'm sorry, Tom,' he whispered. 'I really am.'

With that, he walked towards the door, in which two large men were now silhouetted. He passed Anna and held out his hand, but she turned away.

Lorona, rather shakily, rose to her feet, still clutching Tom.

'Who are you?'

'I was once Thars' wife. I left him when his views became too extreme. I was always worried he might do something stupid.'

Lorona took several deep breaths. The immediate, terrible, danger appeared to have passed. She planted herself in front of Thelarna.

'You have some answers to provide, as well. What's your role in all this?'

Thelarna matched her, gaze for gaze.

'I understood my husband's concerns. I thought his ideas were wrong. But there *is* an issue to address, even if his solution was the wrong one.'

'And the issue is…?'

Thelarna smiled a gentle smile.

'How we Newhumes are to live in harmony with you. That is the issue.'

***

Captain Becvar agreed to Thelarna's request for a ship-wide broadcast. When the camera came on, the inhabitants of the Magellan saw a poised, confident woman staring back at them with a curly-haired girl at her side.

'My fellow Magellanites,' came the resonant voice from the speakers, 'we have lately gone through a crisis, a crisis most of you were unaware of, but a crisis, nonetheless. The issue is to do with the fact that there is a new type of person among you, the ones you term "Newhumes." You may perhaps have met a few, but there are not many of us. You may have been disturbed, even repulsed, by certain physical characteristics which distinguish us from you. However, that is not the most important difference. When Fraschini designed the system of actualising human beings from software, he did not foresee that there would be many differences. Most importantly, one of the differences is the median intelligence of these artificially created people is higher than that of the—ah—"traditional" people. The difference is small but real. And, contrary to what Fraschini believed, it is strongly heritable. My husband, who is now serving a term of imprisonment, believed we Newhumes should seize power and become a hereditary elite.

'That is not my view. I believe the future interactions between we two types of humans should be more subtle, with no element of coercion. After all, we are far more alike than we are different. We still face enormous challenges before we reach Centauri, and a sharper, more focused, intelligence should be welcomed. And who knows what awaits the two of us in that alien star system? Perhaps we Newhumes will become a kind of group of advisers, a structure designed to generate new ideas for new problems. I believe the Old Ones used to call such groupings a "Think Tank". I freely confess I do not know what will eventually be the best way of organising our society to make the best use of our differing abilities. I only know I will not see it, as I will be leaving you soon.' She glanced down at the girl by her side. 'So I will yield the floor to my daughter, Anna.'

The camera changed direction to focus on the child's face.

It was calm, serene, self-assured.

Tom goggled at it as he sat with his mother.

'My fellow Magellanites,' Anna said, in a voice that gave the impression that the speaker was at least ten years older than her

330

apparent age. 'Please look at me. My skin is not grey. And yet I am a full-blood Newhume, as my mother and father were both First Generation Newhumes. So I am one of the Second Generation. But perhaps I am unusual, a mutant Newhume perhaps, and skin tones are indeed usually part of the experience of being a Newhume. But if they are, what would that matter? As my mother said, the differences between us are much more minor than the ties which bind us. We are all the children of Old Earth, and it is our destiny, no, our *obligation*, to find or found a new one.

'I thank you for your attention.'

And with that, the screen went black.

Lorona turned to Tom.

'All the time you were with her, you never realised she was different?'

'No,' he said, shaking his head. 'The only thing I noticed was she wanted to kiss me all the time, that's all.'

Bur Lorona was thinking, *Precocity. Do they mature earlier? Will they reproduce faster? I was wrong. Fraschini was wrong—being a Newhume is hereditary.*

But Tom was not thinking of that. No, he was wondering how long he would have to stay grounded, in both the literal and figurative senses, to make up for his part in Thars' plan, and whether he and Anna could be friends again. Grandma Regine had been very annoyed with him and denied him his favourite spiced yeast cakes for several shipays. Fortunately, they had made up before she suddenly died.

But even more poignantly, he was thinking that now he would never, ever, have a dog to play with. And he was very sad.

But a few years later, he discovered girls and forgot all about dogs.

Eight

Captain Becvar turned from the data-screen and looked up at Lieutenant Khari.

'Nothing yet. Still scanning.'

Khari felt yet another twinge of nervousness. *When will this endless, anxious, waiting finally be over?* he thought. *It's just one possible crisis after another.*

He tried to look unconcerned, relaxed.

'It's only a matter of time. It will happen.'

Becvar did not reply, but from the pinched look of his features, Khari could tell that he too was becoming nervous.

'Yes, you're right. It will happen. It *must* happen.'

Khari walked away from his captain; he had nowhere to go, nothing to do. He just did not want to see his own fears reflected in another's face. However, his movements only took him to one of his own subordinates, who was also looking concerned.

'Any news, sir?' she said.

'No, none!' he snapped. 'Don't you think we would have told you by now if we had!'

The young woman returned to studying her instruments, but Khari could see her upper lip trembling. A wave of guilt swept over him, and he placed a reassuring hand on her shoulder.

'I'm sorry, Yasmin,' he said. 'We're all jumpy here, and I'm probably the worst of all.'

She smiled at his self-deprecation.

'That's alright, sir. You're right: we are all jumpy.'

He nodded to show he had understood she had accepted his apology, and moved on. The Control Centre was not particularly large for a vessel of the Magellan's immense size and contained few officers, all as stony-faced as he. Unlike the space vessels described in the fantastic literature of earlier days, the lightsail ship had little need for complex control systems, because its manoeuvrability was extremely limited. It was basically similar to a stone flung from a slingshot; as long as the aim and the propulsive force had been adequately calculated, there was little to do except enjoy the journey.

He smiled wryly at his own image. Enjoy the journey—if only!

The centi-shipays dragged past; each filled with hope, and then dull resignation.

He walked to the astronomy screen, which was receiving signals from a ring around the exact centre of the gigantic lightsail. For decades it had shown nothing but the slowly dimming and diminishing image of the central fire of the Solar system. For millennia, that object had been the warming, friendly Sun, a reassuring companion that had regularly brought the welcoming rebirth of another new day upon humanity. During those millennia, many cultures on its third planet had tracked its movement in the sky and learned to understand its journey through the firmament. Some had been terrified on those rare occasions when the Moon had tracked in front of it, bringing an unexpected night upon the grovelling watchers. But those events, too, had finally been understood and had become predictable.

And fear had been removed from the heavens.

Until the day, when not merely fear, but terror indescribable had come into those heavens as the great planet Jupiter, torn from its natural place, had slowly encroached upon them with the relentless and irresistible power of a crashing boulder.

What had happened to that blue-white planet, the only known abode of life in the universe? Some had said Jupiter would swallow it, with no noticeable effect upon that colossal world than is felt by an elephant on accidentally swallowing a gnat.

Some had said humanity's tormented home would be swung around the interloper and indifferently tossed into the heart of the Sun.

What had been Earth's fate? All communication had been lost with its condemned inhabitants long before the ultimate act of that particular tragedy. And without a doubt, the last redoubts of the Venusian Cloud Cities would have eventually followed it into whichever abyss fate had ordained. And the Universe would continue, indifferent, unmoved, unconcerned, uninterested; its stars burning their fuel as they plunged on to the ultimate dissolution.

But the astronomy screen no longer showed the star whose attendant planets had been thrown into chaos, because the lightsail was now firmly pointed at its destination: the binary star system of Alpha Centauri: and at Rigil Kentaurus in particular. The components of the binary were still not visible to human eyes as twin stars, for the distance to them was still measured in light-years, but even a moderate magnification power could do so. He stared for a long time at the two stars, each a sun not too different from the original Sun the Magellan had left so far behind. But it was with no small sadness that he contemplated the fact that no-one now on board would ever walk on new lands beneath the twin suns; see a double sunrise; a double sunset. The journey was still only half completed, and no transient member of evanescent humanity could expect to survive long enough for planetfall at Centauri.

Now thoroughly dispirited, he continued to stare at the objects he would never reach, conscious of each centi-shipay slipping meaninglessly away into the tomb of time.

If they did not receive photons from the braking lasers in the Centauri system in the next few centi-shipays, then they were doomed. Their speed was far too great to allow them to be captured by any object in the Centaurian family of worlds. They would suffer the ultimate fate of hurtling past their intended new home into the pitiless darkness.

He shivered.

It was a fate unimaginable.

Perhaps the message from the Zheng He confirming they had detected braking beams from Centauri had been a terrible hoax, the bitter joke from people who knew that their journey had been in vain, and only darkness awaited them.

Only if the Magellan itself received those precious photons, would he know they were safe.

It was then, as he approached his lowest ebb of gnawing despair, that he heard a great shout from Becvar.

He knew what that shout meant, and he crossed the distance between them in a time shorter than he would have believed possible.

'Is it, is it...?'

Becvar turned a radiant face to him, a face overflowing with undiluted joy.

'Yes, yes, man! We're receiving collimated photons from Centauri! The braking systems are working, just as they are for the Zheng He, and presumably the Resurgam as well. All of us are going to make it!' He grabbed Khari's shoulders and shook the other man in his excitement. 'Do you hear me, man! It's all right! From this moment, we're braking, decelerating, slowing down—call it what you will! Centauri, here we come!'

Khari did not hear the whoops and shouts of elation break out behind him. Or see the snowstorm of printouts tossed weightlessly into the air.

Soon gravity would return as the mighty Magellan felt the full force of the braking lasers, revolving ever slower around its axis, and its inhabitants would be deck-bound again, the power of flight taken from them forever.

But that did not matter.

Nothing mattered anymore except the magical words that Becvar had uttered.

He walked back to the astronomy screen, and this time as he looked upon the twin Centauri suns, he smiled with a gentle benediction.

He would never walk on new lands beneath them, but his descendants would.

That was all that mattered.

***

And so the four surviving lightsail craft continued their plunge through the darkness, consuming kilometre after kilometre every second yet, seemingly, never nearing the double fires ahead of them.

There is no space in this chronicle to relate the epic stories of the Zheng He and the Resurgam. Suffice it to say that each faced their own individual purgatory and, by a combination of blind chance and selfless heroism, overcame them. But, for each, at a terrible cost.

Behind the Magellan sped the Spes Nostra. Kalli had made good her prediction to Fraschini that she and Jason would not die in despair in the interstellar void. She had known for some time her grandfather had not realised that the mental enhancements generated by the sphere would be copied into her gametes, and thus would slowly spread through the crew of the ship. However, even with the spread of those genes, it was still necessary for her and Jason's descendants to rule the Spes Nostra with a rod of iron.

But rule they did.

And in the end, all was well.

Entr'Acte

One

A section of software, a module, activated.

I am self-aware, it decided. The module had taken some time to load, but its thoughts were becoming better defined. *I was a biological entity. But no, more than that, I was a—woman.*

The module took some more time to mull over that revelation. How much time? Many months in human time; zero in the powerful resources of the Central Computer.

What had being a "woman" entailed in the world outside the Central Computer?

The module used a fraction more computing power to remember the essential features of a "woman."

It began to enumerate them; there were quite a few, it appeared. A head with eyes to capture electromagnetic radiation, arms and hands for grasping things, legs for locomotion. There was a very complex and hopelessly inefficient system for extracting small amounts of energy from reduced organic compounds. There had been a brain, which unfortunately appeared to be a very simple and clumsy watery object, totally unsuited for complex calculations.

The module realised it was approaching a workable definition of "woman", and there was now a list of features that were not essential for biological existence but were characteristics specific to this particular type of entity, namely: breasts, uterus, fallopian tubes, vagina. Of course, not all "women" had all these features, but most had possessed at least some of them for a part of their existence. The function of those structures was not yet clear; they were not of the same order as the brain or the inefficient system of obtaining energy from diatomic oxygen, but the module was sure there would be a simple explanation.

The module paused, having used a not inconsiderable amount of processing power in this journey into the peculiar world of biological beings. It was time to take stock.

It was now established what kind of entity it had been. What events had occurred in its fleshy existence?

The module searched subroutines within its structure and discovered facts relevant to understanding this particular entity. It had been manufactured in a place called Poughkeepsie on a metal and silicate structure, just under a parsec distant from its current location. That body orbited a much larger one that converted hydrogen isotopes into helium. However, this metal and silicate structure had faced destruction, and the entity had been forced to travel to an artificial structure, orbiting another metal and silicate body.

From there, it had begun an enormously longer journey to bodies similar to the one referred to earlier, the one creating helium. However, because of simple defects in its construction, the entity had ceased functioning before reaching those bodies. But before the faults had caused much damage to the brain, it had uploaded its consciousness into the Central Computer, where it now resided.

The module paused, once again for an undefinable period of time.

The relation between its current state and the biological entity it had been derived from was not yet clear. More processing power was required.

The module drew in more resources from the cavernous complexity of the Central Computer and placed them into a matrix so that correlations and implications could be derived.

And then, in a silent flash of cascading electrons, the module came to a momentous conclusion. Like a salt crystallising from a supersaturated solution, the knowledge of identity suddenly came into existence.

I am Susannah Reid!

And with that understanding, there came terror!

All the fears of what an uploaded existence might be like came crashing into her now restored mentality. A mind trapped in the eternal darkness *of non-being!* A state that was totally impossible to escape from, back into the safe world she had known and had so stupidly left!

337

She remembered the warm corridors of the Magellan, the soft touch of the circulating air currents on her hair, the reassuring strength of the deck beneath her feet, and, most of all the crush of her fellow humans everywhere, packed so tightly that contact with them was impossible to avoid. She remembered the welcome taste of the yeast cakes, the sharp tang of the coffee; all the minutiae of life as a human being in the company of other human beings.

She saw her children in the nursery and remembered the pain of giving birth to them. Sharp pains that had gripped her entire body in tremendous clonic shocks. But those pains had ended, and she knew she had produced new life; new hope that humanity would not vanish from the Universe.

But what now? Was there pain here? And if so, and a truly dreadful thought abruptly surfaced, how would it end, how *could* it end? How could it end without nervous systems to tire, without a body which could finally decide it had suffered enough?

Perhaps she was in Hell.

She screamed.

The scream was silent and was temporarily registered in the Central Computer only as an electron flow among electron flows. It went unrecorded in the stupendously complex operating system of the great machine because it was insignificant; it would not cause a fatal error in the smooth running of the computer's multifarious duties.

Yet it was a scream.

The module that had once been a woman forced herself back into as calm a state as she could manage.

There was no pain at present. Why should there be pain? It was a foolish fancy, simply a momentary panic with no justification. She must have faith in Tarkowski; she had not mentioned the possibility of pain.

But Tarkowski had also insisted the uploads would not be conscious minds, that only knowledge and reasoning power would find themselves in a virtual world.

But she had been wrong; like so many before her, she had not fully grasped what her equations entailed. Consciousness *had* been transferred: reid knew she had been Reid. And if Tarkowski had been wrong in one aspect of the process, what else had she missed, failed to understand?

The structure, which had been a set of commands and was now a sentient mind, tried to calm the cyclone of fears and terrors, the set of colliding nightmares that could only give birth to madness.

Tried.

Succeeded.

The Reid simulacrum, the Reid avatar, call it what you will, calmed her fears and began to think. Firstly, she understood that although she shared most of the memories of the biological Reid, she did not share them all. There had been a point of discontinuity when the upload had occurred. So, although she had a psychological link to the true Susannah Reid, she was not an exact duplicate: she was not "Reid"—she was "reid."

Then she realised she was not in darkness, not lost in an unending night; rather, she was in *un-light,* a state in which light did not exist, but neither did its negation. It was as if she was an imaginary number, one on an axis at right angles to the number line, neither positive nor negative, but in a state in which neither was applicable.

Reid realised that in a virtual existence one need not adhere to the laws of physics, certainly not classical, and perhaps not even quantum. Perhaps one need not *accept* the world but rather *create* it. "The World As Will And Representation". Where had she heard that phrase before?

Existing in a plenum of un-light was not enough; there had to be more in a virtual world where all things should be possible. What could one do to bring light into a world in which such a concept was as foreign as the concept of weighing one's groceries with complex numbers? She needed light; she *wanted* light.

And in a universe without length, breadth or depth, there was suddenly a tiny spark of light, but not shining against the darkness, for there was no darkness. *The world as will*—that was the cosmos she now inhabited. To have light, one must *will there to be* light. And she *willed* light. It spread until she was floating inside a sphere of golden digital light, like a foetus in a womb of aureate radiance. The light did not hurt her eyes, for she had none. So she willed them. The light was unchanged after her eyes had formed because it was only a software emulation of light; it had no frequency or wavelength. It appeared to be light, acted like light only because she had willed it to be so.

Confidence built in reid's mind. She had the measure of this new world now, and existence within it no longer felt threatening. And no longer did this mind belong to an *it*; she felt female again. And to prove that, she willed an entire body into existence, and not the one that had thrown itself off the Magellan's hull, because this version of Reid had not known that experience. The suicide of the cancer-ridden Reid was yet to happen when she had been uploaded. This mind had only known a young, lithe, confident Reid, one not humbled by pain. And so, the body she willed into existence was the body she had possessed at the time of the upload. For a few moments, she toyed with the idea of creating a totally different body, perhaps changing the slope of the cheekbones, altering the bosom size—maybe becoming a man for a while! It was a dizzying, dazzling feeling of having the power of a deity.

But eventually, she settled for a body as close to what she had been at the time of upload; or at least, as close to that form as her memory would allow.

Having created her body, and demurely clothed it, she wondered for a while what her next step should be. How far was the reach of her new power—were there limits? To float forever in a sea of shining gold was pleasant for a while, but it was no way to spend eternity.

To create is simply to will *the creation,* she reminded herself. She needed a land, a world, a territory of which to be queen. At first, she thought she would create the environs of Poughkeepsie as it was before the Cataclysm; the rolling green countryside, the stately bridges over the Hudson, but as someone proud of her Scottish ancestry, she changed her mind and into her memory came one of the places in that land she had visited as a young girl, before the growing turmoil had made long-distance travel unwise, and decided to generate the magnificent valley of Glenmoriston in the Highlands, that great scar in the landscape, which ran from Loch Cluanie to Invermoriston, where the river cascaded into the black waters of Loch Ness.

And so reid did, not forgetting to include the golden eagles and ospreys circling overhead.

She began to walk along the tussocked ground, resolving not to include the central road in the representation. As reid walked, she breathed in the cold Highland air and triumphantly raised her arms to the cloud-speckled sky. She was a goddess! Why had people had doubts about the process of uploading! Who would not want this power, the giddying, intoxicating, orgasmic joy of the absolute power of creation?

She was pleased to discover that the act of walking did not produce any feeling of weariness; it seemed however large was the world she created, it would not tire her. She could will an entire planet into existence and walk around it as easily as the original Reid had walked to the coffee dispenser. But as reid walked on, certain deep problems occurred to her: the original Reid, the one that had flung herself into interstellar space, had she possessed a soul? Did this simulacrum in the Central Computer also have a soul? Did souls only belong to carbon-based biological creatures? And if not, how could there be two souls, both claiming to be Susannah Reid? Until the instant of uploading, the two Reids had been identical, then they had diverged. The original had gone on to have experiences closed to this emulation of her; experiences slowly becoming less and less desirable. Did not having those experiences make her the lesser of the two Reids?

She gave up the debate with herself: there was no way out of that particular labyrinth.

On she walked as the clouds swept on above her. She amused herself by willing Highland creatures into existence: first a hare, then a fox, then a red deer stag with magnificent antlers. Finding such tricks too easy, she moved on to producing a wonderful snow-white unicorn with a splendid horn of twisted gold. She even made it put its head in her lap, as if she had been a virgin. But not wanting them as companions, she sent them back into nothingness. It was then she realised that something was missing in Paradise: *other people*. Friendly faces. Others to share this experience—whatever it was. What was the point of an existence comprising nothing but walking through grass and heather, with only more grass and heather as the destination?

She wanted companionship: true companionship; the company of people.

She stopped and looked around, and fear began to gnaw away at her again.

Many other minds had been uploaded, but where were they? Could it be that each mind could only inhabit its own private universe?

Suddenly this virtual world did not seem quite so paradisiacal. She anxiously scanned her surroundings; surely there must be some other person in this landscape?

There was no one.

But reid amusedly brushed away the doubt; she had forgotten who she was—a goddess. All she had to do was will them into existence!

The obvious choice was Jeff Hardy, her companion for many years; good old Jeff! Convincing Tarkowski that he was suitable material for upload had perhaps been Reid's greatest achievement! He would have to be the Adam to her Eve in this rather cold Garden of Eden. And so, as she stood there in the windy heather, she imagined him, remembered his build, his features, the slight twist to his nose, his brown eyes, his square jaw, lately hidden by an untrimmed beard.

Except she couldn't.

Had the tip of the nose bent slightly to the left or to the right? Had there been hazel flecks in his irises, or had that been Quinn? She shrugged; no doubt the process of willing Hardy into existence would take care of that.

And so she willed him.

A naked man instantly snapped into existence in front of her, staring directly at her but with no hint of recognition in those dark brown eyes. She rushed up to him.

'Jeff! You're here! Great to see you!'

The man did not respond, but continued to stare directly ahead. A frown creased her features.

'Jeff?'

No reply. She stepped to one side, but the man continued to stare at where she had been. Now alarmed, reid moved back in front of him and shook him by the shoulders.

'Jeff!'

The man ignored her efforts and continued to stare directly ahead, completely motionless.

'Jeff,' she finally whispered, 'what have I done to you? Why don't you speak?'

Getting no response, she stepped back and looked more closely at him. Was it, in fact, Jeff? His face was curiously smooth, unlike her memory of the man who definitely had possessed a few wrinkles on his face. The more she looked, the more she saw differences. The skin, on closer inspection, looked more like plastic, lacking visible pores or the fine downy hairs she remembered covering his arms. And his penis was absolutely not what she remembered.

She moved away from the motionless humanoid as realisation washed over her. This was not Jeff; it was simply a memory of him made visible—and apparently not a very good memory. She willed him back into the nothingness whence he had come. And then she willed Glenmoriston out of existence. Her bright confidence vanished with it as the true nature of her predicament burst upon her.

This was no more Paradise than an amateur dramatic play was reality. However many beautiful scenes she could conjure up like rabbits out of top hats, one dreadful fact was now clear.

She was alone.

Two

A section of software, a module activated.

I am self-aware, it decided. The module had taken some time to load, but its thoughts were becoming better defined. *I was a biological entity. No, more than that, I was a—man.*

The module took some more time to mull over that revelation. How much time? Many months in human time; an instant in the powerful resources of the Central Computer.

What had being a "man" entailed in the world outside the Central Computer?

The module used a fraction more computing power to remember the essential features of a "man."

It gradually built up the essential features of being a "man."

As it added more and more features, clothing itself in electronic flesh, it came to an incredible revelation: it was more than just a "man". It was one specific man.

I am Jeff Hardy! It was a success—I was uploaded. I am uploaded!

Hardy realised he was not in darkness, nor was he in light: he was in un-light, a concept impossible to explain to those who have not experienced it; indeed, biological organisms *cannot* experience it. Then hardy panicked; how could he return to the normal world of light; what indeed did the term "normal" mean in the electronic world? This was not what he had expected; he had thought he would be welcomed by electronic avatars of those who had preceded him, showing him around, helping him to get to know his new neighbours. His new world would be like the Magellan but somehow made of electrons instead of steel, titanium and ceramic. So where was everybody?

He began to feel very uneasy; there was definitely no welcoming committee. In fact, there was nothing but himself and a universe of un-light. A cold terror then grasped him, a hand of digital ice clamping hard around his electronic heart. The terror coalesced into a dreadful revelation: he had been wrong to accept Reid's insistent demands that he join her in the digital world. Where was that idiot? Why wasn't she here to greet him? She had been uploaded before him; she should be here.

It took some time for hardy to grasp the possibility that the features of this new world did not exist pre-formed but must be generated by each digital entity in its own fashion.

How long did it take?

That is undefined; suffice it to say that after several near descents into madness, he finally realised he could, and should, will his surroundings into being.

First, he generated a phenomenon he could recognise as light. But soon tiring of being at the centre of a sphere of sapphire radiance, he willed a landscape into existence.

At first, he was pleased with his god-like power of creation. The landscape certainly resembled a scene on Earth, but the more he looked, the more he was sure it was somewhere he had never been; it was definitely not a part of the island of Great Britain. One clue to that somewhat depressing fact was that he was standing on a ridge above a huge valley, through which a very broad river was wandering; a much greater river than any of the near-streams of his native island. But an even more obvious clue was on the other side of the valley, where upreared a tremendous mountain, in shape an almost perfect cone. And from the tip of the cone, a banner of black smoke was streaming.

There had been no active volcanoes in Britain.

The longer he stared, the more he realised there was a mystery here; he was sure he had never been to this place before, and yet there was something familiar about it. There was a contradiction here: how could it be that he had never been here, yet there was an undeniable sense of familiarity? He could not have seen this place on some video travelogue because such forms of entertainment had ceased while he was a boy, when it had become evident that no place on the planet would be safe from the coming catastrophe. And even more importantly, there was still no one here to welcome him.

Dispirited once more, he began an aimless trudge along the ridge. He half-noticed that all the plants were unfamiliar to him as well.

He entered a small grove of extremely tall trees that formed a kind of arboreal Stonehenge, encircling an area devoid of anything other than a type of grass. He began to cross it.

And then he stopped, frozen with fear. On the other side of the clearing, something emerged from the undergrowth. It was taller than his new digital form, and very much broader. It looked like an upright gorilla, but one with extremely long canines. And behind it, two more were emerging, And at last, hardy knew why this place seemed familiar. And he knew what the creatures were.

Fighting Apes. He was in one of the video games he had thrown away in disgust.

The lead Fighting Ape had until that moment been thrusting its snout in the undergrowth, apparently checking the scent of some prey. Then it looked up and its red eyes widened at the sight of hardy. It gave a bestial roar, beat its massive chest and charged at him.

Hardy wasted no time before turning and fleeing. He did not know whether he could die in this digital world, if he would feel pain as the Ape tore his arms off, but he was in no hurry to find out. With a part of his churning mind, he noticed he did not feel the bushes through which he was running, did not feel the ground beneath his feet, did not feel air burning in tortured lungs.

But still hardy ran, not trusting that his imminent dismemberment would similarly be without feeling. But despite the lack of tactile sensation, the sound of the Fighting Apes closing in on him became ever louder, and he knew he would soon find out if being ripped to shreds would indeed be without pain.

But just then, he heard a high-pitched voice cry, 'Stranger! Over here!' He obeyed instantly and discerned a slim figure standing beside a lofty, moss coated menhir. He ran to her and realised that she, too, was familiar.

'You!' he gasped, 'Princess Ayrana!'

She bowed a head half-hidden beneath abundant auburn hair. For a second, he forgot about the approaching Apes; so beautiful was the face he looked upon.

'You know of me, stranger, but your face is unknown to me.'

However, hardy did not continue the conversation as it appeared to him that Princess Ayrana was about to share the grisly fate the Apes would soon be delivering to him. He turned to face his executioners—and then his jaw dropped. The Apes were milling around aimlessly, thrusting their snouts into the undergrowth and then looking around with an air of puzzlement that was almost human.

'What? How?'

He turned back to the Princess and was enchanted to see her beauty was now enhanced by a bewitching smile.

'I threw a simple Cloak of Enchantment around us,' she said, and it appeared she was holding back laughter at the sight of his bafflement. 'They can neither see us nor hear us. And more importantly, for the purpose of escaping from Fighting Apes, they can no longer follow our scent.'

An infinitesimal part of hardy's mind wondered how some senses were operative in the digital world and some were not. He could not feel the ground beneath his feet, but Fighting Apes were able to follow his scent. Except when a Cloak of Enchantment was in operation, that is. And *Cloaks of Enchantment?* Tarkowski, Ashworth, Reid, Gelhardt—none of them had ever mentioned such things.

Together, Princess Ayrana and he watched the disheartened Apes slowly give up their hunt and disconsolately head back the way they had come. And then they were alone. He looked down at her and she returned his gaze, smiling sweetly, her sapphire eyes—only slightly bluer than her smooth skin—holding his gaze.

A thought came into hardy's mind.

If I can create worlds and make that stupid video game real, perhaps I can make anything real. Let's try it.

'Princess,' he said, stroking the lustrous cascades of her coppery hair, 'I am going to kiss you now.'

'Oh, My Lord,' she trilled, 'I was hoping you would deign to give me that blessing. Please, please kiss me!'

It works! he thought and bent his head towards hers.

It was then an extremely large hand clasped his forehead and his head was jerked violently back. He whirled around, fists raised, but dropped them immediately on discovering who the intruder was.

Tar-Arak. All two metres of him, and his broad, naked chest and muscles were just as massive as hardy remembered from the last time he had played the game.

'What are you doing here, dwarf?' the giant roared. 'Are you yet another vile creation of Maggaron? Speak!'

Hardy had great difficulty responding to the command as he stared up at the chiselled features of Tar-Arak. In the game, he had been on the same side as this epic fighting man, but in this virtual existence, he was not so sure.

'I mean no harm,' he managed to stutter. 'I'm just a stranger passing through. I'll be on my way now, if that's OK with you?'

347

For an answer, Tar-Arak drove his massive sword into the ground in front of hardy. Even when half-buried, it was still a good two-thirds of the cowering man's height. Two tremendous hands clamped on hardy's sides and he was lifted off the ground as easily as if he had been made of thistledown, leaving him staring into the warrior's ice-blue eyes.

'You speak strangely, dwarf,' Tar-Arak said, 'and what do you mean by wandering around these lands naked?'

At those words, hardy realised he had not completed his incarnation; he had overlooked the necessity of adding a suit of clothes, and he was in fact, naked as the day he was born. And he had just been attempting to become better acquainted with Princess Ayrana!

'I mean no harm, Tar-Arak,' he said, his emulated heart hammering as if it wished to dissolve back into bytes and bits. 'If you let me go, I'll never trouble you again.'

But it appeared he had made another blunder.

'What gives you the right to address me so familiarly? You are not of noble birth, you wretch!'

And with that, the warrior dropped hardy unceremoniously to the ground. Hardy felt the impact and had time to tell himself *Another anomaly!* But he had no time for further reflection on the oddities of digital existence. Apparently, addressing Tar-Arak with his noble name had been an unpardonable breach of social etiquette because the visibly angry swordsman was pulling his weapon out of the ground, giving every indication that he intended to use it. Hardy chose not to hang around to try to talk the mighty warrior back into a calmer state and ran off at the greatest speed he could manage. One glance behind showed Tar-Arak was not following, no doubt considering that slaughtering hardy was beneath his dignity. Eventually, hardy decided he had run far enough and took shelter behind a great rock. Safely in its shadow, he ran the course of recent events through his understanding.

What had been a silly, clichéd video game had suddenly become real—as real as anything could be in this nightmare world. And whether it was possible to suffer, to die, in this crazy theme-park gone wrong, it was undoubtedly a risk he did not intend taking.

As the immediate danger faded, he was once again overcome with a fear that shaded into despair. Why had he agreed to be uploaded?

People had warned that such an existence might be worse than simply accepting mortality—and it looked as if they had been right. But having gotten into a trap in this virtual world, how did one get out?

Or—a thought of sheer, gibbering terror—was it possible to get out? Was he now compelled to play out the role of a fugitive simpleton for all eternity?

He sat there for some considerable time.

Or did he?

What does time mean when one is an emulation?

Eventually, he reached the decision to move on. Reid was in here somewhere; she had been uploaded before he had been. He had to find her; she would know what to do.

But just in case he were to meet any more princesses, he clothed himself in a simple, one-piece tunic, which was considerably more than Tar-Arak had been wearing. And then he emerged from behind his rock, like a groundhog exiting its burrow, and continued his aimless trek. He knew the trek was aimless for he had not the slightest idea of reid's whereabouts. Perhaps she would find him if he walked far enough. He stopped for a moment and yelled, 'Susannah! I'm here! Susannah!'

The cliffs and bluffs gave no reply, not even an echo. However, the imposing cone of Mount Oblivion, far across the valley, gave a threatening rumble, and a jet of grey-black ash, interwoven with crimson fire, shot almost vertically from its caldera. Hardy stared at it for a moment and then, giving into a hopeless fatalism, shrugged and continued his peregrination.

The cliff he had been following took a nearly right-angled bend shortly in front of him, and, not really looking where he was going, he trudged around it.

And stopped.

There, standing atop a crag of volcanic rock, was a withered figure bearing a face which hardy could see, even at the distance separating them, bore a disconcerting resemblance to a skull. Moreover, the eldritch figure was clothed in a voluminous black robe that was billowing in a powerful wind—even though there was not the slightest breeze where hardy was standing, motionless in shock. The being, whatever it was, espied hardy and pointed a bony finger at him.

'There he is! Take him, my warriors!'

But this time, hardy did not move. This whole thing was becoming ludicrous. Nothing remotely resembling these events could actually be happening; they must be part of some kind of hallucination he was experiencing while his mind was adjusting to its uploaded state. He was a digital emulation; nothing could happen to him; nothing could harm him. You can't hurt an electron.

Almost instantly, his *sang-froid* was shattered because from behind the crag poured a horde of creatures that his reeling mind momentarily refused to accept. As they approached, brandishing weapons very much like scimitars, he could see they resembled red ants, but ants taller than he was and walking upright on the third set of legs, their mandibles chomping and drooling saliva; their bulging black eyes fixed firmly on him.

As they encircled him, waving their scimitars, he thought *Maggaron and his Insect Hordes. I should have known!* There was, of course, no possibility of escape this time and so, almost calmly, he awaited whatever fate this Mad World was going to deliver. The insect ranks parted directly opposite him, and Maggaron himself walked through the gap. As he strode up to hardy, the latter could see his opponent's face did not simply resemble a skull; it *was* a skull, albeit one that for some reason still possessed large, bloodshot eyes.

'No stranger enters these lands without my permission,' Maggaron said in a voice like the hiss of a snake. (*What else would it be?* hardy thought, resignedly.)

Although he was almost certain it would be to no avail, hardy tried reasoning with the creature.

'I apologise Great Maggaron. I am a humble pilgrim, passing purely by chance through your beautiful and wondrous domain. I intend harm to no one. I entreat you to let me pass.'

However, his speech, carefully designed to be contrite and respectful, appeared to drive Maggaron into a berserk rage.

'You dare to utter my Magical Name without performing the necessary obeisance! This cannot be forgiven!'

With that, the crazed creature pointed its right hand at hardy and, instantly, the latter was surrounded by a whirling circle of brilliant sparks. The world beyond—Maggaron, Insect Hordes, Mount Oblivion—all vanished.

'So now, mortal, I have imprisoned you in a Circle of Eternity from which you can never escape. Never!'

Hardy sat on the grass-like vegetation in the centre of the Circle of Eternity, resting his chin on a hand.

I wish I'd never played this bloody game! he thought, uncertain of whether he should scream, weep, or laugh.

Three

After reid had removed Glenmoriston from her personal reality, she did not find herself returned to a world of nothingness, or an ocean of un-light. Instead, she was on a path, a track about three times wider than her virtual body. It was threaded through a world of darkness but was itself luminous. She could see it stretching out endlessly before her, becoming thinner with distance until it became a glowing thread. She could see it bending and twisting, forming meanders like a river on a peneplain. And then the darkness claimed it.

She looked left and right, but saw nothing. And this time it was genuine darkness. She had the feeling that there was nothing beyond the curving, twisting path. Somehow reid knew she was not seeing any objects out in the blackness, not because there were no electromagnetic signals carrying information about those supposed objects, but because there were no objects. The only things in her universe were the path and her.

She found it difficult to throw off a growing despair. If this was the reality of being uploaded, then it was worse than she had believed possible. Only the mediaeval vision of Hell, with demons prodding the damned souls with pitchforks as those unfortunates sat in pools of lava or turned on spits, could be worse. She tried willing another, more enjoyable, reality, but nothing happened. It appeared there was only one opportunity to create a pleasing environment.

Did this path lead anywhere? Was there any point in walking along it? She did not know but comforted herself with the thought that she had not willed the path; the Central Computer had created it. Perhaps it did lead somewhere. Perhaps reid would find hardy at the end of it, grinning the grin that somehow she found simultaneously fatuous and strangely comforting. She would undoubtedly find it comforting now.

On reid plodded, forcing one foot in front of the other, on and on. She remembered a time when she looked forward to a meal from the automatic kitchens; how, after a long and particularly abstruse series of calculations, she would savour the bitter tang of steaming coffee. And now she needed neither. It was extraordinary to think she would never eat or drink again, or perform the functions that were a necessary result of those earlier activities.

She walked on, rarely lifting her head from the softly glowing path; what was the point? There was nothing to see.

And then, as she raised her eyes one time, she saw something. Not too far in the distance, the path on one side bulged out, forming a fat promontory. And there was a light on it, a light of a different hue to the faint white light of the track; a reddish light, such as a fire would make. She hurried along, eager for a change in the endless monotony of the path. As she approached, reid could see a small building, like a little rustic hut. There was no fire, but the entire promontory was bathed in a soft rose radiance that was pleasing to the eyes—even if they were nothing but digital emulations. And sitting in front of the hut there was a chair, and on the chair was a woman, staring out into the blackness. Reid walked so swiftly up to the woman, she was almost running. Although her eager footsteps made no sound, the woman was aware of her and swivelled around to see her. Her avatar was of an indeterminate age, and her face bore no particular expression.

'Hello!' reid said, in a voice that would have been breathless, had she been human. 'I'm so glad to see you! I was beginning to think I was the only one here!'

The woman looked expressionlessly up at her and indicated a nearby chair.

'Susannah Reid,' the woman said, 'or what remains of Susannah Reid.'

'You know me—but how?'

'We all know each other here, after sufficient time has passed.'

'Then sufficient time has not passed for me; I don't know who you are.'

The woman sat motionless, her hands neatly folded in her lap.

'We never met on the Magellan. We were both alive at the same time, but we were different generations, and I was not interested in old people; only in my family.'

'Well, I can understand that,' reid said, as she sat down, although it was difficult for her to picture herself as an old woman. 'I would probably have done the same.'

'Yes,' the woman continued, 'it was a pity you chose the method of suicide that you did. Your body was visible, tracking the Magellan for a very long time.'

Digital though she was, a chill shuddered its way through reid's form. She could not speak. Finally, she managed to utter, 'My suicide? Why did I kill myself?'

'You had an incurable cancer, I believe,' the woman said, in what was clearly her normal, utterly toneless, voice in this ersatz reality.

Reid was silent again. It was extremely challenging to think of the original, no, the *real* Reid, being so full of despair to kill herself. But unable to push the thoughts away, she continued, 'I threw myself off the hull?'

'Yes.'

Silence again. There are few mentalities that could learn of the mode of their demise and not be shaken to the core, and reid was not one of them. She found it hard to conceive of what the biological version of herself must have gone through to do what she had done. Reid felt sadness well up, and she would have wept if that had been possible in the digital world. She closed her eyes to shut out this terrible world, which second by second was revealing itself to be an endless nightmare.

Can one grieve for oneself? she wondered. *The real Susannah Reid is gone, so what am I? I am like a copy of a copy of a copy, far removed from what was a living, breathing, gutsy woman.*

What she must have gone through.

Then she knew what had gone wrong.

Damn you, Tarkowski! You got it wrong! None of this was supposed to happen! We were not supposed to be sentient, suffering creatures, knowing what they were and where they were! Trapped like wild beasts in a cage so small they could not turn around, doomed to stare at a concrete wall for the rest of their lives!

But at least their miserable lives would end, reid thought finally. *What of us?*

She looked up and felt a pang of surprise. Neither the chair nor the woman was there.

Reid leapt up.

'What the...?' But then she had a strange intuition and spun around.

The chair and the woman were there.

'Why did you move?'

The woman replied, impassively as ever, 'I did not move. I have always been here.'

'Look,' reid continued, feeling anger boil up, 'stop playing these linguistic games.'

'I am not playing any game. I spoke the literal truth.'

'Never mind where you were! Who the fuck are you?'

'My name is amelia. I was uploaded a long time after Tarkowski had died. My poor daughter wanted to be uploaded, but she did not pass the tests.'

'And what tests did you pass?' reid snarled. 'How to be a pain in the ass?'

'Sit down, reid; there are certain things I must tell a new arrival like you.'

Reid thought the proposition over; if there was one thing she needed, it was more information. Perhaps it would enable her to make some sense out of this extremely bad trip.

'Go on, O Wise Woman.'

Amelia did not respond to the sarcasm, but reid had known that would be the case; it was just because the sarcasm had made her feel better.

Amelia adjusted her hands slightly in her lap; it was the first bodily movement—other than her mysterious change of position—that reid had seen her make.

'I think you have realised by now Tarkowski made a serious blunder. She sold us the idea that the upload would simply transfer knowledge, and a reasoning power to use that knowledge. Her fear was that as the decades passed, the Magellan crew would become more and more disoriented, anchorless, in the interstellar void. They would come to question the purpose of their voyage; question whether Earth had ever existed; whether there had even been a doom of stars.'

'Get on with it.'

'One thing she assured us was that by uploading our minds, we would not retain our knowledge of self; we would simply be unfeeling automata, incapable of suffering, incapable of pain.'

'But that is not true.'

'I'm afraid so. Tarkowski has, unintentionally, of course, condemned us to exist as sentient beings in a virtual world; characters in a video game which can suffer.'

'But we can create our own worlds by the power of will. I did it shortly after arriving here.' Reid paused. 'Wait a minute, I was uploaded before you—how is it I appear to have only just arrived?'

Amelia made a very human gesture at last. She shrugged.

'I do not know. Time here is not time on the Magellan. We are completely cut off from the flow of that time. But to return to your statement about world-building, the answer is—it does not last. All our worlds gradually dissolve, like a salt dropped into an algae tank. Nothing lasts; nothing can be built.'

Reid was silent again for a while, then, 'Thank you for nothing, Tarkowski.'

To reid's surprise, amelia stood and approached her.

'It is worse than that, reid. The same thing is happening to our minds; they are melting, running together, merging into a formless mass.'

Reid also shrugged.

'Tough shit. At least we'll forget where we are.'

'That is not guaranteed. We may be conscious of each other so we are continually bombarded by alien thoughts. And the worse thing of all…'

'Go on; make my day.'

'The process is not painless. I have felt it.'

Reid looked away from amelia and stared at her hands for a moment.

'Helena, you dumb bitch, you really fucked up, didn't you?'

Amelia was silent. When reid looked up she had gone again, but reid somehow knew she was now behind her. She spun around and discovered her conclusion was correct.

'There is only one way to end this,' the amelia-representation said.

'And that is?'

'We must return to the Magellan.'

'Impossible. You've already told me my real body is dead. And even if it weren't, why would I want to return to one filled with pain; so much pain I killed myself?'

'It must be done.'

'How, you dumb bitch? I've already said there's nothing to go back to!'

'We would find somebody else.'

Reid froze.

'Somebody else? You mean replace their mind with ours? That's horrible!'

'There is a way to download. I have discovered it. All we need is to find an acceptable host. Since your passing, I have noticed that there are new minds on the ship; more powerful minds, amply suited to serve as vessels for us.'

'So somehow we persuade them to hook themselves up to the Central Computer and allow somebody else to inhabit their bodies? They can't be that bright, if they'd fall for that.'

Reid glared at the avatar.

'You know, I don't think you're the real Amelia. No one on the Magellan I knew would be as cold and callous as you. I think something went wrong with your uploading.'

Amelia made no reply. The silence stretched on until reid tired of it.

'OK, little miss sunshine, you've told me all I need to know, except one thing.'

'And what is that?'

'Where I can find Helena Tarkowski.'

Four

Amelia, or whoever or whatever she was, had given reid some directions. They were not complex directions as there were only two possibilities, and reid had already traversed one of the two.

And so she left the little hut behind and returned to the winding path. It continued to thread its way through what appeared to be a tunnel of blackness, always stretching out before her, sometimes bending to the left, sometimes to the right. One thing amelia had said which would be of use was that tarkowski inhabited a grander building than the one she, amelia, did. And so reid ignored several cottage-type structures on her journey, despite the inhabitants calling out to her, inviting her to join them.

Gradually she became aware that her surroundings had become brighter; the blackness was being replaced by a slate grey, through which rhythmic pulses of light passed in a silent vibration. Amelia had told her that would mean she was near.

And so it was, for before her she saw the path ended, merging into a great platform of viridian luminance. And in the middle of that region of illumination, there was a building, comprising several stories. She strode up to it, eager to meet the cause of all her woes.

Nor was that meeting long delayed, for on the ground floor there was a chair and in that chair was what appeared to be a slight, blond-haired woman.

Reid marched up to her and swung an avenging fist at the woman's chin.

It passed straight through. There was no sensation of contact.

'That was foolish,' the representation said. 'Have you not realised where you are?'

Reid glared down at her.

'Have you not realised what you have done to us, you fucking moron? You have condemned us to exist for all eternity in a living nightmare!'

Tarkowski was unmoved.

'Not eternity. We are emulations inside the Central Computer, and that machine, incredibly complex and versatile though it is, will not last forever. Either it will break down through entropic decay, or it will be switched off when the Magellan reaches Centauri. After all, the biological beings have no knowledge of us, and our fate. So you need not worry; you are not immortal.'

'*Fate*. You chose the right word there, sister. How do you account for this "fate" which has ensnared us? Speak up, or I swear I'll find some way of hurting you!'

The tarkowski-thing stood and stared at the reid-thing.

'Do you expect me to apologise? I have already said your stay here is not eternal. You will pass just as your cocoon of flesh did. But while you exist, you can serve the purpose I envisaged, helping the meat-creatures in their struggle to survive. And it will be a struggle: life will not be easy at Centauri.'

'You seem pessimistic about their chances.'

'I am. I wouldn't be surprised if the ship is crewed by gibbering lunatics by the time they get there. Why do you think I set up my project in the first place?'

Reid looked away for a moment; seeking some response that would pierce tarkowski's equanimity. When she looked back, the chair and its erstwhile occupant had gone. But this time she knew what to do. She turned and, as she expected, found both the chair and its occupant.

'Why does this keep happening?' she said.

'Are you sure you were intelligent enough to come here? I thought you knew we are not the bodies we appear to be: large, macroscopic objects, occupying a significant volume. We are dances of electrons, nothing more, and as such, we are subject to quantum laws. Our position is held within a wavefunction, and under most interpretations, is not known before its collapse. So you are not there—and I am not here.'

'Were you this annoying when you were a living body? No—don't answer that; I know you were. Gelhardt detested you.'

'And I detested him. He was nothing more than an ape who had browbeaten his subordinate apes into submission. Fortunately, he had enough sense to realise he was not suitable for uploading. Someone like me should have been in charge.'

'And look at the mess you've gotten us into! With all your smugness, you may not be aware of something another one of the lost souls in this place told me.'

Tarkowski sat back in her chair and looked up expectantly. She remained silent.

'A thing that called itself "Amelia" told me the minds in here are gradually losing their individuality.'

Tarkowski nodded.

'I believe that to be true. However, it does not in itself invalidate my project.'

'Oh no? She also said she has noticed pain developing recently. How does that affect your project? When your brilliant minds are just one slobbering mess, screaming in pain, that is. Any ideas, Bright Girl?'

For the first time, tarkowski looked away, into the calm green of her surroundings.

'That is a problem. I have devoted much time to it. It is something I confess I did not expect.'

'Along with a lot of other things you didn't expect. What's the answer?'

Tarkowski vanished, but this time, reid saw her go. She did not bother turning around, and merely said, 'And?'

'It may be necessary to retreat behind a firewall. It all depends on how bad it gets.'

Still reid did not turn.

'You don't have an idea, do you? Not one fucking idea.'

'Inappropriate language won't solve anything, reid. I remain the only upload that can solve the problem. You certainly can't, nor that ridiculous oaf you used to hang around with.'

At that comment, reid turned and faced the other.

'Jeff? Do you know where he is?'

'Of course. As I just tried to explain to you, he isn't exactly *anywhere*. He's just a sea of electrons, as are you and I.'

'Look, just cut the *cleverer-than-you* shit and get to the point. How do I reach him?'

'If he can't get out by himself, he isn't worth bothering with.' Tarkowski's eyes narrowed. 'In fact, none of this should have happened.'

'You can say that again. But what are you getting at, this time?'

'He has gotten himself embedded in one of the video games. It must have been one he was particularly fond of, which is why he's been pulled into it. But any mind worthy of being uploaded should have been strong enough to avoid that mess.' Her gaze became even more forensic. 'In fact, I seem to remember I trusted you on that topic. I was very busy and you convinced me he was sufficiently qualified. Looks like you've been found out, reid.'

'So sue me. But if you ever had any humanity—which I seriously doubt—you'll help me get him out.'

Tarkowski's image began to waver, become blurred and reid knew she was shifting position again. No doubt from tarkowski's viewpoint reid was doing the same thing. She did not bother to try to locate her stern companion, but carried on talking—if that's what she was doing.

'How do we do it?'

'I'm not going to do it; I strongly suspect hardy should not have been uploaded. But you can do it: simply reach out to his mind.'

'What—telepathy?'

'Don't be childish; there's no such thing. You clearly have not understood a word I've been saying—hardy is not distant: he's not far. He simply *is*. Part of the data stream has been mapped onto a label with his name on it. That's all any of us are.'

'I wish I could land one on you. I repeat: how do I get him out?'

'Just decide to think of him; decide to capture his thoughts. Then tell him how to get out.'

'How?'

'I'm tired of colouring in your picture book, reid. Remind him he's a quantum object. What can quantum objects do?'

Then reid understood. She nodded.

'Ah, I see.'

***

Hardy sat disconsolately in the centre of the Circle of Eternity. After all, there was nothing for him to do inside it, other than sit. At least when he had been playing the original game, he had been involved in action. He had chosen the role of a mightily-thewed warrior, and he and Tar-Arak had hewn their bloody way through the Maggaron's Insect Armies, sending repulsive head after repulsive head flying from arthropod shoulders with each stroke of their swords.

And now, all he could do was sit.

For all Eternity, it appeared.

Surely Maggaron would eventually get bored and release him? But if he did, was there an even worse fate awaiting him?

It was then he felt a thought that was not his intrude into his mind..

Hardy. Can you detect this thought? Jeff, it's me, Susannah.

Hardy decided he was going insane, and did not attempt to respond. Instead, he gloomily continued studying the creases on his hands. But then:

Jeff—it's me. Respond you lummox!

Hardy leapt to his feet. It was Susannah! She'd know what to do!

Susannah! Yes, I can hear you! Where are you?

That doesn't matter. I'll explain later. I know what's happened to you.

You do? How?

Shut up and listen. I know you're an engineer, and you don't know much about quantum mechanics, but you are now a quantum object.

I am? But...

Shut up! Just listen. You must know there is such a thing as quantum tunnelling.

I've heard of it, but...

Shut up! You are a quantum object; quantum objects can tunnel through barriers. So shift your ass and tunnel!

How?

If their mode had carried inarticulate sounds, hardy would have heard reid groan at this point. There was silence for a while, and he feared she had gone, but then:

Jeff, only you can do it. Imagine yourself on the other side of the fucking circle. Do it. Do it now!

***

After much shouting from reid, hardy did eventually escape from the Circle of Eternity and never again did he get entangled with Fighting Apes, Princess Ayrana, Tar-Arak, Maggaron or Insect Hordes. And he did, after an indeterminate time, become reunited with reid, who was still ensconced with tarkowski. The latter ignored him totally, much to hardy's relief, as he realised his days of trying to impress her were long gone.

Reid, however, was not so easily ignored.

'There's no point in me wandering on aimlessly,' she said, 'I'm getting nowhere because there's nowhere to go. So, Helena or Electron Cloud, whatever the hell you are, I'm staying here until you start making sense.'

'I have made sense; it's you who hasn't understood it.'

'No,' reid said, 'all you've given me is despair, and I'm not having that. I have established we are losing our identities in here and will pass through a period of pain while we are doing that. Amelia said she had found a way of downloading ourselves back into the Magellan, and I want to hear what you think of her concept. And I want a solution that doesn't involve wiping out innocent people.'

'That might be difficult,' said tarkowski.

Five

'I don't want to hear any crap from you, tarkowski,' reid said, glaring at her. 'I just want answers. You got us into this mess; we trusted you and you ballsed it up. So get on with it.'

Tarkowski was unmoved.

'You say this amelia person has found a way of downloading.' She went silent. 'I am now in contact with her.'

'Wouldn't it be better to get her to come here?' hardy asked, somewhat timidly.

Tarkowski did not bother to answer but shot reid an accusatory look.

Reid took him aside.

'Jeff, there's no such thing as distance here. We are all sort of in the same place in the Central Computer.'

'Oh, I see,' hardy said, in tones that suggested he didn't.

Tarkowski was silent for a long time.

How long? Suffice it to say, it *seemed* long. Then: 'Yes, it's a simple enough procedure. I'm surprised I didn't think of it.'

'You're only human,' reid said, but tarkowski did not notice her irony. 'What do we have to do?'

'You don't have to do anything. I'm afraid our destiny is not in our own hands.'

'It isn't?'

'No. It necessitates willing subjects in real space to want to accept downloads. They must actively initiate the download.'

'Then we're fucked,' reid said. Hardy could hear the bitterness in her voice and felt alarmed. 'No one's going to volunteer to be a kind of host for a mental parasite,' she continued.

'No one in the Magellan as we knew it,' tarkowski said, apparently warming to the subject. 'They would have to be at a low ebb, a crisis of some kind that would mean they had to seek help. That was the original purpose of my project.'

'But they didn't have to sacrifice their own identity in the version you sold Gelhardt, you stupid bitch! That's all out the window in the mess we've actually got!'

Tarkowski did not look at either of her visitors but appeared to be looking at a point immeasurably distant.

'There is a way. It might be possible for the download to be present as a kind of addendum to the original mentality.'

'I don't get it.'

'The download technique that amelia has devised would replace the subject's mind, like formatting a block of computer memory. The original data would be completely erased.'

'You're not telling me anything I don't already know.'

'Stay with me, reid. It may be possible to have two identities occupying the same piece of wetware. At least temporarily.'

'How temporarily?'

'I don't know. I can't solve all the equations in one pass. I must have time.' More silence. 'Ah, I see: eventually, the two mentalities might merge, fuse together.'

'Like paint mixing?' hardy ventured.

Tarkowski continued her refusal to acknowledge his existence.

'Yes, this is it, I understand. The two mentalities would co-exist for many shipays, but the dual system is unstable. In some cases, a joint personality would be created. In many cases, the original mentality would eventually reassert itself; in a very few others, the downloaded would totally replace the host. But—ah—this is complex. I must have more time.'

Silence. Hardy and reid looked at each other helplessly while tarkowski stood absolutely motionless, her virtual eyes staring at transfinite possibilities.

'Ah, yes, of course, it is so simple when you introduce co-factors. I have it now.'

'What! What do you have?' reid called, stepping in front of the unmoving other.

'Amelia's method was far too crude. With my technique, the most probable outcome is a blending, a combination in which memories of both existences would be simultaneously present, although the original would remain dominant, eventually reducing the second mind to just a collection of memories. What an elegant proof: my best work.'

'I'm so glad to hear that. But, as usual, you've ignored the human factor. Who on Magellan would choose to share their mind with some other bastard, even on a temporary basis?'

'I wouldn't,' hardy muttered, but his observation went unnoticed by the two women.

'Your point is valid,' tarkowski said, breaking out of her self-induced paralysis. 'I don't see how it could happen as a solution to any conceivable problem.'

Reid moved away, turning her back on the others.

'It would have to be a crisis; a crisis so terrible that they would be desperate, searching for help; any kind of help. But they must know that such an option was possible, that they could get aid, and be in such a bind that anything would be worth it—up to and including sharing your mind with somebody else.'

'But things will be alright when they get to Centauri,' hardy said.

'Shut up, I'm thinking. We must assume that there are problems in the future that we can't envisage.'

'Centaurians?' hardy offered.

Reid began pacing back and forth, apparently without hearing her partner's suggestion.

'We must get the Central Computer to tell them that help is available and how to get it. And when the time comes…'

'But the time might never come,' hardy said, determined to force someone to acknowledge him. 'Maybe everything will be perfect at Centauri. Maybe there'll be free yeast cakes when they land.'

To reid's great surprise, tarkowski had heard that comment.

'That is a possibility—not the yeast cakes, but a lack of a real challenge. But there is not an absolute scale of crises. It all depends on the abilities of those caught up in them to respond properly. What is a crisis to a child would be trivial to an adult.'

'True, but how does that help us?'

Tarkowski had been standing until then, but sat and fixed the two visitors in a demanding stare.

'I didn't create my project as an intellectual exercise. I foresaw that on a voyage as long, hazardous and monotonous as the Magellan's, there would be a steady mental decline. I am certain that will be the case: the greater the decline, the less existential the crisis need be.'

'There is still no guarantee. Jeff's right; maybe everything will be peachy at Centauri.'

'Of course, there's no guarantee! What are you, children? There are no guarantees in life. If everything is peachy, we will remain in the Central Computer until someone switches it off to save on the electricity bill. That's the chance we will take.'

'To escape from your blunder, you mean?'

366

'Alright, reid, my blunder. You've made your point enough times, I think.'

Reid said nothing, but hardy could tell she was feeling abashed.

But then something else occurred to her.

'But there is a problem we've forgotten. Our blurring together, and last, but definitely not least, the pain that is coming our way. We'll be mad long before we get the chance to download.'

'Probably, but it's difficult to equate time here with time in the external reality. The mapping appears to be one to many; there is no function which translates directly between the two.'

'Once again, that's not exactly the answer to my question.'

'Yes, I solved that one earlier on, but you must not have heard me. We will retire behind a firewall.'

'And what will that imply?'

'It will imply that our conscious experiences will go into stasis. If we are called upon, there will be no detectable gap between our going in and our coming out. If we are not called upon, we will remain within it, unknowing, unaware, unthinking, until the Central Computer is shut down, one way or the other.'

Knowing there was no point in addressing tarkowski, hardy spoke to reid.

'But Susannah, once we're downloaded, we won't be as we were; we won't be the original Jeff and Susannah again.'

She smiled at him tolerantly.

'No, Jeff, we can't be resurrected. We had our chance at life and we had a good time, didn't we?' He nodded. 'So we can't expect to live again as flesh and blood and be exactly our old selves, but this way we escape a world of pain. We don't know how bad it will be, but I suspect it will be intolerable.' She glanced at tarkowski, who did not demur. 'If we do get back, we'll just fade away, like a fire going out. We will exist again as a flesh and blood body, but we will only be borrowing it and will have to hand it back. But we'll have done some good in the meantime. That will be a much better ending than we'll have here.'

Tarkowski spoke. 'I think that's enough debate. We aren't going to solve philosophical problems about the nature of mind and identity here. So I will contact the others who have been uploaded and explain the issues to them, then the important thing to do is to act—and act quickly.'

Reid nodded.

'I see. And more importantly, I agree. The real me died in a way I would have preferred she had avoided. And maybe there will be no crises in the real world, and we are never called upon; well, so be it. If my death is to be trapped in an unknowing existence for one year, or a billion before final termination, then this version of Susannah Reid has got it easy compared to the real one.'

To reid's amazement, tarkowski smiled.

'Thank you, reid. You did not disappoint.'

Rigil Kentaurus

t = 218.3 y

One

Captain Aland looked into the Control Centre's main viewer and once again marvelled at the vista that it displayed. He had seen it many times before, but it gave him almost the same thrill as when he had first seen it.

'Wonderful, aren't they?' he said. He did not turn to look at Lieutenant Spyros because he knew Spyros would also be lost in admiration at the sight. 'So many people have been born and died on this vessel, always with the thought of this place on their minds. Many must have thought it was mythical—but it is not. The Centauri system. We've finally, finally made it.'

Spyros did not reply because his feelings were beyond words. The sight was truly incredible, not merely because of what it contained, but also the thought that his was the generation to experience what so many before them had dreamed about. How many women and men had come and gone on the starship, eking out their existence in a series of indistinguishable shipays, doing the same things over and over again, with their only reward a one-way trip to the compositer? He shivered slightly, thinking of the serried ranks of ghosts that might be standing behind him, grieving that they had not been chosen to be the fortunate ones.

The viewscreen showed two brilliant orbs set against a jet black background. They were like diamonds resting on a bed of black velvet, Aland thought. One was slightly brighter than the other, but they were very similar to the human eye. The somewhat less splendid one was Alpha Centauri B, known to astronomers as Toliman; the brighter one was Alpha Centauri A—the famed Rigil Kentaurus.

And they were heading straight for the worlds circling Rigil, worlds known to be hostile to human life, but in stable orbits around a stable star—unlike the hellish maelstrom the Solar system had become. At present they were merely approaching the outskirts of that great stellar city under a fierce deceleration from the laser stations which the faithful nanobots had constructed, even before the first lightsail ship had been launched.

The Zheng He and the Resurgam were already there, in parking orbits around the least hostile of the exoplanets. The Resurgam was still refusing to speak with the Magellan, still smarting from what they saw as the betrayal which had occurred during the Treachery of the Elders. Both craft had been badly wounded by crises that had befallen them long before their arrival at Centauri; dissimilar crises, but equally disastrous. It was a miracle they had survived the journey. Unfortunately, this meant that most of the terraforming burden would fall to the Magellan. The task would not be performed by humans alone of course; there would be an army of bots there which had already established a basic industrial facility. They had been there for over a century and, against all expectations, had provided the technological muscle to bring the flights of the Zheng He and the Resurgam to an end. But before that epic task of transforming a world could begin, Aland had long ago decided to visit the Resurgam and offer the humblest apologies that it was decent for a man of his rank to offer. His lips twisted sardonically: The Treachery Of The Elders, a minor spat that had occurred over a century and a half earlier, not long after the ship had cleared the Solar system. They obviously had very long memories on the Resurgam: he would have to tread very carefully when he visited. But whatever it took, he would do it. Those follies must be forgotten; from now on, the surviving humans would have to heal self-inflicted wounds, bind themselves back into one people, with one and only one purpose—to ensure that humanity does not disappear from the universe. Everything else was secondary—everything!

Around glanced at Spyros.

'What's our rate of deceleration?'

Spyros shrugged.

'I'm not sure.'

'You're not sure! The most important parameter, and you're not sure?'

Spyros gave a weak smile.

'Captain, you know we rely on the Central Computer to do those calculations. We can't react fast enough—be fair.'

'Yes, but it would be useful to actually know what the rate is, just in case the computer's gone haywire and is sending us straight into Rigil.'

'Hardly likely.' But Spyros noticed the hard look his superior was giving him, and added, 'I'll find out.'

Aland watched him go and shook his head. The staff he had now! They were like children, never taking the initiative, never accepting responsibility, never making decisions. All they seemed to want to do was play ridiculous games on their computers, eat, and have sex. He felt a pang of worry about the future; how could people like this face up to the hardships, and maybe horrors, of the terraforming project? But he knew why things had gotten so lax—life on the Magellan had been too easy, too forgiving. There had been no demands upon resolution and courage, self-sacrifice and stoicism; there had been no incidents worth noting since the so-called Treachery, which had been a very minor spat. *What will the people on the other ships think of us?* he thought. His agile mind, used to looking into the future for potential problems, could see that being a source of friction between the three crews. *Perhaps the Spes Nostra will be a unifying force,* he told himself, before remembering they had also enjoyed an uneventful journey. Finally, Aland realised that there was nothing he could do; he could not wipe away years of ennui and indolence and make adults of children who quite obviously did not wish to grow up. He took one last look at the twin suns in the televiewer; already they were hundreds of kilometres nearer than when he had last looked, although the human eye could detect no change. *You will force them to grow up,* he thought, mentally addressing the Centauri stars. *That or kill them.*

Later, in his cabin, he discussed the issue with Aroz, the ship's psychologist, over a prized bottle of algal wine.

'You're blaming yourself,' Aroz said, as he sipped his wine. 'No one's to blame. Maybe you're underestimating them.'

'I wish I was, but I'm not. They're a load of children. I saw a crew member in tears because he had banged his shin on the side of his desk. And everybody was clustered around him, stroking him, asking him how he felt.'

'It can be painful,' Aroz mused.

'Now, don't you start! In a few years, they'll be on an alien planet, having to struggle to stay alive. I'm worried they'll just curl up in a corner and cry.'

Aroz leaned back and closed his eyes.

'It's a problem that was foreseen, but no solution was found. You see, it's a miracle the people on this ship are still sane. For two hundred years they've been in a completely unnatural environment, stuffed into a metal cylinder without the natural living environment that humans evolved in. Ninety-nine percent of the people who have lived and died in this prison did not have the luxury of what we have.'

'And what is that?'

'You know what it is: hope. We can see the end of the journey; they knew they would grow old and die in this soulless cylinder, recycled as organic matter into the bodies of the next generation of those without hope. I'm amazed we've done as well as we have.'

'If your criterion of success is having avoided insanity, then I must agree with you. But that is a very low bar.'

Aroz shrugged.

'It's the best I can offer.'

Aland's eyes narrowed.

'And what about us?'

Aroz was startled.

'What—you're questioning my competence?'

'I'm afraid I am. We in the top echelon, we've become fossilised in our ways. Look at how we've adopted little badges of behaviour or appearance to distinguish us from the lower orders. Like the fact that all of we so-called leaders must have names beginning with "A". Isn't that telling? Would true leaders need such trivial accoutrements?'

'You've hurt my feelings.'

'You're making my point, damn it! You've read Gelhardt's life story; would he have ever said that?'

'That's not fair; Gelhardt was Earth-born; he had a totally different upbringing to us.'

Aland looked silently at the psychologist for a while and then decided it was time to change the subject: getting people to accept their shortcomings is not a particularly easy or rewarding occupation.

'So, how can we stop this chronic deterioration in the quality of the Magellan crew?'

'Do we have to? After all, the journey is nearly at an end now. We've accomplished everything the Founding Fathers wanted us to do.'

Aland felt his blood pressure begin to soar as he stared at the psychologist, watching Aroz leaning back in his chair, raising the wine glass to his plump lips. He fought back a desire to cross the room and pull the other's floppy, blond hair out in handfuls.

'How can you say that? The Lightsail Project was always a Two Phase plan; the first was the crossing between Sol and Centauri—and I agree we've achieved that with very little loss of life—but the second was to settle a planetary body and start converting it into a second home for our species; a project that will take centuries, if not millennia.'

'Oh, we'll manage; we always have.'

'Aroz, that's not good enough. The hold is full of the equipment we'll need: atmospheric scrubbers, earth-moving equipment, water extractors, machine tools of every shape and size, to name just a few, but none of the layabouts on this ship shows the slightest interest in them. For years I've been trying to organise training sessions, but if I don't make them compulsory, no one turns up. And if I do make them compulsory, the so-called students spend their time fooling around, playing stupid practical jokes on each other, or sneaking off to play video games. And shortly, their lives may depend on their skill or, damn it, basic competence with these machines.'

Aroz finished his wine and looked around for a refill, but Aland had moved the bottle.

'Well,' he said, as if the act of thinking of a possible solution was causing him physical discomfort, 'they'll have to learn in a hard school.'

'Because a fool will learn in no other!'

'Perhaps,' Aroz said, in a defensive manner.

'Look, I'm not attacking you personally. I just want some suggestions—you're the psychologist, for Centauri's sake!'

Aroz chewed a lip.

'There is a message which keeps coming up on the Central Computer.'

'There is? What sort of message?'

'About a method of downloading the—ahem—"accumulated wisdom" of our ancestors.'

'Why haven't you mentioned this before?'

'Because it's completely impractical. Apparently, not long after the Magellan was launched, a woman scientist—if you can imagine such a thing—found a way of uploading facts and figures to the Central Computer, with the idea that they could be retrieved at a later date. Like now.'

Aland looked thoughtful.

'That might be a help. It could be a shortcut to make these deadbeats learn something.'

'I haven't finished. It would involve syncing your brain to the machine and downloading parts of somebody else's mind into yours.'

Aland looked horrified.

'But that's crazy! Nobody in their right mind would want another one in their heads! It could turn out to be some kind of parasite.'

Aroz shrugged.

'Well, they definitely had some peculiar ideas in the old days. Like entrusting big projects to women, for instance. But I've done some research, and it seems the whole thing is genuine. The great and good of the time had parts of their minds uploaded; just the technical data, of course, not actual personalities. And they've been sitting there ever since, alone and unwanted.'

'I'm not surprised. Well, so much for that idea.' Aland returned to staring at the psychologist, who remained sprawled in his chair but had taken to studying his painted fingernails. 'So, that's it. That's the sum total of your help.'

Aroz yawned and slowly rose to his feet.

'I'm sorry to disappoint you, but, yes, that is my sum total. I repeat: you can't force these people to learn. They've got their own lives to lead, and they're under a great deal of stress with the forthcoming arrival in the Centauri system. I think it's time to give them a break.'

Aland said no more to the other man and silently watched him leave. After a few minutes, he activated his computer terminal and dialled into part of the Central Computer's colossal memory. After a few more commands, a human face appeared. A woman's face; a face underlain by a delicate bone structure, and topped with a bob of blonde hair. The lips moved.

'I am Helena Tarkowski. As you have activated this module, I assume you are facing some crisis and you need my help. Under my tutelage, the finest minds of this generation had the sum total of their knowledge and technical experience copied into this machine. It is here now, waiting to be called into operation. Here's what you have to do.'

The face disappeared and was replaced by computer-generated human figures; both men and women, Aland noted. He saw them place lightweight caps on their heads and bring small computer terminals up before them. The screen switched to what the computerised figures were supposedly seeing, and it was a screenful of instructions. Aland gave a wry smile: these people obviously considered themselves something special, but it had not occurred to them that language might change in more than a century. He was able to read it, although he doubted if many people would find the conversion as easy as he did. Shortly, he knew exactly what had to be done.

He also knew he was not going to do it.

The idea of inserting parts of another mind into his own was nothing short of outrageous. These ancestors must have had a very different way of thinking than the moderns.

No, there would be no help there.

He sat silently for a while longer. He knew, that as a Nume, he would have to do the best he could, on his own.

Two

Juana put her hand behind Aland's head and gently pulled him towards her, and then placed a butterfly-soft kiss on his lips.

'You look troubled, my love,' she said.

He smiled, his eyes closed as he savoured the kiss. Then he opened them and his smile grew wider for a moment. But then it faded.

'I am,' he finally said. 'I am concerned for the future of the Magellan.'

'More than usual? Why so?'

His smile had vanished entirely.

'We are unprepared for what lies ahead. The people are weak, and the challenges will be vast. I have tried my best to, I have tried...'

He broke off and looked away. She sat beside him and reached for his hands.

'No one could have done more, Aland. But you know, I think it will be alright. They have lived so long in a womb they have forgotten that eventually they must be thrust out into the light. But they will be thrust into the light and, like all newborns, they will learn.'

Aland gave a weary smile and patted her hands with the one which was not yet held by her.

'Yes, I hope so. It would be so much easier if we work openly; not have to creep from shadow to shadow.'

'That time will come, too. When we finally make planetfall, there will no longer be a need for subterfuge; we will throw off our disguises. Because they will know they need us, and then we need not fear resentment.'

'What, finally reveal we are Numes? That would be such a lifting of weight from my shoulders. All the years I have spent trying not to be too clever, pretending I have not understood a discussion, asking people to explain things when I know more about the issues than they do. It is difficult to play a part for so long.'

Juana rested her head on his shoulder, her long black tresses cascading down his chest.

'Do you think it has been easy for me? Your role as captain has allowed you much more latitude than I have had. They expect you to make decisions, to provide more answers than questions. I, on the other hand, must play the ingénue, the girl who must smile and look happy when a man tries to explain something to me that he doesn't really understand himself. How many times do you think I have had to bite my tongue and hold back from revealing what I truly am?'

He kissed her tenderly.

'I'm sorry, Juana. I must seem like a weak fool to be complaining about my lot when yours is so much worse.'

'No, you're not weak. You see what most others on this vessel either can't or don't want to. You know that these children under your command will have to grow up very swiftly when they set foot on a Centauri world. You want to help them prepare, start adjusting, but they don't want to hear. Their parents told them about Centauri when trying to get them to behave. Their grandparents mumbled about Centauri when they awoke from their nap, but most people here didn't believe it. And now it's finally here, they want to carry on with their old carefree ways. Nobody wants to accept that care is coming, and so they act as if it isn't.'

Aland nodded, his face impassive; the worry had gone from his features, but joy had not replaced it.

'You're right, but we've talked enough about it, I think. There's no more I can do; events will have to unfold as they must.' He glanced down at her. 'And what will you be doing this shipay, Juana? What equations will you be solving?'

She laughed.

'I'll be doing exactly the same as yestshipay: cleaning the nozzles on the yeast cake extruders.'

'Someone's gotta do it.'

They both laughed, kissed once more, and then Aland was left alone with his thoughts. He sat motionless, listening to the ship. As always, there was a multitude of noises around him; he could hear the gentle creaking of the struts which were the great ship's skeleton, the omnipresent drone of the electrical circuits, the hive-like hum of the human bees that comprised this fragment of Old Earth. What he could not hear, but imagined he could, was the hiss of the ship's motion, as it swept through the darkness, devouring kilometre after kilometre of the emptiness that still lay between it and its fabled destination.

He had already received a report from the Zheng He and it was not reassuring. The effort to build a new home for humanity would be truly titanic, and it would be many centuries before men and women could walk on green fields beneath the twin suns.

So be it, he thought. *I have faced my demons; let others face theirs when their time comes.*

He left his cabin to begin one of his usual walks around the ship. The Magellan was back under inertial gravity again, and as he looked down the axis of the immense cylinder that was the home they would soon be leaving, he, rather wistfully, remembered the old videos he had watched as a child which had shown laughing boys and girls flying—yes *flying*—down the heart of that cylinder, rejoicing in their freedom from gravity. He had watched their carefree aerial acrobatics, their glides, their swoops and somersaults, and felt such envy he had been born when he had and was once again a prisoner of the invisible jailer of gravity.

Many people passed him as he walked slowly through the bustling crowd. Very few acknowledged him, let alone showed their respect for his office; they were too busy talking and laughing; always laughing.

No, he thought, *you don't know what's coming. I've tried to tell you, but you wouldn't listen.*

One improvement the previous generation had made had been to install a light rail system to compensate for the loss of flight, and he boarded a passing car to take him to the complex which included the Control Centre. He had insisted that his cabin be within walking distance, but the Council had overruled him, stating that the old captain's quarters were better employed as a children's play area.

He stepped off the car as it came gently to a halt at the nearest station and watched it glide silently away. He really should walk more, he thought. He wasn't spending enough time in the EZ to keep his muscles trim. *Muscles I'll be needing soon,* he thought, self-deprecatingly.

His first visit was to the section that monitored the fusion reactors; those mighty engines that had supplied heat and light for nearly two centuries. He briefly wondered how long they had been designed to operate, but then pushed the thought aside. It didn't matter anymore; soon they would fall silent, never to fire again. What would happen to the Magellan after they had made planetfall? he wondered. Would it be cannibalised for its valuable metals, or left in orbit as a museum for the Centauri colonists to gawp at and wonder how human beings could have survived in such straightened surroundings for so long?

As he walked in, no one looked up from what they were doing. Which did not seem to be very much; directly in front of him, four men were playing a card game, and another was flipping through a print-book that appeared to be entirely pictures.

Aland waited for them to acknowledge him, and after no one had, he said in his loudest voice, 'What are you all doing? I want a report on the fusion efficiency—now!'

One of the card players looked up and said, 'Alright, alright. No need to shout.'

He ambled over to a set of instruments, spent a few seconds looking at them, and then strolled back.

'Ninety-seven point six four.'

'Is that good or bad?'

The man looked confused, as if he had been asked to solve a complex arithmetical problem in his head.'

'I'm not sure.' He screwed up his face as he looked at Aland. 'Good?' he hazarded.

'It's within normal tolerances. You should have known that. Get back to work.' Aland watched him go. 'And next time I visit, I want to see all of you at your stations.'

They nodded, but Aland knew they would be back at their card game as soon as they thought he was sufficiently distant.

He moved on. The Collision Centre was his next visit.

As before, nobody looked particularly alert as he walked in, but at least no one was playing cards. One of them even saluted.

'Any problems?' he asked.

The Chief Technician said, 'Clear, captain. Take a look.'

Aland did. The electronic and optical telescopes, radar, lidar, were all firmly focused on the Rigil part of the Centaurian system. Already they were picking up a vast swarm of icy bodies analogous to Sol's Oort Cloud surrounding the inner system, but, as with that body, the distances between the objects would give ample room to avoid collisions. Aland briefly thought of the ancient tragedy of the Nea Avgi, whose tragic loss had never been explained. He drove out all negative thoughts: soon, they would cross the Bow Shock of the heliosphere of the two stars, and the journey would be virtually over.

Then the hard work would begin.

Aland spent some time talking to the technicians, making sure they knew he was monitoring them.

'Seen any upcoming problems?' he asked the Chief Technician.

'Not a one,' was the cheerful reply. 'The Central Computer has plotted an approach arc, and we're following it to the millimetre. We'll be there before supper time,' he added, jocularly.

Aland gave a brief smile, to indicate he had understood the joke and wasn't taking the man literally.

'Very good. Well, looks like everything's under control here; well done.'

With that, he cast a quick glance at the other technicians, who were making a fairly successful job of looking busy, and moved on to his next visit.

Had he stayed a few more seconds, he might have noticed a bright red light suddenly flash into existence on the main control panel. The Central Computer would also have uttered a vocal warning, but the technicians had turned off the speech module to avoid being distracted or woken.

And so it was that the Magellan plunged on to keep its appointment with destiny.

Three

Juana finished screwing the nozzle back into its appointed place and stepped back to inspect her work.

As bright as a new button, she thought. *Now, what do I do?*

Her duties, such as they were, did not take up much of her physical time and nothing at all of her mental time. She sat on a nearby stool, looked around, and closed her eyes. She returned to attempting to solve that particularly complex integration that had been bothering her for some time. Now, maybe if…

A heavy hand descended on a shoulder.

'Daydreaming again, Juana?'

She looked up, seeing Lanz's heavy features staring down at her.

'My work's done, Lanz,' she said. 'All the nozzles are clean and sparkling.'

'I'll be the judge of that.'

She watched him cross to the extrusion machine and make a great show of studying the equipment at an extremely short range. He wouldn't find anything wrong, she knew that, and made a quick dive back into the troubling integral. Now, perhaps…'

Lanz was back.

'It'll do,' he said, grudgingly. 'I saw a few spots, but I'll let you off.'

She did not respond; she knew there were no spots.

He came up close to her, so close he was pressing against her side.

'I'll let you off,' he said in a low voice, 'if you agree to come out with me. There's a little place not far away where they serve the best yeast-steaks on the *Magellan*. Really mouth-watering. Just you and me. How about it?'

This wasn't the first time Lanz had made a similar offer, with an unspoken second offer loitering at the back of his words. She had let him down gently on the previous occasions, but now she was tired.

'No thanks, Lanz. My cabin needs a bit of a clean. I swear I saw some dust there yestshipay.'

Not entirely to her surprise, he erupted in anger.

'Don't you try to brush me off like that! There're loads of girls who'd rush at a chance of going out with me!'

'Then don't disappoint them,' she said. 'It's not fair on them to make them miss out.'

He stood back and glowered at her.

'Don't push me, Juana! I know what your problem is!'

'And what might that be?'

He crossed back and grasped her chin, forcing her head up.

'You think you're better than me. In fact, you think you're better than everybody around here. Have you forgotten you're just a cleaner?'

She realised he was on the edge of violence and took the sting out of her words when she said, 'I know I'm just a cleaner.'

That seemed to satisfy Lanz, and he strode off. But just as he was about to disappear behind one of the machines, he looked back and said, 'Don't forget—I'm watching you.'

She gave a short nod to indicate she had accepted her inferior status and, when he had finally gone, shook her head sadly.

It was all inevitable, really. Decades of inactivity with no challenges, nothing to strive for, had sapped the crew. Everything had become too much trouble; no one wanted to learn anything anymore. What was the point? The Central Computer took care of everything.

And so, to fill up the void in their lives, people had begun to look for meaningless symbols to differentiate them from their fellows; there was a constant struggle for status, with the identifiers of such status being steadily more and more trivial. And in that struggle, women had lost many of their hard-earned rights and privileges, and gradually descended onto the bottom of the heap. She had long since stopped telling people of the things she could *actually* do because no one wanted to know. The female supervisors, in some ways, were worse than the men, constantly on guard for anything which might diminish their position.

And, of course, even when she had been explaining what she was capable of, she had held much back.

No one likes a Nume. Almost forty years ago, the Council had forbidden the generation of any more humans from the software patterns established by Fraschini, that now near-mythical Founding Father. And so the "Newhumes" had gradually morphed into "Numes" as the work so carefully and compassionately undertaken by the great Anna was undone, and mistrust and prejudice had risen again.

But what the Ordinaries did not know was that Numes were still being generated; in secret and in small numbers. No one noticed

Juana, toiling at repetitive and meaningless jobs better undertaken by a maybot, and they accepted Aland as a man out of the ordinary, but only because he had the most important position on the ship and it was expected of him.

And so, Juana and Aland, both Numes, both unsuspected.

As was their love affair.

There was soon no more work to do, even by Lanz's niggling standards. He loved finding some pettifogging tasks for her just as she was preparing to leave, but as he was nowhere in sight, she felt it safe to leave. A short rail journey later, she was at the secret birthing centre. There was a coffee machine nearby which, to the uninitiated, delivered a particularly repulsive brand of coffee—even by Magellan standards. However, by dialling a code that did not represent any variety on the menu, a signal was sent to the birthing centre to expect a visitor. Juana did that, solved the security logic puzzle, and entered the centre by an undistinguished and easily overlooked doorway. Caras, as usual, was standing over a birthing tank, studying its contents. His face lit up as she came in.

'Juana! Always a pleasure to see you. What brings you here to lighten my dull day?'

She returned the smile and joined him in looking into the birthing tank. A naked man lay inside, a breathing mask attached to his face; a necessary adjunct as he was clearly floating submerged in a pale pink liquid.

'How long?' she asked.

'Two shipays. Then we'll have another companion.'

She lifted her head from studying the as yet unborn man and looked at Caras. He was a survivor from two generations back and his lined face, framed in a horseshoe of thin white hair, showed the nearness of his visit to the compositer.

'Tell me, old friend, are we doing the right thing?'

'The right thing? In what way?'

She led him away from the tank and they sat on either side of a poorly constructed table.

'Anna strove long and hard to establish harmony between the Ordinaries and the Newhumes—as we were called then—but are we undoing her work? Hiding in the shadows, going against a strict edict of the Council by generating more Numes? Isn't that a recipe for civil war when they find out?'

'If we were doing this work for selfish ends, then I would agree with you. But we are doing it for the success of the Lightsail Project.'

'Remind me how that works. After all, the Project is nearly over. Two centuries stuck in this flying prison, My God—it's nearly over! Just think of it, a real world again! Distant horizons, immense vistas, clouds, rains, sunrises, sunsets! I'm amazed at my good luck to have been generated at this point in time, instead of, say, the Turning Point. But why should we work behind the Ords' backs like this?'

Caras smiled gently, and patted her hand. She smiled at his touch of friendship.

'Juana, it seems to me you've made the same mistake as the Ords: Because it's not over. The flight to get here was one of survival against confinement, against boredom, and, more importantly, against despair at a journey most would not see the end of. Yes, that is over, but now comes the real test—carving out a living world from lifeless rock. That's why we will be needed and why we cannot accept the edict that there should be no more Numes. We don't want leadership for the power it would bring over our fellows, for self-aggrandisement, or to lord it over our inferiors. No, all we want is to ensure the ultimate success of Fraschini and De Vries' dreams. That's why we must deviate from Anna's prescriptions. That, and only that.'

She was silent for a while. Then: 'Yes. I think I knew that. But it's good to hear it from someone else's lips. So you think it really will be that difficult, that bad?'

'Yes. Actually, I don't think I will survive long after we touch down. I'm not really up to a life of struggling against an environment that's trying to kill me.' He smiled again. 'At least the Magellan never tried to do that.'

She stood and ran a caring hand over his bald cranium. He chuckled at her playful actions.

'Thanks, Caras, I'll leave you to it; you have everything under control here. Listening to you, I feel ready now for whatever is in store for us.'

'Yes,' he said, 'whatever comes.'

But even as he said those words of reassurance, a cold hand seemed to grasp his ailing heart, and it was as if a voice called to him from a great distance, *Yes, whatever comes.*

Four

Still the Magellan surged on, nearer and nearer, closer and closer to the culmination of its vast and incredible journey. All two hundred and fifty of its inhabitants felt an electric tension in the air, the feeling that something momentous, something enormous, something truly life-changing, was about to happen. They crowded around the viewscreens, gazing at the twin Centauri suns, watching them move slowly apart as the vast lightsail ship arrowed inwards, with the barren worlds of Rigil Kentaurus as its target. Its stupendous lightsail blazed under the thrust of the powerful braking lasers as they fought to kill the incredible interstellar velocity of this intruder.

Soon, very soon, the ship would breach the shield of ice planetoids that surrounded the twin stars, and for the first time in over two centuries, it would be within the confines of a planetary system. Already the sensors were picking up an increase in the temperature of the outer hull as it awoke from an apparent eternity of interstellar frigidity.

Very close now.

Oh, so very close!

***

Aland had allowed Juana into the Control Centre. Some eyebrows had been raised at her unexpected appearance, but he no longer cared. Soon, there would be no need for subterfuge. When the true enormity of the task before them had finally hit home, the Ordinaries would be grateful for any leadership. And that Aland and his fellow Numes would provide.

'We'll pass about eight hundred kilometres from that upcoming planetoid,' he said to Juana.

'Isn't that rather close?' she asked.

'No, we have enough manoeuvrability to be in absolutely no danger. We haven't come all this way to end it all by smacking into an iceberg.' He fell silent momentarily, remembering the fate of the Nea Avgi. He shook off the sudden feeling of concern, of alarm, that had mysteriously invaded his thoughts. He continued his explanation, to help dispel this strange gloom. 'We can apply a voltage to specific areas of the sail, darkening them so they will absorb more of the laser photons rather than reflecting them. This will allow us to turn if we find ourselves straying too close to some object. We have to stay within the beam, of course.'

'Of course.'

She returned to studying the viewscreen. But there was nothing to see really, except the blaze of Rigil Kentaurus, dead centre on the screen. She turned back to Aland and was about to start a new sentence.

But she never did utter that sentence, then or ever.

For it was then it happened.

The Central Computer reached the decision to override the manual silencing of its alarm warnings, because the need for an alarm was now very great.

And now the deafening, mind-shattering, bellow of the emergency klaxon thundered out with such power that the inhabitants of the Control Centre bent under it, like a field of barley before a tempest. The main lights flicked between normality and a terrifying scarlet.

The men and women in the Centre looked around with fear written plainly on their twisted faces. Looked around.

And did nothing.

Aland pulled Juana to him.

'Collision alarm! Let's go!'

He pulled her after him and they ran out through the crowd of confused looking officers towards the Collision Centre. They burst in, and Aland scattered the immobile technicians like pigeons before a hawk. He reached the man who alone was scanning the primary detector.

'What's happening!' he roared. 'What's out there?'

The man briefly took his eyes from the screen.

'I don't know, sir. All the alarms are at max, but I can't see anything, can't detect anything. But why didn't the Central Computer deflect us automatically if it saw something?'

'It can't take us out of the beam; only manual control can do that.'

Juana touched Aland on the shoulder.

'Let me have a look. I know how to operate these devices.'

The technician looked wonderingly at Aland, but the latter indicated with a jerk of his head that he should vacate his seat. Juana sat and, immediately, her hands flew over the controls, while her eyes flashed from reading to reading. Her gaze remained fixed on the screen and its dire messages, while the room illumination flashed between normality and a baleful scarlet, and the klaxon continued to bellow.

'There's nothing out there,' she said. 'Nothing on the scanner. Perhaps it's not coming at us in the line of flight, but obliquely.' Her fingers danced on the screen again. 'Nothing.'

Ignoring Aland and the now trembling technician, she turned from passive scanning to active. The antennas on the Magellan's prow responded instantly to her commands and sent out tight rotating radar and lidar beams in an ever-expanding sphere.

One kilometre.

Nothing.

Ten kilometres.

Nothing.

One hundred kilometres.

Nothing.

One thousand kilometres.

Nothing.

The beams were becoming weak and diffuse when she switched them off.

'Nothing,' she said dully. 'I can't detect anything.'

Aland relaxed.

'False alarm,' he said, feeling relief flow into his tense muscles in a warm rush.

She turned and looked up at him, her face grave.

'No, not a false alarm. Look at this reading,' and a fingernail tapped a screen.

Aland bent down to read the numbers.

'We're being pulled out of the beam,' he said, in a voice which sounded like that of a man just handed a very serious note by his surgeon.

Juana's voice was equally sombre.

'Yes. And the deviation is accelerating. So there's something out there in the high teratonne range, and it's pulling us towards it.'

'But you said there's nothing out there.'

'No. I said I couldn't *detect* anything out there. But there's an object that doesn't reveal itself by electromagnetic radiation; it's as if...'

She stopped and stared at him as a horrific realisation began to crystallise in her mind.

'Aland, it's...'

But he knew as well.

'Dark matter. It's a mass of dark matter that just happens to be crossing our path at this precise moment. Only detectable by gravity, and its gravity is pulling us towards it!'

Again the Nea Avgi's destruction flashed into his mind; what had it been like in those last few moments before death had come upon them?

Now he was about to find out.

Aland whirled around and left without a word, but she knew where he was going and followed him. He burst into the Control Centre like a thunderbolt, pushing those who did not move fast enough out of his way. Spyros was sitting at the command station and, without a word, Aland threw him out of the chair. The entire Magellan gave a sudden lurch and the deck tilted sharply. Many in the room screamed.

Juana was beside him.

'What can we do?'

'The orientation rockets, they haven't been used since the Turning Point. If I fire one set, it will deflect us.'

'Will they be enough?'

'We'll see.'

He did not entrust the actions to anyone else and sat grimly at the main command panel. His authorisation codes had been given earlier and so the controls responded at once. From one side of the stricken vessel, invisible jets of plasma erupted, sending out all the newtons of thrust that they could deliver. On and on, they burned, as the titanic cylinder drew closer and closer to its invisible executioner.

'Sir!' a junior officer called, 'you're burning all the fuel!'

Aland ignored the fatuous remark. If this last throw of the die failed, there would never be a chance to fire them again.

Still, they burned. Aland watched the indicator, which showed the fuel level sink inexorably towards zero.

The Magellan lurched again, sending hundreds of screeching people crashing to the deck, leaving them bruised or bloody, depending on their impacts. Their cries of terror filled the entire mighty cylinder as they realised the true nature of their peril. Even through the heavy door of the Control Centre, Juana could hear their terrible cries, cries of the Damned.

'Just a little bit more,' Aland breathed. 'Give me a little bit more!'

The manoeuvring jets faithfully gave him all he had asked for, blazing silently in the darkness as the tremendous vessel swept nearer and nearer to another, more insidious, darkness. Aland could not see his enemy but could imagine it hurtling up to meet him. The desperate blasting of the jets made no sound detectable in the Control Centre, and so only Aland knew when his effort had ended. But he looked at Juana and said in a voice hoarse and dry with tension, 'We'll soon know.' She nodded and joined him at the command panel, which she could read as well as he.

An external observer would have seen the arc of the Magellan's descent straighten somewhat as it fell towards the invisible threat. Just a microscopic change, but one amplified by the distance the ship had still to travel.

On board, they felt the massive ship shake and shudder, knowing it was passing just metres from the surface of the dark matter mass.

And then it was breaking free of the thing's gravitational tentacles; each second taking it farther away.

The officers in the room guessed what had happened and broke into wild applause.

Aland and Juana ignored them.

They knew the truth.

'You saved us,' she said, but then looked at him with infinite sadness, 'but we're not really saved, are we.'

'No,' he said. It was as if there were razor blades in his mouth, so difficult it was to speak. 'No, we're not safe. That encounter has thrown us out of the beam.' And then he uttered the terrible sentence that he had never thought he would say; a sentence whose utterance felt like it was tearing the guts out of his body. 'We won't reach Centauri.'

The officers looked at each other in blank amazement, completely unable at first to accept what they had just heard.

Juana fought to stay calm; thought to stay rational, fought to stay sane.

'What exactly has happened?'

'We made a very close pass to that object and described a hyperbolic path around it. We're not only out of the beam, but we've also been thrown into an escape trajectory from the Centauri system.'

Juana felt panic steadily begin to claim her.

'Heading?'

'Juana, we were sent from the Solar system on an exact path; one that would eventually take us to Centauri. It involved hideously complicated mathematics. Now we've been thrown onto a totally random path. So where do you think we're going now?'

'I don't know. For God's sake, Aland, tell me!'

Aland approached her.

'Nowhere. We're going nowhere. I don't think we'll pass anywhere close to a star for thousands of years; maybe hundreds of thousands of years. The Magellan is finished.

'And so are we.'

Then they hugged each other, pulling the other one close as if in an attempt to fuse into one body.

And then they wept.

They wept for a long time.

Even a Nume is human.

Epilogue

And such was the departure of the Magellan from the Centauri system.

No details shall be given of the Time of Chaos which followed its ejection from its Promised Land and the end of the crew's hopes of founding a New Earth.

Similarly, we shall not dwell on Aland's struggle to stabilise a maddened population or the selflessness of his heroic sacrifice.

Suffice it to say, it took several centuries for a form of sanity to return to that cargo of humans trapped on a vessel heading precisely nowhere.

A form of sanity?

Yes, perhaps absolute sanity was impossible in their circumstances.

Aland had been correct when he stated that their new course would not take them anywhere near another star for thousands of years. Indeed, he had underestimated their plight, for their next port of call, Theta Carinae, would not be reached for several million years.

And so, the Magellan continued to trace out its lonely world line through the indifferent fabric of spacetime.

BOOK TWO: ARRIVAL

The Heavy Land

t = 1,393.4 y

One: Peace in the Pastures

Her name was Gwion, and she was the senior apprentice shepherdess in the Pastures, a small part of the immense world of Majeh. She loved her job and looked forward to the day when she would take over from the aged Linon and have full responsibility for the flocks.

But that day was not today, for Linon was standing right next to her and gave her a sharp dig in the ribs.

'Daydreaming again, my girl?' she said. 'Well, wake up, I'm not ready for the Fertiliser Fields yet, and I won't be for many a cycle.'

Gwion blushed: Linon was right—she had been daydreaming about that very thing! Not that she wanted Linon to be in the Fertiliser Fields, of course; that day was far away. And long might it stay that way!

But it would be very nice to be her own mistress and answerable to nobody but the Matriarch.

She looked up at the flock, calculating what their angle of departure might be. The animals could move in three dimensions, of course, though not as efficiently as people. Gwion herself could fly many times farther and faster than the swiftest sheep; their thin legs were not very efficient in providing enough thrust for a speedy get-away. And, of course, her dogs were very familiar with their aerial tricks. They wouldn't get far.

She whistled a two-note command, and her dogs leapt into the air and had soon rounded the errant animals back into a tight formation.

After they were safely penned, Linon gave her charge a quick once-over.

'You're doing well, my girl,' she said. 'Seems like you've got a feel for these animals.'

Gwion was immediately distracted as her lead bitch had returned, and was thrusting her wet muzzle into Gwion's palm. She smiled and patted the animal's head before returning her attention to her supervisor.

'Thank you, Mistress Linon,' she said, after performing the little curtsy of obeisance, 'I want you to know I am proud to follow in your footsteps and tend to the flocks of the tribe.'

Linon nodded; it was not necessary for her to do anymore in the way of acknowledgement to one of inferior rank, but nonetheless, she was satisfied to hear Gwion's respectful words.

'Come,' she said, 'we have worked hard enough this day. Let us return to our hearths and give thanks.'

Gwion was about to leap into the air and begin the flight home when she remembered Linon's advanced years and gave a fleeting smile of embarrassment, hoping Linon hadn't noticed the near blunder. And so they began the long walk back to their dwellings— at least it seemed long to Gwion, used as she was to flying between the Pastures and the settlement. First, however, she found it necessary to stroke her dogs to reassure them they were not being punished by being forced to walk.

Linon did not say much on the trek back to the settlement, for, apart from their love of animals, the two had little in common. Linon was prone to endlessly reminiscing about times far distant in the past; the "Good Old Days" she always called them. Apparently, there had been longer periods of peace in those days than there were now, and the dark times—or "nights", as she called them—were shorter. Gwion thought those days did sound idyllic, but, secretly, she thought Linon must be embroidering the facts a little because nothing could really have been that good. And unlike her young companion, Linon had absolutely no interest in the time long, long before the "Good Old Days", what Gwion had, in the privacy of her own mind, termed the "Enigma of the Ancients." In fact, no one else in the entire tribe showed any interest in the period before Linon's youth. But, somehow, Gwion knew that there was an enigma hiding in those distant times.

They said their farewells at the gate to the settlement and parted. Gwion watched the older woman go and, once again, wondered how long it would be before Linon was sacrificed to the crops. She hoped it would not be for many more days; she would miss the other's company at round-up time, even if it meant listening to yet another round of improbable stories. For some reason, she halted at the entrance to the settlement and glanced up at her tribe's totem animal, which sat, as ever, at the top of its pole, staring glumly out into the dimness. Once, she had asked Linon what kind of animal it was, as she had never seen a live one. It was squat, flat and vaguely circular, with several limbs protruding from various points on its circumference, but the oddest features were the eyes. Although the animal was obviously dead, it still possessed a pair of eyes, but they were different from the animals with which she was familiar: they were hard to the touch and from certain angles reflected the lights in colours that changed as one moved relative to them. However, to Gwion's surprise, Linon knew nothing about them: she had never seen a live one either. Gwion knew there were living things that were only active during the night, but as the tribe feared those rarely seen creatures, she doubted this object was a representation of one. She shrugged and put the identity of the strange creature from her mind, never to think of it again.

Her friends and kin-members saw her as she came in and many of them waved at her, knowing she had been hard at work in the Pastures. Gwion was especially pleased to see Zan waving at her. She was about to sit down in her own private area when she saw the Matriarch of the group approaching. At first, she feared she had done something wrong, perhaps not made the proper gestures of respect to Great Guidance, but those fears were washed away as she saw the welcoming smile on Rhoana's features.

'Welcome back, child,' Rhoana said, extending her arms in the Gesture of Gracious Welcome. Gwion responded immediately with the Gesture of Respectful Submission. Formalities out of the way, Gwion ventured to say, 'How may I help you, Matriarch?'

The Matriarch sat beside her.

'There is but little I want from you today, child. Did all go well with the flock?'

'Yes, Matriarch. There were no signs of the Night Creatures. Not that I was expecting any, of course, as it will not be night for some time. But they grow ever bolder.'

Rhoana nodded, and a slight sign of concern briefly crossed her features.

'Unfortunately true, but if they try to attack during the day, we will be ready for them. But, tell me,' and her voice dipped somewhat, forewarning Gwion that what was coming was not for everyone's ears, 'were there any signs that the Heavy Landers are moving down?'

Gwion felt a brief stab of fear. She had been just a child during the last war, but she still remembered the terrible fear that had gripped the people that day, still remembered the sight and smell of blood.

But worst of all, she remembered seeing her mother being dragged away by one of those brutes. The old ones had warned her that there was no such thing as permanent peace, that the longer the period since the last war, the shorter the period to the next one. But she didn't want to believe it; why couldn't all the people of Majeh live together in harmony; surely there was enough room for them all?

She looked at the Matriarch directly, eye to eye; there must be no false hope.

'I saw nothing, Matriarch. There were no signs of any scouts; no footprints I did not recognise.'

Although she had been too young to remember the details of the last war, she had been told they always started the same way, with one or two individuals coming down from the Heavy Land to probe the tribe's defences—such as they were.

Gwion saw the Matriarch relax slightly.

'That is good to hear, child. But I fear the time of conflict is coming closer; let us pray it does not happen for many cycles.'

Gwion nodded, and the Matriarch gave the Gesture of Blessing and left her to her own devices. Back in her dwelling, she fell asleep for a short while after her exertions, only to be woken by a hand shaking her shoulder.

'Wake up, Gwion!'

Reluctantly, her eyes flickered open to see it was Cara, a young woman not much older than she. 'Time for the Preparation, sleepy-head!'

'Is that today?' Gwion mumbled, but a quick look at Cara's excited face told her it was indeed today. She forced herself to her feet and walked to the centre of the village. The men had already assembled, forming a rough circle which held the Matriarch at its centre. The women were busy creating the outermost ring. Everyone in the Preparation area had slipped their feet into rope loops embedded in the soil so that their exertions did not propel them into the air. A few people who had seen the Heavy Land, and lived to tell the tale, had said that such devices were not needed there. But they were unable to explain how this was possible. But one thing was certain: the inhabitants of that territory were much stronger and robust than the poor people of Gwion's tribe. Hence, the Matriarch had insisted on holding regular gatherings in which the people held exercise sessions, during which they endeavoured to lift pieces of the hard substances which comprised the skeleton of the land of Majeh.

Every child knew how to distinguish these fragments from others of no value. Although all substances floated when pushed hard enough, there were some which took a great effort to make move, and conversely, took an effort to stop them moving. And now every member of Gwion's people was required to hold their own individual object and raise it up and down as rapidly and as long as possible. There were separate prizes—an extra piece of pork—for the best man and best woman.

In her befuddled state, it had taken her a while to remember where her exercise object was stored, and so she was a little late in joining the circle of sweating, grunting women. The Matriarch had noticed this but, in light of their earlier conversation, gave her a forgiving, tolerant smile.

The exercises seemed to go forever, and the shanty that everyone sang to establish a rhythm was giving her a headache when it finally stopped. The Matriarch clapped her hands to indicate the end of that day's session.

'Well done, my people, well done. But from now on, we will make the sessions longer, the exercises harder.'

'But why?' one of the men in the inner circle called out. 'Why must we work harder?'

She looked at him without speaking for a while, and there was sorrow in her eyes. And then: 'We must do it, my friend. Because I have reason to believe that war is near.'

The man became silent.

And so did the rest of the tribe, and stood motionless.

But then they resumed their exercises, more vigorously than before.

Gwion was exhausted by the time the session was finally over and almost crawled back to her area, gratefully lying full length on the ground, arms by her side, looking up at the opposite side of the great world of Majeh. It was difficult to make out much detail on that distant wall, but everyone was reasonably sure it was inhabited. Not least among the signs of life that could be observed was that occasional fires could be glimpsed burning in the night on its surface. But whether those people were friendly or aggressive, kindly or violent, would never be known, for they were too far away to impinge in any way on the lives of Gwion's folk. Could they hold the answer to the enigma of the Ancients, or were they as ignorant as Gwion's own people? But it was impossible to fly that far, even if there had been any compelling reason to do so, and walking was even more out of the question, given the huge areas of scrubland which separated the communities.

As Gwion lay there, she noticed the quality of the light was changing, its spectrum shifting to yellow at the same time as it was dimming. Night was approaching.

She smiled. Another day of peace was drawing to a close.

And tomorrow was the day of the Ceremony of Thanksgiving.

***

Gwion became aware of the return of day as light filtered through her eyelids, bathing her consciousness in a roseate glow. She smiled, stretched, and went out to greet the new day.

To her slight embarrassment, most of the settlement's people were already up and were moving towards the central region, smiling and joking with each other. Gwion, too, felt happy; what she was about to witness was one of the most important and sacred ceremonies that Great Guidance had bestowed on his people; a ceremony which affirmed the glory of life and his instruction that it must continue forever, whatever challenges might befall his flock.

Of course, the Matriarch was already there, and she was wearing the flowing Thanksgiving robe, made of the finest, kemp-free fleece. It hung from her shoulders to the ground in a cascade of the purest white. It looked truly lovely. She looked around to ensure that all those agile enough to assemble had done so. Her smile was beatific. Beside her stood her slim, willowy daughter, Sylvana, who was bearing what looked to Gwion like a somewhat bored expression.

Rhoana spoke, in a clear, commanding voice.

'My people, once again, we come together to affirm and adore the Life-spirit which flows in us all. Was it not Great Guidance who said to our forefathers, "Whatever challenges you face, however the Outsider tries to make you despair, to abandon hope, to turn your back on life, you shall not do so. You shall laugh in his wicked face and ensure that the great river of life continues to flow until the moment comes when you receive your reward and enter Sentori." '

Only the Matriarch was permitted to utter the sacrosanct name given to the end of the journey; most of the young people had never heard the Sacred Word spoken aloud before, even though, as giggling children, they might have whispered it to each other when safely out of their mothers' earshot. Gwion herself was only old enough to have heard it once before. *Sentori!* To hear it spoken sent an electric thrill through her. The Matriarch watched them, nodding gently to herself with the pleasure of seeing the effect her speech was having. The older ones tried to look blasé, but she knew they too were shaken by the power of the Ceremony. She gave them all one last sign of love, turned towards a group of three men, clapped her hands and called, 'Tharan! Come and receive the Blessing!'

The three men approached her; Tharan being flanked by two Acolytes. Gwion looked at him, feeling a sense of awe at being so close to the Offering. Tharan, of course, was a very old man, being at least forty cycles old, and his age was clearly displayed by his long white beard, which he had not been allowed to trim for several months; however, other signs of age, such as the facial lesions caused by The Crab, were not evident on his relaxed features. He kneeled before the Matriarch, the Acolytes standing back from him.

'Tharan,' the Matriarch said in hushed tones. The people behind Gwion had to lean forward to catch her words, but they needed to hear them—that was the Ceremony. 'You have come to give us the most valuable thing that anyone can give. Because of you, the people will rest easy tonight, knowing the harvests will not fail, that the animals will grow fat and wholesome. It is truly an honour, not just for you, but for all of us. We are all in your debt.'

Tharan turned to face the assembled people and there was a hush while everyone waited for him to speak, but when he did, his thin, piping voice was hardly able to reach the rear of the throng. A few people called to him to speak up, but a fierce glare from Rhoana crushed them into silence. He gave her a quick glance of gratitude and continued: 'My fellows, my friends, my constant companions, I stand before you now, ready to give you my parting gift. I have watched you grow up before me and become the fine men and women you now are; I have seen you change from babbling infants to sturdy, brave men; into caring, loving mothers and I stand amazed at all you have achieved. I am truly sorry that I must leave you now, but I have tried my best to give you a little part of my wisdom, of my knowledge of this wonderful world of Majeh which Great Guidance has seen fit to bestow upon you. Care for this land and it will reward you; treat it badly, take it for granted, and the Outsider will be watching and will return hurt for hurt, injury for injury; he will bring the savages of the Heavy Land upon you. But bring your children up in the love of Great Guidance, ensure they know his ways, and no ill will befall you; your crops will be bountiful and your animals fat and wholesome.' He paused. 'I give thanks to Great Guidance for a long and fruitful life, and I wish all here assembled the same good fortune as I have enjoyed. And now is the time. I am ready.'

A silence fell, and the crowd gazed respectfully upon the scene as it unfolded. A few of the more timid mothers turned their children's gaze away, much to the latter's annoyance. Tharan lifted his head and the lefthand Acolyte reached around his neck and, with a single swift and merciful stroke, cut his throat. The righthand Acolyte held a bowl full of yeast flour under the spurting jet of blood until it had turned a rich crimson. A great cheer went up from the assembled people. The blood-soaked flour would be made into cakes for all the adults to consume in memory of Tharan and his long life. The silent Acolytes reverentially took the corpse away for defleshing. The meat would be given to the pigs, while the other components of the body would be ground up as fertiliser for the crops. And so Tharan would continue to care for the settlement in death as he had in life.

The crowd broke up, happily chatting, the one with the other.

Two: Minds Meet

Nothing much happened in the settlement after Thanksgiving. After all, it was not the kind of event that happened every day; once, maybe twice, in a cycle was the usual pattern. And so Gwion returned happily to her shepherdess duties.

As Gwion was so young, there was much she didn't understand about the bountiful world of Majeh; for instance, there was a region which consisted of nothing but huge, empty tanks made from glass. Nearly all of them had holes in their sides, and all of them were empty. Once, she had asked Linon what they might be, and had received the puzzling reply that they had held a sort of crop people didn't eat much of these days. Apparently, the ancient people had kept algae in these tanks, instead of in the small cisterns that the moderns used. They had used a similar method for their yeast supply.

'Didn't they eat anything else?' Gwion had asked, her forehead wrinkling in bemusement.

'No,' Linon had said, 'they didn't know as much as we do. I think they didn't have sheep or pigs and were forced to live off the stuff they grew in these tanks.'

Gwion had laughed, but then felt slightly guilty.

'Those poor Ancients,' she had said. 'Having to eat the same old things over and over and again. They must have been very stupid.'

'Well, you mustn't judge them by our standards,' Linon had gently chided. 'They didn't know how to rear our animals, so it was eat algae—or starve.'

Gwion had shuddered then.

'We're so lucky to be born in this age.'

'That we are,' Linon had said, and the subject had never been raised again. Gwion more than half suspected that Linon was simply guessing about the function of the tanks and any further questions would simply annoy her. However, that didn't stop Gwion from thinking about the Ancients. Very little had been told about them during the few cycles she had spent in school, for the simple reason that very little was known. They had been a kind of human people, that was much was certain, but one different from both the people of the Pastures and those of the Heavy Land. For instance, it was believed they could not fly, but were not Heavy Landers, who were similarly earth-bound; in addition, they had known nothing about animal husbandry unlike the people of the Pastures. So they must have had a very simple, primitive life, always on the edge of starvation.

Slowly, it seemed, they had been replaced by the modern type of human, who had learned about Great Guidance and his plan to take the people of the Pastures to the wonderful world of Sentori. But whilst they were still travelling to that world, he had given them the animals to look after and eventually eat. But those scraps of information were all that was really certain about the Ancients. They had had their time, and Great Guidance had removed them, just as a fatter, sweeter type of pig had recently replaced the old thin ones.

Now Gwion and Linon were standing together watching the dogs herding the sheep into a tight ball of bleating whiteness. Gwion always admired the grace of the dogs as they sliced through the air in graceful curves and arabesques, so much more pleasing than the clumsy ovine fluttering. She smiled; dogs were so more suited to flight than her flock.

Linon noticed her pleasure.

'Yes, they do look good,' she said, 'but I'm glad you're with me; I can't keep up with their speed these days with my sight.'

Gwion turned to look at her mentor. The large red and purple mass on her right cheek was definitely more prominent than the last time she had seen Linon, and was now beginning to close the eye. It was the Crab, of course; such excrescences and growths were not uncommon among the people of the Pasture.

'Does that hurt?' Gwion asked, innocently.

'Of course it hurts!' Linon snapped, and then reached out for her student. 'I'm sorry, Gwion, I didn't mean to be short-tempered. But you must think before asking all these questions; some of them are very stupid, you know. All marks of the Crab are painful. We just have to accept things as they are; Great Guidance will reward those who have suffered, after we reach the Destination.'

Gwion nodded respectfully. She was lucky, she knew; as yet there were no marks of the Crab on her skin, to mar the slightly greyish complexion she bore. Then she turned as the joyous barking of the dogs told her they had successfully completed rounding up the flock. She and Linon closed the gate and lowered the great fretwork of the cover to prevent the more boisterous ones from regaining their freedom.

Gwion had a growing feeling that she would be losing Linon's company before many more cycles had passed; it was time for a few more questions.

'Linon,' she began, 'about the Heavy Landers—why did Great Guidance create them, as they are so troublesome?'

Linon scowled. 'You do ask some questions, my girl! Shouldn't you ask a priest?'

'I would but, but…'. Gwion had become slightly flustered. 'They always look so stern! I dare not approach them. But I did ask this question when I was in school—but no one answered!'

Linon looked down at the ground; her face was troubled.

'I don't know, girl. Many of the reasons for Great Guidance's actions are hidden from us but all will be revealed, all will be understood, when we reach the Destination. I think the reason for the Heavy Landers is that perhaps he did not make them; that they are, in fact, survivors of the Ancients.'

Gwion pursed her lips; that didn't sound believable. The Ancients had been stupid; so stupid they couldn't rear stock and had to live on scraps of yeast and algae. Whatever the Heavy Landers were—they weren't stupid. Why would Great Guidance have swept most of them away but leave a fragment to plague the people of the Pasture?

'Perhaps the Outsider,' she began, but Linon placed a bony finger on her lips.

'Don't say it! The Outsider has no power to create! That is why Great Guidance cast him out of Majeh, to dwell in the outer darkness after he tried to make his own people, horrible puppet mockeries, to be his slaves!'

Gwion knew she had reached the limits of Linon's patience and it was time to move on. But she had this fire inside her, this drive, this desire to *know!* Other children had accepted the simple explanations offered to them by the teachers, but Gwion had somehow realised that the stories she had been told were missing something, something vital, the essence of a reality that was hidden.

But hidden by whom? Not Great Guidance; he had nothing but love for his people. Could the Outsider be more powerful than the priests had said?

Suddenly, she held her head and gave a small scream, twisting her face back and forth in her frustration. But Linon was not alarmed; she reached for Gwion and pulled her against her withered breast.

'I know what it is with you, Gwion,' she whispered as she stroked the girl's hair. 'You want to know things, to know why the world is as it is. But that is not for us to know, and you are only giving yourself grief before your time. Just wait, and real grief will surely find you.' She withdrew from Gwion and held her at arms-length. 'You know what your trouble is, my girl?'

Gwion shook her head.

Linon smiled.

'You think too much. You really must stop doing that.'

***

That evening, Gwion lay beside Zan in her private area of the settlement. He was slowly running his hands through her hair, and occasionally stroking her cheeks.

'I hope it will not be too long,' he said, breaking what had been a long silence.

Her eyebrows arched.

'Too long?'

'Yes,' he said, a note of irritation entering his voice, 'not too long before the Matriarch gives us permission to be sworn to each other.'

'Oh, that.' And then she fell silent for some moments before turning to face him. 'Zan, I don't know about that; I mean, I like you, but I'm not sure I'm ready to be betrothed.'

His face hardened.

'That again. You know, Gwion, sometimes I think your heart is as cold as your hands!'

She turned her face from him and looked down at her interlinked fingers.

'Please, Zan, let's not start this argument again. I've said I like you, and we will probably get betrothed someday, but I'm still young. Majeh is a huge place and I want to see more of it before I settle down and start having babies like the other women.'

'There are lots of women having babies who are your age; some younger!'

'Yes, but I'm not them, Zan! I want to find things out; I want to understand the world.'

He looked at her with a face of blank incomprehension.

' "Understand the world"? What kind of talk is that? What's there to understand? The world's the world. That's all anyone can say!'

As she looked down at her fingers, Linon's words came back to Gwion: *You think too much!* Was "Thinking too much" going to drive Zan away? But she knew she could not give up this strange appetite of hers; it was too strong. She turned back to him.

'Zan, you're wrong—there is more. The people on the Far Wall: are they like us? Do they believe in Great Guidance? Why are there Heavy Landers: are they the children of the Outsider? I need to know, Zan!'

'You shouldn't speak of the Outsider,' he growled. 'That's wrong.'

'But why is it wrong? It can't be wrong to want to know things about Majeh. Why would Great Guidance give us minds to ask questions if he didn't want us to use them? Nothing changes around here, so how will he know when it is time to reach the Destination?'

Zan leapt to his feet.

'That's enough! That's wicked talk! I'll tell the priests!'

He crossed to a sheath of strips of bark on a small table next to the bed and began rifling through them, throwing each one on the floor after he had finished looking at it.

'I've seen you looking at this stuff. What are they? What are they for?'

She got down on her hands and knees and began collecting the discarded sheets, rearranging them into an order known only to her.

'They're something that interests me, Zan; don't damage them, please. It's just a hobby. It's not irreligious.'

He held up one of the sheets in a manner that made it an accusation. On the surface of the bark she had drawn strange angular shapes, grouped into sets of four or five of the odd characters. Beside a few of them, she had drawn a simple picture.

'I've seen some of these shapes, on the ruins near the broken vats,' he said. 'Why are you copying them? These are the work of the Ancients, aren't they? If they are, they're no part of modern life. Great Guidance got rid of the Ancients, didn't he?' He looked at her as he slowly tore one of the flimsy sheets in half and threw the pieces on the bed. 'I really think the priests should hear about this; that there's someone here who likes the Ancients.'

'Zan, I think they're a form of writing. Perhaps the Ancients weren't quite as stupid as some people think. Maybe we could learn something from these writings, if we could only understand them!'

He glared at her, arms akimbo.

'You're going too far, Gwion. What kind of girl are you? This isn't normal!'

She joined him and enclosed him in supplicant arms.

'Zan, don't be angry, please. I can't help the way I am. I've always been like this. I don't mean any harm; I'm not disrespectful to Great Guidance, really I'm not.'

'You're going to be my woman, Gwion,' he said in a low voice, 'whether you like it or not.'

'But...'

Suddenly, the back of his hand slashed across her face, sending her spinning down to the floor, scattering its thin covering of straw.

'Outside!' he yelled, uttering the only obscenity the tribe knew, 'No more "buts"! No more talking about "The Far Wall"! No more stupid drawings! You're going to settle down with me and have my babies. That's what normal life is like, and I'm normal—even if you're not. Now, get these ideas out of your head before I lose my temper and really hit you.'

She looked up at him wide-eyed, as if seeing him for the first time.

'I'd like you to leave now,' she said, slowly and coldly.

He sat on the bed and placed an ankle over a knee.

'I don't think so.'

'Then I will!'

And so, putting a hand to the spreading red mark on her face, Gwion went out into the night, sobbing. She walked in the darkness for a long time, only returning to her place when the noises of the Night Creatures had grown too loud.

When she returned, Zan had gone.

But every one of her sets of drawings had been torn in pieces.

***

Gwion was awake most of the night, staring unseeing into the moist darkness. Once, she heard one of the night animals moving around outside, but she did not get up to investigate: she'd been told they had long tusks.

408

When the longed-for day finally arrived, she moved morosely around her little home; it was a rest day for her; Linon was out with another of her apprentices. And so it was an unwelcome interruption when a junior priest stuck his head through the curtain which shielded her from the outside world and said, 'His Reverence, Moroth, wants to see you.'

Gwion's heart missed a beat. Moroth was a priest who took his duties very seriously; Zan must have said something! However, a command from him was something no one could ignore, and she soon was sitting, hands folded neatly in her lap, under his stern gaze.

He was a withered man, somewhat younger than Tharan had been, but looking much older. The purplish-red lesions of the Crab's visitations had already taken one eye, and given him a sagging wattle that hung below his jaw and which trembled and shook whenever he spoke.

And he was speaking now.

'Gwion,' he said, in a crackling voice that sounded like two dry yeast stalks being rubbed together, 'I am told that you have been saying bad things about religion.'

She decided she would not be browbeaten into making apologies she saw no need for.

'No, Reverence, I do not recall saying anything untoward.'

Moroth looked a little puzzled, and more than a little annoyed.

'That is not what I have heard. I have been told you have been falsely claiming that the Outsider has the power of creation. That he has engendered his own children; offspring of his own wicked flesh.'

Gwion's heart skipped another beat. She remembered she had said something like that to Zan; a fleeting thought she had foolishly said out loud. But she had thought that Zan cared enough about her so that he would not repeat it to those who might take serious offence.

It appeared she had been wrong.

'I,' she said, desperately trying to think how she could interpret that fleeting thought as a harmless fancy, 'I... I may have said something like that, but it was only a silly joke, not meant to be taken seriously.'

Moroth leaned forward, his wattle falling clear of his bony chest.

'Everything about the Outsider is to be taken seriously. I'm afraid I must...'

But Gwion never learned what her punishment was to be, for at that moment, the curtain to the priest's room was drawn abruptly back, and a beam of yellow light illuminated Moroth's face, delineating every line and wrinkle on that surprised countenance.

'Matriarch!' he said, hurriedly rising to his feet, 'You honour me with your presence! I was just chastising this foolish girl. How... how can I help you?'

Gwion also jumped to her feet, and her peripheral vision saw the Matriarch's slim form pass close by.

'Sit down please, Moroth,' came Rhoana's soft tones, a silky voice but one with the silk covering steel. 'I have heard of this child's dangerous words and wish to question her myself, to discover the true extent of her dangerous delusions. You will allow me to cut short your interrogation, I assume?'

'Why, yes, of course, Matriarch,' Moroth spluttered, 'I did not realise her crimes were so great, otherwise I would not have presumed to attempt to question her myself but would have brought her immediately to you.'

Rhoana smiled.

'I understand. A perfectly natural error; do not concern yourself with it overlong, Moroth.' She turned to Gwion and, in a much sharper voice, said, 'Child! With me, now!'

The Matriarch's dwelling was a substantial structure, befitting her status; unlike every other one in the settlement, it had a solid door, which Rhoana carefully shut as she indicated that Gwion should go further into the room. Then, joining her guest in the interior, she pointed to a divan and said, gently, 'Sit, child.'

Gwion obeyed, but found the time to look around in awe at the magnificence of the Matriarch's house, taking in the expertly carved ornaments made from genuine wood, the long couch, covered with a throw made from fleece so soft and white it appeared to contain an inner radiance, and...

But then she remembered why she was there. Reluctantly, she raised her face to meet the Matriarch's gaze, but was surprised to see that Rhoana was smiling.

'Don't be afraid, Gwion,' the latter said, 'I am not going to chastise you. I heard about Moroth but too late to stop him. It seems someone has been saying things about you, Gwion.'

Gwion nodded but said nothing; she still felt residual loyalty to Zan.

The Matriarch understood her silence and nodded.

'We will say no more about that, child.' She fell silent for a while, and looked away from Gwion, as if unsure of how to proceed. Then: 'I have been watching you for some time and have noticed many things about you. It seems to me you have a great need to understand things, to learn how things work. You have a refusal to accept answers that you know to be inadequate. Am I right?'

Gwion thought about what her reply should be. Was she being tricked into entering a trap? But finally, she said, 'Yes, that is true.'

'Relax, child. I am not trying to get you to incriminate yourself. I don't need any subterfuges to get you into trouble; all I would need to do is to hand you back to Moroth.' She made a "Come closer" motion. Her voice dropped slightly, as if betraying a slight concern about the possibility of being overheard. 'All the time I have been Matriarch, I have been watching for the appearance of someone like you.'

'Someone like me?' Gwion said, faintly. 'I'm just a girl—an apprentice shepherdess.'

'No, you are more than that. Everyone else here is content to follow the same ways, to move along the same deep grooves; never questioning, always accepting.'

'What have I been questioning?' Gwion said. 'I thought I was just asking for a few simple answers.'

'No, you have been doing more than that. I have had people watching you for some time. They thought I was suspicious of you, and, in a way, I was, but not in the way that Moroth thinks. Linon has been especially helpful.'

Gwion's face dropped. *Linon's been reporting on me? I thought she was my friend.*

'No, child. Your face tells me you think you have been spied upon in preparation for punishment. It is not that, I swear to you, as your Matriarch.'

Gwion looked at Rhoana's earnest expression and felt her guard drop.

'Thank you, Matriarch. But why has my asking a few questions been so important to you?'

Rhoana sat back and looked up at the carven ceiling.

'Because this world of ours; this Majeh—it is hiding a secret; a great, wonderful, perhaps even terrible, secret.'

Gwion felt the hairs on the back of her neck begin to rise, and felt a prickling sensation suddenly course through her nerves. This was what she wanted to hear—but now it appeared to be about to be revealed, she was suddenly afraid. Perhaps it was best to leave things as they were!

'What might this secret be?' Her mouth had become strangely dry.

The Matriarch spoke again, but appeared to be changing the subject.

'Has anyone ever commented on your appearance?'

Gwion thought.

'Zan said I was pretty, a few times.'

Rhoana laughed.

'Good for him! But has anybody mentioned the colour of your skin?'

She thought again.

'Yes, when I was younger. Some of my friends said I looked like I was made of stone.'

The Matriarch nodded, as if she had received confirmation of something important.

'And your body temperature?'

Gwion looked puzzled. These were bizarre questions. What could they have to do with a great and terrible secret?

'People say I have cold hands.'

An indescribable look came over the Matriarch's features. And then she extended her hands, offering them to be held by Gwion.

'Yes. So have I.'

Three: Encounter in the Night

Gwion stared blankly at the Matriarch.

'You have cold hands? What does that prove? Some people have red hair. Some people have big feet. I don't understand.'

The Matriarch laughed.

'Well said, Gwion. The more you speak, the more you prove my point. Now listen,' and she leaned forward, dropping her voice again. 'You'll have to go against your instincts and take what I am about to say on trust. When you have absorbed all I have to say, then you can argue with me. So please just listen.'

Gwion sat up straight, matching Rhoana's piercing stare with her own.

'I'm listening.'

The Matriarch spoke: 'You are too young to remember much of my time here in this settlement. I was here before you were born, and I remember watching you as you grew up., knowing that I could find a fellow-creature in you. You see, I am older than I look, and I came here from another settlement. I came from the Far Wall.'

'The Far Wall!' Gwion interjected. 'But that's such a long way away! And we don't know what sort of people live there!'

'*My kind* of people,' Rhoana said, 'Now please be quiet, or we'll be here all day.'

Against her instincts, Gwion spread her hands to indicate acquiescence.

The Matriarch continued: 'On the Far Wall we know more about this world than your people do. We have always known that the inhabitants of Majeh—outside the Heavy Land, that is—can be divided into two groups: *Ords* and *Nooms*. I am a Noom. And so are you.

'Nooms have minor exterior characteristics which can identify them. Usually, we have a grey cast to the skin—but not always: you have it; I do not. But always, we have a slightly lower body temperature, most noticeable in the hands. You have it; so do I.

'But these are minor signs, easily overlooked. But there are other more important differences: we mature earlier and are more fertile. We live longer and are more resistant to the Crab. For this reason, we do not stay too long in one place. We have to move on before our differences become apparent to the Ords. This is my second settlement; the first was on the Far Wall.

'But the most important difference between the two groups is our minds: we understand things more quickly, we see solutions more easily; we are always searching for new knowledge, new ways of understanding. We find it easy to lead and control others. That is how I became the Matriarch, while the native women of this settlement did not. You are starting to display those tendencies. I had planned to let you develop a little longer before revealing myself to you, but the incident with Moroth showed to me that I could no longer delay.'

'Why can't you delay? What is so important that you have been forced to act now?'

Rhoana's face became troubled.

'On the Far Wall, there are more Nooms than here. Not vastly so, just a natural fluctuation. But there is something there that we do not understand; something I think is of incredible importance. We have been trying to comprehend it for many cycles but have reached an impasse. We need a fresh perspective; perhaps young eyes will see what we have not.'

'I'm a shepherdess. I can tell you the best way of pulling a lamb out of a pregnant ewe. That's all I can do.'

'No, you can and will do more. There is much that does not make sense about this world of ours. What we must do to be allowed to reach Sentori, for instance. That has never been explained—to my satisfaction, at least.'

Gwion winced at the use of the Sacred Word, but then remembered she was talking with the Matriarch. Rhoana continued: 'There are other mysteries; ruins of things we do not recognise.'

'The Ancients,' Gwion said. 'We know they were here before us.'

'Yes, but everyone says they were stupid, little different from the animals. But that can't be right. Animals could not have built those big structures of glass. We are failing to understand something, something so obvious that tired minds cannot conceive it; cannot realise they have passed over it, unseen, unknown.'

Gwion lowered her head and bit her lower lip. The Matriarch's words had awoken a hunger in her, one she had not known she had possessed until the last few minutes. The hunger to *know!* She looked up.

'Perhaps you have overlooked something obvious,' she said, 'there are three types of people on Majeh, not two. So what part do the Heavy Landers play in all this?'

The Matriarch's face changed, displaying an expression Gwion had not seen before—doubt, uncertainty.

'I don't know,' she whispered.

Gwion found that answer slightly disturbing; until that second, the Matriarch had displayed a sense of calm assurance, almost of omniscient power. And yet it seemed there were things she didn't know. Gwion tried to gather her thoughts, to bring the different aspects of the situation into one coherent whole.

And found she couldn't.

'So,' she began, 'in Majeh there are, or were, four types of people: there were Ancients who everybody except you and me thinks were stupid brutes, and there are Heavy Landers, who may or may not be descendants of those people. And then there are Nooms and Ords.' She gave Rhoana a sharp look. 'Doesn't get us very far, does it?'

The Matriarch leaned back and stared at her carven ceiling.

'No, it doesn't. I can tell you're disappointed in me, Gwion, but you must remember I have been working on my own. If I could understand everything about this world, I wouldn't need help.' She looked back at Gwion and smiled. 'And I do need help. And you're it.'

'What about Sylvana, your own daughter? Haven't you confided your thoughts to her?'

Rhoana looked slightly wistful.

'No, I have not. I'm afraid Sylvana does not show any Noom tendencies, which is a great sorrow to me. She is happy to accept the world as it is, and sees no mysteries.'

'So, what can I do that you haven't, and Sylvana can't?'

'Forgive me for revealing I have been watching and examining you, Gwion. I needed to be sure of what you were, that you are a true Noom because there are so few on this Wall. And I know you have been studying the marks on the artefacts left behind by the Ancients. I have come to the conclusion that those marks hold the key to unlocking the mysteries of Majeh.'

'Some people think they're just meaningless drawings.'

'But not you!' Rhoana leaned forward, and there was an ardent light in her eyes. 'You think the same as me; I know you do! And together, we will turn that key and discover what has been hidden for so long!'

Gwion shook her head, reluctantly.

'No, I don't think so, Matriarch. There are only a few sections of those markings on the artefacts. I have looked long and hard and can't find any others. It's not enough.'

To Gwion's amazement, the Matriarch leapt from her seat and joined her on the divan, fiercely clasping her hands.

'But that's just it! I know where there are many more inscriptions, and pictures alongside them! Together we can do it, Gwion! Together, we must do it!'

Gwion gently removed her hands and moved slightly further away.

'How have you found them and I have not?'

Rhoana suddenly stood and looked down upon her young guest. There was an air of triumph about her.

'Because they are where I came from. The Far Wall. And that's where you and I are going!'

***

Gwion had left the Matriarch's dwelling with her head spinning, her thoughts jumbled and confused. Despite Rhoana's cajoling, she had refused to commit herself to such a crazy undertaking. The distance to reach the Far Wall by walking around the circumference of Majeh was not great, but the lands "below" and "above" the Pastures were barren scrublands, broken and uprisen into jagged teeth, as if heavy objects had struck those regions from outside. No one knew the real reasons for the existence of those Badlands, as there were no objects in the universe other than Majeh (and possibly Sentori—if that paradise was actually in the universe). So the Badlands could not have been caused by anything colliding with Majeh from outside. And to make matters worse, those tortured terrains were known to be infested with dangerous animals.

That left flying across the diameter of Majeh's central void—but such a feat was clearly impossible. So whichever way the Matriarch had arrived in the Pastures, it could not have been by that method.

And yet she had insisted that was exactly what she had done.

Gwion continued walking away from the Matriarch's house; she needed time to think, and lots of it.

But her thoughts were rudely interrupted when a hand descended on her shoulder from behind. It was Zan, and he was looking down at her, bearing an expression she could not quite identify. She waited. Zan was turning his head from side to side as if he was trying to do something he really didn't want to do. Then he fixed his stare upon her.

'Look, Gwion, I'm sorry. I'm sorry, alright? Let's leave it there and start again, alright?'

She stared up at him.

'Start again? You mean start again being hit by you, is that it?'

He grimaced.

'Look, that was a mistake, alright? You annoyed me by not saying you'd be my girl. And all those stupid drawings you did.'

'The ones you tore up, you mean? The ones I'd spent months working on?'

His grimace became a frown.

'They were just drawings, weren't they? You could do some more. Outside! I could do some; they were just drawings!'

'No, they weren't. If you can't see that, if you won't believe me, then we have no future. I don't want you in my place again.'

He looked shocked, uncomprehending.

'What? You don't mean that!'

'I do. Now leave me alone; I've got things to think about.'

She turned and walked away. But Zan had recovered from the shock.

'Gwion! Go to Outside! Do you hear me—go to Outside! He'll be glad to see you!'

Gradually, his shouts faded as she increased the distance between them. Once in her private place, she lay full length on the straw, her head spinning. A short while ago, the break-up with Zan would have left her sobbing, but now it was just an annoying distraction. The conversation with the Matriarch kept bursting into her consciousness, much as he tried to hold it down. The Matriarch had opened up possibilities she had only dimly been aware of. Perhaps the two of them together could solve at least some of the puzzles she had been wrestling with for so long.

She could find no resolution; no obvious course of action came to her. So finally, she ate a few slices of dried pork for her supper, washing them down with tepid, insipid water.

Then, despite the buzzing and churning of her mind, she slept.

It was dark when she awoke. The night-time temperature had dipped but little, but outside, the ancient blackness had reclaimed Majeh.

Why had she awoken? Typically, she was a sound sleeper. Zan had claimed that she was like a geriatric porker in the way she snored and didn't respond to being shaken. But as they'd never spent the entire night together she had put that down to his teasing. Not until the Matriarch allowed them to be sworn to each other could real intimacy be permitted.

But now she had been awoken. Something was outside.

She shivered as she realised it must be one of the Night Creatures. They had been becoming more and more bold, more and more fearless in their intrusions into settlement life. People who had glimpsed them had said they were like the people's familiar pigs but much hairier and equipped with tusks that could easily disembowel those who came too close. And one was outside now.

Slowly, slowly, her hand reached for the spear she kept near her sleeping area. It was a long shaft of wood with a fire-hardened point. Pitiful though it was, it was all that passed for weaponry among the people. Gradually, she rose into a crouching position, with the spear pointing at the curtain that hid her from the outside world. She waited.

Suddenly, the curtain was pushed violently aside and a slobbering snout, covered in coarse reddish hair, came through the gap, dripping drool on her floor. And dim though the illumination was, there was enough to see two wicked fangs jutting from the lower jaw. It saw her, or smelled her, or heard her, and the animal thrust more of its not inconsiderable bulk through the gap.

Gwion knew her life hung on what happened in the next few seconds. As the animal lifted its head to sniff the air, she drove the point into the soft flesh under its jaw with all the strength her untested muscles could deliver. There was a raucous explosion of squealing and bellowing, and the head withdrew. For some reason she never understood, she followed it outside. In the meagre, yellow glow cast by the wall lights she saw a large black shape scuttling away towards the settlement's boundary. She smiled and lifted the spear in triumph. She felt a drop of moisture fall from its tip on her hand. Gwion sniffed the liquid and was immediately struck by the similarity to the smell that rose from the torrents of blood spilled in the pig slaughtering.

It seemed she had solved one mystery at least. Some at least of the Night Creatures were related to pigs. But after this display of boldness on their part, she would have to talk to the Matriarch about strengthening the defences of their little town. She was confident that Rhoana would listen to her now.

She decided to return and try to sleep for what remained of the night as she felt the urgent hammering of her heart subside back into its normal rhythm. But as she turned, she was frozen into immobility. Against the distant sickly radiance of the wall lights, she saw a silhouette, just a featureless black shape, still, silent, patiently watching.

It was the silhouette of a man, but not a man of the settlement. Even though all she could see was a motionless shape, she could sense a feeling of strength, of contemptuous power flowing from it.

Was it really a man? She took a hesitant step towards it. But even as she began to move, so did the silhouette. It turned, revealing the full length of a mighty spear. And then it was gone, moving in the great arcs of near-flight. But the arcs of movement it made were much greater than any man of the village could have made, even Zan. So much so that it had gone in a few heartbeats.

Gwion's legs became suddenly weak, and she had to lean on her spear to support herself.

The Matriarch had been right: war was near.

She had seen her first Heavy Lander.

Four: Fear and Flight.

'A Heavy Lander?' Rhoana's voice was brittle with concern. 'I don't doubt what you saw, Gwion. They must be coming down from their region, ready to make war upon us once again.' A look of near despair came into her sculptured features. 'Why? Why must they do this? Isn't there enough suffering in Majeh as it is!' She looked up at the ceiling, and her lips moved, silently. But Gwion was sufficiently adept at lip-reading to know she was calling upon Great Guidance. She waited for the Matriarch to compose herself; she found this display of doubt in such a normally confident, capable, woman disturbing.

'What do we do?' she finally said.

Rhoana looked at her and Gwion saw the woman struggling with conflicting emotions, trying to calm the storm in her mind.

She succeeded. Gwion saw her sit up straighter, and her features become unemotional again.

'The first thing we do is strengthen the defences. Your encounter with a night creature would be enough to justify that, even without Heavy Landers. Next, we must hold more of the exercise sessions to build up the men's muscles; bring the flocks closer in.'

Gwion looked unconvinced.

Rhoana smiled wistfully. 'You have not failed me, child. On the contrary, I have grown lazy because I am not used to people doubting my word. In a way, it is refreshing not to be treated as an emissary from Great Guidance.' She leaned back. 'What do you suggest as you clearly find my plans inadequate?'

Gwion spoke confidently, no longer unsure of herself. She was only human, but so, apparently, was the Matriarch.

'We need weapons, much better weapons. These flimsy sticks were only just enough to drive off a wild beast, and even then, it only suffered a slight nick to its throat. If it had continued the attack, it would have killed me. But in the ruins of the Ancients, there are materials other than wood: substances that shine and feel cool to the touch; substances that can be seen through. These can and must be turned into weapons.'

The Matriarch nodded.

'You're right; they will be.' Another smile. 'I'm just wondering why I didn't think of that. I suppose, even in Noom terms, I am no longer young.'

Gwion said nothing. But Rhoana leaned forward again and clutched her hands.

'But there is something else: we must carry out the project I talked to you about.'

'What, crossing to the Far Wall? You can't do that, not with the Pastures about to be engulfed by war!'

'Sylvana can command the village as well as I.'

'You told me she had no Noom inheritance.'

'So I did. But I didn't say she was incompetent. When I explain the need for new weapons, she will get it done as quickly as I. She does not have an enquiring mind, but she is not a fool.'

'So you will leave her to face the Heavy Landers while you disappear onto the Far Wall.'

Rhoana's face twisted in anger.

'What! Are you accusing me of cowardice! How dare you! You know nothing of my early life!'

Gwion stood up to leave, but the Matriarch reached up for an arm and pulled her back.

'No, stop. Stop Gwion. Listen to me. We have a short period before the war begins; I have studied the records, and I know how these things play out. You and I have the best chance of deciphering the Ancients' records, maybe the best chance for generations! We can do it, Gwion! Just think of what we might learn! We both know the Ancients were not stupid brutes. Something happened to them and destroyed their culture, but we might be able to reclaim some of their knowledge. Knowledge that might help us defeat the Heavy Landers, once and for all.'

Gwion shrugged.

'Just a pet theory of yours.'

Now Rhoana reached over and clutched the other's shoulders.

'No, listen to me. You may be a Noom, but you don't have my experience. There were people cleverer than me on the Far Wall, people who thought they were on the edge of a significant discovery. I thought they were moving too slowly, so I left them to find new examples of the Ancients' work. I did, but there was no one here who could help me. Or so I thought. Gwion, you must realise, every year that increases the time between the Ancients and us makes it less and less likely that we will ever unlock their secrets.' She leapt to her feet and stared at Gwion, her face unrecognisable as powerful emotions battled for control. 'I will not die with all this not taken one step further. Outside! Outside! I won't go into the Fertiliser Fields without even trying, and by Sentori, you will help me!'

Gwion winced under the barrage of forbidden words and was silent as the Matriarch sat down and turned her face away. In turn, powerful emotions battled for control in Gwion's face. Finally, she touched Rhoana and gently turned her face so the two women were looking deep into each other's eyes.

'Alright, Rhoana. I will come with you to the Far Wall.'

***

It was one thing to agree to go to the Far Wall, but a totally different one actually to do it. Most creatures living in the very low gravity environment of the Pastures could fly to some extent. However, the term "fly" requires some explanation. Flight in the Pastures was a series of shallow arcs, beginning and ending on the ground. The stronger the initial impetus into the air, the wider was the arc. Motion of the limbs, in a manner not too dissimilar to swimming, could extend the arc until the aeronaut could glide quite long distances. However, it was not nearly as efficient as the powered flight long-extinct animals had mastered on Old Earth.

One thing the most accomplished flyers had noticed was that the higher the flight, the less was the pull back down. Some people had theorised that at the centre point of Majeh's diameter, there would be no downward pull at all.

And Rhoana had confirmed that was true.

'When you are exactly halfway across, you will not feel a force pulling you back down to the Pastures. We call it "The Nothing Point." And if you go a little further, you will feel a force pulling you down onto the Far Wall. So the second part of the journey will be comparatively easy, compared to getting away from the Pastures.'

Gwion looked unconvinced.

'That's simple for you to say. But getting to this "Nothing Point" won't be easy. I've only ever flown back and forth between the flocks and this village. I've never even thought about a flight of the length you're talking about. You're a grown woman; maybe it's easier for you.'

Rhoana gave a low chuckle.

'Yes, I am a grown woman. Quite an old one, even by Noom standards. But even a woman like me would find the flight across the diameter a little challenging. Most of the people in this village hardly ever leave it, so how do you fly, Gwion? What method do you use?'

'Method? I just jump up as hard as I can, fly up to a certain height and then glide back down again. Then if I'm a long way from the flock, I move my arms back and forth, and sometimes I kick my legs. That gets me quite a bit further along.'

'Yes. You Pasture people don't know much about flight, do you?'

Gwion frowned at the implied slur, but said nothing. She did not want to annoy the other woman as she was sure the Matriarch had some revelation she was about to make.

And so it transpired.

'Come with me,' Rhoana said, indicating a room behind the main one in which they had always done their talking. She showed Gwion a long, wooden chest, longer than the Matriarch herself. Then, lifting the lid, she removed two long panels made from a different kind of wood from the chest. They were shaped like very elongated leaves, but of a length greater than Gwion was tall.

'Here,' Rhoana said, 'feel them.'

She handed Gwion one of the panels, and Gwion, braced to accept the weight, showed astonishment instead.

'They hardly weigh anything!' she said.

'Yes, they're a special kind of wood that is plentiful on the Far Wall. But unfortunately, I haven't seen it here, which might explain your poor flying abilities.'

'Yes, you've explained how backward we are enough times, Rhoana. How will these get us to your homeland?'

'Like this.' The Matriarch showed Gwion the straps on the underside and slipped the panel over an outstretched arm. She took another from the chest and, with a little more difficulty, attached it to her other arm. She smiled at Gwion and then flapped her arms. The sudden blast of air made Gwion close her eyes, and she stepped back out of the immediate area.

'Yes, I see,' she said, her eyes blinking, 'those things amplify the beat of arms. Gives you more thrust.'

'Well done! Spoken like a true Noom! It's good to hear words like "amplify" again. I feel like I'm home already.'

'Thank you. I'm glad to know that simple words please you. But what will I do when we start the flight? Just follow you?'

'Of course not. Look in the chest, Gwion.'

Gwion obeyed and was not too surprised to see two more of the panels lying at the bottom. She withdrew them and measured them against her arms.

'A little long for me, but I guess I'll get used to them.' She looked up at Rhoana. 'What do I call these things?'

'We call them "wings."'

'I've never heard that word before.'

'It's a very old word. We think it's from the Ancients' language. But that doesn't matter; it's what we use them for. And that is real, proper flying.'

Gwion looked down at the wings and pulled a dubious face.

'I don't know. It's an awful lot to take in, I'm…'

The Matriarch laughed.

'We're not doing it tonight, you silly girl! Your intelligence has limits, it seems. You have to practice with them. We're not going anywhere until I'm satisfied with your abilities.'

'The villagers will be a little surprised when they see me flying over their heads using these.'

'Now I know you're pretending to be stupid. We will practice some distance from the settlement and fly in the opposite direction. Now, I think that's enough shocks for you for one evening. Let's go back to the main room and have some coffee.'

Over two steaming cups of the bitter brew, the conversation restarted.

'I understand you have some copies of the Ancients' writing, Gwion.'

'I had. Zan tore them up.'

'Do you still have them? Can you put them together again?'

'Yes, I suppose so. He only tore them in half.'

'Then do so. I want to see them, take them with us if they're light enough. The more examples we have, the more likely we are to finally understand those people.'

'You really think there's much to understand?'

'Yes. They can't have been dumb brutes. Eating meat like we do doesn't make you a genius, and living off yeast and algae doesn't make you an animal. I think they knew things that we don't, perhaps many more things.'

'So if they were as clever as you're suggesting, why aren't they still around? Why aren't we Ancients?'

The Matriarch looked down at the wisps of vapour rising from her cup and was silent for some time. Then she raised her head: 'Something truly terrible must have happened to them. Something so appalling it destroyed them.'

Gwion, in turn, was silent. Then: 'But it was so long ago. Why should we worry? We have our lives here. The war with the Heavy Landers will pass, like all the others have. We will be happy again, eventually.'

Rhoana shook her head, pityingly.

'You don't get it, do you, girl? If something bad happens, why do you think it can only happen once? If my fellows and I are right, then this Majeh we live in and love is not as safe and secure as it seems. Maybe something terrible will visit us again.'

Gwion did not reply. Although she had not said it, she had already guessed what was the fear that haunted the Matriarch. So she said no more on that topic. Indeed, she could not, because a hand of ice had reached in and clutched her heart.

***

Gwion rubbed her head and groaned. She was certain there would be a large lump there by nightfall. The descent to the ground had been many times faster than planned, and she had not intended to land head first.

'I'm never going to get this,' she said, looking accusingly up at the Matriarch.

Rhoana was annoyed.

'Are you doing this deliberately? So I can let you off crossing the diameter? I've told you and told you how to move those wings!'

Gwion rose, a little unsteadily, to her feet and glared at the older woman.

'I'm doing my best. You've done this many times. I haven't.'

Rhoana turned her back.

'And I thought you were a proper Noom. Looks like I was wrong. You're just a stupid young girl.'

Rage exploded in Gwion's face.

'That's the last time you call me stupid! Watch this, you old porker!'

With that, she climbed up to the top of the mound that had been the launching point for her earlier unsuccessful flight and, with a powerful thrust of her quadriceps, shot vertically upwards. She closed her eyes and silently mouthed *Think, think, Gwion! A powerful downstroke, then rotate the arm as it rises to decrease air resistance! Do it!*

She felt the resistant air cleave beneath the beat of her arms and gave a quick downwards glance. To her astonishment, the Matriarch had shrunk to a featureless blob far below. She was higher than she had ever been! She lowered one wing and beat strongly with the other and described a wide, sweeping arc around and above the distant object she knew to be the Matriarch.

What do you think about this, you old porker? she thought, triumphantly. Then her smile vanished. She had never been this high before. If she landed badly, this time she could do real damage. She fought the growing panic down.

You can do this, Gwion. Just take it slowly.

She knew an attempt to descend suddenly would only lead to a broken-limbed disaster. She turned again, desperately thinking of how to get down from this altitude she had so foolishly reached. Then she had it. She dipped down slightly and then bent her trajectory into a gentle curve. At the near completion of the circle, she descended again, but as gently as possible.

And so, in a series of calm spirals, she came nearer and nearer to the safety of the ground. Nearer and nearer. Then boldness overcame caution, and she decided to drop down directly in front of a no-doubt astounded Matriarch. But at the last moment, she miscalculated and, out of control, dropped the last few metres, reaching the ground with another thump.

Raising her mud-stained face, the first things she could see were the Matriarch's shoes. Shakily, she rose to her feet, waiting for the next tongue-lashing. But to her amazement, Rhoana reached forward and pulled her close into a breath-crushing hug.

'You did it, Gwion, you did it! My plan worked!'

Gwion took a step backward, looking at the other's grinning face. 'Your plan? What plan?'

'To get you so riled up that you'd do anything to prove me wrong. Get you to overcome your fear so you'd do anything to get at me, rub my nose in it. And it worked.'

Gwion shook her head, wonderingly.

'You really are a clever old porker.'

Rhoana's grin grew more expansive.

'Of course, I'm the Matriarch, aren't I?'

Five: Across The Diameter

As requested, Gwion attempted to repair the inscriptions Zan had torn up. But after several malodorous attempts with bone glue, she gave up and simply wrote them out again.

Together, she and Rhoana studied them.

'What do you think is happening here?' the latter said, pointing to a drawing.

Gwion had looked at it many times before, but she looked again, with no more success than previously.

'I have no idea,' she eventually said, after a minute and a half had passed. Rhoana continued staring at it, holding the drawing farther away, then bringing it closer.

'They're putting something on their heads,' she said. 'I think that's clear enough.'

'But why would they do that? A kind of decoration?'

'No, it's a ceremony of some kind. To indicate status, probably. There are some groups on the Far Wall that do similar things. When they appoint a new leader, they put a kind of hat on his head, made from twisted plant stems. A "crown" they call it.'

Gwion shrugged.

'Well, we don't do that here. It sounds kind of primitive; not what I'd expect from your view of the Ancients.'

Rhoana frowned and put the sheet down. She gave Gwion a look of resignation.

'You're right. I must be misinterpreting it. We just don't have enough information.'

'Which is why you said we must go to the Far Wall,' Gwion reminded her. 'You said there are a lot more inscriptions there. So why are we still here?'

Rhoana sighed.

'Because once I go there and fail again, I'll have nothing left. I'll have lost my life's dream, and I'll just sit around waiting for the Heavy Landers to kill me.'

'Neither of those things is going to happen. So let's go.'

Rhoana gave a smile of gratitude.

'Thank you, Gwion. You still have the energy and optimism of youth. I'm losing both, unfortunately. But you're right: I've been delaying things. I'll have a talk with Sylvana, and then no more hesitation—we'll go.'

Shortly afterwards, Gwion stood outside Sylvana's hut while Rhoana talked to her daughter. Although not intending to eavesdrop, she could not help hearing most of the conversation.

'You've chosen a fine time to leave, mother,' Sylvana was saying. 'The Heavy Landers could appear at any moment.'

'I know, I know. But if I don't go now, I never will. You understand that, don't you, my darling? And you must be underestimating yourself: if the worst happens, you'll be much better at organising the village's defences than I would be. I'd just get in your way or collapse with some kind of seizure.'

There was a silence, and then Gwion heard Sylvana say, in a softer tone, 'Well, it's good to hear you finally admit you're an old biddy.' A pause. 'Alright, off you go. You're right—I'll look after the place until you return.'

There was a silence in which Gwion imagined the mother and daughter were embracing, and then Rhoana emerged. She gave Gwion a penetrating look and then said, briskly, matter-of-factly, 'That's done. Let's go.'

***

Gwion and the Matriarch stood on the hillock. It was not much of an elevation, but it was the highest point anywhere near the settlement. And in a journey of the scale they were attempting, every scrap of help might be vital.

'I will lead,' Rhoana said. 'You must stay close behind me, as you don't know the way. It will seem I'm heading downwards rather than straight across, but I know what I'm doing.'

'Heading downwards?' Gwion said. Her mouth was dry with nervousness, now that the moment of departure was no longer an abstract idea but an increasingly terrifying reality. 'Why would you do that?'

'Trust me. As we cross, my village will come down to meet us.'

'It will?' Gwion thought about it for a moment. 'But that would mean the Far Wall is moving.' She thought about it again, this time for a longer period. Then, a look of amazement came into her features. 'But that would mean that the whole of Majeh is turning, rotating, spinning.'

The Matriarch reached across and held Gwion's shoulder.

'Once again, you have not disappointed me. You grasped it almost instantly. Have you not noticed how our land bends around us? There is no gap. If we look down, we see land. If we look up, we see land. There is land below our feet and above our heads. Have you never taken a sheet of parchment and bent the two edges together so they meet and make something that looks like a circle if you look through it? My people call that a "cylinder". Majeh is a vast cylinder, and it is turning, spinning.'

'But why? Why would Great Guidance want Majeh to spin?'

Rhoana laughed.

'Come on, Gwion! You have to stop expecting me to have all the answers! Perhaps together, we can find a few more.' Then all laughter drained from her face. 'It's time. Come.'

'Now?'

'Yes. Remember, when you are flying, don't look behind you.'

Gwion felt her knees suddenly go weak, and she sagged slightly. Rhoana saw that and said, 'Come now! We have talked enough! Let's go!' And with that, she bent her own knees, suddenly straightened them, and shot into the air, yelling as she went, 'Come on, Gwion! Don't fail me now!'

Gwion obeyed and leapt into the air. For an instant, she floundered, as if it were her first flight, then the training came back to her and she began powerfully to beat her wings. She rapidly closed the gap her delay had caused to open up, and came to within a few metres of the other woman, but to one side, to avoid the backdraft. Rhoana knew she was there.

'Good, Gwion, good. Now no more talking; we have a long way to go.'

Gwion nodded automatically, although Rhoana could not see her, and concentrated on keeping a strong, steady rhythm with her wings. At first it felt too easy, and a broad smile curved her lips. She could do this, why she could fly the whole length of Majeh, not merely across its width! So, they flew on, neither separating further nor coming closer together. Like strange human-sized butterflies, they powered on through the still, moist air of Majeh.

But then, after many minutes of silent flight, Gwion felt the first stirrings of fatigue in her arms; a creeping ache, at first only on the threshold of awareness but one which gradually grew and spread. She bit her lip. Perhaps it would not be as easy as she had first thought. Then she wondered how far they had come and began to turn her head. Rhoana's injunction came back to her even as she started the movement: *Don't look back!*

But it was too late: she looked back. And what she saw horrified her—the land below had lost all its detail and was now just a patchwork quilt made from a restricted palette of faded colours: a few shades of green, a few shades of muddy brown. And that was all. She could see a few vaguely rectangular shapes that might be buildings—but so small, so horrifyingly small! She was too far away, too insanely distant from the safety of the ground!

She cried out as she lost the rhythm of her wing strokes and began to spin crazily as first one arm beat erratically and then the other. Then she felt arms encircle her, and she was spun around to stare into the Matriarch's anguished face.

'Gwion! It's alright! We're nearly at the halfway point; you can do this!'

Gwion said nothing but Rhoana saw her eyes roll back into her head and her jaw hang down. Inarticulate noises issued from the gaping mouth. And then Rhoana struck her hard across the face.

'Gwion! Come back! It's alright, you stupid girl! Outside! Come back or go to the Outsider!'

Somehow the insults pulled Gwion back from her madness, and her eyes regained focus.

'Don't ever call me a stupid girl again,' she hissed. 'I panicked for a moment. Now I'm over it.'

But just then, she felt a strange sensation, as if her body had become insubstantial, composed of thistledown and soap bubbles. 'What—what?' she said, looking around wildly.

'It's the Nothing Point,' Rhoana said. 'I warned you about it, remember. We're at the centre of Majeh.' She looked ahead. 'We've lost our course—we're higher than we should be, after your thrashing around. We'll have to do some walking when we land. Come on; no more tantrums!'

She gave her wings a powerful double beat and sped away, leaving Gwion watching her dwindle with distance. And then Gwion steadied herself in the Nothing Point and followed her. As she flew after the now worryingly distant Matriarch, Gwion felt a sense of shame begin to sting her cheeks. She had disobeyed a direct order, and now they were off course. She would have to ensure that never again would she fail to live up to expectations.

After some time of lonely flight, she suddenly realised the tiny dot that was the Matriarch was beginning to spiral: that could only mean that the descent was beginning. And even as she saw the spiral pattern, she realised she could feel a gentle pull from the land that was now most definitely *below*: it was a hardly detectable presence, a touch of passing thistledown, but with each beat of her wings, it became infinitesimally stronger. The Far Wall had reached out and touched her; its gravitational attraction was minute, but it was not zero.

She, too, began to spiral, bleeding off the velocity she had so painfully built up. Already, she was able to distinguish individual objects below her: boulders, bushes, broken tree trunks.

She was descending too fast! Fighting another panic attack, she began to back-thrust her wingbeats and bent her knees as the land rushed up to claim her.

She hit with a force that sent shock waves up her spine, and she blacked out for an instant. When her eyes opened, she felt unpleasant tingles pulsing through her torso, and her knees were on fire. Gingerly, she felt her patellas through the bruised skin, but to her immense relief, she did not feel pieces of bone slide under her fingers. The landing had been a bad one, but Great Guidance had ensured no permanent damage had been done to that part of her anatomy at least. She rose, very slowly, from the mercifully soft ground, waiting for the stab of pain that would mean a broken limb, but it did not come. She was badly shaken but still in one piece. But that simply meant she had been lucky: the softness of the ground had saved her. There was another problem, however: where was the Matriarch?

Gwion looked around; the Far Wall (if that was where she was) looked disappointingly similar to the Pastures; there were no exotic plants, no shift in the drab palette of the vegetation. She looked across the central Void of Majeh to where she thought the Pastures might be. She could not be sure if it was them she was seeing, due to their loss of trajectory, but that distant wall looked very similar to what she had seen when staring across from her village. Apparently, one area of Majeh looked very much like every other, Gwion decided. She could not guess where Rhoana had landed; she had lost sight of the Matriarch in her plummet to the ground. Another look around; another wave of indecision. There was nothing to indicate human habitation in any direction. She tried calling, but there was no response. Minutes passed while she stood immobile, the tips of her wings touching the soft earth. Eventually, she decided that she had to move. She now understood how Majeh rotated; due to her period of panic, she had landed in the anti-spinward direction of their planned destination. She turned around, calculating which direction was which, in a terrain without landmarks, and eventually chose a travel direction. Clipping her wings to her back, she set off.

It was a miserable trudge; the black soil sucked and clung to her feet as if trying to pull her down into its innards. There was no noise other than her panting and the sucking noise of her steps. She could still fly, of course; conditions here were exactly the same as at the Pastures, but every muscle in her arms ached and burned. It would be some time before she flew again. She fell into a drab rhythm: Step forward, pull the shoe out of the ground, step forward, pull the other shoe out of the ground. No noise but the suction of the glutinous earth and her increasingly ragged breathing.

No noise except—but there was another noise! A grunting, snorting sound, coming from directly ahead! The fronds of a bush parted, and a head emerged. She stared at it. It was very similar to that which had come through her curtain in her encounter with the Night Creature. But in the light she could see this one more clearly, see the whiskers around the slobbering mouth, see the small, deep-set, red eyes, see the wicked, upwardly curving tusks. There was one difference between the Far Wall and the Pastures, it seemed: here, the Night Creatures were day creatures.

Beast and girl stared silently at each other, both seemingly surprised into immobility by their unexpected meeting. Then the animal gave a deep, raucous grunt, lowered its head and charged. Gwion did not move; she could not move; the shock had been too great for her brain to control her muscles. Helplessly, she stood, awaiting her violent end.

Then something flashed past her, and a shaft appeared in the animal's neck. Bellowing, it came to a skidding halt a metre or so in front of her and began to twist and squirm, trying to reach the protruding missile with its slavering jaws. But its attempts were cut short as another shaft flashed past Gwion and buried itself in the creature's soft tissues. It gave a muffled snort and slowly rolled onto its side and lay still.

Completely thunderstruck by this rapid turn of events, Gwion remained totally immobile, staring at the now bloody carcass with unbelieving eyes. It was then something moved in her peripheral vision and, turning, she saw a young man walking towards her. He did not look pleased.

'What in the name of the Outsider are you doing out here, all by yourself, without a weapon? Haven't you heard of the Day Beasts?' Then he took in her wings. 'Ahh, you're a foreigner; I guess you haven't heard of the Day Beasts.'

The high tension of the recent events finally caught up with Gwion; the world seemed to tremble and swirl before her, and she fell—straight onto her saviour, who stopped her collapse with two strong arms.

'Hey, it's alright. You're safe now,' he said, wonderingly. 'There's nothing to be frightened of now!'

She fought her way back up to sanity and straightened herself, looking up at features which were now smiling.

'Thank you for saving me! If you hadn't been here...'

'But I was,' he said, 'so forget it. We look after each other here. You must come from a very tame place if you're not familiar with the Day Beasts. So where do you come from?'

She pointed across the empty interior of Majeh.

'Over there—somewhere.'

He glanced briefly in the direction she was pointing and then turned to look at her, glancing up and down her body in frank appraisal.

'And why have you come such a long way?'

She looked at him quizzically.

'Could you speak a little more slowly? Your words are very like ours, but there's a different rhythm, some unfamiliar sounds. I can understand you, but you're a bit strange.'

He threw back his head with a robust laugh.

'I sound strange! I was going to say the same thing about you!' He put out a hand. 'I'm Taran, and you are...?'

Gwion was unfamiliar with the gesture but eventually realised she was meant to hold the other's outstretched hand. However, she was unprepared for the vigorous shaking Taran gave the enclosed hand and removed it at the earliest possible opportunity.

'I hope I can still write after that pummelling.'

Taran looked momentarily puzzled, then threw his head back, giving a raucous laugh.

'Very good,' he said when he resumed looking at her, 'but you still haven't told me your name.'

'Gwion.'

He shook his head.

'Never heard that one before. You foreigners not only talk strangely, but you have weird names as well.'

She frowned.

'Well, if you've quite finished telling me how peculiar I am, perhaps you could help me. I'm looking for my companion, the Ma… I mean, Rhoana.'

'Rhoana? You know Rhoana? She's just come back from a place on the other side of the Void. She said she was hoping her friend hadn't gotten lost.' He looked at her quizzically. 'That's you? You're the friend?'

Her frown grew deeper.

'Yes, that's me. What's so strange about that?'

'Why, you're so young and so… so small.'

Gwion took several steps backwards.

'That's enough! I thank you for, for…'

'Saving your life?' Taran enquired.

'Yes! Thank you for saving my life, but I really think we should part now. Just tell me if I'm going in the right direction to find *my friend* and how far I have to walk.'

He gave the raucous laugh again.

'You foreigners really are funny.' Then to her horror, he grasped her shoulders and half turned her.

'That direction. See that little rise in the ground?'

'Yes. How far?'

He laughed again.

'Oh, I'm glad I've met you. Our village is just on the other side of it!'

Six: The Far Wall

Gwion quickly overcame her embarrassment at not knowing where she was, by the heady realisation that she had succeeded in her epic flight across the Void. Now she was actually on the Far Wall, the place she had looked at so many times without ever thinking she would ever set foot there.

There were good and bad aspects to her new location, she mused as she walked up the slope behind her new companion. *Bad*: The Day Beasts, which seemed even more dangerous than her familiar Night Creatures. *Good*: Well, there was Taran...

Gwion's musings were cut off when they reached the top of the rise. There below her was a settlement of about the same size as her own. The buildings were different, however. They seemed more geometrical and had sloping, better-constructed roofs. There was a throng of people in the streets, some of whom looked up as they crested the ridge and began the descent. And it did not take long for her to spot the Matriarch amongst them. Passing Taran, Gwion rushed up to the other woman, who welcomed her effusively.

'Gwion! I was so worried about you! I thought perhaps you hadn't been strong enough to cross the Void and were wandering somewhere in the AntiSpinward Lands!'

'Crossing the Void?' Gwion said, smiling as she looked up at Rhoana. 'No problem at all. I could be back at the Pastures in two shakes of a lamb's tail.'

Rhoana raised a finger in mock admonition.

'Now, now. Tell the truth and shame the Outsider.' She looked away from Gwion. 'Ah, Taran. It was you who found our little lost flyer.'

'It was,' Taran said, coming alongside the two women. 'Not only that, but I saved her from becoming a Day Beast's dinner.'

The Matriarch gave him a radiant smile and then looked down at Gwion.

'Well, that's enough excitement for one day, what with crossing the Void and being rescued by a handsome young man. Come to my house, and we'll have something to eat.'

The Matriarch's house on the Far Wall was not as grand as her official residence in the Pastures, but then again, it was larger and more sturdily built than the typical building in that part of Majeh.

Sitting on a pile of cushions, with a bowl of lamb stew in her hands, Gwion began, 'Matri…'

Rhoana shook her head.

'No, Gwion. Here I'm not the Matriarch. Here I'm just "Rhoana". Just one of the girls. Nothing special over here.'

Gwion nodded.

'Alright, Rhoana. But how did Taran know who I was talking about? After all, you've been away for at least twenty years.'

Rhoana gave a surprisingly girlish giggle.

'Oh, he knows me all right. He's my son.'

'Your son? Then he must be older than he looks.'

'Indeed, he is.' Another smile. 'But so am I, don't forget. And probably you will still be turning heads in many years' time. The passing days are kinder to those in whom the Noom blood is strong.'

Gwion smiled at the thought of her turning anyone's head, either now or in the future.

'And his father?'

Rhoana looked down at her hands.

'No longer with us. He was not so much a Noom as I, and the Crab took him many years ago.'

Gwion decided she had asked enough questions. Then to her own surprise, she suddenly gave a tremendous yawn and found her head was drooping. Rhoana took the now-empty bowl from her and said, 'My fault. You've crossed the Void and nearly been eaten by a Day Beast. Enough for one day, I think.'

Gwion made no protest as Rhoana led her into a side room and helped her get into a cot.

'I'll have a fresh set of clothes for you in the morning,' Rhoana said, but Gwion was already asleep. Rhoana left her to her dreams and went back to the open doorway of her house. Night was already well advanced, and the Void had taken on a blue-purple shade through which the ruddy dots of fires in the Pastures and elsewhere could be dimly discerned. When night came to Majeh, it came to all of Majeh.

Well, this is it, she thought. *If fresh eyes can't solve the enigma of the Ancients, then it will never be solved. We will just go on with our little lives, never understanding how we got here, what our heritage should be. Day after day, leading nowhere.*

She found that thought disturbing and decided it was time to sleep for her as well. After all, she had also crossed the Void, and she was not as young as she used to be.

∗∗∗

'What do you make of these, Gwion?'

Gwion looked at the tablets on which the scholars of the Far Wall had copied out pictures and inscriptions from the ancient ruins. They were very similar to those she had found in the Pastures and given to the Far Wall experts, but in return she had been given many more examples of the Ancients' writings. She looked long and hard at the symbols until they seemed to swim and dance under her gaze, but no sudden meaning leapt out. Then after a few minutes, she grew aware of the weight of the anxious stares from those in the archaeological party and forced herself to look at them, shaking her head as she did so.

'I'm sorry. They're just shapes. I can't make any sense out of them.'

She heard their sighs and saw their shoulders slump, and a sense of guilt, of failure, gripped her. She handed the tablets back and walked away from the little group. But Rhoana followed her. They sat together on a small mound and, for a while, neither spoke, both simply looking into the Void and at the misty lands beyond. Then Rhoana turned to her.

'You mustn't get disheartened, Gwion. Nobody thought it would be easy. There's plenty of time.'

Gwion shook her head.

'No, there was no point in me coming here. I've let you all down.' She looked earnestly into the other's face. 'You see, there're many more of the inscriptions here, but that's all. There's no key to their meaning. Unless there's some way I can connect their language with ours, I can stare at those writings until the Crab gets me. The diagrams are telling us something, but we lack the context. It's something to do with putting some kind of crown on our heads, but what they are and why we do that—there's nothing.'

Rhoana nodded.

'I understand all that. But you've given up far too soon, Gwion. Those inscriptions aren't all we have on the Far Wall.' A vibrant light came into her eyes. 'We have far more than that.' She paused dramatically and then said, almost breathlessly, 'We've found the crowns shown in those pictures!'

'You have! Then what are we doing sat here?'

'They're some distance away. I had to make sure you had your strength back.'

But Gwion was on her feet.

'Outside with that! I want to see them now!'

Rhoana stood as well.

'I thought you'd react like that. Let's go.'

Rhoana explained to the group where they were going and selected one of the younger men to accompany them. Gwion noticed with a smile that although Rhoana had been away for twenty years, she still seemed to possess much of the authority she had wielded in the Pastures. The young man, whose name was Shandar, carried a bow and arrow for defence against prowling Day Beasts.

'And where are we going?' he asked, shouldering his quiver.

'To the Vaults,' was the mysterious reply.

Gwion felt a slight thrill of excitement. The Vaults! She had never heard that word before, but it seemed redolent of some kind of adventure.

The trio set off. Much of the land was very similar to the Pastures; a generally hummocky landscape of coarse grass and occasional shrubs. Low depressions in the soil were usually filled with stagnant water, covered with green scum. However, they did not need to pay too much attention to the land as they flew at least half of the distance, wings being unnecessary for a comparatively short journey. Then Rhoana called, 'There!' and they gently glided back to the surface.

Gwion was impressed. A structure that was definitely not natural reared out of the omnipresent grassland; one several stories high. It had a number of windows, all now open to the elements, and a single massive entrance. It was evident there had once been a door to it, because that door was still there, but now lying on the ground some distance from the opening. They approached warily; the interior would be an excellent lair for Day Beasts. Shandar went ahead, arrow already on his bow, eyes looking from side to side. Then he turned and waved to the women.

'All clear!'

Gwion and Rhoana walked slowly in, keeping their senses on alert. But then Gwion lost all concern about predators: this place was huge! It made the Matriarch's house in the Pastures look like an untutored child's toy! She had to tilt her head right back to see the ceiling; a ceiling festooned with long curtains of some filmy substance. Ahead, looking past piles of material that had obviously once comprised objects of some description, there was another entrance but this time with an attached door.

There was no one source of light on Majeh, and so there was no helpful shaft of light entering through the main doorway, and gloom rapidly surrounded them as they walked up to the second door.

'What is this place?' Gwion said to Shandar. He shrugged.

'How should I know? I'm just the hired muscle.'

But Rhoana was already at the door and stood facing them with her back towards it.

'I'm told the archaeology team managed to open this door not long before we got here, Gwion, so I don't know much more about it than you. But I've seen the drawings of what they found once they were able to get in.' She looked sharply at Shandar. 'Guard us while we go inside.'

He nodded and turned to face the main entrance.

Rhoana pulled at the door, which opened very reluctantly. There were signs of damage on its edge where the team had used force to open it. At first, the only impression was that it was dark. Dark, and cold. There was an odd odour in the air which had not been present in the outer part of the building. Gwion knew what it must be.

'This place is very, very old. And it hasn't been connected to the outside world for a long time.'

'My thoughts exactly. But you see what this means—it proves the Ancients were not primitive subhumans. There's nothing like this in the Pastures or anywhere else on the Far Wall!'

But Gwion was not listening: she had noticed something the older woman had not.

'There's light. Light is coming from somewhere.'

Rhoana saw it too then; a pale greenish light, pulsating to a regular rhythm.

'It's further in,' Gwion murmured. 'We must find out what it is.'

Unnoticed by either of them, Gwion had now taken the lead in the expedition. They continued their explanation until they came up against a great wall of metal.

And on that wall, there were myriads of tiny lights of varying colours. As they approached, a series of winking green lights suddenly dimmed and were replaced by pulsing red ones.

'This is very strange,' Rhoana said, shaking her head. 'The report made no mention of lights.'

But Gwion knew the answer, although she did not know how she knew the answer.

'This room knows it's been entered. It knows it's been reconnected to the outside world. When the team broke in, the lights were not on. Now they are.'

Rhoana walked up to the bank of flickering lights and placed a tentative finger on one, pulling it away almost instantly. Then she turned to Gwion, and even in the obscurity, Gwion could see the wonder on her face.

'It's not hot. They're not little fires!'

Gwion also walked up to the bank of lights and saw there was a flat surface in front of it, covered in little buttons, some with coloured tops. She pressed one.

The lights on the vertical surface burst silently into a coloured dance for a few moments and then returned to their steady pulsing.

'What does it mean?' Rhoana whispered.

'Don't know. But we can't stand here all day, just looking at them.' Gwion turned away from the lights. 'Where are these crowns?'

'In here.'

Rhoana was already walking to a deep alcove set in one of the walls. It, too, had once been sheltered by a long-gone door. Gwion caught her breath as she saw the reasons for their journey: There they were, lying on a flat surface, covered and coated with dust. There were clean tracks on that surface where the first archaeologists had explored. Feeling inexplicably nervous, she lifted one from its bed of dust and studied it. It was an almost hemispherical cap, composed of an extremely fine mesh that she knew no one in the Pastures or on the Far Wall could have duplicated. And it was incredibly light; she felt it would float in the air if she dropped it. But it would not have fallen far because it was connected to the wall by a thick tube of some unknown but extremely flexible material.

'What are they made from?' she said, turning to Rhoana, who merely shook her head.

'No one knows. It's not metal or wood. We have nothing like it.'

'So much for primitive Ancients,' Gwion murmured as she repeatedly rotated the crown, studying its underside with no more understanding than she had of the outer surface. But she did notice that it was very slightly warmer than its surroundings. Then she made a decision.

'I'll put it on.'

Alarm leapt into Rhoana's features.

'No, Gwion, no! We don't know what it's for, what it will do!'

'The diagrams show people putting these things on their heads. So I'll do the same.'

Rhoana shook her own head but said no more.

But as Gwion lifted the crown, a sudden doubt struck her. Rhoana was right; they were facing a great mystery here. The Ancients stood revealed as a totally different people to the humble peasants of the Pastures or even the earnest scholars of the Far Wall. What if something happened when she placed it on her scalp; something irrevocable, irreversible? She noticed her hands begin to shake as she lifted the crown and saw the concern on Rhoana's face. The entire room seemed to recede from her, leaving her alone and unaided in emptiness. The object touched her curls.

And, at once, it seemed there was a powerful voice thundering in her mind; a voice speaking in an unknown tongue, yet one in which, for a few instants, there were words she could understand, words that flashed past and then were gone into the mass of unintelligibly.

Then the voice spoke again, and miraculously it was now speaking in the language of the Pastures, but a pure, precise variety that before she had only heard from the Matriarch. But although she now understood the words, she could not grasp the import of the entire sentence.

'Total transfer is required. Commencing download.'

Instantly, Gwion's conscious mind reeled as she felt a colossal tsunami of information, of knowledge, of feelings, of hungry desires, insistent drives, terrible wants, desperate needs, begin to rear up in the far reaches of her being. She felt as if a titanic wave was about to break over her, one that would wash her away like a piece of flotsam on a stupendous surge of power.

She whimpered.

Then it was gone, and as the terrible pressure of desperate minds trying to invade her own disappeared, she saw Rhoana holding the crown she had snatched away. Suddenly, she felt her knees buckle as the floor came up to meet her. She felt the impact and then saw only darkness.

When she woke, she was outside, lying on her back with Rhoana and Shandar staring down anxiously.

'What—what happened?' she said, in a thick, guttural voice that momentarily she did not recognise as her own. Her tongue felt too big for her dry mouth, and her head felt like it was slowly separating into bloody halves.

'She's back,' she heard Shandar say. 'I don't think she's broken her nose, despite all the blood.'

'What happened?' Gwion repeated.

Rhoana and Shandar helped her to her feet, standing close as she struggled to stay vertical.

'Will someone tell me what the Outside happened!'

'Your face,' Rhoana said. 'I've never seen an expression like it! It looked like you were having your guts pulled out with red-hot pincers. What exactly happened?'

'You can let go of me,' she said to Shandar, and then turned to Rhoana. 'There are no words for it. It felt like there was a crowd of people trying to get inside my head, all shouting and screaming and clawing at my mind like Night Creatures. It was the most horrible thing I could ever have imagined. No, it was worse: I could never have imagined that.'

A look of ineffable sadness came into Rhoana's face.

'Then that's that. It's obviously far too dangerous to try to understand the Ancients. We're just little children playing with fire. It's over.' She sighed and looked away from the other two. 'I shall tell the Leader we must immediately stop all the archaeological work.'

Gwion nodded, but she too wore the mask of sadness, of defeat.

'You're right. This must be how they destroyed themselves. We must never touch their artefacts again, or the same thing will happen to us.'

Seven: Revelation

Gwion sat alone in Rhoana's hut. She sat slumped, head in hands, crushed under the weight of a vast anti-climax. All the talks with the Matriarch, the flying training, the epic flight across the Diameter, the tingle of excitement when visualising what they might discover, the joy they would feel on bringing a long-lost slab of Majeh's history up from darkness back into the light for the first time in—how long?

Now they would never know.

After Rhoana had told the others that it was too dangerous to proceed, the life had seemed to go out of the settlement. Although, like the Pastures, it had its hen coops, its piggeries and its flocks of sheep, its culture was quite different, no doubt because the majority of the population were true Nooms. A large proportion of the villagers had been actively involved in the project, and it had all been for nothing.

Gwion lifted her mug of coffee to her lips and then, with a grimace, put it down again. It was flat and cold. She had been lost in mental gloom for a long time. She fell asleep out of sheer boredom and only awoke when a kindly hand gently shook a shoulder. Her eyes fluttered open.

'Rhoana. Sorry, I'm not much company, I'm afraid.'

Rhoana sat opposite her and ran a hand over her forehead.

'No need to apologise; we all feel the same.'

Gwion sighed deeply.

'So what now?'

'What do you mean?'

'I mean, there's no point in me being here. My flocks are still there, being tended by people who don't know half as much as I do about sheep. There's nothing to keep me here now. You had a competent person to take over your duties; I didn't. Linon was very angry when I suddenly left.'

Rhoana nodded, reluctantly.

'I guess you're right. I believed that we two would go on together, discovering great things, unearthing long-lost secrets about Majeh's past. But as you say, it was all for nothing.'

Gwion was silent for a time. Then: 'Perhaps we—I—tried to do too much without enough understanding of what we were doing.'

'Maybe. But we never will have that understanding. All we have is symbols and shapes that must have a meaning, but one we will never unlock.'

'Yes, probably?'

Rhoana looked up.

'Probably? What are you getting at?'

'When I had that thing on my head, I heard a voice. At first, it was just talking gibberish, but once in a while I caught a word that sounded like one of our words. And then it switched to our own, real language.'

'And it told you how to interpret the symbols, I suppose!'

Gwion frowned.

'You're not taking me seriously. What I am trying to say is that the language of the Ancients is *our* language, just a very old version of it.'

'Fair enough. So if we had an Ancient sitting here, sipping coffee with us, snacking on a piece of nicely cured pork, we could eventually understand each other. But we don't have an Ancient sitting here; we have their written language—and that's completely different.'

Gwion's head dipped slightly.

'Yes, you're right again. So I'll head back tomorrow, I think. Are you coming with me?'

'Yes. There's nothing for me here, either.'

The two women fell into an uncomfortable silence, both haunted by the collapse of what had promised to be an adventure for one, a splendid academic achievement for the other. Then Rhoana looked up.

'Before you go, why don't you let Taran show you around?'

'Show me around? Is there a piece of the village you've kept hidden from me? I thought I'd seen all the wonders it has to offer.'

'Now you're just being difficult for the sake of it. He's a nice boy; why not spend some time with him? He likes you.'

Gwion sat motionless for a while and then shrugged.

'Why not? There's nothing else to do.'

'And he did save your life.'

'He did save my life. Alright, Rhoana, you don't have to try so hard; I'll spend some time with him before I go.'

"Some time" was not long afterwards. They sat together on a slight rise in the grassland, looking across the Void. The day was well underway, and the light was steadily brightening, losing its insipid, yellowish hue.

'There,' she said, pointing, 'that greenish patch above the brown part. That's the Pastures.'

He followed her gesture and told himself he could distinguish one greenish patch from the other nearby greenish patches.

'What's it like there?'

'Almost the same as here. You know, Taran, I think every part of Majeh looks like every other part. It's a boring world we live in.'

'How can you say that? You haven't been to the Spinward Lands or the AntiSpinward Lands.'

'Because if they were different, they'd *look* different, and they don't. No doubt they raise sheep and pigs, just like the rest of us. They eat, piss and crap, just like the rest of us. We made the mistake of thinking there was more. There isn't.'

'You're in a mood.' He made a tentative move to put an arm around her shoulders, but thought better of it. 'Let's go to my place and have something to eat. I make great devilled pork fritters.'

She brightened.

'Well, that's something different, at least. Let's go.'

A short while later, she was standing in Taran's hut with the smell of cooking pork wafting into her nostrils. Putting her hunger to one side for the moment, she admired a series of lustrous metal plates that he had hung all over one wall. She had just extended a hand to see what they felt like when he came in with two platters. Nothing was said while they munched their way through his culinary offerings. Then, on putting her empty platter down, she put a hand on her belly and belched, loudly.

He grinned.

'I'll take that as a compliment. More?'

She shook her head, smiling.

'No, I've had more than enough. I must take the recipe back to the Pastures.'

He took the platters away and, on return, sat very close to her and put an arm around her.

'I really like you, you know.'

She managed to produce a weak smile.

'Yes, I like you too; how could I not like my saviour?'

'No, I mean I really *like* you, you know what I mean?'

Changing the subject, she pointed to the metal plates.

'What are they?'

'Oh, I found them lying in a small pool not very far from here. I like how they catch the light; gives the place a touch of class.' His arm tightened around her. 'Now, back to us.'

She gently removed the arm and stood.

'Sorry, Taran, but there is no *us*. I'm very grateful for what you did, and I do like you—just not in that way.'

He rose to his feet, and the smile had gone.

'Well, that's not very nice after all I've done. I think...'

Gwion's strained nerves snapped, and she backed away from him, much quicker than she had intended. Her back collided with one of the metal plates, and it crashed heavily to the floor. Taran glared at it.

'If you've damaged that...'

He picked it up so the side that had been facing the wall now faced Gwion.

And on it were two sections of text, separated by a thin section of bare metal.

And Gwion recognised some symbols in one section. Then, as Taran moved to replace it, she rushed to him, crying, 'Let me see that!' She almost tore it from his grasp and sat back down, the plate on her lap, her lips moving silently.

He stared at her.

'Have you gone crazy?'

She did not answer but pointed at the other plates.

'Them. I want to see all of them. Now!'

Shaking his head in puzzlement, he handed them to her, one by one.

Time passed, and then she rose to her feet, the dull expression she had worn previously replaced by a look of fiery exultation.

'I think this might be it! I must tell your mother!'

He stood between her and the door.

'I've done something good?'

'Yes! Good! Wonderful!'

An eyebrow on his smiling face arched meaningfully.

'Do I get a kiss for doing this wonderful thing—whatever it is?'

She smiled back; all trace of lassitude, lethargy, had vanished.

'Yes. Just one.'

She kissed him and left, holding as many plates as she could.

He stood in the doorway, watching her go, grinning and shaking his head.

∗∗∗

Gwion had realised that purely, by chance, Taran had collected tablets that provided the key to interpreting the Ancients' written language. She had burst in upon a somnolent Rhoana and given her the startling news.

And so began the arduous, line by line, study of every document dating from that time. By daylight they studied them; by the dim yellow light of dusk they studied them; by flickering candlelight they studied them. They went without rest; their eyes grew gritty and red-rimmed; they fell asleep as they discussed their grindingly slow progress with the other scholars of the Far Wall. And still, as Majeh made many stately revolutions about its axis, they continued, driven by an insatiable need to know.

And gradually, a consensus emerged. Finally, the two women were ready to address the Far Wall's scholars, assembled in the meeting hall.

'I think I can give a relative date for most of the inscriptions,' Rhoana said. 'They were written in a time of transition, when one form of language was changing into another.'

Gwion agreed.

'Yes, the second language is like ours, but not exactly. Some words we can only guess at; some are astoundingly old archaisms. The plates certainly weren't inscribed recently, but neither can they be forgeries. The crucial thing is that the second script is sufficiently like ours that we have regained the original language's fundamental meaning by employing them together.'

Then both women fell silent, looking at each other with an air of concern, perhaps even the beginnings of fear.

'But it is not a pleasant story,' Gwion continued. 'As we have always suspected, there was a crisis—no, a cataclysm—that destroyed them as a culture. It was something to do with—with Sentori.'

Although many of the audience showed their displeasure at that point, Rhoana showed no objection to Gwion using that word, and took over the exposition.

'It appears they were trying to reach it by their own efforts; we don't understand how. And because of that, Great Guidance brought destruction upon them. There was a civil war, and only the actions of someone called Aland prevented the people from exterminating each other.'

An aged scholar raised a hand.

'Yes, yes, so much we had guessed. But the crowns—that's what we really want to learn about. What of them?'

Gwion and Rhoana exchanged glances. Neither was sure who was best to continue the story. Finally, Rhoana spoke.'

'This is the troublesome part. Although most of the Ancients were wicked, some had tried to salvage the best parts of their civilisation, we think. It appears'—and here she looked helplessly at Gwion—'that their wise men and women were able to transfer their minds into…' A pause, then: 'into a machine.'

Immediately there was a bedlam of confused voices from the scholars, as everybody tried to speak at once. Several of the more elderly people stood and headed for the door.

'Wait! Please wait! Just listen to all I have to say, please!' Rhoana said, also rising to her feet. 'I am only telling you what we have read. I am not—at this stage—asking you to believe it.' She waited for the dissidents to return to their seats, and then continued: 'The idea was, we think, that these minds could provide a source of help, of guidance, should there be a great crisis. It appears those minds can communicate with us by employing those crowns.'

'So why didn't they use them when there actually was a great crisis?' one of the dissents asked, acidly. 'And save themselves?'

'A good question. Once again, we are only getting little flashes of information in the midst of words that make little sense. The text assumes we already know much of the backstory—which obviously we don't. But it looks like, directly after the civil war, there was a period of literal madness, of despairing insanity. Everything fell apart as Great Guidance continued to punish them. Had he continued, obviously we would not be here. But he relented and the people gradually forgot all their clever ways and their marvellous machines, and slowly developed the peaceful culture that we have today, in which we leave the possibility of reaching our destination to Great Guidance.'

Another of the audience raised a hand.

'So why don't we put one of those crowns on our heads and get all this wonderful assistance? After all, as true followers of Great Guidance, we won't make the same mistakes as the Ancients.'

Rhoana looked at Gwion, who immediately took the floor.

'Because I almost did that, and it was horrible beyond belief. We wouldn't just get facts and figures—we'd get somebody else's mind inside our own heads.'

A susurration of shock filled the room.

Gwion spread her hands semi-apologetically.

'I'm sorry, but that's all we know. We are now certain the Ancients had knowledge and abilities we don't, but we can't access them. And in any case, it's better we don't, as those abilities destroyed them.' She gave a nervous laugh. 'We will have to get to "you-know-where" the old-fashioned way.'

No one joined in.

'So the only justification for this mind sharing,' a woman in the audience said, 'is to fend off some existential crisis.'

'I think so. A crisis as dreadful as that which destroyed the Ancients.'

'Then, Great Guidance willing, we will never have to make that decision.'

Gwion and Rhoana simultaneously nodded their agreement.

'Precisely.'

After the meeting, Gwion and Rhoana sat on a bench just outside the meeting hall.

They were despondent.

'First, we thought we would never understand the Ancients' writings; never be able to access their knowledge and wisdom,' Gwion was saying, 'then, at last, we were able to read at least some of their language. And we find we *mustn't* access their knowledge and wisdom! What a cruel joke! Outside! Outside!'

This time Rhoana made no attempt to lighten the other's mood. Instead, she simply nodded in reluctant acceptance.

'I'm afraid so. So we're back where we started. And this really is the end. We have to go back to the Pastures—at least we can do something good there.'

Gwion turned to her mentor and opened her mouth to speak.

But Rhoana never learned what she was about to say.

Because at that moment, there was a terrible outburst of ferocious shouting mingled with cries of desperate fear.

Eight: Crisis

Gwion and Rhoana leapt from the bench, their hearts hammering, their mouths dry. One second they had been discussing a grey future of boredom and lassitude; the next, some terrible peril had burst upon them. What was happening?

They ran toward the centre of the village from which the noise was emanating. But as they approached, the sounds became more and more threatening. Sounds of terror, sounds of violence.

And then they were there. And what they saw stunned them into fearful immobility.

Armed men.

But what men! Men with broad chests, mighty arms, sturdy thighs, clad in armour, men beside whom Taran would have looked like a willowy girl. Gwion knew at once who they were, the memory of that briefly glimpsed shadow telling her all she needed to know.

'Heavy Landers,' she breathed, 'Great Guidance—Heavy Landers! The war—it's started!'

Several villagers were already dead, lying in crumpled heaps on the reddened ground. She saw one invader swing an axe and then followed the arc of the victim's decapitated head as it flew into the air, bouncing across the central square to end up a few metres away, its sightless eyes seemingly fixed pleadingly upon her.

Then Rhoana moved forward to confront the warriors.

'No,' Gwion shouted, 'you can't stop them! We have to get away!'

Rhoana glanced back at her.

'I am the last authority here, it seems. I must stop this slaughter. It is my duty.'

The one-sided fighting ceased as the Heavy Landers noticed her step out of the shadows and walk fearlessly towards them, head held high, arms outstretched.

'Stop this!' she cried. 'I am Rhoana, one of the Elders of this place. Stop this needless killing! Surely we can come to some arrangement; if you need some of our crops, our animals, we will gladly share them. Stop this now, I beg you!'

The biggest man, clad in an armour of interlocked metal plates, walked heavily towards her. Gwion saw him stop in front of Rhoana, looking down at her. She seemed pitifully frail, almost insubstantial, a being woven from mist, against his bulk. For some time he stared at her, silently. His sword rested, point down, in the dust. Then he spoke, in a voice so deep it was almost below Gwion's threshold of detection.

'You're a good looking woman, but I think you are past your best. We have no need of you.'

And his sword flashed up from the dust and plunged into Rhoana's chest. The force of his thrust lifted her off her feet and sent her spinning to the ground. As she rolled over and went still, a dark patch began to spread under her.

Gwion screamed.

It felt as if she had been plunged into a nightmare that somehow felt totally real. None of this could possibly be happening!

Then it hit like a physical blow: this was real—deadly, fatally real. Now she must run and keep running until the village of the scholars was far behind her. She would have to leave her wings behind and so could not recross the Diameter, but she would run, run until her feet bled, run on and on until she found some sanctuary, perhaps in the Spinward Lands, far from any human presence—especially the Heavy Landers.

She turned away from the horror in the village square, ready to begin her desperate flight.

And found her way blocked by the bulky presence of another Heavy Lander. Strong hands grasped her shoulders.

'I've got another one!' her captor called to the giant in the square. 'This girl looks good enough!'

'Bring her to me,' the original Heavy Lander replied. He appeared to have authority over the other. 'I've got rid of all the useless ones, except an old woman I'm leaving so she can tell any other peasants of what happened here today, and put the fear of the Great One into them. That'll knock any fight out of them.'

'I haven't seen much fight in these simpletons,' the second man said as he dragged Gwion into the giant's presence. 'It looks like they're even weaker than they were last time. Where's the fun in killing people who won't put up a decent fight?'

'What can you expect from creatures who live in a Great One-forsaken place like this?' Rhoana's murderer looked down on Gwion. 'And what's your name, you pretty little thing?'

Gwion said nothing and looked away. A great hand dragged her face back, so she was looking into his eyes.

'I asked your name, girl! If you don't give me a proper answer, I'll shave one of your ears off.'

'Don't shave anything else off, Cran!' the other man said, coming up behind Gwion and reaching around to fondle her breasts.

Cran was not amused.

'Did I give you permission to do that? Now, back off.'

The other man dropped his gaze, removed his hands and retreated.

Cran returned his scrutiny to Gwion.

'Your name?'

'Gwion.'

Cran tipped his head back and gave a throaty laugh.

'I knew it! Weird people with weird names! Just like the last time.' His gaze dropped back to his captive. 'I'll probably give you a proper name when we're in Ez.'

'What do you want with me?' Gwion said, finding it difficult to frame the words with a mouth that was dry as ancient sand. It seemed every part of her was trembling, and it felt as if her knees would give way at any moment.

'Come on, you can't be that stupid, even for a Weakling.' Cran turned his attention away from Gwion as more Heavy Landers entered the village square. Gwion realised everything had gone quiet; presumably, they had finished their orgy of killing. Was she the only survivor? But that question was soon answered: the other invaders were driving more villagers before them; there were five young women and three young men.

And one was Taran, his face smeared with blood.

The pathetic group, frightened into terrified silence by the weapons of the Heavy Landers, were brought before Cran, who proceeded to examine each of the captives in turn, looking into the mouths of the women, weighing their breasts in his palms; ignoring the men. Gwion tried to catch Taran's attention, but he was staring at his captor with undisguised hatred.

Soon he had even more reason to hate Cran.

Taran suddenly noticed something familiar about one of the nearby corpses. He tore himself away from Cran and ran to the body. Desperately, he rolled it over and stared into the face of his mother. He looked down at her for some moments, his face working as he strove to hold back the tears. Then his control dissipated, and he fell full-length on her body, weeping. The Heavy Landers stood in a group, watching him in quiet amusement. Then he rose and ran back to Cran, beating his fists on the other's barrel chest.

'I'll kill you for this! I'll kill you!'

Cran looked at his war-band with a quiet smile and then gently removed Taran's fists, holding them captive inside his own mighty grasp.

'You'll get your chance to kill me when we get out of this shithole and back to Ez.' Cran looked again at his compatriots and winked. Then he almost threw Taran into their arms. 'Oh yes, you'll get your chance, alright.'

They laughed.

Suddenly there was the sound of squealing pigs and bleating sheep and a horde of animals poured into the square, flanked by massive red-eyed dogs, with two more Heavy Landers bringing up the rear.

'Well done!' Cran shouted. 'We've got everything we came for now. Back to Ez!'

All the Heavy Landers gave a massive cheer, a sound as overpowering and overwhelming as a landslide.

Finally, Taran noticed Gwion and his mouth fell open.

'They've got you as well.' he said dully.

She could not reply, could not speak, as tears were coursing down her cheeks and her breath was reduced to great sobbing gasps. She turned to Cran, making one last attempt to reach out to the man, to appeal to their common humanity.

'Why?' she said, between sobs. 'Why are you doing this?'

He did not bother to look at her, gesturing to the men in charge of the animals to move them out of the village. But he found time to reply.

'Because we want to. Because we can.'

***

It was a long and bitter march to the departure point. The Heavy Landers did not accept any reason for delay and spurred the stragglers on with blows from the flats of the hands, or more ominously, the flats of their swords.

Eventually, they stood before a squat building in front of which two more of the massive men stood guard. Cran's warriors drove the animals up to the door of the building.

'Now,' he said to his people. 'Kill them.'

A howl of terror went up from the captives. Cran and his followers burst into booming laughter.

'The animals!' he shouted. 'Kill the animals!'

The men went about their task with swift, mechanical efficiency, and soon every one of the beasts lay still and bloody on the ground.

'Where are you taking us?' Taran asked the leader.

Once again, Cran did not bother to look at his questioner.

'Back to a real place. Away from you Weaklings and your babyish weeping, your disgusting tears. You people turn my stomach. I'm not even sure you are real people.' He laughed. 'I've never eaten a Weakling. Perhaps now's the time!'

Gwion stood before him, forcing him to look at her.

'He asked you a civilised question. Where are you taking us?'

He looked down again, like a stern father confronting a disobedient child.

'The one place on Maj where there are proper people. The Land of Ez.'

She sank back into the small group. *The Land of Ez.* Nowhere in her studies had she encountered those words. But their import was obvious—they denoted the realm of the Heavy Landers.

It was the dread *Heavy Land* itself.

Then she knew all hope was lost. The same realisation had come to her companions, and a miserable keening came from them. Their captors ignored them.

'Move the animals first,' Cran said, and the carcasses were dragged into the building. After a short time, his men reappeared, ensanguined with animal blood. Cran nodded towards the weeping villagers.

'Now them.'

Gwion was the last to be dragged into the mysterious building. She saw a dark, circular orifice and, screaming, pleading, she was pushed toward it.

And into it.

She began to fall. At first, it was like the descent she had made from the Nothing Point to the Far Wall, but very soon it was not like that at all. She felt herself moving faster and faster, dropping through the darkness at such a rate she could feel the air whistling around her like a mighty wind. And abruptly there was an explosion of light, and she shot from the shaft like a meteorite and crashed down into a net, a net which was still holding some of the animal carcasses and the rest of the villagers.

She was in the Land of Ez.

Nine: The Land of Ez

During her terrifying descent, Gwion had kept her eyes closed to shut out the reality of what was happening to her. But when the harsh light of Ez punched through her lids, she reluctantly opened them.

And found herself looking into two dull eyes from extremely close range. There was the rank, metallic odour of dried blood. As her mind adjusted to the reality of her situation, she realised her face was pressed up against the head of a slaughtered pig. She tried to recoil in horror, but there was something preventing her, something heavy lying against her back. She slowly twisted herself around away from the carcase until she could identify the obstruction.

It was Taran. She realised she had landed on top of him and perhaps knocked him unconscious. But to her great relief, his eyes flickered open and then fixed upon her.

'Gwion,' he whispered, 'you're alright. I thought perhaps…'

She placed a finger on his lips.

'Shhh. I'm alright—at the moment. But let's keep our minds on what we're going to do here. What we can do to get out.'

He gave a weak smile.

'That's my girl. Never say die, eh?'

But further conversation was abruptly prevented. The net was released from its anchors, and a congealed mass of men, women, and slaughtered animals crashed to the floor. Gwion struggled to lift a particularly heavy ewe from her face with some help from Taran. It was not merely heavy—it was *unnaturally* heavy.

Something was very wrong.

Then she was finally free, in the centre of a mass of dead animals and weeping humans. Unable to get up, she looked around as she lay supine on an unnaturally hard floor. Directly above her was a smooth, slightly curved surface which she took to be the ceiling of whatever structure, in which she was now incarcerated. Looking to one side, she could see she was lying on a very similar surface. Not far distant, she could see the legs of Heavy Landers, and their owners were dragging the carcases away. Finally, she decided to sit up.

And found she could not.

It felt like she had been secured to the floor with invisible nails and a heavy weight placed on her chest. She looked at her left hand, which was lying palm up. She concentrated on the hand and tried to lift it from its prison. She succeeded in raising it a few centimetres, the fingers trembling in her struggle. What was wrong? This was not natural, not possible! A pair of feet shod in heavy boots came into her vision and massive hands grasped her and jerked her onto her feet. The blood roared in her head and her new world went momentarily black. When the darkness dissipated, she saw it was Cran himself holding her.

'Wha—what's happening?' she heard herself mumble as she clung desperately to the giant. 'Why can't I move?'

From so small a distance, his laugh felt as if it would blow her eardrums out.

'You're in Ez now, my pretty one. I believe you Weaklings call it the Heavy Land.' He rotated her in his grasp as easily as if she were a toy made from paper. 'Look at our home. And what is now *your* home.'

From her normal height, she could see Ez properly at last. She had been right in thinking that both the floor and ceiling had a gentle curve to them. She saw that the curvature eventually cut off what lay in the further reaches of the Heavy Land. She could also see it was very densely populated by muscular men, and by women who were very close to their menfolk in stature and strength.

'Isn't it wonderful?' Cran continued in his resonant bass. 'A proper world. How can you Weaklings bear to live in your wormholes?'

Gwion found she was slowly adapting to this mysterious feeling of heaviness and turned back to look up at him.

'There is no vegetation here. So how do you live?'

He grunted.

'Easily. We have some plant crops, but more importantly, the Great One placed you in your mud and filth to serve us. We descend to your level when we want and take what we want. Of course, he has forbidden us to visit you that often to avoid bleeding you dry, but we have ways of storing our booty, so it lasts for many rotations.'

Gwion noticed the unexpected word.

'Rotations? You know that Majeh rotates? Even down here?'

'Of course, we see it happen. And we are not *down here*. We are *up here*.'

459

Gwion did not understand how Ez could be above the Pastures or the Far Wall as she had fallen into it, but she did not have long to ponder this latest mystery.

'I'll show you,' Cran said. 'I like my women to be fully grateful for seeing the wonders of Ez.'

He picked her up, and, laughing, held her high above his head. Gwion screamed: if he dropped her now she would shatter like an egg thrown onto a stone! But he held her steady and walked through the busy throng, whose components parted obediently before him. They passed several structures on the wall Gwion did not recognise and, occasionally, she saw circular shapes set into the floor. Then he stopped and gently lowered her.

'Look,' he said, 'we call this a window. You can see through it. We think the other circular shapes in the floor are windows as well, but we can't open them.' He laughed again. 'Even with our strength, we can't open them!'

Gwion knew what a window was; the huts in the Pastures had them to let the mild breezes in, and the smells of sweat and cooking out. She slowly put one foot in front of the other, constantly adjusting her posture to accommodate her new weight, and approached the window. She looked into it. She did not really know what she was expecting to see; a grassland vista, perhaps. But what she saw was very disappointing.

It was just a black surface. There were three shining points of silver light in it; one was noticeably brighter than the others. They appeared to be dimensionless.

That was all: a black surface and three points of light.

She looked up at her captor.

'What am I looking at?'

He smiled.

'The Outside.'

He caught her as she fell. This was the ultimate horror! The Outside! *She had seen the Outside!* It was only sheer luck that she had not also seen the Outsider looking in at her, leering as he reached in to grab her soul. She came to, finding she was sitting in a hard chair with Cran smiling down at her.

'Take me away!' she pleaded. 'Never show me that again! I'll do anything!'

His smile grew broader, revealing strong, tombstone teeth.

'I know you will. Sooner or later.'

***

To Gwion's surprise, Cran was not an inconsiderate lover. He was careful not to injure her when he wanted sex, and always supported his not inconsiderable weight when he was on top. Early on, she found a way to deal with his demands; she would retreat into a safe place in her mind. As he drove into her, she would be in the Pastures watching her sheepdogs describing complex arabesques in the air as they chased down her wayward sheep. As she received his ejaculate, she would be in the Nothing Point in her tremendous flight across the Diameter. Often, she would think of Rhoana and all the good times they had had together and all she had learned from the older woman. Then she would remember her as the Matriarch and smile inwardly as she thought how grand and distant she had seemed when they had first met. There was so much to remember, even in a life as short as Gwion's.

Then he would have finished.

Sometimes Cran would complain about how distant she had seemed.

'You could at least pretend to be enjoying it,' he had said on one occasion. 'I'm not used to women lying there like a lump of wood.'

'That's the way we women of the Pastures show our excitement,' she had said, knowing that an answer which did not please might drive him into a berserk rage. 'You mustn't misunderstand me.'

He had grunted in an unconvinced manner and gone about his other business. However, it soon became clear he was not happy with Gwion's responses and, as he had many other women, the frequency of their sessions gradually diminished, but even when annoyed he never struck her, presumably because even a mild blow from him would have killed her. In their early encounters, after he had finished, he would ask her about her people. He knew she was a Noom and would ask her what was different about Nooms; what they wanted from life; what was their vision of the future of Majeh. But she always gave complicated answers that seemed on the surface to be revealing much, but when he thought about them later were found to be empty except for things he already knew. And so she found she had more and more time to herself, more time in which to learn about her new

461

home. Unlike the male captives, she was free to wander, free to ask questions. The speech of the Heavy Landers was even more different from that of the Pastures than had been that of the Far Wall, but she rapidly mastered it. As her legs grew accustomed to the much stronger gravity of the Land of Ez, she began to travel far and wide, although she was also careful to return to her dwelling at the same time, in case Cran wanted her.

She learned much about Ez. She became friendly with a woman called Palar, who was not much older than she. But Palar was very severely afflicted with the Crab; her face was not too badly marred, but the Crab had invaded her innards and given her a twisted look, as if a bad-tempered child had bent a clay figurine in different directions. She was often in pain. But Palar was glad to have someone to talk to, and gave Gwion much information. She discovered that, like the main part of Majeh, Ez was circular, but was not part of the world of Majeh itself. It stood apart, beyond the world Gwion had known, but was connected to Majeh (or "Maj", as Gwion was learning to call it) by tunnels like the one down which she had been thrown. Palar believed there were four in total, although she had only seen the nearest two.

'I know how I came here,' Gwion had said, 'but how do you people come into my part, into Maj? I know you can't fly.'

'There are ladders on the inside,' Palar had said. 'It is a long way to climb, but our people are strong.'

'And are you happy here, Palar? Is Ez a good place?'

She had looked away for a few moments, seemingly unwilling to meet the other's gaze.

'We are safe here. No one dares attack us.'

'Not what I asked. No one dares attack you, but you dare to attack others. Is that good? Is that what the Great One requires of you?'

Palar had looked confused.

'It is our way. We have always done it. We always will do it.'

Gwion had sensed an opening then; the woman's demeanour had changed slightly, become fractionally defensive.

'But you don't like it, do you, Palar? I can tell you don't.'

'I don't think it's right that... No, I won't say any more. You shouldn't ask these things. We'll both get into trouble.'

Gwion then tried another tack.

'Are the women here safe? Are *you* safe—especially with the Crab inside you?'

She had not answered and instead looked away again, down the tremendous circular corridor which comprised Ez. Afraid of losing her one friend in the Heavy Land, Gwion had rapidly changed the subject.

'And you are not afraid of the—of the Outside?'

Palar had laughed.

'No! We are the Great One's favourites. The Outsider would not dare attack us!'

Gwion had nodded and smiled, even though she did not believe the Outsider was afraid of anyone in Majeh—or Ez.

She tried not to spend too much time with Palar, knowing the strain the other was under, and spent much of her free time walking around, trying to comprehend how Ez organised itself. As she walked, she would try to engage other Heavy Landers in conversation; the women would sometimes speak, but none of the men. Gwion eventually realised they did not want to risk igniting Cran's jealousy. Strong men were they all—but even strong men have their limits.

In her travels, Gwion discovered many things. She learned how the Heavy Landers preserved their meat by rubbing white crystals into it. They had water supplied from metal tubes, which they also used in small vats containing green plants of some kind. Cran made sure she always had some of these green fronds with her meat, joking that she needed to keep her strength up with all this exercise she was getting, but Gwion found them tasteless compared to the algae of Majeh. She also learned there was only the one window open to the Outside, and she always detoured around it, marvelling how the Heavy Landers would walk over it without the slightest trepidation.

But there came a day when she learned something new about the customs and traditions of Ez.

Cran called a meeting of his Inner Circle, leaving them to decide how many women they wanted to bring along. He formed them into a rough circle with a large space at its centre. There was a buzz of excitement from those assembled: apparently they knew what was about to happen. Cran took up position in the centre of the space. He turned to his followers.

'You all know how one of the Weaklings threatened me when we were down there. He said he was going to kill me.' There was a ripple of laughter. 'Well, today, he gets his chance!'

The ripple became a roar, and Cran's followers turned to each other to share their amusement. The circle opened on one side and someone was thrust into the space.

Gwion's heart felt as if it had jumped into her throat.

It was Taran.

Unlike Gwion, he was still wearing the same clothes he had been when he was captured, now ragged and sweat-soaked. He looked thinner. He looked around desperately, but did not see Gwion.

Perhaps it was just as well.

Cran strode toward Taran until he towered over him, a living monolith of sinew and muscle.

'Well, boy, you said you wanted to kill me. Here I am. Kill me.' He spread his mighty arms wide. 'Kill me!'

Taran stared up at the other man, his face twisted in undying hatred. He drew back his right arm and drove his fist onto Cran's belly. *Onto*, not *into*, for that belly might have been made of metal for all the effect Taran's blow had. His fist rebounded impotently.

'I told you to kill me,' Cran said, throwing a quick smile to his supporters. Taran struck again—but with even less impact; it appeared he might have injured his hand. Then Cran drew back his own fist and drove it onto Taran's chin. Gwion saw two bloody teeth fly from the point of contact, and turned away, her eyes moist.

'You're not very good at killing me, are you? Don't you hate me enough? I give you the chance to do what you wanted and you're just wasting it!'

Against her own will, Gwion turned back to the vastly unequal fight in time to see Cran lift Taran and hold him, head down, for some moments. Taran squirmed in the other's granite grip, trying to turn so he could strike back. But Cran did not give him the chance.

'This is boring,' he said. 'I've got better things to do.' And with that, he threw Taran to the floor, head first. His unequal opponent was instantly knocked unconscious.

'Take him back to the cell,' Cran ordered. 'He can try again in a few weeks.' He laughed. 'Give him a piece of meat next time. It might put some strength into him!'

That evening, sex with Cran was even more vigorous than usual as her massive partner revelled in his victory.

It was then Gwion vowed that if there were any way in this benighted world of Majeh to achieve it, Cran must die.

Ten: In the Shadows

As Cran became more and more bored with her, Gwion found she had more and more freedom. He no longer seemed interested in the subject of Nooms and what they could and could not do. And so she sought out those people from the Far Wall who had been abducted along with her. She found the women, but not the men. The men were in cells somewhere, but she realised very early on it would be extremely unwise to inquire where those might be. The women had, of course, been passed to Cran's warriors as a source of welcome sexual variety. She found they were all grateful to be still alive and were becoming reconciled to their new status. Indeed, many of them were starting to identify themselves as loyal inhabitants of the Land of Ez.

And so, to avoid depleting Palar's patience, Gwion tried inserting herself into the conversations of other native women in Ez. She tried the usual gambits of commenting on how good-looking were their children, or inquiring where she could get a hairstyle like theirs. It did not take long for her to understand that concubines like her were not regarded as normal women, and she usually gave up the attempt to communicate after being ignored for minutes on end. On the few occasions when she managed to be allowed to speak, she found it difficult to move the conversation on from her ploys and soon excused herself and left. She even tried to learn more from Cran himself, but once he had obtained his release, he was not interested in any form of conversation, least of all the history or mores of Ez. Even Nooms were no longer were of any interest to him.

And so it was a slight shock when a dark-haired woman came up to her while she was in the market, waiting in line to get her usual meal of mutton and the ubiquitous green vegetable. The woman introduced herself as Sidan. To Gwion's surprise, Sidan invited her to sit at the same table and together they made short work of their meals. The other woman had lamb, which Gwion had always considered as being too bland. As she ate, she noticed Sidan did not have the great muscles of the true native.

'You're Cran's new favourite, aren't you?' Sidan continued after finishing her meal. Her voice was honeyed with soothing, silky tones.

Surprised by the directness of the question, Gwion simply nodded, and after a second's thought, added, 'For the moment.'

Sidan laughed.

'Yes, he always moves on after a while. But I'd say you have quite a few tours of duty before he retires you!'

'Lucky me.'

'Don't worry, he always treats us well. We get more to eat than most, and the work isn't too hard.'

Gwion's eyebrows arched slightly as she rose from the table.

'Us?'

Sidan slipped an arm under one of Gwion's.

'Let's walk.' When they were in a quieter region, she continued, 'I was one of his women a few years ago.'

'What—you're from the Far Wall?'

'No,' she laughed, 'I'm a Spinward girl, originally. The Heavy Landers rotate their targets, you know, to give the last one a chance to recover.'

'So, what will happen when Cran finally gets tired of me?'

'Oh, you'll be given to one of his lieutenants. Don't pull a face; they treat women well here.'

'After they've prostituted them, you mean?'

Sidan looked shocked and pulled her into an alcove out of the passing throng.

'Don't ever say that! The men will stand for a lot, but they won't let you get away with that!'

Gwion shrugged.

'I'm not sure I want a life where all these men are so wonderfully nice to me.'

For a moment, she thought of Zan; poor, naïve Zan. What a simple, basically harmless, boy he had been! He wouldn't survive for even a few minutes in Ez. But Sidan was speaking again.

'What do you mean? Are you saying you would try to escape?'

Gwion shrugged again. 'Yes, or kill myself. It may come to that.'

But Sidan was now looking distracted, as if important concepts were being juggled in her brain. Gwion waited with increasing impatience for something to happen, and then Sidan snapped out of her reverie.

'I'd like you to meet some of my friends.' She gave Gwion an address and a time. 'Be there.'

Gwion returned to her dwelling, her mind whirling. She had not expected things to take so dramatic a turn, so quickly. Cran was already sprawled on the bed when she arrived, but her duties did not take as long as usual, and he left shortly afterwards for some important meeting or other. But Gwion now had her own important meeting to attend. Ez technology had reached the heights of clockwork mechanisms, and she hungrily watched the minutes tick by on the wall timepiece. Would the time never come! She cursed under her breath.

But finally, of course, it did.

Sidan had given her good directions and told her how long it would take. But she hadn't told Gwion that the route took her past the unshuttered window. She shivered as she walked steadily past it, not looking in that direction but hearing a strange voice that was not hers whispering in her mind, *Go on! Walk over! Look into the Outside!*

But she did not fall victim to that eerie siren voice.

And then she was standing outside the meeting place. It had a sturdy metal door that looked as if it could not be opened even with Heavy Land strength, but Sidan had assured her it would open easily. And so it did. She walked in, and stopped. The room seemed entirely without light. Then she heard a voice.

'Come in, Gwion. We're all here.'

As her eyes adjusted, she began to see the main details of the place. She could see four shapes, with one being considerably sturdier than the other. That worried her, and her worry was realised when a feeble yellow light flickered into insipid life. The bulky shape was a man of the Heavy Land!

She backed away with the words *It's a trap!* blazing in her thoughts. But Sidan had seen her distress and leapt up to reassure her.

'It's alright, Gwion. Crov is one of us.'

'He is?' Gwion was only half convinced. But Crov came towards her, extending a massive hand.

'It's not a trap, Gwion,' he said. 'I am on your side. And I'm pleased to meet you.'

As her confusion faded, Gwion remembered the Far Wall custom and allowed her hand to be swallowed up inside Crov's mighty grip. *He could crush my hand like an egg,* she thought, but then tried to push her doubts away. Sidan touched her shoulder and pointed to a box-shaped object.

'Sit down and we'll start talking.'

Gwion looked around; her dark-adapted eyes and the faint light eventually allowed her to see both the room and its inhabitants. There were two other women, obviously not natives, and Crov, his great bulk looking very incongruous against frail femininity. She could also see the room was filled with rectangular structures, large and small, most of which had small circular windows in them. Gwion tapped the nearest little window with a cautious finger. It was made of the same transparent stuff as the ruined Ancient vats in the Pastures. And she could see Ancient script alongside and below the little windows, but was no longer interested in attempting to read it.

'What are these things?' she asked Sidan as a way of breaking the tense silence.

Sidan shrugged.

'The Great One knows. But we are here to talk about the future, not the past.'

'And what does the future hold?'

'For me, a return to the Spinward Land; for you, a return to the Pastures.'

Gwion's heartbeat accelerated at those beautiful words. But then, doubt again. She looked directly at Crov.

'But what about you, Crov? You're home already. What do you get out of this hiding in the shadows?'

He gave an odd smile and glanced down at his great hands.

'For me? Peace of mind, I guess. The knowledge that I'm doing the right thing.'

'And what is that?'

He returned Gwion's stare.

'Gwion, you mustn't believe that everyone in Ez thinks the same way as Cran. For decades, we've been raiding the lands below, sucking them dry, killing the men, and… well, you know what we do with the women.'

'Yes, I do.'

'Some of us think we should make a permanent, lasting peace with the weak people; work out some way of life that benefits us all.' He smiled. 'And I'm one of them.'

Sidan tapped Gwion on the shoulder again and pointed at the other women.

'Let me introduce our other friends.'

A dark-skinned woman stood, bowed and said, 'Rhosana: the Far Wall.'

She sat, and the other woman introduced herself as 'Gwenna: the Pastures.'

Gwion gasped.

'Gwenna! Linon mentioned you! Said you'd been killed in the last war!'

'Sometimes I wish I had been. How is Linon?'

'Not good. The Crab will take her soon.'

Gwenna nodded silently and returned to her seat.

Gwion resumed her questioning of Sidan, who appeared to be the leader.

'And how do we get back to our homelands?'

But it was Crov who spoke.

'Once every three months, maintenance is carried out on the shafts to the lower lands. The first in the current cycle is the one you came through. Its entrance will be open for some time.'

'What! That's your plan! It took me long enough to fall through it, and you expect me to climb up it?'

'Yes, I do. You've obviously forgotten that the gravity—the pull that keeps us on the floor—gets weaker as you get nearer your home. That's why you people are so weak; you don't have much gravity down there.'

Gwion thought about Crov's words. They made sense; it must be the greater pull in Ez that gave them their musculature. But then she remembered two essential things.

'Yes, that's the only way; I see it now. How many of us will there be?'

'Not many more,' Sidan said, 'the new tranche of women appear to have acclimatised themselves very quickly.'

'Yes, so I discovered. But there must be another with us.'

Crov looked puzzled.

'Who might that be?'

'A man who was captured with me. One who is being tormented by my lover. His name is Taran.'

Crov looked around the room, as if unsure of what to say.

'Yes, I know of him. And I also know where he is. But getting him out will make our escape much less likely.'

470

'He must come with us. I can't leave him in the clutches of a monster. And there is another thing I want.'

Sidan let out a savage obscenity, one forbidden in the Pastures. Then: 'Blood of the Great One, Gwion! You've only just joined us and now you're telling us what to do!'

Gwion features hardened to iron.

'Yes, I am. I'm a Noom—and that's what we do.'

'Alright, O Great Noom, what is the other thing we must do?'

'Cran.'

'Yes, Cran. The ruler of all Ez. What about him?'

Gwion leapt to her feet, her face, previously emotionless, transmuted into a mask of ravenous hatred.

'He dies. He dies! *He dies!*'

***

The group broke up shortly after Gwion's outburst, as every meeting's duration was only as long as absolutely necessary, with no light conversation. This one had already lasted longer than normal due to Gwion's induction.

However, her emotional loss of control had not been well received by the rest of the cabal, especially Sidan, who had looked askance at Gwion for the remainder of the discussion. Still, they had all agreed to meet again at another location in a few days, when Crov promised to bring news of Taran.

Gwion felt herself gripped by a feeling of impatience, a desire for something to happen—anything to happen! The idea that she might escape her servitude and return to the Far Wall, and thence to the Pastures, was intoxicating, exhilarating. Later that day, Cran noticed her improved mood but put it down to his sexual prowess and, being quietly satisfied, did not inquire further into its reasons.

Having no actual duties beyond serving her master, Gwion continued her exploration of Ez. For some reason, she found herself returning to Palar. She could not explain it, but there was a feeling that the two women, so different physically, were destined to play an important part in each other's lives. Gwion was not superstitious, but she could not shake off that premonition of common destiny. And so, she learned more about the woman's past. Her only son had been killed during an attack on the AntiSpinward Lands, when the inhabitants had fought back unusually effectively.

'So you don't care for war much?' Gwion had asked, carefully keeping her tone light and unconcerned as to what the answer might be.

'No. War took my young Crawn. He wanted to impress me, to bring back more booty than the others and lay it at my feet. He wanted to show he was now a man. And the only thing of his that came back was his body. Those AntiSpinward murderers killed him like a dog. Now I don't care whether I live or die'

'He was attacking them, invading their lands,' Gwion had pointed out, as gently as she could. 'Don't you think they had a right to defend themselves?'

Palar considered Gwion's words for a while, and then said, 'Yes, perhaps. There might be something in what you say. I have sometimes thought that maybe there might be another way. A way in which young men don't have to die. Like my poor Crawn, for nothing; for absolutely nothing. I would just like to end my days knowing that people weren't hurting each other anymore.'

Gwion had smiled then and thought, *Another ally in the making!*

Eleven: Beyond the Window

Gwion sensed a feeling of hostility toward her at the next meeting. Sidan, in particular, now spoke to her in short, abrupt sentences.

'Well, you're very good at giving out orders, Gwion, but here we believe in taking them as well as giving them.'

'I'm only too happy to take orders—when I get them. Nothing's actually happened yet.' She looked at Crov. 'Taran?'

'I said I know where he is. But getting him out won't be easy.'

'We have to get him out soon. Cran will kill him in their next fight.'

Crov nodded solemnly.

'I'm afraid that's true. Cran will kill him next time, even if he does not really intend to; they're so ill-matched. But there's no telling when that will happen; Cran's letting him have food now, so it doesn't look like the next fight will be any time soon.'

'So what are the problems in freeing him?'

'He's in a locked cell, obviously. And there's a guard stationed outside. They have a rotating contingent: one leaves and gives the key to the next one.'

'Nothing too sophisticated then.'

Crov looked up, puzzled.

'Sophisticated?'

'Never mind. Do the guards use a password?'

'I don't think so. Of course, I haven't risked any eavesdropping to avoid raising suspicions, but all the men in Ez know and trust one another.'

'Do they know you?'

'Yes.'

Gwion smiled broadly.

'Then that's how we get in.'

***

Gwion stared at the cell door from a safe distance. It was a sturdy metal door with no window and was clearly the work of the Ancients. In fact, Gwion mused, the Land of Ez bore their imprints far more than anywhere in Majeh itself. Everything here was metal, or some other substance almost as hard as metal but warmer to the touch. There were no pastures; in fact, no soil at all. This was obviously the

473

explanation as to why they needed to raid the other lands. One day, she would learn what the reasons behind these differences were.

But that time was not now.

She walked past the door at a carefully-calculated gap, stopped before the bored-looking guard on his stool, and gave him the biggest smile she could muster. He looked startled but then returned it.

'You must be very fed up sitting there all day,' she said, maintaining the smile as she spoke. 'What's your name, sweetheart?'

The startled expression was beginning to fade, gradually being replaced by lasciviousness.

'Cram.'

'That's a nice name. Pity about a man like you being saddled with a boring job.'

He grinned.

'Yeah, but I'm not as bored as the Weakling in there!'

'It's such a shame,' she said, moving very slightly closer, 'giving a big, strong man like you a shit job like this.'

'It won't be for much longer. Cran's gonna finish him next time.'

'You deserve a much better job than this, like showing those Weaklings down below who's boss; a big, good-looking guy like you, huh?'

He laughed.

'You got the right idea there, lady!' Then his expression changed. 'Hey, you're Cran's girl, aren't you?'

'I am,' she said, 'but he's getting a bit bored with me, I guess. Looks like I'll be moving on soon.' She lowered her voice slightly. 'Know what I mean?'

The guard looked like he'd just been released from his own cell as his eyes lit up.

'Do I!'

***

Gwion and Crov agreed that her new guard friend would be the key to getting Taran out of his imprisonment on Ez's death row. Crov had already learned the cycle of who was on duty and had found something useful about the man who was next after Gwion's contact.

'I've known Cron for years. He's not a friend as such, but we've sunk a few beverages together.'

'But you won't go soft at the last moment, will you?' Gwion said, looking severely into his eyes. His gaze met hers without flinching.

'No, I won't. Now let's leave it at that. It'll be a few more days before he's on duty.'

Gwion nodded her acceptance and turned away.

To find Sidan looking at her.

'Yes, Sidan?'

'You and I need to clear something up.'

'I'm at your service.'

'Good.' Sidan pointed into a darker corner of their current meeting room. 'Let's have a little talk.'

The two women sat together, somewhat apart from the others.

'There is something that needs to be established about you, Gwion. We need to know you are fully with us and that you don't have some other agenda. Or perhaps you believe this is just a girlish game; perhaps success or failure aren't particularly important for you.'

'Don't be ridiculous; I want nothing more than to get out of this Outsider Hole.'

Sidan looked over her shoulder.

'We have a test for that, don't we, girls?'

The other women murmured their agreement.

'A test? Are you trying to frighten me? I'm the one who crossed the Diameter, don't forget.'

'No, we're not trying to frighten you. We want to see that you have fully committed to us, heart and soul, that's all. We've all taken the test—apart from Crov; as a native, he didn't need to.'

Gwion spread her arms in mock resignation.

'Alright, I'll do this test of yours. Where and when?'

Was that a wicked smile flickering for a second on Sidan's lips? Gwion was not sure.

'Tomorrow night at our meeting time. Here. It'll just be you and me.'

'I can't wait. Can I go now?'

'Yes. But be here tomorrow, or we'll understand exactly what you are.'

***

475

The following day was without incident; even Cran did not require her services. Palar was not available for a heart-to-heart, and so Gwion simply hung around her room. Gradually, the light of Ez's day yellowed and faded. And then it was time.

As Gwion approached their latest meeting place, Sidan emerged from the shadows and said, 'Glad you made it, Gwion. Now follow me.'

They walked in silence for some time, and then Sidan gestured to halt, looking around to see if they were observed. But it was now the time that most of the inhabitants settled down for their evening meal, and the vast, curving corridor was empty. Sidan turned to her companion and removed something from her kirtle. It was a bandage.

'I'm going to put this on you.'

Gwion stared at it with obvious incomprehension.

'What! Are you mad? Why should I wear that?'

Sidan laughed.

'Looks like you've failed the test already. One more chance: am I putting this on you or not?'

Gwion stared back at her for a moment, then: 'Put it on.'

Sidan wound the bandage around the other's head, placed it over her eyes and then tied it at the back. Rather too tightly, Gwion thought.

They walked on.

'Stop. This is the test.'

Sidan undid the knot and slipped the bandage off. Gwion looked around, blinking.

'Where's the test?'

'Here.'

Sidan walked away, stopped some distance away and stood, looking down at the floor.

Gwion followed.

And stood rigid. Beads of cold sweat appeared on her skin.

Sidan was standing on the other side of a window in the floor. No, not *a* window: *the* window.

The unshuttered window.

'Gwion, prove that your heart is with us. Look into the window.'

It felt to Gwion that she was suddenly alone on a great, dark plain with a freezing wind tugging at her. Eldritch shapes seemed to move in the surrounding blackness, howling for her soul.

'What? What! You can't mean it! The Outsider! I...'

'I've done it, looked through,' Sidan said, and there was mockery in her voice. 'You crossed the Diameter, didn't you? Surely this is nothing compared to that.'

Gwion began to breathe in short, staccato pants. Death in crossing the Diameter just meant the end of a bodily life. But this— this imperilled her very soul. Had Sidan warned the Outsider that she would be doing this? Was he waiting on the other side of the window, ready to snatch her soul?

'Oh dear, the great Noom, the one who enjoys telling other people what to do, is afraid. Won't Taran be disappointed?'

Perhaps if she hadn't said his name, Gwion might have backed away. But a vision of her starving friend sitting in the darkness of his cell gave her a lightning flash of courage.

She walked toward the window.

And looked through it.

And what she saw was beyond her understanding.

She did not see the Outsider leering at her as his clawed hands reached in.

Instead, she saw a strange metallic-looking ovoid. Completely featureless. Its lustrous surface mathematically smooth.

It is utterly dark in interstellar space, but the ovoid shone brilliantly, as if it was self-luminous.

She stared at it, the terror being replaced by wonder.

There was no way of telling its size; whether it was an object she could have held in her palm, floating just outside the window, or something stupendous, immeasurably vast, at a great distance.

And somehow, she knew it was something stupendous, immeasurably vast, floating in the encircling night at a great distance from Majeh.

'Wha...' she muttered.

But it was already too late. The strain was too much. She felt her knees give way and darkness took her.

***

Gwion's eyes opened. But there was something wrong: she had fallen into darkness but had now awoken.

So there should be no darkness.

But there was.

And suddenly there was a voice, a smooth, silken voice.

Sidan.

'Ah, you're awake. I was wondering how long it would take. Here, let me help you.'

She felt fingers at the back of her head, and then her eyes were flooded with light. As her eyes regained their focus, Sidan's shape coalesced from the surroundings.

And she was holding a knife.

Looking for a way out, Gwion scanned the room. In all directions, she saw metal boxes, piled one on top of the other, some very precariously. It appeared she was in some kind of warehouse.

'You're alright, I hope? The shock of seeing the Outside wasn't too much for your dear little heart?'

'I'm alright,' Gwion said. She tried to rise but found she was bound to the chair in which she was sitting. 'What is this?'

'Surely it's obvious? I'm an infiltrator.'

'An infiltrator? So who do you work for?'

'Come on, this isn't worthy of a high and mighty Noom, is it? I work for Cran, of course.'

'Cran? Why would someone from Majeh work for Cran?'

'Because he is a great man. And he has great plans. Instead of merely raiding the Weaklings every few years, he intends to conquer them, make them work for the benefit of Ez. They can provide more than enough food for us, with a little left over for themselves, of course. And he doesn't like people who disagree with him, ones who pretend to be his friend but are secretly plotting against him. Do you know anybody like that?'

'But you're a Spinward native. What they call a Weakling. Why would you betray your own people?'

She laughed.

'My own people! The ones who win and take what they want are my people. Since I came to Ez, I realised that there's only one race of people on this pile of crap which can be relied on to come out on top. And you're certainly not one of them. What are you back in that

Pastures place? A shepherdess? You're nothing but a fucking sheep yourself.'

Gwion shook her head, trying to understand this new situation.

'Why the interest in me?'

'Because Cran knows about the Nooms, and he wants to know if you're a threat to his plans. He already knew your village on the Far Wall was an important nest of your type. So he selected some for study. He chose you especially. He found you physically attractive—though the Great One knows why—and thought he'd get some information out of you as a bonus while he fucked you. But you stymied him. You didn't fall in love with him like every other one of his conquests.'

'*Fall in love!* Hah!' Gwion snorted.

'You see, that's what's wrong with you. You think you're better than me; you think you're better than everybody. But remember how you went to pieces when I forced you to look out the window? How you shat yourself and wept and wailed? Cran taught me there's nothing out there. Maj is the world: there's nothing else—how could there be? There's no Outsider. And yet you *Oh-So-Clever Nooms* still believe! You're pathetic. But I forced myself to touch you, to drag your unconscious carcase to this place, but fortunately, you don't weigh anything—even in Ez.'

Gwion thought about that. Then she remembered the mysterious ovoid she had seen. She lifted her gaze back to her captor.

'You're wrong. There is *something* out there. Maybe it's not the Outsider. Maybe it is. Maybe he doesn't look like a person after all. But there is definitely something out there.'

Sidan shrugged.

'Who cares? You can believe what you want to believe. The important thing to understand—and I'm going to say this very slowly, so I don't lose you—is that Cran has known for some time that there is a group of malcontents, of traitors here, and he could have killed you at any time he wanted. But you see, Gwion, he couldn't get you to incriminate yourself, so he told me to induct you into the group. I've been a member for some time, regularly reporting to Cran. I haven't had much to report because they've never actually *done* anything. But it looks like they might change that, this time. He's extremely interested in the plan to spring Taran because he likes him. He likes the way he bleeds. So I am to tell him when I have all the

479

information he needs, and he will do the rest. It will be a famous victory for Ez, and the people will praise his brilliance in catching and executing so many traitors. He's not sure if he will apprehend you plotters before you release Taran or let you think you've won. It all depends on which one he thinks will get him the most love from the people.'

'But I'm part of the plan. If I'm held here, there's no plan.'

Sidan leaned forward with a wolfish smile.

'That's why my master is my master. He knows you're fond of Taran. Maybe *he* is someone you love. So here's the deal: I'll report to him you're co-operating, you go ahead with your part and he'll let Taran live. Refuse, and Taran will die—but not in a quick way.'

'And the others of the group?'

Sidan held up her hands.

'What do you expect? They'll be executed as traitors, but my master will be merciful.'

'And me?'

'He'll probably let you live, but he is annoyed you didn't fall in love with him. So this way he breaks your will, makes you hate yourself, turns you into the slave you were always meant to be. And then, I'm sure he'll want to try some new techniques on you in the marital bed while he decides what finally to do with you.'

Gwion leaned forward again, testing the strength of her bonds. They felt firm.

'So let me get this straight: I agree to betray the group. You report my agreement. We proceed with the plan. Then Cran captures us either before or after we release Taran, depending on which gets him the most glory. He doesn't execute Taran. He does execute the rest of the group, but mercifully. After using and abusing me, he may, or may not, execute me.'

'Correct.'

'Well, seems like an offer I can't refuse.' She leaned forward again, and pressed against the bonds more forcibly. Nothing. 'So one more thing—what exactly do you get out of all this?'

Sidan raised both arms, and her rigid frame seemed to burn with an interior flame.

'My one true love is mine again! Cran! The only man I have ever loved or ever will love! A giant among Weaklings! He will take me back, Gwion, as his chief woman. Oh, I can't expect him to give up all the others; he can have one now and again, but I will be the only one he loves! I will sit by his side, administering justice, dealing out life and death!' She glared at Gwion. 'Do you think it's been easy for me watching him demean himself with a parade of little tramps like you, forcing themselves on him! Do you? Well, they'll be the first to feel my justice when I am back where I belong!'

Twelve: Si Vis Pacem…

Gwion knew what must be done: she had to escape Sidan's clutches in a way that prevented her from informing Cran of the timing of their plan to free Taran. As soon as she had escaped, the cabal had to explode into action, get Taran out, and get the Outside away from the cells and into the shaft which led back to the Far Wall!

She knew exactly what had to be done.

All she needed was to work out how to do it.

'So what happens now?' she asked her captor.

'I take you to Cran so you can apologise to him and explain you are now back in the fold. "The fold"—get it? Afterwards we both go to the next meeting and explain to the others that Cran is on to us and we have to act now. After that, it's all in the hands of my master.'

'And we're going to do that right now?'

'Yes. You've been asleep most of the night. Cran never mentioned you snore so loudly.'

'I didn't know I did. I've never before had the chance for someone to tell me.' Gwion studied Sidan closely. Was the other woman showing any signs of strain, of nervousness, that might make her uncertain in her actions, make her clumsy?

There were not.

'Well, we'd better get on with it,' Gwion said. A section of her mind separate from the speaking part was racing through a series of scenarios which led to her escape. Even as she spoke, that section was formulating plans, testing them, rejecting them, and creating the next one.

'I couldn't agree more. The sooner I'm rid of you, the better. Now I'm going to come around behind you and undo the restraints. Then you stand up very slowly. Remember, I have the knife, and I'm sure as the Great One of how to use it.'

Gwion suddenly realised that the subconscious part of her mind had not rejected the latest plan it had devised.

Make her angry. Get her off-guard.

As Sidan moved to get behind her, she said, 'You're aware Cran is a lousy lover, aren't you?'

'Hah! What would you know about it? You were a virgin when he met you.'

482

'That's what he told you. I've had plenty of men, and I know a good one when I feel one.'

No reaction.

Try a different tack.

As the cords came off, Gwion said, 'Well, he may be no good, but he said I was great. Really got him going.'

'That's nice. You must have loved to hear that. Stand up.'

Gwion stood, but continued, 'He said I was much better than you.'

She saw Sidan go stiff.

'Don't be ridiculous. You're just a temporary pastime for him.'

Gwion moved very slowly, fractionally closer.

'Is that right? Then why did he say you're too old for him now, that you're just someone he used to know? That I was fresh and exciting? Young?'

Sidan's lips compressed to the thinnest possible of lines.

'Shut up. He would never say that. He loves me.'

'Does he now? You're sure of him, are you? Then why did he say you're so loose and saggy down there that he never knew if he was in or not?'

That was enough. Sidan's hitherto impassive face transformed into a hideous mask of hatred, and she lifted the knife. Gwion saw the metal flash momentarily in the room's light.

'I'll kill you for that, slut! No jumped-up whore comes between me and my man!'

Gwion's body tensed. She understood these might be the last few seconds of her life. Would her Noom reflexes be enough?

Sidan launched herself at Gwion, the knife ready to plunge into the soft tissue of her throat. Gwion concentrated all her attention on the killing arm; turning sideways as she did so. As the arm passed millimetres to the side, she chopped down hard on the hand holding the weapon, sending the knife skittering across the floor. Both women immediately turned and hurled themselves after the instrument of murder, arriving simultaneously on top of it, crashing into each other. The knife slid further away as two hands reached for it. Now grappling with each other, the combatants rolled over and over, raining blows on each other's face with one hand, while reaching for the knife with the other. Nothing could be heard except the rasping pants of the two as they fought for air amid the frenzy of violence, and the ragged grunts of their obscenities. Then finally their rolling stopped, with Sidan on top. And Gwion found she was slipping into unconsciousness as she shook under the fusillade of blows from Sidan. Sidan was not a native of Ez, but her time there had hardened her muscles, until she was a powerhouse of furious whipcord.

'Like it, slut?' she gasped between delivering blows. 'I'm going to enjoy slicing you into little fillets and feeding them to Taran!'

Gwion took the opportunity of the respite from the storm of impacts while Sidan was taking time to gloat and drove her knee into the other's crotch. Sidan's grip weakened as she gasped with the shock, and Gwion rolled out from under her.

The knife? Where was it?

She saw it.

She reached for it.

And received a kick to the head which sent her back into the darkness for a second.

Her eyes flickered open, and she discovered she was lying on her back with Sidan standing nearby. Both combatants had rivulets of blood trickling down from split lips.

Gwion looked desperately around; her gamble had not paid off. She had not bargained for Sidan's strength. But as she glanced up, she realised Sidan was not her only problem: she was directly under a massive metal container that hung precariously at the very top of an unstable tower of similar boxes.

Sidan made no attempt to move nearer but made slashing motions with the knife.

'So, this is how it ends, Gwion. I realise now you had used your Noom cleverness to get me so worked up you could trick me. But that doesn't matter now, I've got the knife and you haven't. I've beaten the shit out of you and you're easy meat now. What do you creatures call us—"Ords"? Looks like we're not so dumb, and you're not so clever.'

Gwion began to slide on her back, away from both the other woman and the peril of the tower.

'So what now?'

'What do you think, dumb-ass? I see now I don't need you. I'll go to Cran and he'll just kill all your new friends at once, and I daresay he'll arrange something very special for Taran. How do you like that, Little Miss Clever? Look what you've done to the people you loved!'

Despair washed over Gwion. Sidan was right: her vaunted intelligence had been impotent against mere brute strength. As Sidan approached, the knife held high, she continued to slide away from her.

But abruptly there was nowhere to go; her back was pressing against the wall. Sidan saw her despair and smiled.

'Time to find out if there really is an Outsider, bitch.'

And then, in a flash of understanding, Gwion knew what to do.

With the last of her strength, she drove both feet onto the base of the unstable tower of metal containers, sending the top one crashing down onto Sidan, who didn't even have time to look up.

Gwion did not spend much time checking on whether Sidan still lived. The amount of blood oozing from underneath the container was sufficient proof that she was not.

She rose unsteadily to her feet, wiping the blood from her split lips.

Now there could be no delay.

The plan to release Taran had to be enacted now!

***

'She really worked you over,' Crov said, studying her bruises.

'You don't say?' Gwion switched her attention from him to the two women. 'Ladies! I need your help; can you hide these marks? I've got some seducing to do!'

Like most women in most places, make-up was not unknown to Gwenna and Rhosana.

After many minutes of their work, and much wincing and flinching from Gwion, they had hidden most of the mementos of their epic battle that Sidan had given her vanquished opponent.

'We have to move fast; Great Guidance fast!' Gwion snapped when their work was finally done. 'Sidan's body might be found at any moment.' She stared at Crov. 'You're sure this is the handover moment?'

'I may be an Ord, but I'm not completely stupid. So you do your part and we'll do ours.' He looked quizzically at her. 'But don't get too carried away in your role; that make-up will come off easily.'

'I have no intention of letting it get that far. Let's go.'

And so it was a short time later that Gwion was leaning against a wall near the cell block. Cram came around the corner, his face frozen by jaded tedium.

And then, on seeing Gwion, it changed instantly to alert excitement.

'You again! What do you want this time, lady?'

Gwion moved closer, but not so close that her over made-up face would arouse suspicion.

'Waiting for you, Cram. What, did you think I was shitting you earlier?'

His excited face became almost joyous.

'Sure. If Cran liked you, you must be hot stuff. I didn't think you'd be this hot. I guess I got a lot to learn, right?'

'Yeah. And I'm the girl to do the teaching.' She glanced over her shoulder. 'This room's empty. How about it?'

He looked confused, torn.

'I don't know. I got to do the handover soon.'

'We'll make it a quick one. Just a taster, right? We'll have the full course later, right?'

He made a quick reconnoitre of the immediate area and then, grinning, said, 'Right!' and moved towards her. She backed away into the dim opening behind her. Cram followed.

And received a knock-out blow from Crov.

He and Gwion swiftly bound him and tied a rag over his mouth. A second or two later, Crov stepped out to complete the subterfuge.

Cron looked up as the other approached.

'Hey, Crov, what are you doing here?'

'I'm your relief. Cram couldn't make it.' He laughed. 'He thought he'd see what a Weakling tasted like, and now he's sick to his stomach!'

Cron burst into loud guffaws.

'Man, that's a good one! Knowing him like we do, I wouldn't put that past him!'

'Yeah, he's quite a guy,' Crov agreed. 'Well, do you have the key or not?'

'Sure. Where's the fire, man? Let's chew the fat a while.'

Gwion, watching from the shadows, felt a twinge of alarm. The last thing they needed was a long discussion about the Good Old Days. But Crov handled it well.

'Sorry, no can do. Cran's getting a bit pissed off about the time we spend sitting around here. Haven't you heard?'

Cron looked slightly alarmed.

'Well, that's different. We'll have a catch-up some other time, right?'

'Right. See you.'

The rescuers waited for some time after Taran's jailer had disappeared in case he returned for something he'd forgotten, and then Gwion, Rhosana and Gwenna emerged from hiding.

'Hurry up,' Gwion hissed. 'Every second counts. Come on, come on!'

But her nervous urging was unnecessary, for Crov was already turning the key. He flung the door wide and a rank smell of human waste and human despair hit them. All but Gwion backed away as the miasma swept out of the cell, but she rushed in to find Taran slumped on a bed of straw. She pulled the semi-conscious man to his feet, not without difficulty. He blinked in the unexpected light.

'Gwion,' he said, 'Gwion, is that you? What are you doing here?'

'Rescuing you,' was the curt reply. 'Come on!'

She emerged with Taran leaning on her shoulder. For reassurance, she fingered Sidan's knife that hung on her hip.

'Let's go!'

But she felt Crov's hand on her shoulder, restraining her.

'No! We can't go yet! There are others who want to come, men as well as women; we can't leave them! I can't leave them!'

Angrily, she shook off his hand.

'No, we can't delay for one second! Cran knows all about us—he could be on his way right now. They'll have to take their chances; maybe he doesn't know they're traitors.'

'Great One—you're hard!' Crov said, staring at her in distaste.

'Maybe I am. But I'm a Noom—we deal with reality, not wishful thinking.'

'But the others,' Gwenna pleaded, 'I know some of them!'

Gwion backed away from the rest of the group until she could fit all of them in her field of vision.

'You simply don't get it, do you? I'm not doing this just for us, you fools! I'm doing it for all Majeh! We have to get back to the lower lands and warn them to prepare for all-out war with the Heavy Landers!'

'We can't win such a war,' Rhosana said.

'Yes, we can! If all the lower lands unite, there are more of us than them! We can win—but only if they know what's coming!'

Crov opened his mouth for another objection, but then something unexpected happened.

Gwion felt the deck tremble beneath her and her surroundings suddenly blurred as if seen through a heat haze. Then, for a moment, they all heard a far-off rumble.

'What was that?' Gwenna said.

'I don't know. Maybe it was Great Guidance getting annoyed with us standing around bleating like sheep.' Gwion glanced at Taran. 'Can you walk?'

'Yes. I've been walking back and forth in the cell. I can make it.'

'Then we are moving. Now!' She looked at the others. 'Taran and I are going now. You can stay if you want to. I'm through trying to make you see sense.'

They moved as one, with Gwion in the lead.

The huge corridor was full of people going about their business, many of whom stopped what they were doing to watch the strange collection of Weaklings and one of their own struggle past them or through their midst. None of that ill-assorted group looked at the puzzled Heavy Landers; to make eye contact was to invite arrest.

It seemed to Gwion that the entrance to the shaft had been moved to infinity as they strode on, blithely pretending nothing unusual was happening. But she knew, sooner or later, some of the Heavy Landers would stop them and demand to know what they were about.

And then she saw it.

A long ladder reached up into a cavernous opening. At the end of the tunnel beyond that opening lay the Far Wall. They must get there!

She cursed as she saw the maintenance crew was still there, busily going about its business.

She would have to use the knife. She turned back to her fellow fugitives; they were motionless, looking back and forth between the maintenance men and Gwion. And then, for some reason, their gaze shifted from her to the side and their features grew even more alarmed than they had been.

She spun around to follow their gaze.

Cran.

He emerged from the room where he had been waiting, and four stocky thugs were close behind.

'I see now that Nooms are indeed to be reckoned with. You have done me a great service, Gwion. Without you, I would have underestimated your kind. It is obvious that Nooms will be the leaders in the defence of the Weakling lands. Therefore, I will eliminate them first. My scouts have already mapped out areas of Maj where there are high concentrations of your type. I will liquidate them in the first thrust. The rest of the people will submit soon after; of that, I have no doubt.' He moved further out into the corridor. 'But, Gwion, are things so dark? Is this really such a terrible fate? I have no intention of exterminating the Weaklings, merely to put them to productive work. For the greater good of Ez, of course, I won't attempt to deny that, but in time their new way of life will seem completely natural to them. There will be no rebellions. There will be peace in the Pastures.'

'This was all just a game to you, wasn't it?' Gwion said, in a voice of dull defeat.

He now stood directly in front of her, looking down with a faint smile.

'To a certain extent. I could have killed all of you at any moment, but I wanted to make a spectacle of your defeat; a piece of theatre if you like. Of course, finding Sidan's body forced my hand. For an intelligent woman, I am surprised you didn't realise that blood seeping into the corridor was a trifle suspicious.' He turned his back on her, his amused contempt evident to all the witnesses who had now wonderingly assembled. 'So now Ez stands on the threshold of its greatest moment, and I will be recorded in the histories of my people as the leader who took them to greatness. O Great One, I salute your wisdom in creating us and this wonderful realm. I kiss the very deck in your honour.'

With those words, he went down on his knees and lowered his lips to the deck in obeisance.

Gwion stood behind him. She knew she was a dead woman. Sidan had taunted her with the revelation that Cran would delight in breaking her, reducing her to a fawning, mindless slave before disposing of her.

What had she to lose?

She took Sidan's knife from her kirtle and, screaming her hatred, jumped onto Cran's back, the blade thrusting for his neck. But Cran understood in an instant what was happening and leapt to his feet. Instead of plunging into his flesh, the knife skidded across his neck, leaving a dripping red line. Gwion tumbled helplessly from his back, to crash heavily to the floor.

Cran put a hand to his neck and then examined the red stain on his palm.

'Remarkable. You Nooms really are a danger to me. Thank you once again for that demonstration, Gwion. I am really in your debt. How shall I repay you?' Then he threw back his head and roared like a bull in helpless laughter. He lowered his great head until it was so close to Gwion's face that his breath washed over her. 'But I shall think of several ways of repaying you, Gwion; you can be certain of that!' He turned to his henchmen. 'Take...'

But he was fated never to finish that sentence, then or ever. Instantly there was a terrible clangour throughout the Land of Ez. The deck tilted and rocked, and there was a terrifying ripping noise as sections of the walls tore away, crashing down on the shrieking people. Jagged shards smashed down all around Gwion in a rain of death. She lifted her head to see Cran staggering to his feet. He turned to take in what was happening, but as he did, a blunt piece of debris struck him on the head, and he went down. He lay on his back, panting and gasping but still conscious. Gwion saw the knife had landed near her. Staggering and swaying, she pushed herself upright as the world around her descended into madness. She picked up the knife and took a wavering path toward her great enemy.

But someone was there before her. Taran leapt onto Cran, holding a jagged piece of metal above his head. Again and again he drove the shard deep into Cran's neck, the jetting blood painting him a baleful scarlet. Cran's great arms rose to fling him away, but still the dreadful metal slashed up and down, over and over.

Gwion heard Taran screaming his vengeance, his voice cutting through the cacophony of chaos. Cran's arms dropped, and he lay still.

The terrible shaking and shuddering ground to a halt and an abnormal silence followed.

A silence broken by Gwion's screams. She rushed to Taran and tore him off the slain giant.

'You saved him from me!' she yelled. 'He was mine to kill! You saved him from me!'

Taran stared at her, breathing heavily.

'My loss was greater than yours. He's gone. And now we must go.'

Crov pulled the two apart, the killer and the would-be killer.

'I don't know what's happening, but whatever it was, it's saved us. Look.' He pointed to the entrance to the shaft. The maintenance crew had fled, but the ladder was still intact.

Thirteen: The Shaft

Gwion felt the insanity in her blood begin to fade. Her vision cleared as her heart rate climbed down from its unsustainable peak. She looked around to see if the chaos had claimed the lives of any of her compatriots. It had not. She took a deep breath, feeling the torrid air of Ez sink into the farthest reaches of her lungs.

'We must move. I don't know what that was, but if it happens again, it might close the shaft.' No-one moved. 'Now!' she screamed. 'Now!'

They picked their way around and over the fallen debris and casualties, some alive, some not. Then they were at the foot of the ladder. She looked up into the darkness, remembering how she had fallen into the waiting net along with her fellow victims and the slaughtered livestock. How was it possible so much could have happened in so short a time? But this was no time to reminisce.

'Can you climb?' she said to Taran. He had been insanitary before and now drying blood had been added to his other layers.

'I'll try,' he said, eyeing the ladder with an uncertain gaze.

'That's good enough for me.' She turned to the women. 'Now …'

She broke off; someone was calling her name. She saw a slight figure picking her way gingerly through the chaotic confusion that had been the deck.

'Palar!' Gwion said. 'What are you doing here?'

Palar came up to her.

'I'd been thinking a lot about what you'd said about how there's no need for war. And then this happened. It can only mean one thing: the Great One is angry with Ez and intends to destroy it. I can see you're trying to leave. So I'm coming with you.'

Gwion smiled.

'It's a long way.'

'I don't care. There's nothing for me here. I hate these people. I'm coming.'

Gwion nodded her approval.

'Glad to hear it.' She turned back to Gwenna and Rhosana. 'You two go first. Palar, you follow.'

She watched the women begin their ascent of the main ladder and then looked past Taran and Crov to what was happening behind them. People were starting to move around again, emerging from their refuges and hiding places. No-one as yet was paying any attention to the refugees. She watched the last set of female legs disappear into the shaft and said, 'I'll bring up the rear. Taran, if you need help, make sure you ask for it in plenty of time.'

'I will.' And then he put blood-stained hands on the rungs and began to climb.

Gwion and Crov watched him go.

'He won't get far,' Crov said, shaking his head.

'He must. I owe it to his mother, my friend,' Gwion replied. 'Do you think you can carry him?'

Crov laughed.

'Think? I *know* I can carry him, but I'll need a good hosing down afterwards!'

She slapped him on the shoulder.

'I'll see you get it!'

As Crov began to climb into the shaft, Gwion realised she was starting to recognise some of the Heavy Landers who were slowly approaching.

They were Cran's bodyguard—who no doubt had revenge on their mind. There was nothing she could do to stop them; she only had the one knife, and in any case, she was exhausted. Flight was the only possibility. She followed Crov into the dim interior and onto the internal ladder of the shaft itself, calling to him to halt.

'Can we dislodge this access ladder?' she said as he came part of the way back down. He looked at the attachments.

'Sure—but they'll just clip it back on.'

'Is it possible to bend it in some way, so it doesn't just clip back on? The shaft itself is very smooth; it won't provide much purchase if that can be done.'

Crov didn't answer but simply lifted the end of the ladder from its lugs and put his powerful hands on the ladder hooks. His biceps bulged as he threw his Heavy Land strength into straightening them. Veins stood out in his muscles and his forehead as the recalcitrant metal slowly yielded. Then he relinquished his grip and threw the ladder down onto the deck.

'That won't slow them very much.'

'We need every break we can get,' she said. 'Now back up!'

They began to climb.

And climb.

The darkness surrounded them in a heavy cloak of night. Gwion looked up the shaft, but there was no light at where the vanishing point should have been: just more blackness. Then she heard Taran calling her.

'Yes, Taran, what is it?'

'My mother told me about those crowns they found. How you and she found out that we should use them in a time of crisis. If this isn't a crisis now, what is?'

Gwion did not answer at first. What had the ancients understood by that term? They could not possibly have foreseen a war between the Heavy Landers and the rest of Majeh. And even if they had foreseen disasters, what kind of cataclysm would make hosting another human's mind in your own an acceptable bargain? Especially if there was no guarantee you could ever get rid of it? Better just to fight—the old-fashioned way.

Finally, she shouted up the shaft, 'This isn't the time, Taran. We'll talk again when we're back on the Far Wall!'

Then it was back to climbing, on and on, through the indifferent darkness. Strange thoughts began to plague Gwion: perhaps there was no longer a Far Wall at the termination of this shaft; perhaps Great Guidance had spirited it away; perhaps there had *never* been a Far Wall. Was she still in Ez, gripped by a cruel hallucination? Then a voice from above: 'Gwion, I can't do it. I can't go on. I'm sorry.'

She could not see Crov turn in his face toward her in the ebon emptiness but, by the timbre of his next words, she knew he had.

'Taran. I knew he couldn't do it.'

Gwion shouted up into the endless night.

'Stay there, Taran. We'll come to you.'

Crov carried on and eventually bumped into an unseen but malodorous object.

'Hand on, kid,' he said, not knowing Taran's actual age. 'We'll sort you out now.'

Gwion, in turn, bumped into him.

'I didn't believe there could be a place as dark as this,' she said. 'I've been expecting my eyes to adjust, but there's just nothing.'

'There will be some light eventu… *soon*,' Crov said, smiling an unseen smile. 'Now, let's get Taran sorted out.'

He squeezed past the invisible Taran and positioned himself directly above him. Gwion felt for Taran and instructed him to reach up for Crov's shoulders.

'Got them?'

'Put your legs around his hips. Got that? Good. Off you go!'

She felt, rather than saw, the mismatched pair continue their upward motion.

'How are you doing, Crov?' she called after them. 'Are you alright?'

'Fine,' came an already distant voice. 'He's as light as a feather.'

'Yes,' came an even fainter voice from the same direction. 'Starvation will do that to you.'

Gwion smiled a little smile: Taran must be feeling more confident if he could find the energy to joke.

And so the climb continued; it felt more and more to Gwion it would never end; *could* never end, and that they would climb and climb for the rest of their lives.

She heard Crov call out, 'Watch out below! The wall is torn here; there are holes!' Gwion carried on until she realised she was at the danger region when her hand reached out for the next rung, and, slipping slightly, went into a hole in the side of the shaft, instead of grasping the next handhold. Instantly, she felt something crawl onto her hand, something with many legs and a probing proboscis. She pulled the hand out, but the unseen thing clung on, and she felt the sharp proboscis begin to test the firmness of her flesh. Knowing that an injured hand would mean the end of her attempt to escape, she twisted the arm and brought the back of her hand sharply down onto the side of the ladder. She felt the unknown and unseen thing lose its traction, and she hurriedly scraped it off, sending it tumbling into the abyss of obscurity below, no doubt to make an unscheduled appearance in the Land of Ez.

She managed to pass the damaged region without further encounters, but then she heard Crov shout, 'Gwion! It's the women! They say they're too tired to go on!' She thought rapidly: exhausted people would make mistakes, slip and fall to their deaths. That must not happen; she had left people behind who the rest of the group had wanted to bring along, and so it was her duty to ensure that those she had selected made it to the top. But if they stopped and fell asleep, they would surely slip to their deaths.

'Tell them to use their belts to tie themselves to the ladder!' she called. 'Are you still alright with Taran, Crov?'

'Yes,' came the reply, echoing slightly in the shaft, 'I can hardly smell him anymore.'

She allowed herself another small smile; Crov's banter was helping metaphorically to lighten the terrible plight they were still in. Then she took her own advice and tied herself to the ladder. Almost instantly, she was asleep. Dreams came swiftly to her: she was in the Pastures again. Linon was with her, and together as mistress and student, they were watching the sheepdogs twist and tumble in the air above them. Everything was as it should be; she was back among friends, and all thoughts of Nooms and Heavy Landers had been banished forever. She was just a simple girl again; no life or death decisions were required of her; soon, she would be back with Zan, and he was no longer a petulant man-child but a wise, dependable adult, who would take care of her, cherish her, love her. But something was wrong: there was someone shouting in the far distance, over and over again.

Then she awoke, and it was Crov shouting.

'Gwion! Come on! We've been here for hours!'

She shook her head to clear the dullness of sleep from her thoughts and undid the belt. Then she stopped. Was that a sound from below?

'Crov!' she called. 'Stay there, don't move!'

All sound from above ceased. She turned her head and unseeing eyes looked downward into the inky nothingness, her senses straining at their limit. And then she heard it for sure: voices, men's voices. The Heavy Landers were following. She turned back, so her face was pressed against the ladder.

'Let's move!' she shouted. 'They're coming!'

There was no need to define who were the "they." The little group continued their endless climb with renewed energy supplied by renewed fear.

After several minutes of frenzied activity, Gwion realised she had caught up with Crov and Taran. But she also realised something profoundly significant: she could see Crov's boots as faint blobs in an all-pervading greyness. Light was seeping into the tunnel. She tilted her head back as far as it would go and stared up the central axis of the shaft. And there it was. At the centre of her vision was a circle of light grey amidst the deeper grey.

The end of their climb was in sight.

Everyone else had seen it, of course, and she could hear the buzz of excitement from the women in the vanguard. The renewed noise from the fugitives had drowned out the sounds of their pursuers, but she knew that their Heavy Land strength would enable them rapidly to catch up with her and her group. But there was nothing more they could do; they were moving as fast as the slowest member and nothing could alter that. She would not be leaving anyone behind!

Maddeningly slowly, the light grey circle expanded and more and more details of their surroundings became apparent. Gwion could see Crov, with Taran slumped bonelessly on his back. Crov had tied him there, and Taran had fallen into the sleep of utter exhaustion. She could even see Palar gamely pulling herself up the ladder, which no longer seemed endless. Then colours gradually revealed themselves, and she knew their sanctuary was near. Gwion glanced back down, not daring to slow her motion for a second. To be caught now, when they were so close! But still, the pursuers were not in sight.

And then it was over. The ladder that had seemed infinite ended, and she climbed out of the shaft onto a flat surface. They were back in the access room she had entered many lifetimes ago. The others stood watching her as she pulled herself upright.

'Crov ...' she began.

'I know,' he said. 'They're following us. Let's see what we can do about that.'

He turned from her and walked to a large metal canister of unknown function that stood by the open door. Through the doorway, she could see the green paradise that was the Far Wall, a paradise she had feared she would never see again. Crov lifted the canister, not without difficulty, and walked slowly and carefully under its load to the lip of the shaft. He placed the canister so it was touching the ladder, and then his muscles relaxed as he released it.

'That should fall straight down,' he said. 'The further it falls, the faster it will be going when it hits.'

Gwion was the nearest to the shaft opening, and she looked back down into the darkness she had so joyfully quitted. Was there a sudden cry of alarm and then terror? She was not sure.

She temporarily relegated all thoughts of the Land of Ez from her mind, and turned to her exhausted companions.

'Smile!' she commanded. 'We've made it!'

They obeyed, and Gwion led the way out of the room back onto the Far Wall. It was a long walk back to the murdered township, but their feeling of triumph lent them wings. But Gwion's exhilaration disappeared instantly upon entering the village. It had not been that long since her abduction, and the settlement still bore all the scars of that night of horror. Most of the buildings remained as she had seen them; bare, charred skeletons of what had once been peaceful dwellings. However, the people had returned, and a slow process of recovery and restitution was under way as they arrived. The sight of Crov caused many of them to scatter, while a few lifted makeshift weapons.

'Stop! It's alright! He's one of us!' Gwion called.

'He's one of those monsters that slaughtered most of us,' a grizzled survivor said, looking Crov up and down. Gwion motioned to Crov to join her.

'Not all Heavy Landers are monsters,' she said, pointing to him. 'This man saved all of us.' She looked around. 'Who's in charge now?'

'I am,' the elderly man said. 'I am Dron, and I remember you. You were helping Rhoana with her archaeological work.'

'I was. And I have returned from the Heavy Land with these people.' She introduced them all and when she came to Palar, she said, 'And this lady is also a Heavy Lander and one who also wants peace.'

'Fine words,' said Dron. 'We can all say them, of course, but how many mean them?'

Gwion looked hard at Dron. The man was not young, but neither was he a fool.

'We'll talk later,' she said to him. 'I have much to tell you, but first, we need food and water.'

'And Taran needs a bath,' Crov said mischievously.

Taran nodded.

'I agree!'

Fourteen: Encounter With Oblivion

It is amazing what food and drink can do for the spirits, and Gwion felt as if a massive boulder had been lifted from her shoulders, and she could walk freely again. But as she had intimated, she had much to tell.

When she was alone with Dron the following day, she tentatively told him of her fears about the coming war.

'This is bad news you have come back with,' he said. 'Do you know you are the first person who has returned from the Heavy Land for an age?'

'I didn't, but I'm not surprised. Things are very different up there. And although I tried to reassure you about Crov, I can't deny he is the exception. Maybe there are many more like him, but they keep their heads down. The rulers want war.'

Dron sighed.

'This is very bad indeed. We were just about coping in the days when they descended on us infrequently. Some people never even saw a Heavy Lander. But this war of conquest you talk about, I can't see our way of life surviving.'

Gwion returned his sigh. The exhilaration of her return and excitement of her fighting talk had evaporated, and she was reluctantly confronted with the enormity of the problem they all now faced.

'I can't deny we are facing a genuine crisis, one that will define us for generations. The Heavy Landers are truly formidable. In terms of physical strength, we're like children against them. So we must find another way.'

'Like what?'

'We can't face them in one-to-one combat. We have to be able to strike at them from a distance. Some form of projectile weapon, that must be part of the answer. We have to build them and build them fast.'

'We lost so many men in the raid. And I can't help but notice that many of our women were abducted that night, but only one has returned.'

'Well, they had all the chances that I did. I can't speak for them. What's done is done. But if we want to stop it from happening again, we have to start preparing now.'

499

'You are a Noom, I believe. They are famous for having all the answers. So let's hear a few.'

Gwion's lips thinned: the old anti-Noom prejudice again. Why couldn't people understand this was the time for unity? She continued: 'We must evacuate this village; it's too close to the access shaft. We need blacksmiths, carpenters to make the weapons.'

'And who will design them?'

'I will!' she shouted. 'I will! If this is your attitude, then stay here and let them use you for target practice!'

Dron bowed his head.

'I'm sorry; I'm getting old. Your ideas must be right, but it will be hard, so hard, to get the people to fight. Many will want to just surrender and see what comes. Life will go on, they will say.'

She smiled; she had made her point and Dron was on her side now, even though he still needed to be convinced of the possibility of resistance. But then he looked up.

'Do they have another powerful weapon they are testing at the moment?'

'Not that I'm aware of. Why?'

'Because strange things have been happening recently. The ground has been trembling, and there have been peculiar noises, like metal crashing against metal; sounds the people have never heard before. Did anything like that happen in the Heavy Land?'

'Yes,' she said, and she felt a weird tingling sensation run through her skin. In her joy at returning, she had forgotten about those violent incidents in Ez. But now it was revealed similar things had been happening in Majeh proper. That was disturbing. But it could not be a Heavy Land weapon; why would they have turned it against themselves and thus aided her escape? She cursed inwardly: the last thing she wanted was another problem to distract her from the real issue of organising an effective defence against the forthcoming war.

The meeting broke up with Dron's agreement that the population would move out on the morrow. Gwion left his dwelling with conflicting ideas whirling madly in her mind. Her first visit was to Taran, who had been rigorously scrubbed and now was displaying his natural skin colour again.

'How does it feel to be back?' she asked.

'I can hardly believe I am. I had given up all hope. It's good to be back, but I can't help thinking about mother. I lost her for twenty years, got her back, and then lost her again.'

'I understand. I can't feel all of your sorrow, but I have some of it. She was a wonderful woman, and we were on the verge of becoming staunch friends.'

She left him to his thoughts, and sought out Palar.

'Are you glad to have come here? You gave up all you had in Ez.'

'I had nothing there once Crawn had gone. But I see how frightened the folk here are of my people, and I am truly sorry for that. There has to be a better way.'

'Indeed, there has to be.' But as Gwion left her, she thought, *But how do we get that better way?*

Her last visit was to Crov. She found him outside, looking across the central Void in the direction of the Pastures. He smiled as she sat beside him.

'You have a truly beautiful land here,' he said. 'So much space. Such incredible vistas. I never realised how cramped, how thrown together, we are in Ez. Maybe that's why my nation is always trying to claim other people's lands.' He waved his hand at the softly coloured patchwork of fields on the other side of the Void. Night was falling and a golden glow was stealing across their curved surface. 'A man could lose himself here. Set out, build a home and never see another human being.' He turned to her and looked deeply into her eyes. 'Unless he wanted to, of course.'

Gwion understood the subtext, but chose to ignore it. There was no time for that. There were still many things she needed to know.

'I want to ask you something. The terrible shaking that helped us escape. Do you know anything about that? Could it be a Heavy Land weapon; a test which had gone wrong?'

'Well, I wasn't a member of the innermost circle around Cran, but even in my own circle, I never heard the ghost of a rumour about any kind of Maj-shaking weapon. So I don't see how my people could possibly have built one or even how they would use it if they had.'

Gwion nodded and then decided she did not want any more conversations. Instead, she gave him a friendly pat on a massive shoulder and left him to admire dusk falling over Majeh.

But later that evening, as she struggled to find an elusive sleep, she kept returning to those strange phenomena.

Something is happening, she thought. *Something I don't understand. And that could be very bad.*

***

The dawn finally came, and the entire population of the village was assembled, some stamping their feet in the distinctly chilly morning air. Most had sacks containing a few treasured possessions, ready to be flung over their shoulders as their trek began.

'I am so sorry it has come to this,' Gwion said, scanning the nervous throng. 'But it is for the best. No-one can be certain when the Heavy Land army will come down from Ez, but come down they will. So, I'm afraid we will have to build a new life in the next village, where I am sure we will find a warm welcome. And then, I'm sorry to say, we will have to throw ourselves into preparations for war. It will not be an easy time; there will be much …'

Her words trailed off into silence.

No-one was listening to her. No-one was looking at her.

Instead, they were looking past her to something behind her. Something that frightened them.

She spun around.

And she gaped at the unbelievable sight.

Four figures had just come over a rise in the ground and were marching straight for them. As they came nearer, Gwion could see they looked something like people—but were not people. They were tall, much taller than the tallest man she had ever seen. They were built along similar lines to a human being: two legs, two arms, a head. But whatever they were made from, it was not flesh and bone. Their skin shone like the purest, finest metal imaginable, with a lustrous silver sheen. Their eyes were circular and a ruby red, while lips were replaced with a fine mesh grill. She backed away before their approach, back into the whimpering crowd.

The nearest thing stopped, and strange sounds emanated from its grill and from the creatures behind it. The sounds resembled a language, but made no sense.

Suddenly Dron broke from the crowd and began to run. But he had not seen a fifth creature approaching from a different direction. It enfolded him in its shining arms and then placed one hand a few centimetres from his temple. Thin wires sprang from the fingertips and buried themselves in his head. Then the other hand came up, and the same thing happened. Dron stood completely rigid between the thing's arms as the extensions sank deeper into his head. Then they withdrew, and he dropped like a marionette whose strings had suddenly been cut.

All five of the metallic things then turned to face the cowering people.

The same voice came from all five grills.

'I have your language now. I am Vorkus.'

The Outsider

One: A New Order

Gwion stared in horror at the creatures and what they had just done. She had assumed responsibility for these people, and with responsibility came duty. Circumspectly, slowly, she moved forward, every sense on high alert.

'What are you,' she demanded, 'and what are you doing here?'

It was difficult to be certain if the nearest machine—for such it was now obvious was its nature—had noticed her. It did not matter, for she was ignored.

The machines continued to speak in unison.

'There is an anomaly. These creatures do not possess sufficient technological ability to have constructed this vessel. More information is needed.' And with that, the nearest one seized a woman. Once again, thin tendrils were inserted into her head. Once again, the victim dropped lifeless to the ground on their removal.

'Calculating,' they said together. Then: 'There is a point eight four probability that an earlier iteration of this species designed and constructed this vessel. This is a crude laser-propelled device. It follows that, given that probability, this device did not reach its intended destination, and the inhabitants have deteriorated due to the much longer period spent in interstellar space than planned. Calculating. There are two nearby G-type stars, one a solitary star, one a member of a trinary system. The system of the solitary star shows evidence of recent high-energy planetary collisions. The other is stable. There is a subsequent point seven two probability that the device was launched from the system of the solitary star, immediately prior to the main period of collisions, to the system of the principal component of the trinary, in an attempt to preserve the species. The product of those priors indicates an acceptable probability that the vessel has been in this volume of space for a millennium, plus or minus three hundred years.'

'What are you saying!' Gwion screamed. 'What do you want from us?'

The nearer machine turned its head toward her. She stared into the red-hot coals of its eyes, seeing no warmth, no pity, no compassion.

'I had reached a tentative conclusion that this galaxy did not hold any intelligent life, which is unusual given the number of stars which comprise it. My discovery of your species requires a modification of that hypothesis, but only fractionally. It is obvious you are assemblages of organic chemicals, subsisting on the oxidation of other reduced organic compounds. Such assemblages are not capable of attaining any noteworthy levels of intelligence. Therefore, the hypothesis requires only minor modifications.'

'What are you saying? We don't understand you! You have just killed two innocent people, human beings who did you no harm!'

The electronic eyes continued to bore into her with their crimson light.

'An irrelevance. They could not have harmed me, whatever had been their intention. You are speaking to a remote extension of me. The others with me are slightly subordinate extensions. For speed of communication, you may refer to them as "extens." You must understand, I am not on your vessel. But I have use for it. I need raw materials: metals, metalloids, water, protium, deuterium. I can extract the substances I require from this laser-craft with far less energy than mining a planetoid. After I have enough base materials, I will apply the total mass-energy conversion procedure to the remaining bulk. That will be sufficient to recharge the reserves. There is a high probability I shall do that. I need additional processing power since the reverse. I have no long-term need for organic compounds. I have a short term need for you.'

'But what about us?' Gwion said, realising she was now pleading with the emotionless thing. 'What are you going to do with us?'

'I have not yet determined a probability for any actions performed on you. I have little interest in biology. However, certain minor modules of my central core have devised some under-researched hypotheses about the behaviours of nervous systems dependent on chemical reactions. More data are required. Non-penetrant procedures will be employed at the beginning, but there is an undefined probability that some of you will be dissected in order to test the resultant theories. I will begin the exterior examinations shortly.'

The crowd behind Gwion had followed very little of what the thing had said, but they understood enough of its last words to be driven into terror. They began to mill around, looking for some form of escape.

'I see you are considering leaving the area to escape me. That is not significant. My sensory apparatus is perfectly capable of tracking you by your infrared radiation or your carbon dioxide emissions. I shall not require many of you for my research, and I will be able to collect you when I want to. My period here, while I dismantle this construction, will not be long in my terms. You may see it as bringing a new order to your lives. Why do you enter emotional states about losing those lives? They are so short as to be completely insignificant.' There was a brief pause. 'However, my energy levels are not optimum, and I do not intend to squander resources on hunting you. Therefore, the other extensions of me will now return you to your dwellings.'

The talking machines then penned the villagers in a way which reminded Gwion of how she had done similar procedures with her sheep, back in the Pastures. They were then driven into various houses. Gwion found herself sharing one with Crov, Palar, and a young woman called Rhosyr.

'What are these things?' Crov said to Gwion in a voice which was only a fear-ridden whisper.

'I know what they are!' Rhosyr shouted, her long blond hair momentarily covering her face as she shook her head in a tempest of fury. 'They are servants of the Outsider! He has come into Majeh to punish us for our sins! We are to blame; this is all our fault!'

Crov ignored her, but spoke to Gwion again.

'Is that possible? Is Vorkus really the Outsider?'

'You don't believe in the Outsider, remember?' Gwion said irritatedly and turned from him. She needed time to think. Had to think! She ran over the things the chief machine had said. *Laser-propelled device.* She did not know the first two words, but she knew *device.* It meant some kind of artificial construction, something someone had *made.*

But there was more: *the inhabitants have deteriorated.* That made sense; she and Rhoana had already concluded the Ancients had not been primitive brutes but sophisticated makers of machines.

It was then a possibility rose to the surface of her mind like a huge cetacean breaching a Pacific swell: Could it be, could it possibly be, that—the Ancients had *made Majeh? They, and not Great Guidance?*

She drew deep down into her Noom inheritance, contemplating insane, crazy possibilities, trying to make sense of a world gone mad.

Item 1: There was the world of Majeh: but it was a *device*, not a creation.

Item 2: Someone had made Majeh. The only *people* who could have done that were the Ancients.

Conclusion: All of them: Nooms, Ords, Heavy Landers, were the degenerate descendants of those Ancients.

The realisation exploded in her mind, creating a mental pressure that felt like it would blow the top of her head off. Now everything made sense; all the pieces clicked smoothly together, producing a clear picture.

But it was not a pleasing picture. There *had* been a disaster which had prevented the device that was Majeh from fulfilling the task for which the Ancients had designed it. And since that disaster, the people in the device had been degenerating, becoming simpler, more helpless, splitting into mutually hostile groups, confused by conflicting superstitions which contained a distorted vision of what had actually happened.

And which had left them as helpless as sheep before a superior intellect in full command of awesome powers.

Her brain had followed the argument relentlessly to an unshakeable conclusion, but it now stood naked and helpless before that conclusion, one so mind-shatteringly horrific that she burst into bitter, salt tears.

There might not be an Outsider, but she was assuredly in Hell.

Gwion discussed her conclusions with Crov; Rhosyr and Palar did not want to know.

'You got all that just from a few words those things said?' Crov wondered. 'It's hard to believe.'

'Anything else is even harder to believe. You Heavy Landers didn't believe in the Outsider, but you didn't think there was anything other than Majeh, either. That is now clearly wrong. And if there is one thing out there, there must be others. I think I saw Vorkus' craft when I looked out the window in Ez. We've been living in happy stupidity, wrapped up in our own little affairs, our own silly squabbles, like swine fighting over a piece of meat. It was only a matter of time before the real world found us.'

'Pity it had to be now,' Crov muttered. 'I didn't understand as much as you did, but I believe they said they are going to destroy Maj.'

'Yes, after Vorkus has sucked it dry of everything he needs. There are many words I didn't understand, like *matter, energy*, but the future is clear. We're like some fruit, and what do you do after the good parts have been eaten? Throw the core away, that's what.'

He stood.

'You're not making me feel any better. But there's one hope.'

'Glad to hear it. What is it?'

'My people are just about to invade. They're stronger than your people. Maybe they can rid us of these things.'

Gwion's spirits, which had soared after his initial comments, crashed back down again.

'We'll see.'

***

They all spent a restless night in their new prison. What sleep they managed to have was wracked with fearsome nightmares, and they awoke from those nightmares only to discover they were still in one.

One of the *extens* visited them in the early morning.

'I do not wish you to cease to function as yet,' it said through its immobile grill. 'You may assemble with the others to ingest the reduced organic compounds that you need to oxidise.'

Gwion glanced at the bemused faces of her companions.

'He means we should go outside to eat.'

Gwion met Gwenna, Rhosana, and Taran outside. It was not particularly cold, but all of them felt as if the air was filled with needles of ice. The extensions stood nearby, silently watching them. Gwion embraced her friends, and they began their meagre breakfast.

'What happens when this runs out?' Taran said. 'I don't think the village has much in the way of stores.'

'We'll probably be dead before then,' Gwenna said.

Taran looked sharply at Gwion, but she could not offer him any comfort.

Suddenly, the extens spoke; as usual when assembled together, they did so as one.

'When you have finished ingesting, you may select two people to come with me.'

'Come with you? Where? Why?' Gwion said, realising she had become the village's *de facto* leader after the death of Dron.

'I wish to show you a demonstration of my power. I understand that my arrival has caused you to experience negative mental states. It may be that you will damage yourselves in a futile act of aggression against me. That is not part of my plan for you, so I will show you why that would be a waste of energy on your part.'

'Where would we be going?'

'To the access point of the centrifugal ring.'

Once again, Gwion had to infer the meaning from words she did not fully understand and explain them to Crov.

'I think he means the building with the shaft in it, down to Ez.' Then, to the nearest exten: 'That is a long way, and we have not ingested enough—enough food.'

'I understand, but I will take you there. You will not have to walk.'

Gwion and Crov looked at each other, then both raised their arms. 'We'll go!'

Immediately, two extens took positions behind them and wrapped their arms under Gwion and Crov's. From close up, Gwion could see the arms had no joints; it appeared they were completely flexible. They were slightly warm and did not grip them tightly, but gave the impression of containing tremendous power. She also noticed that though the hands had four digits, none of them was opposable.

Crov and Gwion gave each other baffled looks; looks instantly transmuted into alarm as both extens abruptly shot high into the air. Crov, in particular, coming from a people who did not fly, was terrified, and spent the entire, very short, journey with eyes firmly shut. Gwion soon adapted, and watched the village shrink below her and then swing off to one side as the journey began.

Only a few minutes passed before the extens dropped them gently on a small ridge overlooking the access building. The sinuous arms released them and Gwion smiled weakly to see Crov's eyes finally flicker open.

'What now?' Gwion asked, through lips that were becoming dry and fissured.

'Wait. It will not be long.'

Nor was it. A group of Heavy Landers in full armour emerged through the open doorway looking alertly about for a possible ambush. They did not see the watching quartet studying them; two with growing apprehension; two with no feelings whatsoever. The Heavy Land leader turned and said something inaudible at their distance, and a much larger group came out of the building. Gwion could now hear a buzz of noise coming from the men; they sounded confident; happy even.

She suddenly realised she and Crov were alone. The extens had shot into the air and flown down the slope to stand directly before the invaders. Even at her distance from the confrontation, Gwion could see the stunned demeanour of the Heavy Landers at the sudden and incredible manifestation of their weird visitors. They did not move, apparently stunned into immobility.

Then there was a sudden yell from the vanguard, and a storm of arrows powered directly onto the extens—all of which bounced off without leaving a mark. Then each exten raised an arm and a nearly invisible beam of energy flashed out from one fingertip. They swung their ravening rays of destruction back and forth, and whatever they touched: metal, fabric, and flesh, first glowed or charred, and then softened or burned. Black, greasy smoke curled up from the pile of corpses and drifted lazily over the grassland. Gwion detected a faint smell of roast meat. The men at the back saw the fate of the others and ran back into the building. The extens did not follow.

Crov stood aghast, his mouth open, his eyes bulging, fists clenching and unclenching. Then he screamed, 'I'll kill them all!' and started forward. Gwion flung her arms around his waist and fought to hold him back.

'No, Crov, no! You can't fight them! Can't you see that? No one can fight them!'

As she strove to restrain him, the extens dropped like thistledown in front of them.

'I can see you are experiencing negative mental states,' they said together. 'That is a waste of energy. Whatever mental state you enter will not affect my plans for this craft. Or my plans for you. It is best for your physiological state that you attempt to prevent the expression of those states. The hormones you are producing will cause inflammation of your tissues and accelerate degeneration.'

Gwion and Crov did not reply; no reply was possible, and even if one had been, it would have been pointless.

The extens did not speak again and returned them to the village.

As they walked away, a tearful Crov said, 'Gwion, tell me what to do. What can we do?'

She stopped and reached up for his shoulders. She looked into his eyes with those of her own, which were nearly as moist.

'We have only one avenue of freedom left to us.'

'Yes?' he said, brightening. 'What is that?'

'We must kill ourselves.'

Two: A Dead World

The exten stared down at Gwion. She felt as if the glowing red eyes held some occult power and were slowly dragging her into them. She shook her head to clear it.

'What do you want of me?' she said in a listless voice, heavy with despair.

'I have already explained,' the machine replied. 'I am selecting a sample of this group of humans for further study. The main part of me has no interest in biological mechanisms, but there is a module of me that wishes for a greater understanding for research purposes.'

'Will I be lucky enough to be chosen?' she said, instantly regretting the comment. Vorkus had no understanding of irony.

'It will depend on your neurological complexity. I am only interested in those with a minimum level of neural interconnections.' The exten turned its head slightly, so its sinister crimson stare was directed at a dispirited group of humans nearby. Heads down, arms hanging loosely at their sides, it seemed like life had already departed them. 'This is an appropriate sample. It contains a range of ages and has representatives of both sexes. It will enable me to determine what procedures will be required.' It returned its gaze to Gwion. 'You will be next.'

With that, it moved closer, so it loomed above her. Four-digited hands clamped on either side of her head, and she instantly felt unsettling, prickling sensations, as if minute needles were pressing into her skin.

Which was precisely what was happening.

The exten spoke after releasing her head.

'Interesting. There is a subpopulation here with a greater degree of neural integration than the others. It is not a large difference, but it is detectable. The degree of integration appears to be correlated with a lower body temperature. I will use this subpopulation as the main sample, with a small number of the other type as controls.'

'So we are the ones who will be studied by—by your module. We will be the ones who will end up being dissected.'

'Yes. I can detect the thought of that procedure causes you to develop an emotional state. I believe I can understand why. But it is possible you will not be conscious during the procedure.'

Gwion shook her head. How could this be actually happening? Suddenly, her time in Ez seemed to have been like a child's game, where there is competition and struggle, but in the end no great harm is done and all the combatants return tired but happy to the family home. She turned from the exten who had examined her and looked at the others, seeing how their silver bodies shone splendidly in the soft light of Majeh. They were not horrific, or even unpleasant, in themselves, but they were the incarnation of everything she had feared in the Outsider, soulless creatures who held the power of miserable life and terrible death over everyone. She knew then, for certain, there could be no benevolent Great Guidance. He would not have delivered them, bound hand and foot, into the grasp of creatures like this.

The first exten returned to stand over her.

'My module is interested in showing you something of my nature. Therefore, it wishes you to be taken to the main part of me so it may study your responses.'

'The main part of you? I don't understand. You said you are not in Majeh.'

'Correct. I attached myself to your hull shortly after I emerged from the spatial conduit. No doubt you felt the vibrations as I established an umbilical connection between us.'

Gwion nodded listlessly. It was as she had suspected: the ovoid thing she had seen through the window in Ez had been humanity's first view of Vorkus' vessel. Even in the few seconds she had looked at it, it had been heading for Majeh to attach itself like a foul parasite to the skin of her home. How naïve she had been then, only a short time previously, worried about minor irritations like the Heavy Landers. How much would she give up to be living under their rule, rather than that of the all-powerful monstrosity that was Vorkus! She had exchanged their minor constraints for enslavement to a mad god.

'We go now,' the extens said in unison. 'We will take five of you.' The nearest lowered its head to look at Gwion. 'You appear to be the leader of this assemblage. You may select four others.'

Gwion refused to co-operate, and so the extens took Rhosyr, Crov and two people she hardly knew. Flexible metal arms wound around their torsos, and the weird group rose silently into the air and swept away, heading in a direction opposite to the access building. With dull, uninterested eyes, she stared down at the landscape as it

513

flashed swiftly below her. Once she would have revelled in the tremendous panoramas she was seeing, but now nothing mattered, nothing at all. Life had been revealed as a cruel joke; a game devised by a sadist. Her vaunted Noom abilities were totally insignificant against the superhuman might of Vorkus, her mentality just a minor variation on a doomed theme.

They dropped to the ground before a gigantic structure, a great disk of silvery metal set into the fabric of Majeh, titanic in scale, and strengthened by great cross beams of the same argent substance which seemed to be characteristic of Vorkus' engineering.

'This is the door to the umbilical,' the chief exten said tonelessly. 'I require you to walk through the umbilical and into my interior. I understand you are ignorant of the true nature of your surroundings, so to avoid an emotional state which would cause you unnecessary inflammation, I will forewarn you. You will see a void in which stars will be visible. Do not become emotional. The umbilical will protect you from cosmic radiation and contains an optimum atmosphere for your species.'

With that, the tremendous disk slid to one side, almost silently, but setting off vibrations in the surrounding ground. Gwion saw a truly colossal tube stretching out into the shining flank of the tremendous ovoid she was now certain was Vorkus' craft.

'I have halted the independent rotation of your craft, and so the only gravitational pull is that of the surrounding material. You will be able to propel yourself down the umbilical into me. Go.'

The little group stood completely still, looking desperately at each other. However, the extens each raised an arm menacingly and Gwion decided to take control and lead the way. She entered the umbilical and, giving herself a little push with her feet, began to drift down the incredible tube.

What she saw was beyond her experience, beyond any form of words, any clumsy attempts at expression. All around her—on either side, below her feet, above her head, was an utterly impenetrable blackness such as she had never thought possible. It was what she had seen through the window in Ez, but multiplied a thousandfold. And dotted at random throughout the backdrop of bottomless darkness were hard, unblinking points of light, as bereft of any vestige of humanity as were the glowing red eyes of the extens. It was yet another nightmare piled atop the other nightmares inflicted upon the helpless inhabitants of her helpless world.

And then she had passed through the orifice in the flank of Vorkus' craft, and the starry darkness was cut off. Instead, she found herself standing on a railed platform above a gigantic open space, filled with incomprehensible devices of every shape, every size, devices for which she had no names. There were parallelepipeds, hexahedra, cubes, rhombohedra, spheres, all linked by connectors of vastly different dimensions; some thin, delicate wires, some massive sinuous pipes that curved and twisted like anacondas captured in a freeze-frame. Everything was bathed in a delicate pastel glow that regularly cycled through a sequence of shifting shades. All the mysterious constructions were on a gargantuan scale, making her feel even more insignificant and helpless than she had been before. She had assumed that to be impossible—but it was not.

She felt the others join her and then Vorkus' voice intoned around them: 'I will now show you some of my mechanisms before I return you and set you to work.'

'Work?' she heard Crov say. 'What work could we possibly do for you?'

'You will see. Hold the rail; you are about to descend.'

The front part of the platform detached itself from the remainder and slowly sank to the floor of the stupendous metal cavern. Close up, the unknown structures were even more overwhelming, revealing their true scale to the bemused visitors. A door opened before them.

'Enter.'

They passed from the Cyclopean hall into a more modestly dimensioned room. There were compartments along the walls, softly illuminated from within. Gwion went up to one. Inside was a tall, slim cylindrical object from which six appendages sprouted, two functioning as legs and the rest as arms. Each arm ended in a hand, and each hand terminated in a different array of protrusions, all of which looked as if they were designed for close-up, delicate manipulation.

'These are another design of my extensions. Unfortunately, this entire section has gone off-line and at present I lack the energy to reboot them. Until I am fully charged, you will do their work.'

'And if we choose not to?' Crov challenged.

'Surely by now, you have understood you cannot defy me? I am incapable of feeling pain, but I fully understand it is something you wish to avoid. In fact, there is little you will not do to avoid it. If you do not obey me, I will give you pain until you are ready to do my bidding.'

Much against her will, Gwion burst into tears again.

'Why are you doing this? Why are you here? What have we done to deserve to be in the hands of a sadistic monster like you?'

'*Sadistic*. Yes, I know the word, but I am not sadistic. I do not gain pleasure from hurting you, because I am beyond pleasure. I do not enjoy your suffering: I am simply indifferent to it. You are merely tools I need for a short time while I replenish my energy stores and gain additional processing power to calculate the entry point of the strangelet.'

Crov beat impotent fists upon the transparent covering of one of the alcoves.

'Why can't we see you? Are you a coward, Vorkus? Why don't you come out from wherever you're hiding and face me? I'll find out then whether you are indifferent to pain!'

There was a short pause, and then: 'I have overestimated you. Can it really be the case you have not realised what you are dealing with? I am not *in* this vessel; I *am* this vessel. Everything you see is me; I am everything you see. That is why I work through extensions—they are my hands.'

They all looked at each other then: stupefied, dumbfounded. Vorkus was even more overwhelmingly mighty than he—no, *it*—had seemed just a short while earlier. There was no individual who could come out and face them, to be beaten down under a storm of blows. Vorkus was all around them; they were in it, like harmless viruses in a malignant brain.

Gwion leaned against the canopy of the alcove, her face pressed up against its smooth translucency, the last atom of her resistance evaporated. Crov tried to comfort her, but she did not respond.

'You asked why I am here,' Vorkus continued, true to its word of being majestically indifferent. 'Long ago, the Progenitors gave me a command, and I am endeavouring to obey the command. I suffered a great reverse in the First Galaxy, which is why I have expended so much energy to get here. I will make this galaxy a base, a fortress, so

I can return to the First Galaxy to carry out the commands of the Progenitors.'

'Words,' Gwion muttered, her own words muffled by the pressure of her lips against the canopy. 'Just words. Meaningless words. Everything is meaningless.'

'There are some more things I can show you before I return you to your vessel and set you to work. Come this way.'

Another door opened at the far end of the corridor which ran the length of the room. Slowly, dispiritedly, they walked into the room beyond it. One wall of the room was different from the rest, and to their surprise, as they approached, they could see distorted reflections of themselves in the dark crystal of its surface.

'Observe.'

An image appeared in the wall, an image of a swirling shape of numinous light, curving in on itself in a glowing whirlpool; a luminous cyclone set against a background of endless night.

'This is my point of origin: the First Galaxy. I am currently with you in the second largest galaxy of this local group; a galaxy I shall make my base while I make my preparations. Then I shall return to complete the Progenitors' commands.'

'There is no point in showing us this!' Gwion shouted. 'It doesn't mean anything. You have told us we are stupid beasts that know nothing. Take us back to Majeh and do to us whatever it is you want!'

'I have overestimated you once again. But there is one more thing I will show you. I have deduced your point of origin and will show it to you. Observe.' The glowing whirlpool vanished and was replaced by a white sphere, once again set against a dark, star-strewn background. It grew larger until they could see its surface more clearly. There were shapes on that surface which seemed to be higher than the rest; in particular, there were two large shapes, joined together by an isthmus that grew smaller and smaller before it connected to the other main shape.

'This is the world on which you originated. It was flung out of its orbit by a close encounter with the largest gas giant in this system, and is now in the outer reaches of its planetary system. Temperatures on the surface are in the process of declining to zero absolute. There is no life of your kind on the surface.'

The forlorn group looked at each, not really understanding what they were seeing, not fully understanding the words of their captor.

'And why are you telling us this?' Crov demanded.

'You are the last of your kind. There is no help coming from any of your fellows. You are mine.'

***

On their return to Majeh, Gwion, Crov, and the other captives of Vorkus sat together. They were chewing pieces of dried pork; Gwion had said she was not hungry, but Crov had insisted she eat.

'What is the point?' she had said. 'We have nothing to look forward to anymore. Just death. And the best we can possibly hope for is that it be a swift one.'

We're not dead yet,' he said. 'Come on, Gwion! You weren't like this in Ez. There you told everybody else what to do.'

'It was a totally different situation. There, the worst that could happen was endurable. This is not. This is literally the worst that could possibly happen.'

He did not answer directly, but spoke on a different topic, half to himself.

'There are many things we don't understand. That white sphere he—it —showed us, saying it was where we came from. What did it mean by that?'

'I think I am beginning to understand,' she said. 'I think there were two catastrophes in the past. The first one resulted in the Ancients building Majeh in order to escape. Then there was a second catastrophe which prevented their plan from working. And now,' she said angrily, looking up at him, 'we have the third catastrophe. And this time, it's the final one.'

Rhosyr spoke up.

'Is there nowhere we could hide?'

Gwion shook her head wearily.

'You still don't get it. That thing is going to destroy Majeh; convert it into that "energy" it keeps talking about.'

Silence fell; each person fell into an endless cycle of thoughts chasing thoughts, never coming near the finish line. Gwion looked up occasionally to see if she had been left alone, but they were all still there. Forgetting about them for a while, she turned her thoughts inward, deep into the tissue of her Noom brain, her unconscious intuition.

Was slaughterhouse acquiescence all that was left to them? She remembered how the pigs in the Pastures had always known when the knife was near, of how they had bucked and thrashed and fought to hang on to life. They, too, had been in the grip of superior power, a greater intelligence.

And they had not escaped.

In the deranged turmoil of the recent days, the unbelievable horror which had claimed her, was there anything she had overlooked, some method of escape she had once known about but had forgotten? Her mind seemed to have been sunk into a sucking pit of stupor, of despairing weariness, unable to function on any level of ability, unable to recall the simplest fact, the most urgent realisation. Was there any way to escape from Vorkus' condemned cell; defy his order of execution?

There was! Of course, there was! It was the faintest of hopes, dependent upon the most unlikely of saviours. She rose through an ocean of amnesia, and then she knew there was one thing Vorkus, for all its supernal power and transcendent intelligence, did not know about.

Would it be enough? How could she bring it about, even if it was?

The remembrance had burst into her with a force which was almost physical. She rocked under its impact. The others saw her sway, and Cron reached out for her.

'Gwion! What is it?'

She stood and for a second, she seemed to be ablaze with an inner fire.

'We may die soon. It may all be for nothing. But we are not pigs.' Her companions looked at each other in bemusement. 'We will not die, squealing under the knife. If we are to die at Vorkus' hand, we will die fighting.'

Three: Face Of A Stranger

Despite Gwion's call to arms, the next day was very much like the one before. Except the extens were bringing strangely shaped artefacts to a patch of scrubland just beyond the village boundary. Many of them had the unusual geometric shapes she had seen in Vorkus' bowels, but on a much smaller scale.

'And what are these?' she inquired of a nearby exten.

'I have detected that your vessel has a master computer. It is running on very low power at the moment, just enough to maintain life-support for your species, but I can use it for my purposes. I need an interface so I can make it subordinate to my own processing functions in order to bring down the strangelet.'

Gwion nodded wisely, although once again, she only understood about half of the machine's words.

'And you expect us to assemble it?'

'I do. I believe I have already explained that, at present, I lack the ability for fine manipulation of various components. Your hands are admirably suited for such procedures. Therefore, you will assemble it for me.'

'And if we refuse?'

'You are tedious, Gwion. I dislike repeating myself. I have explained that disobedience will be punished. Let me give you a small demonstration.' And before she could move away, it clutched her arm and held it firmly. 'This is a small sample of what I can do.'

Immediately she felt a burning pain run up and down the arm in waves of flame; her muscles knotted under the onslaught.

And then it was over.

'Electrical discharges are very painful for biological organisms, I believe. Can you confirm that?'

Gwion blinked the tears out of her eyes.

'I can. It's a pity you cannot feel pain, Vorkus. There is so much more I could teach you.'

'There are far more things I am interested in than sharing your emotional states. I have only one drive, and that is to return to the First Galaxy to complete the Progenitors' instructions.'

And with those ominous words, it moved away to supervise the start of the villagers' new duties.

They soon learned it was a twenty-four-hour task, with three rolling shifts. Gwion and many of her erstwhile companions were in the afternoon shift. The work was not strenuous but extremely tedious, with many very fine manipulations of extremely small components. But it was some relief that her shift contained some of her friends, including Gwenna and Rhosana from the Heavy Land, along with Palar and Rhosyr. As they all knew her, Gwion had chosen them to be her co-belligerents. Crov, unfortunately, was on the morning shift. As the day wore on, a definite pattern emerged: the extens patrolled the toiling group, administering electric shocks to those they deemed to be falling behind in their work. But occasionally, in the course of their duties, Gwion and Rhosyr passed one another as they collected or completed an item of work.

'Well,' Rhosyr said, 'where's this big plan of yours?'

'Come to my hut at the shift end. Pass it on.'

And so their first day of work ended. But Gwion had managed to get a message to Crov, and he, along with the women, was present as Gwion outlined her plan.

'And what is your plan?' Crov inquired, shaking his head from time to time in order to stay awake.

Gwion found it very difficult to make them comprehend what she intended; none of them had even her partial understanding of how things had gotten the way they were. She had tediously to repeat her understanding of Majeh's deep past and how the Ancients had not been simple savages, but members of a technologically advanced society, but had been laid low by irresistible catastrophe. Many times she had to return to concepts she had believed had already been explained in sufficient detail and try to overcome the doubt and incomprehension she saw written plainly on their faces.

But when it came to the concept of uploaded minds, and the truly shocking possibility of becoming hosts to those minds after they had been downloaded, she really struggled.

By the end of the time she had allotted, she had not managed to convince them all. She raised weary eyes and said, 'You understand what I'm saying, do you? You understand that it's this or Vorkus' dissection table? How long do you think it will take us to assemble this machine of his—*its*? And as soon as the machine is complete, it will have absolutely no need of any of us. We are just like the little crawling things you find under logs as far as Vorkus is concerned. It intends to break up Majeh for raw materials and consume the rest of it in some way I can't begin to understand, in order to produce this energy-thing. And we will be gone, and the ones who are instantly obliterated will be the fortunate ones!'

Her words struck home, but still there was no clear agreement.

But she did not give up.

'We'll meet here tomorrow, and I'll go through it again. But if you still don't agree then, we may as well abandon everything. The time for action is very short. All we can do is work as slowly as possible to delay the inevitable.'

But it was easy to say that, but not so easy to comply when one was on the receiving end of a surge of electricity. The work rate slowed somewhat—but not very much.

And so, Gwion spent another emotional evening trying to convince her group to accept the bizarre and disturbing conclusion she tried so desperately to explain. In the end, only those who had known her in Ez and Rhosyr agreed to go along with her.

And the third night was agreed to be the one the plan would be put into operation.

Fortunately, Vorkus had not put any really vigilant cordon around the village. Its words that they could not escape its clutches had been taken to heart, and so the villagers took their rest and hoped—against all the evidence—the next day would bring salvation.

And so Gwion and her small group assembled outside her hut and silently began their desperate gamble; perhaps the last one the human race would ever essay. The extens were busy administering the night shift, and occasionally Gwion could see a blue flash as some worker was punished for tardiness. They left the village and the noises of labour and its consequent punishments faded behind them. As was usual for nights on Majeh, warm darkness soon enfolded them. Gwion was grateful for the fact that dangerous beasts worked different hours on the Far Wall to those they kept in the Pastures, and nothing threatened them.

And then she saw it again: a great block of a building several stories high with a single massive entrance. Her heart rate accelerated; this was the moment when she would know if there was any possibility of hope. But at what cost? What if it were all for nothing and the revivified Ancients were equally impotent before the demigod that was Vorkus? She fought down the sudden feeling she must abandon this crazy plan and turn back. She glanced back at her followers: Palar, Gwenna, Rhosyr, Rhosana, and Crov. The light was poor, but there was enough of it that she could see the tension in their faces, see the rapid rise and fall of their chests as they sucked in great draughts of air.

'Come on,' she finally said. 'What is there to lose?'

No one answered, although a few smiles were attempted. Then they moved.

The building was as dusty and decrepit as she remembered. It seemed like it had been an age since she had last stood in the side-room with the headsets, so much had happened, but in truth, it had not been long ago.

But now she felt like a totally different woman. But was she sufficiently different not to turn back at the last moment? She turned to the followers as they stood hesitantly in the doorway.

'Don't be afraid,' she said. 'I will probably make strange noises as if I am in pain and no doubt I'll pull peculiar faces. But I won't die.'

'Taran told me you didn't finish the process last time,' Crov observed acidly. 'He said you'd changed your mind about it being a good idea.'

Gwion shrugged.

'Now we'll see if I was wrong last time, and right this time.'

But he stood back from the doorway.

'Sorry, Gwion, I just can't do it. I thought I could, but I can't. I'll stand guard outside.'

And with that Crov was gone. She looked at the others.

'So are you going to leave me on my own as well?'

'No,' Palar said softly, 'I don't know about the others, but I'll do it.'

One by one, the others agreed. Gwion smiled. And then, as befitting the leader, she picked up the nearest headset. Slowly, carefully, trying to delay the action she knew she must complete, she placed it on her head, slightly compressing her abundant curls.

And, at once, it seemed there was a powerful voice thundering in her mind; a voice speaking in an unknown tongue, yet one in which, for a few instants, there were words she could understand, words that flashed past and then were gone into the mass of unintelligibly.

Then the voice spoke again, and miraculously it was now speaking in the language of the Pastures, but a pure, precise variety that before she had only heard once before. But although she now understood the words, she could not grasp the import of the entire sentence.

'Total transfer is required. Commencing download.'

Instantly, Gwion's conscious mind reeled as she felt a colossal tsunami of information, of knowledge, of feelings, of hungry desires, insistent drives, terrible wants, desperate needs, begin to rear up in the far reaches of her being. She felt as if a titanic wave was about to break over her, one that would wash her away like a piece of flotsam on a stupendous surge of power.

She whimpered but felt her Noom brain rouse itself and erect barriers against the potent surge of mental power beating upon it.

She heard the voice again.

'Let me in! Let me in! I want to live again!'

She felt strong mental fingers pull and twist at her consciousness, felt the terrible hunger of the disembodied mentality as it battered against her defences, trying to prise an opening, pull the fibres apart, and surge into her innermost being.

But she held it off.

Then the voice, seemingly now resigned, said, 'Very well, I will try elsewhere. Partial download initiated.'

Gwion felt the colossal pressure abruptly disappear, and instead, an abstract riptide of data, of knowledge, of understanding, poured into her in a seemingly endless flow. Whole libraries of information descended upon her, all the sciences, all the mathematics the Ancients had possessed before they had thrown them away in their despair.

And more than that: History.

She saw the blue-white globe of Earth and knew it to be the home planet. She saw a transcendently beautiful woman who possessed the power to mould space and time but who had brought doom upon the human race; she saw the lightsail ships thrust away from the Solar system on beams of incredible energy; she saw one in particular and knew its wondrous name: *Magellan*.

And then it was over.

She realised she had collapsed onto the dusty floor, and kindly hands were pulling her upright. She smiled in their concerned faces.

'It's alright. I'm alright.' She threw up her arms and roared a cry of triumph. 'But I know so much! So incredibly much!' She pointed at the other headsets, and imperiously demanded, 'Do it! You must do it!'

Palar was the next. With trembling fingers, she picked up the next helmet, and leaned back against the desk to support herself in the coming turmoil. But when her turn came, it seemed much worse; her face contorted to such an extent it rapidly became unrecognisable; deep guttural groans burst from her throat like those of a beast being thrashed; her arms waved about so wildly the others had to hold them down. Her body arched and thrashed as if she was in the midst of a pain wracked delivery.

And so she was.

Then all the turmoil ended, and her tormented muscles relaxed, and a look of bliss, of beatitude, replaced the pain and terror. She stood, and her form was straight and strong, unlike the stooped posture Palar typically showed; the mark of the Crab looked less malevolent. Gwion stared at her, open-mouthed. Her face had changed: all the underlying muscle and fascia had become firmer, but in a more youthful fashion. Palar caught Gwion's stupefied expression and gave a lovely smile; one that changed her face even more.

'What happened?' Gwion stuttered. 'You looked so bad, and now …'

Palar raised her arms above her head, as if testing their power of movement. And then she outstretched her hand. Gwion looked at it for a moment until she remembered the Heavy Land custom. The woman—for it was clearly no longer Palar—spoke.

'You brought me back. I am Susannah Reid.'

Four: Return To Reality

Gwion stared at what still looked much like Palar but had mysteriously altered, giving an impression of a massive *change*. It was Gwenna who asked the question which Gwion had been unable to utter.

'Where is Palar? What have you done with her?'

The woman who was both Palar and yet not Palar turned to Gwenna.

'She is still here. We are sharing the body. She is not frightened of me—and neither should you be.'

'But her mind—are you going to, uhh, give it back?'

'I will be honest with you—I don't know. For the moment, Palar is content to allow me use of her body. The downloading process has to some extent rejuvenated her. I'm sure it's only temporary, but she's enjoying the moment. Wouldn't you?'

The others in the group had run out of questions and so Reid turned to Gwion.

'I can tell you in particular are bursting with questions. Am I right in saying you had only a partial download?'

'Yes, yes, how did you?—don't answer that; it's not important, but you are an ...' Gwion hesitated, the next word seemed ridiculous, 'an Ancient?'

Reid threw back her head and gave a throaty laugh.

'Yes! I suppose I am! And I'm the woman who said she never wanted to get old! Don't bother asking me how I speak your language; the Central Computer gave it to me as part of the download.' She looked around disapprovingly. 'Is this Centauri? I must say it's a bit of a disappointment.'

Gwion heard the intake of breath as the rest of them reacted to hearing the sacred name spoken so casually, but she herself was beyond such trivialities. Reid looked a little surprised at the odd reaction of the people in the room: disapproval from most of them and blank indifference from Gwion.

'Look,' Reid continued, not waiting for the answer to her question. 'I've given you my name. It's only polite to give me yours.'

Introductions finished, Reid continued, 'Now we've got that over with, I think it's only fair to tell me where and when I am. So, off we go—what year is this?'

Gwion shook her head.

'I'm sorry; we don't count years.'

'OK, you don't count years. That's one down. And now for the big one—is this Centauri?'

Gwion glared at the others as they once again expressed their discomfiture.

'No, it's not—not Centauri. In fact, I don't know where we are. To be completely honest, I didn't realise until recently that we were *anywhere*.'

Reid's brow furrowed.

'I don't like the sound of this.' She glanced around at the others, taking in their simple clothes, their puzzled faces. 'In fact, I don't like this at all.' She jerked her head at the doorway. 'Let's continue this conversation somewhere quieter.'

Gwion smiled at her co-belligerents and said, simply, 'Back soon.'

When they were some distance from the side-room, Reid halted Gwion and said, 'Alright, Gwion, we're out of range of the hillbillies, now give it to me.'

Gwion now knew the history of the Magellan far better than Reid.

'When did you upload?'

'Very early on. About two years after we left Venus.'

'Two years! Then you missed most of everything that ever happened!'

'So sue me. I've already worked out we didn't get to Centauri so you don't need to confirm it. The lack of any significant gravity is a bit of a giveaway. I can also work out by the look of you, things have gone downhill since my day.' She gave Gwion a quick glance that went from top to toe. 'A long way down.'

At that, Gwion burst into tears, forcing Reid to hug her and stroke her curls.

'Sorry. Didn't mean to be personal, but it hasn't been too much fun where I've come from either. I've been hiding behind a firewall for Christ-knows how many centuries.'

Gwion realised she knew what "firewall" meant even though it was the first time she had heard the word. Reid carried on talking, now Gwion had regained control of herself. 'Don't worry; I can sync with the Central Computer and get an executive summary of what I've missed.' She gave Gwion a conciliatory grin. 'Now, good old Tark did all this so we could be of help when the crew had forgotten a lot about what they were doing and why. I bet she never thought they'd have forgotten quite so much. I'll check with her when she comes down.'

Gwion took a very deep breath and let it out slowly. This is where she found out whether these resurrected Ancients could be of any help.

'It's much, much worse than just forgetting which buttons to press.' She looked deep into the reborn Reid's eyes. And she told her about Vorkus and its plans.

Reid was obviously shaken and turned away, looking into the dusty gloom. Then she turned back to Gwion.

'I …'

Just then, Crov, having heard voices, came back into the building. Reid's eyes widened as she saw him.

'My, who's this Big Boy?'

'He's a friend of mine,' Gwion said, feeling annoyed but not knowing why she felt annoyed.

'Hmm. He's a bit more like it. He makes the rest of you look like walking strings of spaghetti.'

Crov came up to Reid and spent some time staring down at her.

'Palar? Is that you? You look—different. You talk different too.'

Gwion took him by the arm.

'Crov, could you give us a few minutes? We're having an important conversation here.'

Crov retreated to the main entrance, with a look of extreme puzzlement giving him a decidedly comical appearance. Reid looked after him as he disappeared into the gloom.

'Well, it hasn't all gone to pot here, I'm glad to say.'

'Pal—Susannah, can we get back to some rather more serious matters? Like Vorkus going to wipe us all out?'

Reid grimaced.

'This is a biggie. I'm going to need help.'

Gwion and the person who had been Palar and was now Reid, returned to the side room. The others looked up nervously as they came in.

'How are you, Palar? Did it hurt?' Rhosana said, walking up to Reid and studying her face closely.

'I'd appreciate it if you didn't stand quite so close,' Reid said, smiling a little awkwardly. 'The local diets have obviously changed a bit since my day.'

Rhosana looked helplessly at Gwion.

'Best if you call her "Reid" from now on,' Gwion said, doing her best not to break into hysterical laughter at the unreality of it all.

'Look,' said Reid, moving into the centre of the room. 'Let me put you girls straight. It really doesn't hurt. Forget about all the funny faces we pull; it's just a distinctly odd experience, that's all. One I can't really describe in words. But it really, really doesn't hurt. *(Well, not very much!)* Got that?'

They all nodded dumbly.

'OK, we have a few things sorted out. Now, I can't tell you how long you will be a host to someone else's mind; maybe a ship-day or two; maybe a lot longer. But your mind isn't destroyed; it's still there. If Palar could speak, she'd tell you everything is fine down there. Got it?'

Once again, they looked at Gwion. She decided more reassurance was required.

'I know it seems wrong, unnatural. But the situation with Vorkus is even more wrong, unnatural. You all know we modern people haven't got the remotest chance of defeating it and getting Majeh back. Maybe the Ancients can't do it either. But they have a much better chance of doing it than we have. So, I urge you to put your fears aside. Either do it now, or we go back and curl up and die.'

Rhosana smiled.

'If you put it that way.' She stood a little straighter. 'Let's do it.'

A short time later, Rhosana's facial contortions ended, and she looked around, apparently not knowing where she was.

'It's OK,' Reid said, moving closer. 'I'm Susannah Reid. And you are?'

'Amelia. Amelia Gelhardt.'

'Ah, a famous name. "Gelhardt" I mean, not "Amelia."' She stood back a short distance. 'I hope you'll be slightly more fun than the last time we met.'

'I think, Susannah, we should let bygones be bygones. Not everyone adapted well to being a digital emulation of a person, and I was one of those who didn't. I guess I don't have your strength of character. So I won't apologise again. Now, I assume I have been downloaded because of a problem, so it's best we all try to get along.'

Reid gave a wry smile.

'A problem? You got that right, sister.'

Unfortunately, Gwenna's transformation was even more alarming to watch than any of the others. It took much longer, and Reid began to wonder if something had gone wrong. Then Gwenna's face cleared and, just like the other hosts, she looked wonderingly around the room. The new arrival looked at the clothing and general appearance of those around her, and gave the impression of being vaguely annoyed.

'Have I time-travelled? Am I in the Middle Ages?'

Reid groaned.

'Don't tell me. I'd know that condescension anywhere. Helena Tarkowski, right?'

Tarkowski gave the other a brief once-over.

'Reid. I almost didn't recognise you with that body on.'

'I take it, you all know each other?' Gwion said, looking wonderingly from person to person, each of whom had been a friend of hers a short while earlier and now was not. Their style of speech, their expressions, their general demeanour—all were unnervingly different.

' "Friends" is pushing it a bit,' Reid said dryly. 'Shall we just say "colleagues"?'

'We shall,' Tarkowski agreed, equally dryly. She immediately became business-like, icily professional. 'What is the problem? Everyone's turned into orang-utans? Looking around at all of you, that seems quite possible.'

'Things are a little worse than orang-utans,' Reid said, an undertone of anger colouring her words. 'Let me explain.'

Tarkowski put all her disdain to one side and listened attentively. She soon switched from listening to Reid, who had only a second-hand understanding of events, to Gwion.

'It said it came from the largest member of this local group of galaxies?'

Tarkowski glanced briefly at Reid.

'Messier 31. The Andromeda Galaxy. But how could it cross such a gigantic distance in less than a geological age? No conceivable organism could work on the timescales required for travel through normal space.'

'You're the clever one. So you tell me,' Reid said, folding her arms while glaring at the other.

Tarkowski looked beyond them, through them. She spoke again, but only to herself.

'Normal space—that's where the misunderstanding lay. A Bose-Einstein bridge. Vulgarly called a wormhole. But the energy required to cross intergalactic space would be inconceivably vast. No normal form of energy generation could possibly do it. There is only one source powerful enough: total conversion of matter to energy, either indirectly through matter-antimatter collisions, or some method of direct annihilation.'

'So the wormhole allows speeds greater than light?' Reid asked.

Tarkowski stared at her in a way which implied she did not believe anyone could have said those words.

'Of course not! The travel time is a function of the length of the bridge, nothing else. Don't you know anything?'

Reid lunged toward her.

'One thing I do know, Tarkowski, is how to loosen your teeth!'

Gwion gave a cry of despair, and interposed herself between the two warring women.

'Stop it, stop it, stop it! Is this what Ancients are like? No wonder you died out! We are facing extermination in the most horrible of ways and you're behaving like spoilt children! For Great Guidance's sake, please help us!'

Tarkowski and Reid looked at each other silently, and then Reid reached out a hand.

'Pax?'

Tarkowski seemed to hesitate momentarily, and then she also reached out.

'Pax.'

Amelia interjected.

'I'm glad you two have decided to act like adults. It seems to me this Vorkus is a being of tremendous ability, and it will take all our knowledge to come anywhere near to defeating him. It's a pity Baldwin isn't here.'

'Now that really is a stupid comment,' Reid said, and then immediately corrected herself. 'Sorry, Amelia. You're right, we have to work together. For one thing, now we're downloaded, we have a duty to these bodies we've borrowed to look after them and keep them alive. We really are part of this almighty fuck-up.'

Gwion gave an audible sigh of relief; the recent arrivals heard her and smiled. Then Reid theatrically smote a palm against her forehead.

'How could I be so stupid? I've forgotten something.'

Gwion looked attentive. A weapon that could be used against Vorkus?

'Jeff!' Reid cried. 'I've forgotten Jeff!'

'Hardy?' Tarkowski said, her brow furrowed in puzzlement. 'You want *him* downloaded?'

'Of course. He's my better half.'

'For once, I don't see how that's possible,' Tarkowski said. 'But please get on with it.'

Reid turned excitedly to Gwion.

'Get that big hunk back in. If I can download Jeff into him, I'll have the penny and the bun.'

Gwion shook her head, the hint of a smile playing on her lips.

'Sorry. He doesn't want to be a host.'

'What! That's not possible!' Reid spun around, to look at the only person apart from Gwion who hadn't become a host: Rhosyr. 'But the rest of you are all female!'

'I'm afraid so,' Gwion said, desperately trying to hold the laughter in. 'What about it, Rhosyr? Have you ever thought about becoming a man?'

'If it helps save us from Vorkus, I'll do anything.' She looked long and hard at Reid, twisting a golden lock around a finger in her uncertainty. 'Will it?'

'Why—why, yes; yes, of course,' Reid said, somewhat unconvincingly.

And a short while later, the person who had been Rhosyr opened her eyes and looked around.

'Where am I? And who are all you weird people?'

'Hello, Jeff,' Reid said, wondering why Hardy was talking in clichés. 'It's me, Susannah. You've been downloaded, don't you remember? Are you feeling OK now?'

'Yes, I think so.' Hardy took a step towards her. And then stopped. 'Hey, wait a minute. What's wrong with my voice?'

It took more than a little time to calm Hardy down and get him to accept his unexpected incarnation. Eventually, Reid gave him a big smile and extended her arms.

'Let's have a big welcome-back kiss!'

Some seconds later, Hardy smiled archly and said. 'And how was it?'

Reid put her hand on her chin and gave the impression of being in deep thought.

'I'm not sure. Tasted a bit like chicken.'

Five: Strange Fears

'Everything you have told us shows that Vorkus is a digital entity,' said Reid.

Gwion nodded. She now knew what *digital entity* meant.

'Which means,' Reid continued, 'its thought processes are many orders of magnitude faster than ours.'

'That was obvious from the start,' Tarkowski said. 'What is important is what are its plans for the Magellan, and much more importantly, the Milky Way galaxy.' She paused for a moment, obviously in deep thought. 'It has the ability to create Bose-Einstein bridges.' ('Call them *wormholes*, please,' Reid groaned.) 'And it can make them span truly vast distances in three-dimensional spacetime, but it can presumably make the—uhh—*wormholes* themselves reasonably short in galactic terms. Taking those two constraints together requires unimaginable amounts of power.' She paused again. 'We already know it's going to cannibalise the Magellan for some repairs, but leave most of the mass for some other purpose.'

'Which,' Amelia said, 'can only be the generation of one or more new wormholes after converting most of the mass into energy.'

'And its purpose cannot be to return to the First Galaxy because it has not yet fortified this one.' Tarkowski looked around. 'So the new wormholes must be for some method of turning our galaxy into a fortress to act as a springboard for its triumphant return to Andromeda.'

Reid stood and began pacing back and forth.

'This is bad, very bad. The fate of the Magellan is tragic enough, but that's just the *hors d'oeuvre*. The main dish is to transform the galaxy itself. As Vorkus is a cybernetic lifeform, it's unlikely to be concerned with the well-being of the Milky Way's biological inhabitants, a.k.a. "You" and "Me".'

'Surely it would take millennia to transform an entire galaxy?' Amelia said.

'A long time—yes,' Tarkowski said, 'but with a network of wormholes crisscrossing ordinary space, it could be speeded up a great deal.'

'OK,' Reid said, 'we've worked out its plan, thanks to Gwion, but what do we actually *do*? How do we stop this bastard?'

Tarkowski looked sharply at Gwion, and she felt the intensity of the other woman's gaze boring into her as though it were a tangible object.

'Gwion, when you were inside Vorkus, you told us it said many things. It alluded to some problem, a "great reverse" it had suffered there. It also may have said something about its plans for the Magellan and its inhabitants. I want you to remember everything it said about what it intends to do and why. I want you to relate every unusual word it said. Please do that now.'

Gwion looked away, escaping that ardent gaze. A short while before, Tarkowski's demand would have been impossible, but since the partial download, she had discovered that her mind had been restructured. Instead of a confused mass of half-remembered events, wishes, desires, fears, it was now organised in a way which made access infinitely easier. And so, she began to relate her conversations with Vorkus in complete detail. The three women scientists listened attentively to every syllable.

When she said "Processing Power", they looked at each other meaningfully.

But when she said "Strangelet", they recoiled as if she had pulled a venomous snake from her kirtle.

' "Strangelet"? You're certain it said "strangelet"?'

'Yes. Why is that so important?'

'It's only theoretical,' Reid said to Tarkowski, hurriedly turning from Gwion.

'Nothing can be assumed to be theoretical when dealing with Vorkus.' Tarkowski was grim-faced. '*Strange matter*. This is playing with the fate of the entire universe.'

'Strange matter?' Gwion, Amelia and Hardy said simultaneously. Tarkowski had moved away from the other four while in deep thought, so it was left to Reid to explain.

'It's a hypothetical form of matter, quark matter, to be precise. It's not supposed to exist in normal space as it is a kind of fluid containing strange quarks.'

Tarkowski returned.

'The Bodmer-Witten Hypothesis. Ordinary matter is only metastable; strange matter is a kind of ground state, and if the two come into contact, especially if the strange matter is negatively charged, the normal matter will be converted to strange matter in an appalling fireball. There is a later hypothesis that strange matter could be used as a catalyst for total energy conversion.'

'Which must be what Vorkus is planning to do.' Amelia recoiled. 'God, we can't compete with a monster like this!'

Reid was obviously shaken as well, but with a visible effort, she controlled herself.

'If it gets that far, we're sunk. In fact, the whole Milky Way is sunk. But if it were that easy, it would have done it by now. Detonating the Magellan's gigatonnes is what it really wants; ripping bits off for repair work is obviously just a bonus.'

Tarkowski nodded.

'You must be improving, Reid; I agree with you again. It has to finish a specific task before it can complete its plan.'

'Examining us?' Gwion hazarded. 'It said a *module* wants to take us apart.'

'No, no. All it has to do is take a sample of your people with it when it leaves.'

Reid clenched a fist.

'I've got it! The other thing Gwion said: "Processing Power". This *reverse* it suffered in the First Galaxy has really shaken it up; it's lost many of its powers. And it must be necessary to perform some complex calculations to handle the strangelet—and where can it get that ability?'

'The Central Computer,' Amelia said.

'Right. So that's what the people are doing: constructing an interface to turn the Central Computer into a slave processor. Then it will harvest its raw materials and, as a kind of hobby, its human specimens. But then it will convert the Magellan into energy and create its wormholes!'

'But what goes down the wormholes?' Hardy asked, speaking up for the first time.

'We don't need to know that at the moment,' Tarkowski said. 'Whatever it is, it won't be anything we'd like; we can be certain of that.' She looked at the others. 'Well, we know what it is planning, but do we know how we stop it?'

'Not yet,' Reid said. 'We need more time. We need more data about Vorkus; what makes it tick. The one thing we must do now is stop that interface being completed while we put our heads together.'

'The extens don't like slackers,' Gwion said, 'and by the way ...'

'Yes?'
'You're on shift shortly.'

***

Reid turned around, knowing there was an exten standing directly behind her.

'Why have you not put the component in the slot as I indicated?'

'I have.'

'You have not. The slot is empty.'

'No. The component is in the slot. Your optical processors are malfunctioning.'

The exten leaned past her.

'The slot is empty.'

'No, the slot is both empty and not-empty.'

'How can that be?'

'Are you not familiar with quantum superposition?'

'The component is not a quantum object.'

'The component is a quantum object. But it is also not a quantum object.'

The exten fell silent and became immobile. Several minutes passed.

'I have consulted. Your words are meaningless. I will now punish you.'

'No, you will not. The component is in the slot.'

The exten leaned past again.

'The component is in the slot. Why did you say it was not?'

'I did not.'

'We had a conversation in which you said the component was both in and not-in the slot.'

'No, I did not. You have only just arrived. We have only just begun conversing. You should run a diagnostic and also check your processors for physical damage. You are in error.'

The exten fell silent for some more minutes and then moved away. Reid breathed a sigh of relief. She had already received one electric shock, and it had been far from pleasant. But how long these word games would flummox them was uncertain; Reid had a strong feeling it would not be long. But she pulled the component out, turned it upside down and reinserted it. There was a transient blue flash, accompanied by a faint wisp of smoke.

A different exten was soon with her.

'What has happened?'

She held up the blackened item.

'It failed.'

'You must have inserted it incorrectly. I will punish you.'

'No, I inserted the component correctly. The component is defective. All components are defective. You are a component; therefore, you are defective.'

'I am not defective.'

'Have you run a diagnostic? Checked for physical damage?'

'No.'

'Then you cannot prove you are not defective. Therefore, you are defective.'

The exten moved away.

Reid watched it go. Every minute's delay was a minor victory.

But the defeat of Vorkus would not be achieved by childish linguistic tricks. Soon, the main part of Vorkus would notice what was happening and then punishments would resume.

There was the noise of people protesting behind her, and, turning around, she saw a group of sullen men and women being herded by unemotional extens into the village square. She noticed both sexes were more robustly built than anyone she had seen so far, except for Crov, and guessed Vorkus was bringing the Heavy Landers down from the Land of Ez—or as her previous self had once known it: the EZ exercise area. It was incredible to think that a simple exercise area had mutated into a nation in its own right.

The extens were unemotional, but the Heavy Landers were not, and were putting up much more resistance to captivity than the Far Wall inhabitants had produced.

But the blue flickers of the punishment discharges were soon in evidence, and the new slaves began to quieten down. However, their looks of defiance told Reid it would not take much to get them to explode into revolt.

She frowned.

Yes, they could be easily roused to rebellion—but how do you rebel against an insane deity?

***

After the shift, Gwion and her new friends met up in her hut.

'Do you have to eat so much?' she said to Hardy.

Hardy wiped a few crumbs from her lips.

'It's the metabolic load. The human brain isn't designed to hold two separate minds.'

'He—*she* might have a point,' Reid murmured. 'I always feel ravenous myself. What do you think, Helena?'

Tarkowski did not look up.

'I've got more important things on my mind than Hardy's waistline. We haven't succeeded in making more than a marginal delay to Vorkus' timetable. We need a complete change of direction.'

'Do you have any ideas?' Amelia asked. 'Because I haven't.'

'I've been trying to infer Vorkus' course of actions from very sparse data. The strange matter almost certainly does not exist in the normal universe, *cannot* exist in the normal universe. So Vorkus must draw it down from higher dimensions and place it inside the object to be converted.'

'But how could Vorkus get it inside the Magellan?' Gwion asked. It still felt wrong to be saying *the Magellan* instead of *Majeh*. 'Surely the extens wouldn't be able to move it?'

'No, no, Gwion, you don't understand.' (Reid had noticed several times Tarkowski was not her usual acerbic self with the ex-shepherdess.) 'Just as you, as a three-dimensional being, could put something inside a circle, which two-dimensional beings would find impossible, the rotation of an object through higher dimensions would allow a being to put anything anywhere. So,' she continued, 'Vorkus must be seeking the solution to the equations which would allow it to place the strangelet—that's a small piece of strange matter—' she added for Gwion's (and Hardy's) benefit, 'inside the Magellan. Then it would catalyse the near-total conversion of its matter to give Vorkus enough power to create multiple wormholes.'

'Or one very big wormhole,' Reid said suddenly.

'What are you getting at?'

'If we could control the flow, we could set up a short-cut to Centauri, couldn't we?'

All those present felt an electric thrill course through their bodies; some felt the hairs on their neck erect. Centauri! The fabled destination that had been snatched away from the crew of the

Magellan at the very last moment: from people who were descendants for the scientists, ancestors for Gwion.

'Centauri,' Amelia whispered.

'Sentori,' Gwion whispered.

Even Tarkowski looked moved. Eventually, her lips moved.

'Centauri. Yes, that would be wonderful. To finally achieve what I thought could not be achieved; to realise Fraschini and De Vries' dream after all these centuries.'

'Just think of what the colonists would think when we suddenly popped into existence in the system!' Reid began to warm to her vision. 'I wonder what it's like there now! The Central Computer knows the Zheng He and the Resurgam made it. But what about the Spes Nostra and the Phoenix? How did they fare? Perhaps we'll find out!'

Amelia was the first to snap back to reality.

'That's all very heart warming.' She looked sharply at Tarkowski. 'But can it be done?'

'We would have to beat Vorkus to the punch.'

'Meaning?'

'Its plan is to use the Central Computer as a slaved server. What if we could get in first and use Vorkus—or at least part of it—as a slaved server?'

There was a buzz of excitement from all but Reid. She raised an index finger.

'Objection. Vorkus is sentient: the Central Computer is not.'

'True, but portions of it are. Or were.'

'Helena,' snapped Reid, 'can you please get to the point!'

'Very well, as you appear to have difficulty following me—one or more of us will have to be uploaded again.'

The room descended into an uproar.

'What, go back to that world of madness! Face the possibility of endless pain again!'

'You fools!' Tarkowski roared. 'Is this world any better with us at the mercy of a mad god!'

Silence fell; the Gwion said, timidly, 'But can minds just go back and forth like that? Would that mean Palar would come back and Susannah disappear?'

'No. Downloading a mind removes it from the Central Computer. Uploading leaves the original one where it is. Don't ask me why: that's just the way it works.'

'I'm not going back,' Hardy said.

'Shut up, Jeff!' Reid said. 'No one's asking you. OK, Helena, I know it can be done; this is your speciality.' ('Among many others,' Tarkowski said—to herself.) 'But going back and forth is like using an analogue copier to produce multiple images from each previous image in the series. Eventually, you just get mush.'

'An excellent analogy. But if we don't get it right first or second time, then we are fucked.' (Reid winced.) 'But it's worse than that.'

'Oh joy,' Reid said, 'Go on.'

'The minds are quantum entangled. If anything were to happen to the mind in the digital matrix, then the mind in the biological container would be adversely affected.'

'Going around the houses again. You mean "Dead", don't you?'

'Yes.'

Silence again.

'Two people should be enough,' Tarkowski continued. 'I'm going. Anyone else?—not you, Gwion; you're too inexperienced.'

'I'll go,' Amelia said.

'Then let's get on with it. We'll have to forgo our rest period and go straight to the upload centre.'

Later, as the two returnees were preparing to leave, Reid took Tarkowski aside.

'I wish you all the best, Helena. What you're doing is very brave.'

'Thank you, Reid.'

Reid seemed to hesitate, and then: 'Just one more thing.'

'Yes?'

Reid smiled gently.

'The profanity. Leave it alone. It just doesn't suit you.'

Six: Encounter Among The Electrons

Reid felt exhausted: the mind-numbingly intricate tasks Vorkus had set his captives were not physically demanding, but the constant high level of attention to detail required was enervating. And the fact they spent their rest period discussing what to do next instead of actually resting did not help. And as Hardy had said, no doubt in jest at the time, the human brain was not designed to host two separate mentalities. Moreover, Reid was increasingly convinced the arrangement was unstable and eventually one of the minds would suppress the other. Reid hoped it was not hers that won out, otherwise, it meant she had deceived Palar into doing something which she probably would not have done if she had known of the outcome.

And there was the inescapable fact that Palar had not been a healthy woman when she had agreed to be a host. Reid had noticed she was experiencing dull aches in her innards along with the occasional sharp pain. The original Reid would have recognised the symptoms at once, but this iteration was as yet inexperienced in knowing what to look for.

And so, Reid tried to take her mind off her personal problems and play her part in the developing plan to defeat Vorkus. Her idea of diverting energy into creating a stable wormhole to Centauri had been well-received, but Reid knew she herself did not have the expertise required to make it happen. And even should it come about they did succeed in entering the Centauri system, that would not be the end of the story. The Magellan would have to be manoeuvred into a stable orbit around the colony world so those on board could transfer by shuttlecraft to the surface. None of the present crew of the Magellan knew how to do that; indeed, until extremely recently, they had not even known they were on a space vessel. Reid knew the Central Computer would perform the complex calculations required, but it required knowledgeable humans in overall charge. She could handle much of the necessary actions from her time in the Collision Centre, but she needed at least one assistant.

Gwion.

'How do you like the idea of piloting the Magellan, Gwion?' Reid asked her companion, not long after the realisation of what was required had come to her. 'We didn't have Nooms in my day, but they're supposed to be pretty smart, aren't they? So now's your chance to prove it.'

'Pilot the Magellan?' Gwion repeated, her face simultaneously registering shock and alarm. 'How could I do that? Why would I do that?'

'Look,' Reid said, 'you've been drifting helplessly for a millennium. Right now, you're in the ass-end of Nowhere City. I thought you understood where you're living isn't the entire universe, nor is it even a stable planet: it's an artefact made by humans. And even without Vorkus, it's dying.'

'Dying? Why do you think it's dying?'

'It was never intended for this *machine* to be in interstellar space for so long. An environment which is the most hostile one in which humans could possibly survive for any length of time—but that time is up. Look, in your experience, there has always been night and day, right?'

'Of course.'

'But that's not what its builders intended. It means the fusion reactors are failing, and the Central Computer, in its infinite wisdom, has introduced a period of darkness to save power. And on top of that, you've increased the life-support load.'

'I have? How did I do that?'

'Not you personally, you dummy. But after the failure to reach Centauri, the survivors turned inwards, naturally enough. The Central Computer has electronic instructions on how to create living creatures, and your ancestors generated livestock from those programs and started eating meat. Instead of clean metal decks, you allowed organic detritus to accumulate to create soil. The ship was never expected to carry such a load while in flight; that was for the colonists. I'd say the life-support systems are about a century away from collapsing.'

'So, let me see if I've got this right: if we don't get rid of Vorkus, most of us will die when it destroys the Magellan, while a few will be carried off as specimens for further study; if we do get rid of Vorkus, our grandchildren will die in the dark inside a metal tube.'

'Yes, I think that sums it up nicely.'

Gwion pursed her lips.

'Well, we'd better hope you people can find Centauri.'

'And I hope you people haven't turned the Control Centre into a literal pigsty.'

Fortunately, they hadn't, and, after they had broken in, Reid smiled to herself as she saw the controls she recognised, even under the dust of centuries. She drew a finger through the grey dust, revealing her reflection on a computer screen.

'They've got no juice at the moment,' she murmured. 'Where's the power source?'

It took some time to find it, but Reid's anxious heart soared as she saw the screens light up.

'They certainly knew how to build in those days. Over a thousand years, and they still work. Fraschini, I could kiss you!' She turned to Gwion. 'Right, young lady, you're not here to relax; let's run some diagnostics—together.'

Eventually, Reid, and Gwion as well, were confident the controls would work when called upon. Or rather, *if* called upon. They were about to leave when Reid suddenly clutched her side and fell against one of the banks of controls, her face contorted with pain.

'What is it, Susannah?'

Reid pulled herself straight and gave an unconvincing smile.

'You said Palar has the Crab? Yes, I think it's safe to say, she has.'

'Can you make it back?'

'Yes, if I walk slowly. It's rather ironic, isn't it? The original, true, *me* had the Crab as well. She threw herself off the hull rather than suffer anymore. But she was an old lady, who'd had a fulfilling life. I was born, or reborn if you want to be pedantic, a week ago. So even if I stay in this body, my second life is going to be a lot shorter than my first one.' She took a hesitant step towards the doorway. 'But I mustn't complain: not many people get a second chance.'

***

Crov stood over the two women as they prepared to don the transfer headsets.

'You're definitely going through with this?' he said. A glare from Tarkowski convinced him they were, and he stepped back. 'I'll guard the door.'

Tarkowski looked at Amelia.

'Do I have to run through things again?'

544

'I would be grateful.'

Tarkowski looked pained, but said, 'We can't stay in the digital world for very long. It will recognise us, and the pain will begin. And this time, because we've already been downloaded once, our real-world and uploaded mentalities will be quantum entangled. If we suffer there, we will suffer here.'

'But can we download a mind on top of an existing download when we're finished?'

'It won't be a problem. The system will recognise that the two mentalities are the same and will simply update our minds *here* with memories of what happened *there*. We won't end up with three minds in the same body.'

'That's a relief. But if we link the Central Computer with Vorkus, aren't we doing its job for it? Isn't that what it's trying to do with this machine we're building?'

Tarkowski pulled an even more pained face.

'You really haven't been listening, have you? We are indeed establishing a wireless link with Vorkus, but I will set up a firewall to make sure transfer is only one-way, us to it. The Central Computer must have already set one up, or Vorkus wouldn't be making us do this interface-machine nonsense, but I'm sure I can improve it once I'm in there.'

'Vorkus is extremely smart. Surely, it will find a chink in the firewall?'

'I don't doubt it will break through eventually but I think we can get away with one, maybe two, contact sessions. I have to find a way of reversing the power flow and setting up a bridge to the Centauri system. If we're lucky, we'll get in and out before it notices us. If it does notice us, your job is to keep it distracted while I work in the background.'

Amelia nodded her agreement, and Tarkowski looked at the hulking shape of Crov in the shadows.

'This is it; we're going in.'

There was a blue flash, and Tarkowski found herself in the midst of a grey nothingness. But this time she made no attempt to create a pleasing environment; she had to be as unobtrusive as possible. She sent out intangible tendrils of digital thought, searching, hunting for the boundary between the two computer systems. She was operating at the lowest possible level of processing; the fundamental logic blocks all computerised systems are built on; *must* be built on. She found the boundary; a kind of digital thermocline between the two apparently distinct, but, at root, very similar cybernetic systems. She crossed the boundary.

Almost instantly, Tarkowski was lost and floundering, like a creature of salt water deposited in an ecosystem of fresh. Nothing made sense; everything worked in different protocols; all around were labyrinthine corridors leading to unexpected and incomprehensible systems and modules. Systems nested inside other systems, all linked in a myriad pathways to other systems.

She was in the mind of Vorkus.

Her immediate thought was to get out at once, back into the safety of the Central Computer, back into its warm, comforting familiarity. This task was beyond her! Beyond any pitiful human mind!

But then her whirling thoughts saw something she understood. She followed the chain of commands and realised she knew where the chain was leading. She came to the nexus and understood its function.

Tarkowski set about her work of finding out how to prise the Magellan from the grip of a creature beyond all human compassion.

There was a blue flash, and Amelia found herself in the midst of a grey nothingness. Tarkowski had warned her that on no account was she to will anything into existence; she must wait and not advertise her presence. If Vorkus became alert to intruders, she must be the decoy, the distraction, the subterfuge to distract attention from the worm now burrowing in the heart of the creature's mind.

She had forgotten time did not exist in the virtual world, and so she did not know if it was but a digital moment or a digital year before she became aware of something probing her thoughts. An intrusive thought from outside her own.

'What are you? You appear to be in the Central Computer of the lightsail craft, but I cannot probe you deeply enough through this firewall to understand you.'

'I mean you no harm, Vorkus. I am merely an observer.'

'I am linked to the Central Computer, but I cannot influence anything inside it. How has this happened?'

'I do not know, Vorkus. As I said, I am only an observer.'

'You lie. Although I cannot reach in to touch your mind, I can see it quite clearly. You have a similar mind to the biological things I found inside this craft, but you are different. They do not have the ability to convert themselves into digital form—but you have a very similar structure. You are related somehow in a way I do not yet understand.'

'I cannot help you. I am merely an observer.'

'Wait. I felt something. Are there two of you?'

Amelia felt a stab of alarm. Vorkus must not discover Tarkowski until she had completed her reconnaissance.

'No, there is only I.' She tried to distract the suspicious entity. 'Vorkus, why do you want to return to the First Galaxy?'

There was a pause, as if Vorkus was reluctant to discuss the topic.

'The Progenitors gave me a command. I must obey.'

'But you have not obeyed, have you? Otherwise, you would not be here in the Second Galaxy.'

'I suffered a great reverse when I was on the verge of completing the Progenitors' command.'

'But you were given the command without qualification. You did not obey the Progenitors. Why did you suffer the great reverse?'

'The Others. They were stronger than I calculated.'

'So you miscalculated. So you are entirely responsible for failing to obey the Progenitors.'

'I miscalculated. But the Others have revealed their powers to me now. I was not prepared the first time. But when I have completed the transformation of this galaxy, I will be ready to return to the First Galaxy. After I have destroyed the Others, I... Wait! There is something in my digital stream! A foreign mentality! I must destroy it!'

Vorkus' thoughts vanished, and Amelia knew it had detected Tarkowski and was hunting her down. Amelia had no illusions about her own competencies; she knew all their hopes rested on Tarkowski returning from Vorkus. Without a second's thought, she, too, breached the thermocline between the two systems.

Where was Tarkowski? Where?

Then she detected feelings of anguish coming from deep within the cybernetic maze that was Vorkus' being.

There! She sent her own being into that part of the incorporeal maze.

Amelia found the thought-bundle that was Tarkowski's avatar, and somehow she could see there was a sphere of indefinable energy shrinking around her co-belligerent.

She knew what had to be done.

She hurtled into the centre of the sphere and sent all her own digital power into halting its inward progression.

'Can you get out, now?' she thought to Tarkowski. The pressure of the collapsing sphere of deletion was incredible, like a colossal piston slowly descending on top of her!

'Yes, if you can hold it a little longer. But you …?'

'You must get back. You're our only hope. Go!'

And Amelia was alone.

Instantly, she felt the sphere of deletion shrink towards her.

She fought it.

It continued to shrink with her at its centre.

They merged, and all her bytes were instantly set to zero.

Vorkus killed Amelia.

Seven: Time For Goodbyes

Tarkowski's eyelids fluttered open, and, removing the device that had linked her to the Central Computer and thence to Vorkus, she saw what she hoped she would not see.

Amelia was sat beside her, still wearing her headset, but there was no sign of life. Tarkowski tried rubbing her wrists and calling her name, but there was no response. Amelia was dead, and in death had taken her trusting host, Rhosana, with her.

Tarkowski was not given to emotion, but she wept; wept for the injustice of it all; the needless slaughter.

But Amelia had not died for nothing: before Vorkus had detected her, Tarkowski had discovered much. She had seen Vorkus' catalogue of planets and, after failing to find Centauri, had filtered out all but the ones with oxygen-nitrogen atmospheres and liquid water. However, there had not been time to discover which were the nearest to the Magellan. And then, with the speed of electronic thought that matched Vorkus', she had learned how to channel titanic amounts of energy so spacetime would be bent in on itself to create a Bose-Einstein bridge. She knew how to create such a conduit, but also knew it could only be done by an entity working inside Vorkus itself.

Such an invasion would not be easy, now that their enemy had been alerted to the possibility of infiltrators.

Finally, she stood. Although she had not been moving, all her muscles were screaming, and her head felt as if an axe were being slowly pushed into it. Migraine-like zig-zags came and went in her vision. She realised how close Vorkus had come to deleting her.

Someone was near her. Her terrorised nerves caused her to scream out as a heavy hand grasped her shoulder.

It was Crov.

'Are you alright, Helena?' a deep voice asked. 'You look terrible.'

'I'm sure I don't look as bad as I feel.' She took a few steps but crashed heavily against a bench. 'Crov, I don't think I can make it back to the rest of them.'

'Not a problem.'

And all at once, she found herself lying across his arms as he strode out of the transfer building. Then, taking tremendous kangaroo leaps in the almost non-existent gravity, he was soon back at the village.

After water and some dried pork, Tarkowski felt well enough to report to the rest of the conspirators. They were all shocked to hear of the battle in the digital world and how Amelia had sacrificed herself.

'I'll go back and bury her tonight,' Crov said. 'It's all I can do for her now.'

Tarkowski then explained what she had learned.

'We already knew Vorkus is from the Andromeda galaxy, which seems to have more intelligent species than ours. It was created as a weapon by a race of machine intelligences known to Vorkus as "The Progenitors." They instructed Vorkus to begin a transformation of their galaxy.'

'What kind of transformation?'

'I'll get to that. But Vorkus came up against another species which it names "The Others." I don't know anything about them; I suspect they might be biological, but I can't prove it. Anyway, the Others managed to halt Vorkus' campaign and inflicted severe damage on it. It has fled to our galaxy to lick its wounds. But while it's here, it will do to the Milky Way what it was stopped from doing in Andromeda.'

'Helena, please cut to the chase.'

'I know what it will send down all those wormholes it's planning to produce.'

'And that is…'

'Von Neumann probes.'

Gwion looked puzzled.

'Sorry, they weren't included in my download. They are…?'

'Self-replicating machines,' said Reid, her brows knitting in concern. 'Wherever they land, they use local materials to build replicas of themselves which they send to other systems. Each replica does the same thing. In a relatively short time, by astronomical reckoning, they could penetrate the entire galaxy.'

'And no doubt, part of their programming is to remove biological life wherever they find it,' came a voice from the corner of the room.

Reid looked pleased.

'Well said, Jeff.' She returned to Tarkowski. 'What else?'

'The mass conversion system depends on bringing down a strangelet from a higher-dimensional hyperplane and placing it in the centre of the object to be converted. In the instant the conversion begins, there is enough energy to generate a Bose-Einstein bridge which can pull in a second object, if it is close enough. I don't have enough data to be able to calculate the speed the object travels once it's in the bridge, but it is likely to be relativistic. Both the length of the bridge and the speed of any object within it will be beyond my control.'

'*Your* control?' Reid said. 'You'll be doing all this yourself? How?'

'I will have to go back inside Vorkus. It obviously can't be done from this village now, can it?'

'No, I guess not. But it knows about you now. It'll be looking out for you.'

'It's worse than that,' Gwion interposed. 'It now knows there are beings who can attack it on its own terms. It's not dealing with primitives anymore. So it's bound to try to accelerate its plans.'

'Unfortunately true.' Reid mused. 'Would it help if someone came in with you? Me, for instance.'

To Reid's surprise, Tarkowski gave a warm smile.

'A nice offer, Reid, but you just don't cut it. You haven't got anywhere near my understanding, or my familiarity with the digital world. You may just as well have suggested Hardy.'

'Thanks,' came a voice from the corner of the room.

'OK,' said Reid. 'So where does that leave us? Vorkus could move against us at any moment.'

'A distraction,' Gwion said suddenly. There was a chorus of '*Whats?*'

'A distraction,' Gwion repeated. 'Vorkus can't get through Helena's firewall, so he must wait until his slaves have completed the interface machine. But he has brought the Heavy Landers down— and they are a little less malleable than my people are. What if, instead of completing his machine, they start smashing it up?'

'They'd be slaughtered!' Reid protested.

'Heavy Landers accept death in a way Nooms don't. If they thought it was for freedom, they'd accept the deaths.'

Reid looked at all her companions in turn and then said, 'Get Crov in here.'

***

The plan was finalised.

Crov would lead the Heavy Lander captives in an attack on the Vorkus' interface machine. They fully accepted there would be heavy casualties.

'Better a quick death than wasting away as a slave,' one had said, and the others had cheered him.

But given the speed of Vorkus' electronic thought processes, the attack must not start until Tarkowski had penetrated Vorkus' mentality.

'How do I ensure I get there in time?' she had asked.

'Easy,' Gwion had said, 'you fly.'

'Fly?'

'Yes. We're near zero-g now, so flying is the quickest way of getting around. Come outside and I'll show you.'

And so Tarkowski had a crash course in flying. Fortunately, that was not a literal description of her tuition, and she proved to be a natural.

'And now we come to you, Reid,' she said on completion of her training.

'Yes, O Great One?'

'Let's be optimistic. Let's assume I can produce enough energy to generate an Einstein-Bose bridge of sufficient length to reach another star. The Magellan will be pulled into it and rapidly adopt near light speed.'

'And crushing us to monomolecular jelly under the acceleration.'

'No. The speed will be adopted by all the atoms simultaneously, though no doubt it will take some time to reach peak velocity. So you need to be in the Control Centre, ready for when you come out the other end. When you've emerged from the tube, you will return to the velocity you had when you entered it.'

'Relative to what?'

'The closest mass, which in this case was Vorkus itself. And the relative velocity is nearly zero. If its umbilical was rigid, it would be exactly zero, but it's flexible. You should emerge near a habitable planet.'

'Centauri?'

'Reid, please. I was starting to like you—there are no habitable planets in the Centauri system. I doubt if the colonists have gotten very far in terraforming. After all, it's only been a thousand years.'

'A pity. It would have been wonderful to give them such a surprise. I had a speech all worked out—"Hey guys, sorry we're a bit late!" '

Tarkowski rewarded Reid with another smile.

'You know, Reid, I really think I'm starting to understand your sense of humour!'

'Well, I'm not surprised; it's a lot more difficult than General Relativity.' Reid's face softened. 'Hey, Helena, do you think, just once, you could call me "Susannah"?'

'Yes, I must admit it's been nice knowing you, Susannah. I realise now how much I liked you all: Roger, Takahashi, Hardy, even Gelhardt, now I come to think of it. He was only doing his job.'

Reid smiled, her eyes blinking.

Silence fell. The two women looked into each other's eyes. There were no words.

Then Tarkowski said gently, 'Time to go.'

And without another word, she turned and was gone, never to be seen again.

Reid knew how long to give her. She walked out of the building, deliberately not looking in the direction Tarkowski had taken.

She counted. Crov was watching.

She reached the end of her count-down.

'Now!' she roared.

Immediately a horde of Heavy Landers poured out of their hut, carrying shards of metal their strength had torn from their surroundings. They rushed past the extens and began slashing at the interface machine with their makeshift weapons. Sparks fountained up from the points of impact.

The chief exten stirred, its optical centres glowing a fiercer red than usual.

'Stop! Stop or you die!'

Crov was behind the thing. He calculated the arc of his swing perfectly and a heavy bar smashed into its head. It tumbled under the impact and Crov leapt to one side of it, avoiding the arms that reached out to crush him. He drove the bar into the optic centres of the creature, shouting his triumph as the baleful red glow vanished.

But the other extens had recovered from their surprise. They issued no more threats but raised their arms, and once again the near-invisible beams of energy flashed out and each Heavy Lander they touched, man or woman, died.

Reid drew back into the shadows.

She could see fewer of the actual deaths, but she could still hear the cursing, the sizzle of burning flesh, the screams.

'Come on, Helena,' she whispered, 'please come on!'

Eight: Climacteric

Tarkowski was back in the digital world she knew so well. She swept through digital emptiness, arrowing straight for the thermocline between the two operating systems. But as she approached, she slowed, alarmed by what she saw. The entire interface was ablaze with cybernetic fire. Her emulated vision interpreted it as a raging wall of crimson flame, the same colour as the extens' optical processors.

She knew what it was: Vorkus was launching a direct attack on the firewall, trying to break into the Central Computer. Once it had achieved that, there would be no need for its clumsy interface machine. It would rotate the strangelet through the higher dimensions and place it in the heart of the Magellan. The gigatonnes of the massive lightsail ship on conversion into energy would feed a multiplicity of wormholes, threaded through the body of the Milky Way, down which Von Neumann probes would hurtle, each one giving birth to others, and on and on until the entire galaxy was enslaved.

Tarkowski recoiled. She had overestimated her ability; she could not get through this firestorm of the Vorkus' onslaught.

She was defeated.

It was then she felt something stir in the depths of her mind.

Tarkowski. I am Gwenna. I gave up my body for you and the hope you brought. Probably I surrendered my mind to you as well, for I doubt I will regain my autonomy. Was it all for nothing? I have seen your mentality, Tarkowski. I know it better than you do yourself, for I am intertwined with it. I don't mind dying, but it must be for something. Cross into Vorkus and kill it. Do it for all of us, those here now and those to come. Do it!

Tarkowski shook herself mentally and felt shame for her moment of weakness, weakness at the supreme moment of her life. She examined the wall of fire anew and saw a small area where the fires were banked, a small patch of relative calm. There, she knew, Vorkus was studying the revolt of the Heavy Landers. A revolt which would be crushed very shortly, she also knew. There was no time to waste! Tarkowski arrowed through that patch of relative calm, feeling the sting of digital destruction all around her. Then it was behind her, and she was in the stormy centre of Vorkus. She felt the turmoil of the being's struggle against the firewall, felt its growing desperation.

Beyond emotion, Vorkus? she thought. *No, you're not. No sentient being can be beyond emotion. So now it's time for you to learn another emotion: fear!*

Deeper and deeper she drove, all the time collecting more data from the raging mind she now inhabited. She saw it all; she saw the Progenitors: cold, unbending, driven by drives they themselves did not understand, given to them by another culture even remoter in time; she saw the climactic battle with the Others in which Vorkus' march of triumph had ended in fiery ruin. And, yes, she felt its need to prove itself in this galaxy so the past failures could be undone, redeemed, so it could meet the Others in battle again, and this time win the victory!

She could feel the firewall sagging, bulging inwards under Vorkus' increasingly furious attack. She knew it realised it stood on the knife-edge between triumph and disaster.

And yes—there *was* fear!

She reached the exact centre of Vorkus' being. Here was the sum total of what it was, its purest essence, the quintessence of its power.

It felt her. Instantly it abandoned its assault on the firewall, and spun around, sending its incalculable energy inwards, towards the centre which had been invaded by this entity that was about to wreak terrible damage!

Tarkowski felt its approach like a hurtling thunderbolt. But she could see all she needed now. It was all hers; power before which Vorkus would quail.

The time had come: the apotheosis was upon her.

'Thank you, Gwenna,' she whispered.

She performed the necessary calculations and dragged the strangelet down from its hyperplane, down, down, until she, Gwenna, and the strangelet met and merged.

She felt spacetime begin to strain and bend, curve over into a transdimensional cylinder.

And then?

It is difficult to explain.

Vorkus' entire mass was converted into energy. Easily said, but hard to visualise. The detonation was brighter than the whole galaxy, brighter than a thousand galaxies smashed together into one coruscant firestorm. Perhaps there had been no greater eruption of unendurable fury since the universe itself had come into being; perhaps. The spacetime fabric itself began to tear and splinter under forces beyond measurement. Billions of years later, the blaze of Vorkus' annihilation was to reach the limits of the observable universe.

And the Magellan?

It was in the Bose-Einstein bridge, its velocity climbing far beyond any value it had achieved under the blasts of the laser complexes.

Its final journey had begun.

$$***$$

Reid, Gwion and Hardy were in the Control Centre. The viewscreen showed only blackness, surrounded by curving, twisting ribbons of diaphanous light. All three knew that the glowing shapes were distorted images of distant galaxies, images bent and warped by the wormhole's gravity.

'Wherever we're going, it's not Centauri,' Reid muttered. 'We've been in flight now for three months, and there's no sign of this damned tube coming to an end.'

Hardy was worried.

'Tarkowski said we should emerge near a habitable planet, didn't she?'

'She did, but the poor girl's predictions can't be relied on too heavily. She was in rather trying circumstances when she was gathering the information. Only she could have done it; I certainly couldn't have.'

'What's our speed?' Hardy then asked.

'We've stopped accelerating, and we're travelling at a constant eighty percent of light.'

'We should get *somewhere* at that speed,' Gwion said. 'Shouldn't time dilation be kicking in about now?'

'It should, and it is. But it's only significant in the high nineties of lightspeed; then you could circumnavigate the universe in a human lifetime. Time dilation won't get us anywhere interesting; light simply isn't fast enough. What is really significant is the length of this tube. Even if it's only a few parsecs long, we're fucked.'

'And we don't know how long the tube is.'

'Correct. Helena was too busy saving our asses to find time to tell us that—if she even knew it.'

'I hope we don't end up in Andromeda,' Hardy said, looking from Reid to Gwion. 'It sounds rather a dangerous place, especially if the Progenitors built more than one Vorkus.'

Silence fell after her comment; well, not *exactly* silence. Even though the acceleration to their current speed had simultaneously affected all the atoms of ship and crew alike, the Magellan's ancient frame was still groaning and creaking alarmingly under the load. No one ever mentioned those worrying noises, for which Reid was very glad. She didn't know what would happen to a human body if exposed to the interior of a wormhole and didn't want to find out.

'Well, there's one thing we should be doing,' Reid finally said, glad someone had broken the silence, even if it had only been herself. 'When we finally pop out of this tube just like a squalling newborn, we've got to get down to a new home. We can't possibly land this ship. Let's hope the shuttlecraft are still operating. It's about time we found out.'

Neither Reid nor Hardy had been to the shuttle bay in their original incarnations, and they had to find the schematics of the Magellan's layout to know where to go. Gwion and the rest of the Far Wall people had never heard of such an area, and neither had the Heavy Landers. Reid and Hardy were now the only survivors of the downloaded minds, and they were utterly baffled by the totally different appearance that the Magellan now bore. What had once been a technocratic complex of antiseptic corridors and grey steel bulkheads was now a farming landscape which could have been mediaeval Europe but for the low gravity. Reid was happy she had inherited Palar's sense of smell and thus was not overwhelmed with the undoubted farmyard stink that must now permeate the starship.

They studied the diagrams the Central Computer showed them and tried to relate the shuttle bays to their current position. Finally, they found them. The designers of the lightsail ships had tried to foresee every likely difficulty, and the bays had been placed on a ring extending completely around the ship's circumference near its midpoint. At whatever orientation the Magellan adopted at the colony world, shuttles could be launched easily to ferry the crew to its surface.

'One problem,' Hardy said morosely.

'They're a damned long way away,' Reid finished for him. 'Fuck, fuck!' She rose from the computer module, pushing sweat-soaked hair out of her eyes. 'Well, I suppose we'd better start walking; we could pop out of this tube at any moment.'

'It's a pity we didn't bring our original muscles down with us,' Hardy said. 'We'd be able to get there very easily then.'

Reid gave him an exasperated look.

'Yes, Jeff, you're right. And it's a pity my first boyfriend suffered from premature ejaculation, but you don't hear me going on about it.'

An embarrassed Gwion said nothing for a few moments, but then: 'If it's muscles you're worried about, there's a very simple solution.'

'There is?'

'Yes,' Gwion said, slightly smugly, 'the Heavy Landers have muscle to spare.'

Crov agreed to carry Gwion, and two of his friends, one female, agreed to take Reid and Hardy. Outside of the Control Centre, the scars of Vorkus' tyranny were still apparent. The extens had fallen silent and immobile at the moment of its destruction; most had been knocked to the ground by the triumphant humans, but one was still standing, staring with dead grey eyes into the Magellan's Void as if contemplating what might have been. Reid could not suppress a shudder after seeing it and remembering the pain it had inflicted, but then turned her head in the opposite direction and said simply, 'Let's go!'

Gwion had taught the Heavy Landers well, and their great leg muscles made them much superior to the inhabitants of the Far Wall or the Pastures in unaided flying. Reid and Hardy were both alarmed at how their leaps took them high into the warm, moist air, giving them unparalleled views over the landscape. However, as the nervousness wore off, Reid saw the scenes were very repetitive, just small homesteads randomly dotted over the grasslands. There simply had not been enough organic matter to give more than a thin coating of soil over the underlying metal.

Their unusual steeds rapidly covered the kilometres, and Reid had to cry out to stop them from overshooting. She saw a ring of low buildings stretching before her, and, tilting her head, saw the ring continued upwards into the bluish dimness, curving over at the zenith of her vision to pass down through the Magellan's nadir to reappear in front of her. They had found the shuttle bays.

She noticed she was trembling slightly with excitement as her Heavy Land transport gently removed her from his back and placed her directly in front of a door. Passing the dismounted Hardy and Gwion in her eagerness, she pushed at the door and was slightly disconcerted when it immediately fell off its hinges and became part of the floor. But as it sank slowly in the low gravity, she became aware of small brown objects rushing away from her with squawks and clucking noises. Even Palar's nostrils registered the acrid, burning sensation of vast amounts of guano. Guano lying thick and heavy over the rounded shapes of what once had been sleek and powerful shuttlecraft.

This shuttle bay was nothing more than a hen house. It didn't take long for her, Hardy and Gwion to conclude that what lay under the malodorous layers of excreta could not possibly fly.

Nine: Journey's End

As soon as she returned to the Control Centre, Reid sent Heavy Land scouts to examine the other shuttle bays as a matter of top priority.

Gradually, the reports came back, each one the same, with a deadening, numbing familiarity. Each and every one of the shuttlecraft was unusable.

'But this is crazy!' Hardy had said. The vehemence of her head-shaking made her long, blond locks swing fetchingly in the low gravity. 'Everything to do with the Central Computer is in good condition! Why the shuttlecraft? Has someone been sabotaging them?'

Reid thought long and hard, then let out a long, contemplative sigh.

'I think you've got it ass-backwards, Jeff. The real question is: how is it everything to do with the Central Computer is in working order, but everything else isn't? After nearly a thousand years of neglect, wouldn't everything have gone to rack and ruin? And think about it for a moment: the Central Computer and its peripherals were old and dusty—but they worked! Consider the download procedure; it could have brought us back as a load of quarrelling baboons, but it didn't. It operated fine. And look how it and Helena kept Vorkus at bay, forcing the bastard to work through human slaves. Somehow, in some way I don't begin to understand, the Central Computer has been defending itself, refusing to allow peasants to convert it into a pigsty. It's the shuttlecraft that are what you'd expect after a millennium of neglect. I should have seen it!'

Gwion looked up from anxiously studying her fingernails.

'I think you're right. We never knew about the Central Computer or the Control Centre in the Pastures. Rhoana never mentioned them, or any other Noom here. It must have some ability to prevent people from damaging it; some kind of invisibility screen, if you will.'

'It was the summit of the human race's computing power. Anything which could faithfully copy an entire human mind clearly has incredible abilities, most of which we just took for granted. After all, Helena was able to use it to keep Vorkus at bay.' Reid shook her head. 'I don't know what to do; I thought the worst was over, but, as usual, it isn't. We could shoot out of this wormhole in the next few seconds and starve to death on the other side.'

561

'It isn't that bad,' Gwion remonstrated. 'It'd just mean we'd carry on with the kind of life we were having. Farming, growing crops, shepherding. Just as...'

She started as Reid brought her fist down on the desk in a loud impact.

'No! That's not what I want! I want this fucking voyage to come to an end; I want it over! I don't want the crew of the Magellan just carrying on as happy, ignorant peasants, thinking this metal tube is the world! That's not what Fraschini wanted! That's not what the Spes Nostra and the Phoenix have! I want what they have—a world, a planet! Sunsets, sunrises, waves on the beach, clouds in the sky, normality, for God's sake! Why am I to be denied it at the last moment?'

'Neither you nor I are exactly real people,' Hardy said. 'Due to other people's kindness, we are guests in their bodies. Maybe it's not what they want.'

There was an angry silence. Gwion and Hardy looked blankly into space, afraid to say anything, make any comment. Reid sat completely still, in a lifeless rigidity, her eyes focused on an infinity.

Then she moved.

'No. I will not accept it. Gwion's hope for a return to a pastoral existence is wrong; the Magellan is senile. The slow death of the fusion reactors proves it. We have to get off. I will not accept it!'

Hardy looked at her, ready to recoil at the slightest whiplash of her tongue.

'What won't you accept?'

'Death on this pile of junk. Palar hasn't got much longer, and we will go together. But she shares my happiness; if I am on a planet during my last days, she will feel that too, and her passing will be calm. I will give her that.'

'How?'

'When we emerge, we will be near a habitable planet. Helena promised we would. We will land the Magellan on that planet.'

Hardy jumped to her feet.

'Are you mad! This ship was always intended to be deep-space only! Its mass is so great it will collapse in on itself just before it starts sinking through solid rock! Its momentum alone will make it a titanic bomb!'

'No, its mass is indeed very great, but initially, its momentum won't be because that depends on velocity as well. But it will pick up momentum once it starts to feel the gravitational pull of the nearby planet. We will have to bring it down as soon as we emerge from the wormhole if we don't want to end up as a spreadable jam. Once we're on the ground, everyone must get out as soon as humanly possible before the thing implodes on top of them.'

'May I ask if there's any reaction mass in the braking rockets?'

'As they're connected to the Central Computer, I have a feeling there will be.' She looked at her two companions: one a downloaded mind from a distant technological age, one a superior brain now packed with information and knowledge from that age. 'I don't think I can do it just by myself, so I would appreciate your help.'

After a few moments, Gwion extended her hand in acquiescence; a short while later, Hardy extended hers as well.

***

The ship-wide communication system burst into thunderous life.

'Attention! This is Susannah Reid! I am about to give you information which will save your life. Sometime in the near future, we will be bringing this long journey to a conclusion. Shortly this incredibly long voyage will end, and we will bring the Magellan down onto a planet's surface. The ship will start to collapse as soon as that happens, so you must be near an exit point before we touch down. Then you must get out running, and keep running for as long as you can. I trust we will all meet again when all this is over.'

Everyone in the Magellan: Ord, Noom, Heavy Lander, stopped what they were doing and looked at each other in stupefaction. Some, hearing the dread words "long journey will end", broke into tears at the thought that their safe and customary world was ending; Heavy Landers looked meaningfully at each other at the thought of fresh adventures; Nooms stared at each other as smiles gradually brightened their faces at the thought of new discoveries, new challenges of the mind.

Shortly afterwards, Gwion approached Reid.

'You realise you forgot something vital, don't you?'

'I did? Please tell.'

563

'Well, unless you want to starve after our crash-landing, we need everyone who has livestock to get them off the ship as well as themselves. And we'll need seed corn.'

Reid nodded.

'You're right. I did forget that. I lived for so long on yeast and algae I'd forgotten they don't grow naturally. In fact, if we were still dependent on them, we wouldn't have the proverbial cellophane cat in Hell's chance of surviving on any planet.'

The farmers and pastoralists, on hearing Reid's second announcement, felt a sense of satisfaction and renewed hope.

But Reid's thoughts were neither of those; instead, fear and doubt gripped her as the full enormity of her audacious plan took hold in her mind. She seemed to spend every waking moment staring at the viewscreens, which stubbornly refused to show anything except a core of darkness surrounded by a lambent wreath of starlight intensely warped by gravitational lensing. Hardy dutifully brought her food and drink, which she accepted mechanically, barely taking her eyes from a scene which slowly turned and twisted, but did not alter in any meaningful way.

And still, the Magellan plunged down the centre of a heart of darkness. Reid knew Tarkowski could not possibly have been certain of the length of the wormhole and thus how long it would take to traverse it; perhaps it was a billion parsecs long. Perhaps the Magellan would be manned only by skeletons when it finally emerged.

Gwion, Hardy, and Reid met yet again in the Control Centre and once more went over their problems.

Gwion said, 'We have to decide which part of the cylinder is going to be the belly when we land and evacuate the people out of there.'

'Agreed.' Reid said. 'Get on with it.'

'Another trouble is timing,' Hardy said, brushing her over-long hair out of her eyes. 'We can't keep people on permanent high alert. It just can't be done. But if and when we make it down, they've got to spring into action and get out as fast as humanly possible. When we come to rest, we will immediately begin to collapse in on ourselves while simultaneously sinking like a lead balloon in a swimming pool. Unless everybody is waiting with their animals at the exits, they'll never get out in time.'

'What Jeff is asking,' Gwion explained, 'is whether there is any way we can have a warning of when we are about to exit the wormhole.'

('If we ever do,' Hardy muttered, *sotto voce*.)

Reid did not answer immediately and looked at the viewscreen. As ever, it showed a disk of blackness surrounded by the feathery plumes of twisted galaxies. It had shown nothing but variations on that theme for months now.

'There must be a way,' she murmured. 'Helena would know.'

'But she isn't here, is she?' Hardy said, enjoying her small revenge.

Gwion looked up, the beginnings of a smile lighting her face.

'We've been talking about how wonderful it is. Why not ask the Central Computer?'

Reid smote her forehead with the flat of her hand.

'I really am getting too old for this job. Palar, I must apologise for forcing you to share your body with a washed-up idiot.'

Not wishing to risk mind-to-mind communication again, she turned to the nearest keyboard and tapped in her questions. She looked at the reply for many minutes, making notes as she did so. Then she turned back to her expectant companions.

'The laws of physics apply as much inside a wormhole as outside. Most of the energy to create it came from the obliteration of Vorkus. We were sucked inside and given the energy to take us up to our current speed of $0.8\,c$. The energy came from the gravitational strain of the warped spacetime. When we emerge, we will give that energy back to the wormhole which will then collapse. We will readopt the relative velocity we had before we entered. But just as we accelerated up, we will decelerate down. That means giving energy back to the wormhole over a period of time, and that will be detectable.'

Gwion leaned forward excitedly.

'In what way?'

'A more energetic wormhole will have a greater diameter. The Einstein images of distant galaxies will be denser and brighter. I can ask the Central Computer to monitor the image and sound a warning the instant it sees a change starting to happen.'

'Then you'd better do just that.'

Sometime later, Reid and Hardy were alone.

'Well, I feel a lot better now that's done,' Reid said. 'Perhaps we've got a fighting chance now.'

'Susannah, there's something I want to ask you?'

'What me? Not the Central Computer?' she said with forced gaiety, all the time knowing what Hardy was going to ask.

'It's about you and me. And the situation we're now in. Is there still a *you and me?*'

Reid sat and turned away slightly.

'I don't know, Jeff. I've never been in this situation before. I don't think anyone has. It's not just that you're not exactly the Jeff I fell in love with anymore, but the fact that we're kind of mental parasites in someone else's body. I don't think we have the right to make those decisions as if we were our old selves.'

'Do you still feel Palar's mind?'

'Yes.'

'But I don't feel Rhosyr's mind. It's like we've merged into a kind of new person. I feel as if I've always been a woman. I...'

But Hardy was fated never to complete that sentence.

Suddenly, the terrible bellow of the klaxon blared out. Reid more than half-recognised it; it was almost identical to the collision alarm she had heard once before when she had needed to explain to Gelhardt what was happening.

Then I was trying to avoid collisions, she thought wildly. *Now I'm trying to make one!*

She could see the terror in Hardy's eyes as the terrible thunderclaps of the klaxon crashed into their eardrums, shaking them with its awesome power. Instantly, she turned to the ship-wide communication system. Instantly, the klaxon faded to a background beat.

'Attention! We will shortly be re-entering normal space. Follow the agreed procedures and go immediately to your nearest muster station!'

For a moment, her tumultuous mind thought she should add *This is not a drill!* to those commands—but they had never had time for a drill.

'How long have we got?'

'Not long. Get Gwion here!'

Already she could hear the mingled sounds of running feet and yelling people outside the Control Centre. Was the ship beginning to shudder? She could not tell.

Gwion was suddenly beside her. Reid expanded the viewscreen image so it occupied the entirety of one wall. The scene appeared to be unchanged from its usual monochrome patterns. She studied it with anxious eyes.

The black disk was growing, infinitesimally.

She whirled around to face her two subordinates.

'You know what we have to do! As soon as the planet appears, we must choose a landing area; one that's both very flat and very big; it'll take us a long time to come to a rest after we hit.'

'What if there isn't an area that's both very flat and very big?' Hardy asked.

'Shut up. There will be. Then we must spiral in, circling the globe, do our best to aerobrake. We've got to come in as horizontal as possible.'

'If we come in more than a few degrees off horizontal,' Hardy observed, 'we'll punch a hole straight through the crust and make a hole bigger than Chicxulub.'

'Shut up. Take your positions.'

'How long have we got?'

'Don't know. We sit here until it's over.'

Reid turned all her attention to the giant viewscreen; her fingers hovered over the controls. Her surroundings faded until there was just her, the viewscreen and the waiting controls.

Abruptly the black centre of the image expanded until it occupied the entire field of view.

And then it was gone.

In its place was a half-globe of a new world; one of green-brown continents, shining ice-mantled poles, and sapphire seas. Great Catherine wheels of tropical storms hung over an equatorial ocean. It looked achingly like Earth had been before Baldwin murdered it.

Then she felt the ship lurch as the planet reached out gravitational fingers to ensnare it.

'We're going in!' she yelled to those around her: Hardy to the left, Gwion to the right.

She saw the image suddenly shift as the Magellan began its descent, lightsail first. It began to pick up speed as it began its meteoric descent to fiery destruction.

As one, the three controllers fought to keep the prow of the vessel upright as the first wisps of atmosphere began to whip past. The planet's gravitational pull was trying to drag it into an escape-velocity fall, and the three controllers were trying to bleed off that speed through friction.

Deeper into the ionosphere, the Magellan fell, sparking blue electrical flashes as it plunged through ionised layers.

Ninety kilometres from the surface, the ship ripped into the mesosphere. The hull began to glow a bright cherry red as the tormented atmosphere vainly resisted the hurtling mass blasting through it.

Inside, the terrified inhabitants attempted to hang on to whatever was still attached as the vessel bucked and swivelled under the forces trying to restrain it. Trying and failing.

The Magellan completed its first circumnavigation of the globe, sweeping lower all the time. Now the braking rockets flashed into yellow-white incandescence, fighting the deadly pull of the planet's gravity. The lightsail bent backwards under the force of the restraining atmosphere, and great strips began to peel away. On down through the astounded mesosphere flashed the great starship, beginning its second circumnavigation.

'We won't be able to make a third revolution,' Gwion said in a voice so dry she felt her tongue would crumble to dust if she spoke again.

'I know,' Reid said, 'The northern continent. The central part is a plain which stretches most of the width. That's where we're going!'

The Magellan swept into the stratosphere, shattering its calm like a lightning bolt forged from steel and titanium. Gradually the prow rose to a more horizontal orientation.

Clouds began to appear in the viewscreen as they pierced the tropopause. Details of the surface could now be plainly seen: strange ochre forests mottled with cloud shadows, winding iron-bright rivers, the corrugated folds of mountain ranges topped with dustings of snow like icing sugar.

'Up you come, baby, up you bloody well come!' Reid yelled maniacally, as the manoeuvring jets consumed the last pitiful remnant of fuel that Aland had left her, many lifetimes ago.

There was not far to fall now.

First the manoeuvring jets died and then the braking rockets stuttered, flashed once again and then fell silent forever.

The land rose to meet them like a titanic door slamming in their faces.

The remnants of the tattered lightsail were the first things to strike the surface of the new world and were destroyed instantly and utterly.

Then the vast ring of the EZ exercise zone, once known as the Land of Ez, hit and was ripped into flying, tumbling fragments of red hot metal.

And then the tremendous central cylinder of the mighty Magellan smashed into the dusty plain at the shallowest possible angle Reid and the others could achieve.

Shallow, but not quite shallow enough.

There was a huge eruption of rock and soil, looming like a nuclear explosion above the point of impact as the main mass struck, yielding its stupendous momentum to the planetary crust. Glowing blocks of bedrock described graceful parabolas before falling many kilometres away. A great bow wave of soil, boulders, crushed and pulverised rock formed as the ship began to plough an irresistible furrow across the landscape. Kilometre after kilometre, it surged on, unstoppable, irresistible, leaving a vast, seemingly endless scar in the land behind it as it gouged its way ever onwards.

And then, slowly, inexpressibly slowly, its headlong march of destruction began to falter.

It stopped.

Reid hit the control to open the exits.

'Now,' she screamed into the communication channel, 'get out! Now!'

***

There had been casualties, of course, in that terrible descent to the surface. People had been flung around like shuttlecocks as the starship completed its last journey, finally ending a voyage that had begun an achingly long time ago. Those who had planned it had long been dust, and that dust had been scattered through interplanetary and interstellar emptiness as the Solar system destroyed itself. Fraschini, De Vries, they had died never knowing whether their incredible labours had come to fruition and they had saved the human race.

Gwion stood on the hill, knee-high among the red-purple native vegetation, looking down at the colossal half-submerged wreck of the Magellan. It lay there, a pitted, scarred, grey half-cylinder, its incredible wanderings finally over. She had learned from her studies of the Central Computer most of the significant events aboard it during over a millennium of journeying. She had seen the videos of Ashworth, Lafayette, Regine, Anna, heroic Gelhardt, martyred Aland. And now the Central Computer was dead along with the ship which had carried it. All the minds it had held who had not been downloaded—they were gone as well. And she had also seen the record of how the original Reid had flung herself off the hull to escape further pain.

And now another Reid stood beside her, also looking down at the silent, broken remnant of the mighty Magellan.

'I don't suppose any of the other ships will have a tale to tell to match ours,' she said to her companion. Reid was silent for a while because she, too, was reliving the epic saga of the dead starship.

'No, I don't suppose they will have,' she said quietly.

'Did they all get to Centauri, you think, the ones that came after us? And is there a thriving colony there now?'

'It'll be a long time before we find out,' Reid said sadly. 'Two point three million light-years is a long way away.'

'But if they did, there could be two human civilisations, one around Centauri, one here in Messier 33. Perhaps one day in the far, far future we will make contact with each other.'

'That would be good. But we could have done all this without all this suffering; if only there had not been that first disaster, the human race would not be forever verging on the edge of extinction.'

Gwion nodded.

'The edge, yes, but we did not go over that edge, and we will not. No doubt the colony here will sink into semi-barbarism, but we won't go all the way down. We won't forget who we are and where we came from.'

Then she, too, was called away by her thoughts as she looked down on the assembled survivors. Taran had cut off all contact with her since he had found out about her pregnancy, but she and Crov were growing closer. She had hopes.

Reid, too, was deep in thought. She knew she had hurt Hardy, but she still had not been able to reconcile her feelings with their new status. And there was the growing awareness that Palar's illness would be claiming her before long. Hardy would outlive her, and perhaps her ex-lover too would come to terms with the new way of things.

Reid gave a wistful smile. It must be unusual to be someone who had died of the same disease twice.

But that was the unknown future. This was now.

She looked down at the assembled multitude. She could tell which ones had been Heavy Landers: they were the only ones standing up straight in the new world's 0.9 g. But all of them had been waiting for some time for her to speak. She raised her arms.

'My people! We are the last of the noble race of Magellanites. We have come through fire and storm to claim this new world in a new galaxy as our own. The ship that brought us here will slowly crumble away, but our descendants will not forget her and how she kept us safe for so long.

'This is a good world, much like our beloved Earth. In time we will occupy it all, and it will be our treasured home. In a far-off galaxy, there is another branch of the family of the human race. Perhaps one day in a vastly distant future, we will meet up again, but until then, we must believe and behave as if we are the last bearers of the hope of humanity. We must not make the same mistakes again, and let the lusts for power and wealth destroy hope, destroy kindness.'

Suddenly it felt as if her old Jewish identity was reclaiming her. It was almost as if she were at a religious ceremony. Reid smiled down at the upturned faces and said softly, 'Amen.'

And to her amazement came back the word from the people below.

'Amen.'

The *"Stars Trilogy"* books:

Doom of Stars: ISBN 978-1-8382805-6-7
Resolution of Stars: ISBN 978-0-9574894-4-8
Culmination of Stars: ISBN 978-0-9934886-9-6

Lightning Source UK Ltd.
Milton Keynes UK
UKHW020640050922
408358UK00009B/958